PIERCING THE VEIL

BOOK ONE OF THE VEIL SAGA

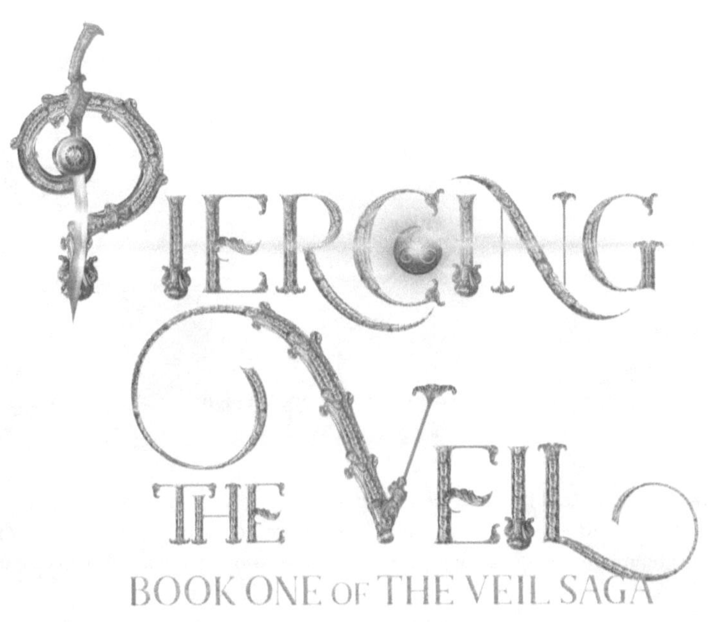

PIERCING THE VEIL

BOOK ONE OF THE VEIL SAGA

STEVEN A. GUGLICH

Book Cover by Autumn M. Birt
Illustrations by Erwin J. Arroza

First Edition: March 31, 2023

Your Wildest Dreams Publishing, LLC
www.stevenguglich.com

To My Children,
Tytus, Kayla, Robert, and Benjamin.
May you always find wonder in the world.

INTRODUCTION

The book you are holding represents a lifelong dream-come-true… a fusion of the wonder and imagination of a child, grown up to find that magic is only make-believe. It unites both the child dreamer and the adult realist, written as a catharsis to reconcile both. It combines fantasy, mythology, mysticism, historical fiction, and various world views to create a story, for young and old, that dares to find hope in a dark world and ignite wonder in the reader.

It is my sincere hope that you find these things and more as you take your first steps into the world of *The Veil Saga.*

Sincerely,
Steven A. Guglich

ACKNOWLEDGMENTS

This book could not exist without some very influential people.

My father, Stanley A. Guglich, was my muse as I grew up. He single-handedly stoked the fires of my imagination by reading fantastic books and introducing me to worlds that I could only dare to imagine.

My high school writing teacher, Mrs. JoAnn Hauptman, gave me the wings to fly and the courage to create worlds of my own imagination. If not for her, I wouldn't have the confidence to even think I could write a story.

My sister, Debra Guglich, taught me unconditional love. Deb believed in me, even when I didn't believe in myself. And despite being the typical big brother who mistreated his little sister, Deb loves me through thick and through thin.

My best friend, Alex Marquez and his wife Ruthie, took me in as family; they saw something in me that I didn't see in myself. Alex and Ruthie encouraged me when I was at my lowest and helped me through some of my toughest times. Alex helped me develop my writing skills. We've written multiple scripts, screenplays, and teleplays together. Maybe one day we'll finish that novel we started.

Most of all, this book would not exist without my wife, Karen. While others have been sources of inspiration and encouragement, Karen became *my* muse. She is the culmination of all those who came before her, encouraging me to do the impossible. On our wedding night we exchanged gifts. Her gift to me was a bound and printed book of all the meanderings, Biblical devotions, and encouragements I had written to her during our courtship. When she presented the book to me, she said, "Steve, you *are* a writer." And she told me that I NEEDED to write more books. She pushed me, despite my busy schedule, to carve out some time each day to write. She is my first alpha reader, eagerly waiting to read the next installment and helping me to understand my characters and their stories in ways I never imagined.

Since embarking on this journey to publication, others have come by my side to help mold *Piercing the Veil* into what it is today. My critique partner, Darrell Pursiful, gave me great insight into developing my characters, and drummed it into my head that real people use contractions when they speak. Darrell is also a language expert and he helped me develop all the rules and mechanics that make up the Elven language.

Jake Parrick was another critique partner in the earliest stages of this book; he helped me to develop the magic system of *The Veil Saga* and joined Darrell in his unbridled campaign to get me to use contractions

I've also enlisted two groups of expert consultants that helped me to brainstorm ideas. Ken Baker, Mike Bogensberger, Anthony Deyarmond, L.D., Jimmy Durst, H.J. Grover IV, Billy Martinez, and Michael Rossano are my *Sci-fi and Fantasy Consultants*. This group, consisting mainly of avid Fantasy and Sci-Fi readers, helped to really flesh out the fantasy cultures and make them seem real. They allowed me to run the strangest ideas by them and tell me their thoughts… and they weren't afraid to tell me if something wouldn't work.

The second group, my *Military Consultants*, consisted of men and woman who have served in the Armed Forces. Wes Houle, Michelle Murray, Paul Turpin, and Mitch Warren helped me to put some realistic touches on scenes that involved military personnel.

My cousin-in-laws, Kei and Stefanie Taniguchi helped me with the parts of the book that take place in Japan, making sure I was sensitive to their culture and that I presented the story in a realistic manner.

I handed over the third draft of this story to my beta readers;

Georgia Carolyn, Zakiya Collupy, Amy Cornell, L.D., H.J. Grover IV, Karen Guglich, Tytus Guglich, Johannah Hayes, Elisha Holliman, Billy Martinez, and Rachel Olson. Let me tell you, this team did not disappoint or hold anything back. They were instrumental in shaping the final manuscript. In fact, I'm sure that they will be surprised at the difference between the draft they read and the final edition you hold today.

Patrick LoBrutto was hired to be my editor for this book. But he became more than that. He became a mentor, challenging me to hone my writing craft and take this story to the next level. His sage advice and foresight helped to not only write this book, but carve the direction of future books in *The Veil Saga*.

Paula Kaledzi, our family's faithful friend, brought this project to life on social media and managed an engaging and successful Kickstarter Campaign.

Autumn Birt, my cover designer, formatter, and friend gave us the gift of her publishing knowledge, walking us through each step and answering all of our newbie questions.

I could fill pages of "thank yous" for others like my Aunt, Roberta, who read the first twenty pages of an earlier draft in 2016 that was nothing more than words crudely pieced together that hardly resembles the final version of the story. In an email from Feb. 3, 2016, Aunt Roberta told me, "Keep writing. The world needs this story."

This story belongs to many people who have encouraged me over the years. And now, *we* get to share that story with you.

CONTENTS

PROLOGUE

1805 B.C.

In the Elder Tree of the elves, in the city of Sayalla, the Sovereign Council of the keshaphim met to discuss the growing problem of the adamu. Rays of sunlight, peering through silhouettes of a thousand leaves streamed in from windows illuminating the ancient oak table. There sat the leaders of the elves, dweorg, alfargnym, koth, and faun. One seat remained empty, but none of the others seemed to notice or care. They argued to no conclusion, predominated by the elders of the dark elves and light elves.

Zohar stood in the shadows, observing, not hiding. He wanted to see for himself, as an outsider looking in, how the existence of the adamu caused much trepidation for the keshaphim. Though the faun and koth said little, the concerned looks upon their faces told Zohar that his plan was a good one.

As the Elven elders argued, Zohar watched the High King of the Dweorg shift uncomfortably in his seat. He scowled at the elves, and Zohar could visibly see the veins on the dweorg's forehead swell with derision. The High King stood from his seat, hefted his war hammer from his side and slammed it down on the large oaken table.

"Enough!" he said, his eyes darted between the factions of elves. "This, we discuss no more! These adamu have caused us all madness. And I, Vrangar, son of Lofarr Dainn, High King of the Dweorg, shall listen no more!"

Vrangar breathed in deeply, leaned forward and placed his open hand flat on the table.

"The adamu have no choice," Vrangar said. "They have no governance of this world; only what we give them. And we will give them what we decide to give them. They blindly follow the goblins; a kind as pathetic as themselves. First, we war against the goblins, and when the adamu see their false gods bloodied in their streets, they will obey us. We will decide where they live and how they live."

"Agreed!" said the faceless Dark Elf, Ejiron. The two other Dark Elves shouted in agreement.

"This," bellowed Vrangar, lifting his war hammer above his head. "This is how rulers govern. We do not talk of pacifying our enemies. We conquer them!"

Doors carved from ancient oak and gilded with gold and silver swung open, interrupting the impassioned dweorg's speech.

Zohar's assistant, Klau, couldn't have had better timing. The koth walked toward the table, his thick tail bobbing behind. In his small arms he carried several large rolls of parchment. Zohar stepped from the shadows, meeting his assistant, and stopped at the empty seat of the Elder of Amyin; his seat.

"Conquer them? Assuredly, we could," said Zohar, placing his hands on the table. His voice calm, yet confident. It matched his dignified demeanor and the nonchalance he wished to convey. "We are, no doubt, capable of annihilating the adamu or forcing them into submission. Yet have we not learned from our very own past?" Zohar paused, waiting for an answer, but none came.

Zohar smiled at his compatriots, knowing once again that his grand entrance had captured their curiosity.

"We—elves, dweorg, alfargnym, faun, and koth—are not like the adamu. We have been endowed with a gift the adamu lack… magic. We have seen the devastation wrought when its use is driven by the desire for conquest. We've learned from this error and to strive to do good with the magic we possess. It's now the adamu's turn to learn. But they must learn without us. We offered our wisdom and they refused it."

Zohar reached for one of the large rolls of parchment his assistant carried. He unrolled it, gently pressing it down on the table. The elf then placed a small smooth stone on each corner to keep the parchment from curling.

"This is what we need to do." He pointed with confidence to the drawing on the parchment. The image began to shimmer and emerge from the paper in a swirling motion, re-forming itself from the two-dimensional drawing into a three-dimensional replica of golden, glittery light; a wheel turned as glyphs engraved around its perimeter glowed with a golden brilliance. From the center of the stone wheel, a shimmering golden curtain appeared. It hung there, drawing the attention of everyone around the table.

"As a people, the keshaphim are content with what we have. We no longer desire to expand our reach. You, the dweorg, have lived in your mountain clanholds since the beginning of time. We elves have built homes where we find comfort. Familiarity. History. And we have invited the like-minded alfargnym and faun to live among us. We saw the plight of the koth and we extended our hands to them to live in peace with us. We will remain content with what we have and we give the rest to the adamu and the goblins. We will protect ourselves behind a veil that we build together. We will remain in obscurity, hidden from their eyes, and we will wait for them to learn the folly of their ways. Until then, we exist only to each other."

PART ONE

CHAPTER I
AN EXCEPTIONALLY ORDINARY MAN

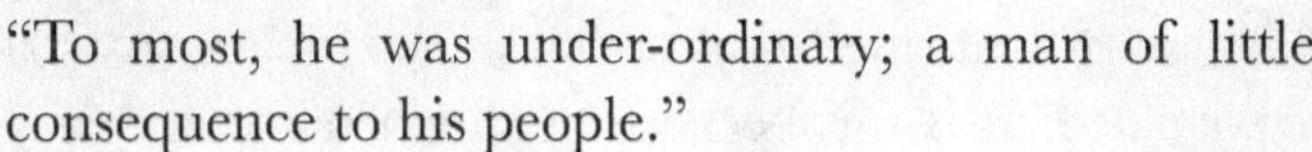

"To most, he was under-ordinary; a man of little consequence to his people."

~ From *The Second Gift Giver Chronicles* compiled by Erwin Albowyn, a Chronicler of the Master Construct, Second Order, an alfargnym of Unterbaum

Present Day

On a warm early summer's day on the bustling streets of New York City, people avoided one another with the skill that only New Yorkers possess. Among the hustle and bustle, one unmoving figure kept watch over a seemingly ordinary human.

Mercurio stood on the sidewalk, busy humans rushing around him. Most of them towered above him, but he was used to that. In some cases, if he wanted to blend in without using his cloak, he could hide among human children. But not today. Today he needed to be unnoticed. The elf stood silent and observing, an unseen watcher hidden in a shroud of magic; the familiar energy of his Veil Cloak surged over his body. The surrounding magic united with his aura and weaved the light around him, making the armor-clad elf invisible to the humans that passed him by. They were completely unaware of his presence, yet they avoided contact with him as if they knew he was there. The cloak's secondary enchantment acted as a deflector, repelling the humans at a subconscious level, causing them to move around him like a river flowing around a large rock.

With humans darting all around him, the elf's eyes focused on his target; a young male sitting on a bench, reading a book. He'd observed this human for weeks and was convinced that this one was indeed worthy of the calling.

This ordinary, plump twenty-eight-year-old man appeared average by most human standards. Perhaps even below average. Jeremy Goodson wore eyeglasses. His round cheeks and belly indicated he ate more than he should. The mustard stain on his blue collared shirt confirmed that conclusion. His brown khaki pants were wrinkled. Was this because he didn't make and care for his own clothing? He did live alone.

Curious.

He didn't remind Mercurio of the other humans he'd met. To his credit, Mercurio had only met a few. Nevertheless, this one was remarkably ordinary. Even his aura, now radiating a steady blue with thinner bands of gold and pink, seemed ordinary.

As Jeremy turned the page of his book, the pink in his aura spiked. He seemed to enjoy whatever it was he was reading.

Could Jeremy Goodson possibly do what Mercurio wanted him to do? Perhaps. With the proper guidance.

In his observations, Mercurio learned Jeremy had lived in New York City all his life. The skills he possessed led him into the odd profession of teaching children who have been promoted to the fourth grade. That was a strange concept. Human children were, for the most part, not taught by their parents. They were sent to schools to be taught by people like Jeremy. Yet, this was where the seemingly unremarkable man showed the remarkable. By human standards, he was an excellent teacher, adored by his students.

Mercurio had watched him at work all day. Today, Jeremy and his students celebrated. The children had been promoted to grade five. Despite the celebration, there was much crying because the children wouldn't see their teacher again. Jeremy himself seemed saddened by this.

When all the children left the school, Jeremy did too. Mercurio followed him, as he had done every day for the past two weeks.

Jeremy sat on one end of the bench at the bus shelter, slouched forward, reading a book. Next to Jeremy sat an older human. His aura was a steady blue and green with splotches of black. Mercurio wondered if the man knew of the cancer that was slowly destroying his body.

Sitting to the elderly man's right was a young woman in her 20s. She brushed her brown hair to the side to adjust the ear bud that played music from the device hidden in her purse. Her aura pulsed green and blue with radiating bands of orange.

Standing to her right was a family. The couple engaged in banter about what they were going to have for dinner. Their two daughters stood quietly, eyes fixed on Jeremy, their auras an intense orange and pink with much smaller bands of blue and green. Both smiled and waved at Jeremy.

Mercurio tensed with anticipation and a grin grew on his ordinarily stoic face. As many times as he saw Jeremy subconsciously do this, it astonished him.

Jeremy glimpsed the two children. His aura intensified as his smile broadened, giving way to the orange and pink to radiate brighter than the blue.

Mercurio watched as the magical energy around Jeremy and the two children swirled together; the magic from Jeremy coaxed their swirling energies toward him. The older child walked over, greeting him without reservation.

He doesn't know he's even doing this, Mercurio thought, shaking his head.

Jeremy put aside his book and sat up. He nodded and said hello to her and then to her younger sister. The younger sister smiled and waved at Jeremy. He smiled and waved back at her.

The mother noticed the interaction and the yellow in her aura quickly faded, replaced by a spike of red. She smiled at Jeremy and apologized as she rushed over to her daughters, grabbed them by their hands, and nodded. Jeremy smiled back and went back to reading his book.

Fascinating! No matter how many times Mercurio saw Jeremy unconsciously change the flow of magic, it amazed him. This was rare among humans. They all walked through a sea of magical energy every day, oblivious to its presence and power. But now and then there were the anomalies, humans who were sensitive to magic.

Throughout history there had been several who felt it but couldn't see it. They knew something was there... something powerful that they couldn't explain. And when they tried to discover it, tried to harness it, most of them went mad. New York seemed to have more occurrences of magic-sensitive humans than anywhere else in the world. Elven mages and alfargnym chroniclers had tried to explain why. But like the human anomalies, New York City itself had a much higher concentration of magical energy than it should have. This was a mystery they couldn't explain.

Jeremy, however, was an anomaly among anomalies: an even rarer type of human who wasn't only sensitive to magic but could change its ebb and flow. He couldn't manipulate it as an elf or alfargnym could. Though among humans, it was a formidable ability that could one day get Jeremy killed—or drive him mad. Mercurio hoped to avoid that.

A human in a typical blue business suit walked up to the bus stop. The man checked his cell phone and took a sideways glance at Jeremy. His aura spiked from pink to blue, and then it shimmered.

Mercurio tensed. *No!*

The shimmer of the man's aura was subtle. To the untrained eye, it wouldn't have been noticeable. But Mercurio knew this could only mean one thing.

Another human showed up at the bus stop. A younger human

male with a backpack. He glanced over at the business executive, and his aura shimmered.

Samyaza! Mercurio profaned to himself.

The bus the humans had all been waiting for pulled up to the curb with a loud screech.

Mercurio ran to the bus stop. He needed to stop them before they got on the bus with Jeremy.

Ever the gentleman, Jeremy waited to get on, letting the others board before he did.

Mercurio growled under his breath. Harnessing magic to increase his speed, he leapt onto the roof of the bus as it pulled away; his Veil Cloak silencing the sound of the impact.

Who are these two? Goblins? Alfargnym? His hope was in the latter, but he needed to know for sure.

The ride took twenty minutes before it stopped where Jeremy normally exited.

Jeremy walked off the bus and the two false humans tailed him.

Mercurio followed them, waiting for Jeremy to turn at 181st Street and Amsterdam Avenue. The tall buildings on either side obstructed the sun and the transition from retail establishments to residential buildings decreased the number of pedestrians. He waited for the most opportune time; confident his cloak would silence any noise. But it wouldn't help explain someone vanishing into thin air. He pounced on the false human wearing the backpack. Wrapping him within the field of his Veil cloak, Mercurio tumbled with him to a space between two parked cars. He straddled the stranger and held his dagger to his heart.

"Who are you?" Mercurio said through gritted teeth.

"Oh my gosh! What… what… what do you want, man? Take my wallet, it's yours. I ain't got—"

"Drop the illusion!" Mercurio applied pressure to the dagger. "Tell me, if I push this blade in any further, will it pierce into your skull? Your throat?"

The deceiver's expression went from false-fear to a pensive smirk.

"I'm going to let you up now. Try to run and I'll send you to the ether. Then I'll go for your partner and I'll see what it knows."

"You're good, Mercurio," the deceiver said. He stood up.

Mercurio held tightly to the false human's sleeve. "Turn it off. Slowly."

The deceiver cautiously reached for his belt. He turned his fingers as if adjusting a knob that wasn't there. The illusion of the young man disappeared. In its place stood a goblin, no taller than Mercurio, dressed in the black, short robes of their sage caste.

"I suspected," Mercurio said. "What are you after?"

"You!" The goblin lunged at Mercurio, catching his arm. With one hand it grabbed him by the wrist. With the other, it wrapped his arm around Mercurio's bicep, attempting to pull the dagger from his grip.

Mercurio held tightly to the hilt and moved in the direction the goblin pulled him. He used the momentum and kept going, flipping the goblin onto the car in front of him, and trying to keep it within the confines of his Veil Cloak.

The goblin clawed at the trunk of the car, trying desperately to crawl away. Mercurio grabbed one of the deceiver's ankles, slowing it down. He slammed the dagger into its calf.

The goblin screamed and turned to kick Mercurio.

Mercurio dodged the kick and yanked the goblin back to him. Grabbing it by the belt, he pulled it closer and held him from behind in a choke hold.

"Why are you here?" Mercurio yelled into the goblin's ear. His cloak absorbed the sound so that no one outside its field heard.

The goblin huffed and struggled to break free. He slammed his elbow back into Mercurio, but the elf's armor absorbed the blows.

"Why are you here?" Mercurio tightened the choke hold.

The goblin huffed, heaving up and down to get its breath back. "I... told... you." It grunted.

"How'd you find me?" Mercurio said.

The goblin pulled forward, lifting Mercurio. They stumbled out from between the two parked cars, out into the street just as a large car careened toward them. Mercurio drew in the magical energy around him, released the goblin, and used the energy and momentum to carry himself over the oncoming car.

A thud and screeching tires drew unwanted attention from the few pedestrians.

Samyaza! Mercurio cursed. He darted to the goblin. It'd been hit by the car, but it still lived. Mercurio pulled his Veil Cloak around them both and thrust his dagger into the goblin's side, sliding it past its ribs and piercing its heart. He pushed harder, twisted, and then removed the knife.

The goblin gasped again, clutching Mercurio's arm. Life left it and his body decayed into a swarm of golden particles, disappearing into the ether.

Mercurio scooped up the goblin's clothing and gear, rolling out of the way as the driver came around the side.

Seeing the smashed headlight with the pool of dark reddish-green blood on the street, the man yelled, "Ay! Dios Mio!" He brought his hands up to his face.

How the humans would explain that, Mercurio didn't know. But he couldn't care about that right now. Humans made up all sorts of unbelievable stories to explain things they didn't know. Now he needed to get to that other goblin before it reached Jeremy.

CHAPTER 2

AN EXTRAORDINARY ENCOUNTER

"Angst and regret could be powerful allies in the life of one who tempers them with hope."

~ From *The Second Gift Giver Chronicles* compiled by Erwin Albowyn, a Chronicler of the Master Construct, Second Order, an alfargnym of Unterbaum

The walk from the bus stop to his apartment in Washington Heights only took Jeremy a few minutes. When he arrived at his building, he followed the usual routine: he checked the mail, threw his book bag on the floor in the entryway and walked into his bedroom to turn on the computer. After that, he didn't have to even think about what he was going to do next. No more papers to grade and no more lessons to plan. It was Friday, and even better, it was the last day of the school year. He was on Summer Break. It was time to relax before he started his job as a camp counselor in a few weeks.

Jeremy dropped his heavy frame into the desk chair. First, he'd check Facebook. After scrolling through his news feed for a few minutes, it was time to escape from this world. He clicked on the

World of Warcraft icon and launched his favorite game. As his character, a Pandaran Warrior, loaded, Jeremy grabbed a half-empty can of day-old Monster Ultra and stretched back in his chair with one arm behind his head.

"Jeremy?" A voice called from behind.

Jeremy violently flailed his chair around, bumping his knee on the computer table. He sprung from his chair and stepped behind it, ready to face the intruder, only to trip on an old empty two-liter bottle of Diet Pepsi and fall backwards into the corner. Jeremy looked towards the open bedroom door where he'd heard the voice. He was ready to yell, "Get out of here!" but stopped when he glimpsed the golden glow in the doorway. Jeremy blinked and then squinted to get a better look. A child stood in his bedroom doorway!

The kid was wearing an absolutely radiant cosplay outfit; shiny emerald armor, a dark green cloak with ornate gold trim. His small, gloved hands moved slowly as he removed the hood, revealing his child-like face and... pointed ears? His pale skin and long blond hair starkly clashed with the brilliance of his chest plate. Around his waist he wore a gold belt that held a sheathed dagger and a few pouches. His armored boots were knee high with the tip of the toe curling upward to a distinct point. Beneath the cloak, he carried a small satchel that hung at his right side.

Jeremy awkwardly and slowly stood up.

After the initial shock, Jeremy relaxed and smiled curiously. He just couldn't escape it. No matter where he went, children sought him out. But this was the first time an under-aged LARPer had broken into his apartment!

"What the he... heck are you doin' kid!? Sneaking up on me like that, you could've gotten yourself hurt." Jeremy said.

Jeremy waited for a response, but the boy just stood there staring at him. There was something off about this kid. That glow unnerved Jeremy.

"How'd you know my name? I haven't seen you around here."

"My name is Mercurio." His voice was rather deep for a kid, with an accent Jeremy couldn't quite place.

"Hmmm… interesting name." Jeremy nodded with false interest. "Is that your real name or your LARPer name?" He waited for an answer, but none came. "Well, you gotta go, kid. I don't want your parents worrying about you." He also didn't want the kid's parents to wonder why a stranger had their child in his apartment. That was the last thing he needed. Jeremy placed his hand on the boy's shoulder to escort him to the door. "Cool outfit, by the way. One of your parents make that for you?"

The unmovable visitor, anchored with a strength Jeremy didn't expect, looked up at him. The boy's aquamarine eyes pierced into Jeremy with an urgency and intensity that sent shivers down his spine. "This is going to seem a bit strange to you. But what I've come to tell you is very important. I am no child. I'm an elf, and I've traveled a long way to speak with you."

Jeremy laughed awkwardly. "Wow, kid, you're um, good at this. And I'd love to LARP with you now, but I think we should find your parents first." He tried to steer the boy around. Jeremy stumbled forward out of the bedroom doorway and braced himself against the hallway wall.

What just happened?

Jeremy turned around, and the boy was no longer in the doorway. The kid was just… he was just there. In a blink, he was gone.

Jeremy peered around the hallway, looking to see if the boy had run into the living room. Nothing.

Strange.

When he turned around, he saw the kid sitting on top of his desk, legs crossed at the ankle and dangling from the edge. Before Jeremy could react, the visitor spoke.

"I'm not here to play games, Jeremy. I have something I want to tell you."

"Uh… way… what? Wait… how'd you do that?"

"I told you. I'm an elf. Now—"

"Wait? I… um… this is crazy!"

"Jeremy, I'm going to be very forthright with you, and you need to listen. I am an Elven Guardian. I am actually here to—"

Jeremy felt that familiar warmth come over him, the kind he

got when he was angry and nervous at the same time. He raised his hands in protest, shaking his head. "Wait… kid, you're not getting what I'm saying… you need to go, now."

"Jeremy, I know this is difficult. Please give me a chance to explain. I think things will be made clearer once you hear what I have to say."

Jeremy slumped onto the bed, rubbing his forehead with one hand and using the other to brace himself. He took a deep breath.

"I'm here because the world has a great need for you." The boy said.

"Man kid, you're good. And this could be fun. But I don't know you or your parents. You really need to go." He leaned forward and pointed at the door.

The kid raised an eyebrow.

Jeremy sighed. "Ok, I'll play along. But just for a few minutes, and then you have to leave." Jeremy smiled, waiting for the would-be-elf to speak.

"Do you remember the first time you wanted to be a teacher?"

"Yeah." Jeremy hesitated, wondering where this strange conversation was growing. "My friends talked me into it because I was so good with kids. I've always known I wanted to work with kids. I just didn't think I could be a teacher."

"And you have felt this way all of your life." Mercurio stated matter-of-factly.

"Yeah. I guess I was about fourteen when I first started to realize I was good with kids. They just seemed to flock around me all the time. I was the only male babysitter I knew."

"See, your gift is with children. You have a bond with them that no one else does. When you look at a child, you see their wonder, their potential, their purity. And you want to preserve that, don't you?" Mercurio said without waiting for Jeremy to answer. "And when a child looks at you, they see something they can only explain as wonder. They're drawn to you. They can see your true heart."

Jeremy stared at the boy. This was getting weird.

The boy reached into his satchel and removed a palm-sized

blue crystal set in a gold disk. It glowed a bluish light that shimmered and transformed into an image.

Jeremy's eyes widened and his mouth gaped as the image moved.

It was Jeremy, when he was fourteen, babysitting twins. The image disappeared and Jeremy found himself there in that moment. He chased after the twin boys as they giggled. He backed them into a corner, and they charged at him, giving him the biggest hug. Then Jeremy was back in his bedroom again. He stood there, slightly disoriented, with his arms wrapped around himself. He shook his head and took a breath to steady himself.

Whoa! "Dude. How… How'd you do that?" Jeremy stammered.

The image shifted. Jeremy was a little older and a counselor at the Campus Day Camp in Alpine, New Jersey. No longer an image, Jeremy found himself there again. Kids of all ages gathered around, clamoring and begging Mr. Hodes, the Camp Director, to let them be in Jeremy's group. Emotions flooded over him. Happiness. Overwhelming happiness.

The emotions slipped away faster than they came, replaced by feelings of disorientation as he found himself back in his bedroom. The light swirled, and the image shifted again.

Jeremy, now seventeen, found himself in Tibbetts Brook Park with his old friends. He hadn't seen these guys in years.

As they walked, two little boys ran up to Jeremy. They must have been four and six. The older boy grabbed Jeremy by the hand and asked him to help them. Their ball had gotten stuck in a tree. Jeremy's friends looked at him, puzzled. Out of all the people in the park, why had these children chosen him to help them?

The image dissolved to an intense light, shifting to another time in Jeremy's life. Now eighteen, he sat at the kitchen table studying for his college math class. His parents were both at work. Jeremy took a swig of his Mountain Dew and got up to go to the bathroom.

Not this day. Jeremy wanted to turn away from this image… this memory. The warmth he felt from the joy of revisiting his youth quickly turned cold. This needed to end now. But he was helpless to stop it. He was trapped within his younger self. He shivered, wanting to stop himself from going into the bathroom. He knew what he'd find in there, and he didn't want to relive this again. But he couldn't stop. He was there and not there. Here in this moment, unaware of what was about to happen, yet completely aware. Nausea gripped him.

"No!" A strangled cry escaped his lips.

Younger Jeremy walked down the hallway to the bathroom. Older Jeremy, trapped within his younger self, pressed his hand firmly against his mouth as tears trickled down his cheek.

The bathroom door appeared. The faint sound of muffled music grew louder with each step; Elvis Presley singing "Jailhouse Rock." Younger Jeremy knocked. There was no answer. He knocked again. Still no answer.

No! Don't open it! He pleaded, but his younger conscious couldn't hear him.

Younger Jeremy tried to push the door open. It wouldn't budge. He pushed again. It opened slightly before it met with resistance. Elvis sang the final refrain as young Jeremy pushed on the door.

Older Jeremy wanted to scream, to do anything to not relive this singular moment of horror, but silence gripped him.

Younger Jeremy pushed a little harder against whatever was blocking the door. It slid with some resistance to open enough for him to get in. He craned his neck through the opening.

On the floor lay his thirteen-year-old sister; motionless, eyes closed.

"Ashley!" She didn't respond. "Ashley!"

He shook her, but there was still no response. Her skin, cold and clammy against Jeremy's warm palm. Jeremy knew what to do. He knew CPR. But Jeremy couldn't think. All he could do was scream for help. None came. Fighting the paralyzing pull of anguish, he forced himself away from his sister and ran to the phone to call "911".

The scene faded. Jeremy's tear-filled eyes opened to see the would-be-elf standing there with his palm closed.

Jeremy gasped and stepped backward until he felt his bed. He sat down, removing his glasses and wiping his eyes.

The boy slid the gold disk back into his satchel and slid off the computer desk. He walked up to Jeremy.

Jeremy didn't need the disk to remember the rest. There'd been nothing the doctors could do. Ashley never regained consciousness. Her organs failed, and she died in the hospital ten days later.

"Jeremy, hear me. You've wanted to change the world since you were a young man. You've wanted to make a difference in the lives of children since your sister died. You—"

Jeremy's anguish morphed into anger.

"Alright! That's enough… this has gone way too far." Jeremy stood up and reached for the boy's shoulders.

He stepped away, avoiding Jeremy's grasp.

"You blame yourself for not saving your sister… for not being there when no one else was." The boy's voice came from behind Jeremy.

Jeremy spun around, still confused and still angered. The boy now sat on the edge of the bed.

"Stop it! How could you…"

The boy pulled out the crystal disk again. The light shimmered, and a still image of Ashley at age twelve appeared. She smiled. She had a beautiful smile. But Jeremy wished he knew then what he knew now. Her eyes reflected the truth that she lived each day. The sadness she tried to overcome. She hid behind that smile.

"Jeremy, your sister took her own life because she didn't want to live in this world."

Jeremy's legs weakened, and he sank to his knees, sobbing.

"The world was a cold, empty place for her," the boy continued. "She saw no hope."

"But I… I was part of that." Jeremy muttered through sobs. "I treated her so… so badly. All she wanted to do was hang out with me." Jeremy tried to stand up, but only managed to point to the image of his sister. His hands trembled… his vision blurred by tears.

"You were only a child yourself. You didn't know she would take her own life."

"No!" Jeremy yelled, pushing himself up. "I took care of every other kid in that neighborhood!" Jeremy turned away from his sister's image. "But I pushed her away and treated her like crap."

"Jeremy," the boy said, putting the crystal disk away. "You didn't know any better." The elf paused. "But you do now. There are so many people out there today who feel like your sister did. And you can help them."

The statement stung. A hard slap reminding him that he could have helped Ashley.

"Help them? How? How can *I* help them?" Jeremy turned and walked towards the doorway.

The boy followed him and placed his small hand on Jeremy's forearm.

Jeremy stopped.

The boy reached up and gently placed his hand on Jeremy's chest, over his heart. "Your gift," he whispered. "That's why I'm here. I want you to come with me so I can show you how to use your gift to bring hope to the world."

CHAPTER 3
FIRST BLOOD

Everything needed to be perfect. Masaru didn't want to take any chances that something could go wrong tonight. He adjusted his prosthetic, sliding it on the inky black sleeve of his arm stump. He pulled tightly on the strap and secured the limb to his shoulder.

Anticipation swarmed around him. He could feel it in his heart, his breath, and his muscles. Masaru closed his eyes, concentrating on his breathing. He guided each breath with the open palm of his flesh hand, moving it out with every exhalation and back with each inhalation. As his breath slowed, so did his heart rate.

He emptied his mind, focusing only on the katana at his side.

Masaru slid his foot back and placed the weight of his squat body on the opposite leg. With his flesh hand on the sheath of his katana, he pushed the hand guard forward with his thumb, readying the deadly blade. He commanded the jet-black polymer fingers of his right hand to wiggle. The digits twitched mechanically, transitioning into a more natural, fluid movement as he calibrated the prosthetic. He reached for the katana. The polymer fingers glanced past their target, the tips tapping the handle and overreaching. Masaru grunted. His mechanical fingers wiggled again, recalibrating, as he prepared to draw the katana a second time.

"Steady. Again." Turtak's raspy voice, calm and assuring, came from the dark corner of the bedroom.

Masaru breathed in and out, black fingers wiggling. His arm moved in a flash, fingers gripping the hilt. Left hand sliding the sheath backward, right hand bringing the blade forward. The majestic sword sprung from the scabbard as his flesh hand came to meet its mechanical counterpart.

Masaru smiled; his arm now fully calibrated. In these moments, when he drew the blade, his mechanical hand seemed to come fully alive. Blade and arm pulsed together, both inorganic, but a living thing when combined.

"Good." Turtak said. "You are almost ready."

Masaru swung the blade overhead, then down and to the right. The muscles of his upper body rippled, contrasting with the black plastic polymer of the neuroprosthetic that replaced his right arm. The harness to stabilize the prosthetic stretched across his hardened chest, giving Masaru the appearance of a modern-day gladiator. All his life Masaru worked to forge his body to the perfection it was now.

He brought his right leg forward, moved his flesh hand from the hilt back to the scabbard and guided the blade back into its sheath.

"Well done." Turtak said. "You are ready. This night you will spill first blood. Dress. And let us do so."

Turtak's words brought a thin smile to Masaru's lips. After all these years of study and training, he was finally ready.

Masaru dressed in black sweatpants and light black boots made for stealth. As he slipped on his black hooded sweatshirt, his heart pumped faster. He breathed in deeply to steady his heartbeat and savor the excitement to fuel his mission. Raising the hood over his head, Masaru covered the brownish-red hair he had grown out over this past year. His fake-parents didn't like it long, but Turtak encouraged him to grow it out because it was more fitting to the culture of his birth. The finishing touches; a mask to cover his beard, a black glove for his left hand, and thermal goggles to hide his eyes

Masaru didn't need the goggles to see any better. He had abnormally excellent night vision. The goggles were only to hide the telltale blue of his non-Japanese eyes. Finally, he strapped his katana back on his belt.

He looked at himself in the mirror to make any final adjustments. His squat body with its broad shoulders and chest broke all stereotypes of the typical small-framed ninja. He smiled under his mask. *A ninja.* The uniform would serve its purpose for tonight's mission. He'd probably never wear it again. Or maybe he would. He tugged on his belt and adjusted his hood. Masaru liked the way he looked; a menacing shadow that no one would see coming or going.

ON THE ROOFTOP, Masaru glanced out over the city he had called his home for the past fifteen years. The bright lights of Tokyo's Nishi Azabu District left very little shadow at night. He darted from rooftop to rooftop, narrowly avoiding city lights and security cameras.

Masaru stopped on one roof and peered over the edge. The target building was just across the way: a luxurious five story structure with a pool and bar on the roof. He counted ten people. Four men, two in bathing suits. Two well dressed, likely bodyguards. The other six were women in various forms of bathing attire. He wouldn't spill their blood. They were only victims of this corrupt society. Masaru looked down and focused on the back door of the building. In the nightclub on the first floor, his unknowing targets sipped their last drinks and danced their last dance.

Masaru waited, Turtak was here somewhere. He always was, but he never showed himself. Never.

The light bulb outside the doorway glowed, and then it didn't. Light from the windows, rooftops, and streetlamps went dark. His vision quickly adjusted to the darkness. The path to the doorway was clear to him now. Once he was on the ground, Masaru pulled his blade from its sheath and moved toward the back door. Stepping one foot over the other, he reached for the knob and opened the door.

Screaming and shouting emanated from within; some out of panic, others to maintain order. It was sheer chaos. Just as Turtak had planned.

Masaru approached, seeing what his prey could not. Two men and a woman ran down the hallway toward the exit. Masaru stepped to the side. Without hesitation, he swung his blade, slicing into the first man. The ease at which the blade glided through flesh and bone surprised him. He knew the katana was the work of a master artisan, but no amount of training had prepared him for this. Masaru's heart pumped with exhilaration. First blood had been spilled. And an evil man had been laid waste.

As the body slumped to the floor, another man ran past him. Masaru swung the blade overhead, turned, and lunged at the man, slicing down and to the left. The blade cut through the man's neck. His head rolled backwards as his body moved forward, falling to the ground.

The woman stumbled and yelped as she felt the blood splatter onto her. She grabbed the wall and rushed toward the back door.

Masaru let her pass. He moved forward, hearing the panic from within.

A man shouted for everyone to calm down. He barked orders for someone to find out what was going on and to get the lights turned on. Two more men came down the hall toward Masaru. A slice to the left felled one. A slice to the right, another. More blood spilled.

———

MASARU RETURNED TO HIS BEDROOM. Silence filled the house. His fake-parents slept in their room, unaware of his nighttime excursion. He removed his goggles and turned the lights on. He couldn't see the blood that soaked into his black clothing, though he could feel its sticky warmth pasting the cloth to his skin.

He removed his katana from its sheath. There was still blood on it. He'd missed a spot when he quickly cleaned it on the rooftop. Turtak wouldn't be happy with his negligence. Masaru didn't want to worry about that now. He was still filled with the thrill of tonight's exercise. No, it wasn't an exercise. This was as real as it could be. He'd taken the first big step to reaching his goal, to fulfill his destiny. Masaru examined his blade, running the fingers of his flesh hand along its razor-sharp edge. He then raised the sword and studied it, moving his gaze from his hand to the blade. Masaru smiled. His first kill. With his hands and his blade, he had taken twenty lives. It wasn't difficult. He knew it wouldn't be. Turtak told him so. He was always right.

"You have done well Masaru." Turtak said. His voice came from somewhere across the room. There was pride in Turtak's voice.

Masaru *had* done well. He smiled, proud of his accomplishment.

"Now, clean your blade properly." The unseen voice chided; the pride gone. "And be sure to clean all the blood left in the scabbard."

Masaru smirked, raising his eyebrows. He pulled out his kit to clean his blade and laughed. Nothing could dull the excitement surging through his body. He had taken the lives of evil men for the first time, and he relished every second of it.

CHAPTER 4

THE MACHINATIONS OF GOBLINS

"The goblins are a duplicitous kind. They can only see their own glory, but they cannot see a world in which all species help one another to prosper."

~ From *The Veiled Happenlore of the Master Construct* compiled by Fulbert Gisilfrid, a Chronicler of the Master Construct, Third Order, an alfargnym of Unterbaum.

High atop the Andes, on a mountain terrace overlooking the jungle, Qannu, the Lord of War, observed the setting sun, but found no solace in it. *Unbind you, Borahsh!* he thought, gritting his teeth and swatting at a stray mosquito. *Why has it come to this?* The goblin warlord sighed. Their empire lay in a state of ruin the likes of which his people have never known. All due to the actions of their ruler. Once a great champion of the Goblin Empire, the formerly mighty and bold Sar Borahsh, now sat on his throne as a corpulent mass of festering flesh.

Borahsh. I would have followed you anywhere. Qannu thought. *But now, instead of leading our people, you spend your days eating, drinking, and plotting revenge.*

Qannu reached for one of the tanned ears that hung from the thin gold chain around his neck. His fingers landed on an elf's ear. He rubbed the leathery prize, remembering those days of glory when he and Borahsh hunted together. But how long had it been? Decades since his people hunted. Many of the soldiers under his command did not wear a prestige necklace. How unfortunate for them to not know the thrill of pursuing the blight and their pitiable allies.

In his lifetime, Qannu had collected seventeen ears; seven elf, five alfargnym, two faun and three human. Borahsh had a similar necklace comprising nine ears; six elf, two alfargnym, and one human.

Perhaps, had Borahsh been able to collect the one ear he desired most, the empire would have risen to glory again. It was that singular elf that consumed Borahsh. Knowing his enemy was still out there drove him mad, and he slaked his desire for vengeance with food and drink. Borahsh was a disgusting and pitiful excuse for a ruler! Qannu gritted his teeth again. This century, under Borahsh's rule, the goblin empire declined more than any war or the tragedy of the Unbinding. The Unbinding had been their initial downfall; a time so dark and devastating. Without reason, and without foreknowledge, the goblins had lost their ability to harness magic. And the elves knew it. They used it to their advantage and attacked relentlessly, decimating the goblin empire until only a remnant stood in what was now Kurgal. The Sar at the time of the Unbinding did all he could to rebuild and give his people hope. Borahsh did nothing but eat. He was hung up on his glory days and hellbent on revenge. And because he couldn't attain either, he became self-indulgent... even by goblin standards.

Qannu shook his head and sighed. If Borahsh only knew what his people thought of him. They often referred to him as Borahsh the Unwise. Others just called him Borahsh the Stupid, or Borahsh the Fat... or Borahsh the Fat and Stupid. Though none would ever dare to say such things in earshot of the Sar or his Excellencies. Borahsh's iron-gripped rule left no room for open dissent, and his famous rage kept the lesser goblins cowed. His reign may have stalled any progress towards goblin-kind gaining a foothold towards world power, but his desire for revenge and his cunning kept him on the throne.

As the Sar's Lord of War, Qannu had tried to reason with Borahsh. He'd tried to focus him and his Excellencies, to think more globally… to think about how they would regain power. But Borahsh wouldn't listen to reason, and his Excellencies only cared for the power they already had. Qannu kept Borahsh safe on his throne, all the while plotting to one day remove him from it. It was an old tactic, but an effective one. Convince your adversary that he's a friend, and when the time was right, it was easier to kill him.

LIGISH RAN, his fists pounding the cobblestone passage, catapulting him forward. *The message must be delivered swiftly.* This could mean a glorious reward or promotion, but first he would need to inform the warlord and get his blessing.

He approached the stone door, sliding to a stop and slamming his fist on the panel to open it. The stone separated into dozens of smaller stones and formed an opening. Sunlight streamed through and Ligish squinted, but didn't slow down. He pounded his fist to the ground and loped swiftly onto the terrace.

Qannu, the Lord of War stood, hands behind his back, staring over the great mountain's edge. The rain forest below bellowed with the sounds of creatures, great and small, flying and crawling, creeping and clawing, drowning out the buzzing of the mosqui-toes that so frequently enjoyed feeding off his people.

Ligish approached the warlord and straightened to stand upright. He trembled a bit in awe of the warlord, before bowing his head and thumping his chest with one fist. "Qannu, Lord of War, we've received a message from the pukas in New York. Sar Borahsh's prize has pierced the Veil!"

Qannu turned, pushing his cape to the side. "Ah. We knew it would only be a matter of time."

Ligish handed the paper to Qannu.

A mosquito landed on the messenger's hand and he jerked it away as the warlord read the message.

Qannu handed the paper back to Ligish. "Take this to the Sar. Then come back to me."

Ligish bowed and returned to all fours. He ran back inside, closing the stone door behind him. *The Sar! I'm going to deliver a message to the Sar!* His heart pounded. Surely the Unbound were influencing this day in his favor. Everyone knew this was the message that the Sar longed to hear. He couldn't believe that he had the honor of delivering it.

Ligish, heart beating with pride, ran through the majestic halls and chambers carved by the hands of his ancestors, up to the passage that led to the pinnacle of Kurgal, the Hall of the Sar.

As he approached the stairs, the path changed from cobblestone to bricks of gold; known as the Path of Judgment and Redemption, so named because only the Sar had the power to grant one or the other.

His emerald skin, covered in sweat, glinted from the fairy lights along the way. Adrenaline surging through Ligish's veins propelled him up the stairs to the entrance. He stared up at the massive sculpture that surrounded the bronze and iron doors that led to the Hall of the Sar. Hewn by the hands of his predecessors, the sculpture depicted the goblin caste system. The stone taotie on the left represented the warrior caste. The stone naga on the right represented the religious caste. Above them, with its talons resting on the top of the two columns, was the stone dragon; the totem of the goblin royal caste. And below it all, kneeling stone goblins with heads bowed, and outstretched hands holding gold bricks, formed the stairs. Ligish gazed at the kneeling stone goblins, feeling a kindred with them. He too was a servant of the high bloods. His gaze shifted to the two warriors guarding the doors. Encased in ornate bronze-steel armor, they held their polearms at their side, guarding their great and mighty Sar. *I'd make a great warrior.* Ligish thought proudly. He was strong and fast. He took a deep breath and bolted up the stairs.

The warriors opened the massive doors and the brilliance of the Hall of the Sar shone upon him. Illuminated by a series of fairy lamps along its perimeters and amplified by a large, polished metal ring inset into the stone walls, the throne room was as bright as if it were lit by sunlight.

The golden bricks glittered, as did the bronze armor of the twelve warriors that stood reverently along the Path of Judgment and Redemption. The Lord of War chose these warriors, known as the Sar's Fang, to protect the Sar and His Excellencies. They were the empire's mightiest. *Maybe I could be one of them someday?* Ligish thought.

The messenger dared not slow his pace. This was his chance to impress the Sar. Ligish ran down the path, past the Sar's Gallery of Glory; a decorative wall with three glass cases. On display was the Sar's armor, his collection of weapons, and other prizes obtained when he held the title of Lord of War. Ligish heard tales of the Sar's Gallery of Glory and all that it once held; the Great Axe of the Troll King Garg, the Hammer of Thor, the Elven Cloak of Taharlev iyl Orindin, the Sword of Shotef iyl Brid, and several alfargnym artifices. Most of those items were long gone. Some had been used in experiments. They gave others to pukas to be used in service to the Sar. All he knew for certain was that the ring; the one that had earned Sar Borahsh his reputation, must still be on display. Perhaps he'd be given the honor of seeing it?

A wailing moan from Ligish's left caught his attention. *The Sar's Bane.* Ligish shivered, running past the ten seven-foot spikes protruding from the ground.

A lone goblin hung on one pike, moaning in agony. The shaft piercing her abdomen and the cross piece holding her halfway down the pike so that the Sar could watch her suffer. Carved channels in the ground collected her blood to be used in the sages' experiments below. *What must she have done to deserve such punishment?*

Ligish shivered and turned his gaze from her, pushing himself toward his destination.

Three stone stairs, the length of the dais, led to the throne itself. Four more members of the Sar's Fang stood guard at the foot of the stairs. Ligish stopped there, bowed his head, thumped his chest, and looked back up, waiting to be acknowledged. He'd never been so close to the Sar.

A wall of glowing quartz bathed the Sar and his throne in dazzling light. Borahsh, the Sar of the Goblin Empire, sat upon cushions and pillows that lay atop the massive skull of an ancient ally; the long dead dragon Garghmang. Sar Borahsh heaved a great sigh and the red stone eyes of the Sar's pendant sparkled.

Below the throne, to either side of the dragon's snout, Sar Borahsh's Excellencies sat. His Excellency, Alfash, the Sar's adviser to Borahsh's left, slowly stood, rolled his eyes, and opened his mouth to speak.

The doorway to the left of the throne burst open and the delicious smell of roast meat wafted in, exciting the Excellencies into a cacophony of stomping and yelling. They cheered on the servants and hurried them to deliver the food.

Ligish watched as two goblin servants carried a multi-tiered table of food to the throne. The upper tier was the Sar's. It fit perfectly over the dragon skull's snout. The servants moved with a grace and skill that reminded Ligish of the human acrobats he once saw at one of the monitoring stations.

Sar Borahsh scooped up one of the roasted cave birds, clamped his gnarled teeth down on its neck, and ripped its head off. Blood and juices sprayed from the bird carcass as the Sar wrenched the head from the body. He slurped at the delectable bodily fluids, taking more in than his mouth had room for. It splattered on his robes, blending in with the stains left from an earlier meal. He crunched down on the skull and more fluids dribbled from his mouth and onto his royal robes marring them with more grease, blood, saliva.

The Sar took a sloppy swig of his drink, then slammed his

goblet down. He made eye contact with Ligish and cleared his throat to get his Excellencies' attention.

Ligish fought off a chill and waited for the moment he'd be able to deliver this delicious news.

His Excellency Alfash stood up; his robes soiled with food and drink. He was shorter than any goblin Ligish had ever met. But what he lacked in height, he made up for in girth. He continued to chew and use his tongue to collect any further bits of whatever organ of cave bird he was chewing on. When he was content with the job he had done, he sighed and looked at Ligish. "Speak to your Sar, The Great and Mighty Borahsh," Alfash intoned.

Ligish opened his mouth to speak, but two servants who appeared in the left archway distracted him. The servants exchanged wide-eyed glances, and their green complexion turned pallid.

Ligish swallowed and drew in as much air as he could. "Great and Mighty Borahsh. I have news that will be of great interest to you."

"News?" Sar Borahsh said, licking his lips and grabbing his golden, jewel encrusted goblet to take another drink.

"Great and Mighty Borahsh, Sar of the Goblins... the elf, Mercurio, has left the Veil."

The Sar's eyes widened, and liquid spewed from his mouth as he choked. Mead and barely chewed fowl flesh rained down on the table below.

His Excellency, Ubarat, the Sar's other adviser, sprung from his seat and backed away from the table. Borahsh choked a little more, gagging on bits of bird that were still in his mouth. He forcibly spit the remaining chunks out, struggling under his own weight to stand up. The Sar pushed the heavy wooden table away. Two servants rushed out. The table and its contents lunged forward, beginning their descent towards the polished stone of the dais. One servant dove for the platter, another for the goblet. The table slammed on the floor, reverberating through the room. Both servants missed their targets. Plates, goblets, and various other dinnerware clanked as they hit the floor and danced on the dais.

"This is it," Borahsh mumbled as he struggled to stand.

Ligish proudly straightened. He'd done it. He was the goblin that delivered the message that Sar Borahsh longed to hear.

The Sar grabbed the scepter that lay at his side and used it to stagger to his feet, teetering and wavering as he traversed the obstacle of pillows along the narrow brim of the dragon skull's snout.

Two more servants ran in carrying a small staircase. They weaved around their fellow-servants and any falling or already fallen dinner items, darting to the left of His Excellency, Alfash. They quickly placed the stairs against the left side of the skull throne. One servant took her place on the right of the stairs and the other quickly ascended. The servant took Sar Borahsh's hand and helped to steady him as he reached the first rise of the stairs.

Once stable, the Sar pushed his servant away. The servant gracefully tumbled and landed to the left of the staircase. Both stair servants, in unison, raised their arms to support their Sar as he began his lumbered descent. Sar Borahsh grabbed the hand of his servant on the left. In his other hand he clung to his scepter, limping down each rise. When he reached the bottom, he pushed the servant away. The two followed him as the Sar began his walk to the edge of the dais.

"Mercurio!" He limped forward, dragging his right leg, nursing an old wound. He huffed to catch his breath. "Mercurio... I... want... him... dead!" The words took every last breath to belt out. He slammed his scepter on the floor and inhaled. "Send... my best warriors... to bring him... to me!"

CHAPTER 5
HOPE BEYOND THE VEIL

"Hope is the muse of perseverance."
~ An alfargnym proverb

An amalgamation of anguish, disbelief, and shock rattled Jeremy's mind as Mercurio's words echoed through his head. *I want you to come with me so I can show you how to use your gift to bring hope to the world.*

"Hope?" Jeremy asked, removing his hands from his tear-stained face. "Me? I…"

Mercurio laid a comforting hand on Jeremy's forearm.

"Hope is a peculiar thing, Jeremy." Mercurio said. "People, human and elves alike, can find it in the most unlikely places. If they're looking. Sometimes it just takes someone with hope to show them where to look."

"And you expect *me* to show them?" Jeremy asked, still hopelessly puzzled. *What's happening here?* He tried not to think about his sister much. It was too painful. He'd become good at not thinking about her, and now it was all fresh again, like he re-lived that day twelve years ago. He could feel her still warm body in his arms…

the cold tile beneath his bare feet… the sound of the dripping water drowned out by his beating heart and screams for help.

Jeremy heaved a sigh. *Oh Ashley! Why'd you do it?* He knew the answer to that question. He wanted to scream. He wanted to cry again, but most of all he wished the day would just end.

"Ashley…" Jeremy sobbed, bringing his hand up to his face, he pushed under his glasses to wipe his tears. *I did love you. I'm sorry I never showed you I did. I'm sorry.* "I'm sorry." He continued to sob.

"Hope, Jeremy, is very powerful." Mercurio said. "I see that I am going to need to convince you a bit more before we go."

Jeremy shook his head. He wanted to say something, he just didn't know what to say. *What does this elf want with me? Do I really want to know? Did I just acknowledge the fact that I am talking to an elf?*

Jeremy studied Mercurio. That faint glow emanating from the elf's face and hands. A soft, pale, golden glow. *What was that all about?* How could someone who looked like a kid seem so wise? The elf was as tall as one of Jeremy's 4th grade students. He couldn't have been over four and a half feet tall.

"It is strange for me as well, Jeremy." Mercurio said, leaning back on the bed, his legs clasped at the ankles.

Did he just read my mind? Jeremy wondered.

"I, for one, didn't ever think I'd find hope in humanity." Mercurio continued. "I was raised to believe that humans were hope-*less*." He leaned forward, clasping his hands together. Then turned his face to the window. "Humans caused so much damage to the world. We tried to warn them, but they just wouldn't listen."

Jeremy, still numb from this afternoon's experience, found his curiosity piqued. "Warn them about what?"

Mercurio turned again to meet Jeremy's gaze. "The world was once a very different place. My people and others like us. They—"

"Others like you?" Jeremy said, leaning forward in the chair.

"There are many differences between the peoples that live on this world. Among them are my people, the elves. Your people, the humans. There are alfargnym; what you might call gnomes. There are others too, but we haven't the time for that lesson. You'll learn of the many differences another time. However, for now you need to know that the biggest differences between my people and yours are two things; lifespan and what you would call magic. Humans are the most short-lived of the peoples who inhabit this world. Humans also lack access to magic."

"Lack access to magic?" The phrase sounded odd to Jeremy.

"Jeremy," Mercurio sighed and shook his head. "I knew you'd be most curious, but we haven't the time for all your questions. I want you to understand my purpose for coming to you."

This roller coaster of an afternoon exhausted Jeremy. He had so many questions he wanted… *needed* to be answered. But those would have to wait. He resolved to the fact that now all he could do was listen. "All right," Jeremy leaned back in his chair again.

"Centuries ago, there was nothing that divided the people of this world, other than selfishness. We existed and interacted with one another. My people were the first to come to live on this world, yours were the latest. We tried to help humanity avoid the same mistakes we made. Stubborn and selfish, humans persisted to take more than what was theirs and destroy what they didn't understand."

Jeremy shifted forward as the elf told his story. He couldn't help but wonder, how could all of this be going on without his people knowing?

"Jeremy, pay close attention. This is the part you must hear and understand." Mercurio said.

Jeremy snapped out of his mental meandering and nodded.

"When it was clear to us that the humans were on the brink of war, we wanted nothing to do with them and we hid ourselves away. We hid our very lands so that no human would ever be able to find us. And for many centuries, humanity never knew of our existence. But there was one. One human who showed my people that hope existed among your own kind."

Mercurio pulled out his crystal disk once again. It glowed, and the light shimmered. "I'd like to introduce you to him."

Jeremy watched as the light faded until all he saw was darkness.

CHAPTER 6
A SLIVER OF HOPE

"Like all adamu, he could only see with a narrow mind."

~ From *The Gift Giver Chronicles* compiled by Volcdegen Vigdis, a Chronicler of the Master Construct, First Order, an alfargnym of Unterbaum

A.D. 311

Jeremy flailed in the darkness, desperately trying to find something familiar. A horrible stench filled his nostrils, and he brought his hands up to cover his face. His mind swirled; his stomach churned. He pressed harder against his mouth, hoping his lunch wouldn't make its way back up.

Where am I? The sewer? He brought one hand down to feel around in the darkness. He found a damp, stone wall.

Someone groaned not too far from him. Jeremy jumped. His very presence was immediately drawn to the man. An indescribable connection; this man was uncomfortable… frail… tired. Jeremy could *feel* those things emanating from him.

Jeremy's eyes adjusted, aided by the faint light in the distance.

Less than five feet away, a disheveled bearded man on the cold stone floor. Startled, Jeremy backed up to the wall.

The man knelt on calloused knees, head down and arms at his side, palms open; cold and alone in the darkness.

Jeremy somehow knew he was in a prison. This man was a prisoner!

It was an odd feeling of awe and dread at the same time... as if he was in two places at once. He knew this place but had never been here. He knew this man, but he didn't know who he was.

This prison... it used to be filled with people. In his head, Jeremy could see them. They had all, in some way, been comforted by the disheveled prisoner. Then, one by one, they were taken away. Flashes of crying women and children struck Jeremy. Men trying to protect them. Beaten, bloodied, dragged away. Jeremy cringed, grabbing for the wall. And now, all that was left was this man... this poor, bedraggled man. They'd come for him twice, whipping him in the public square, and then returning him to this cell. An example to the others. They wanted to break this man's faith, and when it didn't break, his followers paid the price. Anguish washed over Jeremy, and he and the man shivered at the same time.

Jeremy jerked his head back; memories that were not his own flashed within his mind. Roman soldiers kicked in wooden doors, dragging people from their homes.

Their Emperor, Diocletian, had gone mad and ordered the persecution of anyone who denounced the gods of Rome and followed the one they called the Christ.

Memories that weren't Jeremy's evoked the anguish he shared with the prisoner. He mourned for each person who once occupied this cell. Each day, new Christ-followers were thrown in with the man and others were taken out, never to be seen again. He tried to intervene, to fight back. Sometimes he got in a good punch, but the soldiers were too strong and too many.

But this man had no doubts about what he believed to be true. And he paid dearly for it. They made an example of him, beating him... waiting for him to recant, but the man just would not.

After each beating, they took several other prisoners away.

"Lord, God, spare us. Help your children, please," the lone prisoner prayed as others screamed in nearby cells. He continued to pray even as their wailing turned to silence.

A burst of bright light caused Jeremy to wince. When he opened his eyes, he was no longer in the cell. His eyes were fixed on a mother desperately holding her child. Other men and women stood around; their faces panic stricken. In the distance, multitudes chanted for blood. *This was madness!* Jeremy swallowed and stepped backwards. He shielded his face, but he couldn't drown out the cheers of thousands of people as the soldiers released starving lions. Innocent men, women, and children screamed, clutching their loved ones. Jeremy gasped, holding his arms tightly in front of his face as he continued to step backwards.

"Please make it stop!" He yelled.

A bright light flashed. Jeremy continued to pant. The sound of the crowd changed. They weren't chanting anymore. But he could hear murmuring. Jeremy pulled his arms away from his face and opened his eyes. He was outside. People gathered all around. Roman soldiers surrounded them.

Crack!

Jeremy jumped and spun around. The lone prisoner: his hands bound and tied to a post in the center thrashed as the whip struck him. Jeremy held his hand to his throbbing head and tried to steady his breathing. The whip cracked again and Jeremy simultaneously felt the pain as the whip stung the man's flesh. Jeremy shuddered with each crack of the whip and the fiery pain that followed each stroke.

Flash!

Jeremy jerked as the bright light vanished. He stumbled backwards and felt the familiar damp stone of the cell. He squinted, waiting for his eyes to adjust to the darkness. The putrid smell accosted him again, and he held his hand to his nose and mouth as he searched the cell for the prisoner. The man wasn't here. Jeremy heard footsteps. Torchlight from down the hall slowly illuminated the cell with each footfall. The soldiers carrying the prisoner stopped at the entrance of the cell, hefted the man in and locked the door as the prisoner fell to the ground.

He shivered from fever in the icy darkness. Jeremy wanted to reach out and help him, but he knew that this wasn't real… wasn't the present. It was like the memories he re-experienced of his own life, only now it was someone else's. *Who is this man?* Jeremy, fighting the foul stench of the cell, slowed his breathing and concentrated on the man. The prisoner's feelings, a miasma of anguish and despair and something more. *Hope?* There it was. Despite misery and pain, this man still had hope. The guards thought he'd die; wagered on it. *Why didn't he die? Why wouldn't he just tell them what they wanted to hear?*

After months, the man had lost track of time. The whippings seemed to have gone on forever. And then they stopped. They no longer took him outside. They just beat him here in his cell, every day. They spit on him and commanded him to recant. He'd pray as the soldiers struck him with their clubs. He prayed for them to stop. But they didn't. Not until their breath heaved from the exertion and their clubs became too heavy to raise. *How did this man survive?*

Each day the prisoner wondered if it would be his day to go to the arena. Sometimes he thought the guards were teasing him by bringing him closer to the exit of his cell. Then they'd just dropped him back down and beat him again. *Why?* The man wondered. Some days he wished it could be over. Some days he was tempted to recant. But he couldn't… he wouldn't.

When he prayed, it was mostly for his persecution to end. Though sometimes he remembered to pray for the souls of the soldiers. None were kind to him. He asked his God to deliver them. He understood they were wrong. They'd been led astray by a deranged man who feared that the Christ-followers would one day rise up against him. *Why would they ever do that?* The prisoner wondered. The Christ taught love and peace, not conquest. Diocletian didn't understand. The prisoner didn't pray for the emperor anymore. He could rot in hell.

Footsteps drew Jeremy's attention from the man. *Not again. Not another beating.* Jeremy didn't know how much more of this he could take.

The soldiers stood at the door of the cell. They grabbed the prisoner under his arms and dragged him toward the cell door. Jeremy expected the soldiers to drop him and begin beating him with their clubs. They didn't. The prisoner groaned as they dragged him from the filthy cell. Confused, he struggled to lift his head. The man didn't know exactly how long it had been, but today was the day he had prayed for. His heart beat stronger. Relief was coming, albeit at the mouths of lions. His time of persecution would be over.

The soldiers dragged the prisoner down the corridor, scraping his uncovered feet against the dirty ground. The man's relief of his impending death washed over Jeremy, as did the pain of being dragged through the prison. The prisoner saw the sliver of light streaming through the ceiling grate at the other end of the hall-way. The anticipation of feeling sunlight on his skin caused his heart to flutter more. He was grateful the soldiers hadn't chosen to take him to the lions at night. The sun never shined in his cell. His heart raced.

They dragged him down one more hallway and then the door creaked open. Light! Brilliant, warm, and beautiful sunlight washed in like a wave. The warmth of the sun felt wonderful on the man's skin. Despite the pain, he couldn't help but summon a faint smile. His eyes tightly shut, he wanted to open them, but knew he couldn't yet.

The man breathed in his first taste of fresh air in years; air free of the foul stench of sewage, blood, and unwashed bodies. The simple pleasure caused his eyes to well up. But before he could savor it, the soldiers hefted him up one more time by his arms and tossed him.

"You're free, *Christian,*" one soldier called down with a sneer. "Get out of here." Jeremy sprinted through the door before both guards spun and closed it behind them.

The man lay face down on a cobbled street. Blood from a gash on his forehead ran down the side of his face. Taking a deep breath of the fresh air, the prisoner summoned the remaining strength he had and flopped on his back. The sun seared through his eyelids.

Free? he thought, incredulous, fearing a cruel joke. Jeremy heard the beating of the man's heart hammering in his ears and his stomach churned again.

A nearby blacksmith's hammer rang on an anvil. Jeremy and the prisoner simultaneously flinched. The man struggled to raise a hand as if to ward off the blow his traumatized mind said must come. It didn't come. He took another deep and wondrous breath. He lay still, sun caressing his pale, filthy skin.

Free. Thank you, Lord.

Light surrounded Jeremy again. He quickly drew his arms up to cover his eyes. The light subsided and Jeremy peeked through his arms. He now stood in a room. The former prisoner lay in a bed, his face clean. The pain of his wounds and hunger had forced the man to sleep.

Jeremy gradually unshielded his eyes.

The man stirred, and the aches and pains of his stiffened body rippled through Jeremy. His eyes slowly opened, blinking at the effort it took to examine his surroundings. He took a sluggish, painful look around the small room and was surprised to find himself in a bed. An actual soft bed with warm blankets.

He didn't remember eating, but his stomach was full and his head didn't feel as bad as it did before, though it pained him to move.

The man eased himself out of the bed and shuffled across the room to the windows past Jeremy.

Jeremy marveled at his present circumstances. He knew this was some sort of magic caused by the elf's crystal disc. But it was unlike anything he'd ever experienced. It was one thing to relive your own past, but this was someone else's. He was here in this strange place, centuries before his own birth.

And yet, he knew he really wasn't. He could see, smell, touch and hear everything as if he was really there. And he could feel and experience what this man had experienced. But the logical part of his mind knew that he was still at home sitting on his bed.

The man stood at the window, reveling in his freedom. The sun shined, but the buildings obscured its rays. He could still feel its warmth. *Home!* Not home in his own bed, but in the city he loved. He took another full breath, and smiled, enjoying air, not stale and tainted with the smell of human waste, but the familiar aromas of baking bread, of horses, and the salt of the ocean. All of it, just as he remembered.

He brought his hand to his heart and felt soft, clean cloth. The man looked down to see what he was wearing. A tunic. A clean, soft, white tunic. The rags of the past decade were gone.

He lifted his hands to feel his face. The dried blood was gone, and someone had trimmed his beard. The right side of his face was still swollen, but not nearly as bad as before. It didn't hurt so much to open his eyes. Glancing again out the window, he felt the freedom calling to him. He wondered how many days it had been since he was released. And who had taken him in? *Where were they now?*

He walked outside to the busy streets.

Jeremy followed him.

Joy and pride swelled in the man's heart. This was his city. He looked up at the sky, trying to orient himself. He wanted to go to the town square, to the church.

Though the people were busy, several stopped and gasped, holding their hands to their mouths. Others tilted their heads as if struggling to recognize him. The man gave them no time to greet him. There was something not quite right about the city. Sure, there were many changes, but something disturbed him.

Making his way down the streets, he took it all in. The buildings... the people. Much had changed, but much remained the same. He was home and he couldn't be more excited. The man approached the center of town and froze. His brow tightened and his nostrils flared. He stood in front of a building where his church once stood. In its place was a new building, a temple, but it was not to his God. They had dedicated it to another.

An angry wave of heat pulsed through Jeremy's body.

The man stared up at the temple, clenching his fists. His jaw tightened.

A woman stopped next to the man. Her eyes grew wide and she brought her free hand to her face. "Confessor!" she gasped.

A man next to her stopped with the same incredulity. "Is it really him?"

The passersby stopped one by one, all with the same look of shocked recognition. A crowd gathered around the former prisoner.

"Nikolaos?" A woman said.

Faint recognition flickered in the man's mind.

Murmurs grew in volume. The man turned from the temple to the gathering crowd.

"Nikolaos! Bishop Nikolaos has returned home!" Someone shouted.

CHAPTER 7
TO HELL'S FIRE

A.D. 311

Nikolaos? Jeremy fixated on the name as another flash disoriented him. His eyes opened and he found himself in the familiar town square. The bright sun turned dim, shifting lower in the sky. Dozens of people gathered here. The square had been decorated for a celebration with lanterns and streamers. Tables were placed along its perimeter, set with delicacies of food and drink. Musicians played merry songs. People passed pitchers of wine. Others danced. *Myra…* he knew this city. No. Jeremy didn't know it. The man… Nikolaos knew the city… his city. *Nikolaos? Myra? No! It couldn't be!*

A strange notion tugged at Jeremy's conscience, drawing him directly to Nikolaos. The man's weary body called for rest. He walked through the crowd of merrymakers, each one patting him on the back and smiling, as he made his way to the side to sit at a small table. Jeremy followed him, feeling the man's rage from within; all directed at the pagan temple that stood where his old church once did. There was no place to escape its view, so Nikolaos sat alone in the shadow of the Temple of Artemis. He seethed with anger and disappointment, withdrawing to a place of comfort as he prayed for guidance.

God, what am I to do? He wondered. His home, their place of worship, had been destroyed. And in its place was a temple of the enemy.

The townsfolk didn't know how Nikolaos felt. They were only glad to have their friend back among them. Even the priests of Artemis were there celebrating Nikolaos' return.

Nikolaos clenched his fists and gritted his teeth. A wave of heat washed over Jeremy and he could literally feel the man's rage.

Fools, the bishop thought.

Jeremy shivered. That odd sensation of bilocation sat uneasily with him. This was another human being. His private thoughts and feelings. It didn't feel right.

"Mercurio!" Jeremy said, stepping back, and jerking his hands to his mouth. Could Nikolaos hear him? The man didn't react. He just angrily stared at the temple and Jeremy heard his thoughts again. *Do they think I'll sit idly by and watch as the people of Myra worship demons?*

"Mercurio?" Jeremy said again. "I don't want to be here. I don't want to see this anymore," he said, stepping backwards and looking left and right for some way to exit.

Jeremy, just relax and watch. Mercurio whispered in Jeremy's head.

"This doesn't feel right. I'm intruding on this man's thoughts. And I don't feel safe in here knowing my body's out there."

There is still much for you to see. Mercurio said.

Jeremy sighed and focused his attention back on the man. *Fine.*

Nikolaos shifted his eyes from the temple to the crowd, and his expression softened. Empathy… care… compassion for the towns-folk slowly seeped in. Today, for the sake of the people he loved, Nikolaos resolved to celebrate with them. He would *not* let that temple be a constant reminder that his people had turned their hearts to a false god.

Tomorrow, however, would be a day the priests of Artemis would never forget.

Jeremy studied Nikolaos as he watched the townsfolk.

This man was Saint Nikolaos. The legend. Or was he? Jeremy still wasn't sure how any of this was relevant. He was nothing like Jeremy had ever read or imagined. Jeremy stood several inches taller than Nikolaos. His skin, though paled from years of impris-onment, had a ruddy hue that would have hidden any rosy cheeks. The only thing remotely similar to stories he heard as a kid was Nikolaos' graying beard. To be fair, the man had spent the last ten years in prison being beaten and eating slop, but still, Jeremy found it hard to imagine this man being the legend he had loved as a child.

Another pang of concern from Nikolaos disrupted Jeremy's study of the man.

With no church, Nikolaos no longer had a home. The man wondered how they would ever rebuild. *Lord, I know not what to do.*

An elderly man with a cane hobbled over to the table, inter-rupting Nikolaos' melancholy prayer. The man said nothing. He hefted a small pouch onto the table. Coins jingled as his aged fingers pushed it toward Nikolaos. He looked up at the gray-haired man smiling at him.

"Ovidius?" Nikolaos said.

"I always knew it was you, Bishop," the elderly man said.

Nikolaos raised an eyebrow.

"This is rightfully yours. Please take it."

Nikolaos carefully opened the pouch and silver coins slid out. More than Jeremy cared to count.

"Ovidius I—"

"Bishop, please use this to help build our new church. Besides, I know you gave it to me and my daughters, never expecting a return."

"Ovidius, thank you. But I—"

"Bishop, what you did for my family those many years ago I could never repay." The old man removed his hat and wrung it in his hands. His nose wrinkled, and he continued. "My eldest daughter and her husband care for me in my old age. We live here in Myra now." Ovidius paused again, tears forming. His voice now strained. "Bishop, I have grandchildren. I never thought… If it weren't for your kindness, we'd be dead."

Before Nikolaos could reply, others came. They too placed sacks of coins on the table. Each one thanked him for some act of kindness Nikolaos had long forgotten. The crowd gathered round him soon overshadowed the Temple of Artemis. Their actions quelled his melancholy, and Jeremy felt hope pushing its way into Nikolaos' heart.

Those who had turned away from the church, reminded of the love and kindness shown to them by their bishop, had returned.

Jeremy blinked as another flash disoriented him. He pushed his fingers under his glasses and rubbed his eyes to adjust. A wave of images cluttered his mind, as if he were quickly flipping through the pictures on his cell phone. Nikolaos and his people rebuilt the church in Myra. The scars on his face healed. Dressed in the red robes of his office as Bishop, he stood outside the Temple of Artemis, preaching against its pagan ways. He loved the people of Myra, but his time in prison had hardened him. He was less tolerant of those who didn't follow his God. And to his dismay, many people in Myra had strayed away from the true faith.

The Temple of Artemis was a constant reminder of his time in prison. He was furious that they had allowed this place of pagan worship in his city. It wasn't the only place of false worship in Myra. Smaller temples and shrines were in operation. People wore amulets they claimed were magical. Others had even taken to bringing statues and other idols into their homes. Nikolaos declared war from the pulpit and took to the streets, preaching and praying against those who worshiped the false gods. His primary target had been the priests and followers of Artemis. Once they fell, the others wouldn't be far behind.

A flash of golden light replaced the onslaught of images. Jeremy found himself floating… above the city! Below him, the city of Myra shook and people scattered.

Waves, large and fearsome, pounded the shipping port. The rocky hillside the city sat upon crumbled, destroying many homes and warehouses below. The Temple of Artemis crumbled from the might of the shaking earth.

Nikolaos rushed through the city, pulling survivors from the rubble and giving aid to those who had suffered.

A flash and Jeremy stood in Nikolaos' church. Survivors, in various states of confusion and need for medical attention, lay out on blankets in the sanctuary.

Nikolaos sat with an injured farmer, holding his hand, and praying over him. A woman, sitting opposite Nikolaos, used a wet cloth to wipe the blood from the farmer's face.

The church doors creaked open.

Nikolaos looked up from his prayer to see who had entered. He saw Hekataios and Damasos, the two surviving priests of Artemis.

They approached him, pensive and nervous. The three men met in the center of the church. Before Nikolaos could speak, Hekataios put up a submissive hand.

"Nikolaos, we have no place to go."

Nikolaos' scowl only grew tighter. Years of torture at the hands of those that worshiped false gods caused his face to tighten into a snarl. He reached out, grabbing the scruff of Hekataios' robe in his left hand, and that of Damasos' in his right. Nikolaos spun the two men around and dragged them back to the door, throwing them both out onto the street.

"Go to hell's fire," Nikolaos muttered, "which has been lit for you by the Devil himself!" He slammed the door and turned to go back to the others who needed help.

Jeremy's jaw dropped. This was the man that was going to show him how to bring hope to the world?

CHAPTER 8

THE LESSONS BEGIN

"The alfargnym seem more intelligent and more adept with magic than the dweorg. Though, they are both equally erroneous in their odd beliefs, believing in that which they cannot see or possibly know. They claim that a being called Odin created them and made the mountains for them."

~ From *The Annals of Meital iyl Sayalla*, 1st Lore Keeper of Sayalla

Masaru couldn't sleep. How could he? Twelve years… no, more like all twenty years of his life had been devoted to preparing him for this. Tonight had only been a step, but it was a big one. He had perfectly executed all his training in a real-life mission. How could he sleep after all that?

Turtak assured him he needed to rest because they still had more work to do. When he finally fell asleep, his stomach woke him a few hours later. *Bacon.* Betrayed by his nose, Masaru gave in to his stomach's persistent groans and he crawled out of bed.

After strapping on his prosthetic arm, he calibrated it by trying to pick up a marble from his desk. He only needed two tries before it was fully calibrated. Masaru pulled on a pair of plaid pajama pants and an Imagine Dragons t-shirt. He followed his nose to the dining room.

His fake-parents sat at the table, while Sora, their maid, cooked breakfast in the kitchen. Will had his nose in *The Japan Times*. Val stared at the TV in the other room before noticing Masaru walk in.

"Ru." Said his fake-mother, getting up from her seat. "Good morning." She leaned down, wrapping her arms around him to give him a hug. Japanese people didn't hug much, and he liked it that way. He wished the Hagens had adopted that custom.

His fake-father looked up and smiled at him.

"Sora-san!" He yelled into the kitchen. "Masaru is awake and ready to eat."

These people tried. They were good parents. But they weren't really his parents. They knew nothing about who he really was.

Masaru sat down after halfheartedly returning Val's hug.

"So, what are we up to today?" Will asked.

"Camping, remember?"

"Yeah. That's right. What time are you meeting the guys?"

There were no guys. He told his parents that he wanted to go on a camping trip with his friends to celebrate his twentieth birthday. He didn't really have any friends. Masaru was the short white kid with one arm. Some shunned him altogether. Others made fun of him. And a small few pitied him. Goro fit into the latter category. He didn't want Goro's pity. Just his alibi.

Masaru didn't know when his actual birthday was. But the Hagens always celebrated it on the day they had found him. He'd been adopted by William and Val Hagen, Americans with Scandinavian roots, living in Japan. The Hagens found Masaru wrapped in cloth and freezing to death in the Koli National Park in Finland. He couldn't have been more than a few weeks old. After almost two years of paperwork and red tape, they were able to adopt him.

Will and his business partner, Hitoshi Sano, started a small robotics company in Japan. Fresh out of college, Will graduated from M.I.T. where he met Hitoshi. With the help of Hitoshi's parents, they created NovaSan Robotics.

Will placed his hand on Masaru's jet-black prosthetic. Artificial nerve receptors registered the touch to Masaru's brain.

"How's this design working for you?" Will asked.

"Good." Masaru grabbed for a fork, tensing the muscles above his stump and sending the impulses to the prosthetic. "Works real well." He flashed a disingenuous smile at Will.

When the Hagens adopted Masaru, Will started a division of NovaSan dedicated to prosthetics. Masaru wore the latest and most advanced neuroprosthetic arm NovaSan designed. Will boasted that it was the most advanced in the world. They worked with doctors to develop a neuro-synaptic implant that felt more realistic to the user. Masaru had this model for about a year now, and he'd learned to control it well. Will's team was very impressed with his progress.

"The next update, we'll get a coat of artificial flesh on there so it won't stand out so much." Will said.

Masaru nodded his head, hiding his disinterest. He didn't want to hide his prosthetic arm. It intimidated people, and he liked that.

The news report on the twenty-inch screen sitting in the next room caught Masaru's attention. "Dad, turn this up."

Will looked at him, cocking an eyebrow.

"Please," Masaru added.

Will grabbed the remote from beside his plate and turned the volume up.

A female reporter stood outside the building Masaru had infiltrated last night. Police cars and a border of police tape stood behind her.

"… at least twenty dead. All men." Said the reporter. "Several witnesses escaped unharmed. And we're told that none of them saw what happened. Authorities are not saying, but there's quite a bit of speculation that a much-anticipated Yakuza war between the Yamaguchi-gumi and Sumiyoshi-ka has escalated."

"Oh my!" Val interrupted. "That's not too far from here."

"No," Will agreed. "It's not." He sighed. "I'm gonna talk to Hitoshi. It may be a good time to move the company to the U.S."

"You're just trading one problem for another, Hon," Val said.

Sora emerged from the kitchen holding a plate of eggs, bacon, home fries and toast.

"Masaru-kun! Here is breakfast for growing boy!" She smiled as she laid the plate down.

Growing boy? Masaru hadn't gained an inch in more than two years. He'd always been shorter than any of the other kids. He'd been 4'5" since he was sixteen. Somehow, Sora thought he'd still grow.

Sora had been with the Hagen family before Masaru was adopted. She was like a grandmother to him. Her own family died in the aftermath of the economic crisis of the nineties. Sora was "rescued" by the Hagen family and given a room and salary.

As fond as he was of Sora, Masaru didn't even look at the plump old Japanese woman. His eyes were glued to the screen. He had inadvertently made the news. His work had been attributed to a gang war. No matter. He didn't need to be credited for the spilling of blood in the eyes of man. Last night's adventure was merely an exercise in killing. He needed to know what it would feel like to stab his sword into a man knowing that it was by his will, by his muscle, that they would breathe their last breaths. Turtak's words prepared him.

"Life cannot be taken with hesitation. Your mind must be clear of doubt. And once the death of your enemy comes by your own hand, you must have no remorse. For life to advance, life must be taken."

The Yakuza Masaru killed last night weren't innocent. They too had spilled blood. They had taken lives, but only to advance their own. Masaru wouldn't do the same. He wouldn't claim his birthright out of selfish pride or advancement. No. He wouldn't be like those in power who did what they did for only themselves.

The world would know the steel of his blade, but only because they needed to know. They needed their eyes opened. They—

Sora tapped him on the shoulder. "Masaru-kun! Eat."

He turned his gaze from the TV and looked at her. Her face was so wrinkled you couldn't tell which lines were from age or from that kindly smile she always had.

She reached out and ruffled his beard. "And when you going to shave this thing? You look like old man." Sora laughed.

Masaru attempted a halfhearted smile and returned his attention to his breakfast.

"TAKE ONLY WHAT YOU NEED. The journey is long." Turtak said from the shadows. "Once the Hagens realize you are not coming back, they will cut off your credit card. Travel lightly. Get money as often as you can."

Masaru trusted Turtak more than anyone. The Hagens served a purpose, but the unseen voice was the one Masaru followed. He knew Turtak was real. His tone and inflection were different from Masaru's own inner and spoken voice. It was an audible voice that always spoke from somewhere in the shadows, but only when Masaru was alone. They had their own secret language. The voice had been there ever since he could remember. Masaru once told the Hagens about the voice. They were concerned but excused it as an imaginary friend.

"They could not possibly understand." Turtak told him when he was eight years old. "They are not your real parents." He frequently reminded Masaru of that fact ever since he could remember. When he was five, his parents had the adoption talk with him, and they confirmed what the unseen voice had already told him.

When he was ten, Masaru asked questions about why he couldn't see Turtak.

"Your life with the Hagens will be brief." Turtak said. "You have a destiny that far exceeds anything the Hagens can offer you.

I will be with you beyond your life here. But for now, I must only be a shadow. One day, I will reveal myself to you. When I do, you will know it is the day you will fulfill your destiny."

Masaru packed lightly with only a change of clothes and a few essentials. He knew that once he left, the only things he'd have of his old life would be the ever-present voice of Turtak and his katana.

Hamayoshi Sensei taught him how to use the blade, but it was Turtak who taught him to master it. Masaru had worked with Hamayoshi Sensei since he was eight years old. He wanted to start earlier. An obsession imposed by Turtak, Masaru begged Will to find him a kenjutsu teacher. However, Hamayoshi Sensei would not take him until he was eight. Will offered him extra money to start at six. Hamayoshi Sensei wouldn't be bought, and Turtak became his true master. He taught Masaru the basics and had him prepare his body to wield the katana; a task that was difficult with a prosthetic arm. Masaru was determined, and he learned to wield the blade using five different prosthetics. Each new one would force him to re-learn each technique. Each time, Turtak pushed him to train harder and faster.

Hamayoshi Sensei began his formal training in *Shin Munin Ryu* when Masaru was eight. From Sensei he learned the katana and several other weapons. He also learned several unarmed fighting and defensive techniques. It was Turtak who took his training to a higher level. He taught Masaru other ways to fight, to sneak silently, to hide within the shadows. Turtak made him a powerful warrior. No one else knew this. But everyone would soon know. Every aspect of his life had been carefully orchestrated so that he could one day claim his birthright.

Masaru finished packing the last of his gear. He had two bags. One, a knapsack with all the essentials he would need for survival. The other, a duffel containing only his sleeping bag and his katana. Once he made it to the mountains, he'd rearrange everything and move his katana to its rightful place at his side.

The goodbye had been more emotional than Masaru had expected. The Hagens hugged him, told him to be safe, and said they'd see him in a few weeks. They would not. This was a permanent goodbye they were unaware of. The next time they saw him, he'd likely be on television. He imagined the shock on their faces once they realized it was him. As doubt and feelings of loss stirred in him, Masaru gently pushed Val away. He couldn't worry about the Hagens. His time with them had come to an end.

CHAPTER 9
CONTRADICTION AND CONFLICT

"Nikolaos delighted in their laughter, marveled at their innocence, and was saddened by their misfortune. He'd sit for hours and watch the children as they played around the fountain in the public square."

~ From *The Gift Giver Chronicles* compiled by Volcdegen Vigdis, a Chronicler of the Master Construct, First Order, an alfargnym of Unterbaum

The flash of the crystal disk sent Jeremy's mind swirling. Head spinning, nausea overtaking his stomach, Jeremy stepped backward and sat on his bed.

Mercurio stared up at him; chin and eyebrow raised as if he were checking to see if Jeremy would say or do something.

All Jeremy wanted was some Tylenol. The familiar surroundings of his bedroom didn't ease the discomfort of his head and stomach. "What are you trying to do to me?" Jeremy said.

"I'm trying to give you some context to why I'm here and why I believe your particular magical gifting will be useful."

"But I don't get it." Jeremy removed his glasses and massaged his forehead, trying to ease his headache. "You're showing me… no, you're taking me into the life of this man who's so bitter he threw two people out in the street because they didn't believe same as him. He's a hypocrite! How is this even relevant?"

"Your people also call this man Santa Claus." Mercurio said.

"Eh, well… no, technically not. Santa is based, very loosely based, on this guy. But I guess that depends on the culture."

"You believe you know much of Nikolaos, do you?" Mercurio said, crossing his arms and staring up at Jeremy.

"Well, yeah. Every year I do 'Christmas Around the World' with my class. We start on December 6th, which is Saint Nicholas Day, and we start with some German traditions. I have the kids put their shoes in the hallway and then Mr. Albert, the janitor, comes by sometime during the day jingling his keys and putting oranges in the kids' shoes. My students love it. Then each day after that we do a different tradition."

Mercurio smiled fondly, as if he'd been reminded of something long forgotten. "Nikolaos' story didn't end where we left off. There's much more you need to know."

"Please. My head is killing me. Can't you just tell me the rest?"

"Would you truly believe me if I told you? Would it not be better to see for yourself?"

Jeremy sighed and grabbed his head. "At this point, I think I'd believe anything. But, I guess I'd like to see for myself. Isn't there a way to not do that flashy thing?"

"No. I had not suspected the mimstone would have this effect on you. But I could make the transition easier with healing magic. May I put my hands upon your head?" Mercurio asked.

Jeremy laughed a little inside. What an odd question. But it certainly fit the strange events of the day. "Sure. If it'll help."

"Here, hold the mimstone." Mercurio said, handing him the crystal disk. Mercurio climbed onto the bed and stood behind Jeremy. He placed the tips of his fingers on Jeremy's temples.

"Now close your eyes, listen, and focus on the words." Mercurio said.

Jeremy closed his eyes and gently floated in a void of darkness.

"Time did little to heal the physical and emotional scars that Nikolaos gained during his imprisonment." A kindly, gentle voice much different from Mercurio's spoke in his head. It had a different accent. Jeremy couldn't place it. "Though he had cleansed the City of Myra of those who worshiped other gods, there was always something that angered him. His faith was strong, but his intolerance for those that did not follow his God was strong too."

Faint images of an angry Nikolaos appeared in Jeremy's mind. Nikolaos yelling. Nikolaos arguing; quickly replaced with images of the bishop coming home exhausted and filled with frustration and despair.

"He spent most of his days on the streets of Myra, visiting people, helping them, and sharing stories about the one he called God. On days when he was particularly stressed, he'd sit in the town square and whittle. It became more of a way to ease his nerves and keep his hands busy while he thought. Occasionally children played by the fountain in the square. He came to enjoy listening to them. Their laughter always put a smile on his face."

In his mind's eye, Jeremy saw Nikolaos sitting on the edge of a fountain in the square. Children gathered around him and he smiled, nodding to each child as they approached.

"His duties as the Bishop of Myra often called him away from the people he loved."

The bishop and several others dressed in similar robes sat in a semicircle in the sanctuary of a church. Nikolaos sneered; his eyes glued to one man. Anger, once again, seethed from Nikolaos, penetrating Jeremy's psyche.

The bishop waved for his chance to speak and stood when the council granted him permission.

"The man, Arius, has sinned against our Lord, and we have entertained this sin far too long. We listen as he vomits lies. Our Lord, the Christ, told the Apostles that he and the Father are one! I didn't endure my time in prison for a lie. And I—"

"Bishop Nikolaos," Arius interrupted. His voice dripped with condescension. Sitting three seats down from Nikolaos, the blasphemer stood. "You speak as a man renowned for his preaching and his work in the ministry of Jesus Christ. Yet, may I remind you that we all were imprisoned because—"

Nikolaos slammed his hand against the wooden pew and it echoed through the church. With a clenched fist he dashed toward Arius.

"Bishop, I…" Arius stepped back.

Nikolaos reached up and grabbed the collar of his own robe, tearing it and revealing the scars on his back and chest that he'd received at the hands of his torturers.

Jeremy winced at the sight. The flesh looked as if it had been raked over, being torn up, down, left and right.

"I didn't endure these scars for a mere man! We," Nikolaos raised his voice, pointing at the other clergy gathered around the table. "*We* didn't have our flesh ripped from our backs because we believed that the Christ was just a man!"

Arius stepped backwards as Nikolaos drew closer.

"The Apostle John made it clear when the Christ revealed his own divinity to him. In the beginning was the Word, and the Word was with God and the Word *was* God. Anything more you say of the Christ and who he is, lessens him. If we can't all agree that the Christ is God, then we mock what he has done—"

"What do you mean by 'God'?" Arius said.

"God from God, light from light, true God from true God, begotten not made."

"Bishop, I—

"No more of your lies, Arius! We sit here for weeks debating and discussing what most of us agree to be true. Instead of ministering to the people, we sit here and wag our tongues, letting our ears be tickled by this blasphemer!"

"Bishop, I—" Arius interrupted again and Nikolaos raised his open hand to stop him.

"We must agree on the truth and go back to the business of our Lord."

"Bishop," Arius finally interjected, "I too suffered for my beliefs. I—"

Nikolaos closed his hand into a clenched fist. And with it, he struck Arius in the face, sending the man back into his seat.

The crowd of clergy gasped.

Jeremy stared at Nikolaos. This man was a hypocrite! It was like all the other supposed Christians in the world who said one thing, but did another. People like this were why Jeremy struggled with his own thoughts about God.

Nikolaos turned and straightened his robes as he walked back to his seat. Still standing, he took in a breath to calm himself and then faced his startled peers.

"Let us stand firm now and make our beliefs official as ones united in Christ." Nikolaos said.

Jeremy felt the mimstone pulse in the palm of his hand. Darkness replaced the scene and Jeremy floated in its tranquility with only the other voice guiding him.

"They did not vote that day." The unfamiliar voice of the mimstone said in Jeremy's head. "Instead, Nikolaos was removed and placed in jail again. His name stricken from the official council record, he sat in a cell for weeks until the council concluded. He would have been removed from his office as bishop were it not for his reputation and the love of the people he served. Nikolaos was pardoned for his outburst and given a stern reprimand before being sent home to Myra."

The darkness dissipated, and the hazy view of Nikolaos formed in front of Jeremy. The bishop smiled, happy to be home and ministering to the people of Myra.

"This was where Nikolaos belonged, among his beloved people," the mimstone continued. "Not in meetings debating doctrine. The emotional scars of his persecution and the anger that came from them lessened over the years. He thanked his God for this, but he also thanked his God for the children of Myra. They played a vital role in his healing."

The mimstone pulsed and Jeremy stood in the familiar surroundings of the town square with Nikolaos sitting by the fountain. Children gathered around the bishop. His contemplative expression turned into a smile as he greeted each one by name.

"Nikolaos delighted in their laughter, marveled at their innocence, and was saddened by their misfortune," the mimstone said. "He'd sit for hours and watch the children as they played around the fountain in the public square. His forays there were no longer just a side visit to rest and be contemplative. They became a part of his daily routine. And as those children grew, he served them as adults."

The children laughed and played in the square. Jeremy felt the concern and worry dissipate from Nikolaos. The sounds of the children and the flowing water of the fountain gently massaged away all tension from the man's mind.

Jeremy smiled. "I know where this is going," he said as Nikolaos opened his satchel and produced a small knife and a block of wood. Surrounded by the laughter of children all around him, Nikolaos grinned and worked the wood with his knife.

Jeremy watched with anxious intensity as the bishop's old hands turned the block of wood into an intricate representation of an animal. *A horse?* Jeremy stepped closer, his curiosity mounting. Nikolaos placed his finished creation beside him on the edge of the fountain. It stood on all fours, its elongated neck with flowing mane holding its head up proudly. The detail was magnificent.

A little girl ran up to him. Nikolaos greeted her with a nod and a smile. His eyes seemed to follow hers, peeking down from the corner of his eyes, his smile broadening. He picked up the wooden horse and handed it to the little girl.

Jeremy couldn't see her face, but he felt the rush of joy emanate from her, infecting Nikolaos and causing his spirit to lift more than before.

"This singular event gave Nikolaos an idea," the mimstone said. The image faded into a cloudy haze, replaced by other similar events with Nikolaos and the children. "He began a tradition of giving his carvings to the boys and girls. Sometimes he'd give them directly to the children. Sometimes he'd arrive at the fountain before them and display the carvings in a scene."

The changing images settled on a crowd of children gathered

around Nikolaos. He waved his left hand and directed the children to the carvings he had placed on the side of the fountain. A wooden family and several animals. *A manger scene!* Jeremy recognized the familiar imagery. The only piece missing was that of the baby Jesus.

"The family traveled a long way to the town of Bethlehem." Nikolaos said, pointing to the carvings of Mary and Joseph. "Yet, they could find no place to stay. The inn was full. Thankfully a kindly man allowed them to spend the night in his stables. The woman, named Mary, birthed her child there." Nikolaos brought out his right hand, clenched closed. He opened it, revealing the small carving of a baby.

The children exclaimed with "oohs" and "ahhs", each clamoring to get a good view.

"It was the children!" Jeremy opened his eyes, severing his connection to the mimstone. "They changed Nikolaos."

"Precisely," Mercurio jumped down from the bed and walked to the window. He stood beside it and peeked out through the curtain.

"What's wrong?" Jeremy said.

"I sensed magic. Someone other than us is manipulating magic. I think they're in the structure across from this one, but I'm unsure."

"It could be nothing, right?" Jeremy walked up to the window and peeked out from the opposite side.

"If someone is manipulating magic outside the Veil, it's more likely for no good. I find it suspicious that they chose now to do so. We need to leave."

"What? I still don't understand why. You've shown me a lot of cool stuff, and I'm grateful. But, I still don't understand why you want me to go with you?"

Mercurio exhaled an angry puff of air and glowered at Jeremy. "Samyaza! Why are you being so stubborn?" Mercurio said, closing the blinds.

"Sam who? Stubborn? I'm being stubborn? How is me not wanting to go with a stranger who happens to be an elf, stubborn?

I'm not buying this 'come with me if you want to live' stuff until I know what's going on?" Jeremy walked back to his bed.

"I never said 'come with me if you want to live'. I'm sure whomever it is across the way is more likely looking for me." Mercurio said.

"Looking for you? Why?"

"Jeremy, I'm afraid there is too much to tell you in one day. If you want to know more about Nikolaos, we may continue with the mimstone for now. And then we may leave."

Jeremy stared at the elf, feeling slightly agitated that he was so confident he would go with him.

The notification chime on Jeremy's cell phone dinged and vibrated on the desk.

Mercurio shot an angry stare at the phone.

Jeremy snatched the phone and read the text from his friend, Zelda.

You coming? We got a raid scheduled in fifteen minutes!

He looked at the time: 3:45pm

Oh brother! Now she's scheduling raids for me? Zelda was the last person he needed to deal with right now. If she found out that Jeremy knew a real elf, then she'd be even more infatuated with him! Using his thumbs, he swiftly texted her back. *Not today. I'm busy with something else.*

"Jeremy, I do not wish to rush you, but we've little time for distractions. I'll show you more so that you can understand why I want you to come with me."

Jeremy stared at the elf. All this was just… just crazy. He wasn't about to leave with this guy, but he was willing to see more. "Cool." Jeremy said, switching his phone off and resuming his position on the edge of the bed.

CHAPTER 10

ACQUISITIONS

"Man will sell himself to the highest bidder. I only hope for man's sake, that the kindest ones have the most money."

~ Khodar iyl Juyir, Elven Elder of Juyir,

J ason Jaeger ran up the stairs of the old apartment building, skipping every other step without breaking a sweat and growing more excited with each stride. Tufts, and Decoudreau followed closely behind him. This mission would be the highlight of his career and the catalyst to his retirement. A twelve-year veteran of the Marine Corps, Staff Sergeant Jason Jaeger enlisted as a Basic Reconnaissance Marine and served with the 1st Recon Battalion before his final deployment to Afghanistan with the Marine Special Operations Command. Ambushed in a firefight with Taliban soldiers pretending to be Afghan Police, Jaeger and two of his men were killed in action. At least that was the official story. The unofficial story was something Jaeger still had difficulty wrapping his head around.

He'd woken to find himself in a hospital. An older man with glasses, a long black leather coat and matching fedora stood at his bedside staring down at him with a smug grin. The stranger's hands rested on a beautifully carved off-white walking stick with a gold handle.

"Staff Sergeant Jaeger," the stranger said, still smiling. "I'm going to make you and your men very rich."

That was six years ago. The man, Thaddaios Wyllt, had kept his promise. Under Wyllt's employ they were paid handsomely and promised bonuses with the completion of each mission. Staff Sergeant Jaeger became the leader of Thaddaios Wyllt's Search & Acquire Team.

For six years Jaeger led his men in ops all over the world, chasing down the fantastic, the unbelievable, and the downright strange. They relied on intel from Wyllt's Research Team. At first Jaeger thought Wyllt was just some rich, eccentric loon. His first mission changed all that. Tasked to recover an old staff from a small town in Russia, Jaeger and his men survived a firefight with Russian contractors only to be bested by an old Russian mobster with a staff that brought lightning down on them. It'd been an eye-opening experience for Jaeger. He and his men withdrew before any of them were struck. Jaeger phoned Wyllt to tell him what went down and the man laughed.

"Mr. Jaeger, I see you met Vigo Popov and his big stick. But you forget, you're not playing in the little leagues anymore. You've moved up. You're in the big leagues, and you play for Thaddaios Wyllt now. And when I send a team out to play, I send them out prepared. You Marines are tough, combat hardened warriors. That's why I chose you. But I also understand that you haven't played in the big leagues yet. Despite how you're feeling now, I would've been remiss had I just told you that I'm sending you to retrieve the Khatvanga of Shiva; a magical staff that controls lightning. You wouldn't have believed me. Though, for the amount of money I'm paying you, I'm sure you would've humored me, am I right?" He didn't let Jaeger answer. "So, I made sure you were prepared. When ol' Vigo used the Khatvanga to bring lightning down on you, none of you were struck, correct?" He didn't wait for Jaeger's answer again. "That's because your cammies are custom made for the type of work I hired you to do. They're made from gnome-spun garntier fur and Elven silk. I'm sure you noticed how lightweight they are. Not only are they naturally lightweight, they're also water repellent and fire resistant. Listen to me. I sound like a clothing salesman." He laughed again. "But I digress. The buttons, however, and I hope you feel lucky knowing this, are the last remaining… well, I should say the last known set of Elven anti-dragon buttons. I'm sure that's not what the elves called them. They probably had some fanciful name when they were created thousands of years ago, but nonetheless, I had them added to your cammies, not to protect you from dragons, but to protect you from the elements… acid, fire, lightning, poison, etcetera. You see where I'm going with this? You and your men, Mr. Jaeger, are virtually invulnerable. I say virtually, so it doesn't go to your head and you get any fanciful ideas about betraying me. That would *not* go well for you. Anyway, the Khatvanga is ready for the taking. Just walk up to ol' Vigo and shoot him in the head before you take the Khatvanga from his grubby little hands. He'll know you work for me, and I don't want a petty little war getting in the way of any other acquisitions that might come up."

When Wyllt hung up the phone, Jaeger found himself dumbstruck and conflicted. The boss had just unloaded a whole lot of crazy on him. But it wasn't just the magic mumbo jumbo that caught Jaeger off guard. Jaeger wasn't a cold-blooded murderer. Yeah, the Corps had taught him how to neutralize an enemy. But in the Corps, he fought for his country. He considered himself a patriot. He was willing to die for his country… and he did. That's when the cold, dark truth really hit him. Sure, he knew what he'd gotten himself into when he took Wyllt's deal. He knew his life as a Marine was over. Sure, he boasted with his brothers in arms and said, "Once a Marine, always a Marine." But this was different. How had it been so easy for his country to let him die and be hired by Wyllt? He'd wrestled with those questions for a while now. But that day, hiding in a shack in some rat hole Russian village, it hit him hard. He could've walked away right then and there. He knew Tufts and Decoudreau would've followed and never looked back. He wasn't afraid that Wyllt would retaliate if they just disappeared. This wasn't a fear of death, this was a fear of what he had become… or would become. He could do as Wyllt said and kill Popov. He'd done it before. Long range kills, close-quarter kills, hand-to-hand combat kills. He was no stranger to them. In hindsight, his dilemma seemed silly. He was going to kill a man for a magic stick, and he was going to get paid a lot of money for it.

That day the three Marines learned the truth about who they were. They belonged to Thaddaios Wyllt, and they were unstoppable.

Over the past six years they made a lot of cash flying all over the world and retrieving dozens of items that did some weird stuff; rings that shoot fire, boots that cause a person to move quickly, magic wands, capes of invisibility, gloves that gave the wearer super strength, and so much more. And Wyllt owned it all.

They had a pretty good success rate for retrieving items. But when it came to the thing Wyllt wanted most, it always turned out to be a soup sandwich.

Thaddaios Wyllt, a self-proclaimed purveyor of magical antiquities, believed in the existence of elves, goblins, gnomes, and anything else you might find on a pimply-faced nerd's bookshelf. Wyllt had an intelligence network across the globe dedicated to researching the existence of these creatures. Why he wanted to meet these creatures, Jaeger never knew. He really didn't care whether Wyllt wanted to dissect them or have a beer with them. This was where the big bonuses came in.

Today's intel seemed to be more promising than any other. It didn't come from the overweight geek squad Wyllt called his Intelligence Division. It came straight from Jau, the boss's right hand; you could bet on that kind of information. Jaeger certainly was. Once they secured their target and brought it back to Wyllt, that'd be it. They'd be set. They'd get their promised bonus, and then they'd be done. No more chasing shadows and legends. And no more dealing with the eccentric Thaddaios Wyllt or Jau; that thing he relied on. The thought of that goblin gave him the creeps. And that was hard to do to Jaeger. He'd seen a lot as a Marine, and even before that growing up on the streets of Bed Stuy. But the day Wyllt introduced him to that goblin thing, that was it. The encounter gave him nightmares for days. Had it not been for the money Wyllt paid him and his crew, Jaeger would've walked a long time ago.

The hardened military contractor, with all his experience, never quite understood his employer's obsession, but it was a job… a very well-paying job. His crew put boots on the ground on every continent, chasing leads and retrieving items for this man. This was the first time in a long time Wyllt sent them after an elf. The last time was three years ago. The intel hadn't come from Wyllt's creature companion, but the boss had been fairly certain they'd find one at some run-down monastery in Argentina, of all places. Jaeger clenched his jaw, thinking about the waste of time traveling by multiple planes and driving through mosquito-ridden jungles. When they got there, they found nothing. Just some local legends and a whole lot of nonsense. He hadn't ever put eyes on an elf, and neither had his two men. Each time they'd show up to the reported site, they'd find nothing. Either there was no such thing as elves and their employer was delusional, or elves were really good at evading capture. But Wyllt's thirst for trying to find these creatures seemed unquenchable. It wasn't just elves. They chased all sorts of creatures. Wyllt was certain of their existence. Jaeger found it difficult to doubt his boss's belief. Wyllt sent them to some strange places, and they recovered some really inexplicable stuff over the years.

Then there was the undeniable fact that the boss's second was a goblin. An honest to goodness, genuine, green skin, three-foot-tall goblin with freaky eyes. Those pupil-less, black eyes were the worst. Jaeger would never forget the day he met Jau. The thing walked into the room with the boss. He even wore a nice three-piece suit with a crimson tie. Wyllt sat down and Jau stood next to him.

"Gentlemen," Wyllt said in that calm, proper, well-educated

voice of his. "This is Jau'Asar. But you can call him Jau. You do what he says. He answers to me. You answer to him. Do that and you'll go far in my organization."

Jaeger's phone vibrated in his pocket as they crossed from the second floor to the landing leading to the third. He pulled the phone out and saw *Brooklyn Bagel* on the caller I.D. Jaeger answered it.

"Yes, sir?"

"Have you arrived at the location?"

"Roger. We're 'cross from the target." Jaeger replied. "We'll set up surveillance in an apartment over here. Then we'll keep ya posted."

"Very good. This should prove to be quite the educational experience for you. Call Jau when you've finished setting up the surveillance. He'll tell you what to look out for."

"Copy that."

"Oh, and Jaeger?"

"Yes, sir?"

"Don't try to impress me by capturing the elf. I assure you, you won't capture him. Your target is the young man. Wait until the elf leaves before you apprehend him."

Jaeger wanted to curse. This was supposed to be their big score.

"Roger that." Jaeger said, not showing his disappointment.

"Good. I'm making chicken confit tonight. I'll have Jorey or Simmons bring you some."

"Roger that."

Jaeger slipped the phone back in his pocket as he and his men arrived at the third floor.

So much for retirement. Jaeger thought. If he even dared to try to catch the elf and the target got away, he could forget about ever getting a bonus from Wyllt. He'd be lucky to even still have a job. On the bright side, he was grateful that it wasn't Jau who called him. He hated when that thing called. The problem was that Jau didn't just call. He insisted on using FaceTime, and Jaeger hated to look that thing in the eyes. *Probably why he does it. He knows I hate it,* Jaeger thought.

They approached the apartment. Tufts, all six-foot-seven of him, positioned himself to the left of the door. The mountainous man stood there in that navy blue five-thousand-dollar suit. In the hall of the old middle-class apartment building with its 1950s architecture, peeling paint, and dim lighting, he stood out like a two-thousand-pound gorilla in a shopping mall. Jaeger used to resent Wyllt for making them all wear the expensive suits. He much preferred the custom Dragon Cammies they wore on other missions. It was hard to remain inconspicuous when you wore expensive designer suits and drove around in a fancy car. But Wyllt insisted. And Jaeger and his crew adapted.

Decoudreau, on the other hand, looked more comfortable in his suit. His chestnut skin and dreads tied in a ponytail combined with the Oakley sunglasses, red tie, and blue Brioni suit made him look like a high-end fashion model. Decoudreau, unlike Jaeger, appreciated the clothing expense account and custom tailoring that came with their job. The Haitian smiled, peering over his dark sunglasses, and took his place to the right of the door.

Jaeger, in his dark gray suit, swiped a stray lock of dirty blond hair to the side and stood in the center facing the door. He knocked, put his hand on his hip, set his jaw, gritted his teeth and stared intently at the peephole; Jaeger's best attempt to look like Detective Sippowitz from *NYPD Blue*. He loved that show back in high school.

Thirty seconds passed, and Jaeger knocked again.

"I'm comin'," said the man inside the apartment.

After a count of ten, they heard the shifting of the peephole cover.

"What'd ya want?"

Jaeger raised a stolen NYPD Detective badge. "Detective Richard Evans, NYPD. I need to ask you some questions about your downstairs neighbor."

Jaeger had perfected that line. Anyone could pretend to be a cop. But an *NYPD* cop, they're a whole different breed. The opening line was an important one that needed to be delivered with a calm bravado. Easy for Jaeger. He was born and raised in NYC. He had the accent.

As the man closed the peephole, removed the security chain, and unlocked the deadbolt, Jaeger readied himself. The door hadn't been open farther than two inches before Jaeger pushed it in. He grabbed the man and easily placed him into a rear-naked choke, squeezing tight against the man's throat so that he couldn't scream.

Tufts raised a small cylindrical wand and aimed it at the man. "*Yashan.*" Tufts said.

The man went limp. Jaeger dragged him through the apartment and dumped him down into the recliner. The TV blared with the sound and images of an old western starring Audie Murphy, decked out in his light blue shirt, black bolo tie, and tan cowboy hat. *Destry.* The boss had gotten him hooked on Westerns. He'd often have one on in the background when they discussed business. Jaeger found the remote and killed it.

"All clear." Decoudreau said, coming out of the bedroom. His tight dreadlocks swayed as he propped himself beside the window frame and peered out. He removed his sunglasses and looked for their target across the street.

Tufts disappeared into the kitchen.

"I got eyes on the target." Decoudreau said. He had a Creole accent that Jaeger sometimes wondered about. The man didn't speak much. And in the fourteen years he served under Jaeger, Corporal Franklyn Decoudreau never spoke about his home.

The corporal grabbed his large black case and began setting up the equipment. The laptop's screen loaded while Decoudreau set up the small wireless HD camera, pointing it at the window. The parabolic microphone came next.

Decoudreau pulled a chair from the small dining room and sat down in front of the screen.

"All clear." Tufts said, appearing from the kitchen carrying several empty beer cans and a half-eaten sandwich. He placed two of the beer cans on the floor next to the recliner and a third on the end table next to the sleeping man. The finishing touch; the half-eaten sandwich placed in the man's hand, laying in his lap.

Jaeger and Tufts stood behind Decoudreau, staring intently at the screen.

Decoudreau moved the cursor to open the surveillance apps. The video came up on the screen, followed by the ambient noise of the apartment across the way. There were no voices.

"Well, I'll be." Jaeger muttered.

On the screen, they saw the elf. The creature looked like a child standing next to the overweight young man sitting on the edge of his bed. The elf walked over to the window and closed the blinds.

CHAPTER II

THE ROAD NOT TAKEN

"I often ponder, was High King Vrangar right when he proposed that we kill every living goblin? Perhaps humanity would have been better for it." Said Elder Jeris iyl Fistrata

"No, I think not. They would have become their own gods." Replied Elder Corsicur iyl Amyin.

~ From *The Chronicles of the Sovereign Council*, Volume 379, written by Dagmar Kundolhip, Chronicler of the First Order, an Alfargnym of Unterbaum–Circa A.D. 1741

A.D. 341

The darkness of the crystal waxed to light. Jeremy stood outside. The warm air blew gently against him, carrying with it the earthy smell of damp leaves and moss. He blinked and squinted to adjust his eyes. Faint sunlight shining through the canopy of trees revealed an old unpaved road winding through the wilderness. Ahead of him he heard the pounding of horse's hoofs as Nikolaos and his two guards approached.

Nikolaos' horse stopped. The guard sitting on his right pointed up the road.

With the horses now silent, Jeremy heard scuffling and strange noises behind him. He turned. His eyes widened, his mouth opened, and a gasp of horror escaped as he slowly stepped backward to the side of the road.

"Galenos, what is it?" Nikolaos asked.

"Bishop, I'm unsure. It looks to be children," said one of the guards.

"Children?" Nikolaos asked.

Galenos didn't respond.

Nikolaos nudged his horse to amble forward.

"Your Grace!" The other guard said with a harsh whisper.

Nikolaos ignored him and continued to move forward. As he drew closer, Jeremy heard a similar gasp of horror from Nikolaos.

The nightmarish scene appeared to be right from the pages of Grimm's Darkest Fairy Tales. Three strange, grotesque creatures clad in ornate bronze armor. Hairless. Green skin. Long pointed ears. Pug inhuman faces with sharp, gnarled teeth. Short in stature, yet monstrous in appearance. Each carried a pole with a sword-like blade at one end.

At each of their sides, a monstrous armor-clad beast bared its teeth at Nikolaos and his guards.

Jeremy knew without a doubt that the bipedal creatures were the foul goblins of myth and legend. But he'd never seen anything like the four-legged beasts that stood beside each goblin. Their hulking shoulders neared the height of their masters' heads.

To the right of the road, two of the goblins used the pole end of their swords to hold down a child while their beasts stood ready to pounce at Nikolaos. To the left, another goblin stood over a little girl, holding a blade to her throat. The creature snapped its head up and fixed its eyes on Nikolaos. It yelled something unintelligible with a guttural voice that sent shivers down Jeremy's spine.

Its beast crept forward slowly with its eyes fixed on Nikolaos.

The bishop ignored the threat as well as the aches and pains of his old and tired body, heaved himself off his horse and carelessly ran to rescue the children.

"Your Grace, no!" The other guard pleaded, jumping off his horse and grasping Nikolaos by his right shoulder. Galenos followed, stepping in front of the bishop.

Nikolaos halted; his face taut in an angry scowl. "We must help them!"

The bowlegged goblin and his beast slowly approached Nikolaos. Holding its pole-sword point forward, it took one cautious step at a time, weaving its head left to right, never unlocking its gaze. Beside him the creature crept forward, ready to attack. They stopped ten feet away from the bishop, blocking the path to his companions. This goblin was dressed differently than the other two. The armor was similar, but the pauldrons weren't as big, and it had a dark purple cape that fluttered as the creature moved. Its weapon was unique; more cleaver-like, but still with a short, pole handle.

The two goblins to the right lifted the pole end of their swords up and turned to face Nikolaos. One moved forward a few steps. The other held its position with its foot on the chest of the unmoving child.

The three goblins stood apelike with bowed legs, all facing Nikolaos.

The goblin in purple curled its lipless mouth into a taunting smile as if it were daring Nikolaos to approach him.

"Galenos," Nikolaos said, pointing to the two other creatures.

"No, your Grace." Galenos placed his hand on Nikolaos' chest, pushing him back further.

The caped goblin yelled again, and the other two stepped forward; their beasts following.

The other guard stepped in front of Nikolaos. The goblin leader pulled its sword up and took a defensive stance as his minions slowly crept forward.

"Linos, be careful." Nikolaos said to his guard.

The goblin leader eyed him, but quickly returned his gaze to Linos. It charged.

Linos deflected the creature's blade with his own.

Nikolaos flinched at the clang of steel striking steel. He stepped to the left; his eyes focused on the girl. The blades clashed a second time and Nikolaos pushed himself forward. With each step, Nikolaos used his staff to propel himself closer to the girl.

The bishop didn't see the creature coming straight at him. Jeremy yelled, to no avail as the creature bowled into Nikolaos, taking him to the ground with the grace of a lion taking down a gazelle.

Linos swirled around and jabbed his sword down into the beast's back.

The creature howled in agony.

Linos let out a blood-curdling scream as the goblin sliced clear through his calf.

Jeremy looked away, hiding his gaze from the blood, but he couldn't shut his ears from the man's screams.

Nikolaos grabbed his staff and pushed himself up with a swiftness Jeremy didn't think was possible for the old man.

Linos lay on the ground. The caped goblin held its blood-stained sword above Linos, taunting him.

The bishop lunged toward the goblin and swung his staff down. The crook connected with the goblin's skull. The creature fell to the ground and didn't move. Unsatisfied with a single blow, Nikolaos repeatedly brought his staff down on the goblin's head.

Jeremy watched in horror, wanting to turn away but he couldn't.

A golden, shimmering light leaked from the goblin's wounds.

Nikolaos heaved a deep, shock inspired breath and stepped away from the goblin.

Dark reddish-green blood glistened from the light as it pooled around the goblin's body. The golden light continued to escape, spreading over its body until all flesh and bone dissipated like a cloud of dust being blown away by a soft wind. All that remained was the goblin's armor and weapons lying in a pool of reddish-green blood.

What in the world just happened? Jeremy wondered as he watched the last wisps of golden light disappear.

Nikolaos blinked and shook his head, his eyes fixed on the goblin's remains until the sound of steel clashing on steel drew his attention. The bishop looked up, searching for his guards, but his eyes were drawn to the movement of one lone creature standing amid the chaos. Galenos lay still at the goblin's side. A fallen and unmoving goblin lay beside him. The other two beasts lay in a bloody mess, barely breathing.

The lone goblin turned away from Galenos' bloodied body toward the child. The boy slowly sat up and pitched to the left. He brought his hand up to support his head and winced.

"No!" Nikolaos yelled, charging at the creature. Old wounds and old tired muscles no longer slowed him. He had to help that child.

The lone goblin, wide eyed, ran in the opposite direction. It hunched over; weapon now slung on his back. It used its arms like an ape to run faster into the woods.

Nikolaos stopped and watched it lope away and disappear into the woods. He then glanced over at the bloodied, lifeless body of Galenos. Nikolaos' lungs burned as he tried to draw in more air. Bracing himself by leaning into his staff, he turned and looked to Linos. The guard barely moved.

Jeremy wiped the sweat from his brow and placed his other hand over his thumping chest. *This was like living in a movie.*

Nikolaos' head spun and his heart raced. His chest heaved mightily to draw in more air. He couldn't wrap his mind around what had just happened. He didn't know what to do. With one hand on his forehead and the other still clutching his staff the bishop hobbled over to Linos, still writhing from some unseen wound.

Jeremy followed but stopped short at the sight of Linos' leg separated from his body. He shuddered. The taste of bile seeped into his throat, and he quickly brought his hand up to cover his eyes. He swallowed and then breathed in deeply, feeling faint. His head throbbed and his attention was drawn back to Nikolaos. Taking in another deep breath, he unveiled his eyes and looked to the bishop.

Nikolaos, kneeling beside Linos, grabbed his friend's hand. Cold and clammy, Linos' fingers trembled in Nikolaos' palm. The bishop glanced down at his friend's severed limb. There was so much blood and more still flowing out.

"Linos, I'm here." Nikolaos said, placing his other hand on the man's forehead.

The guard's chest drew in shallow breaths and his expression was seemingly fixed in that second of horror when his leg was displaced from his body. Linos stared straight out as if something sinister hung above him.

"Oh, Linos. I am… I…" Nikolaos had seen death approach before. But his experience didn't make it any easier to see his young friend so close to it. He knew he should pray, but he wasn't ready to say goodbye.

Nikolaos' eyes wandered to the small carved boat hanging from Linos' neck. Holding the dying man's hand with one hand, the bishop used his other to grab the tiny boat. A faint smile forced its way onto his saddened face.

"Fishers of men." Nikolaos whispered.

A tear ran down his cheek and disappeared into his fluffy white beard.

Linos' eyes fluttered. His chest heaved, struggling to draw in air.

"Linos," Nikolaos said, drawing in a deep breath to steady himself. "The blessing of our Lord, God and Savior Jesus Christ," he stifled a sob and continued, "…be upon you for the healing of the soul and body, now and ever, and unto ages of ages. Amen."

Linos' grip tightened on Nikolaos' hand and then relaxed. His chest no longer moved. His lifeless face fixed in that last moment of agony with eyes still open. Nikolaos moved his hand from the man's forehead, over Linos' eyes, and gently closed them.

The bishop looked back over his shoulder and glanced once

again at Galenos. He had hoped to see some sign of life, even though he knew Galenos was dead too. An empty numbness washed over him. He didn't know how to respond. These men gave their lives for his protection. They weren't merely his guards. These were men he worked with and cared for. Men he had broken bread with on many occasions. Men he had known since they were children. These men were his family.

Jeremy sighed and looked around, taking in the entire scene. The once pleasant smell of the tranquil forest was now tainted with metal and acetone. Blood and death surrounded him and in the middle of it all kneeled the man known as Saint Nicholas. Jeremy felt sorry for the man. More so, he felt his sorrow and confusion at what had just taken place.

An uneasy groan distracted Jeremy's pondering of the situation and Nikolaos' prayer.

The children! Jeremy heard the voice of Nikolaos echo in his head.

Nikolaos grabbed his staff, hefted himself up, and hobbled over to the child.

Jeremy followed.

Nikolaos knelt beside the boy.

"Child, are you alright?" he asked, gently placing his hand on the boy's shoulder.

The boy looked oddly familiar to Jeremy.

The child ignored Nikolaos and slowly pulled himself up from the ground. The boy looked around until his eyes rested on his friend. With one hand guarding his ribcage, the boy used the other to push Nikolaos away and walk towards the other child.

Nikolaos and Jeremy followed.

"Child, you're injured. Let me help you." Nikolaos said.

The boy squatted down next to the girl. He cupped his hand under his friend's neck and pulled her onto his lap. The unconscious girl's head rolled over and with the aid of what little sunlight was left, Jeremy saw blood on the right side of her head. Nikolaos leaned over for a closer look. Nikolaos and Jeremy gasped. The child's ear had been cut off!

The boy spoke to her in a language Jeremy didn't recognize.

Nikolaos' shock from seeing the wound added to his surprise at the boy's strange speech and mannerisms. It wasn't the concern in what the boy spoke of that troubled Nikolaos. He couldn't have been more than six or seven years old, but his voice was deeper, like that of a young man.

The unconscious girl blinked, her eyes growing wider as she stared at Nikolaos looming behind the boy.

She tried to move away, but all she could do was wince.

The boy spoke again, trying to calm his friend.

"Listen to me child," Nikolaos spoke softly and slowly, but urgently. "Your friend seems to be quite injured. The closest town is my home, about a day's travel west." He moved himself to a squatting position and put his hand underneath the child to lift her. "Come with me and we can have the monks at the abbey look at her."

The boy grabbed Nikolaos' arm.

"No, adamu…" the boy said. "You've done enough. I'll tend to my friend's wellbeing. You just stay out of the way until then." The boy now spoke in a language that both Jeremy and Nikolaos understood.

Nikolaos furrowed his brow. His sentiment echoing Jeremy's. The boy must have been speaking in Nikolaos native language of Greek. Somehow, Jeremy could understand. It was as if he was hearing the child's voice through Nikolaos. Which would explain why he didn't understand the child when he spoke the other language to his friend.

Nikolaos pulled his hand back from under the unconscious girl's head. Taking a few steps away, he watched as the boy walked with certainty toward the armor of the goblin Nikolaos had killed.

Drawing a knife from his belt, the boy cut the cape from the armor.

"Child, your friend is badly injured and in need of medicine. The monks at the abbey are quite good at what they do. You need…" Nikolaos noticed something odd about the boy. In all the chaos he hadn't seen it before and neither had Jeremy. The boy's ears were pointed.

"Mercurio!" Jeremy said. His face cracked from the shock. *He's not a boy! He's Mercurio!*

He looked down at the unconscious girl, and her remaining ear was pointed too. *They're both elves!*

Jeremy turned and looked at Nikolaos, who watched Mercurio cut the purple cape into strips. Nikolaos still thought they were children… odd children. Their mannerisms, their clothing, everything about them was unusual. They both wore beautiful cloaks with ornate stitching. The taller of the two, Mercurio, wore a forest green shirt with black pants, green boots… odd-looking boots that curled at the toe-tip. The girl wore a long dark green tunic, lined with white fur. Under the tunic she wore a light green shirt. A white silk scarf, now stained with blood, covered her neck from her collar to her chin. Her boots were black with gold embroidery that looked like the designs had been etched into the leather. And they had that curious curl at the toe-tip, too. But Nikolaos found their ears more curious than anything else.

"Your ears…" Nikolaos stammered, "they are unlike anything I have seen."

Mercurio shook his head and sighed with agitation. He knelt beside his friend and wrapped the cloth around her head. Little spots of blood darkened the deep purple of the cloth as he secured it.

"You shouldn't have interfered with us! Now we're all in grave danger." Mercurio glanced over at the remains of the goblin whom he'd cut the strips of purple cloth from. Then he used his knife to point at its armor. "Did you kill that one?"

Nikolaos sighed, looking at the lifeless armor. "I did," Nikolaos whispered. "I tried to save…"

"You don't know what you've done." Mercurio stood up and walked toward the dead goblin's armor. "You should've never let the other one get away!" He stopped and took a deep breath before turning to face Nikolaos. "I have no time to explain things to you." The elf walked back over and knelt beside his friend. "We must first get Ellesmere well and fit for travel." He kept one hand on his friend's head. With the other he pointed at Nikolaos and then brought his fist to his chest. "And then it is you who must come with us."

"What?" Nikolaos' forehead furrowed.

Mercurio snapped his head toward Nikolaos. "I have no time for your questions, adamu. You want to help… just do as I say. Now, come here and hold Ellesmere's head up so I can give her an elixir."

Jeremy raised his eyebrows unsure of what to make of this situation.

Nikolaos, however, stared, slack jawed and dumbfounded by Mercurio's harsh words. He paused, unsure if he should do as the elf said.

"Now, adamu!"

Nikolaos glowered at the elf, but held his tongue. He decided his best option now was to comply. He moved over, gently grabbing the unconscious girl's head and placing it on his lap.

Mercurio ran to a small satchel on the side of the road and removed a tiny, round bottle. He raced to his friend's side. Uncorking the bottle, he held it steady and began to slowly pour it into her mouth, reassuring her in their strange language.

As he turned his concerned look from his friend to Nikolaos, Mercurio's features hardened into a scowl. "I don't know what to say to you, adamu." He shook his head. "You're ignorant of the events you have stumbled upon today. Those creatures won't rest until they've avenged their leader's death. You killed someone important to them and you let that other one get away. You can be sure that once he returns, your life will be over."

"What? What are…"

"Enough questions, adamu. Just listen and do as I say."

"Boy, if you haven't forgotten, I saved your lives!"

"I am *not* a boy!" Mercurio shouted as he stood, slamming the cork back into the elixir bottle. "You would do well to know that, adamu. I'm an elf. And—"

"Elf? What—" He had never heard that word before.

"I told you I'd explain everything… later," Mercurio said. "You adamu are so arrogant and stubborn. Close your mouth and listen to what I have to say, or you will surely die at the hands of those bloodthirsty creatures." He nodded toward the empty goblin armor.

Jeremy raised his hand to his mouth and bit the inside of his lip.

Nikolaos' eyes tightened and his nostrils flared. *Who is this boy… this elf… to speak to me in such a way after I just saved his life, and his friend's life too?* He took a deep breath, trying to calm himself. He needed to know more, and if not saying anything helped with that, then he'd swallow his pride and listen. He sighed and nodded at Mercurio.

"Very well, adamu." The elf turned his back to Nikolaos and headed toward the goblin armor. "As I said before, by saving our lives you've put your own life in danger. Those creatures are called goblins."

"Goblins? And you're an elf?" Nikolaos questioned.

"Adamu, your mouth is open again. Close it and listen."

"Whoa!" Jeremy gasped. *Mercurio is hardcore.*

The elf shook his head and then walked over to the armor that belonged to the goblin Nikolaos had killed. "They'll stop at nothing now to avenge the death of their leader."

He rolled the chest piece over to the front. Staring down at the ground, his eyes grew wide, and he shook his head. Mercurio reached down and picked up a pendant. The elf swallowed and shook his head again. He held the necklace up to Nikolaos. "You see? It's much worse than I feared."

Jeremy walked closer to get a look at the necklace. The silver and gold pendant, hanging from a thick chain, was shaped like a claw wrapped around a golden dragon's head. Its jeweled eyes of red glittered even in the sparse light.

"This goblin you killed was of high blood. He may have even been next in line to rule." The elf shook his head again. "You've no choice. If you're to live out your life, you must come under the protection of my people. We'll bring you to a place where the goblins can't reach you."

"Wait," Nikolaos heard enough. "That's impossible. I have responsibilities… I have duties to the people of my town. I can't just—"

"It is by your choice. But know this, if you don't, you put their lives in danger as well." He walked toward Nikolaos. "Anyone around, when the goblins find you, will be used to exact revenge. The goblins will bind you to a chair and make you watch as they viciously torture your family and friends. They'll beg for mercy, but no mercy will come until they breathe their last agonizing breath. And when they finally die, those goblins will put you through the same torture. Your pain will be so intense you'll welcome death. Is that what you wish?"

Jeremy gritted his teeth and cringed at the thought.

The color drained from Nikolaos' face as he swallowed. The thought of harm coming to anyone he loved, especially the children of Myra, was too much for him to take. Tears welled up in his eyes. He sighed. "I will… go with you."

"You will," said Mercurio matter-of-factly as he ran back to the side of the road and hefted the satchel. "Make yourself useful and pick up Ellesmere. She should be fit for travel now. And let's put those horses of yours to good use."

Nikolaos woefully lifted the injured elf and carried her over to his horse. Laying Ellesmere gently down on the horse's back, Nikolaos turned to Mercurio.

"My name is Nikolaos," he said somberly.

Gathering the rest of their gear, the elf turned toward Nikolaos.

"I am called Mercurio. Let's go."

CHAPTER 12

NO TURNING BACK

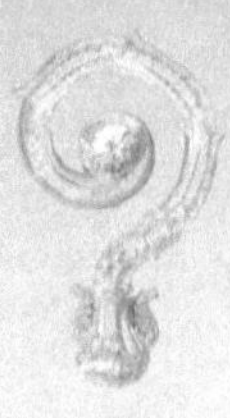

"Nikolaos grumbled incessantly on their journey. And with good reason; his frail body ached from travel and his heart broke from the people he left behind."

~ From *The Gift Giver Chronicles* compiled by Volcdegen Vigdis, a Chronicler of the Master Construct, First Order, an alfargnym of Unterbaum

A.D. 343

"They traveled throughout the day, making their way closer to the Veil," the voice of the mimstone echoed in the darkness. Jeremy listened to its calming voice, but his heart still raced. The events of the last flash were nothing short of incredible. If Jeremy hadn't experienced it, he'd never have believed it.

"Mercurio's only concern was getting Ellesmere home," the voice of the mimstone continued. "He cared not whether Nikolaos followed them or fell off his horse. And Nikolaos; his thoughts were on the day's events. Losing Galenos and Linos weighed heavily on him. Exhaustion made its home in every muscle and bone of his body. The former Bishop of Myra was relieved when Mercurio called for them to stop and rest for the night."

Jeremy stepped out of the mimstone's darkness and into a moonlit clearing surrounded by silhouetted trees. Nikolaos sat atop his horse, struggling against exhaustion and soreness, and deciding whether it was worth the effort to dismount. Giving in, he eased himself down. He placed his hands on the back of his hips and stretched, letting out a moan as his tired old bones cracked.

Mercurio turned and looked at Nikolaos. The elf's eyebrows raised, and his lips pursed. The look said it all. He had somehow offended Mercurio again! *Can I do nothing right in this creature's eyes?*

"Get Ellesmere and anything else you want off the horses while I set up," Mercurio whispered. "We will rest here for the night."

Why is Mercurio so mean to Nikolaos? Jeremy wondered.

Nikolaos' eyes felt heavy as he considered the daunting task of lifting the girl and unpacking. He just wanted to sleep. But, in the back of his mind, he feared he couldn't sleep. He still had so many unanswered questions.

"We have no time for you to just stand there." Mercurio snapped at Nikolaos. "Take Ellesmere to that tree over there with the widespread branches. We'll sleep under it."

Jeremy watched Nikolaos as he unpacked and gently laid Ellesmere on a bedroll beneath the tree. None of this made sense. Curiosity replaced his pity for Nikolaos and his own trepidation over the situation. Jeremy needed to know more. He wanted to know how this whole thing played out and how *he* fit into all of this.

Mercurio returned with an armful of wood. The elf said nothing to Nikolaos and set straight to assembling the wood into a small nest within a circle of rocks.

Nikolaos slumped down against the tree and watched Mercurio use his bare hands to set fire to the wood.

Nikolaos rubbed his eyes, straining to see if there was anything more to what the elf was doing. It amazed Jeremy. But it freaked Nikolaos out. The man leaned forward, squinting at the fire. How could he start the fire with no tinder and kindle? *Was this magic? Was this the Devil's work?* Nikolaos wondered. But these elves didn't seem to be devils, nor did they seem to be angels or anything else he had ever studied. This bothered Nikolaos. He wanted to know more but feared asking questions. He hoped that if he kept quiet for a while Mercurio would be more amiable to talking.

After dinner, Mercurio checked on Ellesmere one last time before turning in.

Loneliness pushed the sadness and anguish away from Nikolaos. He had never felt more alone in his entire life. Jeremy found that strange because the man had spent so many years alone in prison. But at least then he had some idea of what was going on. He had been persecuted for his faith. But what was this? Why was this happening? Nikolaos closed his eyes and turned his face skyward. *God, where are you in all this?* The bishop waited for an answer, but none came. With a deep breath of despair, Nikolaos hefted himself up and retreated to his bedroll. He laid down thinking that he could never fall asleep. He had too many questions.

Nikolaos was wrong. The shock of the day's events combined with being awake for more hours than he was used to had exhausted him. He had no trouble falling asleep.

A LIGHT FLASHED, and the night quickly turned to day. Nikolaos, still asleep, lay on his side resting comfortably.

Whispering voices drew Jeremy's attention away from the man.

Mercurio and Ellesmere sat cross-legged by the campfire. The two elves chatted as Mercurio gently stoked the embers with a stick. Dizziness, accompanied by a thick, numb feeling in his head, came upon Jeremy as the words the elves spoke sounded strange and foreign at first and then became clear and identifiable.

"We have no choice." Mercurio whispered, shaking his head.

"We'll figure this out." Ellesmere said. Her voice, soft and winsome, just as Jeremy had imagined it would be.

The uneasiness dissipated as Jeremy gingerly shook his head. Behind him, he heard Nikolaos grumble. He turned to see the man grab his staff, use it to stand up and hobble over to the elves.

"It's good to see that you're awake." Nikolaos smiled at the girl.

"It is good to be awake." Ellesmere smiled back.

Nikolaos took a seat across from Mercurio and Ellesmere, crossing his legs and wriggling his torso to ease the soreness from his old muscles.

"That language you were speaking. I don't think I have heard it before."

"Indeed, you haven't." Mercurio snapped, not even looking at Nikolaos. "Your ears were never meant to hear it."

Ellesmere raised her eyebrows and looked disapprovingly at Mercurio. She then turned back to Nikolaos. "It's Elvish. Our native language. We were just discussing how we would get you through the Veil."

"Veil?" Nikolaos said.

"The Veil separates our lands from your lands," Ellesmere said. She spoke robustly for someone who had lost an ear, and gotten the life beaten out of her only twelve hours earlier. "There are different Elven Cities on the other side of the Veil. I'm from the Northern city, called Orindin. Mercurio lives in one of the Southern Elven cities, called Sayalla."

Jeremy tilted his head to the side and raised an eyebrow. *Is she talking about some sort of portal to another land?*

Mercurio shot Ellesmere a disapproving look.

"He's going to find out eventually. Why not just tell him now?" Ellesmere responded sheepishly.

"How have I never seen or heard of your people before?" Nikolaos said, directing the question to Ellesmere.

Before Ellesmere could answer, Mercurio stood up and looked at Nikolaos. An icy stare bore into the man. "Do you think we are such fools that we would associate ourselves with a people who are so destructive?" Mercurio sneered and walked toward Nikolaos. "We've chosen to conceal ourselves from your kind so that your ways would not poison ours." The elf leaned over, coming face to face with Nikolaos. "You adamu do not know about the world… you're all so selfish… self-centered, that you deem yourselves the authority on everything! We elves, and many other keshaphim, have been around far longer than you."

"Mercurio," Ellesmere interrupted, "he doesn't know. We are probably the first keshaphim he can remember."

Geeze! Jeremy thought. *What brought that on?*

"Forgive me," Nikolaos said sarcastically. His jaw tightened and his cheeks flushed with anger. His compassion and tolerance for this creature slipped away. "I am sorry that my presence and my lack of knowledge is so upsetting to you, Mercurio!" Nikolaos stood up. He towered over the elf and flung his hands into the air. "What more do you want of me? I saved your life, only to discover that I have placed my own life and the lives of those I care for in danger. I'm trusting you to lead me to safety… what more do you want of me?"

"What more do I want of you, adamu?" Mercurio puffed out his chest and stood on the tips of his toes, engaging Nikolaos. "I want you and all the other adamu to stop taking what is *not* yours… to stop harming one another out of selfish desires. Sometimes I don't know what is worse, adamu or goblins!"

"You incorrigible little creature!" Nikolaos yelled as he leaned down to bring his face closer to Mercurio's. "Don't cast judgment on me based upon your misguided view of my people. *I* stopped to help *you*." Nikolaos shoved his finger at Mercurio. "*I* didn't have to, but *you* needed help. I've devoted my entire life to helping other people by serving my God! You treat me as if I'm supposed to know something about you or these goblins. I've never met anyone like *you* or them, so stop treating me like I am supposed to know of things that I have never even heard of!"

Nikolaos turned away from Mercurio and headed back to his bedroll.

The elf stood silent; his face frozen in a contemptuous sneer.

"When you are ready to leave, let me know and I'll be ready," Nikolaos said. He paused and turned around. "My name is Nikolaos, *not* Adam!"

Mercurio huffed and scampered off in the opposite direction.

Ellesmere put her hand to her forehead and sighed.

Jeremy stared at the girl, feeling more sorry for her than he did for Mercurio and Nikolaos. He felt his attention being pulled back toward the man.

Nikolaos stewed for a few minutes before the guilt of his outburst overcame him. *God forgive me,* he prayed. *I am at a loss on this journey. I struggle to see your will in it, and I need patience and wisdom to see this journey through.*

The thundering stomp of hooves hitting earth startled Nikolaos and Jeremy. They looked over and saw the horses running off into the woods.

Mercurio stood silently by, watching them scamper off.

Nikolaos stood up from his stump; confusion and anger washed over him. He clenched his fists and turned to Mercurio.

"Now how are—"

"We had to let them go," Ellesmere said. "They will not travel well where we are going."

"We are leaving." Mercurio walked across the clearing and disappeared into the forest.

Nikolaos looked around. A forlorn Ellesmere stood there watching Mercurio. The campsite was clear of all debris, including the fire and the patch of earth beneath it. Fresh grass stood in its place. The goblin's gear was gone as well. They weren't on the horses when Mercurio sent them off. *What had they done with everything?*

"Nikolaos, come," Ellesmere said. "We must go." She ran to catch up with Mercurio.

Nikolaos sighed, looking up at the sky.

CHAPTER 13
THE ROAD TO SAYALLA

"What was it that allowed the Gift Giver to push on? Hope? Or was he just a stubborn adamu? Mercurio claimed that there was no adamu like Nikolaos."
~ From *The Gift Giver Chronicles* compiled by Volcdegen Vigdis, a Chronicler of the Master Construct, First Order, an alfargnym of Unterbaum

A.D. 343

The voice of the mimstone continued to tell its tale. "Mercurio, Ellesmere, and Nikolaos traveled the unpaved wilderness. For the adamu, it felt as if they had walked for days. Each footstep intensified his discomfort. His body ached. His lips parched. And his head throbbed. Yet, the disheartened bishop pressed on."

The light unfolded around Jeremy. He stood behind young Mercurio. Nikolaos and Ellesmere beside him. They all stared down at a beautifully hand-drawn map. It was written in the elves' language, but Jeremy could somehow understand it.

Mercurio pointed to a faint golden circle that glowed among a forest of hand drawn trees.

Ellesmere nodded.

Mercurio then pointed to another icon on the map. A gold, glowing circle with three curved lines radiating from the center labeled "Gatehouse." Jeremy had seen that symbol before. *Celtic? Or maybe Greek?* He wondered. *A triskele, that's what it's called.* But he couldn't remember much about it or where he'd seen it.

A line appeared between the glowing triskele and the circle. Several glowing icons appeared above the line. Mercurio touched the gatehouse symbol, and it glowed. Above the symbol the words "Arnburk Eileifr, Artificer of the Veil, Fourth Order" appeared.

Ellesmere nodded again.

Mercurio folded the map and placed it back in his satchel.

"How much further?" Nikolaos asked.

"We're almost there." Mercurio said. "The gatehouse is very close."

"A house… delightful. I'm rather hungry and quite parched."

"Don't get comfortable." Mercurio said. "We won't be staying there. It's the door through the Veil."

"If we can't see the Veil, how will we know it's there?"

Mercurio ignored Nikolaos and kept walking.

"The Veil uses magic to keep it hidden." Ellesmere said. "You could never find it. We just know where to look." Ellesmere smiled and reached into Mercurio's satchel, grabbing the map and unfolding it again.

Mercurio sneered at Ellesmere with disapproval, but he did nothing to stop her.

"This," she said, pointing to the faint golden circle, "is me. The map reads my aura and knows where I am." She moved her finger over to the triskele. "This is where the entrance to the Veil is. When Mercurio touched the Veil glyph, the map showed him which direction to go and how far away it is."

"GPS?" Jeremy said, smiling. "Elves have their own GPS."

"How far away is it?" Nikolaos asked.

"Less than five hundred paces." Ellesmere said.

Ellesmere folded the map up again and returned it to her friend's satchel. Mercurio led the way and Ellesmere slowed her pace, walking next to Nikolaos.

"Nikolaos, I need you to hear me carefully." Ellesmere said, gently placing her hand on the man's forearm. "The Veil is just over that way." She pointed to a path overgrown with thistle. "As we draw closer to the gatehouse, it's going to get harder for you. You're going to want to run away from it. You must trust me and keep following us. Do you understand?"

"Yes, I think so." But Nikolaos really didn't. Jeremy felt the uneasiness and uncertainty emanating from him. None of this made sense to either of them. But what choice did Nikolaos have? His life was in the hands of these elves.

"Just keep following us." Ellesmere reminded him.

Nikolaos followed the two elves down the old path and abruptly stopped. He jerked his head to the left.

Jeremy shivered as a wave of fear surged over him.

"What was that?" Nikolaos whispered.

"Nothing, Nikolaos." Ellesmere said. "Just keep following us."

Nikolaos cocked his head, raised an eyebrow and looked suspiciously at her. *There's something up the path. They needed to stop. Was it a bear? Wolves? More of those goblins?* A sense of foreboding washed over Jeremy and Nikolaos. *This isn't good.* Nikolaos' heart pounded against his chest. These creatures were going to get him killed. He needed to turn back.

"Ellesmere," Nikolaos whispered. "We need to turn around."

"Nikolaos, remember what I told you. What you're feeling is not real. Just keep walking."

Easier said than done. Could this magic be playing tricks on his mind? If so, his heart and mind were in league together. His heart beat faster. His mind yelled for him to run the other way. Nikolaos brought his hand to his chest, his breathing shallow. His body flushed with warmth. He closed his eyes and tried to steady his breath before taking a step. *Oh, dear God, help me.* He took a small step forward, one hand clutching his staff, the other moving from his chest to clutch the neckline of his robes, hoping to cool down from the stifling heat.

Jeremy pulled at his collar with one hand and massaged his head with the other.

Nikolaos saw something out of the corner of his eyes. It darted from one tree to the other. He stopped again and swallowed. They were so far away from civilization; bandits might have a camp out here. And if they caught him, he'd be dead anyway. Or worse: there could be more of those goblin creatures out here. He needed to turn back, now!

"Nikolaos." Ellesmere said. Her voice steady and comforting. "Stay with us. You'll be safe as long as you follow us."

Safe? This place didn't seem safe at all! Ellesmere's warning rang in his ears. *You have to trust me and keep following us.* He swallowed, attempting to suppress his fear. Trusting her, Nikolaos raised his trembling hand and wiped the sweat from his brow. He needed to get out of here. If he didn't, he'd surely die. Where was he? If he died here, no one would ever find him. He needed to move on… needed to reach the Veil. He didn't belong here and he knew it. He was going to die right here on this path. His mind swirled, his head throbbed, his eyes hurt. His thoughts collided with one another, and Nikolaos stopped. He needed to turn around.

Mercurio halted and turned toward him. "Just keep walking."

"Ellesmere… we shouldn't be here! We must turn around!" Nikolaos frantically whispered. "We've been walking for hours, and…"

"Be still," Mercurio said. "We are precisely where we need to be."

Jeremy braced himself against a tree. The dysphoria was too much. His head throbbed, his heart pounded, and he felt hotter than a day at the beach in August.

Confusion and uncertainty joined in with fear and Nikolaos' torment increased. His eyes, wide with panic, desperately searched for a place to run. He didn't know where he was. One word, among the disorienting thoughts of terror echoed through his mind… *Veil. Veil?* He thought. *They keep talking about a veil.*

"Veil? What is this Veil you keep mentioning?" He repeated his earlier question.

"Nikolaos?" Ellesmere said. "Mind what I have told you. What you are feeling isn't real. We are going to take care of you. Just keep following us, no matter what. I promise you. We're almost there."

It's not real, Nikolaos thought. He held his trembling hand to his throbbing head. Bursts of white light danced around him. *None of this is real. I have to stop. I have to turn back.* Nikolaos stopped and turned around. Ellesmere grabbed him by the hand. Nikolaos tugged on the elf's hand. *I have to leave here.* Nikolaos wanted to yell, but he couldn't. He felt the elf tug back… pulling him toward the danger. *What is wrong with her?*

"Nikolaos, you must summon all your strength and push through. Please follow me. As bad as you feel now, it will be worse if the goblins find you."

Nikolaos stopped again. Dizzy. His head spun. Or did it? He couldn't tell. He thought he might vomit. He clung tightly to his staff and looked up for guidance. All he saw were the trees. They surrounded him, their branches reaching for him with twisted, long-fingered claws.

Jeremy jerked away from the tree he'd been clinging to and he stumbled toward Ellesmere.

Nikolaos cringed and looked for some place to run, but they were everywhere, and they were going to kill him. Sweat plastered his hair and his skin prickled. With nowhere to run, Nikolaos stood frozen, desperately trying to catch his breath, eyes pinched tightly.

"Nikolaos, please." Ellesmere said, trying to lead Nikolaos by the hand toward Mercurio.

Nikolaos took another deep breath. He asked God for strength.

He heard Ellesmere's voice again. "Nikolaos, it's all right. Just follow us."

Follow you? He wanted to say, but he only thought it. Unable to make his mouth work. He tried again. *Follow you? I don't even know where we're going. Oh dear God, I don't know where we're going.* The words wouldn't come out. Nikolaos opened his eyes and forced his lungs to breathe deeply. Despite every inclination to run in the other direction, he stepped forward. His feet felt shackled.

Ellesmere guided Nikolaos toward the danger. He used his staff to push forward and take another step… and then another, and another. All the while praying to God for strength.

Jeremy, however, froze with fear. Try as he might, he couldn't cause his legs to step forward. Every feeling and every fear Nikolaos felt, Jeremy experienced as well. Through wide eyes, Jeremy watched as Nikolaos pushed himself forward as if he were facing a torrent of mighty wind.

Jeremy winced and closed his eyes as a bright, white light washed over the scene. It faded, along with Jeremy's vertigo, leaving only the dull headache and sticky warmth of his body. Jeremy inhaled, finding himself in a small clearing free of the Veil's torment. A small, ramshackle house surrounded by stately oaks sat quaintly on the right. To the rear a small well completed the picturesque scene.

"The gatehouse!" Mercurio yelled.

Jeremy turned and saw Mercurio, followed by Ellesmere and the beleaguered Nikolaos. His breathing labored, sweat poured down his face, and his eyes barely opened.

Nikolaos tried to push forward, the end of his journey only being a mere thirty feet away. But the rushing fear was strongest now. So strong that his head and heart pounded in unison. His stomach threatened to push itself up his gullet and out of his mouth.

Jeremy felt the odd sensation of knowing… of understanding what Nikolaos experienced, but he was being spared the full onslaught.

A bird fluttered around Nikolaos' head. He tried to pull away from it and almost lost his balance. It looped around his head a few more times. *A purple bird?* Or was it an insect? It circled around again, making his nausea even worse. He opened his eyes wide to get a better look, but it fluttered around his head so fast he couldn't be sure of what he saw.

Jeremy stepped forward, curious to see what it was.

The creature completed one more circle around Nikolaos' head and flew off. He was sure it wasn't a bird now. The purple fluttering, translucent dragonfly-like wings and two long legs reminded him of something else. *Was that a fairy?* Jeremy wondered.

Nikolaos blinked and took another deep breath before digging his staff into the ground to push forward. The fear and discomfort overwhelmed him. Nikolaos fell to his knees and teetered forward, crashing to the ground.

Jeremy brought his hand to his mouth and let out a gasp. His connection to Nikolaos faded.

Ellesmere knelt next to Nikolaos and brushed the hair away from his face. She held a comforting hand on his shoulder.

A gentle inner tugging drew Jeremy's attention away from the fallen bishop, shifting to Mercurio.

Jeremy could feel the elf's indifference toward Nikolaos. Mercurio continued toward the house and stopped twenty feet away from it.

"Arnburk!" He shouted.

Nothing.

Where was that alfargnym? Jeremy heard Mercurio say to himself. "Arnburk!" Mercurio shouted again. "We need you to part the Veil."

Seconds later, a shutter in the house opened revealing the face of a disheveled old man. Jeremy's eyes were drawn to the large, bulbous nose surrounded by his small, round, bearded face. Despite being covered in dirt, it was apparent that his beard and hair were white. On top of his head, he wore a ragged, floppy brown hat.

Is that a gnome? Jeremy wondered. But somehow, he knew it was called an alfargnym.

The purple-winged fairy that checked on them earlier flittered above the little man before landing on his head. It stood there, looking curiously at the elves.

The alfargnym stroked his scraggly beard, studying Mercurio and Ellesmere, eyes crinkling as he surveyed them. He looked past them and stared at the unconscious Nikolaos.

"What be that?" Asked the alfargnym, nodding his head toward Nikolaos.

"It is a long story, Arnburk," said Mercurio, agitated. "We must take this adamu through the Veil for his protection."

"When the cosmic ash falls!" Arnburk shouted.

"He killed a goblin high-blood." Mercurio said.

The shutter slammed close. Seconds later, the doors of the house opened, and the old, scraggly alfargnym wobbled out. The fairy followed closely behind him. Arnburk was shorter than Mercurio and Ellesmere. He wore a long, tattered dark blue tunic tied at the waist with a thick leather belt holding pouches and a dagger.

"Garm's embrace, children! What do you think you're doing?" Arnburk said gruffly, scolding them. His head bobbled back and forth between the elves and the unconscious Nikolaos.

"I already told you we have to bring him through with us." Mercurio said.

"And I'm telling you, you have no headship! No, in fact I'm going to tell you that you've a crack in your brain case, elf!" Arnburk shook his head.

Mercurio sighed, looked down and crossed his arms. Arnburk was right. They could go and come through the Veil as they pleased. But they didn't have the authority to bring an adamu through the Veil. In fact, they could be in trouble for even bringing Nikolaos to the gatehouse. Mercurio looked to Ellesmere for help.

Ellesmere stood up and shrugged.

This was a problem. Or was it? Did they really need to take this fool adamu back with them? He really wasn't their concern. Mercurio wrestled with what to do. They could drag him back to the Veil's perimeter and leave him—he was as good as dead anyway. And even if he somehow made it back to his home, the goblins would come for him. The image of Nikolaos sitting tied up in his own home as he watched goblins flay his family was too disturbing for Mercurio. He sighed as he thought of his mother teaching him the fourth tenet of the Iyl'Sel'wyn. *What is good for all, is right; what is good for one, is wrong.*

"Ah! Samyaza, do not find me!" Mercurio profaned. He sighed and clenched his fists. "Hear me Arnburk. This adamu didn't just kill *one* goblin. He killed *two*, and one of them was a prince."

Arnburk raised an eyebrow and brought his finger to his beard. He scowled at the two elves, eyebrows furrowed as he contemplated and calculated the ramifications of this additional information.

"You may go," Arnburk said, pointing at Mercurio. He gestured toward Nikolaos. "But he may not."

The alfargnym's answer agitated Mercurio. But he couldn't fault Arnburk for following the law. Mercurio turned to Ellesmere.

"You're going to have to go to the council. I'll stay here with him. Bring back a letter with the council's seal. It's the only way we can bring the adamu through."

"I feared as much," replied Ellesmere.

The friends hugged, and Ellesmere hurried off with Arnburk toward the house.

"Hurry back. I don't fancy having to spend much longer with this adamu."

Mercurio looked over at the unconscious Nikolaos. *Actually,* the elf thought, *if he stays like this it won't be so bad.*

CHAPTER 14

A LESSON IN INDEPENDENCE

"The dweorg and the alfargnym will not relent. They believe us to be beings they call the *Ljosalfar*. They say we are the guardians of this world. Our leaders have denied this claim and have chosen to leave these primitive peoples. The elves shall not make claim to the land of the dweorg and the alfargnym."

~ From *The Annals of Meital iyl Sayalla*, 1st Lore Keeper of Sayalla

Masaru took the train from Tokyo to Sakaiminato. Following the directions given to him by Turtak, he made his way to the port to catch the ferry. Though he hadn't heard the voice of his guide since earlier this morning, Masaru recalled the directions perfectly.

He arrived at the ferry docks with enough time to purchase his tickets and watch as members of the Moscow State Circus unloaded caged tigers and bears. Masaru eyed the tiger, sympathizing with the caged creature. He knew that feeling. Created for more than life in a non-place, filled with raw, wild power only to be forced not to use it. He had been that caged creature once, but not anymore.

Before boarding the ferry, he slipped into the restroom, locked the door, and removed his katana from his bag. Masaru pulled the blade from its sheath and held it, taking a minute to savor its magnificence. He closed his eyes and breathed deeply. He loved this weapon. He'd trained so hard over the years, and it had become an extension of him. Masaru opened his eyes and sighed again as he slipped the katana into a black garbage bag, wrapped it up tightly, and reluctantly shoved it into the trash can. As always, Masaru did exactly as Turtak instructed. Early that morning, the voice had given him these instructions and assured Masaru that he'd find his precious katana again once he was in Russia. He trusted Turtak. If he said it would be there, it would.

The idea of not having his sword with him was unsettling. It was no ordinary *shinken katana*. He'd begged his fake parents for it, which was Turtak's idea. He insisted that Masaru be a part of the forging of his own sword. In the end, the sword cost the Hagens sixty thousand dollars. But that ensured that Masaru would be involved in the weapon's creation. Masaru would apprentice under Yoshikazu Yoshihara, the son of renowned Master Swordsmith Yoshindo Yoshihara. It seemed a hard decision for the Hagens to spend that kind of money. Turtak listened in on the Hagens' private conversation. They discussed the purchase to exhaustion. They had the money, but it was still quite the investment. In the end they rationalized that Masaru never asked for much and reasoned that maybe learning more about the Japanese culture would help him fit in better. At the age of twelve he had proven himself to be remarkable with the sword. Masaru had convinced them of the merits in learning the art of sword making and having a katana that he himself made. The education card was always a trump card in the Hagens' case.

The process took three months. Despite Masaru's prosthetic, he was able to be involved at every step. When they were complete, Masaru had a katana that was unlike any the master swordsmiths had ever made. Rather than using traditional

Japanese icons, Masaru used traditional Norse icons. For the tsuba, the blade guard, he used a symbol shown to him by Turtak. He awoke one morning and found the drawing of five interlocking triangles with the Hammer of Thor behind the triangles. He didn't know what it meant, but Turtak assured him he would one day.

Masaru boarded the ferry. A musty smell composed of the ocean combined with decades of cigarette smoke greeted him as he walked inside. It was strangely foreign to him, decorated with Russian influences, rather than Japanese. Orange paint that matched the color of the ship's rusty hull covered the lower half of the walls. Paintings of lush forests stood out from the dirty white paint that covered the upper portion. He'd booked a private room for the two days' travel to Vladivostok.

***

THE VOYAGE across the Sea of Japan had been uneventful. They docked in Vladivostok on Sunday afternoon. Within a few days, the Hagens would see the purchases on the credit card and know that he'd left Japan. They'd be worried, but they'd never be able to find him.

Masaru made his way through customs and immigration and then followed Turtak's directions to retrieve his katana from the restroom. It was exactly where he said it would be. With the katana was a fake Russian I.D. with his pictures on it, a new credit card, a stack of rubles, and the ownership papers and keys for a Suzuki V-Strom 1050 motorcycle. Masaru wrapped the katana within his sleeping bag and exited the restroom.

Not far from the port building, Masaru found the motorcycle parked on the streets. Sleek, with its black and gray chassis and off-road tires, Masaru could not help but feel excited to ride it.

He drove several miles along the coast, enjoying the cool tranquility of his newfound freedom. Tiny ships in the distance slowly made their way across Amur Bay. Masaru stopped to watch one, mesmerized by the cool ocean breeze that danced against his skin and through his hair, drowning out the tiny boat's engines.

"You will go many miles to your destination," Turtak said.

The unseen voice jarred Masaru.

"Your journey serves two purposes. One, it is a means to a destination. Two, it is a trial of your true measure. I will test you to your brink. If you fail, your life will mean nothing, and you will not hear from me again."

The thought of not having the voice to guide him sent shivers down his spine. "You would leave me?"

"You are an instrument forged by my tutelage for a purpose beyond your comprehension. In claiming your birthright, you will change the world forever. But if you fail, then I must find another. Our mission is too important."

"I will not fail."

"Then let us begin."

Masaru rode for several days over mountains, across lakes and rivers, into the cold Russian wilderness. The frigid air didn't bother him. Not like it would anyone else who was only wearing a helmet and a hoodie in below freezing temperatures. He didn't know how cold it was, but it felt invigorating.

The journey was an unfamiliar experience for Masaru. Turtak taught him to hunt for his food, and how to identify edible foliage. He slept in the wild, under the stars.

At the peak of a mountain where Masaru camped for the night, he noticed something strange. In the light covering of snow he found small, four-toed footprints.

In all the years he'd known Turtak, there had been very few physical signs of his presence. An occasional note or drawing, but mainly any sign of Turtak had been audible, but not omnipresent. It emanated from one place in the room or another, but never seemed to come from the same place for too long.

Looking out at the snow, rock, and trees that spread for miles, Masaru breathed in the crisp mountain air. The Hagens had expected him back yesterday. With no word from him they must be worried sick. By now they knew he hadn't gone camping. The authorities could probably trace him as far as Vladivostok. In some small way, he felt sorry for them. But he couldn't think about them now. Their memories only served as distractions, and he still had a long journey ahead of him.

He wished Turtak would be more open with him. There'd been little communication between them since Masaru started this journey. The more he thought about all this mystery and Turtak's flippant statement to replace him if he failed, the more he became angered. He wanted to stomp his feet or lash out with his blade. But Turtak's training kicked in. *Anger only clouds judgment and keeps one from his truth path.* Masaru took a deep breath, exhaling the anger with each breath until he was calm again.

"Who are you?" Masaru asked, staring at the idyllic view of the countryside.

There was no answer.

"I know there's more to you. I saw your footprints. Who are you?" He asked again.

"Masaru," Turtak hesitated. "I am your guide, your teacher, and your only true ally. I always have been."

Masaru turned in the voice's direction. It appeared to be standing ten feet away. There was no snow there, just a large rock.

"Then why won't you reveal yourself to me?"

"It's not time. Soon though, but it is not time now. You have a long way to go."

Masaru didn't like the answer. He wanted more. But there was no doubt in intentions where Turtak was concerned. He led him this far. Turtak told him things no one else ever told him. Everyone else lied to him. Even the doctors. They all pretended that he was human. They said he was human, just different. One doctor told him he had some form of hypochondroplasia no doctor had seen before. They explained to the Hagens that Masaru's type of dwarfism was unique. During their testing, they also discovered that he had elevated levels of gold in his blood. They couldn't explain any of it other than he was a human born with multiple birth defects that would make his life difficult.

Masaru not only lived, he excelled. He was a straight "A"

student. An excellent athlete. There was nothing Masaru couldn't do that any human could. He had to give credit to Turtak. The voice was his ever-present guide and encourager, always assuring him when others just worried.

"Masaru," Turtak once told him, "you are not human. You are beyond human. No human doctor will understand what you are and how special you are. The elements that flow through your blood give you strength and skill beyond human capability."

When he was ten years old, Turtak told him how he had given him to the Hagens.

"I found you, an infant, crying and alone in the cold. Abandoned by your people because you were born with only one arm. I could have taken you anywhere. I took you to the Hagens. And without him knowing, I convinced William Hagen to use his knowledge to make you a new arm. From the day you first learned to crawl, your training began, and I anointed you with the Blood of the Taotie. You were born for war, and I made sure you had all you needed to become the warrior our peoples need."

Masaru had to trust Turtak. He had taken care of him more than anyone else in his life. Masaru was not human. He could live with that. But those footprints he'd seen in the snow, they weren't human either. Four toes? Turtak often used the phrase "our peoples" when he referred to the two of them.

"Are our people the same?" Masaru asked, his gaze still fixed on the view.

"We were not born of the same people. But we share the Blood of the Taotie."

Taotie? When he was ten, that word just seemed like any other word. He hadn't asked about it. Several years later he saw a Japanese manga called *Toutetsu,* which was based on the Chinese legend of the taotie. Two years after that, when visiting China with the Hagens, he saw ancient artwork depicting the taotie. He never asked Turtak about it, but he figured now was a good time to get those answers.

"What do you mean when you say we are Blood of the Taotie?"

"Masaru," Turtak laughed, "you have so many questions today."

"I've had a lot to think about since leaving Japan." Masaru said.

"The taotie were a race of fierce warriors. They were allies to my people. They showed no mercy to their enemy."

"And where are the taotie now?" Masaru said.

"All perished long, long ago. They died fighting the blight who used trickery to bring upon the taotie's demise."

The blight? The more questions were answered, newer questions came up. Masaru could tell that Turtak didn't want to answer any more questions. He stepped forward and began his descent down the mountain.

CHAPTER 15

THE HEART OF THE VEIL

> "Mercurio believed that Nikolaos was a warrior. He had been taught by his father that warriors were not to be honored."
>
> ~ From *The Gift Giver Chronicles* compiled by Volcdegen Vigdis, a Chronicler of the Master Construct, First Order, an alfargnym of Unterbaum

A.D. 343

As the darkness of the mimstone changed to light, the eyes of the fallen bishop opened. Jeremy's head still pounded, but he didn't know if it was from the mimstone or from the empathy he felt for Nikolaos.

The bishop heaved a deep breath as he awoke. The nausea and fear hit him like a hammer plunging a spike into wood. He gasped for air, writhing in discomfort. Nikolaos tried to roll over but his body wouldn't cooperate. Fear, pain, and sore muscles paralyzed him.

"You're awake. I'm surprised." Mercurio said, staring down at him. "You're quite the warrior."

Nikolaos tried to speak… tried to look up at the elf, but he couldn't.

"Be still," Mercurio said, unconcerned. "Ellesmere will be back soon, and this will be over."

Nikolaos groaned.

Mercurio dragged Nikolaos by the pits of his arms and propped the man up against the tree. The elf's strength was impressive for someone his size. He squatted by the bishop's head, pushing him up to a seated position.

Nikolaos squinted groggily. He jerked away, seeing the alfargnym for the first time.

Arnburk held out a small bowl with both hands. "I've longed to try this," he raised his bushy eyebrows and smirked. "I ofttimes give this to the wilder that wander too close to the Veil. It doesn't all take way the effects, but it do make light of them. I eked a wee bit of honey to sweeten it up." The alfargnym brought the bowl to Nikolaos' mouth and helped him drink. "Slow like."

"You may drink of it, Nikolaos. It'll help you." Mercurio said.

Nikolaos had no choice but to sip the sweet concoction, taking shallow breaths in between sips. *What is this?* Nikolaos wondered. The fear increased again, and Nikolaos jerked at its sudden intensity. He pulled his head away.

The alfargnym withdrew the bowl.

This will kill me! Nikolaos thought.

"Nikolaos, your fear is unfounded. You've come this far. You must continue to fight it." Mercurio said.

Nikolaos didn't respond. His eyelids fought to stay open.

Mercurio used his free hand to grab the bowl from Arnburk. He forced it to Nikolaos' lips and used his other hand to hold Nikolaos' head.

Try as he might, Nikolaos couldn't fight any longer. The sweet, warm liquid flowed gently across his dry tongue and he swallowed.

Mercurio let up in between sips until the bowl was empty.

Nikolaos waxed and waned between consciousness and unconsciousness.

"Give the adamu more when his stirring is less and his waking is more." Arnburk said, handing a plugged bottle to Mercurio.

"I will." Mercurio said without glancing at Arnburk or the bottle.

Jeremy sat against a tree across the path from Nikolaos. He watched as Mercurio continued to pace and Arnburk sat and observed Nikolaos. Using what looked like a small piece of charcoal, the alfargnym wrote his observations out on a piece of parchment. He made note of each time Nikolaos stirred.

After about ten minutes, Nikolaos kept his eyes open longer, staring down at the alfargnym before closing his eyes again. Another ten minutes and his lucidity lasted longer and longer.

Jeremy watched Arnburk curiously. He was an odd little man in both speech and mannerisms. Nikolaos felt sorry for him. But Jeremy thought otherwise. Sure, he looked a mess with his tattered blue tunic. And with the number of holes in his hat, Jeremy wondered why he even wore it. He was more fascinating than pitiable. Clean Arnburk up, slap a conical hat on his head, and he'd make a great stand in for a garden gnome.

Nikolaos coughed, drawing Jeremy's attention back to him. He cleared his throat and swallowed before straining to speak. "Are you… an elf too?"

The scraggly alfargnym smiled.

"Not hardly," he replied. "I'm an alfargnym of the Artificer's House. Name's Arnburk."

Nikolaos scrunched his nose and raised an eyebrow.

"I care for this gatehouse and part the Veil for those who wish to enter."

Mercurio crossed his arms and scowled at Arnburk.

The alfargnym cocked his head slightly and smirked at Mercurio, as if he were taunting him. "I'm not one to care for what others think."

The elf, still scowling, turned away.

Arnburk continued. "Most elves be loving behestments and laws and all that other rightfulness stuffs. I prefer solitude and doing what I want."

"Might as well be a svartalgnym!" Mercurio spit.

"Aye, keep your tongue in." Arnburk smiled at Mercurio and then turned back to Nikolaos. "It was we alfargnym what constructed the Veil, so it is we who uphold it. My kind live all over the Master Construct, making certain the Veil artifice are in fine working condition. And keeping the likes of your kind from getting close to it. I been here twenty-two years, and you're the first adamu I ever met."

Mercurio shook his head and glowered at Arnburk. The elf acted as if the alfargnym were giving away state secrets.

"Asking?" Arnburk said, scrunching his furry eyebrows and furling his lips. "I only said, I've not spoken to an adamu before."

Mercurio shook his head again and walked away.

"I must go." Arnburk said, grumbling as he rose to his feet. "Keep sipping the blendish stirring." He nodded to a ceramic bottle sitting beside Nikolaos. "Slow like. I have no knowledge what that minglestuffs can do to an adamu."

"Thank you." Nikolaos said, swallowing to moisten his dry mouth.

The bishop watched the alfargnym walk to the house and disappear through the door. He then turned his head slowly, still fighting aches, pain, and exhaustion.

Mercurio continued to pace back and forth.

Nikolaos hoped the elf would sit and talk with him, but after a while of staring at the pacing elf, Nikolaos fell asleep.

Jeremy focused on Mercurio, and once again the empathy he felt shifted to the elf.

"Hmmm…" Jeremy said. *I wonder if I can control this?*

He experimented by focusing his attention on Nikolaos again. He felt a tugging within his mind, and all of Nikolaos' exhaustion and subconscious emotions came upon him like a weight. Despite feeling exhausted and uneasy, Jeremy uttered an excited, "Yes!" *I can control it. This just keeps getting better.* He shifted empathy back to Mercurio and the exhaustion faded, replaced by apprehension and impatience. The elf picked up a stick and held it forward as if it was a sword.

Mercurio cleared his mind and focused on the sword stances he had learned from his father. He knew them well, but his thoughts constantly pulled him back to the events of the past few days. This adamu perplexed him. Old and frail, yet he fought with ferocity. And his constant questions! If curiosity could be dispelled, Mercurio would surely use all measure of magic to quell this adamu. And what was taking Ellesmere so long? Six hours had passed since she left.

"Six hours!" Jeremy blurted. *How can that be? It only feels like I've been here an hour at the most.* Pangs of panic niggled their way in as Jeremy wondered what was happening in his bedroom at this very moment.

"Jeremy, just focus." He heard the present-day Mercurio say. Jeremy sighed and reluctantly focused his attention back on the young elf.

Unable to concentrate on the sword forms, Mercurio tossed the stick to the side and moved to sit under the tree next to Jeremy. *Where was Ellesmere?* He wondered. *She should have been back by now.* This was not good. They were going to be in so much trouble. Mercurio shuddered. When his father found out, Mercurio feared he'd never be accepted as a Swordsworn. He and Ellesmere had ruined everything.

"Samyaza take her and her curiosity!" Mercurio blurted, slamming his fist into the side of his satchel. A pang of guilt immediately seeped in and Mercurio closed his eyes. He breathed in deeply and commanded the surrounding magic to settle his aura. *I will be a Swordsworn. It might take longer than I wanted, but I will be a Swordsworn.* He grabbed his satchel and produced a scroll. Mercurio fingered the well-worn paper and read it again.

Sahmel Advises

I, Sahmel iyl Sayalla, have traveled through all Veilpoints, and based on observation, I offer my advice to those young who make their first journey through the Veil. Heed these things and you will return safely.

Observe, but never interact with adamu. You may be tempted to do so, especially with their children, but do not give in to your temptation.

Do not take from the adamu. They have many treasures, but they do not belong to you.

Only visit one adamu settlement on any given trip. It is far too easy to stray too far from a Veilpoint.

Always return through the same Veilpoint you entered.

Mercurio slammed the scroll down and huffed with aggravation. He folded the scroll and shoved it back into his pack. He crossed his arms and looked with disdain at Nikolaos.

A faint flicker of colors startled Jeremy. Somehow he knew that Mercurio was focusing on Nikolaos' aura, but he himself couldn't see it the way Mercurio did. In his mind he heard Mercurio use the word *hila*, but he knew it meant aura.

The adamu's aura bewildered Mercurio. Reds, purples, grays, blues, yellows. The intensity of the black and yellow was most disconcerting. The two hues bled together, shifting frequently into ochre. He didn't know what any of it meant. It differed from an elf's aura. Not quite as vibrant and not as erratic. Though this adamu seemed to be under an inordinate amount of stress and discomfort. Perhaps that's what the predominant ochre of his aura indicated?

The adamu had indeed been under much stress these past few days. Mercurio had caused some of that stress. If adamu weren't so irksome, he would've treated Nikolaos better. But that really wasn't what bothered Mercurio about the adamu. He'd done nothing to them. In fact, Nikolaos saved their lives. Mercurio had never met an adamu. He'd seen them… watched them… heard stories about them. He knew firsthand the misery and destruction the adamu could bring.

A brief flicker jarred Jeremy and he flinched.

Mercurio's mother screamed for him to run as a Roman soldier grabbed her by the waist.

Mercurio forced the memory away, and it vanished from Jeremy's mind. The elf sighed and stared intently at Nikolaos. Looking back at the past few days, he could tell Nikolaos was not like the other adamu. Mercurio walked toward the sleeping bishop.

Nikolaos slowly opened his eyes halfway and looked up at Mercurio.

"I suppose I do owe you some gratitude," Mercurio said, taking in a deep breath and shaking his head. "Those goblins would've killed us."

Nikolaos looked up at Mercurio through eyes he struggled to keep open. "You are welcome," he said, forcing a grateful smile.

"Once we take you to the Council of Elders, I can't be sure of what will happen." Mercurio explained. "You'll perhaps be sent to live in one of the more remote Elven cities. At least that is what I would suggest. That is where you'll be safest."

"Are these goblins as evil as you say they are? Will they honestly do the things you say?" Nikolaos asked.

A good question, Jeremy thought. He often wondered about the concept of pure evil. *Could every goblin be evil? Are there any good goblins?*

"Nikolaos, I cannot emphasize enough the evil that resides within their hearts. They will stop at nothing to exact revenge, especially since it was a goblin prince you killed. When word of your deed reaches the Goblin Sar, every one of them will try to find you. If the Sar deems it eternal, the vengeance decree will last beyond his death and be carried on by each new Sar until you're dead. As long as you live, they will hunt for you. That is why I'd suggest a more remote region for your asylum. Perhaps the Northern city, Orindin, where Ellesmere is from. The goblins would most likely never look there because there are no surrounding adamu settlements for them to search for you."

"But how will I live there? What will I do with my life in the company of elves?"

"Is it not customary for old warriors such as yourself to retire from war? And let your younger warriors go to battle?"

Nikolaos scrunched his eyes and wrinkled his nose. "An old warrior like me?" The bishop painfully chuckled.

"Are you not old for an adamu? Your hair and beard are white, and your face is wrinkled."

Nikolaos tried to laugh, but his discomfort made it difficult.

"Mercurio, I am indeed old. But I'm no warrior. I'm a bishop."

Mercurio returned a perplexed stare. "Not a warrior? You traveled with two young warriors and fought beside them. You commanded them in battle and you yourself slew a goblin prince."

"Those young men…" Nikolaos paused and his smile faded. "They were my guards. They were there to protect me when I travel. They weren't seeking war, nor was I. If anything, we were seeking peace."

"Ah. I think I see. They were your guardians. And you are not a warrior, but a peacemaker?"

"I'm a bishop. I am… I was the spiritual leader of my city."

"Ah. An elder. I see." Mercurio said. "But I don't know what you mean by spiritual leader."

Nikolaos pondered before he spoke.

"I teach people about God. I help people when they're in need."

"My mother told me of these gods you adamu follow."

"Not gods. God. One God." Nikolaos corrected.

"*You* follow one god. Other adamu follow more than one. Your kind has been deceived by goblins. They once hid themselves among you, pretending to be your gods. And you adamu blindly followed them. It seems confusing to me." Mercurio shook his head. "You adamu always complicate things."

Deceived by goblins? Jeremy found that statement… disturbing. What did Mercurio mean by that? Was it the same thing in the modern world? How could people be deceived into thinking that goblins were gods?

"Why do you call me adamu?" Nikolaos changed the subject.

"You are an adamu. I'm an elf."

"We call ourselves man."

"Different words, same meaning." Mercurio said. He then

cocked his head toward the house. He could feel Ellesmere's presence.

"Is something wrong?" Nikolaos asked.

Mercurio jumped to his feet. "The Veil has been parted."

Jeremy stood up and watched Mercurio run to the house, leaving Nikolaos behind.

Where had Ellesmere gone? Nikolaos wondered. In the amazement of having a genuine conversation with Mercurio, he had forgotten to even ask what had happened to her.

Ellesmere, followed by Arnburk, and the purple fairy, emerged from the house. She raised a scroll above her head.

"Good tidings!" she said. "The elders have given Nikolaos permission to pass through the Veil."

They wasted no time. The trio packed their belongings and headed toward the house. Ellesmere stood by Nikolaos' side, helping him walk.

He still felt weak. His stomach turned and twisted, but he pushed on. The fear lingered, calling from the house. It whispered to him. An unintelligible, but foreboding whisper. He didn't want to go anywhere near it. With one hand on Ellesmere's shoulder and his other hand on his staff, the former bishop of Myra ambled toward the house.

The trio followed Arnburk inside. Nikolaos bent to fit through the door, his back straining from the effort. A musty odor greeted him, and his nose wrinkled to prevent a sneeze. His eyes took in the simple room with a single glance: two small cots, a small table and chairs, and a set of cupboards. The wooden floor creaked under the weight of Nikolaos. Hunched over, crammed in, and still fighting off the effects of the Veil, Nikolaos wanted to just lay down and curl up into a ball.

From out of the shadows, a slightly thinner, yet equally scraggly alfargnym walked toward the table.

Nikolaos jerked backwards and withdrew.

Ellesmere comforted him by squeezing his hand and forearm and giving him an assuring nod.

The thinner alfargnym moved the chairs away from the table and placed them against the far wall.

Arnburk opened the cupboard, reached in and pulled something.

A creaking, mechanical sound emanated from the walls and floor. Whirring and whizzing from some unseen mechanical contraption filled the room.

The floor beneath the table tilted on one side and the table it held stayed in place. *Was it nailed to the floor? Or was this magic?* Nikolaos dared not ask for fear of appearing the fool.

He watched intently as the moving floor revealed a secret passage down a large staircase.

Arnburk closed the cupboard door and opened another one. He produced a small scepter-like object. The handle was wood, inlaid with gold designs. He waved his hand over the glass orb at its tip and it glowed brightly. He handed it to Nikolaos, who reluctantly accepted it.

"Odin guide your way," Arnburk said.

Nikolaos examined the object. The base of the handle; a uniform gold inlay over the wooden shaft. Just above that, a golden design of flames reached all the way to the top, where they formed a base for the glowing orb.

Jeremy felt a wave of wonder wash from him to Nikolaos.

The purple-winged fairy flitted around Nikolaos' head again and then hovered between his face and the glowing orb. It stared, nodding its head from side to side and bobbing it back and forth, looking at the orb, then at Nikolaos' face.

Nikolaos stared back at the flittering creature and then switched his gaze back to the torch. He held his hand over the glowing orb. It produced no heat and felt cool to the touch.

Ellesmere looked up at Nikolaos and smiled. "If you are amazed at that, you'll truly be amazed when you get to Sayalla."

Despite what he had seen these past few days, everything seemed to get stranger and stranger. He couldn't even imagine what he would see in the land of the elves.

The other alfargnym hobbled over to the stairs and descended.

Mercurio followed behind him. Arnburk stayed close to the cupboard and motioned Nikolaos to go. Ellesmere helped Nikolaos down each step.

The size of the staircase surprised Nikolaos. "Such a large staircase for such small people," Nikolaos said in wonder.

"Elves and alfargnym aren't the only ones who used this passage," said the unnamed alfargnym, annoyed, as if Nikolaos should know.

"Um, my name is Nikolaos. And thank…"

"Don't care… don't want to know. Just follow the elves."

The alfargnym, the elves, and Nikolaos walked down the long flight of stairs into the darkness, lit only by the steady glowing light of the flameless torch. Nikolaos was grateful for the torch, but even with it, he could barely see anything. From the staircase above, Nikolaos heard the gentle rumble of the secret door sliding back in place. *This is it.* His life, as he knew it, had ended.

The dark staircase led them down hundreds of feet below the Earth's surface. The air turned from fresh and warm to stale and cool. The light of the flameless torch revealed a stairwell and stairs made of finely carved stone. It curved into a spiral that made Nikolaos even more dizzy with each step.

Nearing the end of the staircase, a faint light intensified as they came closer to the bottom. With only a few steps left, they came to a brightly lit circular chamber. Nikolaos' eyes opened wide and his mouth followed. In the center, a shimmering golden curtain of light dispersed into three concentric swirls, radiating from the center of the golden disk. Golden sparkles, like tiny stars, waxed and waned in the darker golden streams of light. On the wall, opposite the curtain of light, hung a wooden sign, written in a language Nikolaos didn't understand.

Beside the disk was a contraption of wheels within wheels. Strange symbols were etched around each wheel's perimeter. Protruding from the side of the contraption were two gold rods. The unfriendly alfargnym grabbed the golden rods and the shimmering field grew in intensity. The room blazed with golden brilliance.

"It's set and ready for you," said the alfargnym.

Mercurio walked into the light and disappeared.

"Nikolaos, you'll go through next," Ellesmere said. "Don't worry, you won't feel a thing. Just walk through and you'll see Mercurio on the other side."

Nikolaos took a deep breath and stepped into the shimmering light.

CHAPTER 16

CITY OF WONDER

"The Veil is one of the most uneath artifices created. Its inworkings and structure are a onefoldly work of elven, alfargnym, and dweorg wrights and crafters."
~ From *The Veiled Happenlore of the Master Construct* compiled by Fulbert Gisilfrid, a Chronicler of the Master Construct, Third Order, an alfargnym of Unterbaum.

A.D. 342

Jeremy blinked and the brilliant, shimmering curtain of the Veil stood before him. The younger Mercurio beside him. The room was different… nicer. Fresh air replaced the musty smell. The walls, made of bright gold bricks and trimmed with contoured white stone crown molding, reminded him of something he might have seen in an ancient history book.

Behind him, on the wall, hung a white stone sign with Elvish lettering that read "Sayalla".

Mercurio, arms crossed, waited for Nikolaos to come through

the Veil. *What will the council say of all this? Worst of all, what will my father say?*

A smiling alfargnym stood beside Mercurio. He wore a blue conical hat and matching vest. His hands, tightly wrapped around a wrench-like tool, nervously squeezed it with excitement. There was a familiarity between them. But something about the alfargnym aggravated Mercurio.

From within the shimmering curtain of golden light, a hand carefully reached out, searching for whatever it might find. Nikolaos timidly stepped through the Veil. He placed his free hand on his stomach, the other clutching his staff, he breathed a sigh of relief and looked around. His eyes fixed on the alfargnym who grinned at him with a smile that was barely dwarfed by his bulbous nose.

Nikolaos stepped away from the golden circle below the shimmering curtain and greeted the alfargnym.

"Peace to you. My name is Nikolaos."

"Wonder of creation!" The alfargnym turned to Mercurio. "He's real… and a big one at that!"

"Yes, he is," Mercurio said flatly under a displeased sigh.

"Hail, Nikolaos." The alfargnym said, nodding his head and still smiling. "My name is Geirmund Archenbald, an Artificer of the Master Construct, Wright of the First Order, an alfargnym of Unterbaum."

Geirmund slowly circled around Nikolaos; his eyes wide, his mouth an open smile. He stopped in front of the man, extended his pointer finger and gently touched Nikolaos' staff.

"I am unbelieving! There's an adamu on this side of the Veil!" Geirmund said. "In my gatehouse! My gatehouse. I'm greatly unbelieving, Mercurio. And you of all elves brought him here. You're on the wrong side of this mess," he said laughing.

"It wasn't something I wanted to do," Mercurio responded just as Ellesmere walked through the curtain.

"Ellesmere!" Geirmund shouted, waddling over and hugging the elf. "I'm unbelieving! You brought a real adamu to this side of the Veil. This is a historic day. I think I shall petition my Clan Lord to speak to the council and declare it a holiday."

"You will not," Mercurio snapped. "This is just an ordinary adamu. His presence here will make no difference to anyone. He's just going to live the rest of his days here."

"Ohhh… that's right," Geirmund's smile turned to a frown. "Adamu don't live too long. But still. He's the first. He's the first adamu to enter Sayalla, or any keshaphim city for that matter."

"Hear me now, Geirmund," Mercurio admonished. "He's here because he's in danger! We will *not* be celebrating his coming for years to come. He won't be remembered by anyone, because no one is to know that he's here."

Geirmund recoiled slightly.

"He will be in hiding, and you'll not tell anyone that you saw this adamu!"

"Whoa! Guess you were wrong there." Jeremy laughed, trying to solicit a response from the present-day Mercurio. But there was no reply.

"Umm, umm…" Geirmund stammered.

"Enough talk," Mercurio said, turning away from the artificer. "Take us upstairs so we can be on our way."

The deflated alfargnym complied. Mercurio followed him. Nikolaos stepped up the first rise and Ellesmere stopped him.

"Nikolaos, you're going to have to stay hidden."

Mercurio stopped at the third rise and turned to see why Ellesmere stopped.

"Put this on," Ellesmere said, handing Nikolaos her Veil Cloak.

That cloak. Mercurio thought, sighing. Their cloaks were more trouble than they were worth. He watched Nikolaos fumble with the clasp. It reminded him of when Ellesmere first put it on herself. A fiftieth birthday gift from her parents; the day that marked her passing into adulthood. *In hindsight,* Mercurio thought, *this was such a foolish tradition.* These cloaks gave his people a false sense of security. How foolish they were to travel into the Adamu-lands thinking they were safe in their cloaks. Mercurio's mother had taken him a few times to observe the adamu. She had been cautious, and his mother's wisdom tempered his excitement. When it had come time for Ellesmere to visit the Adamulands for the first time, Mercurio volunteered to be the one to take her. *What a fool I was.* Ellesmere was so excited to go, even more than Mercurio. She couldn't stop talking about everything she wanted to see. Mercurio tried to prepare her, just as his mother had prepared him each time they pierced the Veil. Their cloaks should have kept them hidden. But those goblins rode nian. The vile beasts must have outed them while they walked through the forest.

Nikolaos' struggle to clasp the cloak snapped Mercurio back to the present. *This isn't good.* Other keshaphim were sure to notice the big lumbering adamu. When Nikolaos finally got the cloak on, he looked ridiculous. But it would have to do.

Jeremy smiled at the sight of the large man in the elf's small cloak. The white Elven silk contrasted against Nikolaos' dirty, red robes.

"Now put on the cowl." Ellesmere instructed. "And keep it over your head and hide as much of your face as you can."

Nikolaos did as he was told, and then he vanished.

"Good," Ellesmere said, holding out her hand toward Nikolaos. "It's working. Remember, keep the cowl on. We can't see you. Hand me your staff."

Nikolaos hesitated and then placed the shaft in her outstretched hand. She grasped it. He let go, and the bishop's staff appeared.

"Good, now you hold on to the shaft so I can guide you."

"Ellesmere, what is this? What are you speaking about?" Nikolaos said.

"The cloak. It'll keep you hidden from some, but not all…" She paused. "I'm not sure how to describe the different kinds that live here. We use the word keshaphim. I don't know the word in your language. Perhaps the closest might be *daimon*, but I'm unsure."

"I'm not sure either, because I still don't quite understand what you are. How is it you speak Greek so well, yet you can't tell me what this word means?"

Ellesmere cocked her head to the left, thinking. "I guess there's no word in your language to describe us." She shrugged.

"Enough of the questions, Nikolaos." Mercurio said. "We must go. You'll need to be silent, so that Ellesmere does not appear out of wits talking to someone who isn't there."

"I'll try to explain it later." Ellesmere said. "But you are about to see for yourself." She smiled.

Jeremy followed them as they climbed the staircase. Unlike the one below the ramshackle house, this passage was lit by flameless torches held in decorative sconces interspersed at intervals. As he walked up the stairs, Nikolaos rubbed his hand along the smooth bricks and up to the sconces holding flameless torches. The craftsmanship was not only beautiful with its intricate gold vine and leaf design, but it was also unlike anything Nikolaos had ever seen.

The arduous climb left Nikolaos nearly breathless as they reached the top. He heard voices; strange voices talking in a language or languages that he couldn't understand.

The top of the stairs led to a small room with an archway. Beyond the archway, Nikolaos came upon a display that sent him staggering back.

"Whoa!" Jeremy gasped. Goosebumps danced across the back of his neck. He paused, taking in the grandeur before him. A vast room, brilliantly lit. Creatures of all shapes, hues, and sizes walking everywhere, in every direction. His own excitement, combined with Nikolaos' astonishment, was too much for him to take. His heart raced. He felt lightheaded. He took a deep breath and braced himself against the archway, unable to take his eyes off the scene.

The creatures all appeared to be about their own business. Some were talking to companions. Others hurried toward destinations unknown. The grand hall reminded Jeremy of the hub at Grand Central Station, only far more elegant.

He swallowed, trying to take in every delicate detail. Jeremy gasped, bringing his hands to his mouth. He could easily pick the elves out of the crowd. Just outside the archway were three of them. Two appeared to be guards. One wearing a green tunic and a floppy green hat stood on a ladder, polishing a sconce. Standing below the elf, Jeremy saw a creature that took his breath away. It was unlike any he'd seen so far. Perhaps as tall as Mercurio, it stood on massive, animal-like clawed feet and used its thick, long tail for balance. Most frightening of all was the creature's long snout, sharp teeth, and horns. Jeremy stared at the large reptile with astonishment equal to Nikolaos. He scratched his head, wondering what it was. *Is that a dragon? A velociraptor?*

The creature held the ladder for the elf and didn't seem a danger to anyone. In fact, it seemed as if it were there to help. It wore a pack around the front of its body. The creature used its thin fingers to reach into the pack and grab an orb, like the ones he'd seen glowing in the sconces below.

The elf took the orb and exchanged it with one that was in the sconce he had been polishing. When he placed the orb on the sconce, it glowed. The soft light gleamed enough to highlight the light and dark green stripes of the creature's skin.

A koth. The word came to him and he knew instantly that this creature was called a koth.

He could see several other kinds of fae in the grand hall. They all seemed vaguely familiar to Jeremy. Some similar in size to the elves. Some smaller. Others taller. Fairies fluttered around the chamber, darting between, around, and over the other occupants.

Jeremy's eyes fixed on another creature he'd never seen before. A strange little one, maybe eighteen inches tall, with purple fur that shimmered with golden light. It looked like a cross between a monkey, a cartoon troll, and a Furby! There were several of these small, furry, ear-less creatures. Some walked on two legs beside elf or faun companions, while others were carried. Some had purple fur of varying shades, and others had red and brown fur. Jeremy counted seven different ones. *Are they some kind of pet?*

Krodin. These creatures were called krodin. Jeremy smiled, marveling at the mimstone's ability to convey information. He wondered what more the magical stone could do.

Aside from the large hall's occupants, the sheer grandeur of it astounded Jeremy. Six carved archways identical to the one they stood in lined the other side of the oblong hall. Large wooden doors hung on either of the opposite sides of the hall. As creatures exited and entered through the doorway, Jeremy could see daylight streaming through. The upper perimeter, lined with stained glass, allowed more daylight to flood through the windows.

High above the ground, in the center of the great hall, hung a magnificent chandelier with eight arms, each in the shape of a small dragon. From each one's mouth a modest flame flickered. Together they lit the center of the hall. A long chain attached to a circular hub that looped around the curled tails of each reptile held the chandelier in place.

Each archway shared sconces on either side. Guards stood between each arch. They wore beautiful bronze armor that seemed to be molded perfectly to their bodies. The rounded bronze helmets covered their heads but left the face exposed. Unfamiliar etchings and designs adorned the armor. On the upper right side of the chest plate, they each wore an identical symbol that Jeremy couldn't make out from this distance.

He watched as a guard across the way greeted a faun carrying a small harp. A mixture of man and beast, from the waist up the faun appeared to be a human despite the grayish-white goat-like horns on his head that contrasted with his mahogany brown hair. Below the waist, thick fur that matched the hair on his head covered his legs. And where feet should be, the creature had haunches and black hooves. It wore a dark blue shirt that buttoned three-quarters of the way, exposing a patch of hair on his chest. A strip of blue cloth hung from his waist by a rope.

Jeremy giggled, thinking of Mr. Tumnus from *The Chronicles of Narnia.*

A talkative female elf walked beside the faun. In her arms she carried a contented krodin. The elf and faun appeared to be following a green-clad alfargnym through the archway.

Jeremy caught sight of a fairy that crossed the archway and approached Nikolaos. It zipped around the man's head, making a giggling noise. Seconds later, another fluttered around him. No bigger than Jeremy's hand, the fairies circled Nikolaos' head several times. They wore no clothing and had no noticeable genitalia. But their human-like features surprised Jeremy. Tiny fingers attached to tiny arms extended out as if they wanted to hug Nikolaos. Before the embrace came, they shot off, kicking their long svelte legs and making another few loops around his head. The two fairies were nearly identical except for their skin color; one blue, and the other purple. Each glowed with a faint light in their respective colors.

The blue one stopped and alighted in front of Nikolaos' face. Its long, flowing blue hair shimmered and waved as if it was under water. Its facial features were strikingly beautiful and very human-like, save for its stark, pupil-less black eyes. It stared at Nikolaos and smiled.

The man stared back at the fairy with an awestruck smile.

"Samyaza!" Mercurio yelled. "The fairies are drawn to him!"

"Wonder! They're drawn to his wonder!" Ellesmere exclaimed. "I feared this."

Before the elves could respond, two more of the flittering creatures showed up and circled around Nikolaos. He pulled off his hood to get a better look at the fairies.

The din of the bustling promenade beyond the archway slowly dulled. Jeremy looked out to see what was going on.

A chain reaction of startled and speechless fae turned to a whispering stand still as they gawked at the sight of the man.

Nikolaos quickly pulled the hood back on again and wafted his hand in front of his face to clear away the fairies.

"Ah… Samyaza, do not take me!" Mercurio said. "Go and get a covered wagon and pull it up to the back," he told Ellesmere. "We can't walk through the streets of Sayalla with everyone seeing this adamu."

"There is no need for that," said the elf guarding the archway.

"The council has sent a dispatch to escort you and the adamu to the Hall of Na'Sim."

Mercurio looked over at Ellesmere. Embarrassed at forgetting to tell him that one detail she turned her eyes downward and flashed him an awkward smile.

The set of large wooden doors on the left opened, and a regiment of Elven soldiers entered.

Nikolaos took a deep breath as panic set in. He saw the soldiers, but heard no sound as they approached. No clanging of armor or the stomping of armored feet. They were as quiet as mice. The menacing soldiers closed in on him. Some carried spears, and others held swords.

Jeremy felt pangs of panic radiate from the man.

Nikolaos clung to his staff as memories flooded in. Flashes of Roman soldiers marching through Myra kicking in doors appeared in Jeremy's mind. One soldier grabbed Nikolaos. He fought back, but they beat him down with clubs.

Nikolaos gasped for air and the fairies flew away.

The army of Elven soldiers stopped outside the archway and formed a perimeter that blocked the gawking crowd from seeing Nikolaos.

A soldier walked up to Mercurio, and Ellesmere. He stood out as their leader, distinguished by his green cape and green pauldrons. Jeremy glimpsed the curious looking ornament on the upper part of their chests. It reminded him of a badge; a large circular-cut emerald, set in silver, and held in place by tiny silver leaves. Behind the setting hung two swords.

"You'll follow me. We have a carriage waiting for you outside."

CHAPTER 17
THE COUNCIL OF NINE

"When Janek iyl Nadal, the Dark Elf Elder first laid eyes on Nikolaos, he wanted to kill the man himself. He found it an affront to the Veil Accords that a human should set foot on Elven soil. "

~ From *The Gift Giver Chronicles* compiled by Volcdegen Vigdis, a Chronicler of the Master Construct, First Order, an alfargnym of Unterbaum

A.D. 342

The wagon eased forward without a jerk, surprising Nikolaos. He'd expected to be jostled in the cramped quarters. It made very little noise, unlike the carpentum and chariots he was accustomed to in Rome and Myra. *Are we being pulled by a horse?* He didn't hear the familiar clopping. *Perhaps we are being carried? No.* He didn't feel as if someone had lifted them like they were being carried in a palanquin. *Strange.*

Jeremy wondered the same thing. It wasn't quite like being in a car or truck, and it didn't remind him of the horse-drawn hayrides he had been on.

Mercurio sat with his arms crossed, deep in thought; his eyes turned down and his jaw clenched into an angry frown.

Nikolaos looked as uncomfortable and cramped as an adult in a child-sized blanket fort. He tried to peer through a tiny crack in the wagon's curtain, but anything he could see went by in a blur.

Jeremy couldn't make anything out either. But he imagined being in an Elven town with other buildings as magnificent as the one he had just exited. His imagination ran wild picturing fantastic creatures and stunning structures. But all he saw were the two elves, Nikolaos, and the faint stream of light coming through the crack in the curtain.

Outside the wagon, an orchestra of sounds and a symphony of smells only served to fuel his imagination. Birds chirped. Voices spoke unknown languages. The clanking of tools and the shifting and shuffling of everyday objects joined with the scent of fresh bread, roasting meat, wildflowers, and grass. Strangely absent though was the sound of horses and wagon wheels rolling. The timbre of the orchestra changed as the trickling of water joined in. The wagon tilted slightly upward and the sound of steady, rushing water became more prevalent. As the wagon arched its way back down, the sounds slowly returned to the normal din of city life.

The gurgle of the river distracted him, serving to amplify his curiosity. Where were they? Were they even still on Earth?

The cart stopped. Nikolaos grunted. His discomfort heightened with alarm when the back of the wagon opened.

Two long lines of bronze-clad soldiers led to a doorway… a peculiar-looking doorway. *A doorway into a tree?*

Ellesmere and Mercurio hopped out first. Nikolaos craned his aching neck out of the wagon and was immediately greeted by a flittering pink fairy. She swooshed around his head; arms wide as if absorbing some unseen energy. Nikolaos tried to ignore the creature and work out the kinks in his shoulders. He slowly stepped down from the wagon, leaning on his staff for balance and arching backwards to stretch his sore muscles.

Jeremy peeked his head out of the wagon and he froze in awe

of this new sight before him: a tree so massive it seemed the size of a skyscraper. He looked around slowly, wanting to absorb every aspect of the splendor before him. His mouth grew into a wide smile with each unfamiliar sight.

This is incredible!

Walkways and outcroppings of rooms along the tree's immense branches connected to other trees in what appeared to be a city unlike anything Nikolaos and Jeremy had ever seen. Images of New York City and Chicago surfaced in Jeremy's mind, and the beauty and architecture of this Elven city rivaled even those.

The great city's canopy allowed faint rays of crepuscular light to stream through, illuminating levels upon levels of various shaped rooms.

From walkways and windows, elves and other creatures peered down at Nikolaos. Some smiled. Others stared with wide-eyed wonder.

Nikolaos returned that same sentiment of amazement as he took in the wonders. How strange it must be for this man to see these things. Jeremy had the advantage of having read fantasy and science fiction books and he had seen special effects in movies and TV. He lived in New York City with all its grand architecture, old and new. But Nikolaos had never even seen a skyscraper.

Three more fluttering fairies appeared and circled around Nikolaos' head.

"Nikolaos, come," Ellesmere said.

He walked toward the tall double doors that lead into the massive tree, past lines of soldiers. Two guards, holding polearms, stood beside the doors. As Nikolaos approached, the doors opened, though no one attended them. Grateful that he would not have to bend over to enter, Nikolaos crossed the spacious threshold into a large well-lit room. The inner walls rippled with column-like limbs connected to roots that gripped the gargantuan tree in place. Several columns sprouted vine-like protrusions that wrapped around flameless glowing sconces. Two more guards stood to the rear. The room itself was unadorned, save for a large round platform in the center. Made from wood overlaid with gold vines and leaves arranged in an ornate pattern, the pedestal stood as high as a stair step. Gilded leaves of varying size folded over the platform's edge in evenly dispersed increments along its perimeter.

The two guards in the rear stepped forward and onto the pedestal.

Ellesmere gently pulled Nikolaos' arm, guiding him.

Mercurio stepped up, followed by Jeremy, Nikolaos and Ellesmere.

Jeremy and Nikolaos looked up and found that most of the tree's inside was hollow. The ceiling was at least thirty feet from the pedestal. A set of odd-looking doors, set within the side of the tree, twenty feet up, caught Jeremy's attention.

Strange. Jeremy looked down and up again. *He smiled. This must be some sort of elevator.*

A tapping and clicking sound from the sides diverted Jeremy's attention. The guard had placed the dull end of his polearm into a recess by his feet. The pedestal gently rose.

Nikolaos nearly lost his balance. He used his staff and Ellesmere's shoulder to steady himself.

They slowly ascended. Nikolaos took a deep breath, and, with eyes wide and mouth agape, he looked down as the ground grew more distant. The platform moved with an ease and fluidity that never wavered in one direction or another. Yet Nikolaos felt uneasy. The strange feeling of moving upward as the inner shaft narrowed unnerved him further.

Nikolaos closed his eyes and took another deep breath. Any moment now he was going to meet a group of beings who would decide his fate. In his heart he feared these people even more than he feared the Council of Bishops.

He opened his eyes and removed his hand from Ellesmere's shoulder. Nikolaos straightened his robes. They were tattered and filthy. He looked at his hand and it too was dirty. Lifting his hand to his face, he felt the accumulated grime of the past two days. His beard felt hard and caked with dirt and... *I hope that isn't blood.* He was about to meet Elven royalty, and he looked as if he didn't care about his own appearance. He looked over at the two elves. The frail-looking, childlike creatures looked as disheveled and dirty as he did: a stark contrast to the polished bronze armor of the Elven soldiers standing on either side of them.

The pedestal slowly came to a stop, fitting snugly within the trees' inner perimeter. It fit so perfectly the platform looked like it was the floor. Large double doors, matching the designs on the pedestal, stood in front of them.

The doors opened, and Nikolaos slowly walked into the room, leaning on his staff with every footstep.

Jeremy followed him into the room, and his jaw dropped. Should he have been surprised at the grandeur of the Elven Court of Elders? He gasped, taking in the splendor of this room with its high ceiling, its grand architecture, and opulent decor.

They stood on a massively wide tree branch, at least six feet across. To the branch's left and right, planks of polished dark-brown hardwood made up the rest of the large chamber's floor.

Sitting on a platform six feet off the floor sat nine… beings. Six he recognized as elves. Three were clad all in black, their faces hidden by menacing masks. An aura of golden light surrounded all of them, though it was fainter on those in black.

These nine elves would be the ones that decided the fate of Nikolaos. The elders sat in an ornate configuration of branches woven together to create nine identical high-backed, throne-like chairs. At the crest of each chair back, ensconced by vine-like branches, inlaid a distinct gemstone. Each of the elders dressed differently; all elegant and imposing in their own way.

They stared at Nikolaos, studying him as if he were some strange new creature. None frightened the man more than the faceless ones. He couldn't see their eyes, yet they appeared to be staring at him… not at him, but through him into his very soul. Each wore a unique mask. One had eye slits and swirled circular patterns etched into its surface. Another's was overlaid with iron, giving it the appearance of a beast with large fangs. The third one resembled a face frozen with stoic resignation. These three had the appearance of demons. Nikolaos averted his gaze and looked up. *God of Heaven and Earth, help your servant, please.*

Nikolaos and Jeremy turned their attention to the six brightly dressed elves. These six elders had a youthful appearance, like the older Mercurio. Each of them, though dressed somewhat differently, had a regal bearing that bordered on angelic. Their skin... their very countenance seemed to glow with golden radiance, just like Mercurio when Jeremy first met him. Jeremy turned to the young Mercurio, standing in front of Nikolaos. *Strange.* He didn't glow like his older self.

The elders continued to scrutinize Nikolaos. The silence deepened until it took on a life of its own. It lay heavy on Nikolaos; an oppressive thing that gripped him around the chest and made it hard to breathe. He shivered under the intensity of their gaze.

Fear... worry... doubt; it all slammed into Jeremy. The weight of all that had occurred in the last three days compounded at that very moment. The attack. The long journey here. The knowledge that Nikolaos would never see his loved ones again. Had God forsaken him? Nikolaos could no longer meet the elders' intense gaze. He shut his eyes. After taking a deep breath, he opened them again, this time staring into the light that streamed through four open windows behind the elders.

Green drapes held open by curved branches adorned each one. Outside, varied hues of brown and green leaves rustled ever so slightly with the wind.

Between each pair of windows, a tapestry hung. Nikolaos' eyes drew to the green one in the center. Sunlight reflected off the gold and silver embroidery that formed a diamond shaped twinkling star on the center panel. Gemstones, matching each of the ones on the nine thrones, made up the star's perimeter.

"You are Nikolaos?" Asked the elf in the center chair, his voice gentle and its cadence slow. He spoke in Greek. Each word carried with it an air of wisdom, and when he spoke, he spoke with a calm authority that put Nikolaos at some ease. Yet, he found himself unable to speak. He wanted to reply, but he was in awe of the power and majesty that this creature emanated. Dressed in indigo and green, accented with silver, this elf appeared regal yet youthful. A band of silver leaves held back his long, golden hair. Around his slim neck he wore a silver pendant with an emerald gem that matched the one on the back of his throne.

The elder turned to Ellesmere, "Does this adamu speak?" He asked in Elvish.

"Elder Avisjai, he speaks," Ellesmere responded in Greek and gently placed her hand on Nikolaos' forearm. "I believe he's nervous."

Nikolaos swallowed and cleared his throat. "Yes," responded Nikolaos, bobbing his head. "Yes, your highness, my name is Nikolaos."

"Welcome to our city, Sayalla."

"Th… thank you." Nikolaos said.

"We are grateful for your service to our kind." Avisjai continued.

"I especially am grateful." Another of the Elders spoke. This one wore a long, floppy green cloth hat with the point hanging to the side. It was like the one that Ellesmere wore. Its fluffy white brim hid most of the elder's short, brown hair. To Jeremy, it looked like some fancy-looking Christmas hat. The elder's shirt was green with puffy sleeves and a frilled collar that hung over his ice blue vest. He had the same pendant as the others, only his gemstone was a light bluish green. "I am Laven. Ellesmere is my daughter, and you saved her life."

"I only—" Nikolaos said.

"Nevertheless," Laven said, raising his hand. "We owe you a debt of gratitude. And the least we can do is offer you our protection. I am the Elder of the northern city of Orindin. You shall be safe living there with us. Our city is small, but you will find it comfortable. And, although you are our guest, it is our hope that you will become a member of our community. My people have already begun constructing a house for you that would accommodate your size."

What? That's it? No discussion? Was he supposed to say thank you and leave?

"Forgive me," Nikolaos said and then paused, thinking of what to say. "I… hmmm… I am thankful for your protection and hospitality." He swallowed. "I will do my part as a member of your community."

"Very well then." Laven said. "Ellesmere, you will escort Nikolaos and show him his new home."

The pedestal guards turned, as did Mercurio and Ellesmere. Nikolaos followed.

"Mercurio…" Elder Avisjai called. He then said something in their language.

The trio stopped and turned.

Jeremy shifted his empathy to Mercurio. A pulse of trepidation hit him.

"Your father wishes to see you, immediately."

Mercurio's brows pulled together as he lowered his head. The elf turned and headed back toward the exit.

Jeremy didn't need the mimstone's magic to sense Mercurio's apprehension.

When they left the tree, the wagon awaited them. Nikolaos laid his staff inside and crawled in, careful not to bump his head.

Jeremy followed.

A well of emotions warred in Nikolaos. He was concerned for Mercurio. But he was equally concerned for himself. His presence here caused a hardship for the elves, especially Mercurio. But he didn't understand why. The elder, Laven, was grateful that Nikolaos intervened. Look where that got him; one-way passage to the frozen north. He'd never see his people again. Never would he carve another toy for a child. Never would he again pray with his friends when they needed help. Nikolaos sighed, then swallowed. A tear formed, but he fought against any joining it.

Jeremy looked away, feeling sorry for the man. Outside the wagon he caught sight of Ellesmere and Mercurio standing in front of the gargantuan tree. Ellesmere placed a consoling hand on Mercurio's shoulder as she spoke to him. Mercurio sighed and pursed his lips. Ellesmere reached out and drew her friend in for a hug. Mercurio reciprocated. They broke the embrace and Ellesmere hopped into the carriage.

"Let us be off," she said, smiling at Nikolaos.

The guard closed the curtain on the wagon and it lurched forward.

"Ellesmere, tell me about your home." Nikolaos said.

The elf smiled. "Orindin… is a strange paradise, Nikolaos. It is unlike any of the other Elven cities. I cannot compare it to any adamu cities, though it is quite different than the two I've seen. But you shall see very soon."

"How long will the journey be?"

"Oh, minutes," Ellesmere smiled again.

"You said it was up in the north."

"Indeed. We'll be there shortly. We're going back to the Heart of the Veil. There we'll go through the gate that connects Sayalla to Orindin."

"Ellesmere. This confuses me," Nikolaos said. "We walked so far from my homeland, to that old house, and then we walked through that… that, light and everything there… here is different. I can feel the change in climate. It's not as humid here and it's slightly cooler."

"Let me explain. You live, um, you lived in a place you called Asia. When we pierced the Veil to Sayalla, it led us to the land you call Germania. That is where we are now."

Jeremy pushed his fingers beneath his glasses to massage his eyes and forehead, trying to wrap his mind around the conversation.

"How is that possible? That would be thousands of miles traveled in a single pace!"

The carriage stopped.

"So, we aren't on another plane or a planet. We're in Germany?" Jeremy said, but no one responded.

"You have much to learn, my new friend," Ellesmere said.

The flap of the wagon opened, and they were back at what Ellesmere called the Heart of the Veil.

Inside, soldiers surrounded Nikolaos and escorted him through an archway. Crowds of fae gathered behind the wall of soldiers, attempting to catch a peek at the oddity known as Nikolaos.

They descended the staircase beyond the archway. In the chamber at the bottom of the stairs, two alfargnym greeted Nikolaos.

One of them moved into position next to the ornate disk in the chamber's center. He placed his hands on two gold rods and in seconds the shimmering curtain appeared, increasing in intensity and bathing the room in golden light.

Ellesmere and Nikolaos stood at the Veil's entrance. The elf looked up at Nikolaos and smiled. "I'll see you in Orindin," Ellesmere said as she walked through the curtain of light.

Nikolaos inhaled and smiled.

Flashes of Nikolaos' memory appeared to Jeremy. He sat at a table, eating. Three other bishops joined him.

"What will you do when your body no longer allows you to serve?" One bishop asked.

"I shall live comfortably in a small house, on a beach where I will fish for my own supper."

Nikolaos' mind wandered as the others discussed their retirement. How do these men not understand the scriptures? He wondered. *I shall serve my Lord all the days until my body does not allow me to serve.* He had always assumed he would serve the people of Myra until he died.

He gazed into the golden curtain, took a deep breath, and stepped through the Veil.

CHAPTER 18
MERCURIO'S LAMENT

> "Alas! How dreary would be the world if there was no Santa Claus! There would be no childlike faith then, no poetry, no romance to make tolerable this existence."
> ~ Francis P. Church

Present Day

The light surrounded Jeremy, and he returned to his bedroom. A wave of disorientation dizzied him as his eyes opened and he shifted back to the reality of the present. He removed his glasses, rubbed his eyes, and took a deep breath.

"Whoa!" Jeremy said, steadying himself with his hand against the edge of the bed.

"And the rest is, as you humans are fond of saying… history," Mercurio said, stepping down from the bed.

Jeremy rubbed his head and looked up at Mercurio. "It's incredible. I saw it and I still can't believe it."

Mercurio smiled.

"So, do you want me to go with you to meet Nikolaos? Is that what this is all about?"

Mercurio tilted his head downward and paused. "Not precisely."

"What then?"

"There is more I'll show you, but I wanted to give your mind some rest before we continued. Perhaps you should get some water to drink."

"I thought you were in a hurry." Jeremy glanced over at the digital Batman clock on his nightstand. He furrowed his brow and did a double take. "What the? It can't only be 4:07?"

"Your device is not wrong." Mercurio said.

"What?" Jeremy stood up and walked over to the digital clock. He held out the mimstone. "It… it felt like I was… I mean, I know we were outside the gatehouse for at least an hour."

Mercurio muffled a laugh. "What you experience daily works on temporal properties. What the mimstone shows are merely memories… collective memories pieced together to show truths of the past. Alfargnym are quite good at creating artifices that show truths. When one uses a mimstone, the information travels to the mind at a speed that far exceeds visual perception."

Jeremy rubbed his head again. "No wonder my heads killing me. You shoved years of information into my brain in less than twenty minutes."

Mercurio smiled. "Drink. I will tell you more before I show you more."

Jeremy reached over to his nightstand, grabbing the half-empty twenty-ounce bottle of Diet Pepsi. He unscrewed the lid and chugged the lukewarm and slightly flat cola.

"Ellesmere went to the Council of Elders to get approval for what we all know as Santa's Christmas Eve visits and to get the enchanted equipment we would need to pull it all off. Then she came to see me," Mercurio said, as he walked to the window and peeked around the curtain. "To my surprise, she told me their ridiculous plan to deliver gifts to all the children of the world. I wanted nothing to do with it at first." The elf laughed and faced

Jeremy. "However, Ellesmere knew me well. She spoke to my conscience and convinced me to be a part of her plan. In hindsight, it wasn't terribly hard to convince me. I didn't want to admit it to myself back then, but Nikolaos didn't just save my life, he changed it. He was the first human that I ever trusted. His heart and his actions had convinced me way before Ellesmere ever did."

Jeremy scratched his head. "This is absolutely amazing." He smiled with wide-eyed astonishment. "All these years... but how? And what changed? Where's Nikolaos now?"

Mercurio's demeanor shifted. A frown replaced his thoughtful smile. The elf turned his gaze away from Jeremy and sighed. "That is, unfortunately, my greatest failure." He faced the window.

An awkward silence filled the room. Jeremy wanted to say something, but he didn't know what to say.

Mercurio looked up, his back still to Jeremy. The elf moved the curtain, peeked out the window, and sighed again. "Many things had to be worked out before Nikolaos' dream could ever come to fruition. They planned almost everything: from the reindeer to the sleigh, to the day in which all of this would take place." Mercurio let go of the curtain and walked toward Jeremy. "The Elders of each Elven Commonwealth came together and created the enchantments that allowed Nikolaos to become the legend you know him as. I was given permission to train along with two other fledgling Swordsworn to be the Gift Giver's Guard." He laughed and smiled. "That's what we were called. The Gift Giver's Guard. I knew Ellesmere's plan to help Nikolaos and let him leave the protection of Orindin was foolish. But I also knew that if the council approved her plan, they were going to do it with or without me. Laven was quite convincing. He persuaded the council to agree to everything on Ellesmere's list in hopes that Nikolaos would be the one to curb humanity's penchant for destruction and open the Veil for all the world." Mercurio climbed back up on the bed and sat down. "They knew it would take some time for Nikolaos to do so, and he would therefore need to be protected from the goblins. I begged my father to allow me to complete my Swordsworn training in Orindin as one of the Gift Giver's Guard. As the *Tsir'azzelqān* of the Swordsworn, only he could make it so."

"Zeer what?" Jeremy asked.

"*Tsir'azzelqān*. My father's title. It's Elvish. It doesn't translate well to English. *Tsir'azzelqān* literally means Lord of the Field of Swords. He was the leader of all who take the oath of the Swordsworn. It was his responsibility to protect the nine Elven cities from any outside forces. And when he heard that I'd come in contact with a human and I wanted to bring him through the Veil, he was furious. I was certain my future as a Swordsworn had ended that day. He adamantly denied Ellesmere's request to bring Nikolaos through the Veil. It was Laven who convinced the council to overrule my father. And when the council made their decision to carry out Nikolaos' plan, my father had no choice but to assign his best guardian to lead and train the Gift Giver's Guard. Our training was difficult, unlike anything the other Swordsworn trained for. Our sole purpose was to protect one man from goblins. We planned for every possible attack."

Mercurio continued to pace back and forth as he told the story.

"Whenever Nikolaos left Orindin, we traveled with him. And just as I knew it would happen, the Goblin Sar discovered what we were up to each Christmas Eve. He sent many to kill Nikolaos. Every Christmas Eve, some group of foolish goblins looking to find favor with their Sar tried to take Nikolaos' life. Hundreds of years went by. Goblin Sars died, and the next would take up the oath to kill Nikolaos. We kept them at bay, and Nikolaos made all of his deliveries."

"Over the years the Christmas Eve attacks became bolder, and in greater number. Although Nikolaos had the protection of his enchantments, at one point I wanted Nikolaos to wear armor. But he refused. It was quite comical. 'Me, wear armor? You would have me clunking about in armor?' Mercurio placed his hands on his belly as if it were round and imitated his old friend. He followed it up with Nikolaos' familiar deep, three-part laugh.

"Wait," interjected Jeremy. "He really laughed like that?"

"Indeed, he did. There are many stories about Nikolaos that your people have wrong. But some ring true."

"Wow!" Jeremy said, shaking his head. "So, what happened?"

Mercurio took another deep breath and then turned to Jeremy. He pointed at him and wagged his finger. "December 24th, 1803. We were in the town of Poughkeepsie, New York."

CHAPTER 19
UP ON THE HOUSETOP

"A many happenings have changed our shared world, but none so much as the happenings of December 24th, 1803."

~ From *The Veiled Happenlore of the Master Construct* compiled by Fulbert Gisilfrid, a Chronicler of the Master Construct, Third Order, an alfargnym of Unterbaum.

A.D. 1803

The light unfolded around Jeremy. He stood on a rooftop, unaffected by the chill air of the winter night. Gently falling snowflakes slowly drifted down from gray clouds hiding the luminous moon. He looked around at the distinctly Dutch homestead surrounded by large, barren, dark gray trees. Golden, bean-like seed pods glistened with moonlight reflected off the surrounding snow-covered landscape. The characteristic barn-like roof of the Dutch Colonial home, with its broad, slightly sloped double-pitch top, was flat enough for Jeremy to walk on.

He stepped forward, wanting to get his bearings better, but a wave of anxiety washed over him as he peered over the roof's edge. Jeremy wasn't afraid of heights, but the fact that he was at least thirty feet off the ground, on a snow-covered roof, set off all sorts of red flags. He knew he could taste, feel, and smell while under the influence of the mimstone. He wondered if he could get hurt too. Jeremy took a breath, trying to calm himself.

A wintry wind rustled the leafless branches all around. Jeremy steadied himself and took another deep breath. From the corner of his eye he saw movement. He looked across at the barn and only noticed the branches of the surrounding trees swaying with the wind. A shiver ran up his spine. Not from the cold. Though he wasn't wearing a jacket or coat, only the short-sleeved collared shirt and khakis he'd worn to school that day. Despite the cold winter night, he remained warm. And he was thankful for that. He hated the cold and having to bundle up in layers every winter. He caught another flash of movement in his periphery. He turned again to the barn and watched as one of the pale bean-like seed pods detached from a tree and tumbled to the ground, landing in the snow beside the barn with the myriad of others that had gone before it.

Why am I here? Jeremy wondered. *Why'd Mercurio bring me here?* He spread out his arms, holding his palms upward, and stuck out his tongue, catching a few snowflakes on its tip. The light gray snow clouds parted, and the pale light of the waxing gibbous moon revealed an object in the dark blue of the night sky. Jeremy crinkled his eyes and pushed his glasses back up the bridge of his nose. He smiled, spying the silhouette of a sleigh pulled by eight reindeer.

As the sleigh drew closer, Nikolaos pulled lightly on the reins as the magic-enhanced reindeer and the sleigh came to a smooth stop on the rooftop.

In all his red and white glory, Nicholas sat in the sleigh surrounded by his guards. They were dressed in sleek emerald armor with matching gold-trimmed cloaks. Each wore a gold badge in the shape of a crook on the left side of their chest.

Mercurio, perched beside Nikolaos, quickly scanned the area.

Jeremy was immediately drawn to the elf; apprehension, excitement, and joy emanated from him as he looked around for the familiar enemy that had not yet shown themselves this night.

Yardin, one of the Gift Giver's Guard, sprung out of the sleigh, tapped the side of his nose, and in a flurry of dazzling, shimmering golden motes darted down the chimney.

Denever, another of Nikolaos' guard, hopped from the sleigh and off the rooftop, making his way to the barn across from the house. He took position on the barn's roof, surveyed the area, and signaled the all-clear with a wave of his hand.

Jeremy smiled, a joy-filled grin beaming with wonder. He couldn't believe his eyes. As far as life moments go, this was the greatest. It superseded his first kiss, high school and college graduation, and the **XBOX** One he received from his parents for his 18th birthday. Santa Claus was real, and he was about to see him in action.

Jeremy watched as the Gift Giver climbed out of his sleigh and hoisted his magical sack over his back. With a smile, Nikolaos raised his right index finger to the side of his nose and descended the chimney in a tornado of shimmering gold.

Yardin followed behind.

Mercurio stood watch, perched on the top of the sleigh. Nikolaos' other guards, Hamion and Ihrdren, stood beside the chimney, ready to escort Nikolaos back to the sleigh.

The sound of a window opening alerted Mercurio. He turned and looked to Denever, who lay in the shadow of a tree on the barn's rooftop.

Another human awake. That's the third one tonight. Denever said, using his uniform's communication enchantment to relay the info directly into Mercurio's head.

Mercurio smiled. He never worried about humans seeing any of them. He knew they wouldn't remember any of this once Nikolaos and the team left.

A sense of pride washed over Mercurio. He'd built this team; trained these guardians and delivered millions of toys over several centuries. And his friendship with the man that had saved him so long ago had grown to something more like a brother. He'd learned so much from Nikolaos.

Goblins! Denever warned.

Jeremy jumped and turned to look at Denever.

They're crawling up the side, still caught in the temporal displacement. Denever relayed. *We should be done before—*

Jeremy stumbled as he watched an arrow pierce Denever's head. The elf staggered backwards, slipped, and fell to the ground.

It can't be goblins! Mercurio said to his team.

Four goblins swiftly approached.

How could this be? How could they be within the temporal field?

Mercurio looked behind. They were climbing up from every direction. Their bronze battle armor glistened in the moonlight as they ran on all fours toward the sleigh.

Mercurio looked left, then right.

Jeremy darted for the sleigh, grabbed onto the side, and hefted himself inside. Breathing heavily, heart pumping, Jeremy braced himself behind the windshield, next to Mercurio.

Goblins surrounded them. Four approached the chimney from the left where Hamion stood guard, sword drawn. Four others slowly approached Ihrdren. The two guardians backed up toward each other until each could protect the other's back.

Another four goblins approached the sleigh from the front, and four more from the back.

Mercurio commanded his sword to his hand. The sword released from its sheath on Mercurio's back and met his grasp as he reached backward. The guardian stepped up onto the seat, taking the higher ground.

Metallic clanging drew Jeremy's attention back to Ihrdren and Hamion.

Ihrdren parried the blade of one goblin, and with his free hand he released a shimmering bluish-gold sphere of energy that slammed into another. The energy dispersed upon impact, sending surges over the creature's body, causing it to convulse and cry out in agony.

More energy spheres whizzed by, slamming into goblins, sending them sliding across the rooftop. Jeremy watched as one convulsing goblin slid down the slope and over the edge. He turned back to see another and gasped as he saw the white snow turn blood red and the unresponsive body of Ihrdren slide off the roof.

Jeremy frantically searched for Hamion. The elf parried the blades of five attackers. He moved as effortlessly as the wind and faster than humanly possible.

Mercurio leapt from the sleigh towards Hamion, over a goblin's head. The guardian spun around as his feet touched the rooftop, slicing his blade through the arm of a goblin. The amputated limb fell to the rooftop and rolled off the side, leaving a trail of emerald blood behind. The goblin screamed, turning around before he fell silent. His slumped body followed its arm and rolled off the side.

Hamion backed up to the chimney. Goblin blades slashed at him. He blocked two. A third poleblade jabbed into his calf, and Hamion buckled. One on his left jabbed its blade into his side. One on the right hit his other flank. The other jabbed low a second time, hitting his knee and pressing in, nearly severing Hamion's leg. Another goblin used his pole end to push the fallen guardian down the slope.

Jeremy swallowed back a wave of nausea and sunk into the sleigh's footwell. He couldn't watch anymore. There was so much blood! Each clang of steel on steel caused him to cringe. Despite the nausea and dizziness, Jeremy had to see what happened next. He took a deep breath and hefted himself up to find Mercurio surrounded by goblins. Their emerald skin glowing eerily in the moonlight. Each pointed a polearm at the elf, glaring through the metallic toothed maw of their beast-like bronze helmets. One jabbed his blade at Mercurio's feet. He jumped, moving like lightning and avoiding the blade. From behind, another swiped at the elf, and the guardian spun, catching the pole with his free hand and slicing the goblin's neck with his sword. Decapitating his attacker, he continued through with the motion until his sword grazed over another goblin's pauldron and into its neck.

From behind, a blade swung toward Mercurio's head. The elf turned his neck just enough to avoid the polearm's edge. Using the leverage of the beheaded goblin's pole, Mercurio vaulted himself up and over his attacker's weapon. In mid-air, the elf kicked his attacker in the face, sending him backward and tumbling off the side of the roof.

Mercurio landed on his feet and faced the five remaining goblins.

An arrow hit Mercurio in the back, bouncing off his armor and distracting him enough for a goblin to lunge at him. Mercurio twisted to avoid the blade's edge, but the charging goblin knocked him off balance, allowing another to hit Mercurio in the left thigh. The armor stopped the blade from penetrating, but the impact knocked him to his knee, and they were on him. One goblin returned his polearm to his back and grabbed Mercurio by the back of his neck and pushed him to the rooftop. Two more grabbed his sword arm.

Another two climbed onto the roof and dove for Mercurio's arm.

Jeremy gasped; his knuckles turning white from holding the windshield's edge so tightly.

Mercurio released magical energy from his left hand and caused it to coalesce into an orb. It smashed into a goblin's chest and pushed him. The orb lost its shape and crackling blue and gold energy spread across the creature's chest. The goblin convulsed and screamed as the power of the orb burned every cell in his body.

Mercurio lifted his right leg up to stand again. He released magical energy into his sword. It glowed with golden-fiery flames. The goblins holding his sword arm jumped back.

Mercurio tried to stand, but another goblin grabbed his right leg and pulled it out from under him, sending him back to his knees. He raised his flaming sword.

The goblin holding him by the neck strained, pushing

Mercurio back down to the rooftop. It straddled the elf, forcing its weight down on his lower back and knocking the wind out of Mercurio.

The goblin pulled a curved, rectangular box from its belt and pushed it against the back of Mercurio's neck. It clamped on like a partial neck-brace.

Two needle-like pricks jabbed into Mercurio's neck. The flame of his sword instantly extinguished.

Jeremy felt a wave of fear and confusion overcome Mercurio. It was as if a part of him had suddenly vanished.

The goblins were quick to grab his arms again. The one holding Mercurio by his neck pushed him flat against the rooftop, his warm cheek meeting the cold snow.

A goblin secured Mercurio's legs. Another stepped on his hand and pried the guardian's sword away.

The goblin holding Mercurio by the back of the neck used his other hand to tear off the elf's helmet.

Mercurio felt the pressure on the back of his neck ease up. The goblin no longer pushed on him, but the box was still attached. It grabbed Mercurio's hair, pulling his head up. It placed a small dagger at the elf's throat, applying enough pressure to be felt but not enough to pierce flesh.

Jeremy watched in horror as the goblins positioned Mercurio so that he could see the sleigh and the chimney.

Two goblin warriors stood beside the chimney where Hamion and Ihrdren once stood, their polearms ready for anyone who came out. Two more goblin warriors stood beside the sleigh.

Mercurio blinked wildly, straining to see something. His fear heightening to panic. The goblins had done something to him; something they'd never done before. They had cut off his access to magic! Mercurio squeezed his fists tightly, summoning the magical energy to form around him. None came.

"Yardin!" he yelled, trying to activate the communication device in his uniform. *Yardin! Execute Escape Plan Zayn!*

Jeremy felt Mercurio's panic level rise as he realized the communication enchantment did not work either.

The goblin tugged on Mercurio's hair. "I have a message from my Sar," said the goblin from behind. Its voice, raspy and controlled, it brought its lipless mouth close to Mercurio's ear. "His wish is for you to see your human pet die at the hands of goblins."

Yardin materialized from the chimney.

Mercurio opened his mouth to yell as the goblins swung their blades. One pierced Yardin's stomach. The other sliced through his neck. His head rolled off his body, teetered on the chimney's edge and dispersed into a myriad of golden motes like a cloud of dust diffusing into the cold air.

Jeremy closed his eyes and swallowed hard, fighting the dryness of his mouth.

The surrounding air changed, and he heard a *thunk*. He opened his eyes. He was no longer in the sleigh.

Nikolaos stood in a living room by a fireplace. Two other elves Jeremy hadn't seen before stood beside Nikolaos' open sack. They weren't armored like the others, but they were dressed in simple clothes like he'd seen Ellesmere and her father wear.

The two elves peered up at Nikolaos; their faces gaunt with panic.

Nikolaos grabbed his toy sack and stepped backward away from the fireplace. "Quickly!" The Gift Giver pointed to the open mouth of the sack.

Nikolaos took a deep breath. He and the elves had planned for this. He was told this could happen, but he never expected it to. In his head he heard the voice of Mercurio from their training. *If you panic, you perish. You must follow the plan, no matter what happens, always follow the plan.*

Mercurio, Nikolaos said, trying to communicate with his guardian. *Mercurio, we need to evacuate. Plan Zayn. Yes? Mercurio?*

A twang of panic emanated from Nikolaos. *Could Mercurio be dead?*

Glass shattered from a nearby room. Nikolaos recoiled and turned, readying himself for whatever was coming his way.

"Mommy!" cried a voice from somewhere in the house.

Screams followed more breaking glass. An infant wailed. A man's muffled voice yelled out. More screams; several children screaming. A mother crying out for her child.

Shards of splintering glass exploded from the window near Nikolaos. He brought his hands up to cover his face, just as he caught sight of the creatures entering through the broken window.

Two climbed in and charged at Nikolaos.

"Mira! Omer! Quickly!" Nikolaos yelled.

The two elves scuttled and climbed into the sack.

One goblin, his polearm still hung from his back, pounced on Nikolaos' back, clawing for his neck. A wave of energy emanated from the man, and the goblin was repelled with a force equal to its own. It slammed against the wall and slumped to the floor.

Another grabbed hold of his leg, and Nikolaos kicked it before its grasp was complete. It fell to the side, rolled several feet away, and sprung to a standing, defensive position.

Several more goblins entered the living room.

Jeremy grabbed the sides of his head, wanting desperately to cover his eyes. But he couldn't look away.

Six more goblins surrounded Nikolaos, poleswords drawn and pointing at him.

If you panic, you perish.

Nikolaos placed his finger beside his nose, and he disappeared.

He and Jeremy reappeared on the rooftop of the barn. An arrow flew towards him, struck the magical field surrounding Nikolaos, and fell inches away from his feet.

Nikolaos looked at the tree only ten feet away. Aided by his enchanted ring, he could see a goblin perched within its branches, nocking another arrow.

Nikolaos raised his finger to his nose, and instantly transported to the tree. He grabbed the goblin's head and smashed it into the tree's trunk, several times, before he dropped the foul creature. It struck the ground and lay unconscious.

Nikolaos steadied himself in the tree and surveyed the scene. He could not believe the profusion of goblins; they brought an entire army this year. His breathing shallow, Nikolaos sat with his back against the trunk to collect his thoughts and balance his breathing.

He remembered his training, though. Given this scenario, he was to use the remaining magic in the ring to get him to the nearest gatehouse.

Nikolaos could barely see the reindeer and sled on the rooftop. He assumed Mercurio and the other guardians were up there, but feared they may already be dead. He couldn't leave without knowing if they were still alive. Nikolaos climbed down from the tree and walked toward the house.

Jeremy looked across the road and concentrated on Mercurio. His empathy shifted as did his location and he stood on the roof of the house, beside the chimney. He watched as Nikolaos walked from the back of the barn, out into the open.

The Gift Giver stopped in the middle of the dirt road between the barn and the house and stood with his hands on his hips. He breathed in and then shouted.

"I believe it is me you seek!"

The goblins turned toward Nikolaos.

"Nikolaos! Run!" Mercurio yelled out.

The goblins holding the elf down pressed harder.

Four goblins leapt off the house.

"Follow me!" A goblin yelled from behind.

Nikolaos disappeared.

Jeremy turned to see Mercurio struggling to get free. A shimmering vortex of golden light materialized beside the elf. Within the vortex, Nikolaos kicked the goblin holding Mercurio's right arm. The goblin fell backwards and scrambled to keep his footing.

"No, Nikolaos!" Mercurio yelled. "Plan Zayn!"

Four goblins charged at Nikolaos. A wave of energy launched them off the roof.

Nikolaos disappeared and reappeared on the left side of Mercurio. He slammed his fist into the face of the goblin holding Mercurio's arm.

The goblin flinched but didn't let go.

Nikolaos punched him again. The goblin's head whipped to the other side, but it still held on.

Nikolaos pulled his leg back to kick the goblin.

Another goblin grabbed onto him, followed by three more. They held tightly as if hugging him, using their own weight, rather than force to bring Nikolaos down. Four more goblins approached slowly and added their weight to the melee. The man struggled to break free, but the weight was too much. He lost his balance and crashed to the snow-covered rooftop.

Nikolaos continued to struggle, but there were too many of them. Mercurio watched helplessly, only feet away. Several other goblins climbed onto the roof from all directions.

Jeremy's gut twisted. He knew he was only here to observe, and nothing he did would make a difference. But he desperately wanted to jump in. He felt so helpless.

One more goblin hefted himself onto the roof. He didn't run like the others. He approached with a subtle, confident gait; his silhouette giving way as he neared Nikolaos. His purple cape fluttered in the cool, steady air. This goblin was different; taller and paler than the others. He wore no helmet. His bald head, illuminated by the moon, gave him an eerie green visage. His breastplate was black, like obsidian. And in its center was the gold dragon head crest of goblin royalty. The red eyes of the dragon sparkled in the moonlight. A strange necklace of shriveled leather dangled above the crest. A sheathed sword hung at his side.

Nikolaos grunted as the goblin stepped onto his back.

He looked down at Mercurio and sneered. Then placed his hands on the thin gold chain that hung from his neck; a collection of ears, some pointed and others round. He touched a pointed one and eagerly rubbed it between his thumb and index finger.

With wide eyes that glowed in the moonlight, he continued to stare at Mercurio. A gnarled, toothy smile grew as he embraced the hilt of his sword and slid the cleaver-like blade out. Steadying his grip, he placed his other hand on the hilt, raised the blade above his head and let it linger menacingly above Nikolaos. Its edge glistened in the moonlight.

"I've waited for this day," snarled the goblin leader. "The Vengeance Decree ends tonight."

The goblin plunged the sword down toward the back of Nikolaos' head.

A burst of magical energy surged from the Gift Giver's ring and spread over his body. The force of magic exploded into the surrounding goblins.

The leader catapulted into the air, over the sleigh. He lost his grip on the sword and it fell point-down onto the roof, inches away from Jeremy.

Jeremy jerked. Wide-eyed and heart beating madly, he took a deep breath.

The goblin leader landed with a thud and slid across the roof, off the peak's edge.

The two holding Nikolaos' arms went tumbling off the side of the roof. One holding his right leg slammed backward, hitting the chimney.

The goblin on Nikolaos' left leg careened into the lead reindeer, who snorted at the abrupt intrusion. It scooped the goblin up with its antlers and threw it off the roof.

Nikolaos hefted himself up from the snowy rooftop and ran towards Mercurio.

"Yes!" Jeremy shouted, slumping forward with relief.

The goblins not directly in the magical surge's wake slowly approached him. Nikolaos punched at one, but it dodged, and with gingerly grace, it wrapped its arms around the man's forearm.

Nikolaos slammed his fist into the clinging goblin. It grunted but held tightly.

Several other goblins crawled onto the man. Jeremy cringed as the goblins creeped forward and all slowly piled on to Nikolaos, sending him crashing to the rooftop again, this time only several inches from Mercurio. The two companions were now face to face.

"No!" Jeremy cried.

"The ring!" Shouted the goblin straddling Mercurio. "The

ring is enchanted. It protects the human!"

The bald head of the goblin leader appeared over the edge. He hefted himself back onto the roof and headed straight towards Nikolaos and Mercurio.

"Ahhh…" said the goblin leader, readjusting his armor. "The elves have done well to protect their pet. But this night, human, the red of your blood will cover the stain you brought upon my family."

The goblin leader walked up to his underling sitting on Nikolaos' right arm.

Jeremy followed his gaze as the goblin leader peered down at Nikolaos' trembling fist; the ring secured tightly in its grasp.

The goblin squatted down, squinting its eyes and shifting his head from left to right, studying the ring. It made a guttural, growling noise.

Jeremy trembled, wondering if they would try to pry the man's fingers open?

Mercurio hoped they'd try. It would activate the ring's protection again, and this time he'd be in the surge's wake.

"Go to Hunzuu." The goblin leader stood and pointed to the road below. "Tell him to make me something to put this human to sleep."

Mercurio's face betrayed his stoic demeanor. His eyes grew wide with despair. He swallowed nervously, trying not to show his worry.

"Why not just poison him, my warlord?" asked the goblin holding down Nikolaos' right arm.

"His ring protects him from harm, I doubt it protects him from sleep." The leader replied, smiling, and nodding at Mercurio.

The creature was correct. Mercurio returned its smile with a scowl, not wanting to give the goblin leader the satisfaction he wanted.

Two goblins ran off into the night to do their leader's bidding.

The goblin warlord squatted beside Nikolaos' face. A goblin held the Gift Giver's cheek to the snow-covered roof.

"You don't even know what you've done, do you, human?" The goblin warlord snarled as he carefully brushed Nikolaos' hat off his head.

"Please, let my friend go and do with me what you want." Nikolaos pleaded.

The goblin leader laughed. A bold, raucous laugh.

"I hate you more than I hate these elves. You're in no position to bargain with me or tell me your demands." He spit into Nikolaus' face and rose to his feet. "Innan, that was his name. You didn't know that, did you?" He slammed his foot to the rooftop and kicked snow into the man's face. "That day you took Innan's life, that was the day you gave every goblin warlord his purpose! A human! A pitiful waste of flesh took the life of a goblin." He slammed his hand against his breastplate and turned back to Nikolaos. "And not just any goblin, the Sar's son. The heir to the throne. The stories say he was trying to impress his father, the Sar Enzuna. He thought if he brought back an elf's ears, the Sar would see him as a warrior and worthy to receive the throne. He wasn't going to kill those elves! He just wanted their ears!" The goblin yelled, thrashing his cape away and stomping his foot in front of Nikolaos. He leaned over and yelled into his face. "On that day you incurred the wrath of the Sar Enzuna and every Sar thereafter! Your debt has been passed from generation to generation!" He straightened and composed himself, turning his gaze to Mercurio. "My father has dreamed of collecting that debt and seeing your miserable human head sitting on a spike and dripping with blood in the center of his chamber." He took two steps toward Mercurio. "Now look at me elf."

The goblin holding Mercurio's hair pulled tightly, aiming the elf's face at the warlord.

"You will live," the goblin leader said. "You will tell all your kind who it was that spilled the blood of your prized human. Remember my name, elf. I am Borahsh, The Lord of War, son of Sar Belshunu, and I am collecting the debt owed to the goblin empire."

The goblin's word stung Mercurio like hot coals upon his feet.

It was his job to protect Nikolaos, and he'd failed. But the Gift Giver still had his ring. As long as that ring was on Nikolaos' finger, he'd be safe. He had to do something… but it was already too late. A goblin returned with a wineskin and handed it to his leader.

Borahsh grabbed the wineskin from his minion, withdrew his sword, and stooped down next to Mercurio. He held the blade to the back of the elf's neck and turned to Nikolaos.

"Try to escape, and the elf will be unbound," Borahsh said to Nikolaos.

"No! Nikolaos, do not give in to these deceivers!" Mercurio yelled.

"Turn him over," Borahsh commanded.

The ten goblins it took to hold Nikolaos down forced him onto his back. When the man was securely held, Borahsh sat on Nikolaos' chest. The goblin smiled and stared hungrily at his prey. He then shoved the spout of the wineskin into his mouth. Nikolaos tried to shake it away, but the goblins held his head tightly in place. He tried to keep his mouth clenched closed, but the liquid seeped in, and he choked. As he opened his mouth to cough, Borahsh squeezed more of it into his mouth. He choked again, and Borahsh let up before squeezing more in and emptying the rest of the wineskin.

Borahsh sneered at Nikolaos.

Jeremy couldn't look. He raised his hands to his face, turned around, and then turned back again, curiosity overcoming trepidation.

Nikolaos' contorted; strained muscles tight with resolve slowly eased, and he went limp.

The goblin holding his head let go. Nikolaos lay still.

"No!" Mercurio screamed.

Borahsh's smile widened and Mercurio begged for him to stop.

Jeremy swallowed and stepped back. He brought one hand to his mouth and the other to his head. *This can't be happening… this couldn't be what happened.*

Borahsh stood up and tossed the wineskin.

All this. Jeremy thought. *This is what it all led up to. This is why—*

"No!" Mercurio yelled. "No! Don't do this!" His screaming continued as the smiling Borahsh knelt down, removing the ring from Nikolaos' finger.

"Hmmm…" Borahsh held the ring up and studied it. "This should prove interesting." He wiggled the three fingers on his left hand and then slid the ring over each one. Finding it too big, he placed it on his thumb and flashed Mercurio a satisfied grin. He then removed a dagger from his belt and taunted the elf by running the tips of his emerald fingers along the edge. Borahsh turned the blade slowly, moving the dagger toward Nikolaos, and resting the point upright against the man's forehead.

Borahsh gingerly pushed on the dagger's pommel and watched Mercurio's face as the tip pierced through the layers of skin, just pricking it enough to make blood slowly trickle out.

Borahsh laughed. "Delightful," he said slowly and methodically as he slid the tip of his blade down the side of Nikolaos' face. Its touch was faint, not yet drawing more blood.

Borahsh slowly eased the dagger's point down Nikolaos' neck and then down the side of his body as if he were caressing the man with the tip of his finger. He stopped at Nikolaos' right flank and then looked at Mercurio. The goblin's smile grew more sinister as he cupped his hand around the pummel of the dagger and slowly forced it into Nikolaos' side.

Mercurio screamed.

The reindeer groaned and stomped their hooves. The goblins surrounding them grabbed the reins and held them in place.

Borahsh let out a cackling, guttural laugh. He removed the dagger and repeated the same torturous procedure, blood dripping from the blade as he crept the tip along Nikolaos' left side. Borahsh repeated the same unhurried process of slowly sinking the blade into the man's flesh.

As the dagger pierced Nikolaos' left flank, the reindeer grew more agitated.

The incantation! That's it! Mercurio thought. With a final breath,

Mercurio yelled, "Ho, Swiftfoot! Ho, Dancer! Ho, Littlefox and Prancer! Ho, Longhair and Passion! Quickly! Ho, Oh Thunder and Lightning!"

Borahsh jerked his head up and glared at Mercurio.

"From the rooftop and through the Veil! Dash away! Dash away now! All, dash away!" Mercurio shouted.

A wave of energy emanated from all sides of the sleigh, passing through every living being in a one-mile radius. The reindeer beat their hooves to the roof and took off, knocking the two startled goblins beside them down and rolling off the roof.

Borahsh, face rigid with anger, clenched his teeth and yelled out in frustration. "Nooooooo!"

The reindeer flew into the night sky, disappearing as they sped further away.

The goblins on the roof gently swayed, eyes slowly blinking, unaffected by the sight of the reindeer taking flight or their leader's enraged roar.

Only Borahsh, who possessed Nikolaos' ring, was unaffected by the spell Mercurio unleashed.

Mercurio sprung to his feet, sending the stupefied goblin on his back into the one holding his left leg. The box it held to the back of the elf's neck fell, hit the roof and rolled off with the two goblins.

Mercurio slammed his fists into the two goblins holding his arms. They lost their footing and fell to the same fate as their brethren.

Jeremy jumped backwards and steadied himself by holding onto the chimney's edge. Before him, seven entranced goblins stood idly by as four others went off the roof.

The enraged goblin leader surveyed the scene.

Mercurio poised for battle. His blue eyes fixed in an icy stare blinked, and the elf wavered slightly as if he had just been struck with something. He shook his head, trying to shake away whatever was happening to him. He looked down at his hands, turning them slowly before making them into fists. Mercurio's knuckles shimmered and golden light surrounded each fist.

Borahsh's face tightened into an intense snarl.

Mercurio braced for the goblin's charge. But Borahsh's eyes moved from Mercurio to Nikolaos. He raised his dagger and leapt at his long-awaited prize.

Mercurio thrust upward, meeting the goblin in midair, and tackling him to the rooftop. The impact activated the ring's defenses, and Mercurio bolted backward. He recovered with a tuck and roll, turning around swiftly to once again engage Borahsh.

The goblin leader drew composure from his rage and faced Mercurio. He placed his dagger back in its sheath, withdrew his sword, and slashed at Mercurio.

The elf stepped to the side, gingerly grasped the goblin's shoulder and twisted himself carefully onto Borahsh's back.

The goblin thrashed around, trying to buck the elf from his back. But Mercurio held firmly, desperately trying not to activate the ring's defenses. Borahsh slipped on the icy snow and they fell to the rooftop. Mercurio shook loose of Borahsh and they rolled down the side and over the edge.

"No!" Jeremy yelled. He carefully hurried away from the chimney to see what happened.

Somehow Mercurio had managed to grab onto the eave. Borahsh had slipped and now clung to Mercurio's midsection. The elf pulled in magical energy, increasing his strength so he could hold on with one hand and use the momentum to shake Borahsh free of his waist. He slammed the goblin several times against the side of the house, but the ring protected him from any damage.

Mercurio reached up with his other arm, grabbed the eave, and swung Borahsh even harder against the house. After three swings, he felt the goblin slip. He swung harder, let go with one hand, and used the force of the swing and his enhanced strength to grab hold of Borahsh's wrist, prying him from his waist.

Summoning more magical energy, Mercurio swung Borahsh like a rag doll and repeatedly slammed him against the house. The force of each slam didn't do any damage to the goblin, but disoriented him and...

The ring slipped off, tumbled through the air, slammed against the house, and into the snow-covered shrubs below.

A horrified Borahsh frantically reached out for the ring that wasn't there.

Mercurio swung Borahsh upward, slamming him onto the roof.

The warlord cringed at the impact and loss of air.

Mercurio swung himself up and landed on the roof. He extended his hand, held it for several seconds. Jeremy heard a clanging sound from below. The guardian's sword flew up, whizzed past Jeremy, and into Mercurio's hand. He readied the weapon and charged at Borahsh.

Borahsh spun and swept Mercurio's leg, sending him back over the side.

The warlord pushed himself up and ran to retrieve his sword.

Mercurio grabbed the eave and pulled himself back up again.

A twinge of dizziness hit Mercurio. Then his muscles tensed. He recognized it as magic fatigue. But he hadn't used enough to bring it on so quickly. Mercurio stopped drawing in magic to maintain his increased strength and lunged for Borahsh.

The goblin rolled, avoiding the sword to his gut, but not his thigh.

Mercurio's Elven blade pierced through muscle, slicing downward until it hit the bone, just above the knee. He pushed the blade further in, severing tendon and cartilage.

Borahsh lurched in pain, losing his balance.

The momentum freed the sword, and green blood poured from the wound.

Borahsh stumbled to regain his footing, but the combination of the pain, the roof's pitch, and the freshly fallen snow sent him falling face forward and sliding down the side of the roof. His eyes wide with rage, he clawed for a handhold and slowly came to a stop at the edge. He snarled and pushed himself back toward the elf.

Mercurio drew the magical energy into his hand, formed a charge orb, and released it. It struck Borahsh in the head and sent him reeling backwards off the roof. The goblin fell to the ground below and Borahsh cried out from the searing pain.

The dizziness returned. Mercurio forced more air into his lungs, closed his eyes and concentrated on the magic field around him. The magic was abundant, but his body seemed to be sluggishly drawing from it. That goblin injected something into him, some sort of inhibitor. But what? He'd never heard of anything like this. Not since the Unbinding, but that only affected the goblins. He couldn't worry about any of that now. He needed to get Nikolaos out of here.

Mercurio opened his eyes and surveyed the scene. The four other goblins remained stupefied. He knew it wouldn't last long, and even though they wouldn't remember anything that happened in the last four hours, he didn't want to be around when they saw him and Nikolaos.

The guardian knelt beside Nikolaos, grabbed hold of his arm and placed the Gift Giver's finger beside his nose.

Nothing happened.

Mercurio sighed and gritted his teeth. *The ring!*

The guardian stood and paced. He glanced at Nikolaos. Dark red bloodstains on the Gift Giver's flank contrasted with the lighter red of his coat.

What am I going to do?

Time was running out. The spell wouldn't keep the goblins and the humans stunned for much longer. Mercurio tugged at Nikolaos' unmoving body, trying to figure out how he was going to lift him, but the man was too heavy. And he was too weak. Mercurio had overextended himself.

The elf looked around. There was no place to go. There was nothing for him to do. His heart pounded against chest and his breathing shallowed. He closed his eyes. *If you panic, you will perish.* He heard his father's voice in his head. He opened his eyes.

Mercurio laid his hands on the left side wound. He strained to manipulate the magical energy around the wound, though it was too deep, and he was so exhausted. The goblin's dagger hadn't pierced through the other side, but it was deep enough to have damaged organs. This was beyond Mercurio's training. Nikolaos needed a true healer.

Perhaps he could transport Nikolaos using the vortex spell? But that could take too long. The nearest gatehouse was almost a hundred miles away, and the vortex spell only had a range of a hundred feet. Besides, if he channeled any more energy, he himself might pass out. But if he didn't go very far, he might make it. He was the only one left. The sleigh was gone along with… no. Nikolaos' sack was still here somewhere.

"Mira and Omer!" He sprang to his feet.

Where could it be? He wondered, walking to the roof's edge. He channeled enough magic to jump off the roof.

The scene flashed and Jeremy was in the living room of the house. He shook off the disorienting sensation of being in two places at once and used the wall to steady himself.

Mercurio walked in and stopped at the living room's entrance.

A spellbound man in a nightcap and gown stood, expressionless, before him. His eyes glassed over, and his mouth slightly open, he gently swayed in place. Mercurio paid him no mind.

Two entranced goblins wavered in place by the window.

Mercurio surveyed the area, spotting Nikolaos' sack beside the fallen Christmas tree.

The elf walked over to retrieve it and then stopped. A puddle of blood to the side of the tree caught his attention. It wasn't goblin blood.

Mercurio rushed to the tree and pushed it.

Mira and Omer's clothing lay there. They had returned to the ether.

"No!" Mercurio stood up and kicked the tree. He stood there for a moment, holding his head and trying to think of his next move.

Through the broken window, Mercurio peered at the barn across the way. They could hide in there. That might give him enough time to find the ring.

Mercurio grabbed Nikolaos' bag and walked toward the front door.

The flash of light disoriented Jeremy again. His eyes blinked, trying to adjust. He closed them and slowly opened his eyes to find he was in the barn. Three horses stirred from within the stalls as the light of a golden vortex appeared and dissipated, revealing Mercurio and Nikolaos.

Mercurio gently laid Nikolaos' head down on the cold dirt floor. The elf breathed in deeply, trying to fight off the effects of magic fatigue. He had to think quickly. He looked at the wagon by the barn's entrance, then to the tack on the wall, and then at the horses.

He cursed himself for not depositing them in the wagon bed. How was he going to get Nikolaos out of here? They could stay hidden, but when the goblins awoke they would surely look in the barn. This was only a temporary reprieve. He pushed himself, straining from fatigue. His vision spun as he stood. That settled it. He would not be able to manipulate magic for a while.

Steadying himself, he placed Nikolaos' bag beside the fallen Gift Giver, and went to the door. Mercurio opened it slowly and peered out. Several stupefied goblins stood outside the house. He didn't see Borahsh.

Maybe the fall broke the deceiver's neck.

Jeremy followed as Mercurio stepped outside and walked to the bushes where he had seen the ring land. The elf desperately searched to no avail. He stood up and glared angrily around, looking for signs of the goblin leader. A trail of blood pointed to the rear of the house.

Did Borahsh get the ring already?

He looked back at the barn, then at the stunned goblins; two at the door. Two more at the edge of the house. He wondered how many were inside.

Mercurio hefted himself up on the windowsill and spotted the man frozen in place at the entrance to the living room.

Mercurio studied the man, then looked to the rear of the house, and then back at the barn where Nikolaos lay dying. He didn't have time to hunt down Borahsh. He needed to get Nikolaos in the wagon and tack the horses, all before the spell wore off. He had no choice.

The guardian used his cloak to push in the remaining broken glass and wood. Hopping inside, he ran over to the man.

Jeremy watched from outside.

Mercurio removed a mimstone from his belt pouch and raised it to the man's face. He spoke a few words in Elvish, and the mimstone began to glow, becoming brighter with each second. Mercurio uttered another phrase. The mimstone flashed and grew dark again.

The man blinked and gently shook his head.

"Sir," Mercurio said. "I need your help.

CHAPTER 20
HOPE UNDONE

"We know not to whom we are indebted for the following description of that unwearied patron of children — that homely, but delightful personification of parental kindness — Sante Claus, his costume and his equipage, as he goes about visiting the fire-sides of this happy land, laden with Christmas bounties; but, from whomsoever it may have come, we give thanks for it."

Words preceding the first printing of *A Visit from St. Nicholas* in the Troy Sentinel on December 23rd, 1823

A.D. 1803

"Do *not* panic," Mercurio said. "We are *not* here to harm you. But there are evil creatures here who will." He pointed to the destruction all around; broken windows, upturned furniture, and the two spellbound goblins slowly wavering in place.

169

The human stared at the scene, holding his hands up defensively. He gasped at the first sight of a goblin.

"I've little time to explain. Therefore, I'll be forthwith. My name is Mercurio. I'm here with the one you call Saint Nicholas. We were attacked, and our attackers are still around. I need your help to get Nikolaos to safety. Please, help me."

The man's eyes darted about the room, as if seeking an escape from the chaos. His lips parted, and his tongue quickly wet them. Mercurio thought he might speak, but the man only let out an unintelligent burble.

"Sir, please. Nikolaos will surely die without your help." Mercurio said.

"Uh..." The man bobbed his head back and forth between Mercurio and the nearest goblin. "What is... uh..." The man stammered, placing his hands on the side of his head to rub his temples. "I, I..." He swallowed and caught his breath, moving one hand to his chest and the other over his mouth. He stepped backwards.

"Sir, I cannot do this without you." Mercurio said desperately.

"They... they... I don't understand."

"Please, help me." Mercurio pleaded. He grabbed the man by his hand. "Come with me. I'll show you."

As Mercurio guided the man past two goblins, the man stared at one with horror.

"They're still here, but..."

"Yes. They're under a spell. The spell will only last a little longer. I need your..."

"No. Wait," the man said, pulling away from Mercurio. He ran back toward the house.

"No, sir. Please..." Mercurio begged.

The man ran back inside, and Mercurio placed his hands over his face. He stumbled into the doorway and held onto the door frame. Uncertainty, dread, and fear spoke to the elf. All his training had failed him. He ran through each scenario they had practiced over the years. None accounted for him being the sole survivor of an attack with Nikolaos lying near death in the stables of a human.

Samyaza, Nikolaos! You should have left. Mercurio balled one hand into a fist and slammed it into his other hand. *You should have followed the plan!* None of the scenarios accounted for Nikolaos not following the plan!

He needed to get out of here before the spell wore off. But how? If he manipulated any more magic, he could fall unconscious too. He'd have to risk it. He'd wrap themselves in a blanket and use the vortex to get them as far from here as he could. If he passed out, he'd wake up eventually. But Nikolaos' wounds were so severe. He couldn't wait that long. Mercurio slammed his fist into the door.

The man ran up to Mercurio.

"My family… they're in some kind of trance. They won't wake. And those… those creatures. They're everywhere. They're bewitched as well. I, I don't…"

"It's the spell. It won't last much longer. We must be swift."

"My family? What will happen to them when…" he trailed off and placed his hand over his mouth.

"We'll get them out of here too. We just need to get Nikolaos some help."

The man's brow furrowed, and he looked down at Mercurio. "I'm not leaving my family here."

"Hear me," Mercurio said impatiently. "Nikolaos is wounded. He's in your barn. I need to get him in your wagon, but I can't lift him! Go to the barn and get the horses ready. I'll bring your family there."

The man hesitated.

"I promise you. I'll keep your family safe."

The man shook his head, sighed, and reluctantly ran off to the barn.

Mercurio entered the home and ran up the stairs.

Jeremy followed him down a hallway to the first room.

The guardian entered a bedroom.

Jeremy paused, startled by the scene before him.

A woman holding an infant.

A small boy clutching the woman's leg.

A goblin standing by the window.

Another goblin, only a few feet away from the woman.

Spellbound, they all wavered like fronds of grass caressed by a gentle breeze. Their faces void of emotion. Their heads moved slightly, and their eyes slowly blinked as if waking from a long sleep.

Mercurio removed his dagger from his belt and thrust it into the unprotected throat of the goblin closest to the woman. It gasped and its eyes opened wide. The guardian withdrew his blade from the creature's neck, and it slumped to the floor. He dashed to the one by the window and jabbed the dagger into its neck. It gasped and fell to the floor. Mercurio removed the dagger and used the cloth of the goblin's sash to wipe the blood before putting the blade back in its scabbard.

The guardian ran to the woman and child. He placed his bloodstained hand on her shoulder, eased himself close to the boy and guided them out the door as the gurgling sounds of goblins drowning in their blood betrayed the silence.

Mercurio escorted the mother and son back to the barn, silently coaxing them along the way by pushing gently on their shoulders.

They entered the barn, and the man jumped, startled by the doors opening. He dropped the harness and grunted as he leaned over to pick it up. "How much time do we have before they awake?"

"Less than ten minutes."

The human froze. "Ten minutes? We'll not make it. It'll take me at least fifteen to harness the horses."

"Do it quietly," Mercurio said, guiding his wards to the wagon. "They don't know we're in here."

"My sons, Charles and Sidney," the man's face became gaunt. "You didn't bring them…"

Mercurio sighed. "I'll go back. Ready the wagon."

Mercurio unsheathed his dagger and ran toward the house. As he passed the four waking goblins, he stabbed each one.

Goosebumps danced along the back of Jeremy's neck as he watched the guardian in action. Even without magic, he moved with the grace of a ballet dancer and the intensity of Bruce Lee. He was too fast for Jeremy to catch up to.

Jeremy entered the house and sluggishly walked up the stairs. He found Mercurio standing still in the middle of the hallway.

The elf's eyes were closed, his breath and heart rate slow. He drew in a small amount of magic to enhance his senses. He listened. The wind blew gently. Leaves rustled. The roof creaked. Heartbeats, quick and steady. He had to separate the goblin beats from the human ones. Two sets, one slower than the other. He stepped forward, moving silently, he followed the sound of the quicker heartbeat. Both heartbeats in the same room. The faster heartbeat came from under the bed. Mercurio knelt, peered under the bed and found a cowering boy with his hands over his face. The guardian pulled the child from his hiding place, the effects of the spell making him unresistant.

Mercurio tried placing the boy on his feet, but he couldn't stand. He let him be while he searched out the heartbeat from within the closet. He opened the door. Another boy, almost as tall as Mercurio, stood in the corner. His back turned and his hands covered his face.

Mercurio walked the boy from the closet to the door. He then bent down and lifted the smaller boy over his shoulders, opened the bedroom door and guided the taller boy out.

Jeremy followed the elf into the stables. The woman, the baby, and the smallest boy were still in a stupor. The man pulled tightly on the straps of the horse rigging and looked up at Mercurio. He sighed with relief as he saw his children. He nodded a thank you and continued his work.

Jeremy swallowed, wondering if this family would survive the night.

Mercurio laid the boy in the well of the wagon's footboard and then darted to the barn door to assess the situation. He didn't see any movement. But he knew Borahsh was still out there some-where. And there were other goblins he hadn't killed.

The door of the house opened. A groggy goblin emerged, turning his head left and right. Another walked out behind him.

Mercurio sighed and looked back at the man and his family. While the man feverishly worked, his family woke from their stupor. The boy clutched tighter to his mother. The infant cooed. Mercurio looked at Nikolaos. He could use the vortex and get Nikolaos away from here now. No. He couldn't leave this family in the hands of the goblins.

Samyaza, do not take me!

"Papa."

Mercurio snapped his head towards the little boy. He then looked at the man.

The man rushed to his son.

"Sidney, shhh. I need you to be absolutely quiet."

"But Papa, why…"

"Henry?" The woman said, staring at her husband, her eyes still heavy from the spell.

"Oh, dear," the man said. He stood and gathered his family around him. "I can't explain to you what is happening. We are in grave danger and I need you to do exactly what I say."

"Henry, you're scaring…"

"Jane!" He added a gruffness to his whisper. "Please do as I say. Take the children and put them in the wagon."

The woman noticed Mercurio by the door. She squinted, staring at him, and then looked to her husband.

Henry nodded and turned to his oldest son. He placed his hands on his shoulders and drew him closer. "Charles, I need you to keep the children quiet in the wagon. Can you do that?"

Charles looked at his father. He appeared to be fighting back tears. "Yes, Papa."

"Jane, give the children to Charles and help me harness the horses."

The family did as Henry said.

Mercurio peered out the door again. Three goblins lingered in the center of the road between the barn and the house.

"Emesh! Lahar!" Borahsh yelled from the side of the house. He clung to the corner, hobbling forward. "Find them! Search everywhere!"

Mercurio breathed a heavy sigh. *I will not panic. I will not perish.*

The guardian watched as the goblins searched the perimeter of the house. His eyes landed on the footprints in the snow that lead from the house to the barn. His heart raced again as one goblin noticed the footprints.

Mercurio rushed over to Henry.

"Hear me," he whispered with urgency. "They will find us soon. I need to slow them. Do *not* wait for me. If I'm able, I will catch up to you. But the second you're finished getting the horses ready, get Nikolaos in the wagon and leave here as if you were a bolt of lightning. Do you understand?"

The man swallowed and nodded. "Yes."

"Take Nikolaos to whoever it is who can help him and do *not* tarry."

Mercurio placed the cowl of his cloak over his head and disappeared to all but Jeremy. The guardian raised his arm and placed his hand on the hilt of his sword. He struggled to remove it without the aid of magic. He brought his other hand up to meet the hilt, and he sprung forward, retracing his footprints. When he came upon the first goblin, he didn't stop. He brought the sword to the side and sliced through the goblin's neck. He didn't slow to watch the head roll away from the body as it slumped to the ground and dissipated into golden light.

Mercurio continued forward, doing the same as he came upon a second goblin emerging from the house. He stopped beside the door, waiting and watching. His eyes focused on the barn.

Jeremy stood on the dirt road between the barn and the house, watching Mercurio and wincing at every sound he heard from the goblins in the house, thinking that an attack was imminent. It was nerve-racking. But Mercurio stood guard, unwavering. The entire time he kept his focus on the barn.

The barn doors swung open. The horses burst forth, pulling the wagon and its occupants in a thunderous run that rivaled the noise of the ransacking goblins. The wagon swerved on the dirt road and passed the farmhouse.

Mercurio pulled in magical energy, propelling himself into the air and into the passing wagon.

Jeremy blinked and found himself sitting in the wagon at Nikolaos' feet. Disoriented, he rubbed his eyes with one hand and grabbed onto the side of the wagon with the other.

Several goblins ran from the house, jumped to all fours and chased after them. They looked like a troop of chimpanzees, but their speed was no match for the horses.

A lumbering figure hobbled from the farmhouse doorway to the middle of the dirt road. He let out a blood-curdling scream.

As the farmhouse and barn grew smaller in the distance, Mercurio sighed and slumped down next to Nikolaos. He would soon be able to rest.

THE HORSES and wagon slowed after twenty minutes. They came to a church, its steeple illuminated by the moonlight, reflecting off the snow on the roof. Henry directed the horses to pull the wagon around the back of the church, off the main road.

Mercurio, Henry and the man's wife carried Nikolaos inside, down a flight of stairs, through a corridor, and into a storage room. Charles carried the baby, and the other boys followed.

"Jane, take the children and wait for me up in the sanctuary."

"Henry…" she said, her face worn with concern.

"Jane, take them up to the sanctuary now," the man said urgently.

The woman huddled the children and ushered them through the door, but not before giving her husband a disapproving look.

With his family out of the room, Henry pushed on a wall in the basement, revealing a secret door and another room.

Darkness filled the room until a flickering candle came on in the distance.

"Ruth," the man whispered loudly into the darkness, "we need help."

From the darkness, the candle came forward, revealing a dark-skinned woman. She wore a long blue and gray dress, with a gray apron and a matching kerchief around her head.

"Mr. Livingston, my word. It's the middle of the night!"

"There's been an accident. This man and his," he paused, looking at Mercurio. "… his friend are wounded."

"I'm fine," Mercurio said, "it is he who needs help, please."

Two more candles flickered in the back of the room. Several other dark-skinned men and women came forward. Ruth knelt and placed her ear to Nikolaos' lips. She looked up at Henry and shook her head. The others also knelt down to help. They quickly removed the bloody blanket and Nikolaos' bloodstained coat. Ruth put her ear to the man's chest.

"Mr. Livingston. I'm afraid this man is gone."

Mercurio pushed his way forward. "Gone? What do you mean gone?"

"I mean, he's dead. He ain't alive no more."

I knew it. I knew this was how the night was going to end. Jeremy said to himself, hanging his head and wishing it weren't so. This was why he was here. This was what Mercurio wanted him to see.

"No!" Mercurio knelt and grabbed Nikolaos by the collar. "No! He can't be dead!" He shook him. "You can't be dead." Mercurio let go of the collar and placed his ear to Nikolaos' mouth. He felt nothing. No air from his nose or breath from his lips.

"Nikolaos?" Mercurio moved his ear away. He took a second to look at his lifeless friend. "No!" The guardian drew in magic, and sent it into Nikolaos, urgently trying to heal the wounds. He could see the organs and the damage to them, but he didn't know enough about human anatomy to do anything. He continued anyway, desperately commanding the magic to knit together the wounds. His head spinning, and his muscles burning, Mercurio teetered backwards, bracing himself with his hands.

The guardian stared blankly at his friend. He slowly brought his trembling right hand forward and placed it on Nikolaos' still chest.

"Nikolaos," Mercurio, whispered. He touched Nikolaos' cheek. It was cold. "My friend, I'm sorry. I'm so sorry." He leaned forward and threw his small hands around Nikolaos' head, hugging his neck. Mercurio held his cheek to his friend's and a single tear made its way from Mercurio's face to Nikolaos'. "Nikolaos… no… you can't be dead… this can't be over… the children, Nikolaos… the children." Mercurio sobbed.

"Mr. Livingston, who is this man?" Ruth asked quietly.

"Ruth," Henry sighed, "I do believe that this is Saint Nicholas."

The room remained quiet and solemn as Mercurio hugged his friend for the last time.

After a few minutes, Henry placed his hand on the elf's shoulder. "I'm sorry," he said. "Is there anything else we can do to help you?"

Mercurio stood up and took a deep breath as he adjusted his cloak and armor. He looked up at Henry.

"We need to return to your home and be sure the goblins left no sign for anyone to wake up to."

"You stay here with your friend. I'll see to that task. You've been through enough."

Mercurio thought about it for a moment. He didn't want to leave Nikolaos, and he was exhausted.

"You must promise to take care of everything. Be meticulous. Leave nothing out of the ordinary for anyone to find. And then you must burn it all. Place it all in your barn and burn it down. I will give you enough in precious jewels and metals for you to purchase another barn. Promise me, you will save nothing."

Henry nodded. "I give you my word." He turned and headed for the door.

"Henry?" Mercurio called to him.

Henry turned and looked back at the elf.

"I am sorry you and your family had to be a part of all this."

Henry nodded.

"You should wait awhile," Mercurio said. "Sunrise isn't for a few more hours. Give the goblins some time to thoroughly search before they decide to head back."

Mercurio sat down next to Nikolaos' body and leaned against the wall.

Henry joined him.

Jeremy sat and leaned against the wall opposite Mercurio. He felt numb… out of place. Saint Nicholas lay dead before him, and he had so many questions. But he was fairly certain of one thing, there could only be one reason Mercurio was showing him all this. *Why me? Why would he want me to be a part of all this? He can't possibly want me to replace Nikolaos.*

Ruth placed an old blanket around Mercurio's shoulders.

The elf stared at Nikolaos' lifeless, blanket covered body, illuminated by the flickering light of Henry's candle.

"I cannot fathom what has happened here this night." Henry said to Mercurio. "And you owe me no explanation."

"Your people called him Saint Nicholas. And by the definition of the word, he was indeed a saint. The world has lost a great man this day." Mercurio shared his fond memories of Nikolaos. Jeremy listened. There were moments of reminiscing and moments of silent contemplation. At first, it seemed a much-needed catharsis for Mercurio. But it soon transitioned to regret.

"You can't blame yourself," Henry said.

Mercurio pulled at the hem of the blanket. "There is no one else to blame. My entire life has been dedicated to protecting Nikolaos."

"The fault lies only with those creatures. You did everything you…"

"If only I had thought of the incantation sooner."

"I… I don't understand," Henry said.

"It's why all of you were in the stupor. It's the spell I told you about. The words are Greek, so that Nikolaos could easily say them. We tried Elvish, but Nikolaos had difficulty with it, especially since we used the names he had given to the reindeer." Mercurio sighed. "Ho, Swiftfoot! Ho, Dancer." He uttered the words without fervor or zeal. "Ho, Littlefox and Prancer. Ho, Longhair and Passion. Quickly. Ho, O Thunder and Lightning. From the rooftop and through the Veil. Dash away. Dash away now. All, dash away. I'd say that's a somewhat strained translation. No matter." Mercurio sighed again, shaking his head. "I had thought of every way the goblins could have attacked us. Every possible way. We practiced. I knew they'd try to attack us in larger numbers one day. I just don't know why we didn't see them coming! And I don't understand why I couldn't harness the magic. Those goblins did something, I just don't know what." He rubbed his hands on the back of his neck.

WHEN MERCURIO AWOKE, he looked around.

Ruth lay beside him. She sat up and stared curiously at the elf.

In all the events leading Mercurio here, he hadn't taken the time to even consider where he was or who these other humans were that lived in here. "What is this place?"

"A place for us to hide." Ruth responded matter-of-factly.

"Hide from what?" Mercurio furrowed his brow.

"From the white folk. Not the white folk like Mr. Livingston. He good white folk. But there are wicked white folk. Mr. Livingston and other good white-folk help to hide us here until the next wagon come. Then we'll go where we'll be free."

"The underground railroad!" Jeremy said, surprised.

"Free?" Mercurio said.

"Where the wicked white man don't beat us and force us to work for him."

Wicked white men? Flashes of Mercurio's memories appeared in Jeremy's mind. Roman soldiers beating and rounding up other people. An elf among them; a female elf. They hit her on the head with a club and carried her away. Mercurio, hidden in a Veil cloak, reaching out for her, crying out.

Mercurio inhaled and shook his head. The images disappeared. His eyes fell upon his friend's body. Nikolaos was different. Nikolaos showed the elves that there was good in humanity.

Jeremy looked around at the cramped space. Eight people shared this tiny dark room. Hiding, hoping to one day be free. *So much for hope in humanity*, he thought, shaking his head at the sad state of these people. *The underground railroad?* His thoughts drifted away from Mercurio's conversation with Ruth. *Could one of these people be Harriet Tubman?* Remembering his history, he concluded it was too early for the famed underground railroad. The mimstone told him that this was 1803, and he remembered that the underground railroad wasn't organized until the middle of the 1800s. He couldn't remember when Harriet Tubman was born, but he thought she probably wasn't even born yet. This must be one of those precursor abolitionists groups that became a part of the more organized underground railroad. Jeremy wanted to know more… more about these people hiding here and the man helping them. He looked at Ruth, wondering what her story was. But the mimstone didn't reveal any more about her.

"You look like a child," Ruth said. She stared at Mercurio with squinting eyes. "But you don't act like no child I ever seen."

Mercurio smiled. Nikolaos thought he was a child, once. And so did Jeremy.

Jeremy laughed.

"I'm no child. I'm an elf."

"A elf?" Ruth said, cocking her head backwards with her eyebrow raised.

"My people. We are elves. You are humans."

Ruth's jaw went slack and her eyes lit with wonder. "You are Emere? My grandmother told us of your folk."

Mercurio smiled.

The secret door slid open and Henry entered.

"I brought you some food," he said, handing a basket to Ruth. "Merry Christmas."

Merry Christmas. Not hardly. Mercurio thought, standing and removing the blanket from around his shoulders. He laid it on the floor beside Ruth.

"Henry, may I take your horses and wagon? I will gladly give you more than enough to purchase new ones."

"Of course. But I will go with you and…"

"No," Mercurio said. "What you've done, I cannot thank you enough for. Alas, you cannot go where I'm going. It is forbidden."

CHAPTER 21

HOPE UNFURLED

"If you find that not many of the things you asked for have come, and not perhaps quite so many as sometimes, remember that this Christmas all over the world there are a terrible number of poor and starving people."

~ From *Letters from Father Christmas* by J.R.R. Tolkien,

Present Day

Jeremy floated in the dark tranquility of the mimstone.

"The trek back to Orindin was uneventful for Mercurio," the mimstone spoke. "He'd taken Henry's wagon as far as he could go, resting along the way, and waiting for the full effects of the goblins' foul deed to wear off. To this day, no one knows what the goblins used to temporarily block Mercurio from using magic."

Jeremy opened his eyes and focused on the faded gray carpet of his bedroom floor. He sat on the edge of his bed. In his mind, he scrambled to form a complete thought, but he could only think of the horror he'd just witnessed.

"Henry couldn't forget what he saw that night." Mercurio said. "And he and millions of other parents all over the world couldn't let Christmas die in the hearts of their children."

Mercurio turned away from the window and faced Jeremy. "Parents awoke to find no Christmas presents for their children from Saint Nicholas. So they did what any parent who didn't wish to break their child's heart would do. They furiously scrambled to get presents under the tree so that they could say they were from Saint Nicholas. And most have been doing so ever since."

All these years. All this time. Santa… Saint Nicholas was real. "My Dad… he…" Jeremy mumbled. "My Dad wanted us to believe in Santa Claus so much. He would tell us these crazy stories, trying to get us to believe every year."

"Jeremy," Mercurio said. "I have watched the world grow deeper in darkness and hate. I have watched humans and other species wage war and do unspeakable things. This world needs to find hope in again. They need to know that there is someone out there who cares for them… who shows them love, no matter what. It may be too late for many. But we can bring hope to a new generation. That's what Nikolaos did. He knew the key to reviving hope in his people was through the children. He brought out the best in everyone with a single act of love and kindness… a gift. The world needs that again… the world needs Santa Claus."

Silence took the room.

Wait a minute, Jeremy thought. "Nikolaos failed!" Jeremy said, rising from the bed.

"What?" Mercurio asked, puzzled.

"He failed!" Jeremy walked to the door. "You said he brought hope. How do you explain the countless wars that happened in his lifetime?"

"Jeremy—"

"And um, what about all of those people that made the world a living hell for others?"

"Jeremy—"

"Like Attila the Hun, Ivan the Terrible, Vlad the Impaler—"

"Jeremy… I don't—"

"Oh, and what about Oliver Cromwell and Genghis Khan and Robespierre? Did they all get coal in their stockings?"

"No. Nikolaos never did that. That was something parents made up. But Jeremy, you—"

"No, Mercurio. You listen. Seriously… you want me to just pick up where Nikolaos left off and just keep doing the same thing, even though it didn't make a difference? That's the definition of insanity!"

Mercurio stared at Jeremy, silent for a moment. "He did make a difference. He did. I saw it. I saw the looks on the children's faces. The love they felt when they opened their gifts. And there were countless other humans in the world who went on to do great things. I do not, nor will I ever know why those humans you mentioned chose to do such evil. But I do know there are good people who went on to do great things because of the kindness shown to them by Nikolaos. People like George Washington, Jesper Montenegro, Luscious Bean, Queen Nanny, Fyodor Rtishchev, Halima Sharma, Gaius Sophilus, and so many others! I could go on."

"The only one of those people I've ever heard of is George Washington."

"Precisely right. They were good people who did good things in their community. They may have not been famous in the sense that your history books chronicled their deeds, but they showed love and kindness to their family and neighbors. Jeremy, Nikolaos didn't fail. Even in his death he left a legacy of good. Henry Livingston, the man who helped me that night Nikolaos died. Have you heard of him before this day?"

"No. I've never heard of him. Should I have?"

"'Twas the night before Christmas," Mercurio paused and cleared his throat, and with a smile, he continued. "…when all through the house, not a creature was stirring, not even a mouse; The stockings were hung by the chimney with care, in *hopes* that Saint Nicholas soon would be there."

The elf smiled mischievously at Jeremy.

Jeremy cocked his head and raised his right eyebrow. "A Visit from St. Nicholas by Clement Clarke Moore. I read that poem to my students every year at Christmas time."

"Henry Livingston penned that poem two days after Nikolaos died. He composed it as a gift to his children. A way to preserve in their hearts what Nikolaos stood for. How it came to be known as being written by Clement Moore is a rather long story. The short of it is, out of a promise Henry made to me the poem remained a story he only shared with his family. It was after he died that the poem became popular. You see Jeremy, at the very heart of what Nikolaos did, he gave hope that an act of kindness had power to brighten someone's day. And I know you believe it too. I want to give you the power to magnify that belief. I want you to become Santa Claus."

Wait a minute! Jeremy raised his head and eyebrow. He looked back at Mercurio. "What about the goblins?"

"Well," Mercurio said, pausing. "That is still a problem. But it's nothing we can't handle."

Jeremy stiffened. "What?"

"Well, I'm sure by now they know that I've pierced the Veil. They are after *me* this time. Their vendetta is not with you. You'll have your own Gift Giver's Guard that will not include me. You'll be safe."

Jeremy rubbed his forehead. "I can't believe I am even considering this! What am I going to tell everyone? My parents? My students?"

"Jeremy, you can't tell them anything. They can't know where you are because they can never come there. You can't even send them letters."

"What? That's crazy. They won't know what happened to me? They'll think I died."

"Precisely. That's all part of the mystery. At first they won't know what happened to you. Then, after your first Christmas Eve, the magic will spread beyond the Veil, and those you love will know in their hearts what happened. They won't be able to explain it, but they will have peace in their hearts and know that you are well."

"What? That sounds ridiculous! I don't think you quite understand how things work in the real world these days. My parents will be frantic. They'll have police looking for me everywhere. They'll be questioning everyone I know. I can't put everyone through that. The police have better things to do than look for me."

Mercurio looked to the window again, his face tight as he considered Jeremy's concern.

"If I leave now, my mom and dad are gonna be heartbroken! They already lost one child; you're asking me to make them go through that again? No thanks."

"Jeremy," Mercurio said, turning to face him. "I shouldn't be doing this. Pack up anything that is important to you and then go see your parents and tell them. But they must be sworn to secrecy. They'll have to tell everyone something else, but they can never reveal who you have become and where you went."

Jeremy laughed. "So, you want me to go and tell my parents that I am leaving them, my job, my apartment… everything, so that I can become Santa Claus? Do you know how crazy that sounds? They'll never believe me."

Mercurio glowered at Jeremy.

"What? Did you think this was going to be easy? Did you think you'd just say, 'come with me if you want to be Santa Claus' and I'd just pack up and go? Come on, you've gotta be over a thousand years old! You had to have thought this through."

"Honestly, Jeremy," Mercurio shrugged. "My main concern was how I would get you to the gatehouse. I believe that will not be a problem."

"Yeah, but the only way this is going to work is if you come with me to my parents' house and show them some magic. Otherwise, I'm gonna end up being admitted for observation."

"Oh, Jeremy," Mercurio shook his head. "The more of your people that know about this, the more difficult it will be to keep this all a secret. Besides, we are not supposed to go around revealing our kind to humans. It is forbidden. Alas, I see no other choice here. Very well. I will meet your parents."

———

JEREMY SPENT the next half-hour packing his bags. He didn't know what to bring with him. It didn't help that Mercurio kept rushing him and telling him to only take what he absolutely needed. He told Jeremy that everything else, including clothing, would be provided for him in Orindin. He squeezed his laptop, a few books, and some of his favorite t-shirts into a backpack and small wheeled suitcase. And underwear. He thought it would be strange to have elves making his underwear.

Mercurio left him with instructions to go directly to his parents' house. The elf couldn't go with him, because he had to be sure no one was following them. However, he assured Jeremy that he would meet him there.

———

MERCURIO PERCHED on the rooftop's edge, the hood of his cloak drawn, hiding him from anyone who might see him in the daylight.

Jeremy left the apartment building and turned down the busy sidewalk.

Numerous cars moved up and down the street while dozens of others sat parked along the curbs. Two children repeatedly bounced and threw an orange ball through a ladder hanging from the side of the apartment building. A young couple argued on the corner. Another couple walked hand in hand. Three men emerged from the apartment building across the street. Several other lone humans walked purposefully to their destinations.

Mercurio scanned the scene below, looking for any disturbances in their auras. Most of the humans had orange and blue emanating from their aura. Only a few had the characteristic vibrancy of red and orange, showing someone on alert. There were five total. The young couple had flares of pink and black as well. The other three, the men who exited the building across the street, produced synchronous pulsing waves of orange and red. But none of their auras shimmered. *Where was the other goblin?*

One man, muscular with dirty blond hair and dark gray clothing, pointed down the street in the opposite direction of Jeremy. He appeared to be giving orders to the tall thin, dark-skinned man whose thick black hair was tied into a ponytail.

The dark-skinned man ran in the opposite direction, while the leader and a hulking troll-like man walked across the street towards Jeremy. Mercurio feared this would happen.

He turned to look for the dark-skinned man and saw him getting into a black car.

Mercurio dashed down the side of the building and onto the sidewalk. He dodged around several pedestrians and leapt onto the hood of the car, his cloak absorbing the sound of the impact.

The man pulled the car into the street.

Mercurio braced himself, placing his palms face-down on the hood. Harnessing the magical energy all around him, he concentrated the magic into the engine, hyper-accelerating the molecules and rapidly raising the vehicle's temperature. He felt the heat rise through the hood and he somersaulted backwards onto the roof.

Smoke and steam rose from the hood and the car came to a halt.

Almost immediately the car behind honked, causing a dissonant chain reaction of trumpet-like blasts that echoed through the cavernous street.

Mercurio stood up on the car's roof and fixed his eyes on his new ward. Jeremy was just about to reach the corner. He stopped and turned, looking back at the rising smoke and honking cars.

Keep going, Jeremy! Don't stop, Mercurio thought.

The dark-skinned man opened the door and threw up his hands in frustration. He slammed his hand on the roof and turned to the cars honking behind him. "What you want me to do, brah?"

Mercurio leapt off the hood and darted down the street

toward the other two men, who stopped to look behind at the commotion. As he drew closer, Mercurio saw his next target. The two kids playing with the orange ball.

Mercurio raised his hand, manipulating the magical energy all around, sending a ripple towards the ball, just enough to loosen it from the boy's grip.

The ball bounced to the ground, and the boy reached out to grab it. Mercurio pushed the ball to its left and sent it speeding through the air. The ball slammed into the side of the leader's head, knocking him off balance. The man tumbled to the ground.

The boys ran off around the corner.

The big man crouched down and placed his hands on the leader's shoulders.

Mercurio ran up to Jeremy and grabbed him by the arm, startling him.

"Jeremy, quickly. Get to your parents' house and don't stop for anything else."

Before Jeremy could speak, Mercurio released his arm and ran back to the two men.

The leader was still in pain, clutching his left ear. The troll-like man held onto his arm.

"Tufts, don't let him get out of your sight." The leader said urgently, wafting his hand in Jeremy's direction.

The big man walked toward Jeremy while the leader, still holding his head, staggered to the stalled car.

How do I stop this man without being seen or bringing harm to anyone else?

Tufts maintained a reasonable distance as he followed Jeremy around the corner.

Mercurio searched for a way to stop this man. More parked cars, apartment buildings, pedestrians, and a disheveled man asleep beside a fire hydrant.

Jeremy stopped and reached into his pocket to give something to the disheveled man.

Jeremy! I said keep going!

The guardian looked up at the variety of open windows. This

gave him an idea. He had to choose the correct one, and he needed to time it just right. Mercurio reduced the gravity around him and ran swiftly past the big man and several other pedestrians. He scaled the side of the building and climbed into the open window.

There was no one there, but a woman's voice drifted in from another room.

"Oye, Barbara. If I'm not cookin' I'm doin' laundry. I swear, I think these kids change their clothes every few hours!"

Mercurio looked around for something heavy, but not too heavy. His eyes narrowed on a white ceramic pot housing a lush green plant. Medium-sized, it was just right. He snatched it and took it to the window ledge.

As Tufts passed the window, Mercurio manipulated the magical energy around the pot and hurled it towards the big man. It landed directly in front of him, smashing to the ground.

The big man stopped and looked up, confused.

In the same instant, Mercurio focused on the valve of the fire hydrant and caused it to burst open. Water sprayed out of the side, barely missing Tufts, but enough to saturate the disheveled man. He jumped up, clutching on to Tufts and yelling something unintelligible.

The big man snarled and shoved the vagrant back into the stream of water. The man glared back at him and walked away.

The elf darted out through the window, down the side of the building, and bowled into the back of Tufts's legs, sending him crashing to the ground.

As the big man groaned and rolled around on the sidewalk, Mercurio concentrated on the magic around a squirrel sitting in a tree several feet away. He moved the squirrel as if it was jumping from the tree onto the sidewalk and towards the big man. A convenient opening at the cuff of the man's damp pants served as the perfect entry. Mercurio pulled the rodent up the man's leg and let it go.

The squirrel frantically scratched around, looking for a way out.

Tufts tried to escape the frightening prospect of the damage the creature could do. He awkwardly shook his leg, wincing with each movement, as the bulge in his pants wiggled agitatedly.

Tufts continued to frantically shake his leg trying to liberate the angry squirrel. The squirrel ran out and ran back up the tree as far as it could go.

The fire hydrant and the large man rolling on the ground had caused more of a distraction as people made their way around the massive puddle forming on the sidewalk.

Tufts hobbled, bracing himself against each car, slowly making his way back toward his leader.

The leader and the dark-skinned man had moved the car over to the side, but it still blocked much of the street. A police officer directed traffic around the car as the leader and dark-skinned man had the hood open, studying the steaming, smoking engine.

When the leader saw Tufts, he smacked the edge of the car and shot him an aggravated glance.

"What happened?" The leader demanded.

"I'm not really sure. A lot of weird stuff. I need an ice pack."

"You lost him? Seriously? You lost him? How? Ah, forget about it." He turned to the dark-skin man. "Decoudreau, see if you can get an address for this kid's parents."

Mercurio nodded his head. He couldn't believe the tenacity of these men. He needed to get to Jeremy's parents' place quickly, but first he had to disable their devices just to be on the safe side.

CHAPTER 22
MEET THE PARENTS

"Guilt can only be pacified through forgiveness or payment. Both are determined by the wronged. Within the Iyl'Sel'wyn, it is always best to extend forgiveness."

~ Elven Wisdom from *The Second Annals of Wisdom*

When Jeremy arrived at his parents' house, he stood on the cement sidewalk and stared at the lawn-less, two-story house. Now painted brick red, he remembered when it was gray. His Dad and his uncle spent a weekend painting it that dark, brick red color. His Mom hated it. "If we wanted brick red," she said, "we would've bought a brick house." Jeremy smiled at the memory.

What was he going to tell them? How was he going to tell them? *Maybe this isn't such a good idea*, he wondered. This was just too incredible. There had to be someone else who could… who could… Jeremy couldn't even say the words, it sounded so ridiculous.

He felt a gentle touch on his forearm, and he flinched away.

"Shall we go in?" He heard Mercurio's voice.

We shall not! Was what Jeremy wanted to say. Instead, he just sighed and fumbled for his keys. He slowly took the keys from his pocket to the door.

"I should probably ring the bell. They're not expecting me… us."

How embarrassing that'd be if his dad was sitting around in his underwear and Mercurio saw him.

"Good idea," Mercurio said.

"So, how do we do this?" Jeremy asked.

"Simple. You tell them the truth. And I will remove my cowl and reveal myself—"

"Giving my parents a heart attack, resulting in an ambulance ride to the hospital."

"Are your parents ill at heart? Perhaps—"

"No, no… I was just being sarcastic. I doubt both of them will have a heart attack." Jeremy said sarcastically as he pushed the button to ring the doorbell.

He looked down where he thought Mercurio was and then back at the door.

It seemed an eternity before the door swung open. The faint sound of Sinatra singing "Luck Be a Lady" streamed through the doorway.

"Jeremy! You surprised us." His mom said. She held the door open, standing there in her bright green muumuu-looking, housedress.

"Come in," Mom said.

Jeremy put on his best fake smile and walked in. He gave his mom a hug.

"Why'd you bring your luggage with you?"

"You're not moving back in, are you?" His dad yelled from upstairs, laughing.

Jeremy parked his suitcase against the wall and laid his backpack beside it. He followed his mom upstairs and greeted his dad with a hug when they reached the top.

"So, what's going on?" Dad said.

"I wanted to talk to you guys about something."

"Are you needing to move back in?" Mom said.

"No. Something else."

They walked into the dining room to the familiar scene of an oblong table covered in newspapers and a closed box of Entenmann's blueberry pie sitting in the center. Frank Sinatra concluded his final stanza, and the opening melody of Nat King Cole's "Unforgettable" came on. Jeremy's mom sat at her seat in front of the pile of newspapers. Dad went into the kitchen, and Jeremy sat in the seat across from his mom.

"You want a drink, son?" Dad called from the kitchen.

"No. No thanks."

"How about some blueberry pie?" Mom asked.

"No. I'm good."

Nat King Cole belted out the refrain of his legendary song.

"Alexa, volume two." Mom said, smiling. "I love this thing." She tapped on the black cylindrical speaker with the glowing blue light ring next to her.

Nat continued to sing, only lower now.

Jeremy's dad walked in from the kitchen with a glass of diet tonic water and stood in the doorway. Both parents stared awkwardly at Jeremy.

"So, um…" Jeremy stammered. "So, I got this job offer I'm really considering."

"Oh?" Said Dad.

Mom continued to stare and smile.

"Yeah," Jeremy said. "It's a great offer, but if I take it, I'm gonna have to move, uh, up north."

"Really?" Said Dad.

Mom still stared.

"Yeah, but it's quite—"

"Moths and rust!" Mercurio shouted, taking his cowl off and revealing himself.

Dad's glass crashed to the floor.

———

Mercurio's impromptu reveal made everything easier, at least after the initial shock wore off. Jeremy's dad kept repeating the same question over and over again. "You're going to be Santa Claus?" In fact, he seemed more excited than Jeremy. Mom didn't say much. She listened as Mercurio and Jeremy explained what was going on, but her face remained frozen with eyes wide and mouth closed.

"Jeremy, we need to go," Mercurio said, urgency in his voice.

Jeremy stood up from the kitchen table and bent over to Mercurio.

"Is everything okay?" He whispered. "Did someone find us?"

"The longer we stay here, the more likely someone will," Mercurio whispered back.

Jeremy turned and looked at his parents. Dad smiled, standing behind Mom with his hand on her shoulder. Mom still had the same shocked expression.

Jeremy couldn't imagine endangering his parents. They needed to get out of there.

"Well, Mom, Dad… we need to go." Jeremy said nervously. He reached out, extending his arms towards his mom for a hug.

"No!" Mom said. "This is crazy! You can't just leave and… and… go with some strange man-child to the North Pole!"

"Man-child?" Mercurio scrunched his face, staring at her.

"Man-child?" Jeremy said, "Mom, he's an elf. He's not—"

"I don't care what he is!" Mom threw her hands up. "Or what he can do with his magic tricks!"

"Honey…" Dad said consolingly and placed his hand on her shoulder.

"You just can't…" Her angry scowl softened, and her eyes turned down as she sobbed. "… leave us. You can't." She sunk down into her chair.

Jeremy's heart sank. "Oh Mom, I'm not gonna be gone for good." He walked over and pulled his mom up for a hug. "And I'll visit. Maybe I can even send the ol' sled by and pick you guys up."

"That'd be great!" Dad said.

Mercurio let out an exasperated sigh and vigorously shook his head.

Jeremy shrugged slightly in his mom's embrace, lifting his eyebrows and mouthing, "What do you want me to do?"

"Wouldn't that be nice, Honey? I'd love to see the North Pole." Dad said.

Mercurio placed his hand on his forehead and let out another exasperated sigh.

"Oh, Martin," Mom said, slowly pulling away from Jeremy. "How can we… how can this be? Do you hear yourself? Us at the North Pole on vacation? In a town of elfs?"

"Elves, Honey. They're called elves."

Mom wiped the tears from her eyes. "Jeremy, are you sure about this? I just—"

"Mom. I know it sounds crazy. I know it looks crazy. But, um… just think of it as a sabbatical."

"Oh, Jeremy!" She embraced her son; a difficult, bittersweet embrace.

I don't know when I'll be back. When will I see them again? Well, now that my parents know what's going on, I'm sure I could convince the elves to let me call. Oh, but what if they don't have cell service or internet? No internet. That's gonna be tough.

Mom squeezed him a little tighter. And Dad joined in.

"Alrighty Mom, we really need to go." Jeremy said.

Jeremy walked to the door, followed by his parents. He looked at his dad. He was still smiling. Jeremy half-smiled back. Dad reached out, and they hugged.

"I'm proud of you, son. So proud of you."

"Thanks, Dad. But I haven't really done anything yet."

Dad pulled away from the hug and held Jeremy by the shoulders. He looked down at his son, smile wide and eyes glistening through thick dark-rimmed glasses.

"Son, I'm proud of you because you're willing to see this through. You're answering a call. Not just to help a few people or even a large group of people. What you're doing will help the whole world! Jeremy, this is incredible." He shook his head and his smile never wavered. "My son."

"Dad. I'm a little scared."

"You better be!" Dad laughed. "If you weren't, I might be worried."

Mercurio tugged on Jeremy's shirt. He looked down at the elf, who glowered back at him with eyes that shifted toward the door.

Jeremy hugged his parents quickly and kissed them one last time before hefting his backpack on. He grabbed his suitcase and opened the door.

Mercurio raised his cowl and disappeared.

Jeremy stepped through the doorway and looked at his parents one more time.

"I'll be looking for you in the sky on Christmas Eve." Dad said.

Jeremy nodded and began his walk back down the block to catch the bus.

"Martin?" Mom said. "Is our son crazy?"

"No." Dad said.

"Then are we crazy?" Mom asked.

Jeremy giggled and shook his head.

THE ARGOSY

> "The two most important days in your life are the day you are born and the day you find out why."
> ~ Mark Twain.

On the bus ride back to Manhattan, Jeremy stood in the back, holding onto the handrail and traversing it back and forth. There were plenty of seats this time of day going into Manhattan, but how could he possibly sit? His life was about to change in unimaginable ways and self-doubt put a damper on the excitement.

An elderly couple eyed him. The gentleman looked at Jeremy and the surrounding empty seats as if to say, "Relax, sit down. You're making us nervous with all the pacing."

Nervous! Sheesh! How could he not be nervous? There was so much he needed to do. But the feeling that he was the wrong person for the job scratched away at the back of his mind. He was just a teacher. And what Mercurio was asking him to do was… was beyond his capabilities.

He slung his backpack onto an empty seat, sat down next to it and looked out the window at the busy streets. So many people.

And they were all oblivious to what Jeremy experienced today. All caught up in their own existence, trying to make their way in the world. Though most put up the stoic front New Yorkers were famous for, Jeremy saw past their facade. Beyond the mask of dauntless determination, there was something there. Or, more correctly, there was something not there. He glanced over at the elderly couple. The man's hand sat tenderly on his wife's knee; both glancing out the window. He turned and looked at Jeremy. And there it was. Beyond the glass of his tortoise-shell spectacles, despair and sadness. Just like Ashley.

Jeremy shivered and swallowed. He turned away from the man and looked out the window again. The bus slowed around the corner. A group of pedestrians stood at the crosswalk and Jeremy saw the very same thing in their eyes too.

What's happening to me? How come I never noticed this before? Jeremy sighed and took out his cell phone. He clicked on the camera app and looked into his own eyes. And there it was. Faint, but recognizable, he too was lost.

Oh, God... Jeremy sighed, shaking his head. How was he any different from anyone else? What right did he have to take up Nikolaos' cause? If he did, he'd be nothing more than a hypocrite.

A distant giggle disturbed his thoughts, and Jeremy looked up from his phone.

Toward the center front of the bus, two small eyes and a set of dimpled cheeks peered out from the back of a seat. The child stared curiously at Jeremy and grew more excited when he realized he had noticed him.

Jeremy smiled back. In that instant, the hopelessness and self-pity dissipated.

The child waved at him and Jeremy waved back.

Nikolaos was right. *The children.* Jeremy may not be able to help everyone, but he'd certainly be able to help the children. Resolved to what he must do, Jeremy emailed a letter of resignation to his principal and another to the summer camp. He used the "job offer he couldn't refuse" excuse. He texted his friends and let them know he had the opportunity to travel the world on sabbatical, and he'd be gone awhile.

It only took ten minutes before his text and Facebook notifications started blowing up with well wishes, congratulations, and questions about what countries he'd be in and when.

It took a bus ride, a subway ride, and a five-minute walk to get from his parents' house in Yonkers to the location Mercurio said to meet him. The elf had given him directions to meet at the Argosy Book Store in midtown Manhattan.

The bookstore wasn't difficult to find. It stood out amid the concrete landscape; a deep brown, wooden-framed storefront; its entrance preceded by an open-air alcove with display cases to its left and right and bookshelves at its rear. An antique wooden table filled with books sat in the center. The round sign outside the alcove read: "Old and Rare Prints, Books, Maps". Another sign boasted, "New York City's Oldest Bookstore."

Inside, stacks and stacks of books as far as the eye could see lined the walls and floor. Above the stacks were pictures and maps. On any other day Jeremy would have loved to explore this place.

"May I help you?" asked a round-faced gentleman. His balding head and thick-framed glasses reminded Jeremy of the stereotypical bookseller. He wasn't far from what Jeremy expected to find working here.

Mercurio had given Jeremy specific instructions. He was to ask for Edgar and only Edgar. Once he met Edgar, he was supposed to ask him if he had a first edition of Lewis Carroll's "The Pruning of the Tumtum Tree."

Jeremy swallowed and licked his lips nervously.

"Um, I'm looking for a first edition of…" He stopped and realized he forgot to ask for Edgar. "I, um… is Edgar here?"

"I'm Edgar," the gentleman kindly replied, pointing to a tag hanging from a brown lanyard around his neck.

"Oh, OK. Um, I'm looking for a first edition of…" He paused and apprehensively looked around to see if anyone else was watching. There were several other people in the store, but no one paid any mind to Jeremy or Edgar. Then he arched his head forward toward Edgar's ear and nervously whispered, "The Pruning of the Tumtum Tree." He had forgotten to mention the author, and nervously repeated himself. "Um… by Lewis Carroll…"

Edgar smiled.

"Oh. Yes. Right this way." The man had a calm and assuring manner.

Edgar led Jeremy toward the back of the store, down a staircase to a brightly lit basement filled with more books.

"We have over 48,000 books in this basement alone," Edgar said, leading Jeremy deeper into the store, past wall-to-wall bookshelves.

The rattling wheels of Jeremy's suitcase drew the attention of a gray-haired woman with her hair in a bun. She turned from one stack and squinted at Jeremy through high-point half-rimmed glasses.

"Here we are," Edgar said, diverting Jeremy's attention to an old wooden door.

Edgar produced an antiquated skeleton key and unlocked the door.

"Come. Come this way," Edgar said, leading Jeremy into a small storage room filled with more books, some on shelves, some on tables. The room, though ordinary, gave Jeremy the creeps. There was something odd about it, something foreboding that made him feel as if he should leave… right now.

The bookseller extended his index finger towards Jeremy as if he had just remembered something. He began shuffling through his pockets.

"Ah!" Edgar said. His eyes grew wide, and a smile appeared as he pulled a small glowing stone out of his pocket and held it up to Jeremy. "Here it is."

The green, speckled stone glowed dimly.

"Please take this," Edgar instructed.

Jeremy cocked his head, perplexed by the glowing stone. He hesitantly took it and examined it further.

The foreboding feeling went away, and Jeremy's natural

curiosity piqued again. *The Veil. I must be near it,* he thought to himself and smiled.

"Ah good," Edgar said, turning. He then reached for another set of keys from his pocket and walked to the back corner of the room.

There was a door that Jeremy hadn't noticed when he first walked in.

Edgar unlocked the door and pulled it open. The musky aroma of antiquity wafted in.

Jeremy smiled nervously with anticipation. *This is so cool!*

"Come," Edgar called, waving Jeremy over to the door.

The doorway led down a flight of dimly lit old stone stairs to another locked door.

Edgar used his key to unlock it. Jeremy followed the bookseller into the room, and Edgar closed the door, locking it behind him.

The image of Edgar disappeared, and in its place appeared a gnome. He stood a good two feet shorter than he did as the bookseller, yet he had the same round face. Only this Edgar's nose and cheeks were bigger. Gone were the glasses, white shirt and beige pants. He now wore a brimless blue conical cap, matching blue vest, and black boots.

The gnome smiled and extended his hand. "You must be Jeremy."

"Um, yes. Yes, I am," Jeremy said, still clutching the glowing stone. He placed it in his pocket and shook the gnome's hand.

"So, you're the one Mercurio has been talking about. This is going to be great. Just great. I'm so happy to meet you."

"Same here. Um, so, I'm guessing you're the gatekeeper?"

"Yes! Welcome to the Gate at Argosy." he said, raising his arms.

"A gnome named Edgar," Jeremy stated matter-of-factly, looking around the damp, stone room. Once more, there were shelves covering every wall, each one filled with books. But no Veil.

"Oh no. Pardon me. Edgar's my covert name. My real name is Bartleby Gasto, Artificer, Veil Wright of the First Order, and

Alfargnym of Unterbaum. And I am so pleased to have you in my gatehouse!"

Jeremy looked down at the exuberant gnome and smiled. "Can I ask you something?"

"Of course. Anything."

"You're a gnome, right?"

"I'm a Veil Wright."

"Huh?" Jeremy raised his left eyebrow.

"A Veil Wright. W-R-I-G-H-T. Like an engineer. That is my profession. I maintain this gatehouse."

"Um, no… that's not what I mean." Jeremy said flustered. "You're a gnome. But you call yourself an alfargnym?"

"A gnome. An alfargnym. A leprechaun. All the same." Bartleby smiled. "Gnome is what we've become known as these past few centuries. We prefer to be called alfargnym, but I'm afraid we've never been quite assertive enough with our peoples' true name. This century I'm a gnome. Perhaps next, my children will be called something different."

Jeremy contemplated this for a moment. How strange that one race of people should be called so many different names. *And where did the name gnome come from?* He wondered.

"You must be excited," Bartleby interrupted Jeremy's thoughts.

Excited? That's one way to put it.

"Well, yeah… I am excited. But I'm also terrified! Today I met an elf and a gnome, and I was asked to become Santa Claus!"

"Yes, yes… Mercurio told me about you. I can't wait until everyone else finds out. It's so hard to keep a secret! Especially one this size." The gnome laughed.

"What about—"

The rumbling sound of mechanical pulleys and wood sliding on stone diverted Jeremy's attention. The bookshelves on the far wall opened outward to reveal another brightly lit room with wood panel walls. Mercurio walked in, followed by another elf and one of the unusual reptilian creatures.

Jeremy stepped backward at the site of the fearsome looking

reptile. He had seen glimpses of these creatures while under the influence of the mimstone. Though seeing it with his own eyes was mind blowing; raptor-like, standing on two large clawed feet, only slightly taller than Mercurio. Its skin, silvery white with deep brown, almost black, irregular stripes, reminded Jeremy of a birch tree. He appeared to be some kind of dinosaur! A living, breathing dinosaur! The pointed teeth of its lower jaw overlapped onto the upper jaw. Its horns, protruding from its brow, had glyph-like etchings and an ornamented silver band around each one.

The creature stared back at Jeremy with its right eye turned toward him, a yellow reptilian eye, unblinking. Jeremy couldn't pull his gaze away from this majestic creature. It was beautiful and terrifying at the same time.

It wore what looked to Jeremy like a fancy harness… or was it a vest… or a backpack? *It couldn't be a backpack*, Jeremy thought. The red cloth pack hanging from the creature's front was held in place with black leather straps and ornamented silver rings. The creature carried a stack of neatly folded brown cloth. Resting on it was a small, lacquered wood box with etchings all around.

"Jeremy, allow me to introduce to you some others who are going to help you." Mercurio pointed to the other elf, redirecting Jeremy's gaze away from the reptilian. "This is Ee'azar. He will be assigned to you as your assistant, guide, and bodyguard."

Jeremy's heart fluttered at the idea that he needed a body-guard. "Bodyguard? What do I need a bodyguard for? You said…"

"It's merely a precaution," Ee'azar interjected. "Whether or not the goblins pursue the Gift Giver, as long as there is a Gift Giver, there will always be a Gift Giver's Guard." He walked toward Jeremy. "And may I say, I am honored to meet you."

Jeremy's chest tightened as Ee'azar extended his hand. He didn't know whether to be more intimidated by the reptilian crea-ture or by this elf. Clad in green and gold contoured armor he looked like a hardcore superhero. On the upper left of his chest was a badge-like symbol consisting of a squiggly crook and a sword. On his back, obscured slightly by his green cloak, he carried his sword. Jeremy sensed something powerful about this elf. Ee'azar exuded an air of ultimate confidence. He stood in a way that appeared casual but poised, as if he could spring into action at any moment. And he didn't have that glow about him like Mercurio, that softened the older elf's appearance. Ee'azar's features seemed as if he had been chiseled with that hawk-like nose and square jaw.

Ee'azar looked at his own hand and then at Jeremy's. "I'm sorry. I was led to believe this is how humans greeted."

"Um, yeah," Jeremy quickly wiped his hand against his leg to remove the sweat before extending it. "Yes. It is. This is just so strange for me."

"I completely understand," Ee'azar said. He smiled at Jeremy, but his cold, brown eyes only briefly met Jeremy's. Instead, they scanned the room as if he expected someone else to arrive.

Mercurio continued as Jeremy and Ee'azar shook hands. "As far as he being your bodyguard. It's better to be proactive, rather than reactive. Besides, Jeremy, you're going to encounter many things that you won't be able to explain. Ee'azar is the new captain of the Gift Giver's Guard. He'll tell you what is safe and what isn't safe. He'll also see that your sled is prepped and ready to go."

Mercurio walked over to the reptilian creature, wafting his hand in front of it. "And this is Birch. He is a koth."

Jeremy swallowed nervously again and licked his lips as the creature bowed his head slightly and extended the cloth and wooden box toward him.

"These are for you." Mercurio said. "One is merely a precaution, and the other is a gift from Birch."

The words "gift" and "Birch" jarred Jeremy. "A gift?" he asked, hesitating.

"Go ahead, Jeremy." Mercurio flashed an assuring smile and nodded at the koth.

Jeremy nervously took the cloth and the box from the creature. He laid the cloth over his arm and gently opened the box. On a fluffy setting of red silk sat a quartz-like round stone with blood red veins running through it from top to bottom.

"Go ahead, put it on." Mercurio said.

"It's kinda girly, isn't it?" Jeremy said, raising an eyebrow and pursing his lips.

Mercurio smiled. "Just put it on."

Jeremy pulled the silver chain attached to the stone and lifted it from the box. He placed it around his neck.

A pleasure to meet and serve you, Gift Giver.

Jeremy flinched and stepped backwards, almost dropping the box. A voice… the voice had come from within his own mind. It was a deep voice that had an accent similar to Mercurio's.

Birch lifted his head and nodded once more, still staring at Jeremy.

Mercurio, Ee'azar, and Bartleby all smiled at him.

"This is how Birch will communicate with you," Mercurio said. "The necklace is his koth stone. However, we don't have time to explain how it works. You'll have plenty of time later, and much more to learn."

Jeremy smiled at the creature. *This is so cool,* he thought to himself. "Wait! If I can hear what he says in my head, can he read my mind?"

"No, Jeremy," Mercurio said. "Only what you intend for him to receive."

Just speak to me as you would anyone else. I will show you how to mind-cast with me another time. Birch said in Jeremy's head.

Jeremy shook his head, amazed.

"Birch will serve you in many ways. He will tend to your clothes, clean your home, run errands for you. Anything you ask, Birch will do. You'll find that he will take good care of you," Mercurio said.

Jeremy laughed and looked between Mercurio and the fearsome reptile. "He's my butler?"

"And much, much more," Mercurio said.

Now this is interesting, Jeremy thought. *I have an elf as a bodyguard and a dinosaur as a butler? This is my life now?*

Mercurio took the brown cloth from Jeremy's arm and unfolded it.

"You're going to need to wear this robe. We can't walk through Sayalla to get to the Court of the Elders with you. We're going to have to be much more clandestine so as not to draw any attention to you."

"So this will make me invisible?" Jeremy asked as Mercurio helped him put on the robe.

"I'm afraid that we don't have that luxury. The Council of Elders has increased the restrictions on enchanted items. They are almost impossible to take beyond the Veil. Everything I bring through must be registered on either side. I could wear my own cloak, but to bring another with me would have certainly aroused suspicion."

Jeremy adjusted the robe, and Mercurio stood back to look at him. It felt tight around his belly and didn't quite cover his sneakers.

"This won't work," Ee'azar said, looking Jeremy up and down. "He'll just need to stay hidden. The guards trust you and they'll only be checking for items, not beings."

"At least they aren't now. But after today that might just change," Bartleby said.

Mercurio shot the gnome a scathing look.

"What do you mean?" Jeremy asked.

"It's been quite a while since a human has visited Sayalla," Mercurio said, still looking Jeremy over. "It will take some getting used to." The elf shook his head and glanced over at Ee'azar.

Ee'azar shook his head in agreement.

"He's right. This isn't going to work. You're too tall, Jeremy," Mercurio said. "You'll just need to stay hidden."

"Wait. I don't understand why we have to hide? Isn't everyone expecting me?"

Mercurio ignored Jeremy and continued his discussion with Ee'azar. However, they were now speaking in another language.

"You guys are starting to freak me out," Jeremy said.

Mercurio continued to ignore him. He and Ee'azar were no

longer conversing. The older elf looked around the room, as if he were counting all the books.

"Bartleby, we'll need more books, I think." Mercurio said.

The gnome nodded.

Mercurio pulled off his backpack and withdrew a folded sack of red velvet with gold stitching. He unfolded it and uncinched the gold braided rope that held it closed. Opened, it looked to be about three feet in diameter.

Jeremy's eyes grew wide, and a smile took shape. Awestruck, he pointed at the sack. He recognized it from the mimstone. "Is that what I think it is?"

Mercurio smiled back at Jeremy and nodded. "Indeed, it is… Nicholas' Christmas Eve Sack." He laid the bag on the ground and flattened it so that the opening faced the ceiling. "Birch, you enter first and we'll start handing you books."

Birch stepped into the opened mouth of the flattened sack. He reached back and grabbed his tail, making sure it didn't hang over the edge. Mercurio, aided by Ee'azar, brought the sack up to the koth's waist. It was a tight fit, but the mouth of the sack seemed to adjust to the wide girth of Birch's hips. When the sack was snug, Birch appeared to take a step down, followed by another.

Jeremy watched in rapt wonder as the koth became fully immersed within the sack. "Whoa! It's like a TARDIS in there!"

Bartleby flashed Jeremy a smile, nodding as he handed a small stack of books to Mercurio. The elf placed the books into the sack, and they disappeared.

"Jeremy, we're going to need your help as well." Mercurio said.

Jeremy shook his head, diverting his attention to Mercurio.

Mercurio nodded toward the sack.

Before grabbing any of the books, Jeremy had to look. He slowly peeked over the edge of the sack but all he saw was darkness. Shaking his head, he took a step backwards and began helping the elves fill the sack.

———

After a little more than an hour, the book storage room was empty, and all its contents, and more, miraculously placed within the sack.

"Alright Jeremy. It's your turn," Mercurio said.

Jeremy looked at the elf and nervously sighed.

"You'll step in and you'll feel the ground," Mercurio explained. "Then move your foot forward and you'll feel a step down. Just carefully keep walking down until you're all the way in."

"I don't really understand what's going to happen to me." Jeremy peered into the infinite darkness of the sack's mouth. The concept of entering this magical sack terrified him.

"Jeremy, it's difficult to explain, but simple to experience. The simple answer is you will not feel any discomfort. You won't even feel like you're in a sack. You'll be in a room filled with books, and Birch will be there with you."

"So, it's like a portal to somewhere else?"

"Precisely," Mercurio responded.

"So why can't I just travel through the bag to where we need to go?"

"It's not quite like that, Jeremy." Mercurio said. "It's a portal that leads to a room that is neither here nor there, but in between. There is only one place to enter and exit from. When you exit, it will be in the place of the sack's physical location in the universe."

"That's just freaky," Jeremy said, shaking his head. "And if I try to get out while you're carrying it?"

"You cannot. It can only be opened from the outside," Mercurio said solemnly.

Jeremy's eyes widened as his mood went from awestruck wonder to outright fear. "So, you're saying that I'm stuck in there until someone opens it? What if something happens to you and no one opens it?"

"It was made for precisely that. We could not allow any one item to have infinite powers. With magic, there has to be limits. Otherwise, the temptation to use magic for personal gain and power would be overwhelming. When the elders created the enchantments for Nikolaos, they insisted on limitations. They wouldn't permit a sack that could traverse space like a Veilpoint. Militarily, it would prove to be a powerful offensive weapon. And that just couldn't be allowed."

"That doesn't make me any more comfortable going in there." Jeremy said, shaking his head. "I mean, even the TARDIS had an emergency exit!"

"Ah, yes!" Bartleby said. "But the TARDIS is a vehicle, used to travel around in time and space. You can't do that with this sack."

Jeremy raised an eyebrow and smiled at Bartleby. "You watch Dr. Who?"

"Oh, yes. It's a wonderful show. I really like David Tenant's Doctor the best."

"Me too. That episode where he used the pocket watch and became a human and fell in love. Dude… I felt so bad for him."

"Yes! Family of Blood! That was actually a two-parter. The first—"

Mercurio crossed his arms and let out an exasperated sigh. "Jeremy. Do you two really think we have time to sit here and discuss this? We must be going."

Jeremy took a deep breath and looked nervously into the blackness of the sack again.

"If we are to continue Nikolaos' legacy, we're going to have to trust one another." Mercurio said.

"I'm from New York. Trust doesn't come easily for New York-ers." Jeremy took a deep breath. "I guess I'm going in."

Mercurio smiled.

Jeremy hoisted his left leg into the sack. He felt the ground beneath. He sighed and licked his lips before creeping his right foot forward. Reaching with his toes he felt the edge of a step.

This is so weird!

His body seemed to be in two places at once, though he could only see the storage room. A wave of dizziness hit Jeremy. He took a deep breath and stepped down with his right foot. He paused to look around, breathing in to overcome the vertigo. Then his left foot. It was like going down the stairs in the darkness of an unfamiliar place. Only now his eyes were wide open. He could see everything and everyone else clearly, except his own feet.

Mercurio nodded.

Jeremy swallowed and took the next step, followed by another, until he was no longer in the storage room of the Argosy Bookstore.

CHAPTER 24

NEITHER HERE, NOR THERE

"As despicable as blood magic is, one can only wonder what life would be like without the koth who willingly serve the Iyl'Sel'wyn."

~ From *The Elven Annals of the Koth*, Circa 4,321 B.C.

J eremy descended the small set of stairs and found himself in a very ordinary room. Plain wooden walls. More shelves. A few large wooden tables. A small table and a tall cabinet in one corner. And piles of books everywhere. Not at all like a TARDIS.

He looked up at the mouth of the sack. It was like a window—or more like a round, opened trap door—several feet above his head. Outside was the ceiling of the storage room in the basement of the Argosy Bookstore. He could also see Mercurio's arm and shoulder.

Mercurio turned and cinched the sack closed, making the trap door and staircase instantly and completely disappear.

Jeremy swallowed and turned to find the reptile… the koth standing before him. He forced a smile.

"Um, hello."

Greetings, Gift Giver. Birch said.

Was the koth smiling too? Jeremy couldn't really tell. Birch's mouth seemed to curve slightly at the base of his long snout.

Would you like a drink? There is water and juice in the cupboard.

It was so strange to hear another voice in his head. He'd have a tough time getting used to this.

"Um, yes. Juice, please." Jeremy replied, surveying the room again. How odd, he thought. It was so ordinary. The books they'd placed in the sack were in various piles, some on the floor towards the back corner and some in small stacks on the workbenches.

"What is this place?" Jeremy asked, still looking around.

I am unsure. I've not been here before.

"If they pick up the sack, we aren't gonna get tossed around, right?" He paused but didn't wait for the koth to answer. "No, that wouldn't make sense."

Jeremy remembered the two elves that were killed outside of the sack from his mimstone experience. He couldn't remember their names, but he remembered something about them being Nikolaos' helpers. The presents must be stored down here. But the room didn't look big enough to hold that many presents. *I wonder if the room increases in size as you add stuff to it?*

Birch walked over holding a small platter with a ceramic goblet. He spoke in Jeremy's head as he handed him the drink. *Mercurio said the room is between here and there. I believe it exists outside of the natural world. Where it specifically is, I do not know.*

Jeremy took a sip from the goblet. The liquid tasted sweet, like fruit punch. He walked around the room, sliding his hand along the workbenches and the shelves. He grabbed a book from one workbench: *The Red Badge of Courage* by Stephen Crane. It was an old book in excellent condition. He wondered how much something like this was worth. Holding the book at his side, Jeremy strolled across the room to the small table and chairs. The height reminded him of the small group table he had in his classroom; just the right size for fourth graders, but an adult could easily sit at as well. He placed the goblet on the table and sat down in one of the small chairs.

"So, we just sit around here until someone opens the sack?"

Yes. But we can pass the time by becoming acquainted with one another, Birch said.

"Ok. Have a seat," Jeremy said.

The koth raised his left brow, looked at the chair, and then back at Jeremy again.

Jeremy realized Birch couldn't sit in a chair made for humans and elves. His tail was too long, and his legs were too short.

Awkward! Jeremy thought as he stood up and walked back toward where the entrance once was.

"Um, so… what's your story? How'd you become a butler?"

A butler? I've never been referred to as a butler before. Birch responded, shuffling towards Jeremy. *However, I do know what you mean. I come from a long line of servants. My carefather and his carefather before him served the Swordsworn. My carefather served Mercurio. I served Mercurio, and he has asked me to now serve you.*

"As long as you're not going by the Serling recipe, *To Serve Man.*" Jeremy smiled.

Birch cocked his head and raised his scaly brow.

Jeremy laughed and changed the subject. "And you serve willingly?"

Oh yes, of course. It is the honor of my people to serve.

Jeremy looked the koth over. Though he was shorter than Jeremy, he was quite a frightening creature. He looked as if he could do quite a bit of damage, especially with the long claw on each foot. He remembered the scene from *Jurassic Park* when the paleontologist explained how a velociraptor might use such a claw. Jeremy shuddered at the thought of being trapped in here with such a creature.

"Do your people have some sort of Stockholm syndrome or something?"

I do not understand this reference.

"In my world—"

We share the same world, Gift Giver, Birch interjected.

"Um, yeah… I mean in my culture we refer to prisoners who become attached to their captors as having Stockholm Syndrome. Something like that."

Birch tilted his head.

Jeremy rushed to further clarify. "By attached I mean devoted, I guess. I'm not sure I can explain it."

I am understanding you to mean that you are asking me if my people serve because we have been mentally damaged by the elves during wartime. Is this correct?

Jeremy gave Birch a perplexed look. He thought about the koth's interpretation. It was quite insightful.

"Yeah, that's what I'm asking."

The answer is no, Gift Giver. My people, they were created to serve. It gives us satisfaction. Indeed, it is chemical satisfaction; I suppose. Like most species, we have hormones. For us, a hormone is released that makes us feel good when we are serving. When we are not serving, my people become… unmotivated.

"Created? You mean like by a god? You believe your god created you this way?"

No. Not a god. We have no god, nor do we believe in any of the multitude of pantheons that other kinds believe in. We were created by the goblins.

Jeremy snapped his head back. "Seriously?"

I make no jest or duplicity in what I say. It is well documented that goblins created us to serve them. They fashioned us for war. But they used my people for other things as well. The elves freed us from the goblins' subjugation. We tried, with the help of the elves, to live autonomously. But without direction, we are not motivated. The elves aided us in finding ways for us to enjoy our freedom and be useful in our shared commonwealth.

Goblins? Jeremy thought. *How could they create something like Birch?* He gave the creature another puzzled glance.

The stairway appeared, and Jeremy jumped back.

Quickly! Birch shouted in Jeremy's head. He waved his hands for him to follow him. *You must quietly hide over here.*

"Hide?" Jeremy jumped from his chair. "Why? What am I hiding from?"

Hurry. The koth led him to a shelf in the far corner. There was no actual place to hide, but the koth pointed to the floor.

Here, sit here and make no sound. Birch said.

Confused, Jeremy did as he was told. The piles of books, arrangement of workbenches, and the distance obscured his view of the stairs and the trapdoor. Was that their plan? To hide him in plain sight?

Jeremy heard Mercurio speaking an unfamiliar language. Then he heard footsteps, followed by a stranger's voice.

Jeremy's heart pounded. He had no idea what was going on, but it was clear that if the stranger found him, there'd be trouble. He tried to keep his breath controlled. Huddled in a ball, arms wrapped around his knees, his belly made it difficult to breathe. But he dared not move. What was only a minute or so seemed like hours.

He heard footsteps on the stairs. Were they leaving or were there more coming in?

The sack has been closed, Birch said.

Jeremy adjusted his head and slowly glanced up at Birch. He released his held breath.

"Can… I get up… now?" Jeremy struggled.

By all means, Birch said.

Birch extended his muscular arm and Jeremy grabbed on. His smooth skin had the feel of saran wrap. He had only four digits; three long fingers and an opposable thumb. With great strength, Birch easily and gently pulled Jeremy up.

"Thank you," Jeremy said.

It is my pleasure, Gift Giver.

"What was that all about?" Jeremy asked.

The guardians had to make sure we did not bring any enchanted or unallowed items into the city, Birch said.

"So, we're in Sh.. Sa…" He couldn't remember the name.

Sayalla.

"Sayalla, that's right. That's an Elven city?" Jeremy said, brushing himself off.

It is more than that. Though it is governed by elves. Therein live elves, alfargnym, fauns, koth, and fairies.

"It must be pretty big, huh?"

Oh, very big.

"So, now what happens?" Jeremy asked.

I am unsure, Gift Giver. Mercurio said we were going to see the Council of Elders. It should not take us much longer to get there.

"I don't understand. Those guards didn't do such a great job of looking for anything. We could have filled the cupboard with stuff. They didn't even check there."

Elves are a trusting people. If an elf tells another elf something, it is taken as truth. To not do so goes against the Iyl'Sel'wyn; the law of the elves.

Jeremy considered this. If Mercurio lied to the guards, he broke the law. "I just don't get it. Why are we doing all this sneaking around? Didn't Mercurio get permission for me to see the council?" He walked back to the table where he left the book earlier.

It would appear not, Gift Giver. I was not told the plan. Only to serve you. And, if I know Mercurio as well as I think I do, his actions are indeed what he deems best as a Swordsworn Guardian of the elves.

Jeremy sat down at the table and looked around the room again. Things weren't adding up. If the council was unaware of his coming, then Mercurio must have some other plan. But what? Once they met with the council, would he then go to the North Pole? It was July. Were they planning for him to make his first run this Christmas? If so, the elves must be getting ready. He bit his lower lip and let out a pensive "Hmm…"

Jeremy looked up at Birch again and smiled. This creature… this koth was growing on him. Despite the fact that this dinosaur looked like he could eviscerate him in seconds, there was something genuine and comforting about him. Birch was really fascinating. *Created by goblins? What was that all about?*

"So, you…"

Not I. My people. It was over—

"Wait. Did you just read my mind? You said you couldn't do that."

I did not. Birch responded matter-of-factly. *Did you not direct a question toward me?*

"Um, yes. I guess I did. But I thought it first."

Our way of communication with non-koth can be confusing. I will teach you to master it. Shall I continue to answer your question? I do not believe we have time for a communication lesson now.

"Um, yes. Please," Jeremy said, a little more at ease.

"Seven millennia ago, when they created my people. We—"

"Seven millennia?" Jeremy gasped. "As in seven thousand years ago?"

Yes. My people were made for war, to fight against the dweorg, elves, and trolls. Using blood magic, goblin sages created us from dragons and other creatures. They placed within us a yearning to serve. Additionally, they desired for us to work strategically on the battlefield. They insured this with the koth stone. Birch pointed to the necklace he had given Jeremy earlier. *This we are born with.*

Jeremy clutched the necklace and let out an awe-inspired gasp. "What?" Jeremy examined the crystal with newfound amazement.

It grows in our eggs with us, at the base of our necks. And when we are three months old, the stone falls off. The goblins would place our stones in a band, controlling twelve koth at one time. The elves put an end to that. They gave my ancestors their stones back and the right to give those stones to someone of their choosing. This continues to this day.

"And you allow them to be your master?"

We do not use the term master. The elves taught us that the term master implied more than what we were. We serve. They receive our service. There is no human word for what this is. Those we serve are called pa'kach in the Elven tongue.

"Pa'kach," Jeremy repeated.

Yes. It means as I said. The koth serve. Pa'kach receive our service. In many ways, it is a symbiotic relationship. We koth feel complete when we serve. And our pa'kach receive the help they need to do whatever it is they do.

"What if your stone were given to someone who was evil? Would you steal or kill if they told you to?" Jeremy asked.

Our stones do not give our pa'kach total control over us. We can disobey. But when we do, we become physically ill. We no longer feel complete. This is rare, as my kind seek only to give our stones to those who have proven worthy. The elves and our carefathers help us decide, but the final decision is ours. When we give our stone to someone, it allows us to do two things. He held up two of his three fingers. *Koth stones make communication between koth and pa'kach faster. They also help to create a bond between us. Over time, the bond increases.*

"OK, but that doesn't answer my question. If your pa'kach asked you to do something wrong, would you?"

You are my pa'kach. Would you ask me to do evil?

Jeremy sighed, furrowed his brow, and raised his hand to his chin. Birch wasn't answering his question.

"I wouldn't. But what if I wasn't your pa'kach? What if a goblin took this stone from me?" Jeremy asked, clutching the pendant around his neck.

Each koth is his own. The elves showed us this. I would as soon wither than serve evil. Though my desire to serve is strong; it can be denied.

"Wow," Jeremy said.

It is more difficult for a young koth to deny his pa'kach. Birch continued. *The bond is strong. A young koth may learn to do evil and thus become evil too.*

The stairs appeared. Jeremy jumped to his feet and ran toward his hiding place.

Elven feet appeared on the stairs just as Jeremy crouched between the bookcases and folded his legs up to his chest.

"Birch. Jeremy," Mercurio said. "It is time."

CHAPTER 25

BEFORE THE NINE

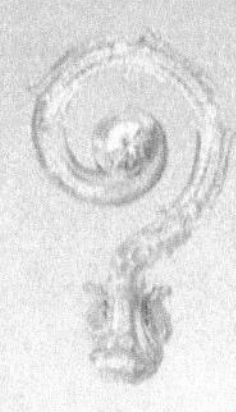

"He was the first to help us all communicate through the spoken word. And he was the first to use those very words to corrupt our people. Samyaza iyl Sayalla was the first born of darkness."

~ From *The Elven Annals of Discord*, Circa 9,800 B.C.

"Jeremy?" Mercurio said. "Are you listening to me?"

Jeremy directed his attention from the sack's opening and turned to Mercurio, who stood beside him.

"Jeremy, you will need to follow these directions exactly, so hear me. Do *not* address any members of the council directly. Only speak when spoken to. Tell them the truth. Do *not* hide anything about yourself from them. Do you understand?"

Not completely, Jeremy thought. But he could comply despite his increasing anxiety. Jeremy's mouth felt dry. His heart pounded faster. He raised his trembling hands and stared at them. *I can do this. I can do this.*

"Jeremy, do you understand?" Mercurio said.

"Um, yes… yeah, I do. I'll… I'll be fine."

"Wait at the bottom of the stairs. When I call for you, come quickly, but not too quickly. I don't want you stumbling into the court."

Right. I don't want to stumble into the court either.

"And," Mercurio said, "One more thing. Do *not* stare at the Dark Ones."

"The Dark Ones?" Jeremy gulped.

Mercurio turned and stepped onto the first rise of the staircase. "Wait here until I summon you."

Birch stood beside Jeremy.

There are three factions of Dark Elves. Each has a representative on the council. You will know them because they will be dressed in dark clothing and you will not see their faces, Birch said.

Jeremy swallowed, remembering the ones that frightened Nikolaos. "Good to know. Thanks."

The sack cinched closed and the stairs disappeared.

"Birch, I gotta tell ya, I'm really nervous," Jeremy said.

Why? Birch asked.

"Why, um… this is it, man." Jeremy said, pacing. His hands waved erratically as he spoke. "I don't really know what's going to happen. This whole thing is crazy. I was really excited there for a while after I got used to the idea of becoming, um, you know…" He still couldn't bring himself to say Santa Claus.

The Gift Giver? Birch said.

"Yeah, the Gift Giver. But, uh, I don't understand this whole sneaking around thing. There's something Mercurio's not telling me."

I have known Mercurio all my life. If he isn't telling you something, it's because he is trying to protect you.

"Protect me? From what? Ya know Birch, that doesn't make me feel any better." Jeremy wiped a bead of sweat from his forehead.

Is there anything I can do for you? Birch said.

"No," Jeremy sighed. "I'm just going to stand here and wait." He stopped and faced the spot where the stairs would appear. His stomach churned, and he placed his hand on it, hoping that would stop the uneasiness.

I shall wait with you, Birch said.

Jeremy nervously shifted his weight from his left leg to his right. "Don't speak until spoken to. Don't look at the Dark Ones."

The seconds dragged on.

"This is nerve-racking!" Jeremy turned and paced.

I could sing for you. Birch said.

Jeremy pivoted and furrowed his brow. He slid his glasses down and peered at Birch over the rims. "Sing? You can sing?"

Koth are known for the calming effects of their singing. Carefathers sing frequently to soothe hatchlings. We will occasionally sing for our pa'kach.

Why not? Jeremy thought. *It can't get any stranger than it already is.* "Sure."

From the sharp-toothed maw of Birch's snout came a melodious trill. Soft and varying in pitch, the koth's eerie yet peaceful song caught Jeremy's attention. He cocked an eyebrow and smiled at Birch. The song reminded him somewhat of a bird's, but not as high pitched and with varying tempo and notes.

As Birch trilled the gentle melody, the tension in Jeremy's body seemed to ease and a calmness came over him.

One day… the goblin will prowl no more… Birch continued to produce the musical sound with his snout, but the words he sang through mindcasting. It was such an odd, but peaceful experience. The koth's singing voice was remarkable, reminiscent of Nat King Cole.

The troll… and dragon will cease their roar…

The stairs appeared, startling Jeremy and raising his heart rate again. Birch stopped his song and turned to face the entrance.

"Jeremy, it's time. Come up here." Mercurio said.

Jeremy took a deep breath and approached the stairs. Sunlight streamed in from the sack's opening, and all Jeremy could see was Mercurio's silhouette.

He took the first few steps up slowly.

Don't speak unless spoken to. He took another step.

Tell the truth, don't hide anything about myself. Another step.

Don't look at the Dark Ones. Another step.

Another step and his head crested the opening. Bright sunlight gave way to the Court of Elders. Jeremy squinted, feeling a touch of vertigo as the sheer grandeur of the court came into view. He grabbed the side of the bag. Ee'azar gently took his hand. Jeremy closed his eyes and took a breath, pausing at the top to get his bearings. Ee'azar gently tugged on his hand and Jeremy opened his eyes again, stepping out of the sack into the majestic hall.

He heard gasps of shock and disapproval from all around. They only intensified the vertigo. Jeremy's head wobbled. His stomach tightened, and he swallowed to quell any further discomfort.

"Mercurio! What have you done?" A voice yelled out. Jeremy couldn't tell from whom. But it was strange. He heard unfamiliar words with his ears, but in his head he heard the words in English.

Jeremy held his hand to his head, took a deep breath and closed his eyes again.

"Honored Ones, allow me…" Mercurio said.

"Mercurio, your reputation may indeed precede you and allow you some leniency from time to time. But this day, you have surpassed that limit!" Another voice said.

I have to do this. I can't fail. I can't make a fool of myself. I am… I am… Jeremy struggled to believe that he could do what Mercurio said he could. But if he gave up now, he'd never know if he could truly bring hope to the world as the Gift Giver. *I am the Gift Giver.* He opened his eyes. The vertigo eased.

Jeremy faced the nine elders. Around each of their necks hung a jeweled pendant; each jewel different. The three Dark Elves sat to the left. Jeremy could see their shadowy clothing and faceless masks out of the corner of his eye. He dared not look at them. He tried to focus on the elder in the center, but a different one caught his attention: the smallest of the nine and the only noticeable female on the council. She sat on the right, opposite the Dark Elves. In contrast to them, the small elf wore a light green dress with fluffy white trim and a floppy white hat to match. Her face taut with anger; she stared not at Jeremy, but at Mercurio. Jeremy noticed that the elf's right ear was missing.

Ellesmere! Like Mercurio, she had hardly aged. The only real difference was the glow each of them had.

"Mercurio," Ellesmere said through clenched teeth. "Why have you brought this *human* before the Council of Elders?"

She spoke in Elvish. Jeremy heard the strange language audibly. But in his head, he heard the words in English. Jeremy turned and looked at Birch, who nodded. Somehow the koth was making it so that Jeremy could understand Elvish.

"My old friend, I have found what we have been searching for these many years." Mercurio said with excitement. "I would like to introduce you to Jeremy Goodson." He used both of his hands to direct the Elders to look at Jeremy.

Jeremy was unsure of what to do. He stood shaking nervously, with a smile, waiting for the elves to applaud or give some sort of accolade.

Ellesmere stood up from her seat and slammed the end of her staff on the wooden floor. "You've gone too far, Mercurio!"

"Peace!" The elder in the center demanded. "We are a council of peace."

What in the world is going on here? Jeremy wondered. It was as if the elders knew nothing about him. He glanced over at Mercurio, and his suspicions were confirmed. Mercurio looked at him with apologetic eyes.

"Mercurio of Sayalla. Explain yourself," the elder in the center demanded.

"Elders, I have brought Jeremy Goodson to you because he possesses a gift even greater than Nikolaos. It is unlike anything I've ever seen. He can become the Gift Giver."

"This is preposterous!" said the elder directly to the right of the one in the center. "You act as if this is some prophetic find you have come across."

"There is no such prophecy," the center elder said.

"Respectfully, Elder Shirgha of Sayalla, you are correct,"

Mercurio said. "There is no prophecy. This is not about prophecy. Nikolaos left a void in the world…"

"A human void," yelled the Dark Elf wearing the topaz pendant. "And they are not our concern! The Veil Accord says so. Their kind may be gone in another generation."

"With respect, Elder Golyath of Sudal, that is precisely why we need another Gift Giver."

"They are not our concern!" Golyath said.

"Honored Ones, we have been searching for someone who possesses the same qualities as Nikolaos once did." Mercurio said.

"We?" Ellesmere cut in. "There is no 'we'! You've taken this upon yourself. An errand of Samyaza!"

Several other members of the council gasped at Ellesmere's statement.

She took a deep breath and adjusted her tunic. She looked over at the elder in the center and nodded.

"Mercurio, because of our friendship and history, I will speak with you privately. Come with me," she demanded.

Ellesmere followed a guard to the back of the chamber. Mercurio walked up the stairs behind the elders' thrones, where he met Ellesmere. The guard opened the door on the left and the two elves entered.

Jeremy nervously shut his eyes and took a deep breath.

"Stay calm." Ee'azar whispered.

When Jeremy opened his eyes, the remaining elders were still staring at him. He shivered, wanting to hide himself. Jeremy looked around, trying to find something—anything to focus on that didn't meet his gaze with one of the elders. The court had changed little from the time Nikolaos first came here. Slight differences in décor, and the guards' armor was different. All the elders were different too. His eyes landed on the ornate tapestries that hung behind the elders. The one on the left caught his attention. It depicted a battle between elves and goblins.

The door in the rear of the chamber opened again.

Are they done already?

He expected Mercurio and Ellesmere to walk in, but his gaze

was instantly drawn to the elf that emerged. Everything else in the room seemed to fade away as she entered. Unlike any elf he had seen here or through the mimstone, this elf was more captivating. She was taller than the other elves by at least six inches. Her light brown skin, like an almond, and deep brown curly hair set her apart from anyone else there. She glided with purpose, her dark green, calf length dress gently flowing as she made her way towards the elders. Her attire matched that of Ellesmere's, complete with the floppy green, white fur-trimmed hat and curly-toe boots to match. She stopped at the elder in the center and bowed her head slightly. The elf maiden said something Jeremy couldn't hear, and then she handed the elder a piece of paper. The elder accepted it and read it. As he read, the woman turned and glanced at Jeremy. He felt his heart jump. Though it lasted only a few seconds, he felt as if he had been lost in her green eyes for an eternity. *Who is this elf-woman?* Jeremy wondered.

I advise that you do not pay any further attention to her. Birch's voice broke into his thoughts. *She is yilchaga.* The word did not translate well from koth brain to human brain and from Elvish to English.

Yilchaga? Jeremy asked, looking at the koth.

There was no reply. Birch turned his head.

You are trying to mindcast with me. I will show you how to do so one day. However, I must reiterate. Pay no attention to the yilchaga. It will look unfavorable on your part.

The elf maiden walked to the rear of the chamber and disappeared into the doorway she had first emerged.

No! Jeremy didn't want her to leave. There was something about her—

The door on the left opened again.

The guard, followed by Ellesmere and Mercurio, walked out.

His mind drifted away from the girl as he watched Mercurio walk in behind Ellesmere. Neither looked at each other. Neither looked happy. Hairs stood up on the back of Jeremy's neck and he shivered. The down-turned look on Mercurio's face only amplified his uncertainty.

Mercurio made his way back down to Jeremy. Ellesmere sat on her throne.

"Elders," Ellesmere said. Her icy voice snapped Jeremy back to reality. "Mercurio has shared his heart with me. He proposes that this human, Jeremy Goodson, be given the same enchantments that were given to Nikolaos, the Gift Giver."

There was a pause followed by murmuring and looks of confusion among the Elders.

"I, Ellesmere, Elder of Orindin, propose that we do *not* honor this request."

Ellesmere's words knocked the wind out of Jeremy. What was going on here? He looked to Mercurio for direction, but the elf's sad eyes were fixed on Ellesmere.

"I, Kafir, Elder of Nadal," spoke the Dark Elf furthest on the left, "agree with Ellesmere of Orindin. We say no to Mercurio's proposal."

One by one, the elders cast their vote. It was unanimous. They would not grant Mercurio's request.

"But wait," Jeremy stammered, looking up at the Elders. "Wait, a minute. Why?"

"Jeremy, no," Mercurio raised his open palm.

"I came all this way for nothing?" Jeremy said to the elders, ignoring Mercurio. "Why?"

"Jeremy Goodson," Ellesmere said, speaking in English. "The Council of Elders owes you no explanation. You shall be returned to where Mercurio found you."

"Mercurio," Elder Shirgha said. "You will return Jeremy Goodson to his home and immediately come before the council for punishment proceedings. The Council of Elders is dismissed."

The elders rose from their thrones and followed the guards to the rear door.

"Wait, a minute. This isn't right!" Jeremy said.

"Jeremy," Mercurio grabbed him by the arm again. "We're done here." Mercurio led Jeremy, Ee'azar, and Birch out through the double doors and onto the platform.

"Mercurio, I don't understand what just happened?" Jeremy said.

The guard placed the shaft of his polearm in the pedestal's recess, turned the shaft, and they descended.

"What is there to understand? The council made their decision."

"But why? You... you said... I could make things better for everyone. But you never bothered to ask the elders for permission in the first place? Why would you do that? I, I... don't understand why you would go through all this trouble?"

"Jeremy, I thought that once they met you they'd give their approval. At the very least, that they'd want to get to know you before making a decision. I knew it was going to be hard to convince them, and I never thought that they would make their decision so hastily."

"Well, so what do we do now?"

"Now? Now we go home. You go back to being a teacher. And the world continues to decay without hope."

"No! Come on! You convinced me! Why can't you convince them to reconsider?"

"It doesn't work that way, Jeremy. Once the council has dismissed, the standing is final."

"Well, who cares what the council thinks!"

Mercurio turned back toward Jeremy and raised his hands to stop him from talking further. "Jeremy—" He said, eyeing the guards and giving Jeremy a stern look.

"Let's show them. We'll do it all ourselves and then they'll see that the world needs us."

"Jeremy, I don't think you understand. This—"

"Well then, help me understand! I can't go back to my normal life knowing that all this exists and that I can't be a part of it. Let's just do it without the council!"

Mercurio glanced nervously at the guards. "Jeremy, we cannot. They are the only ones who can make this work."

"What do you mean?"

"We must have the council's permission to create the enchantments that are needed to make it all work. Without the enchantments, you're just a mortal."

"Okay, so there's got to be someone else who can make the enchantments? A wizard or a witch?"

Mercurio stared at Jeremy with a conflicted smile. "Enchantments can only be made with permission from the full Council of Elders," he said, shaking his head.

The pedestal reached the bottom and rested in the entry hall.

"That's the way it's always been," Mercurio stepped down.

Birch and Ee'azar followed.

"For Nikolaos to do everything he did, he had four enchanted items." Mercurio continued. "The elders commissioned the creation of the Gift Giver's Sleigh, the reindeer's harness, the sack, and most importantly, his ring. Nikolaos' ring bound all the enchantments together. Not only did it protect him, it allowed him to manipulate magic with gestures and incantations so that he could drive the sleigh, command the reindeer, enter homes, alter the temporal field, and see even deeper into the hearts of children. Without them, you're just a human."

"And you asked the council to make new enchantments for me?"

"Yes, and they said no."

Mercurio looked up at Jeremy and paused for a moment. "It's time to go, Jeremy. I need to pierce the Veil before dark."

Jeremy hesitantly stepped down from the pedestal.

Mercurio walked to the front doors.

"They're sending a carriage to take you back to the Heart of the Veil," the guard said.

As they waited, Jeremy paced. An idea formed. He grabbed Mercurio by the shoulders and gently spun him around. "Mercurio," he whispered as he leaned down to look the elf in his eyes. "Where are the enchantments that Nicholas used?"

"The sleigh and the reindeer are back in Orindin. I still have the sack here. But they are all useless to you without the ring."

"Ok, so where *is* the ring?" Jeremy asked.

"I can only assume that Borahsh still has the ring." Mercurio said. "Goblins are notorious collectors. They use items and body parts of enemies to boast of their accomplishments."

Jeremy cringed, remembering the ring of ears around Borahsh's neck. "Is there any way we can get the ring from Borahsh?"

"No, Jeremy. That would be impossible," Mercurio said, pushing the door open a crack. "We don't go to Kurgal for any reason. The goblin kingdom is…" Mercurio paused and shuddered. "… it's evil. I have no other words to describe it. It's just evil, and we don't want to go there."

Jeremy raised his hand to his forehead and rubbed. "I just don't understand why the elders are making this so hard!"

Mercurio closed the door and turned back to him. "Jeremy, let me help you understand. The night that Nikolaos died was one of the greatest tragedies in all of history… on both sides of the Veil. I blamed myself. Ellesmere blamed herself. The Elders blamed themselves. That night they swore never to commission another enchantment for a human. In fact, they put more regulations in place to make it harder for anyone to make or possess an enchantment. The elders even commissioned a group of Swordsworn to retrieve any that were lost or stolen. You must understand that enchantments are powerful, and power corrupts even the most kindhearted."

"It didn't corrupt Nikolaos, did it?" Jeremy said.

"I told you before, Nikolaos was different. He… used the power he had for good. But that's just it. The power may not have corrupted Nikolaos to do evil, but it did corrupt his sense of immortality. He wasn't immortal, but he acted as if he was. And in the end, that's what got him killed. The elders vowed that another enchantment would never be made and that another human would never be put in harm's way by the false security of an enchanted item. I assumed that when I brought you before the council, they would change their mind… that they would see that it was time. And I was wrong. We are done. The carriage is here. Let's get you home."

Mercurio walked back to the door.

"Mercurio, wait!" Jeremy yelled. "Just wait. What if we went and got the ring ourselves?"

Mercurio stopped and turned around again, shaking his head. "Jeremy, I just told you we are not going to Kurgal. You cannot, and you will *not* even think about getting that ring. I am Swordsworn with centuries of training, and I would not be foolhardy enough to invade the goblin kingdom."

"I didn't say anything about invading. We can sneak in and steal the ring. You and Ee'azar can teach me everything I need to know and more."

Mercurio shot Jeremy a stern look. "Look at you, Jeremy!" He pulled on the part of Jeremy's shirt that was overhanging his belly. "Look at you! You're an overweight schoolteacher with 28 years of life! You're a child! I'm sorry that I ever filled your head with notions of grandeur. But we're done! You *are* going home, now!"

Jeremy stood defiantly with his arms crossed.

"No! I'm not leaving! If you won't train me, then I'll find someone else. Ee'azar, what about you?"

"I cannot." Ee'azar shook his head.

"Enough of this." Mercurio turned around, lifted his hand toward Jeremy's face, and twisted his fingers.

CHAPTER 26
IN A MIRROR DIMLY

Jeremy awoke, disoriented. He sat up and looked around the room. The twilight of the moon above the New York skyline cast a faint glow through his bedroom window that illuminated his apartment. The realization of what happened hit him hard. It was over.

"Oh! Very funny, Mercurio!" He yelled out as if the elf was still there. "Trying to make me think it was all just a dream!"

Jeremy threw the blankets back over his head with a grunt. He laid there, sulking, casting angry thoughts at the elf who had betrayed him.

Mercurio, you can't just come into my life and change everything and then expect me to just go back to normal. Tomorrow I'll go back to the Argosy and demand that gnome let me through the Veil. I'll keep coming back.

Then a thought struck him. What if next time they just erased his memories? *I'd forget everything I saw. Magic would just be make-believe again.* The realization caused him to sit back up. He looked around the room at the ordinariness that was his. His computer, that allowed him to pretend to wield a sword and live in a world of magic. His bookshelf filled with science fiction and fantasy books; more gateways to realms of make-believe.

Swinging his feet over the side of his bed, he stood and shuffled into his living room, dragging the blanket with him and knocking his pillow to the floor. He wanted desperately to be back with Mercurio and the others. To be the person they wanted him to be. Even now the notion seemed ridiculous. Was he crazy to even consider the possibility that he could have been… dare he say it… *Santa Claus? How ridiculous!* He questioned the reality of the last twenty-four hours several times. *Was I just dreaming? No. No. It was real. I was there. It was real.*

Jeremy walked over to his living room window. The sun had just begun to inch its way over Manhattan. The New York skyline at sunrise and sunset was one of Jeremy's favorite sights. There was a breathtaking beauty in it… it seemed magical at one time. This morning, it didn't. He found no solace in the silhouette of glowing buildings amid the orange and azure sky. How could there ever be again? Jeremy had tasted something amazing and wonderful… real magic! How could anything ever come close to that again?

He sighed and placed his hands in his pockets. He felt something in one of them and he pulled it out to see what it was. The familiar green glow of the speckled stone pushed at Jeremy's despair making way for a small glimmer of hope.

The stone? Why? Why hadn't they taken it from him? *Did they forget?* This was it. This was the key back through the Veil.

He felt for the koth stone around his neck. That was gone. But why not the other stone?

He turned away from the window and dashed back into his bedroom. Mercurio surely didn't forget to take the stone from him. It had to be a signal of some sort. But what? Was he supposed to go back to the Argosy? *Should I go now? Or am I supposed to wait?* He turned back to the door and then back around toward his computer. *Maybe I can figure out where the gatehouse in Germany is. Or maybe I don't even need to go to the gatehouse. Maybe I can just find where Sayalla is and walk there from… from where?*

Jeremy sat down at his computer. The desktop screen loaded, and Jeremy stared at the icons. He didn't even know where to begin. He clicked on the Chrome icon, watched the browser load and stared at the search engine window. *I don't know anything about Germany.* But his dad did. He was stationed there, in the army, before Jeremy was born. His thoughts drifted to his parents. What was he going to tell his parents now? Should he even contact them? They'd be at his apartment any day now anyway to clean it up and put all of his belongings in storage. And his mom would be delighted that he was home. But he knew that there'd be a small part of his Dad that would be disappointed.

That last embrace they shared. There was something about the way his Dad took the news that seemed odd to Jeremy. It was as if his Dad had been relieved that he was leaving for the North Pole to become Santa Claus. Like he'd been waiting to hear this all his life. He remembered something his Dad used to say, "If you truly believe, it is no fairy tale." Jeremy wanted to believe, to believe in magic, and fantasy, and Santa Claus. But as he got older reality made the fantastic less believable; just because you believed in something, didn't make it real or true. Reality was reality, and no matter how much he wanted to believe in fairy tales, they weren't true. That was until yesterday.

A single day.

Jeremy had lived a lifetime of adventure in that one day. Meeting elves, and gnomes, and a dinosaur, or whatever Birch was. What was he going to tell his parents? Jeremy decided to wait to call them. He'd have to figure out what he was going to do.

The cursor in the blank search bar window continued to blink, waiting for Jeremy to type something.

A knock on the door disrupted Jeremy's thoughts. He glanced at his clock. *5:06am. Who could be here this early?* He walked to the door and looked through the peephole. A well-built man in his thirties with dirty blond hair, wearing a gray suit stood there, hands on his hips.

Who could that be?

"Who is it?" he asked.

"Detective Richard Evans, NYPD," he said, flashing a badge up to the peephole. "I need to ask ya some questions about your downstairs neighbor."

Great! Now what? Jeremy released the deadbolt.

He turned the doorknob and felt the door push open from outside. The detective slipped in and around Jeremy faster than he could react. Adrenaline spiked through Jeremy's body, but not fast enough. The detective had him in a headlock.

A huge hulking man swept in and pointed something at him.

"*Yashan*," said the big man.

Jeremy's body went limp.

His eyes fluttered.

A third man walked in.

Jeremy willed his eyes to stay open, but his muscles wouldn't cooperate. His eyelids, despite the rush of adrenaline, blinked wildly.

A tall, dark-skinned man with waving dreadlocks smiled as he walked past.

Jeremy's eyelids grew heavier, as did the rest of his body. Every muscle weakened. His weight was now fully held by the detective. His body fought against his will, and his will was no match. There was darkness, and then there was silence.

CHAPTER 27
DON'T KILL
THE MESSENGER

"In the happening following the fall of the Goblin Empire, Ziusudra, the 31st Goblin Emperor, changed the empire's focus from that of undoing the Unbinding, to rebuilding their army. In 440 B.C. all males were drafted into the goblin army. The females remained thrall, but they were given berths previously held by male thrall."

~ From *The Veiled Happenlore of the Master Construct* compiled by Fulbert Gisilfrid, a Chronicler of the Master Construct, Third Order, an alfargnym of Unterbaum.

Borahsh stood in his Gallery of Glory. He rested his hands on the glass display case, but his forlorn gaze was upon the wall that displayed his armor. He hadn't worn it in decades. Beside the armor was his sword; his father's sword before him, handed down generations. He'd give anything to wield its magnificence again. He'd give anything to thrust it into Mercurio's heart.

The Sar sighed and turned his gaze downward to the display

case he'd braced himself on. Borahsh ran his chubby, gnarled fingers over the glass and gazed in. Three red silk pillows rested within. The first pillow held an Elven Dagger finely crafted of gold, steel, and obsidian. In its pummel rested an onyx stone; the jeweled symbol of the Dark Elf City of Nadal. Borahsh's father had used that very dagger to take the life of its owner, the Dark Elf Elder, Sidion. This was his father's prize.

Borahsh then turned to the center pillow. Beneath the glass, a ring sat on a pillow. This was Borahsh's prize; the Ring of Nikolaos. To Borahsh, this ring told the story of his glory; the day he fulfilled the empire's vengeance decree and took the life of Nikolaos the Gift Giver.

His finger danced on the glass with delight, and Borahsh made a guttural purring sound. He looked at the third pillow and smiled. "My vengeance decree with Mercurio is close to being fulfilled," he muttered under his breath and turned around to face his throne. "Mercurio's head will sit upon a stake in my Bane and I will place his sword in my collection."

"I am delighted for you, my almighty Sar," said the portly Alfash, looking up at Borahsh.

"Yes, I too am pleased for you," Ubarat agreed.

Borahsh dragged his gimp leg over to the center of the hall, just before the steps that led up to his throne. He stood for a moment and stared up at his throne. He turned and looked at the first pike in his Bane. Then back at his throne. "Right here! Right here!" Borahsh pointed to the spot where he stood. "This is where I'll mount his head. I'll sit on my throne and watch it rot each day. Alfash, how long do you think it will be before it rots?"

"Um, several days Lord, perhaps a long week." Alfash said.

"Ubarat, I'll place you in charge of Mercurio's head. See that my servants prepare a special pike to be placed, right here, in the center. I'll have it set away from the others. The final piece of vengeance for all to see and for me to delight in."

Ubarat smiled a delightfully disgusting smile and wafted his way over to his Sar.

"As soon as the head arrives, I want it mounted right away. If it arrives when I sleep, I want to be woken up and I want to see it hanging from the pike right here in the center of my throne chamber. It deserves a special place. Assure me that you will have that done."

"Borahsh, Sar of the Goblin Empire. You will delight in the expediency of my service."

Borahsh lifted his hand to his mouth and smiled. "Hmmmm. But even better. If he arrives alive! Then I can watch him suffer for days. Alfash, you'll see to that. If Mercurio is captured alive, you will make sure the sage keep him alive for a long, tantalizing torture."

"By all means, Lord Borahsh. By all..." He trailed off when the doors opened.

A messenger entered the throne room.

"Halt!" Yelled Alfash. "Sar Borahsh will see no one unless he is seated on his throne!"

Alfash's words echoed throughout the throne room, followed by the clanging of poleswords as the Sar's Fang crossed their weapons and blocked the messenger from entering.

"I need to hear this," Borahsh said, as he limped up the three stairs to the dais. Two servants darted in and assisted their Sar up the stairs to his dragon skull throne. The room was silent save for the moaning and gasping of Borahsh as he painstakingly walked up the stairs and took his seat.

Alfash and Ubarat took their place beside the Sar's throne. Borahsh adjusted his robes and then waved his hand at Alfash, indicating that he was ready.

"You may enter and approach Borahsh, the Mighty Sar of the Goblin Empire!" Alfash announced.

The messenger carried a rolled-up piece of paper. He stopped at the steps, bowed his head, brought his fist to his chest, and looked up at Borahsh. "My Sar, the Great and Mighty Borahsh. I have news from Jau'Asar."

"Yes!" Borahsh arched forward. "Does he have Mercurio's head?"

"N... n... no, My King. Jau'Asar sends news that Mercurio went behind the Veil again."

Borahsh smashed his fist on one of his pillows. He reached for his staff and used it to lift himself up. He staggered slightly, trying to regain his balance.

Two servants ran in carrying the small set of stairs.

"My Sar," the messenger stammered. "Jau'Asar wishes to assure you that he has everything under control."

Making his way down the stairs as fast as his corpulent frame would allow, he huffed and puffed with every push. The two servants stood in their assigned positions beside the stairs to help their sar steady himself.

"Under control?" He took a deep breath. "He let Mercurio slip away!" Another gasp for air. "My servants are incompetent!" Borahsh pushed himself towards the messenger, stepping down one step, dragging his gimp leg behind. "All of you!"

The Sar reached out and grabbed the messenger by the hood. He tugged and dragged him up each step; every labored step sending pain up his leg. He strained to breathe, but the fuel of his anger pushed him beyond normal tolerance. Ubarat and Alfash were quick to assist.

"M...m...my... s... s... Sar.... There is... m...m...m... more." The messenger attempted to speak further. But it was too late for him. Borahsh's anger made him deaf to everything except his own thoughts.

They pulled the messenger up the last rise and threw him to the ground. Borahsh lifted his scepter-staff and slammed it into the messenger's face. Alfash and Ubarat joined in with kicks and stomps. The messenger whimpered and cried out with each strike.

"I am displeased by more delays and failures!" Borahsh yelled, driving his scepter into the messenger's skull. "We are goblins!" Despite the effort, he continued beating the messenger. "I... am the slayer of Nikolaos... the Gift Giver!" He heaved a deep breath and swung the scepter into the side of his victim's head. More bone crunched as the blow severed the skull from its spine.

"I am Borahsh... Sar of the Goblin Empire! And I demand...

the respect owed to me. Mercurio… must die!" Borahsh turned away from the bloodbath and struggled to take a long, deep breath. He steadied himself on his scepter-staff and called out into the chamber. "Is there no goblin… skilled enough to do this for me?" His voice echoed.

The Sar slumped forward and rested on his bloodied scepter-staff, breathing haggardly. His advisers continued to beat on the messenger.

Borahsh dragged himself back to his throne stairs. His servants had to push him up and help him sit on the throne's cushions. Blood dripped from his scepter, his robe, and his face.

"My Sar," Alfash said with labored breath. "Would you… like… this… impaled upon your Bane… or… disposed of?"

The Sar breathed deeply, unable to answer. He pointed to the pikes on the side of his throne chamber.

"Guards… place… this in… the Sar's… Bane." Alfash then turned to the Sar's servants. "Send… maidstock… to clean up this… mess."

The Sar's Fang were quick to scoop up the body of the dead messenger and haul it down the dais steps to the closest spike. Heaving it above their heads, they skewered the bloodied body with a tug, pulling it down to rest on the crossbeam.

"My Sar," Ubarat said proudly. He held a rolled-up paper above his head. "I found something of interest that the messenger brought with him." He unrolled the paper and began reading it.

"It says here that Jau'Asar and the human have a plan to pierce the Veil."

Borahsh leaned forward, still panting.

"Pierce… the Veil?" he said. "Why… didn't… the messenger say so… in the first place?"

CHAPTER 28

BREAKFAST WITH EPIPHANIES

"The New York Mets Baseball cap that Jeremy wore was a gift from his father. It told me that Jeremy was not a fan of the Mets, but he wore it because he loved his father. The cap also told me that Jeremy wore it so that people didn't recognize when he went somewhere he might be recognized by his peers."

~ From *The Second Gift Giver Chronicles* compiled by Erwin Albowyn, a Chronicler of the Master Construct, Second Order, an alfargnym of Unterbaum

Jeremy's body tingled. His neck strained, trying to support the weight of his head. He opened and shut his eyes, but only darkness remained. A tinny and low melody caught his attention. He could barely make out the words. He moved his hands to feel around, but they wouldn't move. His arms moved, but his hands… were bound. *Where am I?*

"Livin' just to find emotion…" The music grew louder and clearer. And it all came back to him as the iconic voice of Steve Perry belted out the chorus of Journey's timeless hit.

That cop.

The detective… the other men.

The detective's arm tight around his neck.

Jeremy took a deep breath, remembering the last things he saw before it all went dark. The warmth and smell of his unbrushed teeth lingered around his face. Journey continued to blast in the background. His heart raced. Jeremy flailed his head, hoping to escape the darkness. He gasped, feeling the warmth of his breath wash over his face again. Momentum pushed him forward and back again. The floor vibrated slightly under his feet. He was sitting in a car… maybe a truck? Sensation and realization returned as his heart beat madly. He wasn't in darkness. There was something covering his head. He jerked forward, trying to move… trying to separate his hands… to remove the bag from around his head.

A hand braced against his chest. Jeremy jerked and froze. Someone else was sitting beside him. An elbow jabbed into him. The hand on his chest pushed him back against the seat. The guitar riff faded in the background, and Steve Perry's vocal crescendo faded with it.

"Just relax, kid." It sounded like the detective. "We're almost there."

Almost there? Almost where? He wanted to speak, but his mouth wouldn't cooperate. Fear held it shut and had taken control of his entire body. The hand on his chest. The voice. The moving car. He took shallow breaths so that he could try to gain some control. The bag on his head made it difficult, but he knew he needed to concentrate. He needed to get control of himself before he hyperventilated.

Where am I? Why? He couldn't gain control of his breathing. All he wanted to do was run. His bowels tensed and tightened. His bladder ached. Oh no. *I am not going to pee in my pants! No!*

The heat of his own breath continued to fill the bag. Sweat teemed from every pore.

"Please!" Jeremy shouted. He found his voice. "Please. I didn't do anything. Please, just let me out of here."

"Just relax, kid." It sounded like the detective's voice again. "You ain't got nothin' to worry about. We're just gonna ask ya a few questions and then will put ya back where we got ya."

What is going on? Jeremy's mind raced in dozens of directions. Where was he? What were they going to do with him? What questions could he possibly answer for them? Why him? Where were they going? His uneasiness increased, and he began to hyperventilate and squirm.

"Take it easy, kid," the detective said again. "I don't want to have to hurt ya." The detective's voice was smooth, yet stern. He sounded like he was from Brooklyn.

Jeremy took a deep breath and attempted to calm himself. He didn't want the detective to hurt him. *Take it easy,* he repeated it to himself. *Take it easy.*

The car pulled to a stop, and Jeremy wondered if this had anything to do with his visit to… he couldn't remember the name of the Elven city.

The door opened, and Jeremy felt the warm summer air waft into the car. A hand grabbed the back of his head, and another gripped his shoulder, guiding him out of the vehicle. They eased him forward, one of them gripping him by the arm. Jeremy's feet shuffled close together. He was afraid to take bigger steps.

"Stairs." Someone with a foreign accent said. Jeremy shuffled a little more and the tips of his sneakers tapped something. He lifted his feet and felt the next rise. He was wearing his sneakers. They must have put them on him while he was unconscious. *Considerate kidnappers.*

He walked up four steps and then forward. The air changed. No longer humid, but cool. They were inside now. *Inside what?* Jeremy continued to shuffle his feet, afraid of the next step not only out of fear of tripping, but fear of where they were taking him. He felt the floor change from carpet to smooth tile as he stepped forward and turned around. He heard the whirring of electronic doors closing, followed by a sudden lurch upward. *An elevator.*

What if these guys are some sort of clean-up crew for the elves? Maybe

Mercurio did forget to get the stone from him? Maybe these guys were going to erase his memory? He imagined being taken to a room where elves awaited him, his kidnappers removing the bag and strapping him to a table. The elves grabbing him by his head like some version of a Vulcan mind meld and then using their magic to erase everything that happened over the last twenty-four hours. The thought saddened and frightened him at the same time. He didn't want to forget.

The elevator came to a stop, and the doors whirred open. Someone pushed him forward. The floor changed again. A confusing array of smells greeted him; bacon, onions, and a variety of other delicious aromas. *Where am I?*

"Ah! Jeremy!" A man's voice came from in front of him. "Our guest has arrived. Delightful." The unfamiliar voice sounded sophisticated and had an eerie calm to it.

They guided Jeremy forward.

"Sit. Sit," the unfamiliar voice said.

They pushed him into a chair… a stool. They pulled the black sack off his head and the bright light caused him to blink and squint. Without his glasses, things appeared blurry as his eyes adjusted to the light. Jeremy saw a hazy blur of what appeared to be a kitchen and several people standing around.

"Jeremy, I am delighted to have you here," the distinguished sounding blur behind the kitchen counter said.

The man behind Jeremy flicked open a pocketknife, cut the bindings from his wrists, and handed Jeremy his glasses.

He put them on, and everything came into focus.

He sat in a stark white open-concept apartment. Everything was white: the floors, the walls, the kitchen cabinets, the furniture. Some furniture had a strip of either black or silver. Pressed up against the far wall, a large glass display case sat on a rectangular table. Illuminated by recessed lighting from above, Jeremy noticed a stone tablet with glyph-like markings. Above the display, a short sword hung on the wall.

Large glass windows lined the back of the apartment. A grand view of the New York City skyline at dawn sparkled through perfectly polished glass. He could see the Chrysler Building not far away. They must have been pretty high up. Judging by the grandeur of the place, he figured he was in a penthouse.

His kidnappers stood around him. The detective to his right stood at attention with his hands clasped in front of him. The tall, dark-skinned man in Oakley sunglasses sported dreadlocks tied into a ponytail. He stood awfully close behind him, giving Jeremy no room to run. And the hulking man stood further back by the elevator, standing at attention like the detective.

Jeremy sat at a mostly white café-height counter with hints of gray marbling. On the other side, a well-dressed older man in blue slacks, a blue pin-striped vest, and a light blue shirt, wearing a pristine white apron, smiled at Jeremy. He wore horn-rimmed glasses that amplified his mint green eyes. His graying brown hair was absent from the top of his head but kept short around the sides and back. The man smiled at Jeremy; hands clasped in front of him.

"Jeremy, you have no idea what a delight it is to have you here today." The man spoke with an eerie confidence; slowly, with a refined drawl, inflecting words to draw them out longer. His accent was distinctly American, but there was something there that almost made him sound British.

Jeremy didn't know what to say. This was not at all what he expected.

The distinguished man reached forward and grabbed a chef's knife from the table.

"Jeremy, there are several ways in life to get what you want from people." The man sliced up a handful of black olives. "Some pleasant. Some not so pleasant. My dear ol' Mom always said, you catch more flies with honey than you do with vinegar." He looked up and smiled at Jeremy, nonchalantly pointing the knife at him as if it were his own finger. "I've always adored my Mom, so I like to try things her way first. And if that doesn't work out, then I have other ways of getting what I want."

Jeremy swallowed. His mouth felt as if someone had dried it out with paper towels.

The man continued to chop as he peeked up at Jeremy. A sly smile appeared as if to say, "You've no place to run. You're right where I want you."

Jeremy nervously licked his lips.

"The interesting thing about that ol' American proverb Mom used to say is that in its true essence, it's a complete fallacy." The man laughed. "One of the best fly traps is a jar with vinegar on the bottom and honey along the sides. Imagine that." He laughed again. "The flies, lured in by the smell of the vinegar…" He was quite animated, the knife glinting in the bright light as it passed this way and that way; his eyes expressive, and his smile genuine as he told the story. "… vinegar smells like rotting fruit to them, which they adore, by the way, and they're tricked into going higher up the jar where the sides are coated with honey, and they get stuck on it. The whole notion is turned up on its ear! The basic meaning of the saying however remains the same… if you want people to do what you want, be nice to them."

Jeremy found the man's exuberance frightening. He spoke to him as if they were old friends.

"Do you like *shakshuka*?"

Jeremy stared at the man. Was he supposed to answer the question? *Shack-what?* He had no idea.

"You strike me as the type who likes to eat. I like to eat too. Am I right?" He looked over the counter and glanced at Jeremy's round belly and then to his own, not nearly as big and round as Jeremy's.

Jeremy still didn't know what to say.

The man picked up the knife again and some sprigs of green leaf. He placed the herb on a cutting board and chopped it up into little pieces. "You're going to like this, Jeremy. Shakshuka is a delightful North African dish. I was in Israel a few years back, in the city of Jaffa, and lo-and-behold I see this grungy looking hole in the wall. Imagine a run-down building in the Middle East and there's this distinctly American looking sign on it in big letters, written in English… Dr. Shakshuka."

Holding the knife in one hand and his palm open in the other, he held both arms up and leaned back slightly, pumping his hands back and forth as if to emulate a blinking sign.

"Imagine that: Dr. Shakshuka. As I get closer, the smell coming from this dive is just heavenly! So, I have to try some for me and my boys here, and I tell you… it did not disappoint! It's the kind of place you'd find Guy Fieri if he did *Diners, Drive-Ins and Dives* in the Middle East. So, I'm there and I just have to get this recipe. I go up to the owner… a delightful man named Bino Gabsu. I know, it's a strange name, but I'm sure you're no stranger to strange names. Anyway, I digress. I pay Bino a thousand U.S. dollars right then and there to show me how to make his shakshuka. So here I am, in the middle of this dive in Israel, cooking up shakshuka for Bino's customers. It was a trip. An experience I'll not soon forget. But since then, I tried a few variations of my own. This one's a simple variation with bacon. You can't go wrong with bacon, am I right?"

Jeremy nodded nervously.

The man turned and removed the lid from a cast-iron pan on the stove. Steaming vapors rose from the pan, intensifying the already delicious aroma that filled the room. The man placed the lid on the counter and grabbed a soup spoon. He used it to bring a small portion of the liquid to his mouth. He blew on and it used his other hand to wave the vapors toward him. The man inhaled and then took the spoon into his mouth.

"Ah!" The man said. "Delightful." He laid the spoon on the counter and picked up a white china plate in one hand and a larger serving spoon in the other. Scooping up a portion of poached egg, surrounded by a chunky tomato sauce, he laid it gently in the center of the plate. He placed the serving spoon down and sprinkled some small pieces of bacon on top, followed by olives, and the green herb. The man completed each plating with a flawlessly biased cut of French bread.

He repeated the procedure six more times as he spoke. "I have two secret ingredients in my shakshuka. The sauce is not only made with tomatoes and onion, there's a teaspoon of harissa in there as well. It gives it that extra kick you're going to taste in a minute. The other secret ingredient is the bacon. But I use the bacon fat as well when I make the sauce. Of course you have to first cut your bacon into lardons and then render down the fat."

The man paused as if an idea struck him. "Pancetta! Hmmm… I bet some pancetta in place of the bacon would go well, too. I'll have to remember that for next time."

Jeremy had no idea what the man was talking about, nor did he care. He just wanted to get out of there alive. The food smelled delicious. But how could anyone expect him to want to eat after being abducted and held against his will? This man had to be insane.

As the pretentious man plated each dish, the light caught the collection of rings on his fingers; each distinctly different.

"I'll tell you something else about this dish," the man said as he sprinkled the herb over the last plate. "These Paleo nuts and their anti-bread craze have brought shakshuka into the limelight in the past few years. But here's the thing. You have all of this amazing flavor in the sauce and there is no way you're going to get it all with just a fork… not even a spoon. So, a good slice of rustic bread is what every plate of shakshuka should have. I serve mine with a slice of baguette from Caputo's."

He lifted the first plate and slid it in front of Jeremy, followed by a polished fork and a butter knife.

As the chef handed out each plate, a shorter man wearing a black suit poured orange juice into champagne glasses and handed one to each person.

Where'd he come from? Jeremy wondered. He hadn't seen him before.

The distinguished man crossed his arms and leaned slightly to the right. He tilted his head and looked over his horn-rimmed glasses, smiling at Jeremy.

Jeremy sat there. All eyes on him. Was he supposed to just start eating?

"Come, Jeremy. I can't wait to see what you think," the chef said.

Jeremy picked up the fork and knife, placing the knife in his right hand. He nervously prodded at the perfectly cooked egg yolk and watched as it oozed out across the white and into the red sauce. Before scooping up a bite, Jeremy looked around to see if everyone was still watching him. They were. He scooped up a piece of egg and some chunky tomato sauce. As he raised it to his mouth, the chef's smile grew wider.

The shak-whatever was delicious. Under normal circumstances, Jeremy would have really enjoyed this. Under the scrutiny of five men holding him hostage, not so much.

"It's good, right?"

"Yes," Jeremy said, chewing. "It's very good."

"Excellent." The chef smiled, slapped his hands together and turned to pick up his own plate. He brought it over to the counter and stood opposite Jeremy, quickly digging into his own portion. "Now, I've told you my secrets. Now you tell me yours."

Jeremy gulped and almost choked on his food. "Secrets?"

"I do like to cut to the chase," the man said, chewing lightly on his food.

The other men chowed down, creating a symphony of food chewing likened to nails on a chalkboard.

"Tell me about your recent trip?" The man said.

"Recent trip?"

The man laughed, his mouth closed, he placed his bowl on the counter. Bringing his napkin to his mouth, he dabbed it against the left corner.

"Jeremy, let's not pretend we don't know what the other is talking about." The smile quickly disappeared, and the man's face grew more intense. He looked down at Jeremy, cocked his head slightly to the right, and stared at him. Piercing light green eyes paralyzed Jeremy as if two fists had grabbed him by the collar and held him against a wall.

"You went to the other side of the Veil. What I want to know is why and how?"

As if on cue, Jeremy heard footsteps from across the room. The noise broke the intensity of the man's stare, and Jeremy moved his eyes in the footsteps' direction. It had come from the living room. Something moved along the backside of the couch. The top of a pale green, hairless head with pointed ears glided through in stark contrast to the white of the walls and furniture. As it drew closer, it disappeared amid the cabinetry of the kitchen and reappeared from behind the bald man.

A short, hideous creature dressed in a modern black pinstriped suit with a blood-red tie and white shirt stood there smiling a toothy grin.

The man pulled his gaze from Jeremy and turned toward the creature.

"Jau, you're late for breakfast," he said, walking to the counter and grabbing the last of the plates. He bent over slightly and handed it to the creature.

The servant handed the goblin a glass of juice.

"I do like to make an entrance," the goblin said; his voice raspy with a foreign accent Jeremy couldn't place.

"Jau, Jeremy was just about to tell us how and why he crossed through the Veil."

Jeremy looked down at the plate. He couldn't look at the man or his goblin companion. The man's eyes were intense enough, but the goblin's were creepy. Dark, without pupils, they seemed to look at Jeremy, yet not at Jeremy. It was very unnerving.

"Jeremy, my patience and kindness grows thin," the man said as he leaned over the counter. "I expect every word you say to me to be truth. And let me warn you…" The man barely moved as he spoke.

Jeremy looked up only to see the man's lips move.

"…if you do lie to me, I'll know, and you will *not* like my response to those who lie to me."

Jeremy swallowed; his mouth still dry. "Um, what do you want to know?"

"I already know that you've gone through the Veil. What I want to know is how and why?"

"Sir, I…"

"Eh, eh, eh…," the stranger said, waving his left pointer carefully at Jeremy. "The truth."

Jeremy sighed. "I… I was invited by an elf. He brought me through to see…"

"He brought you through, where?"

"Through the Veil."

"Jeremy, I happen to know you're a pretty smart guy. So you and I are not going to have this tête-à-tête as if it were some sort of dance. I invited you to breakfast, but I didn't invite you to waltz. Just tell me the location of where you entered the Veil."

The Argosy? Jeremy swallowed. Surrounded by goons. A strange man was interrogating him. And he had just met his first goblin. As scared as he was, Jeremy had read enough stories to know that he had information this man wanted. He could either freely give that information, or he could barter with it. The question was whether he was willing to accept any discomfort in the bargaining process.

"Mr. um," He realized the man had never given his name.

The man perked up and looked at Jeremy. "Forgive me, Jeremy. I never introduced myself. My name is Thaddaios Wyllt." The man smiled, a grin that under normal circumstances would be perceived as warm and inviting. But it intimidated Jeremy enough that he felt his buttock muscles tighten.

"Um… Mr. Um…"

"Wyllt." The man nodded and smiled. "As in a flower that wilts from lack of water. But spelled W-Y-L-L-T. Wyllt. It's a very old surname."

"Mr. Wyllt, seeing that I have some information you are looking for… um, would you mind answering some questions for me?"

Wyllt stood motionless, staring at Jeremy, boring those light green eyes through him. The room was silent, with everyone staring at Thaddaios Wyllt, waiting to see what he'd do. What seemed like an eternity frozen in time was finally disrupted as the man's eyebrows slowly crinkled and a new smile formed.

Wyllt flung his arms up, and Jeremy jumped backwards into the tall, dark-skinned man. "Look at this, gentlemen, the boy wants to play." Wyllt said, looking at his henchmen and pointing his hands toward Jeremy.

No one moved.

The goblin snickered.

"Listen." Wyllt paused and crossed his arms. "Jeremy, you surprised me. And I don't surprise easily. Your bravado has impressed me. I tell you what, ask me three questions."

"Only three questions?"

"You wanted to play a game. So, let's play. I'm confident that the result will be the same anyway, and I do love a good game. Three questions. Go." Wyllt smiled.

"Ok… ok. Three questions." Jeremy thought hard on this. He didn't want to be the fool who asked a direct question that he really didn't mean to ask. *He wants to know where the gatehouse is. Why? Well, it's obvious he wants to go to the magic side of the Veil. Magic side? Is that what they called it? Or was it the Enchanted side?* He realized Mercurio had never referred to either side with a specific name. Either way, why does this guy want to go to Mercurio's side? *That's the real question.*

"Ok… um… Why is it… um. Ok, here we go. What reason do you want to go to the Enchanted Lands?"

"Enchanted Lands?" Wyllt smiled and looked at Jau.

The goblin snickered again, chewing on a spoonful of shakshuka.

"That is a very clever and well thought out question, Jeremy." Wyllt said. "I'm a procurer of goods and services of the more esoteric variety. Crossing the Veil and entering 'the Enchanted lands', as you call them, presents far more opportunities for someone in my business than the dreadful side of the Veil we live on. That's my reason for wanting to go to the *Enchanted Lands*." He smiled and drew out the last of his words.

Jeremy nervously tapped his fingers against the cold marble countertop, carefully wording his next question. *Opportunities? He said the Enchanted Lands will have more opportunities for him. But that seems foolish. He can't actually believe that the elves would just let him waltz through the Veil and take what he wanted. And, he must not know how the*

Veil works. Even if I told him where to go, he'd never be able to get in. The Veil wouldn't let him. Wait a minute! He thought. Jeremy stopped the tapping and looked at Wyllt.

How did he know that I even went to the Enchanted Lands? If he doesn't know where the gatehouse is, how could he even know that I went there?

"Ok… next question. How… how did you know that I've been to the Enchanted Lands?"

"That is a good question, Jeremy. Let me think about answering that one carefully." Wyllt took off his glasses and placed an ear-rest tip in his mouth. The man's piercing green eyes shimmered in the light.

"Jeremy, I have to say that I'm just a tad bit disappointed in you. The answer to that question is quite obvious. My associates have been following you and your elf friend around for some time now. He's a clever one. Managed to give us a slip there, so we weren't able to follow either of you to the gatehouse. So you see the answer to your second question is simple… you just told me you did."

Jeremy wanted to curse. He felt like he was playing chess. Wyllt was clever enough to feed Jeremy just the right amount of information to make him over think it or ask a foolish question. But Jeremy had played his fair share of chess. This was more like poker. Wyllt didn't answer Jeremy's question. He dodged around it. He bluffed. One final question. *Gotta keep my poker face. Should I ask him about the goblin or should I ask him if he was planning on doing harm to anyone when he crossed into the Enchanted Lands? What about something more personal? Like who he really is and how he knows so much about magic. Should I ask him more about that? No, that'd be a wasted question. I'll call your bluff…*

"If I show you where the gatehouse is, will you promise to take me with you?"

… and I'll raise the stakes.

CHAPTER 29

THE SPLENDOR
OF MAGIC

"My first impressions of the human wizard called Thaddaios Wyllt was that of a duplicitous scoundrel out to sooth his own selfish desires."

~ From *The Second Gift Giver Chronicles* compiled by Erwin Albowyn, a Chronicler of the Master Construct, Second Order, an alfargnym of Unterbaum

Thaddaios Wyllt howled a hard, raucous laugh. Jeremy didn't think the question was funny at all. As the man chortled, he placed his hand on his belly as if his gut was going to spill out.

"Jau, I do believe our guest has tasted the splendor of magic and wants more."

"Don't we all?" Jau said, shaking his head wistfully,

"He's got an itch I believe he can't scratch on this side of the Veil." Wyllt laughed out loud.

Wyllt's henchman stood at ease, unaffected by their boss' laughter.

The goblin didn't seem all that amused either. "Wyllt," Jau

said, "you have no idea. To be a goblin cursed without magic is the worst curse of all. The blight saw to that."

Cursed without magic? What's that supposed to mean?

Wyllt regained some control and shook his head at the goblin. "Oh Jau, elves meddle in everything. It's their nature. I swear, they're always trying to find ways to inject their perceived self-righteousness into everyone else's business. Am I right?"

"This is true, this is why we call them blight," Jau said, shaking his head.

There was a dynamic here that Jeremy couldn't figure out. What was the relationship between the goblin and Wyllt? At first, he thought Jau was one of Wyllt's henchmen. He wasn't so sure now. They acted differently. More like friends or partners. Regardless, he knew he needed to get back to the Enchanted Lands, and Wyllt could be his only ticket. If he cooperated, maybe he could go with them and let the elves sort it out. They'd probably have this guy and his crew arrested, or whatever they do with bad guys.

"So, do I get to go with you or not?" Jeremy said.

Wyllt's smile disappeared, and he pursed his lips before speaking. "No."

"Why not?" Jeremy said.

"That, my boy, is a fourth question," he said pointing his finger at Jeremy. "And I only permitted you three. However, I do like you." He said reaching over the counter and patting Jeremy on his cheek. "I do like you."

Jeremy wanted to pull away, but he didn't want to offend or make him angry.

"What would be your reason for wanting to go?"

"Well, I… uh." Jeremy didn't know what to say. Either he told him the truth, or he made something up. *I'm supposed to be the new Santa Claus.* Oh yeah, that would go over real well. He could just hear them all laughing at the ridiculousness of that statement. But he had to tell them something. Either way, Jeremy had a feeling that this partnership would not bode well for him or for the people who inhabited the Enchanted Lands. "Ummm… well, I have—"

"It doesn't really matter. You're not going. Now, just tell me where the gatehouse is before I send my boys to pick up your parents."

Jeremy gulped and stared wide-eyed at Wyllt. The man stared back—an icy hard stare that told Jeremy that Wyllt wasn't kidding. Jeremy's heart raced again.

"Mr. Jaeger and the others aren't really into the torture thing. They're more of a quick bullet to the head kind-of-guys. Jau, on the other hand, would delight in flaying them right here in front of you. Though, knowing Jau, I'm sure he'd begin by slicing their ears off first. Am I right, Jau?"

"Oh yes. I'd enjoy adding a few more to my collection." The goblin displayed a grotesque, sharp-toothed grin.

"You… you… you wouldn't…" Jeremy stammered. He couldn't get the words out.

"I would. I told you, Jeremy. There are two ways to get what you want from a person. You can treat them nicely and hope that they reciprocate. Or you make them so excruciatingly miserable that they can't help but tell you what you want. I prepared you a delightful meal. We had our fun, and it was nice. But Mom's approach didn't work with you. You have a bravado that I wouldn't have expected from someone like you. But, breakfast is over, and we need to move on. So, do I have my men pick up your parents or do you just want to tell me where the gatehouse is?"

Checkmate. Jeremy's shoulders slumped and he brought his hands to his face. The vision of his parents tied up to a chair as the goblin, holding a sharp knife, made his way towards them was too much to imagine. Jeremy couldn't bear the thought. He had no choice. He'd have to tell them. He sighed, pulling his hands away from his face.

"It's at the—"

The elevator doors slid open.

Jeremy turned.

A glowing yellow sphere hurtled toward the detective. The space around the sphere rippled in its wake. The detective reached for his gun as the sphere struck him in the shoulder. Rippling yellow light dissipated over his body. He convulsed and fell to the ground. His gun tumbled out of his hand and crashed to the floor with him.

Another sphere followed closely behind on a course for the guy with dreadlocks. He too swerved around and tried to reach for his gun but met with the same fate as the detective.

Jeremy felt a hand grab him by his shirt and yank him onto the counter. His plate slid with him as he went over the side and crashed to the ground, shattering into pieces and splattering tomato sauce, egg, and shards of china onto Jeremy's face. His shoulder hit the tiled kitchen floor hard, and his glasses slid off. Jeremy grunted as his breath rushed out of him.

Wyllt and Jau crouched behind the counter. Wyllt's hand remained clenched around Jeremy's collar. He yanked Jeremy to a crouching position and locked eyes with him. Even without his glasses, Wyllt's menacing, icy stare sent shivers down Jeremy's spine.

"Jeremy," Wyllt said with confidence, unperturbed by the situation. "You're going to get us out of this."

The sound of smashing glass and thuds of bodies falling to the floor came from the other side of the counter. Then there was silence.

"Jau'Asar!" Said a familiar voice.

Mercurio! Jeremy's heart soared.

"This is wrong, Jau'Asar. You know you can't possibly win here. Give me the human and I'll let you return to Kurgal unharmed," Mercurio said.

Wyllt looked at Jau and shook his head. Then he nodded in the direction of the kitchen entrance that led to the living room.

Jau nodded and crawled away.

Wyllt tugged on Jeremy's collar, snapping him around into a headlock. He hefted Jeremy up to face Mercurio. The man's fist slammed into Jeremy's head. He could feel the curve of one of Wyllt's rings pressing against his temple.

Jeremy squinted to see Mercurio standing in the elevator's doorway, sword drawn and a glowing yellow orb in his hand.

Another figure stood to Mercurio's left and slightly in front of him. *Ee'azar?*

Wyllt pushed harder against Jeremy's temple. The metal of the ring stung.

"Do you recognize this ring, Mercurio?" Wyllt said; his voice still calm.

Mercurio didn't flinch or pause to look at it.

"No, I can't say that I do. Just let Jeremy go."

"This ring, Mercurio, is the fabled Ring of Ra."

"Is that supposed to mean something to me?" Mercurio asked.

"Oh, Mercurio. I'm disappointed. Your reputation precedes you, and I thought for sure you'd know of this ring."

"You dabble in things you don't understand!" Mercurio shouted.

"You see, Jeremy," Wyllt said, loud enough for Mercurio to hear. "This is what Jau and I were talking about. This self-right-eous, know-it-all, controlling attitude of elves. They think that because they live longer they know everything. But from my perspective, if this elf is so smart, he'd know that the Ring of Ra commands the power of the sun. And if he knew that, he'd know that you're one thought away from your face being melted off."

Jeremy gulped, his Adam's apple rubbing against Wyllt's fore-arm. "I don't want to die. Please." Jeremy begged.

"I'm willing to bargain with you, Mercurio," Wyllt said. "All I want is passage to your side of the Veil."

"Samyaza! You must be insane!"

"I've been called worse," Wyllt responded.

"What makes you think I have any such authority or that any of my people would ever grant such a request? The Veil exists for a reason, Wyllt. And you are part of that reason."

"All I want is passage. Just grant me—"

Wyllt's grip tightened around Jeremy's neck, jerking him back-wards. His fist pulled away from Jeremy's head.

Jeremy gagged.

Ee'azar leaped with superhuman speed over the counter and slipped himself between Wyllt and Jeremy.

Wyllt's grip on Jeremy eased. Ee'azar pushed him to the side and Jeremy rolled on the floor and against a cabinet. He straightened and crawled on all fours, feeling around for his glasses. He found them and quickly placed them back on. Jeremy looked over and saw a perfectly round hole in the floor, the size of a manhole. Wyllt's hands held onto the side and dangled over the floor below.

Ee'azar kicked Wyllt in the face and stomped on his hand. The man let go and fell.

Two elves climbed out of the hole. They wore the same dark green cloaks, and green and gold armor as Ee'azar.

Ee'azar helped Jeremy to his feet.

Jeremy peered into the hole. Wyllt was lay prone on the floor below, moving slowly, trying to push himself up.

The man looked up through the hole and stared at Jeremy with eyes that spoke one word: vengeance!

Jeremy swallowed.

Another man with a gun strapped to his back rushed over to Wyllt and began helping him up.

One elf reached into the hole and grabbed something. The hole disappeared. The floor was back to normal as if it had never been touched.

"Quickly!" Yelled Mercurio. "We need to get out of the building before Wyllt assembles his troops."

"Troops?" Jeremy swallowed, raising his hand to his forehead.

"Yes. This entire building is filled with Wyllt's private mercenaries."

Ee'azar grabbed tightly to Jeremy, holding him by the arm. He reached up and touched the side of his nose. A shimmering, golden vortex quickly surrounded them. In a blink, the kitchen disappeared.

Light rushed in from every direction, blinding Jeremy. Warm wind blew against his body. He felt Ee'azar push him forward. Jeremy's eyes adjusted and he saw the faint outline of the New York City Skyline partially obscured by a gray brick wall and the black tar of the roof.

Ee'azar clung to Jeremy's arm, urgently pulling him forward. Mercurio walked beside him, the other two elves behind them.

The door from behind burst open, and Jeremy jumped.

Sounds of gunfire erupted. Ee'azar pulled Jeremy faster, quickening their pace to a run.

Jeremy looked back. Several mercenaries fired at them with automatic weapons. The elves behind Jeremy held their hands forward. Bullets hit all around them, shimmering and falling to the ground, unable to hit their targets.

Now what? How do we get off the roof? Jeremy wondered, gasping for breath. He couldn't run anymore. He needed to stop, but Ee'azar wouldn't relent. They were heading toward the edge.

Oh no! Please don't tell me we are going to jump! Jeremy didn't care if they could fly or levitate, he didn't want to jump off the roof.

"Where… where are… we… going?"

"Away from here," Mercurio said.

Ee'azar stopped short and reached out, placing his hand on something that wasn't there.

"Watch your step," Ee'azar said, grabbing Jeremy's leg and lifting it on to an invisible foot rail.

With a step up and a shove from Ee'azar and Mercurio, Jeremy found himself in the seat of a large ornate sleigh.

He sat up, looking over the sleigh's dashboard he saw eight reindeer.

Jeremy breathed a hefty breath, powered equally by exhaustion and awe.

"This is…"

"Yes," Mercurio said as he stepped in, "this is Nikolas's sleigh."

Another barrage of gunfire startled Jeremy. He turned just as the mercenaries fired and advanced. The bullets had the same effect as before.

The two other elves climbed aboard, taking their seats in the rear.

The mercenaries stopped and lowered their guns. Only twenty

feet away, they stared at the sleigh in shock. *Can they see it?* Jeremy didn't think so. They appeared to be looking past it.

"Sit back," Mercurio said, grabbing the reins.

Jeremy obeyed and watched as Mercurio took control. With a loud voice and a flick of the reins, Mercurio shouted the incantation.

A flash of golden light emanated from the sleigh and radiated in all directions. The reindeer lurched forward and trotted before reaching a full run toward the rooftop's edge.

Jeremy knew what was about to happen, but it didn't change the way his heart sank into his stomach as the reindeer jumped over the side of the roof and pulled the sleigh into the sky.

THE MIDDLE OF NOWHERE

"The Gift Giver's sleigh was a marvel of Elven ingenuity and alfargnym engineering. The ingenuity was in the use of reindeer-like b'hemayal as a magical conductor."

~ From *The Gift Giver Chronicles* compiled by Volcdegen Vigdis, a Chronicler of the Master Construct, First Order, an alfargnym of Unterbaum

They soared high above the Rockies at 20,000 feet, slowing down as they approached their destination. A bluish-gray haze surrounded them on all sides; the sleigh's integrity field protected the passengers from the sub-zero temperatures, stabilized the air pressure, and smoothed out any unexpected turbulence.

Mercurio held the reins in gloved hands and looked over at Jeremy. The human gripped the side of the sleigh and smiled in wide-eyed fascination at the scenery below. Mercurio hadn't said a word to him since they left New York. The fact of the matter was that he didn't know what to say. With all his centuries of experience and wisdom, Mercurio had still made a mess of things. Once again, he thought he had anticipated every likely scenario. He purposely left Jeremy with the frithstone, knowing that he'd try to come back. He figured that he'd draw the council's attention and someone else could see what an extraordinary human Jeremy was. It was risky and it could have easily failed, but it was his last attempt at bringing the Gift Giver back to the world.

Wyllt. Mercurio thought. *He was the unexpected variable that botched it all.* Mercurio underestimated the man's tenacity. Too many people know about the Veil now. Too many people knew about Jeremy. They couldn't go back to Sayalla or any other Elven city.

When they reached western Colorado, Mercurio steered the b'hemayal south and urged them towards their descent.

Jeremy looked over at Mercurio with a puzzled look on his face.

"Colorado?"

"Yes," Mercurio said.

"Why?"

"There's a gatehouse there. We're going to need someplace safe to stay until we can figure out what to do," Mercurio responded curtly, his aggravation now turning to Jeremy.

"Another gatehouse? Wow. How many of them are there?"

"They're all over the world." Mercurio knew that Jeremy was going to keep asking questions. He couldn't blame him. But he was in no mood to answer them or give history and geography lessons.

"Gaviryl," Mercurio called to one of the other guardians.

"Yes, Palgen?" Gaviryl replied from behind him.

"Birch is expected to meet us at Zahl's Gate, correct?" Mercurio already knew the answer but used the question to distract Jeremy.

"Yes, as you requested, Palgen."

"Good. Give Jeremy his Blood Stone."

Gaviryl reached into a small satchel at his side and produced the familiar pendant. He passed it to Jeremy.

Jeremy took it. "Thank you," he said as he placed the chain around his neck.

"Palgen? Why do you call him Palgen?" Jeremy asked Gaviryl, loud enough for Mercurio to hear.

"It's an Elven term. Similar to how your military ranks its individuals. It means 'the one with authority over you.' Mercurio has authority over this team. He is our Palgen."

"Kinda like a Captain?" Jeremy asked.

"Yes. In some ways. The idea is the same. Our group is small. Just the four of us, including Mercurio. He assembled us a few months ago to reform the Gift Giver's Guard in anticipation of your arrival."

"Really? So we're gonna go ahead with the plan? Awesome!"

"No!" Mercurio yelled. "We are not. The only thing we are going to do now is keep you safe. And I haven't figured that out yet. So just hold your tongue of any further questions." He turned away, not wanting to see Jeremy's disappointment. "I'll let you know when and what we're doing."

Mercurio imagined the sullen look on Jeremy's face. But what was he to do? This was already further out of hand than he ever expected. He had to get things back under control.

MERCURIO LANDED the sleigh in a valley. A small log cabin sat in a picturesque view of a lush green clearing surrounded by trees and snow-capped mountains in the background.

Jeremy wondered if they were within the Veil's perimeter, but he dared not ask. He touched the small bulge in his pocket, making sure that the stone was still there.

Mercurio was obviously not in the mood to answer questions. Jeremy was apparently just along for the ride.

The door of the log cabin slammed open and a small… man? Gnome… shuffled out. He wore an old wide-brimmed hat and what appeared to be ski goggles. He carried something in his hands, holding it like a rifle, pointing it at Jeremy and the others.

Ee'azar stood in front of Jeremy.

"What in Odin's fury do you elves think you're doing?" The

gnome yelled, walking closer. The tip of the weapon became clearer as he approached. A red jewel, resting in a gold setting, aimed right at Jeremy's head.

Jeremy swallowed.

The gnome waved his weapon around as he continued to berate the elves. "You can't be landing that here—and you certainly can't be bringing *that* here, either." He jabbed the staff toward Jeremy.

Mercurio responded to the gnome in a language Jeremy didn't understand.

The gnome held up a hand. "English, elf! I want that trespassing human to know that he's no more worthy to be here than he is to be standing in Odin's dung pile."

"Forgive us, Gatekeeper Eginoff." Mercurio said as he slowly exited the sleigh. "I am Mercurio iyl Sayalla. We're seeking a temporary place to hide this human. He is in danger…"

"Spare me the story, tender face. This is a gatehouse. It isn't a sanctuary for wayward men and elves."

The gnome's appearance matched his surly nature. He wore what looked like an old beat up prospector's hat that had actually seen the first Gold Rush. His vest and shirt were a slovenly, dirt encrusted patchwork of denim, burlap, and various other cloths. Slung over his shoulder was a bandolier-style belt of pouches and tools. He wore a pair of polarized ski-goggles that covered his eyes. But his cheeks, nose, and dark beard were as dirty as they could get. Jeremy could barely tell the color of this guy's skin or beard.

"Please hear me and understand. An associate of ours was supposed to meet us here." Mercurio glanced at Gaviryl, whose expression revealed concern.

"Hear me, elf. My gatehouse, my rules. Now—" The gnome paused, then cocked his head and turned back toward the cabin. "Well, it seems my gatehouse is a busy one today." He turned back towards Mercurio. "Get back in that flying menagerie of yours and find another gatehouse."

The gnome turned and walked back to the cabin. "Don't be here when I get back!" He slammed the door.

"That has to be Birch coming through the Veil. Though I don't understand why he's not already here," Mercurio said, shaking his head. "Jeremy, let me know the second Birch contacts you."

"So, what was that all about?" Jeremy said, stepping out of the sleigh. The three other elves followed.

Mercurio ignored Jeremy and walked away from the sleigh.

"Palgen, what are we going to do? Find another gatehouse?" Ee'azar asked.

"We could. However, I'm unsure if we'll meet with better reception anywhere else. We need a remote location, protected by the Veil where no one will bother us for a few days. We'll just need to be more convincing with Eginoff."

Gift Giver. I am here, though Eginoff the gatekeeper is not pleased with my arrival.

"Birch is here. He says the gatekeeper's not happy."

"We'll just wait and see. I'm going to try approaching Eginoff with different leverage." Mercurio smiled and then turned to Gaviryl and the other elf, Jar'iyu.

"While we're negotiating, you two scout out the area. We're going to need a place to set up camp. I doubt negotiations will get us permission to stay in the cabin."

Gaviryl and Jar'iyu ran off as the cabin door slammed open again.

"Alright. Who does this goblin-spawn belong to?" The gnome said, gesturing at Birch and walking toward them.

"He doesn't belong to anyone," Jeremy retorted.

Mercurio held up a hand to stop Jeremy from speaking.

"Ah, come on! You gave the koth to a human!" Eginoff said.

Jeremy knew he needed to keep his mouth closed, but he surely didn't want to.

"Gatekeeper. As I said, I am Mercurio iyl Sayalla. I am a Palgen Swordsworn of the Gray Guard. A new Gift Giver has been found.

Arrangements are being made for his transfer to Orindin. However, there has been a breach of the Gate at Argosy. We need to keep the new Gift Giver safe until the situation in New York is taken care of."

"I couldn't care less about your plans. You got no writ. I want you gone," the gnome said gruffly, switching the staff to his other hand and pointing it upward.

"As I was saying, gatekeeper, we just need to stay someplace safe within the confines of the Veil. We'll set up camp and you won't even know we're here unless we need to go through the Veil. Now," Mercurio continued, "once all this is settled, I may be able to see to it that you get posted at the least frequented gatehouse."

"Fladebert's?" Eginoff perked up. "You can do that?" The gnome grew excited.

"I didn't say I could. But I do have influence among those who can. We won't be in your way. We'll just set up a camp not too far from here."

"Fine. I don't want anyone around my cabin. No questions, no borrowing things. Keep to yourself. Do that and put in a good word for my transfer, and you can stay."

"Agreed." Mercurio said.

———

That evening Jeremy and the four elves gathered around a campfire. He and Ee'azar sat on a large, heavy log that Birch had carried to the campsite himself. Gaviryl and Jar'iyu sat on another log across from them. It took all four elves to carry that one.

Unperturbed by the heat of the fire, Birch turned the spit that held the skinned carcass of their dinner. The koth was a remarkable creature; strong, smart, and resourceful. Jeremy was glad that Birch was on his side.

Behind them sat a spacious leather tent with a pointed top. It reminded Jeremy of something he'd seen at a carnival.

They had spent the day setting up the camp with the supplies that Birch brought through the Veil. Now it was time to eat. Jar'iyu had gone hunting and gathering, coming back with two rabbits and a variety of vegetation. Jeremy had never eaten rabbit before.

After all the excitement in the last few days, the last thing he had eaten was the bite of that shack-stuff Wyllt made him. The more he smelled the roasting meat, the hungrier he'd become. He actually felt like he could relax a little and eat. He was safe. And Mercurio had assured him that his parents were being protected by more guardians.

Mercurio sat by Jeremy and interrupted his hunger-induced daze. The elf looked up at him. His eyes could not hide his concern.

"Jeremy, I'm afraid I've come to a decision," Mercurio said.

Jeremy furrowed his eyes, cocked his head and looked down at the elf. His heart beat just a bit faster.

"We have but one thing to do. We need to go to Kurgal and get Nikolaos' Ring."

END PART 1

PART TWO

CHAPTER 31
IN THE WAITING

> "Morag iyl Juyir is one of the most celebrated and most infamous elves in history. It was his spell, using blood magic, that caused the fall of the Goblin Empire. The Unbinding was released in 574 B.C. Morag left Juyir that same year and was never seen again."
>
> ~ From *The Veiled Happenlore of the Master Construct* compiled by Fulbert Gisilfrid, a Chronicler of the Master Construct, Third Order, an alfargnym of Unterbaum.

The miasma of gasoline smoke and the hum of engines filled the valley. Swarms of mosquitoes, unaffected by the haze, perched on Masaru's bare flesh. He ignored their breakfast at his expense, focusing his attention on the men digging into the side of the land. The noise of the engine pumps filled the river valley, making it much easier for Masaru to sneak around and get a better view. The pumps propelled water through hoses, creating powerful water cannons that melted away the ancient permafrost. A great cavernous hole torn into the hillside made way for men to enter. Masaru counted thirteen men who worked here. Most were within the cavern now. A handful of others worked inland and were rarely seen.

Over the past three days, Masaru made his way steadily north following Turtak's instructions. He had to abandon the motorcycle several hours ago and hike his way to this location to stop these men. But he didn't know why. And he had no idea what these men were digging for.

"Man cannot yet discover the truth about this world. One day you'll be the one to show it to them. But this day, there are men whose blood you must spill," Turtak said.

Masaru watched from across the decimated and silt-filled river as one man emerged from the cavern triumphantly carrying what appeared to be a very large tusk. Two other workers followed. The excited man showed the others what he found. Two more came out to see the man's treasure.

"What is that?" Masaru said.

"A mammoth's tusk." Turtak said.

"You want me to kill these men because they found a mammoth tusk?"

"No, Masaru. There is more."

Another man emerged from the cavern. He yelled with even more excitement, calling for the others to come back in.

Masaru couldn't quite make out what he was saying. He was too far away.

Other workers ran in from the forest, making their way toward the cavern's entrance.

"Masaru. Go now! Let no one leave here alive."

Masaru stood up and rushed out of the forest. The mosquitoes feasting on him flew away as he picked up speed. He bounded down the side of the riverbank, leaping across and drawing his katana as he landed.

A man, running towards the cavern, stopped. He looked at Masaru, squinted, and lurched his head back. "Who… what are you doing here?" He spoke in Russian.

Masaru could speak and understand Russian. It was one of

the many languages Turtak had encouraged him to learn. He had no intention of speaking it now. Masaru launched himself up the riverbank at the man. His katana slid under the man's rib cage and into his heart. His eyes opened wide as Masaru withdrew the sword. The man flopped to the muddy ground.

Other workers continued to run toward the entrance of the cavern, unaware of Masaru or their fallen comrade.

At the cavern's mouth a man shouted, frantically waving his hand. "Hurry… you've got to see this. We'll all be rich," he yelled.

Masaru darted after the men, slicing through two before the others spotted him. The startled men scattered. He went after the ones that ran away from the cavern, killing them before they could escape. The others, he hoped, were still in the cavern where he could trap them.

A loud bang echoed through the valley followed by a hot searing pain in his left shoulder. Masaru staggered back a few steps. Adrenaline and training refocused him, helping to mask the pain. He turned and looked up to see a man standing at the cavern's entrance pointing a pistol at him. The man lurched forward and his eyes went wide with terror. He tumbled to the ground and rolled down the man-made hillside.

Turtak? Masaru wondered. The pain in his shoulder and the imminence of the situation didn't allow him to continue to ponder what had killed that man. He suppressed the pain in his shoulder with controlled breathing and made his way to the cavern's entrance. It was barely four feet around. He had to duck to enter. As the workers tried to escape, Masaru killed each one.

Curious, he made his way to the end of the tunnel to see the source of their jubilation. The nozzle of the water cannon lay on the ground; a steady jet of water stripped away the lower part of the cavern and revealed stone and metal. Masaru moved closer, following the exposed stone. The men had blasted a large section of the permafrost away, exposing a ten-foot section of a wall and the top of a doorway. The doorway was still filled with millennia-old mud. At the edge of the doorway a small chunk had been carved out. At its base was a partially exposed rod. A weapon perhaps?

Masaru squatted and reached for it. His shoulder radiated a blast of pain, reminding him of the wound. The bullet had grazed his deltoid. A little further over and it would have done a lot more damage. Masaru needed to bandage it before he lost any more blood. The pain of the wound didn't bother him as much as the wonder of what these men had uncovered. He reached for the rod again.

"Leave it," Turtak said. "Tend your wound and then bury what has been unearthed."

This is getting old. Masaru gritted his teeth and took one last glance at the rod before standing. It was too old and worn to identify.

Masaru exited the cavern and rifled through the camp for something to bandage himself with. He found a vodka bottle with just enough left in it to pour over the wound. He then made a poultice from surrounding vegetation. Another lesson he had learned from Turtak.

"What is this place?" Masaru said, applying pressure to his wound.

There was no answer.

Did that mean Turtak was ignoring him? Or was he not here?

Masaru spent the rest of the day collecting the bodies. When he came across the man with the gun, he examined him, noticing a stab wound that went clear through the back and out of the front. Turtak had used a blade to kill this man. *Interesting.*

He piled all the bodies up at the back of the cavern, against the exposed wall and doorway. *Curious.* He wanted to keep digging. He wanted to see for himself what was in there. But he'd never go against Turtak. He had given Masaru specific instructions to make the camp look like it never existed.

With the bodies piled against the wall, he used the water cannon to blast away at the cavern's ceiling, hoping to release enough mud and silt to cover the bodies and the wall.

By the end of the day, Masaru had covered as much as he

could without exposing anymore of the wall or compromising the structural integrity of the cavern. He hoped it would be good enough until winter came.

There was still more to do, but he was hungry and tired. He'd camp here for the night, eating the dead men's food and sleeping in one of their tents. This way, if he had missed any or if suppliers came through, he'd be able to finish them off as well.

IN THE MORNING, Masaru woke before sunrise. Over the past week he'd been training himself to sleep with his prosthetic arm. It was a difficult task at first, but his discipline won over, and he slept better each night. Now he only took off the prosthetic to bathe and clean its parts. Even though he didn't need to, he preferred recalibrating it each morning, just to make sure it was working optimally. This morning he did so by picking up a spoon so he could eat breakfast.

He heaped a spoonful of cold beans into his mouth and listened. Silence.

"You there?"

"I am always here," Turtak said.

"What is that supposed to mean?"

"Just because I don't always answer, does not mean I'm not there. I am with you always, Masaru, though I will not be forever. Our paths will diverge once you reach your destination."

"What am I doing here?"

"Training."

"Training?"

"You still have much to learn, Masaru. In fact, your most difficult lesson still lies ahead."

"And what lesson is that?"

"You must learn defeat."

Masaru looked up and cocked his head in the voice's direction. "How is that a lesson? I'm not supposed to win every time?"

"You've never known defeat. You've conquered everything ever thrown at you. You've never failed a test. You've—"

"I don't understand," Masaru said. He threw down the half-full can of beans and stood up. "You taught me to be diligent. Everything I've ever accomplished is because you taught me to work hard… to push myself. That's why I passed all my exams—"

"But you've never been defeated. You've never lost a fight, whether it was through competition or life and death. It is one thing to win when you are superior to your opponent. It is another to face an opponent and learn defeat."

"I know defeat. I've lost at games. Sensei has beaten me. I—"

"Masaru, you don't know of what I speak because you have never experienced it. You must continue to trust me. You must know defeat. You must know what it is to face death itself."

"I just got shot in the shoulder! And you killed the guy before he could pull the trigger again! I would have died if you hadn't stabbed him."

"And what did you learn from getting shot?"

"It hurts!"

"And?"

Masaru thought about what happened. He didn't see the guy with the gun because he turned his back on the men that were closest to the cavern. But if he didn't, the other two would have gotten away. What was he supposed to do?

"I should have made sure there were no other threats before I went after the two that were running away."

Turtak remained silent.

Was that the right answer? Masaru sighed, a bit out of anger but more so because he knew there was nothing more he could say. He simply had to trust Turtak. He decided to change the subject. "What is this place?"

"It is old and has not been seen by the eyes of any creature for several millennia. It was once the home of the goblin empire. Beneath this mud and loam lies the once great city of Badtibirra, lost to war… lost to the Dark Elves."

"Goblins? In all these years, you've never mentioned goblins and Dark Elves. Why now? What are we doing?"

"I have never lied to you, Masaru. Though I have withheld information from you. There is a time frame for your training, an order to which you must learn things. You didn't master the katana before you mastered its first kata. This is so that you learn patience, above all."

"Am I a goblin?"

Turtak laughed. A rare sound.

Silence. Masaru waited patiently for an answer.

"You are not," Turtak finally said. "You will know soon what you are. But that will be a lesson you learn after you learn true defeat."

Anger swelled in Masaru again. Why wouldn't Turtak just tell him everything now? It'd sure make things easier. Masaru took a deep breath, steeling his nerves, banishing his anger.

"I don't understand why you won't just tell me what we're doing. Where are we going?" The breathing technique was no longer working. He cursed in Japanese, kicked the bean can and sent it hurtling across the campsite. "Why all this secrecy? Just tell me what we're doing already!"

Only the sounds of nature remained; mosquitoes buzzed, birds chirped, the wind slowly blew through the trees, and the river trickled past the campsite.

Masaru gritted his teeth. The muscles of his flesh arm and shoulders tensed. Turtak's unresponsiveness only fed his anger.

"Well, answer me!"

"Everything is a lesson," Turtak said; his voice calm. "One day, Masaru, you will be a great leader. You will command armies and govern an empire. And you will not have every answer you wish at your whim. There is much to learn in the waiting. Patience. Wisdom. Control. It is good that you desire to know the why and will of things. In the waiting, you must look at the clues all around you and weigh them against your knowledge. Make conclusions. But be patient in the waiting, for everything will eventually be revealed. This is an ongoing lesson, one you will practice daily along with other lessons. Patience is a lesson that complements all others. Soon, you will understand what there is to learn in defeat. Exercise patience, and that lesson will be easier to learn."

Masaru unclenched his fists and exhaled.

"Are there still goblins that exist today?" Masaru asked.

"Yes. Goblins still exist. As do elves, alfargnym, dweorg and other creatures you are unaware of. Goblins no longer live in the north. After their defeat at the hands of the Dark Elves, those that survived retreated to the southern kingdom with their sar."

There was more Masaru wanted to ask. What are Dark Elves? Was Turtak a goblin? An elf? He'd finished breakfast, and he needed to tear down the rest of the camp before anyone else arrived. He would ask those questions later.

Masaru began by filling the entryway of the cavern with dead branches and tree trunks. He then scooped as much mud as he could into buckets. Using a thick tree trunk, he carried two buckets at a time over his shoulders. The bullet wound throbbed, but it hadn't impeded him much. *Strange.* He thought a bullet wound would be far worse. In fact, it bothered him significantly less this morning than it did last night. Turtak's poultice was a wonder.

Masaru attempted to hide the entryway as best he could, pouring and slapping mud over it, then dried dirt and some leaves.

His next task involved collecting all the equipment in the area and disposing of it. He loaded it all into the five boats. Masaru hitched two at a time to one boat and brought them down river, about an hour away from the dig site. Then he sent them at full speed, crashing into the river's edge. He kept one boat for himself.

The end of an exhausting day had come. His shoulders ached now more than ever. He went to change his bandage and found that the wound had closed. A small red circle, tender to the touch, remained. *Wow! That is some poultice,* he thought again. He didn't bother putting on a fresh bandage. Instead, he feasted on two cans of hash and went to sleep.

After waiting at the campsite for a few days, Masaru was convinced that no one else was coming. He loaded up the remaining supplies and took the last remaining boat down the river, heading east. Heading towards his next lesson... to learn defeat.

LAMENTATIONS

> "Words change the ebb and flow of magic and therefore have the power of life and death. They are a Lawsworn's greatest tools."
>
> ~ Stahjhue iyl Orindin, Elder of Orindin, A.D. 789 to A.D. 1650

Ellesmere had returned to Orindin after the council meeting… after she'd done one of the hardest things she'd ever done as an elder. For the past three days, she took to walking during the *Time of Rest*, to clear her mind. And each day she seemed to find herself here, outside the old house, staring up at the human-sized door.

"Oh Nikolaos," she sighed and placed her hand on the crook-shaped symbol carved into the door; the Gift Giver's symbol. She remembered the first time she'd seen it, when Nikolaos had rescued her and Mercurio.

That fateful day she had begged Mercurio to see just one more human town.

No, Ellesmere! Mercurio's rebuke echoed in her mind. *We are not visiting another adamu town today.* But she pressured him, and he relented. They traveled too far from the gatehouse. Mercurio was sure they were being followed. She didn't believe him. They pressed on and found the next adamu city; larger and more spectacular than the first. Sitting on the edge of a cliff, the city overlooked the ocean.

The crashing waves, the smell of the sea, and the vast openness called to her. It was nothing like the small, enclosed village Ellesmere had lived in all her life or any of the Elven cities she had ever visited. The land of the adamu was breathtaking. She had to get a better look. Peering out from behind a tree, she felt Mercurio yank her away, into the forest, toward the gatehouse.

"Goblins!" Mercurio yelled. "They're riding nian. They must have sensed our presence!"

Ellesmere shivered, remembering the rest of that day. They ran for miles, and she couldn't run any longer. She felt the goblin's hands on her shoulder as it pulled her away from Mercurio. They tumbled to the ground.

"Ellesmere!" Mercurio shouted.

The goblin straddled her from the back and pushed her head to the ground. She breathed in dirt. Her heart pounded. She struggled, but the goblin held her in place.

"I'll have the first ear of the hunt!" The goblin yelled.

The icy edge of the blade touched her skull, and she felt it slowly slice into the back of her ear. The stinging burn of the blade's edge cut into her flesh.

Her mouth, dry from inhaling dirt, couldn't push out a scream. The warm blood trickled down to her neck. She coughed. No matter how hard she struggled, the goblin held her head in place and continued to slice her ear from her skull. Ellesmere wasn't strong enough to resist. The panic and fear paralyzed her, and that was all she could remember until she saw Nikolaos' smiling face for the first time. He had a beautiful smile.

Caught between the regrets of the present and fond memories of her friend, Ellesmere pushed open the old door and entered Nikolaos' house. She couldn't bring herself to enter for the last few centuries. She'd almost gone in yesterday, but the memories were too painful. Memories she'd long pushed to the side. Memories she wanted to forget, but never could. She, Mercurio, and Nikolaos had shared something wonderful, something that ended in tragedy and despair. And it was all her fault.

She stood in the doorway and sighed. The house had not been touched in over a century. But it was exactly how she remembered it. Nikolaos' old journal lay undisturbed on the table. And that old wooden cross that caused her friend so much turmoil hung on the wall in the center of the room. It was one of the few things in the cottage that Nikolaos made with his own hands.

She remembered Nikolaos staring up at that cross and how angry it would make him. She could never understand why he kept it there. And when pressed, he'd tell her that he didn't know how to serve his god here in Orindin. They'd had their fair share of theological debates, and Nikolaos never wavered from what he believed. But he lamented. He wanted to do more with the life he had remaining. And finally, one afternoon about six months after he'd come to live there, everything changed. Nikolaos came to terms with his new life, and he was determined to spend it serving his god by serving the people of Orindin.

In their daily talks during *The Time of Rest*, before Nikolaos left to whittle and tell stories to the children, he'd often wonder what it'd be like to spread that same joy to all the children of the world. That's when Ellesmere had the idea.

She remembered that day so long ago, standing outside her father's home, pacing back and forth, eager to tell her father her idea. But apprehension held her at bay. How could she disturb the Elder of Orindin during the time of day when he prepared the words for Last Feast?

Her plan took shape that afternoon as she left Nikolaos' house. Something the man said struck a chord, and she couldn't stop thinking about helping him.

Ellesmere approached her father's door, but before she could knock, fear gripped her. What would he say? Laven had already done enough to fix his daughter's mistake. How could she ask him to do any more? Guilt joined fear, and Ellesmere turned away from the door, her eyes falling on the Resting Tree. Beneath the great oak, Nikolaos sat on a bench surrounded by the children of Orindin.

A wave of guilt washed over Ellesmere.

I should've listened to Mercurio.

She could live without an ear, but she couldn't live with the remorse of knowing that Nikolaos was now paying the price of her curiosity.

Ellesmere could never repay Nikolaos for saving her. Never. Two other men had lost their lives that day.

Guilt gave way to sadness. Ellesmere turned her head and rested it against her father's door. *I never asked Nikolaos about the guardians he traveled with. How sad it must have been for him.*

She pulled her head away from the door and glanced over at Nikolaos again. The man whittled away at a block of wood as he told one of his fantastic stories. The children waited eagerly for him to finish.

The Gift Giver. That's what the children of Orindin called him. They loved Nikolaos. Ellesmere smiled, watching her friend whittle away at the wood, wondering what he was going to make. And then she remembered why she was sitting outside her father's door.

She'd come here for a reason. An idea kindled when Nikolaos spoke about wanting to help the children of the world. It took form as Ellesmere watched Nikolaos walk to the Resting Tree to visit with the children of Orindin. But without her father's approval and help, her idea would never come to be.

Ellesmere closed her eyes, breathed in a bit of magic, and pushed herself away from the door. She paused and knocked. Her heart pounded against her chest, seeming to intensify as each second passed.

The door opened. "Why, Little Heart!" Laven exclaimed, reaching out and touching his daughter on her cheeks. "It is rest." He gently pulled Ellesmere's head close and leaned over to kiss her on the forehead. "What reason do you have to disturb my thoughts?"

"Father… I… I must speak with you," she said. He let go of her and Ellesmere walked inside.

Her father's krodin waddled up to her.

"Yewly!" Ellesmere said. She bent over to pick up the gray-furred creature and scratch it on its head.

Yewly gurgled and bent its beak-like snout to smile.

Ellesmere's nerves settled as she stroked the creature.

Laven watched his daughter suspiciously. He cleared his throat and raised an eyebrow.

Ellesmere tightened her hug around Yewly. The creature groaned in contentment.

She cleared her throat. "I have an idea," she said, straightening and looking her father in the eyes. "And I can't wait for a more opportune time to share it with you."

Laven looked at Ellesmere, eyebrow raised, head tilted slightly back, his aura intensifying to crimson.

She wilted slightly from that all-too-familiar look of arrogant concern that her father was famous for; a look not only reserved for his children, but anyone he deemed to be treading in uncomfortable territory.

Unable to look him in the eyes any longer, she turned away. "Father, Nikolaos is a good and just adamu. He's not a warrior. He wants to change his people. It is as our forebears tried to do in Israel and Egypt… change the minds of the adamu and lead them away from warring with one another. He doesn't want…" Ellesmere caught herself babbling. Her father's unchanging demeanor confirmed her self-doubt.

"We need to aid Nikolaos in helping his people. We need to help him visit the children of the world and give them gifts."

Laven's eyebrows furrowed further up his brow.

Ellesmere sighed. Now that the words had left her mouth, she couldn't believe how utterly foolish she sounded. *Oh, Samyaza has surely found me!*

Ellesmere paced, trying to clear her thoughts and not seem like a babbling fool. She drew in more magic as she inhaled; the energy's potency enhanced by the krodin in her arms. She did as her father taught her to do. Ellesmere exhaled and used the surrounding magic to soften her aura, pushing away the crimson bands with tranquil blue ones. "We have among us this rare adamu. One of courage and integrity. One of compassion. It's these virtues that we admire in ourselves, yes?" She turned, facing her father, and she looked deeply into his concerned blue eyes. "I believe this adamu can inspire his people to change for the better. How can we let this opportunity escape us? Is this not our world as well?"

Laven sighed a terrible, awful, lingering sigh. He nodded his head and looked into his daughter's eyes. Ellesmere had rarely seen this look. It was not dismissive but concerned. The elder's aura confirmed that, softening from a crimson to a vibrant blue.

"Little Heart, I'll need to think on this. What you want to do will require more than just my help, but that of the entire council," Laven said, walking his daughter to the door.

Ellesmere was dumbstruck by her father's reaction. *He would actually consider it!*

That night at the evening meal, her father's speech caused quite a stir.

"Elves of Orindin," Laven said. His voice carried with it the full sincerity and weight of his authority. "Tonight, I speak to you, not to encourage you, but to encourage you to rise and be a part of something greater than our village… greater than what we hold sacred behind the Veil. We have among us one who was once a stranger but is now a part of our community. Some of you call him friend. Our children call him Gift Giver. To my own daughter, he has become family."

While her father spoke, Ellesmere kept her eyes on Nikolaos. As he did every night, the man ate and listened to Laven's words. At the mention of his title from the Orindin children, Nikolaos paused with his spoon halfway to his mouth. He took one last bite and leaned forward, listening more intently.

"Nikolaos has come to Orindin because he chose to act to save the lives of others with little regard for his own. He sits here, a hunted adamu in hiding. And once again, his thoughts and desires are not for his own life, but for the lives of others. My daughter came for my ears this day, and I reluctantly gave them to her. When she shared with me her heart, and the heart of her friend, my reluctance waned. Nikolaos is not content with just helping the folk of Orindin, or even the village from where he came. He has a desire to bring joy to every village of the world, be they keshaphim or not. And I, for one, wish to stand behind him in this desire."

Ellesmere's heart fluttered when she saw Nikolaos' mouth fall open.

"The world can be a terrible place," Laven said, his voice more somber. "What it needs is more joy… more love. And we can be the ones who help Nikolaos bring joy and love to the people of our shared world."

Ellesmere's smile widened, looking around at the crowd. They no longer stared at their elder, but all eyes were now on Nikolaos.

Blinking back tears, Nikolaos crinkled his nose and lifted a knuckle to wipe his eye.

"Tomorrow," the elder continued, "the Great Hall will open at day start, and we shall not work. When Telteva sounds her horn, we will plan. I'm imploring each of you to come here with ideas to help Nikolaos bring joy to the world."

Laven sat down and the hall erupted in unprecedented discussion.

As Ellesmere scanned the hall, she caught Nikolaos' eye. She smiled a humble grin. Nikolaos dried his eyes with his sleeve and smiled back.

That was many centuries ago. Another lifetime. Ellesmere sighed at the distant memory and her thoughts turned to Mercurio and the night he returned to Orindin alone. The night the Gift Giver had died.

CHAPTER 33
SPITE OF THY PAST DISTRESS

"B'hemayal are very similar to what humans call Peary caribou. Though b'hemayal are smaller and stockier than any other breed of caribou. They are also the only known breed of caribou to be biomagical."

~ From *The Veiled Happenlore of the Master Construct* compiled by Fulbert Gisilfrid, a Chronicler of the Master Construct, Third Order, an alfargnym of Unterbaum

After her daily walk around Orindin, Ellesmere returned home and sat on the old couch. Her mind still on Mercurio, she sighed once more and pulled the blanket onto her lap. The more she thought about what Mercurio had done, it seemed as if Samyaza himself had orchestrated the plan. What else could explain the madness behind his actions? Mercurio had still not returned, and to make matters worse, Nikolaos' sledge was gone too. It was obvious to Ellesmere that Mercurio had not heeded the decision of the council. But why?

Why would he destroy his reputation and face banishment to reincarnate the Gift Giver?

After centuries of living with the guilt of Nikolaos' exile and his eventual death, Ellesmere could never consent to another Gift Giver. Mercurio reminded her of all the good Nikolaos had done. He pleaded with her to at least meet this human. But how could she? Humanity was depraved and on the brink of extinction. The Earth would be better off without humans. She kicked off the blanket and hung her feet over the edge of the couch. *Humans!* For all she cared, they could go extinct and take the goblins along with them. She doubted she'd see such a thing in her lifetime. But she was fine with that. She'd continue to pave the way for her people to pick up the pieces once the humans destroyed themselves.

Ellesmere was the first female elder in the history of her people. She was humble enough to not consider that an impressive feat, but still proud that her people felt she would be the best fit to replace her father. There were other elves who could have been appointed Elder of Orindin. When her father's flesh could no longer contain his essence, her people made it clear that it was Ellesmere that they wanted to lead them. At that time, Nikolaos was still alive, and things were very different. So much had changed in the last two centuries, and the town of Orindin had suffered more so than any other Elven community. Ellesmere had little time to mourn the death of Nikolaos. She had to lead her people. And that meant making hard decisions. Orindin could no longer be known as the home of the Gift Giver. Her initial instinct was to tear down Nikolaos' house and the toy workshop. But each time she thought about it, she found herself standing outside Orindin's largest buildings, staring up at them. She couldn't do it. It was all that was left of the human that had changed her life.

She declared they leave each structure as is and no one be permitted to enter. At one of her nightly speeches, she declared Nikolaos' house and workshop a reminder that there were still humans capable of good.

"The people of Orindin were privy to something wonderful," Ellesmere told her people, standing at the table her father once occupied. "We saw that humanity was capable of more than just evil. We will leave be the home of Nikolaos the Gift Giver and the workshop filled with his gifts of hope. It will stand as a reminder as we wait for the day when elves and humans exist together for the good of all."

What a hypocrite. Ellesmere sighed as she remembered her own words. Why hadn't she remembered them when Mercurio and the human stood before the council only days earlier? She had been furious with Mercurio, and her anger clouded her wisdom. But Mercurio… he took this whole thing upon himself! She stomped and clenched her fists.

Ezzy walked in from the kitchen area, holding a cup of tea. Another reminder of humanity. Not only was the tea made by humans in Sri Lanka, but Ezzy too carried a sliver of humanity.

Ellesmere smiled at the girl. She shook her head and placed her hand to her mouth. What was she going to do?

Ezzy returned the smile. "Your heart is troubled, immatina," she said, handing the cup of hot tea to Ellesmere. She then sat on the couch, legs crossed at the ankles, and stared at her adopted mother.

"Oh, Little Heart, you have no idea."

"I don't," Ezzy said. "But my ears work just fine. You've used them before, you're welcome to them again."

Ellesmere smiled and sat beside the tall girl. She held the cup of tea in her lap, staring down at the steam rising from the light brown liquid that reminded her of Ezzy's skin.

What can I say to this child? Ellesmere wondered. *Dare I cast my burdens upon her? She already knows everything else. But she's a mere child and—*

"I may have not known Nikolaos. But I know you," Ezzy said. "And I've listened to every story you've ever told me and the other children about him. Your heart sings when you tell his tales. And when you speak of Mercurio, now that is a different story. You've always loved him, but the two of you never married—"

"Ezzy!" Ellesmere looked up at her and scoffed. "None of this has a thing to do with my feelings toward Mercurio."

"Immatina, you know that isn't true. I'd say it has everything to do with your feelings." She cleared her throat, raised her right eyebrow, and recited. "Too late thou shalt repent. The base injustice thou hast done my love. Yes, thou shalt know, spite of thy past distress, and all those ills, which thou so long hast mourned; heaven has no rage, like love to hatred turned, nor hell a fury, like a woman scorned."

Ellesmere pursed her lips and scoffed again. "Child, do not recite poetry to me. This trouble is beyond your wisdom. Leave me and let me think upon this, as is my station. If I need your ears, I will call for you."

Ezzy smiled. "Yes, immatina." She stood up and walked away, disappearing beyond the walls of the library.

Ellesmere sighed, shaking her head. "That child. She's been nothing but muscle her entire life." Her thoughts fondly wandered to the little girl that once was Ezzy. Now in her fiftieth year, she was mature. Were she not *yilchaga*, she'd be preparing for her *rishonam assa*. Ellesmere had given Ezzy a dress, rather than the traditional Veil cloak, as a gift for her fiftieth birthday. She sensed some bitterness from the girl, but Ezzy would never say anything. Ellesmere had always made it clear who Ezzy was and what it meant to be *yilchaga*. As an elder, she had mixed feelings about the way her people treated the pitied ones. She had only known two in her long lifetime; Ezzy and one adopted by the Elder of Juyir some seven hundred years ago. Neither of them had any choice in their birth. It wasn't their fault. Yet, her people treated them as if they didn't exist. That's why most *yilchaga* ended up in the care of elders. No one else would have them. *Unfortunate children.*

Ellesmere had experienced so much in her lifetime. And now, in the years she was expected to ready the mantle of Orindin for another, she had to deal with Mercurio.

She sighed again. *Stubborn guardian. What had he gotten himself into?* And why had he not yet returned? More importantly, what was she going to do about it?

Ellesmere sat on her couch, sipping tea, contemplating these questions until there was a knock on her door. Who would disturb her during rest?

Minutes later, Ezzy, followed by one of Orindin's guardians, entered the library.

"Immatina. I'm sorry to disturb your thoughts. Haym is here. He has a message regarding *your* Mercurio." Ezzy smiled.

Ellesmere shot her a sneer at her use of the word *your*. She stood up and approached the guardian.

"Thank you Haym. What have you learned?" Ellesmere said.

"Elder, Mercurio and several of the other members of the Gray Guard set up camp within the Veil at Zahl's Gate."

"What are they doing there?"

"We're not sure. But we surmise they're hiding the human there. He'd been taken by one of the wizards. Someone named Thaddaios Wyllt. A formidable one, at number two on the list. Mercurio and the other guardians rescued the human. That's why the sledge is missing. The Tsir 'azzelqān decided not to have him or the others pursued. And the alfargnym have appointed a chronicler. Should Mercurio return, the council will be called, and he will be brought before them."

"A chronicler!" Ellesmere paced back and forth. "This has become far more than it should ever have." She looked up at Ezzy and then walked to her desk. "Haym, thank you for bringing this to me. Continue to monitor the situation and let me know if anything changes."

Haym bowed his head, turned, and exited.

Ellesmere sat at her desk, removed a pen and piece of paper, and began to write. When she finished writing, she folded the paper and placed it in an envelope. She then turned and called out.

"Ezzy! Come here, please."

Ezzy entered the room. "Yes immatina?"

"We need to send word to the council. I think it's time you had your *rishonam assa*."

CHAPTER 34

AN INCURABLE RASH

"What Jeremy lacked in physical prowess he made up for, in abundance, with kindness. Though some might characterize this as timidity, I would characterize this as meekness. For meekness can be defined as strength under control."

~ From *The Second Gift Giver Chronicles* compiled by Erwin Albowyn, a Chronicler of the Master Construct, Second Order, an alfargnym of Unterbaum.

The glint of Mercurio's blade alerted Jeremy to his location. He turned and swung at the elf, only to find air.

Leaping with inhuman speed, blade held above his head, Mercurio came straight down at him.

Jeremy swerved to the right, but he was no match for the veteran sword master. The blade sliced through the air and stopped centimeters away from severing Jeremy's lower leg at the knee.

Jeremy sighed, disappointed in himself... again.

"We need to think about what we're doing here," Mercurio said.

"I'll get it. I promise," Jeremy said.

"We've been working on this for over a week now. The outcome is always the same."

"I just need to practice more," Jeremy patted his gut. "I can tell that I've already lost weight. I'm getting faster and stronger every day. Maybe we just need to practice some offensive moves for a while."

"Absolutely not!" Ee'azar stepped in. "You are the Gift Giver. The Gift Giver cannot fight."

Mercurio shook his head, looking disappointed. "Hear me, Ee'azar. We've discussed this before. The first Gift Giver killed a fully armored goblin high-blood. Don't fall prey to idealistic tales perpetuated by our people. Humans have done a fine job of that on their own."

"Palgen, is it not our responsibility to protect the Gift Giver?" Ee'azar asked.

"Indeed. But I failed to protect Nikolaos," Mercurio said. "As the Gift Giver's Guard, we trained, trying to protect Nikolaos from every likely scenario. But we never taught him to fight as we do. Only to run. In the end, he didn't run. His love for me and the other guardians led him to fight… untrained. I often wonder how that night may have gone if Nikolaos had a weapon and he knew how to wield it." Mercurio walked toward Jeremy. "By allowing Jeremy to only train defensively, we're crippling him. And by seeing him as different, you're crippling him. He needs to train as a Swordsworn. He needs to work as hard as we do."

Ee'azar sighed. "I will do as you command, Palgen."

"We will move on to offensive training," Mercurio said,

"Yes!" Jeremy said, pumping his fist. "I've always wanted to learn to use a sword."

"Jeremy, you need to understand something. You cannot have any romantic ideals about the sword. It is one thing to protect yourself in battle. It is another to actively go into battle. Despite their despicable nature, goblins are still living beings. When you battle one, you'll see its eyes. You'll see its own struggle to survive… to kill or be killed. And you'll need to take its life without the slightest hesitation, because if you don't, it will surely take yours."

Jeremy hesitated and swallowed before answering. "I can do that." Though he wasn't convinced he could. Not for lack of trying. He was willing to commit to the discipline it took to become… to become what? A warrior? That sounded so… so strange. Becoming Santa Claus was ludicrous enough. But now, he was actually accepting the fantastic notion of becoming a real, tried-and-true sword-wielding warrior. The thought was both exhilarating and frightening.

A wooden staff landed at his feet.

"Let's begin with the staff. We'll work up to the sword. And tonight, you'll hunt with Ee'azar and Gaviryl. They'll teach you how to use the bow." Mercurio said.

Jeremy pulled off his baseball cap and used his forearm to wipe the sweat from his brow before bending over to pick up the staff.

Mercurio stepped on the staff, pushing it back to the ground.

Jeremy looked up and raised an eyebrow, confused.

"Let's start with being mindful of everything around you. Train yourself to be alert. Head up. Eyes searching, always anticipating—"

Mercurio turned around, reached for his sword, and faced Eginoff's cabin. He stood with his weapon ready.

Ee'azar, Gaviryl, and Jar'iyu surrounded Jeremy, weapons ready.

They stood thirty feet away from the cabin in a clearing that served as their training ground. Over the past week they spent most of the day in the clearing. They had only seen Eginoff a few times. Birch had gone through the Veil twice for supplies. Other than that, there had been very little movement from the cabin.

Jeremy stood up and walked to stand behind Mercurio. The other elves drew closer, flanking him on all sides.

The cabin door creaked open, and the noonday sun grabbed

on to something. Beautiful streams of prismatic light flared. Jeremy squinted and used the brim of his hat to block the glare, still watching the cabin with great curiosity.

The prismatic light shifted, creating a silhouette of the creature that held the radiance over its head. Emerging fully from the cabin, it hobbled towards Jeremy and his guardians. Behind it, another taller silhouette followed. This was unmistakably a koth.

Mercurio let out a soft grunt. "I suspected as much." He lowered his sword.

"A chronicler?" Ee'azar said. "They've sent a chronicler?" He too lowered his sword.

The creatures drew closer, and Jeremy could make out more of their features. A gnome. Not Eginoff. And the koth wasn't Birch. He was back at the tent preparing lunch.

Jeremy swallowed and continued to squint to get a better view.

Dressed in a light blue, pinstriped tunic with a purple sash that matched his conical hat, this gnome appeared to be much cleaner than Eginoff. He carried a wooden staff with a crystal orb on top; the source of the radiance. The sunlight also caught the gold etching that bedazzled the rim of the gnome's hat.

The koth, larger than Birch, walked behind the gnome. He wore a purple scarf around his neck that matched the gnome's tunic and hat. His skin, a mottled green and brown, was in stark contrast to Birch's. From his white horns, purple and blue feathers hung from black braids attached to gold bands. He wore a pack that overflowed with items on the front and sides.

"Erwin." Mercurio shook his head and returned his sword to its sheath.

Something about the way Mercurio clenched his jaw and shook his head told Jeremy that the elf was irritated by the sight of this gnome.

"Why are you here?" Mercurio said.

The gnome's smile grew wide as he and the koth approached Mercurio.

"Mercurio," the gnome said. "Come now, old friend. What

sort of chronicler would I be if I were not here to record the momentous exploits of the new Gift Giver and his Guard?"

Gaviryl stepped forward, his eyes open wide with awe. "The Chronicler's House sent you here?"

"Cut off his head, and he shall not die," Mercurio muttered, shaking his head.

"Palgen?" Gaviryl said.

"It's of no use to dissuade him. Erwin is a rash that even our greatest healers couldn't cure." Mercurio laughed.

"Mercurio," the gnome snickered. "I will receive that as a compliment to my extraordinary abilities as a chronicler."

"And you," Mercurio smiled and waved his hand at the koth, "You still following this old puffer around?"

The koth nodded.

"Puffer?" The gnome feigned insult by placing his hand on his chest. "You wound me." He let out a raucous belly laugh, grabbing onto his staff with both hands to keep from falling over.

Jeremy stared at the elf and the gnome, both now engaged in a fit of laughter. This was perhaps the oddest display he'd seen since he'd met Mercurio.

"How about you guys fill me in here? Is this guy like some sort of reporter?" Jeremy asked.

"No, Jeremy." Mercurio composed himself. "Erwin is a gifted chronicler. Among his kind, the chroniclers are responsible for recording history. My question, however, is how did he know we were here and that there was a new Gift Giver?"

Erwin's smile widened. "First, allow me to introduce myself to the new Gift Giver. I am Erwin Albowyn, a Chronicler of the Master Construct, Second Order, an alfargnym of Unterbaum." He extended his hand.

Jeremy hesitated and looked to Mercurio.

"Is my gesture of greeting incorrect? Don't you shake the hands of new acquaintances? I thought I guessed correctly of your origin."

Mercurio nodded to Jeremy.

Jeremy extended his hand and shook Erwin's.

"Sorry. Yeah. You're right. I guess I'm just a little… overwhelmed."

"No need. My renown should be no greater than any of my brethren. Interact with me as you would a friend."

Mercurio laughed and shook his head. "He's not overwhelmed by your presence, Erwin. He's overwhelmed by the situation he's in. And you being here only compounds that."

"Ah! No bother. Just pretend I'm not here. I'm an observer. My assistant, Grath, and I will simply be in the background. If I have questions, I will ask them during mealtimes, for the most part."

"You still haven't told me how you knew we were here," Mercurio said.

"To paraphrase a famous human storyteller, it was elementary, my dear Mercurio. First, I believe you have underestimated the impact you've had on recent events in Sayalla. You brought a human before the council. Surely you had to know that would cause quite some agitation. And not only that, but you asked them to commission a new Gift Giver. Your name is on the lips of every citizen of Sayalla, and by now on those of the other cities as well."

Mercurio's demeanor hardened as he listened to the gnome tell his tale. What was he thinking? Would this change anything?

"Second," Erwin continued. "You've been gone for a while now, and the only sign of you has been the comings and goings of your assistant, Birch. And as koth go, Birch's coloration is not inconspicuous. You've stirred the proverbial pot, my good friend, and the Chronicler's House wants it documented. It was my good fortune that they assigned me to do so."

"Good fortune?" Mercurio said. "I think not. More Good grace, as they know our history together."

"So, what does this mean for us? Does it change anything?" Jeremy said.

Mercurio looked up at Jeremy. "That depends on the extent to which Erwin decides he's willing to follow us," Mercurio said. Then he crossed his arms and turned his gaze back to Erwin. An intense gaze, his eyes locked with the gnome's. "Erwin, you need to know that we're going to Kurgal."

"Ah! I see," said the chronicler. He raised a hand from his hip and placed it on his beard. "I wondered how you were going to transform this young man into the Gift Giver without the Ring of Nikolaos."

"It's the only way. And I surmise, at this point, Jeremy already has a price on his head. It's better to do the unexpected and take the fight to them."

"Wait! What?" Jeremy stepped back; eyes wide with surprise. "Price on my head?"

"Jeremy, what did you think was happening here?" Mercurio said. "You may not have killed a goblin prince. But you've upset someone who by human standards would be considered very powerful. You know the location of the Gate at Argosy. And you're the first human to cross the Veil in over three hundred years. You're valuable, and I doubt the goblins and their human wizards will hesitate to make your life miserable without our protection."

"Yeah, well… I knew that already. But I didn't think they'd put a price on my head. Are there like bounty hunters out there looking for me?"

Erwin laughed.

"Not quite," Mercurio said. "There are various small factions of humans who think themselves wizards and will stop at nothing to know what you know. You have to understand, I would not be taking you into Kurgal if I didn't think you'd have a better chance of survival with Nikolaos' ring."

Jeremy swallowed. He wasn't sure how to take this information. Some part of him already knew this, but it hadn't sunk in until Mercurio laid it all out. His biggest worry had been his parents, even though Mercurio assured him that he had Elven Guardians watching over them. Wyllt had his parents under constant surveillance. Mercurio said that this was a good thing, because that meant Wyllt didn't know where Jeremy was. And that could be used to their advantage. Unlike Mercurio, Ee'azar and

Gaviryl had a much better understanding of modern life outside the Veil. They designed an elaborate plan of misdirection for anyone looking for Jeremy. Postcards from all over the world would arrive at his parents' house. Emails routed through dozens of IP addresses would be sent. All sending Wyllt and his men on wild goose chases. The only thing Jeremy couldn't do was go on social media.

Jeremy's thoughts turned away from his parents and back to the conversation Erwin and Mercurio were having.

"… if that were the case, you'd just find someplace within the Veil to hide Jeremy and his parents so that they'd never be seen again. But, part of this is also your only way to bring back the Gift Giver," Erwin said to Mercurio. "If you have the Ring of Nikolaos and you give it to Jeremy, you think the council would reinstate the Gift Giver's yearly flight. That's your gambit, correct?"

Jeremy waited for Mercurio to answer, but the elf kept an icy, emotionless lock on Erwin.

"This is by my choice," Jeremy interrupted. "I'm the one that asked for this."

"Why?" Erwin asked. "Why would you be willing to put yourself in danger for this?"

"I don't know… it's complicated." Jeremy searched for the right words. "When I was a kid, my dad had this big coffee mug with a picture of John Wayne on it. My Dad loved John Wayne. Do you know who that is?"

"Yes." Erwin smiled.

"Well, to my dad, John Wayne was a hero. We'd watch his movies together every now and then. But my Dad once told me he wasn't just a hero in the movies. He was a man of honor and integrity, someone who stood up for what's right. Someone you could count on to do the right thing. My Dad must have had that John Wayne coffee mug for years, and I had never noticed, until I was about ten years old. There was this quote inside the rim. It said, 'Courage is being scared to death–but saddling up anyway.' I didn't really understand that quote for a long time. There are all sorts of people in the world, many willing to die for their ideals.

I've spent my whole life imagining what it would be like to be a hero… to be a champion of an ideal. And now I have the opportunity to do just that. I'm scared to death." Jeremy smiled awkwardly. "But if I'm not willing to die for it, truly willing to die for it, then what kind of champion would I really be?"

"And what ideal is it you are willing to die for, Jeremy?" Erwin asked.

Jeremy hesitated, remembering the false look on his sister's face. The same look that so many other people had, trying to hide their despair. "Hope." He paused, letting that word marinate. "Hope. Isn't that what we all want? To know that there's good in the world. That somebody out there cares about us. That someone is willing to die so that others can live?" Jeremy paused and looked at Mercurio. This elf believed in him. *He thinks I can really do this.* Jeremy turned back to Erwin. "You're a historian, Erwin. So, write this. The Gift Giver must be willing to die so that others may know that there is hope. Nikolaos of Myra died bringing hope to the world. Jeremy Goodson was willing to die too. And in doing so, he and his guardians journeyed to Kurgal to retrieve the Ring of Nikolaos. That's how you need to start your chronicle."

Erwin, still smiling, turned to Mercurio. "I believe him."

Mercurio nodded and smiled.

Jeremy smiled back. He felt as if he had been supercharged with energy. He was ready for anything. And he didn't want to stop now. "So, let's get training."

"Just one thing before we continue," Mercurio said. "Can we just call it Nikolaos' ring and not The Ring of Nikolaos? That just makes it sound so…" he struggled for the word. "…pretentious."

Erwin giggled; a contagious chortle that spread quickly among the misbegotten band. It felt good to laugh. The muscles of Jeremy's abdomen tightened, and his jaw muscles followed. Jeremy grabbed his belly and tried not to fall to the ground. He couldn't remember the last time he had laughed so hard.

CHAPTER 35

THE ABSOLUTE TRUTH

"The Swordsworn take an oath to protect the peoples of their city and of the Elven nation as a whole. In doing so, they dedicate their lives to this oath and to the mastery of their sword. Mercurio was the finest sword master I have ever met."

~ From *The Second Gift Giver Chronicles* compiled by Erwin Albowyn, a Chronicler of the Master Construct, Second Order, an alfargnym of Unterbaum.

Jeremy fought through the soreness in his shoulders and arms to lift the spoonful of strangely sweet and savory venison stew. Exhaustion fought with every muscle in his body, but it wouldn't win against the iron will of Jeremy's stomach.

It seemed strange that the log he sat on felt comfortable. Though he'd give it up in a heartbeat for his recliner. Thoughts of the soft, warm chair brought longing to his heart as he savored the stew. He wished he could be in his cozy apartment watching a good movie or binge watching something. No such luxuries here.

He had a log to sit on, a sleeping bag to slumber in, and the forest to do his business in. The luster of camping out in the Veil-protected wilderness of Colorado had waned after a week and Jeremy was more homesick than ever. It wasn't the company as much as it was the discomfort of outdoor living. The company wasn't bad at all, and he had learned so much. The elves worked mostly on combat techniques with him, and Birch gave him a crash course in history.

With Erwin's arrival yesterday, Jeremy's life took an even more complicated twist. It wasn't enough to be training all day long, but now he had to answer all these questions every time he took a break.

Jeremy took another spoonful of stew and looked out into the darkness of the woods. All was dark save for a few lights and the barely visible sparkling explosions of fireworks. The Fourth of July had come without notice until now. Absent were the hot dogs and burgers cooking on the grill and his aunts, uncles, and cousins talking about the current state of major league baseball. He didn't miss that. And he certainly didn't miss the plethora of questions about who Jeremy was dating, if at all. *No.* There was no one in Jeremy's life who put a sparkle in his eye or brought a smile to his face. There was that elf girl he saw a few weeks back in Sayalla. She was stunning and so far out of his league that Jeremy might as well be a rock. He tried bringing her up to the elves and Birch a few times, but they got all freaked out. *What was it that Birch had called her? A yilchaga? Was she not an elf? Or is a yilchaga a type of elf?*

Jeremy turned his gaze from the distant fireworks, back to his merry band sitting around the campfire. A motley bunch of unlikely adventurers. It was like the role-playing games he played, but this was real. Four Elven warriors, two ferocious looking but docile reptilian servants, and a gnome… *would Erwin be considered a bard?* He really didn't know what Erwin could do, other than write and illustrate. To his surprise, the gnome chronicler didn't only record history through the written word, but also through beautiful illustrations. Jeremy was uncomfortable as the subject of Erwin's drawings. Earlier that day, Erwin had shown him a sketch from his training session. He had captured the intensity of Jeremy's face as Ee'azar taught him to use the staff.

Jeremy took another spoonful of stew and settled his gaze on Mercurio. An elf! How long would it take for this to feel normal? He looked so young, but Mercurio was almost two millennia old. And when he spoke with Jeremy, his wisdom transcended his youthful appearance. He changed Jeremy's life and taught him so much in the short time they knew each other. Mercurio was the wise sage. Jeremy's ancient mentor. His Obi Wan Kenobi. Despite what he already learned, Jeremy still had so many questions. Every answer seemed to lead to more questions. And Mercurio always seemed to have all the answers.

"What about the Tooth Fairy?" Jeremy asked.

Mercurio's smile straightened as his eyebrows furrowed. "What?"

"What about the Tooth Fairy? Is she real too?"

"Jeremy, don't be ridiculous," Mercurio said, shaking his head.

"So, should I just assume that there isn't an Easter Bunny or Bogeyman either?"

That brought a smile to Mercurio's face as he chewed on a spoonful of stew.

Erwin laughed and Ee'azar, Gaviryl and Jar'iyu joined in.

"Yes, you can be sure they're not real." Mercurio said. "The Easter Bunny and Tooth Fairy are completely made up by human imagination. Whereas the Bogeyman, though that term is not used among my people, there is some credence to the notion of the Bogeyman, even in my own culture. Many elves believe in Samyaza, the First Born of Darkness. Various myths and legends tell of how he was the first to do evil against his own people. He was banished. And in his exile, he discovered immortality. Some believe that he lurks in the shadows and manipulates us into doing what is wrong."

"And did Samyaza lead you, Mercurio, into bringing Jeremy here?" Erwin said, a big grin lighting up his face.

Mercurio smiled back. "You jest, Erwin. And to those who

believe, Samyaza is not one to invoke in jest. Good thing I don't believe in such fairy tales."

Fairy tales? Jeremy couldn't help but smile. Was this the proverbial pot calling the kettle black?

"As for your people, Jeremy," Mercurio continued. "Goblins have intervened in humanity since man first came to this world. But they're not the only ones. Keshaphim of all kinds have crossed from our side of the Veil to yours and have caused untold terror and trickery. Goblins are by far the most troublesome. Some have even revealed themselves completely, such as the one that you saw with Thaddaios Wyllt."

"But why? What's the point?"

"Control and power," Mercurio said as he laid his bowl down on the ground and reclined backwards against the log.

"Goblins have always wanted to be the lords of this world. They've manipulated themselves into power for many millennia," Erwin interjected. "Long before men. Goblins were the demise of trolls and dragons. And if the elves had not intervened, humanity would have most likely fallen at their hands as well."

"Seriously? Goblins are that powerful?"

"At one time they were even more powerful," Mercurio said.

"Oh, Mercurio. Do allow me to tell this story," Erwin pleaded.

"By all means chronicler. Storytelling is your specialty, not mine."

"Ah, very well," Erwin said, laying his bowl beside him. He rubbed his hands together and smiled. "At the dawn of some of humanity's greatest empires, the goblins were orchestrating and manipulating. They were once great mages, wielding magic as their most powerful tool. Unbridled in their use of magic, they created abominations to seize power. They tainted the blood of Odin's creations and used them to become the gods of man."

"So, you're saying that Odin was real but other gods were just goblins pretending to be gods?" Jeremy stared incredulously at Erwin.

"That is an entirely different topic. And a matter of debate," Erwin said.

Jeremy frowned. "Ok. So, what happened with the goblins?"

"Mosquitoes!" Erwin said menacingly.

Mercurio laughed.

"What?" Jeremy said.

"Mosquitoes," Erwin repeated. "A dark time, this was for the keshaphim. We—"

"Keshaphim?" Jeremy asked. He heard them use this word several times over the past few weeks. They had used it often when they referred to themselves, but he didn't exactly know what it meant.

"Yes, those whose existence is based on magical energy. Keshaphim are those whose flesh is powered by magic. And this allows us to manipulate the magical energy that is around us. See, you are not keshaphim. Your flesh is powered by electrical energy. You cannot manipulate magic."

Mercurio raised an eyebrow and looked at Jeremy, smiling. "You'd be surprised."

Erwin looked at Mercurio, eyebrows furrowed, and head cocked. "What? He is…" Erwin trailed off, unable to finish his sentence.

"Indeed," Mercurio said.

Erwin cocked his head back and sighed, giving Mercurio another incredulous stare.

"What are you guys saying but not saying?" Jeremy asked, looking back and forth at them.

They ignored Jeremy.

"To what degree?" Erwin asked.

"The highest I've ever seen. It is quite remarkable," Mercurio said.

"Come on guys, what are you talking about?" Jeremy pleaded.

Erwin shook his head and then glanced back over to Jeremy. "Forgive me, Gift Giver. I had no idea."

"No idea what?"

"No idea that you are gifted! You are a true *a'shaf*! Do you descend from the Basque?"

"Um, What? Someone just tell what you guys are talking about."

Erwin turned to Mercurio again. "He doesn't know?"

Mercurio shook his head.

"Rare are you among your own kind. To wield magic at your whim has only been a gift possessed by a handful of humans. To not know you can do this, how can that be?"

"It is indeed rare. Your gift only seems to work around children," Mercurio said.

"Only around children?" Erwin's face puckered, sending his brow to the brim of his hat.

"What do you mean?" Jeremy said.

"Your desire to help and teach children is so strong that you unconsciously command the surrounding magic to draw children to you."

"So, you're saying the reason children are always flocking around me is because I'm using magic to control them?"

"Control is not really the word I would use to describe what you do. All beings are surrounded by magic, and each being resonates at a specific and unique frequency. You, Jeremy, are able to unconsciously manipulate your frequency and affect the surrounding magic. When you see a child, you feel strong emotion towards them. You want to help them and your aura, what we call the resonant frequency around you, uses magic to interact with the aura of children. Your aura mingles with theirs and it attunes it to a frequency of joy and wonder. The children are awestruck. They see, in their hearts, a greatness... a wonder... and they want to be around you."

Erwin stared wide eyed at Jeremy. "Fascinating."

"Indeed," Mercurio replied. "I've not seen anything like it before."

"Wait, what about Nikolaos? Wasn't he like me?" Jeremy asked.

"No. He was not," Mercurio said. "He loved children, but he didn't draw them to himself like you do. Children were drawn to him because he went to them. He dearly loved children, but he was not like you."

Jeremy looked at Mercurio with disbelief. *How could this be?* When one question was answered, more popped up. *Now that I know I am using magic, can I learn to harness it? Can I do more with it?* He placed his bowl down and stood up.

"Can you teach me how to use magic?"

Mercurio stood, meeting Jeremy and placing his hand on his arm. "I'm afraid it doesn't quite work like that. Magic is not used, it is manipulated. What you do is at a subconscious level. I wouldn't even know where to begin to teach you, or if it was even possible to do more than you already do."

Jeremy looked to Erwin.

"I too am not an expert on all things magical. I'm a chronicler, and my magic is limited to truth and understanding."

"Huh?" Jeremy cocked his head and raised an eyebrow at Erwin. "How can there be anything magical about truth and understanding?"

"Ah, good questions you ask. In your own history, you have a saying, 'In war, the first casualty is truth.' Never a more profound statement that transcends even war. How does one know the truth when two sides see things differently? You see, I, as a chronicler, have a responsibility to record what is true… the absolute truth, not the interpreted truth. I can ask you, Jeremy, what you first experienced when you came to Sayalla. And you can tell me what you remember, and how you think you felt. And you can omit feelings to avoid embarrassment or say phrases to make yourself appear to be more than you are. If I recorded what you said, there could be ambiguity as to the truth. But, if I studied your aura and watched it shift, I could discern your true feelings. If I asked the trees what they observed or the shoes upon your feet what it is they experienced, I would get an unbiased truth, for things of their nature never lie."

Jeremy tilted his glasses, furrowed his brow, and looked over the rim at the gnome. "So, you're saying that you can talk to things and they talk back to you?"

"I talk, and I listen."

"You can talk to my sneakers?"

"I manipulate the magic around an object using words in the form of a question. And then I can see what that object experienced. Sometimes I will also touch an object to see what it has experienced."

"Oh. I see." Jeremy said, sitting back down. "I've heard of something like that before. It's called psycho… psy… something or other. I can't remember."

"I believe the word you are searching for is psychometry," Erwin said. "However, that is a human term. Some humans claim to speak with the inanimate or non-sentient. I've never met a human who could. What I have seen is humans with impressive skills of observation pretend to use magic to commune with plants or objects; going to great lengths of dramatics to falsely give the impression of knowing the truth. You see, it goes back to what I said earlier. Truth, as is beauty, is in the beholder's eye. Furthermore, as we speak I can see your aura shift and I know whether or not you're lying, or uncomfortable, or embarrassed, or excited. Of course, I'm not an expert on reading human auras, but I have several tomes to consult as I chronicle our conversations."

Jeremy shifted uncomfortably.

"As I record your journey, Gift Giver, it will be absolute. Your fear, your dishonesty, your insecurities, and your strengths will all be captured, and the world will know the truth of Jeremy Goodson's journey to become the Gift Giver."

Jeremy swallowed. *How disturbing! How intrusive!*

"Of course, there is always room for some author's notes where I can share my opinion."

CHAPTER 36

WELCOME TO NEW YORK

"An atrocity against our people has been committed. Kafziel iyl Chaggai and Roni iyl Chaggai have taken the daughters of the Adamu and now a half-breed grows in the womb of the Adamu females. The elders are unable to explain how this was possible without blessing or magic. Elder Sachar iyl Chaggai has ordered that the elves responsible for this be brought before the council."

~ From *The Annals of the Adamu* by T'siyba Iyl Chaggai, Circa 3,822 B.C.

Ellesmere paced back and forth. *Samyaza has gotten to me too! First Mercurio! Now me!* She growled. *I can't do this.*

Ezzy hefted the loaded backpack over her shoulder. "Are we ready to go?" Her voice quivered with nervous enthusiasm.

Ellesmere looked up at the girl. She stood there, beaming, dressed in a new outfit made for her *rishonam assa*. The tailor had done a fine job on the cloak; an icy light blue with white and gold trim that matched the trim of her white tunic. Having it made wasn't a hard sell to the council. Ellesmere needed a break to digest all that happened, and she wanted to travel outside the Veil to do so. In their minds it wasn't so much a *rishonam assa* for Ezzy, but a much-needed break for Ellesmere. Everyone knew that wherever Ellesmere went for the past fifty years, the *yilchaga* went too.

She smiled at Ezzy. She couldn't cancel now. The child's aura was practically saturated with red and orange. The thought of disappointing her caused Ellesmere's heart to ache. She loved this child as her own. It saddened her to see how others treated Ezzy. They walked by her as if she didn't exist. They only spoke with her when they needed to speak with Ellesmere. It was a terrible practice of her people, but Ellesmere hadn't been able to do anything about it. She tried once and the council wouldn't even listen. Just as they didn't listen to Mercurio. Just like *she* didn't listen to Mercurio.

Ellesmere sighed and widened her smile for Ezzy. "Child, we are indeed ready. Our first stop will be New York. I want you to try this food they have, called pizza."

"I know what pizza is," Ezzy smirked.

"Ah, Little Heart. It is one thing to read about pizza in your books and artifices. It is another to eat pizza anywhere in the world. But, one does not truly know pizza until she has eaten pizza in New York City. The humans rave about it. I had it several years before you were born. It is most delicious."

"Well, since you put it like that, let's go and have pizza," Ezzy said, wafting her arm toward the door.

"Off we go," Ellesmere said, nodding. She walked to the door and grabbed her hat and walking staff.

They walked across the path from Ellesmere's house to the gatehouse where they were greeted by Hamjil, one of Ellesmere's guardians. He too was dressed in travel gear; green boots, gray trousers, and a green tunic covered by a brown vest. He wore his travel sack under his green and gold Veil cloak; the hilt of his sword peeking from behind the cloak. As Ellesmere approached, Hamjil bowed his head and placed his hands on his belt.

"Elder, I look forward to accompanying you," Hamjil said.

"Good," Ellesmere said. "Tell me, have you ever had pizza?" She continued her walk toward the gatehouse.

Hamjil opened the door. "No, Elder. I have not had the pleasure."

Ellesmere and Ezzy entered the gatehouse. Hamjil followed.

ELLESMERE STEPPED THROUGH THE SHIMMERING, golden Veil into the lower level of the Argosy Bookstore.

"Greetings, traveler, and welcome to..." Bartleby's eyes grew wide as he focused on Ellesmere.

She caught his quick glance at the side of her head where her ear had once been. Her hair covered the wound, but everyone knew it was there.

"Um... Elder Ellesmere. I wasn't expecting you. Um..." His eyes shifted to Hamjil, who had stepped through before Ellesmere. He raised his eyebrow in disapproval and then turned back to Ellesmere.

"Stop fussing, gatekeeper. I'm no different from anyone else who comes through this gatehouse."

"Um, yes... um welcome to..."

Ezzy stepped in from the Veil.

Bartleby did a double take as he watched her walk in.

"My, um, I wasn't expecting so many of you. Um, welcome to New York. But I should have known—

"Thank you, gatekeeper. I don't travel through the Veil very often; in fact it's been about sixty years since I've been here. There was another gatekeeper here at that time."

"Oh yes. That was Gordon. He hasn't worked here in twenty years."

"And you are?"

"Oh, forgive me, Elder. I'm Bartleby Gasto, Artificer, Veil Wright of the First Order, an Alfargnym of Unterbaum. Welcome to New York."

Ellesmere sighed. "You've already welcomed us. But thank you. We'll be eating here this evening. We'd like a pepperoni pizza and enough root beer for all of us, including yourself. When you return, we'd like you to join us. I have some questions for you regarding the human you let through this gatehouse."

Bartleby's eyes went wide again as he swallowed nervously.

"Elder, I didn't know…"

"Gatekeeper. I'd rather not stand here all evening. Please take us to the dining room and then bring us the pizza and root beer."

Bartleby stiffened and turned around. "This way, please."

Halfway up the stairs, the gatekeeper stopped and turned to her. "Um, Elder. Will you be needing lodging here tonight?"

"No. We'll eat, explore the city for a bit, and then head to another gatehouse. Though, while you're out getting the pizza, I will need a private communication room."

"As you wish. I'll have supper delivered from Patsy's Pizzeria."

Ellesmere, Ezzy, and Hamjil followed Bartleby up a flight of stairs, through a door, and into a vestibule containing three other doors. The walls and doors were all wooden and resembled the architecture of Sayalla. A chandelier with eight curved arms, each displaying a bird balancing an orb light lit the room. It was just as Ellesmere remembered.

Ezzy looked around but seemed unimpressed.

"Elder," Bartleby said, pointing to the door on the left. "Through that door. The communication room will be the first room on the right. No one else is staying here at this time, so you will have all the privacy you need."

"Thank you," Ellesmere nodded.

Bartleby led them through the door on the right. They entered a large hall, lit by two chandeliers, identical to the one in the vestibule. The walls, covered with wood paneling made to resemble the Great Halls of Sayalla, had additional orb light sconces on the walls. The room was bright despite being window-less and hundreds of feet below ground.

Seven round tables, each with six chairs, sat in the center of the room. Bartleby walked over to the first table and pulled out a chair for Ellesmere.

She sat and pointed to the chair next to her for Ezzy to sit down.

Ezzy pulled off her pack and laid it on the floor beside her chair.

"I'll be back in less than sixty minutes. Hopefully sooner," Bartleby said, pulling out a cell phone from the small pouch on his waist. His thumbs danced across the screen and he exited without looking where he was going.

Hamjil removed his pack and sat across from Ellesmere.

"What is this place?" Ezzy asked.

"The Argosy Dining Hall," Ellesmere said.

"I can see that it's a dining hall. But why here? And where is here?"

"Many of the gatehouses in the larger human cities have amenities to enhance our visits. Rather than waiting for a place to close or taking food without asking—"

"You mean stealing food," Ezzy said.

"It's traditional to leave something of value in return. So, it's not stealing. It's taking without asking." Ellesmere folded her hands in her lap.

"Semantics," Ezzy said.

"Do you care to know the answer to your question? Or would you prefer to discuss semantics?"

"Please. I would like to know what this place is and where we are exactly."

"As I said, rather than taking without asking, we built these dining halls in several of the gatehouses so that we could enjoy the local cuisine," Ellesmere said.

"I don't understand why we don't just use illusory devices like the alfargnym. Then we could just go to the places ourselves."

"We could. We just don't. Part of *rishonam assa* is the excitement of sneaking around. Part of it is not interfering. And..."

"Not interfering? Immatina, our people have interfered with

humanity before the Veil was even up. What difference would it make if we wore Veil cloaks or Illusory Belts?"

"Child, you have so many questions tonight. But I must excuse myself for a short span. I have other business to tend to before our pizza and root beer arrive."

"Other business?" Ezzy frowned.

"Nothing that concerns you. Hamjil, you will stay here with Ezzy. Feel free to speak with her. She will not rub off on you."

"Immatina!" Ezzy scowled.

"I…" Hamjil's eyes grew wide with discomfort.

"Ezzy, my apologies. I just didn't want it to be awkward while I was gone."

"I… um…" Hamjil stammered.

"Awkward? You didn't want it to be awkward? It's awkward now!" Ezzy said.

"I… um…" Hamjil continued.

"I'm sorry," Ellesmere said getting up and pushing her chair back in. "Please. Just feel free to talk to her."

"Um, I…"

"Don't bother," Ezzy said, reaching into her backpack. "I'll just read while you're gone. You don't need to *pity* me with forced conversation."

"Oh, Ezzy," Ellesmere said, sighing and walking away from the table.

That child! Ellesmere thought. *Hmmm. I can't rightly call her a child anymore. This is her rishonam assa. Yet still, she can be so petulant.* Before exiting, Ellesmere glanced back. Hamjil sat awkwardly, glancing from side to side. Ezzy sulked; her face turned down into a book. But Ellesmere had more pressing matters. The child… Ezzy, would get over it.

Ellesmere went to the communication room. Orb lights, held in sconces on the wood-paneled walls, brightened as she walked in. A mimstone and logbook sat on the table.

Ellesmere paused, sighing. *Just how did Mercurio discover the human?* She knew his name was Jeremy, but something fought within her against calling him by his given name. Would it make him more real? Would she start to feel compassion for him?

She sat down at the desk and flipped through the logbook, looking for Mercurio's name. He'd been here several times over the past six months. Each time he recorded the reason as "scouting". This would be reasonable for someone of the Gray Guard. Normally, it would have been a scout, not the Palgen of the Gray Guard.

Ellesmere traced through the record book, back to February. Mercurio's first entry was listed as a meeting with Wendulf Myrgjol.

Ellesmere placed her fingertips on the surface of the mimstone. The image of an alfargnym appeared. In her mind, she heard a voice.

Wendulf Myrgjol, a Chronicler of the Master Construct, First Order, an alfargnym of Unterbaum. Wendulf works with the Gray Guard. He is stationed at the Museum of Natural History in New York. Wendulf has taken on the human alter-ego of Doctor Barry Melvin, a historian and curator at the museum. He gathers intelligence pertaining to information and/or human contact with enchanted items and/or keshaphim.

"Hmmm," Ellesmere said. *It would make sense for the Gray Guard to work with Wendulf. But why Mercurio? Why not one of his underlings?*

Ellesmere went back to the logbook, this time looking for Wendulf's name. Prior to Mercurio, he met with an elf named Gaviryl, a Gray Guard scout.

Gaviryl must have found something that Mercurio felt needed his attention. *Was that something Jeremy?* There was only one way to find out. She needed to speak with Wendulf.

She glanced at her pocket watch. It was 6:35pm in New York City. She wondered where she might find Wendulf at this hour.

Ellesmere exited the communication room and went back to the dining hall.

She found Ezzy reading and Hamjil pacing back and forth.

Ezzy ignored Ellesmere as she entered and took a seat.

Ellesmere stared at the girl.

Ezzy arched her brow, taking a quick glance at Ellesmere before returning to the book.

"Really, Ezzy? You're not planning on spending the rest of your *rishonam assa* angry with me, are you?"

Ezzy glanced up again, sighed, and then placed her book on the table.

"Really?" Ezzy said. "I don't understand what we're doing here. Why bother with giving me a *rishonam assa* if everyone is still going to treat me differently anyway?"

"You know very well why. We cannot change your lineage any more than I can change mine. What you make of this trip is up to you. I for one am looking forward to all of it. After we have pizza and root beer, I am going to show you one of the strangest places in all of New York. It's called the Museum of Natural History."

CHAPTER 37

BEST LAID PLANS

"Ee'azar was a dedicated Guardian who idolized Mercurio from a young age. When Mercurio recruited him for the Gray Guard, Ee'azar was unaware that he was being trained to become the leader of the new Gift Giver's Guard."

~ From *The Second Gift Giver Chronicles* compiled by Erwin Albowyn, a Chronicler of the Master Construct, Second Order, an alfargnym of Unterbaum

Mercurio observed from afar as Jeremy clumsily swung the staff at Ee'azar and missed for the tenth time. He had worked so hard over the past week to learn to use that staff. But he might as well have been a koth trying to use a bow and arrow.

Mercurio felt Erwin's gaze shift from Jeremy to him. The chronicler walked up from behind and stood beside Mercurio.

"What are you doing?" Erwin said.

Mercurio sensed concern and doubt in his friend's question. He sighed again.

"I'm trying to train a child to kill a goblin," Mercurio said.

"Precisely. This exercise is futile, even for you, my friend. Jeremy Goodson will surely lose his life in Kurgal."

"Did you not hear him? He's willing to die for this."

"And you're willing to let him? Can you live with the death of two Gift Givers?"

That stung. Despite how much time had passed, there wasn't a day that went by that Mercurio didn't think about Nikolaos. He wanted to snap at the chronicler, but he gritted his teeth and held back a harsh rebuttal.

"I've no intention of letting Jeremy die. That's why he's training differently than Nikolaos."

Erwin shook his head. "But he'll never survive Kurgal. He'll die there."

"He's not going to Kurgal," Mercurio said, eyes still on Jeremy.

Erwin furrowed his eyebrows and looked up at Mercurio. "I've always liked you, Mercurio. You're one of the few elves I know so well that I know so little about. But this," Erwin said, pointing to Jeremy, "is a fool's errand. Whether or not you like it, when you make a decision to do something, it affects everyone and everything around you. You're trying to minimize the chaos by keeping the plan to yourself. The more people you tell your plan to, the number of probable outcomes increases because the actions of each person involved affects everyone and everything around them."

"You're thinking too hard, Erwin."

"On the contrary. I can't imagine how hard you've been thinking to pull this off without sharing it with anyone, not even your own team. You've planned this whole thing. You knew how Ellesmere would respond. You knew the only way to make this happen was to make Jeremy known to as many people as possible. Get everyone talking about it. Odin's Fury! Did you know I'd be involved?"

"I knew they'd send a chronicler. I couldn't be sure they'd send you."

"Oh, Mercurio," Erwin said, shaking his head. "How long have you been planning this?"

Mercurio pursed his lips and sighed. "About a century. I've been looking for someone like Nikolaos for a long time. I've searched the streets of dozens of cities, looking... studying; coming close a few times. I thought I found a good prospect in Denmark, but he had a family, and it would've been too complicated. He went on to create Lego, so it was a good thing I didn't recruit him. There were a few others, but for one reason or another, it just didn't seem right. A decade ago, I had the idea to use the Gray Guard to help me in my search."

"Forgive my bumptiousness, but you've got a crack in your braincase! I can't believe you've been plotting all this for so long! You used the Gray Guard as your own personal intelligence service!"

"Erwin, it's simple really. The world needs hope. And the Gift Giver gave that. His memory still brings hope to this very day. Imagine what a living Gift Giver would do."

"If you've no intention of bringing Jeremy to Kurgal, then why all this training?" Erwin threw his hands into the air and thrust them towards Eginoff's house. "Just go and get the Ring of Nicholas and let's be on with this."

"I already told you. First, Jeremy has to want this. Second, I'll not make the same mistake as I did before. The Gift Giver needs to know how to defend himself."

"So, now what?"

"Wyllt will stop at nothing to find him. And by now I'm sure Borahsh knows about Jeremy. I imagine they're using all their available resources to find him. So, this is what I need your assistance in."

Erwin cocked his head and raised an eyebrow, looking up at Mercurio.

Mercurio kept his eyes on Jeremy but smiled, knowing that he had piqued Erwin's interest.

Jeremy swung his staff at Ee'azar. The elf dodged, grabbed the tip of the staff and used his body weight to pull the staff forward and kick Jeremy in the stomach. He jerked from the blow and fell to the ground.

"You're incorrigible, Mercurio," Erwin said.

"I know," Mercurio sighed. "I've put a lot of thought into this. It hasn't been a perfect plan. I wasn't counting on Thaddaios Wyllt's involvement." He watched Jeremy pick himself and the staff up. He immediately took his battle stance and faced Ee'azar once again.

"Just how do I 'fit in' to your plan?"

"If I tell him that he's not going with me to Kurgal, he'll argue with me the whole time."

Jeremy whirled around with his staff and once again missed hitting Ee'azar. The guardian slipped his leg under Jeremy's leg, tripping him and sending him to the ground again.

"I think it would be far better if we departed discreetly. We'll leave after breakfast tomorrow. You'll take Jeremy for a walk to the edge of the Veil under the pretense of interviewing him. The Gift Giver's Guard will take the sledge and leave. You should be far enough away where the incantation won't affect you. But once you get back to the campsite and Jeremy sees us gone, you'll need to explain to him why we left."

"My intuition tells me you're trying to avoid confrontation with Jeremy. Well and done, I know you prefer your confrontation with charge orbs and swords, rather than with words. I'll take care of Jeremy while you're gone."

"Thank you."

"How many days will you need?"

"Give us three."

"And," Erwin said, clearing his throat nervously, "if you should not return, what then?"

"Then you'll be responsible for taking care of Jeremy and his parents. The guardians at his parents' house will stay there until I contact them. Jar'iyu has been keeping them updated on things. I'll have Jar'iyu tell you the incantation to unlock his laptop and the information on how to contact the other guardians."

"Very well."

"And you'll figure out what to do with them after that, right?" Mercurio said.

"Well, I can't use your name anymore. You've reached the extent of your reputation. Even if you pull this off, it's quite likely that you'll be exiled. I'll have to appeal to my clan lord first. Nevertheless, just be sure to return safely. I don't want to imagine what will happen if you don't." Erwin shuddered and grimaced.

"Good. It's all settled. I'll let the other guardians know and we'll depart after breakfast tomorrow."

Erwin placed his hand on Mercurio's shoulder. "May the speed of Thor, the wisdom of Odin, and the cunning of Loki be upon you, my friend."

Mercurio smiled and sighed. *And may Samyaza not take me.*

CHAPTER 38
A NIGHT AT THE MUSEUM

"The serpents of old returned. From their earthen dens they awoke. We saw them and in our hearts we knew them, but in our minds they had been forgotten. The sight of the winged serpents brought us to our knees and the bitter cold of unknown fear caused us to wail. We knew not why, we only knew that we should. That which we called death had now taken form."

~ From the *Elven Annals of Discord*, Circa 7,778 B.C.

Ezzy stared up at the giant mammoth skeleton, shaking her head in disbelief. "Immatina, have you ever seen one of these things in real life?"

Ellesmere tsked. "Little Heart, you know very well I haven't. My age isn't a secret to you, and your knowledge, I'm sure, is formidable where natural history is concerned."

Ezzy laughed. "It's beautiful. This whole building is beautiful!" Ezzy whirled around. Her cloak fanned out as she completed the twirl and ran across to the mastodon skeleton.

Ellesmere, Hamjil, and Wendulf all watched the excited girl.

Ellesmere smiled, pleased that Ezzy was having such a delightful time.

"Well," Wendulf said, "if you're enjoying this, wait until you see the ninety-four-foot blue whale in the Hall of Ocean Life. It's not as impressive as a leviathan, but if you've never seen one of them, you'll love the blue whale."

"Yes!" Ezzy said. "I can't wait to see it. But first, I need to know more about this mastodon." She leaned forward, reading the plaque in front of the skeleton.

"Take your time, Ezzy. We have the place to ourselves." Ellesmere said. She paused for a moment, watching the girl dart toward another plaque.

"Wendulf, I'm also here on council affairs. I'm sure word has gotten to you regarding the human that pierced the Veil."

The alfargnym smiled a broad, uneasy grin. His eyes darted up toward his brimless, purple, conical hat. "Ah," he said, folding his hands together and licking his lips. "Yes. I do know a bit about that."

"Tell me. Why is it that Mercurio, the *Palgen* of the Gray Guard, visited you about this?"

"Elder, I presumed you knew." Wendulf waved his hands around awkwardly and then folded them at his chest. "It's a most fascinating account. One I would scarce believe if I hadn't been the one to see it with my own eyes."

The chronicler brought his folded hands to his mouth and nibbled on his thumb before continuing. "It was January 17th of this year. Normally, I'd be about my job cataloging new items and searching the shared museum databases for anything out of the ordinary. But I was hungry, and I just had a hankering for a dirty water dog. As Odin would have it, I didn't exit from the employee entrance because I was delivering some paperwork upstairs. And as I'm leaving the museum, I noticed a group of children being led by this human adult. That's not so unusual. We have children visit the museum every day; large groups of them on a weekly basis. But there was something very unusual about this man. His aura was drawing the children to him. And not only the group of children he was with, but others in the museum. They were more interested in this man than they were the *Tyrannosaurus rex* skeleton! This piqued my curiosity, so I went up to him and recorded his name and the group he was with. When I reported it to Gaviryl, my usual contact in the Gray Guard, he investigated. Two weeks later I'm visited by the Palgen of the Gray Guard himself! He asks me to tell him everything about what I saw. He wanted aura colors, names, magic flow patterns. We must have spent hours going over everything."

"And that's it? Did he tell you why he was interested in this human?"

"Forgive me for saying, Elder, but I think it was rather obvious. It's not very common that you find such an anomaly."

"Yes, I'm aware of that. But why Mercurio? Why not one of the other Gray Guard?"

Ellesmere knew the answer. She just wanted to see if Mercurio had told anyone else what he was up to.

"He didn't say," Wendulf shrugged. "And I didn't insist."

"This is why we're here?" Ezzy interrupted.

Ellesmere hadn't noticed her approach. But she could hear the hurt in her voice.

"This is my *rishonam assa*? You're trying to find Mercurio? And I'm just an excuse—"

"Ezzy, I'm quite capable of doing two things at once. You—"

"Why didn't you just tell me? I would've been fine with it. But you should have—"

"Little Heart, I'm an Elder of the Elven Council. You know how busy I am. And this business with Mercurio is Elder Council business. It doesn't concern you. Your *rishonam assa* is what should concern you. Go and enjoy these exhibits. We'll be leaving soon."

Ezzy took a deep breath and glared at Ellesmere before forcefully exhaling and turning around. She stomped her foot and walked across the room.

Ellesmere sighed and turned her attention back to Wendulf. "Is there anymore you can tell me about this human?"

"Only that I've never seen so many children react so adoringly toward one man. If it weren't for the parents of the other children paying such close attention, they would've started following along with his group."

"You did well to report this, Wendulf. Thank you," Ellesmere said. She paused and looked at Ezzy again. The girl was squatting, looking at a fossilized mammoth tooth encased in epoxy resin. She seemed to beam with curiosity, her aura radiating between bands of pink and orange, with a slight band of red around the inner-most band. Ezzy was still angry with her.

THEY EXPLORED the museum for another two hours before Ellesmere announced they needed to go. They made their way back to the Argosy through the ever-buzzing nightlife of New York City. Cloaked in a shroud of magic, Ezzy marveled at each passerby.

Ellesmere couldn't help but think about what to do next. She knew where Jeremy and Mercurio were, but she wasn't ready to confront them yet. She couldn't understand why Mercurio hadn't come to the council before going through all the trouble of smuggling him through the Veil. Surely, he knew that wouldn't go well. He had to have known how she would react. She pondered that for a second. *He did know! That's why he did it. This is all part of his plan. So why did they go through Zahl's Gate?* She couldn't think of any reason.

When they arrived at the Argosy Bookstore, Bartleby greeted them at the door.

"Welcome back. Did you have a good time?" The alfargnym said.

Ellesmere glanced at Ezzy, waiting for her to speak. She nodded, prodding her to answer.

"Yes," Ezzy said reluctantly. She wasn't used to having idle conversation with anyone but Ellesmere. "It was... beyond my expectations. I've seen pictures in books and on the internet and even in mimstones, but this was incredible."

Bartleby nodded. "New York City has a magic of its own. What was your favorite part?"

Ezzy looked at Ellesmere out of the corner of her eye. She waited for another encouraging nod and Ellesmere gave it to her. Alfargnym didn't place the same stigma on *yilchaga* as elves. There weren't any alfargnym in Orindin, so this was a rare treat for her.

"The people!" Ezzy said. "They're all so different and colorful. Their clothes and their skin and their hair. And they're all so… so… different!" She smiled.

"They are," he said. "You wouldn't believe the kinds that come into this store and the things they are interested in. It is amazing."

Ezzy shook her head, still smiling.

Ellesmere permitted herself to smile at Ezzy and Bartleby. It was nice to see the girl interacting with someone else. "It's getting late," She interrupted. "I think we'll stay here for the night, after all. Please show us to our rooms and then I would have a word with you in the Communication Room."

They made their way down to the lower levels of the Argosy. Another alfargnym walked out from the door leading to the guest rooms. When he saw Ellesmere, he stood to the side and leaned forward with his head bowed.

"Elder, welcome to New York," he said.

"Thank you," Ellesmere said.

"I am Blicger Sigrund, Artificer, Veil Wright of the Second Order, an Alfargnym of Unterbaum. And I am at your service."

"A pleasure to meet you. Thank you for maintaining this gate-house so well. You and Bartleby have an exemplary station."

The two alfargnym smiled.

"As soon as Bartleby shows us to our rooms, I would like to meet with the two of you in the Communication Room."

"Well and done," Blicger said, opening the door for them to enter the hall.

Bartleby showed Ellesmere to their room, and Hamjil to his.

"Ezzy, I will return shortly. Try to go to sleep."

Ezzy smiled. "Immatina?"

Ellesmere stopped in the doorway and turned back to the girl.

"I'm sorry," Ezzy said. Her expression and the light green of her aura showed her sincerity. "Thank you for bringing me here."

Ellesmere smiled at her. "You're welcome, Little Heart. Now get some sleep."

She shut the door and walked down the hall to the Communication Room.

Blicger and Bartleby stood against the back wall, hands clasped at their stomachs.

"How may we help you, Elder?" Bartleby said.

Ellesmere sat at the table and turned the chair toward the alfargnym.

"Tell me, why would anyone wish to go to Zahl's Gate?"

The alfargnym looked at one another, puzzled.

Bartleby shrugged. "I'm not sure. There's nothing there anymore."

"Used to be a Dark Elf stronghold," Blicger said. "But that's been long gone."

Bartleby shook his head in agreement. "The only reason there's a Veilpoint there is because the elders at the time expected Colorado to grow from there. With the growing population of Native Americans there, they figured we'd need easy access to observe them. But the rest, is as they say, history. The humans didn't expand there as much as expected. So we just left the Veilpoint over the old Saraph stronghold, just so they wouldn't find it."

"All that I could have gleaned from a mimstone," Ellesmere said.

Bartleby shrugged. "It's just the Veilpoint, the gatehouse, and wilderness. There's nothing more there. I'm not sure who the gatekeeper there is. I could find out for you."

"No. I can do that myself," Ellesmere said, nodding to the

mimstone on the desk. She pondered the information. *Nothing there. Why would Mercurio go there?*

"You're sure there is nothing more than the Veilpoint and the gatehouse? What of the stronghold?"

"Most of it was destroyed and filled in. The base was used to make the Veil chamber. I assure you, it isn't of any interest or significance."

"Must be the gatekeeper," Ellesmere said aloud to herself as she reached for the mimstone. When she touched the stone, the information appeared instantly in her mind.

Eginoff Vragin, Artificer, Veil Wright of the Fourth Order. Gatekeeper of Zahl's Gate in the human territory of Colorado.

Ellesmere sifted through the information on Eginoff and Zahl's Gate, finding nothing of any note or importance. She sat back in the chair and pondered it all. She'd forgotten about the two alfargnym standing there until one of them coughed. Ellesmere took a deep breath and stood up.

"Gatekeepers, thank you for your time. I'm going to sleep now. Do you have any recommendations for breakfast?"

"You can't go wrong with some bagels and *schmear*." Blicger said.

The alfargnym spoke to her in Elvish. But that was a word she'd never heard.

"*Schmear?*" Ellesmere said. "Is that an English word?"

"It's a Yiddish colloquial word for a type of spreadable cheese, popular here in the city. It's derived from cows' milk. Sometimes it's called cream cheese. It's very good. I like mine on an onion bagel with lox," Bartleby said.

"Lox?" Ellesmere said, raising an eyebrow.

"Um, another Yiddish word. It's just smoked salmon," Bartleby said.

"I like a good everything bagel with veggie schmear." Blicger said.

"Very well," Ellesmere said, opening the door. "Bring us bagels and *schmear* for breakfast. But none of that coffee New Yorkers are fond of. I shudder what it might do to Ezzy."

"Well and done. We'll bring in an assortment of bagels and schmear from Ess-a-Bagel. You'll enjoy it, you will," Blicger said.

"Thank you." Ellesmere exited and walked to her room, pondering her next move.

<h1 style="text-align:center">CHAPTER 39
NO HERO
TO BE FOUND</h1>

"The Second Gift Giver, despite his intelligence, passion, and kindness possessed a naivete that blinded him to the true intentions of others. It was his good fortune that he had someone with the truth-seeing abilities that I possess."

~ From *The Second Gift Giver Chronicles* compiled by Erwin Albowyn, a Chronicler of the Master Construct, Second Order, an alfargnym of Unterbaum

"I can't believe you! All of you! All this training, for nothing! How—"

"Jeremy, it's for the better," Erwin said.

It's best this way. You are safer, Birch said.

Jeremy swung around and looked menacingly at Birch. "You too?" He yelled. "Didn't any of you hear me? Didn't you hear what I said when I told you that I had to do this? I had to be the one to reclaim Nicholas' ring. You plant these ideas in my head, making me think I could be something… someone who… who…" He wanted to say a *hero*. A real-life hero. A way of appeasing the guilt he felt over his sister's death. But his anger gave way to that guilt and clouded his thinking. Jeremy threw his staff, and it made a loud cracking echo as it hit the campsite log.

"Jeremy!" Erwin snapped, now clenching his own fists. "There is a very strong possibility that you would die in Kurgal. And the guardians may have died trying to protect you. What difference does it make who reclaims the ring? You'll possess it, nonetheless. And with its power you'll be far more protected than you'd be without it."

Jeremy turned away from Erwin. The gnome was right. How could he have been so stupid as to think that he could've survived a hoard of goblins? He wasn't a warrior! He was a wannabe, just as he had been all his life. But he wanted so much to be the hero. And, in his pride, he wanted Erwin's chronicles to tell of the fat kid from Yonkers who became a warrior and reclaimed the Ring of Nicholas. *What an idiot!* He smacked himself on his forehead.

"You don't understand," Jeremy sighed. "I need some time to think. Just leave me alone for a little while." Jeremy walked off, numb and confused. He knew that he had no right to be angry. And he didn't know whether he was angrier at Mercurio and Erwin or himself. Mercurio would surely get the ring, and then they'd be back on track. But he still felt angry and realized that there was another emotion in play. He felt betrayed. Mercurio, once again, had filled his head with glory and grandeur and once again, Jeremy was left alone.

He walked further into the woods with his thoughts.

AFTER A FEW HOURS of walking in circles, Jeremy walked back to the campsite and sat on the log beside the campfire tended by Birch.

It is good to see you again, Gift Giver. Birch said.

"I'm sorry I was angry before," Jeremy said, leaning down and plucking a long blade of grass that grew beside the log.

I've already forgiven your outburst. Birch stirred the freshly made stew.

"Where's Erwin and Grath?" Jeremy asked.

Erwin resides in his tent and Grath followed you. He's not too far behind.

"Followed me? I didn't even hear him." Jeremy was surprised at first, but he was more concerned about Mercurio's plan. "So, what's Mercurio's plan to get the ring?"

They will sneak into Kurgal, find Nicholas' ring, and then bring it to you.

"That simple, eh?" Jeremy said, shaking his head.

It will not be simple, Gift Giver. The ring is most likely in the throne room of Borahsh, the Sar of Goblins.

"Well how long will it take? And what are we supposed to do in the meantime?"

"Three days," Erwin said emerging from his tent, only twenty feet from the campfire, "Mercurio wishes for us to wait three days for them to return."

"What if Mercurio doesn't return?"

Erwin paled and looked down before answering. "You and your parents will have no choice but to go to Orindin so that you can be protected from Wyllt."

Jeremy smirked and let out a disgusted *hmph.* "So that's what you guys do? Orindin is just a refuge for wayward humans?"

"Only once, Jeremy. But the facts remain the same. You and your parents won't be safe on your side of the Veil," Erwin said somberly.

Jeremy remembered what it was like for Nicholas in Orindin. How bad could that be? Life in an Elven town? Perhaps he could even start a school there or something. He knew his Dad would enjoy working with the Elven crafters. But the realization of what could have been was too powerful. And the thought of Mercurio and the others dying at the hands of the goblins was not at all settling.

"And what about Mercurio and Ee'azar and the other Guardians?"

Erwin stood silently somber for a moment. Jeremy could tell

that Erwin knew the answer. The gnome was trying to spare Jeremy.

"If they don't return… it means they're dead."

Stunned silence filled the forest as if everything collectively held a breath at Erwin's statement.

"I shudder to think of what would happen to them if they were unsuccessful," Erwin said. "Borahsh would see to it they suffered many long days. And their blood would be siphoned for experimentation." The gnome shook with disgust.

"Experimentation?"

"Sadly. The goblins have no boundaries. Their sages are notorious for using keshaphim in all sorts of experiments. The ancestors of our friends, Birch and Grath, are products of their earlier experimentation. Who knows what they would do with the technology they have now!"

"And the elders would just leave them there? No rescue team?"

"Oh no, I'm afraid not. They'd never sanction a rescue for someone who intentionally went against their wishes. Mercurio, sadly, even if he survives will likely be exiled."

"They'd just let him and the others die?"

"Jeremy, there are laws. Laws that have been broken. And you know as well as I do, there are punishments for lawbreakers. Among the elves, the most common is exile… life outside the Veil with no option to ever return."

Jeremy glowered at Erwin as if this was all his fault. He knew it wasn't, but these rules, laws, and restrictions they all had were so frustrating. Black and white and no room for gray. No discussions, they just had to accept it or leave. Jeremy sighed and shifted his gaze to the fraying grass blade he'd been fiddling with.

"Jeremy, I think it's best if we just wait and see what happens. Mercurio asked for three days. We should give him that. We can pass the time by working on your chronicle together," Erwin said.

CHAPTER 40

A LESSON IN DEFEAT

Dweorg society can be summed up with the lore of innangard and utangard. All that is dweorg, is innangard. Innangard can also be used to mean *within the mountain.* The term utangard is used to refer to anything not dweorg… *anything out of the mountain.*

~ From *The Veiled Happenlore of the Master Construct* compiled by Fulbert Gisilfrid, a Chronicler of the Master Construct, Third Order, an alfargnym of Unterbaum.

Masaru had to ditch the motorcycle a week ago and hike from the buried ruins of Badtibirra to… to where? Turtak still hadn't told him where he was going. But the time he spent in the wilderness, learning to survive off the land, unlocked something in Masaru. His true nature had been shackled to a civilization that was not his own. He was free and Masaru understood what he truly was. He was a warrior. But, there were things he missed. A soft bed. Bread. And believe it or not, the news. After being away for three weeks now, he was curious to know what was going on in the world.

Masaru hadn't seen another soul for eight days. The occasional rabbit, birds, even a bear, but not one person. The forest he'd been hiking through seemed endless until today. At the edge of the forest, Masaru saw a small town about a hundred and fifty meters from the forest's edge. Tall trees surrounded it on all sides, hidden away from the rest of the world. Its walls were tall and made from strips of overlapping metal, like a steel roof, but painted white. A taller, barbed-wire fence surrounded the inside walls and towers. This town was well fortified.

"Tonight, Masaru," Turtak said. "I will not be with you. Men will come from within those walls. When darkness comes, your final lesson will begin. You must not let any man leave here."

Masaru looked again toward the town. He thought he saw movement on one tower. He pulled a pair of binoculars from his pack and focused on the left tower.

A guard wearing blue and gray urban camo and carrying an assault rifle paced from the front of the tower.

"What is this place?" Masaru asked.

"A prison. It houses some of this land's most dangerous criminals."

"Is someone planning a break? You want me to stop them?"

"I want you to stop the men as they try to escape. You will have five hours to prepare. There will be several explosions. Several will come from outside the walls."

"Shouldn't we try to stop the explosions?"

"No. You are to stop the men who escape. Spend your time now scouting. Determine your vantage point."

As always, Masaru did as he was told. He spent the day scouting the area. He found a road that cut through the forest, leading up to the prison. The road too was hidden by tall trees. He climbed a tree and studied the prison from overhead. He counted eight towers along the wall. The outer wall surrounded the entire prison complex. He counted six buildings inside; two larger, three-story buildings separated by smaller buildings of varying size. The inside perimeter contained a large barbed-wire fence. As far as he could tell, there was only one way in and one way out. An outer gate led to an inner alley, fenced on both sides leading up to the inner gate.

Beyond the prison, less than half a kilometer away, he saw several houses. *That must be where the people who work in the prison live.* This place was so far away from anywhere, the workers had to live here as well.

Masaru looked at the entrance to the prison again and decided that this was the best vantage point. He climbed down and continued his reconnaissance before returning to the tree at dusk.

As nightfall came, the temperature dropped and lights came on at each watchtower.

The first explosion rocked the nearby village as a burst of light, and smoke came from its direction. It was followed by a second explosion not far from the first. A third one came from within the prison, followed by a fourth and fifth.

Masaru braced himself in the tree, watching the outer gate just in time to see the sixth and seventh explosions take out the inner and outer gates. Twisted metal rocketed through the air in several directions. A single smoldering chunk landed only centimeters from him.

A flash of light from the road leading to the prison caught Masaru's eye. He snapped his head to look. A flaming truck barreled down the dirt road from the worker housing and crashed into the outer metal fence. Flames engulfed the truck, licking their way towards the opening it had made.

Chaos, Masaru thought. And in the distraction of chaos, evil men would slip by their guards. His eyes were unmoving, focused on the newly opened entrance to the prison. He climbed down from the tree and sprinted towards the entrance; the gate only lit by the flames of the smoldering truck.

The truck exploded. The concussive wave knocked Masaru backwards.

His head spun. His ears rung. He only saw white light. Masaru eased himself up from the ground, teetering from the imbalance in his equilibrium, he almost fell to the ground again.

There was no voice to encourage him. All he could hear was the echoing after-effect of the explosion.

He breathed deeply and blinked. His vision returned. Blurred, hazy images of flickering light and the outline of the prison's white walls came into focus.

Sounds penetrated the echoing in his ears: yelling and screaming. It was indistinct among the chaos. The rat-a-tat of gunfire added to the discord. Hazy images of men approached the exit, their forms silhouetted by the flickering fires. This was it.

Masaru breathed in again and withdrew his katana. The blade shimmered, the flickering firelight dancing along its finely polished steel edge. He set himself in battle stance, six meters away from the entrance.

The image of four men, all dressed in black, became clear as they ran to escape. They held makeshift clubs. Behind them, the silhouettes of more men. The one in front held his hand back to stop the other three.

The leader, a beefy man with short black hair, stared at Masaru. He clenched his jaw and his brow drew together.

"We are leaving!" The man shouted in Russian. He turned to the left, heading toward the worker housing. The three men behind him followed.

Masaru leapt forward, slicing into the prisoner closest to him, connecting with the flesh and bone of the man's shoulder, then bringing the sword out, around and down to strike the man's leg.

The prisoner screamed in agony.

The other prisoners faced Masaru, brandishing their makeshift clubs.

One prisoner cursed at him.

Masaru answered with a swift strike at the man.

The prisoner raised his metal pipe and blocked the blade.

The other two men closed in on Masaru.

Masaru turned, dodging a blow from a wooden plank on the left and bending forward to evade another from the man on the right. He stepped away from the three, resetting his stance to the rear of the prisoner on the left.

The prisoner spun around, deflecting another swipe of Masaru's sword. The other stepped towards Masaru, trying to flank him on the right while his comrade with the wooden plank tried to flank him on the left.

Masaru lunged and swiped at the three, each man deflecting his blade and tightening the flank they made around him.

Masaru spun his sword around, crouching. The blade met one of the prisoner's legs.

The man stepped forward. The part of his leg from the knee down stayed in place and he toppled to the ground.

Masaru kicked at the falling man, giving himself some distance. He then stepped backward.

More men appeared around him.

"What is this?" One man yelled.

Another replied with a curse.

"Wait," another man said.

Masaru couldn't tell where the voice came from. More men surrounded him; ten armed with planks of wood, metal pipes, and legs from broken furniture.

A prisoner made his way forward, pushing himself beyond the perimeter of the men who circled around Masaru. The newcomer laughed.

"This is the man from the letter!" The man's grizzled voice sounded as if he was shocked.

Letter? Masaru cocked his head back, putting most of his focus on this man, while still using his skills to make sure no one attacked him from the side or rear.

"We can't kill him." The man dug into his black prisoner's jacket and produced a piece of paper. He looked it over carefully. Raising his eyebrow, his smile grew wider. He looked up at Masaru. The man was missing his front tooth on top. He tossed the paper on the ground.

Masaru didn't take his eyes off the man.

"But we can beat him until he begs us to kill him." The man's smile grew wider. He brought his metal pipe up and placed the upper part in the palm of his hand. Then he slowly stepped toward Masaru.

The other prisoners closed in.

Masaru brought his katana close as he braced himself. He tumbled to the right, rolling backward and slamming into the legs of a nearby prisoner. Coming out of the tumble, he sprung to his feet and ran toward the forest. There were too many to fight. What was Turtak thinking? *This was suicide!* There was no way Masaru could take on these many men. He was good, and he was confident in his abilities. But he was also smart. Perhaps if he had been trained to use a bow or a rifle, he could have picked them off one by one from a distance.

You must learn defeat. Turtak's words echoed in Masaru's mind.

He felt a pain in his right leg. His knee buckled, and he went down. The prisoners came upon him. Masaru couldn't get his sword free. He couldn't deflect the blows from the clubs and kicks. Pain, searing pain in each of his sides caused him to jerk to the left and the right, trying to protect himself. His grip loosened from his katana. A kick slammed into his head and his vision faded into darkness.

CHAPTER 41

WHAT'S A YILCHAGA?

"Hadar iyl Nadal found the human in a field of death. Hundreds of humans, slaughtered by their own in an attempt to eradicate a culture. The humans use words like *genocide* and *ethnic cleansing* to describe such atrocities against their own kind. But all Hadar saw was a people in need of help."

~ From the *Chronicles of the Yilchaga, Volume 3* compiled by Frambold Chlodovech, a Chronicler of the Master Construct, First Order, an Alfargnym of Unterbaum

Erwin Albowyn, a Chronicler of the Master Construct, Second Order, an alfargnym of Unterbaum, sat upon the familiar campsite log waiting for Jeremy to return. In one hand he grasped a mimstone. In the other, he held Jeremy's unoccupied shoe. As Erwin waited for Jeremy to return, he decided to learn more about the human. He drew in some magic and sent it flowing into every atom of the shoe.

When Jeremy went before the Council of Elders, what did he say to them? The answer to his question slowly appeared in his mind as if it was a vivid memory he himself had experienced. He saw the Court of Elders; each elder sitting in their seats, eyes on Jeremy. He smelled the familiar clean air of Sayalla; the sweet smells of the oak trees, the baking goods, and the smell of Jeremy. Not a malodorous scent, but a musty, human scent. Jeremy became agitated by each elder's response not to grant Mercurio's request. Jeremy protested, and Mercurio rushed him to the exit.

Erwin stored those memories in the mimstone. *Go back.* He commanded the magic. *Did he say anything else before that?*

The *yilchaga* appeared. Jeremy's heart fluttered and raced. She was stunning. Unlike anyone Jeremy had seen before. Jeremy looked at Birch and then back again to the *yilchaga*. Erwin focused his gaze upon her.

Ah! Now there is something. She is equally fascinated by Jeremy. She—

The thwack of wood disrupted Erwin, and he opened his eyes to see Jeremy looking at him. Jeremy narrowed his eyes and shook his head slightly.

"That's just weird. Someone should draw a picture of you holding my Chuck like that," Jeremy said as he took a seat on the log. His stave lay next to him; the source of the noise that disrupted Erwin. He wished Jeremy would gently lay his stave down instead of dropping it.

"If I had my phone, I'd take a picture of you," Jeremy said.

"If you only knew the strangeness I've seen," Erwin snickered. He then reached for his sketchbook and began to draw the *yilchaga*.

Birch and Grath shuffled into the campsite carrying an assortment of vegetables and sweet bread.

Just lay a portion for me on the log. I'll eat momentarily, Erwin mindcasted to Grath.

Gladly. Grath's bellowing voice echoed in Erwin's head.

Birch handed Jeremy a similar plate, and the Gift Giver happily took it.

Jeremy looked down at the plate and then back at Birch. "Carrots, onions, and cookies?"

There was silence as Birch mindcasted to Jeremy.

"Thanks. Something sweet will be nice," Jeremy said, biting into the sweet bread.

Grath lumbered away and disappeared into their tent.

"Don't you think it's about time for you to learn how to mind-cast with Birch? It's a very useful skill," Erwin said.

"I suppose. I've just been concentrating mostly on getting in shape and learning to fight."

"Today, I think it's best for you to take a break from weapons training and focus on mindcasting with Birch."

Jeremy rolled his eyes and frowned at Birch. "Birch agrees with you," he said. "I have to admit, it kinda freaks me out."

"There's nothing for you to be concerned about. Birch will not see or hear anything that you don't purposely wish to share with him. That's why you need to learn the skill. He can't read your mind. You have to share, or cast, your thoughts to him."

"Fine. I'll learn today. Right after lunch," he mumbled through a mouthful of carrot, "if that's alright with you, Birch?"

Birch nodded.

"Whatcha drawing now?" Jeremy asked.

"I'm going to show you as soon as I'm done."

Erwin stroked his pencil to the paper a few more times, cocked his head back and to the side, searching his memory to make sure that he had the girl's hair correct. Once he was satisfied, he turned the sketchpad around and showed Jeremy.

Jeremy's eyes widened, and he started choking on the carrot. "Tha… that's her."

"Indeed," Erwin said.

"Wait, a minute. I was told we're not supposed to be talking about her and you're sitting here drawing a picture of her?"

"Stuff and nonsense, Jeremy. The elves told you to not talk about her."

"Birch did too."

"Well, he was only telling you so you wouldn't have to hear it from the elves."

"Why are you drawing her?"

"I wanted to talk to you about her," Erwin smiled.

"I don't know anything about her. I only saw her that one time."

"Yes, but you felt something for her. The proverbial 'love at first sight.'" Erwin said, smiling again.

Jeremy nervously lowered his head and rubbed the side of his face. "I wouldn't go that far. I, uh—"

"Jeremy, remember, it'd be very difficult for you to hide the truth from me."

"Well, I don't know if I love her! I just met her, for crying out loud!" Jeremy stood up and walked to the other side of the campsite.

"Jeremy, the truth is, you do love her. You are just not willing to admit it to yourself and anyone else. And when I say love, I mean that you feel a powerful attraction to her. Romantic love. I wouldn't say it was quite at the unconditional love level."

"Geez, man. This is awkward," Jeremy said, his eyes turned away from Erwin.

"Jeremy, truth is not always comfortable."

The human turned back around and faced Erwin. "Why do you keep saying my name every time you say something to me? It's not like anyone else is here. Man, it's annoying."

Erwin laughed. "You may feel that way, but I believe you're trying to avoid the discussion about the girl."

"Geez. You *are* relentless! What was it Mercurio said about you? You're like a rash that won't go away, or something like that."

Erwin laughed again. "Jeremy, I'm asking you about her because she is a part of your story. I don't know if you two will ever meet again. But I do know she feels similarly about you and if you two were—"

"Wait! What? She feels what?" Jeremy's voice cracked. He walked back to the log and sat beside Erwin.

"She feels as you do. A romantic attraction. And, should you meet again, I want to get everything about this first part correct for your chronicle."

"She does, huh? Wow." Jeremy awkwardly smiled and ran his fingers through his hair. "So who is she and why wouldn't anyone answer my questions about her?" Jeremy snapped his head towards Birch. "No. I don't really care what Mercurio and the others think right now. I want to know who she is." Jeremy turned and faced Erwin.

"Her name is Ezichi, or as she likes to be called, Ezzy. However, as she is *yilchaga*, it is forbidden to chronicle her story. I only know because my instructor, Frambold Chlodovech, a Chronicler of the Master Construct, First Order, chronicled the story of her father. You're a kind of a loophole here." Erwin laughed.

"Ezzy, huh?" Jeremy tilted his head.

"Yes, it is a name from her mother's people, the Igbo."

"Wait. OK. Wait. Igbo? Then what's a *yilchaga*? And why is it forbidden to write about her?" Jeremy said, placing his face in his hands and rubbing his temples.

Erwin sighed. The thought of working this *yilchaga* into Jeremy's chronicle made him giddy. The elves and their antiquated beliefs had made this young lady virtually non-existent. But because she appeared in the would-be Gift Givers chronicle, Erwin had an opportunity… no, not just an opportunity, but an obligation to chronicle the truth. "When the elves met man, there were several Elven males who fell in love with human women. Not only was this considered taboo, it was worse when the first women became pregnant with the children of elves. No woman has ever survived childbirth with a child of Elven blood. The very idea became heresy… it became an abomination. Those elves who engaged in such acts were banished. These incidents are rare because the punishment is so steep. Fifty-four years ago. Hadar iyl Nadal, fell in love with an Igbo woman."

"Igbo woman? What's an Igbo?" Jeremy said.

"Among the humans in Africa, the Igbo are native to the land you call Nigeria."

"Oh! Igbo are humans!"

Erwin laughed. It amazed him how little humans knew of their own kind.

"People; whether human, elf, or goblin, are sadly capable of epic atrocities because of differences in opinion. The Igbo of Nigeria killed thousands of their own people because one among them had different ideals. He led a terrible pogrom across his country, killing entire villages. What a sad and horrific time it was. For the Dark Elves living in Nadal, what you would call Southeastern Nigeria, it was too close to home. Dark Elves, who visited the land of humans, found nothing but devastation. One of those Dark Elves, Hadar iyl Nadal, was a healer among his people. And though he had nothing more than a curiosity about the Igbo, it became an obsession for him to help those left for dead. He spent more time searching through the devastated villages, helping the survivors. And that is when he met and fell in love with Adaeze Obi. She was—"

"Wait. Wait," Jeremy raised an eyebrow, let out a little laugh, and pointed to the sketch of Ezzy. "You're saying this girl is a half-elf?"

Erwin furrowed his brow before responding. "We don't use that term. The elves call these offspring of humans and elves, *yilchaga*. It means 'pitied one.'"

"'Pitied one?'" Jeremy's face crinkled with disapproval. "Are you serious?"

"Most certainly. Jeremy, you must understand. The elves are a proud people who live by their laws. It is an abomination to them for humans and elves to have a romantic interest in one another. They don't blame Ezzy for her parents' actions. Rather than being excommunicated like her father, she is given mercy. The elves pity her and allow her to live among them."

"Her mother died?"

"Yes, in childbirth."

"Didn't her father know that she'd die if she got pregnant?"

"He must have. But he was a healer. He thought, foolishly, that he could save her." Erwin said.

"So, what happened?"

"Hadar, distraught over the death of Adaeze, returned to Nadal. He was immediately detained and brought before the council to face exile. He begged the Council of Elders to spare his daughter a life of isolation. Hadar knew he could not return her to the Igbo. And any life with him outside the Veil would be very lonely. She had her father's ears and therefore could not blend in among the humans. The council was silent and resolute at first. Not even his own people of Nadal were willing to allow a *yilchaga* to live among them. It was Elder Ellesmere of Orindin that agreed to take the child."

"Wait," Jeremy laughed nervously. "So, what you're saying is that she's basically Ellesmere's adopted daughter?"

"Yes. I would say that is a somewhat fair summary. However, she is still *yilchaga*. She is not considered at all equal, but I surmise that the people of Orindin treat her well. They are generally—"

Grath charged out of the tent. *Someone has pierced the Veil.*

Startled by the charging koth, Jeremy jumped from his seat.

Erwin swung around; eyes wide with concern.

Birch's head snapped up and he looked directly at Eginoff's house.

Grath stopped short, next to Erwin.

Birch stood in front of Jeremy.

Erwin peered from behind Grath, looking puzzled. "Who could that be?"

Jeremy reached down, grabbed his staff and stood, battle ready, behind Birch.

CHAPTER 42

ARRESTED DEVELOPMENT

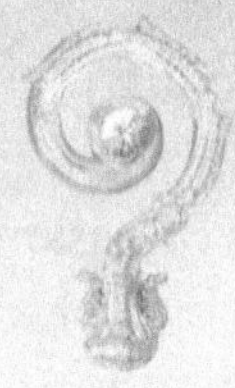

"Jeremy's mind was occupied by the guilt of his sister's death more than he wanted anyone to know. He didn't realize how many life decisions he made just to appease that guilt. In fact, he became a teacher not directly because of his gift, but to make up for the way he mistreated his sister."

~ From *The Second Gift Giver Chronicles* compiled by Erwin Albowyn, a Chronicler of the Master Construct, Second Order, an alfargnym of Unterbaum

Jeremy wiped the sweat from his brow as they waited to see who'd come through the Veil. Could it be Mercurio and the other guardians? Another visitor? Or a group of guardians sent to arrest them?

"Shouldn't we hide?" Jeremy whispered.

No one answered. Their full attention was on the door of Eginoff's tiny cottage. It opened slowly, and an elf appeared. He wasn't wearing armor, but he did have a sword on his back, sticking out from beneath his green and gold cloak.

A guardian? *They're here to arrest us.* Jeremy gasped. He exchanged a worried glance with Erwin, hoping the gnome would provide some direction.

Erwin's gaze remained on the guardian, who stood in the doorway, scanning the area, before settling his sights on Jeremy.

Jeremy swallowed.

"Palgen Mercurio of the Gray Guard. Are you here?" The guardian shouted.

"No. He's not," Erwin said.

"I see the human. Where are the guardians who brought him here?"

"On whose authority are you asking?" Erwin said.

"I am here on the authority of Elder Ellesmere wyn Orindin." He stepped forward and cautiously ambled toward them.

"For what purpose?" Erwin shouted to the guardian.

The door swung open. An elf, who was unmistakably Ellesmere, stomped out. She held her staff in front of her and used it to walk swiftly toward them. "Where is Mercurio?" she shouted.

The guardian kept pace with her.

Erwin's eyes grew wide. He stepped forward several paces to meet her and bowed his head. "Elder, as I told the guardian, Mercurio isn't here."

"Chronicler," Ellesmere said, standing only a few feet away now, "as you know very well, I am aware of all that has transpired in bringing the human here. I need to speak with Mercurio."

Jeremy and Erwin exchanged a worried glance. Neither of them knew what to say.

The gnome turned his gaze downward, spinning his pencil between his fingers. "Elder... he's gone to Kurgal."

"Kurgal?" Ellesmere said, bringing her hand to her mouth. "Surely Samyaza has taken him. That fool!"

Jeremy noticed movement at the door of Eginoff's house. Someone else was here. A head of curly brown hair and dazzling emerald eyes peered out of the doorway.

Ezzy! Jeremy said to himself. His staff slipped from his fingers and fell to the ground. If it made a noise or anyone reacted to it, Jeremy didn't know. He was captivated by the elf girl he'd seen in Sayalla. The very person he and Erwin had just been talking about. She walked out of the house toward them. *Gosh, she's beautiful.*

This will only make matters worse for you, Gift Giver. Birch said.

Birch's voice jarred Jeremy. The words at first didn't register, and Jeremy hesitated. When they finally did, he stopped staring at the girl and shot a frustrated look at Birch.

Ellesmere sighed and shifted her gaze from Erwin to Jeremy. "Jeremy Goodson, why did Mercurio bring you here?"

Jeremy furrowed his brow, giving Ellesmere a puzzled look. There was too much going on. He couldn't concentrate.

"Jeremy," she said sternly, "answer me."

To ditch me, he wanted to say out loud, but he wasn't sure what to say to her.

Ezzy slowly walked up behind Ellesmere. She looked around, searching, unimpressed until her eyes settled on Jeremy. She smiled.

Jeremy swallowed. His eyes darted between the girl's and Ellesmere's.

"Um…" he said.

"Jeremy was brought here for training," Erwin said.

Ellesmere pursed her lips and scowled at Erwin. "Hear me. If Mercurio has gone to Kurgal…" She trailed off as her voice cracked. Her gaze turned downward, and she brought her hand to her chest. She steadied herself on her staff and then walked over to the log, turning her back to Jeremy and Erwin.

The girl followed and placed a comforting arm around Ellesmere.

"Oh Ezzy," Ellesmere stammered. "Mercurio has placed himself in such danger. All for this human."

Jeremy scrunched his face and took a step toward Ellesmere.

The guardian stepped in front of him, blocking his elder.

Jeremy looked down at the guardian and gritted his teeth. He then directed his gaze to Ellesmere.

"He didn't do this for me," Jeremy said. "He did this because he believes in what you started with Nikolaos." He made his way around to face her.

The guardian matched step for step, blocking Jeremy from getting closer. But now he could look her in the face.

"Ellesmere, I know everything that happened. Mercurio shared the whole story with me. You started all of this. You helped Nikolaos become the Gift Giver."

Ellesmere lowered her head and grabbed the hem of her tunic. She picked at the white fur and sobbed.

Ezzy pulled Ellesmere to her chest and began stroking her hair. "Immatina. It'll be alright. We'll figure it out. We always do."

"You can send reinforcements to help Mercurio," Jeremy said.

Ellesmere didn't look at Jeremy right away. She stared at the ground for a few seconds and then took a deep breath.

"I cannot," Ellesmere said.

"Why?"

"Jeremy," Erwin interjected. "I told you why."

"But she's here now. She's an Elder. She knows what's going on."

"But he went against the council. If he returns, he'll be exiled." Erwin said.

"No," Jeremy said, "you don't know that."

"He's correct," Ellesmere said.

"Has the council made a formal decision on this?" Jeremy asked.

"No, Mercurio was supposed to return when he brought you home. He never returned," Ellesmere said.

"Did the council formally decide to banish him?"

"No. But we all know the law. It's just a formality," Ellesmere said.

"So punishment can be carried out by anyone in Sayalla before someone in authority passes judgment?"

Ellesmere looked up at Jeremy. Her brow scrunched, studying Jeremy as if she were looking for more.

"I'm not sure how things work where you're from," Jeremy

said. "Where I'm from, we have this thing called innocent until proven guilty in a court of law."

"Jeremy," Erwin scolded, "the Elder doesn't need a lesson from you on the American judicial system."

Jeremy stared at Erwin. He didn't know how to respond to that.

Ellesmere said nothing.

"I'm just trying to understand how your system works. If an elf steals from someone, what is the punishment?" Jeremy said.

"His accusers would bring him before his Elder, and if they had evidence to support their claim, the thief would be exiled," Erwin said.

"Who makes that decision?"

"The elder. An Elder's word is binding."

"Has anyone brought Mercurio to an Elder for dispute?"

"No," Ellesmere said.

"Are you making the decision to banish him?"

"No, I'm not his Elder," she replied. "Besides, he defied the entire Elder Council. Someone would need to bring him before the council."

"Great! So, bring him before the council. Send a group of guardians to arrest him. At least he'll still be alive."

Ellesmere's brow knitted together, and she bored into Jeremy. "Stop it child!" Ellesmere shot up from the log. "You do not know what you're speaking of!"

Jeremy stepped backwards.

Ezzy stood up with Ellesmere and held her arm.

"Jeremy Goodson," Ellesmere said, "I cannot do any of these things, you ask. I am but one Elder. If Mercurio returns to Sayalla, he will be brought before the council. It is that simple."

Erwin stepped forward and looked up at Jeremy. "It's not our way to pursue those who place themselves in danger on the other side of the Veil. Everyone knows that if they pierce the Veil, they are solely responsible for their actions, unless their actions bring attention to magic or threaten the existence of the Veil. And that is not the case here. Mercurio has only placed himself and the other guardians in danger."

"So, he's on his own?"

"Yes." Ellesmere sighed and sat down again.

"He said to give him three days. And if he didn't return…" Erwin hesitated. "Then I am to bring Jeremy and his parents to you for protection."

Ellesmere shot Erwin a disapproving look and then sighed. "Of course." She glanced over at the elf girl and her demeanor softened. "It's what Nikolaos would have wanted."

"So, we just sit here and wait? That's it?" Jeremy said.

The others said nothing.

"I can't just do that," Jeremy said, throwing his hands up.

"Three days," Erwin said.

"Fine," Jeremy poked his finger toward Erwin. "But I'm telling you all now, that I'm making a plan. In fact, I'm making several plans. Plan A, Plan B, Plan C… as many as it takes. But if Mercurio and the others aren't back here in three days, I'm going with one of my plans and you can either help me or not."

CHAPTER 43
A LESSON IN BETRAYAL

"Badtibirra was the capital of the Goblin Empire. Forged by the sweat of the goblins' lower caste, it would have been considered one of the Wonders of the Pre-Human world. After the Unbinding, the city was destroyed by the elves in 4,232 B.C."

~ From *The Veiled Happenlore of the Master Construct* compiled by Fulbert Gisilfrid, a Chronicler of the Master Construct, Third Order, an alfargnym of Unterbaum.

Masaru eased his swollen eyes open and he was immediately aware of every pain in his body. The searing pain in his side made it difficult to breathe. But his right side hurt the most. Despite the ache in his nose he could smell the faint odor of engine grease and gasoline.

Through swollen eyes, he saw the escapees, only three meters away, gathered in a loose huddle. Surrounding them were several old vehicles and tools. They were in a large garage.

Masaru tried to move. Cold steel across his bare chest and shoulders held him in place. He looked down and found himself chained to a chair; one end of the chain wrapped around his shoulders, chest and neck. The other end was attached to a pulley over his head. Rope bound his legs and lap to the chair. His arms… his arm! *My prosthetic!* His left arm was bound to the chair by a rope. The stump of his right arm hung there, unsecured. Masaru breathed in slowly, attempting to avoid any panic. Where was his prosthetic? He had to think of a way out of this. But to think clearly, he needed to remain calm.

"He's awake," someone to his left yelled out in Russian.

The escapees from the huddle stopped talking. Their leader made his way to the front and walked closer to Masaru.

"Ah, good. You've woken up." He tilted his head and looked curiously at Masaru. "Tell me, who are you?"

Masaru said nothing. He clenched his teeth and stared at his captor.

"You don't want to explain? Fine. Let's play." The leader waved his fingers for someone to come forward.

An escapee rolled a portable battery charger over.

"I'll admit. I've never used one of these before. But I think it'll be fun to see what it does to you. There's a label here that says 'Danger'. I'm sure it will be very painful." He laughed.

The escapee plugged the charger in and flipped a switch. The machine slowly hummed.

The leader put on a pair of rubber gloves and picked up the charging clamps.

Another of the escapees doused Masaru with a bucket of cold water. It felt good, almost invigorating. But he knew what would come next. Jolts of electricity would surge through his body, affecting his nervous system and causing him to convulse.

The leader took the charging clamps and touched them to Masaru's chest, one clamp on each pectoral.

Electricity surged all around Masaru's body, and he gritted his teeth to brace against the impending pain. He felt a tingling in his muscles. A warm sensation came over his body. But no pain. It felt… uncomfortable, like entering a sweltering furnace.

"Is it working?" The leader asked.

"I think it is," an escapee said.

The leader pushed the alligator clamps harder onto Masaru's chest.

Masaru winced from the heat and discomfort. His skin flushed and a wave of nausea hit, but still no pain. It was obvious by the leader's puzzled face that this was not the reaction he was looking for.

The leader pulled the clamps away.

"Humph!" He said, throwing the clamps to the floor and removing the rubber gloves.

"Yuri," an older prisoner stepped forward. "I've been tortured by something like this before, and that's not what happened to me. It nearly killed me."

"The machine must be malfunctioning. Turn it off, Vlad. There are other ways to make this little man talk."

The leader stared at Masaru and then waved his fingers again to call someone forward. "Nick. The hoist."

A large muscular man disappeared beyond Masaru. He felt the chain around his neck tighten. And then, he heard the voice…

"Masaru," Turtak whispered.

Masaru jerked forward, invigorated.

"Be brave," Turtak said.

Masaru felt Turtak's warm breath against his ear.

The chain grew tighter around his neck and the back legs of the chair came slightly off the ground.

The leader held his hand up.

"So, tell me who you are and why I cannot kill you?" The leader said.

"Masaru. Tell him nothing," Turtak said.

Masaru gulped and strained his neck so that he could speak. "Why?" He said in their secret language, straining to get his words out. "Why… is this… happening to me?"

The escapees furrowed their brows at one another.

"What?" One escapee said. "What did he say?"

"Stay the course, Masaru," Turtak said. "Death will not claim you this night. He will try. But I will not let him."

"Vadim. You speak seven languages, right?" The leader asked in Russian. "Did you understand him?"

"No. Sounds like garbles to me. Maybe he's delirious?" Vadim said.

"Idiot! What good are you?" The leader said.

The chain grew tighter around Masaru's neck as the back legs of the chair rose higher off the floor.

The leader walked closer to Masaru and grabbed him by his broad chin.

"You are a strange looking little man. Like a dwarf." The leader laughed.

The other prisoners laughed with him.

"If you won't tell me who you are, then tell me why I have this letter and your picture?" The leader let go of Masaru's chin and reached into his jacket. "I wake up this morning with a letter in my cell. This is what it says. 'Tonight you will be free. The gates of this prison will be open. But there is one who will try to stop you. He is the one in the picture. Stop him. Do not kill him. Hold him and wait for further instructions.' It's a strange letter to find, no?"

The leader paced, looking at the letter and picture. He turned back towards Masaru and held the photo up to his face.

Masaru's eyes strained to open. They focused on the picture. *No!* His eyes grew wider as the realization of the image sunk in. It was a photo of him from six months ago. A candid shot of him practicing with his katana.

"This *is* you, little man. You're shorter than the man you fight in the picture, and I see your robot arm. In all my years I have not met anyone like you. I've killed seven men, and I have hurt countless others. The men I killed, I killed because I was told to. There is always one to answer to. Only this time, I don't know who I answer to. Why did I receive this strange letter? Why did you try to kill me? It's a shame you killed some of my friends today. Men that I've come to know as brothers. You killed. I don't know why. Tell me why!" He slapped Masaru.

Masaru said nothing. He strained to breathe, gulping and licking his lips to squeeze more air in.

The chain drew tighter. The chair lifted higher; the front legs barely touched the ground.

The leader continued his soul piercing, unrelenting, angry stare. He watched as Masaru struggled to breathe, muscles straining. He watched as Masaru, starved for oxygen, drew a last breath and closed his eyes.

CHAPTER 44

IS THE ENEMY OF MY ENEMY MY FRIEND?

"He snores. I can only equate it to the sound that swine make when they are rooting out truffles."
~ From *The Second Gift Giver Chronicles* compiled by Erwin Albowyn, a Chronicler of the Master Construct, Second Order, an alfargnym of Unterbaum

Jeremy paced back and forth. Three days and no word from Mercurio or the other guardians. Erwin and Ellesmere tried not to show their worry, but their skills at deception were lacking. The night before, during dinner, Jeremy proposed several plans to rescue the Gift Giver's Guard, all of which Erwin and Ellesmere shot down. They treated Jeremy like a child, and he hated that. But none of them had any ideas.

Jeremy distracted himself by continuing his combat training. He had no one to instruct him, but he was diligent to practice what he'd been taught. When he wasn't training, Erwin interviewed him. He and Ezzy made eye contact a few times. They exchanged a few smiles, but no words. She spent most of her time with Ellesmere or reading. He could never glimpse the book title of what she was reading, but she sure read a lot. Jeremy caught her a few times watching him as he practiced the stances he learned with the staff. He wanted to talk to her, but he had no idea what to say, especially since Ellesmere and Hamjil were always around. Ellesmere said little to him. She'd ask the occasional question, and he'd answer, but Erwin used up any of Jeremy's free time asking him questions or talking to his stuff. He hated when Erwin talked to his stuff.

Jeremy took a deep breath as he wiped the sweat from his brow. He caught a glimpse of Eginoff peeking out the window, staring ominously at him. Jeremy turned away, shaking his head. *Why does that gnome hate me so much?*

Out of the corner of his eye, he saw movement around the campsite. Ellesmere and Ezzy emerged from their tent. Hamjil greeted them.

He caught Ezzy's eye, and she smiled at him again.

Ellesmere said something to her and they walked off into the woods.

He didn't understand Ellesmere. She seemed genuinely concerned about Mercurio. Would she really just leave him without help? Erwin told him that if the goblins captured Mercurio, they'd torture him for days. Was he being tortured at this very moment while they all sat around camping?

That thought haunted Jeremy most of the night. He'd hoped to wake up and find Mercurio back. Now, the third day was about to end and there was no sign of him. If Erwin thought Jeremy was going to just comply and go live out the rest of his life at the North Pole, he was mistaken.

Erwin peeked out of his tent and looked at Jeremy. The old gnome's eyes drooped heavy with worry.

"They're not back!" Jeremy shouted, walking toward the tent.

Erwin slowly emerged and walked to meet him.

"Listen, Erwin. I've been thinking. There's nothing you can do that'll stop me from finding a way to help Mercurio!"

The gnome sighed with aggravation. "Jeremy, you're showing

your immaturity again. We have yet to turn away from the sun. There is still time."

"Come on, Erwin! You know they're not coming back. Something happened! They failed. And I'll tell you right now, I'm not going to go and just live my life at the North Pole! You said Kurgal is in Ecuador, in the Andes Mountains, right? So, there's got to be something…"

"Jeremy, the council will surely provide for you and your family. You have nothing to worry about."

"Nothing to worry about? I'm not worried about myself right now! Mercurio is my friend. Mistake or not, I'm not just going to roll over and leave him to die!"

"Let's not be hasty. Thaddaios Wyllt is still looking for you. You have no choice. You and your parents must retire in Orindin."

"No choice?" Jeremy yelled. "What are you going to do? Use your magic and knock me out like Mercurio did? Take me against my will? Kidnap me?"

"Jeremy, it's the most logical way to keep you and your family safe. Whether or not you like it, you have made an enemy out of Thaddaios Wyllt. Don't you wish to keep your parents safe?"

Thaddaios Wyllt? Hmmm… Jeremy thought. *My enemy?*

"Erwin, let me ask you something. Do you seriously think Mercurio is coming back?"

Erwin's cheeks paled, and his eyes darted to the left. "I cannot be certain."

"OK. And neither can I. So, let me ask you this. If you could help Mercurio… if you could save him from dying in Kurgal, would you?"

Erwin's eyes widened, and he frowned at the question. "Well, of course I would! By all means!"

"Well, then, we both want the same thing. So, will you at least hear me out with an open mind?"

Erwin hesitated. He looked at Grath and Birch, who were preparing dinner. Neither met his gaze. He sighed and looked back at Jeremy. "Very well."

"Mercurio said three days. So, if they're not back by morning, we'll discuss a plan to rescue them."

Erwin nodded hesitantly.

It was good enough for Jeremy. He'd take the rest of the time he had left to work on his plan and find a way to convince Ellesmere to listen as well.

Jeremy nodded off just after 3:00am, waking only a few hours later as the dawn sun lit up the campsite. He pushed himself up and darted out of the tent, hoping to see Mercurio or any sign that he and the others had returned. Nothing had changed since the night before. Jeremy sighed and stretched.

Birch and Grath lay on opposite sides of a nearby log. They had set up a makeshift bed, placing cushions on top to accommodate their saurian anatomy. Birch opened an eye and peered at Jeremy. He then lifted his head and pushed himself backwards and off the log.

Good morning, Gift Giver. I shall prepare breakfast. Birch said.

"Thanks, Birch. I'm not really hungry, but it'd probably be a good thing to have some food in us when we go over the plan. I'd like you in on the plan too." Jeremy said.

Of course.

A bleary-eyed Erwin emerged from his tent. He looked to Jeremy.

Jeremy shook his head.

Erwin sighed and walked toward him. "Well then, I suppose it's time for me to listen to your plan."

"Sounds good, Erwin. I want Ellesmere, Ezzy, Birch and Grath in on it, so we'll discuss it over breakfast."

Jeremy cupped his hands around his steaming mug of coffee and stared at Birch. The koth gnawed on a deer's haunch. It was a strange sight. By now Jeremy thought he'd be used to the way Birch ate. But watching the mild-mannered koth eat was mesmerizing; the full haunch rested between his hands, and he gently, with the briefest sound, nibbled away at it. Grath sat next to Birch doing the same. Jeremy expected to see them tear into it like a raptor ripped savagely into its prey.

The others sat quietly on the logs, eating the savory porridge Birch had prepared for them. The tension was tangible. They were all worried about Mercurio and the other guardians.

"OK," Jeremy said, breaking the silence. "So, here's what I'm thinking."

Erwin chewed on the spoonful he'd just taken and stared intently at Jeremy. Birch and Grath set their venison haunches down and listened. Ezzy placed her bowl in her lap and smiled at Jeremy. Ellesmere, however, seemed a bit agitated. She turned her head away from him and sighed.

"I know this is going to sound crazy, but I really want you to hear me out. Ya know how they say that the enemy of my enemy is my friend?"

"Who says that?" Erwin asked.

Jeremy cocked his head back, a little shocked by the question. "Um, I don't know. I just heard it before. But, it's..."

"You don't know who said it, but you're quoting it?" Erwin said.

"Listen, I don't care who said it. I'm just taking the words at their face value..."

"The words you quote are actually from the Arthashastra, a Sanskrit document written several thousand years ago."

Jeremy placed his hand on his forehead and grunted a sigh.

"A more direct translation," Erwin continued, "would be, 'Is the enemy of my enemy my friend, or my enemy?' The modern version, in which you quote, comes from your second World War. Winston Churchill uttered this phrase in a speech to his allies of the United States and Russia. Some say it was your Theodore Roosevelt who quoted it, but I can assure you that it was indeed your Winston Churchill who said it." Erwin smiled enthusiastically at Jeremy.

Jeremy swallowed, sighed again and pursed his lips together, expecting Erwin to say more. The gnome did not.

"Thank you, Wikipedia! But as I was—"

Erwin slapped the log and laughed, a hard belly laugh.

Ezzy giggled, placing her hand over her mouth.

"Ah, ha, ho! I see what you said!" Erwin continued to chortle, almost choking on whatever bits of food he had left in his mouth. "Jeremy, that is funny."

"Um, thanks." Jeremy nodded. "But seriously. Thaddaios Wyllt is our enemy, right?"

Erwin's smile disappeared, and his eyes grew wide. "Jeremy!" The gnome stood up. "Surely you're not contemplating that we ally ourselves with that man?"

Ellesmere snapped her head around and stared at Erwin, and then at Jeremy.

"You said you'd listen," Jeremy pointed at Erwin. He then turned to Birch. "He said he would listen to my plan, right?"

Birch nodded his head.

"Very well," Erwin sighed, sitting back down. "Continue."

"I'm not *implying* that we team up with Thaddaios Wyllt, I'm actually saying it. Here's why. You've never had a conversation with Wyllt, have you?"

"No. But I'm aware of his reputation. He's despicable."

Ellesmere tightened her eyes and stared at Jeremy, listening more intently.

"Yeah, but listen. When I spoke with him, he just wanted magic items. He wants the power that they give him. He's been led to believe that the elves have all the magic. But you said that the goblins have all sorts of magical stuff in Kurgal. I don't think Wyllt knows that. Can you imagine how he'll react when he finds out that his supposed partner, that goblin he works with, has been holding out on him?"

Erwin scrunched his face in derision. "Hmmm… your entire

plan supposes Wyllt doesn't know about Kurgal and what the goblins have?"

"True, but Wyllt said he wanted to go through the Veil because he wants magic items. What if he didn't have to go through the Veil? We tell him about Kurgal and then we lead him there. He's got an army of trained mercenaries and who knows what other magic he has."

"This makes me uneasy, Jeremy," Erwin said.

"The thought of Mercurio, Ee'azar, Gaviryl and Jar'iyu being tortured for several days makes me uneasy."

Erwin sighed.

"At least let me call Wyllt on a cell phone. You gotta have some way to make it untraceable, right?"

"Jeremy, this is madness," Erwin said, crossing his arms.

"No," Ellesmere said, "let him speak."

Erwin slowly turned his head to face Ellesmere. A slow, shocked expression formed on his face.

Jeremy was surprised too, but he was on a roll and he didn't want to stop.

"Didn't Jar'iyu say that he was using a laptop to send emails and stuff? Surely that's gotta already be set up to re-route locations. If we used that, then we could use a voice-over-IP service like Skype to make a call."

"How would we know if it's secure?" Erwin asked.

"Jar'iyu already said it was. Now we just need to find a way to get Wyllt's number."

"I'd have to go back to Sayalla and see if I could find someone that…"

"No! Wait. It's simpler than that. If he's trying to find me and he's tracking my emails and social media presence, all we need to do is send an email with a way to contact us."

Jeremy jumped up and ran to the tent. He searched through the supplies and found Jar'iyu's laptop. The small, sleek design reminded him of a MacBook Air, only this was flatter and dark green with gold trim.

Running out of the tent, he raised it above his head. "Got it!"

Jeremy sat on the log next to Erwin and opened the laptop. He furrowed his eyebrows, admiring the computer's sleek design. The keyboard was similar in configuration to ones Jeremy was used to, though the keys all had unique characters. The entire keyboard was gold with symbols engraved on each key. He wondered if the layout was QWERTY. If so, he could easily figure out what each symbol meant. But at this point he couldn't tell which button did what.

"They are not very common this side of the Veil. Used mainly by the Elven Defense Force," Erwin said.

"Do you know how to use this thing? I don't even know how to turn it on," Jeremy said.

Jeremy looked up from the keyboard and noted the hesitation in Erwin's face.

"What are you not telling me?" Jeremy asked.

Erwin swallowed and pursed his lips. "It's magic protected. There isn't a button to turn it on. It can only be turned on by its owner or by the proper incantation. And it's powered by its user."

"Powered by its user? What does that even mean?"

"Keshaphim are conduits for the magical energy in the universe. The energy flows through us and into the device, providing it with power."

"So, what you're saying is that I can't use it?"

"I'm afraid not, Jeremy."

Jeremy slammed the screen cover closed and handed it to Erwin.

"Do you know how to use it?" Jeremy asked.

Erwin took the laptop and opened it.

"I do not," Erwin said. "But I do know the incantation and I'm sure if I speak with it long enough, I can figure it out."

Jeremy stood behind the chronicler and watched the blank screen.

Erwin stared at the laptop, then looked at it from all angles.

"Oh, is that how you work?" He mumbled. "Interesting."

"I know how to use it," Ezzy said.

Jeremy looked up, excited to hear her voice. "You do?"

Ellesmere said nothing but continued to watch intently.

"By all means," Erwin handed her the laptop. "I'll tell you the incantation."

Ezzy took the laptop from him and sat back down next to Ellesmere. "OK. I'm ready."

Erwin muttered something in a language that sounded mostly gibberish. Ezzy repeated it. The screen's illumination slowly intensified, highlighting her smile and the subtle chestnut of her cheeks.

Jeremy's mind went blank as he became lost in this feeling he couldn't explain. Ezzy was beautiful, but there was more. She possessed a beauty that went beyond the physical, as if Jeremy could feel her very soul.

"I'm in," Ezzy said.

Erwin nudged Jeremy and nodded his head in the girl's direction.

Jeremy exhaled, feeling as if he were being woken from a dream. He frowned nervously at Erwin and then made his way over to stand behind Ezzy.

The characters on the keyboard glowed with the screen. A circular symbol, resembling the badge he had seen the guardians in Sayalla wearing, cut away and the desktop appeared. A series of icons and a pull-down menu lined the left of the screen. It wasn't quite Windows, but it was similar. *Maybe it's Linux based?*

"OK. Do you know how to load up Gmail?" Jeremy said.

"No," Ezzy said. "But if you tell me the URL, I can get there."

Jeremy gave Ezzy the information, and her fingers quickly tapped the keyboard.

Erwin nervously watched Jeremy and sighed.

"What?" Jeremy said with a hint of aggravation.

"Jeremy, your entire plan is based on a supposition. What if you're wrong?"

"How could I be wrong?" Jeremy said smiling.

"Quite easily, I'm afraid."

"But we've got something that Wyllt doesn't have." Jeremy's smile widened.

"What would that be?"

"A walking lie detector!"

"Oh, Jeremy," Erwin shook his head. "It doesn't quite work that way."

"You won't be able to tell if Wyllt is lying?" Jeremy said.

"Not precisely. Not without speaking with the objects who were present in the truth."

"Hmm," Jeremy signed and bit his lip. "Not precisely? You mean you'd need the objects around him to verify that what he says is true?"

"No. That's not what I mean. I'll be able to tell whether he's surprised at what you say and whether he's hiding something. I'll even know if he believes what he says is true. But I won't know the exact truth until it's verified by the objects who have lived in that truth."

"Ah. I see." He really didn't understand. But he didn't have time for a lesson on gnomish truthfinding. "Well, that's good enough for me. Let's do this."

"Let's do this, you say? You truly believe your plan will work?" Erwin said nervously.

"You would know, wouldn't you?" Jeremy smiled.

Erwin frowned and opened his mouth to speak.

"Truly," Ellesmere said. "It's the only viable plan. All others would involve the council or someone who doesn't already know about any of this. And if this wizard and the goblins go to war with one another, it is not our affair."

Erwin exhaled again, nervously rubbing his forehead.

"What do I do now?" Ezzy said.

"I'll give you my account info," Jeremy said, pointing to the login window.

This was going to work. Jeremy felt it in his bones. A ripple of excitement shot up his spine as he relayed the information for Ezzy to type.

CHAPTER 45
A FOOL, A MADMAN, OR A GENIUS?

"Some might find it strange that the stoic Elder Ellesmere of Orindin placed her hope in a human again. She might never admit it, but she saw in Jeremy the same hope she saw in Nikolaos. And her love for Mercurio only fueled her desire to help Jeremy. Guilt played a big part. It's funny how love and hope can often be made known by guilt."

~ From *The Second Gift Giver Chronicles* compiled by Erwin Albowyn, a Chronicler of the Master Construct, Second Order, an alfargnym of Unterbaum

"That should do it," Jeremy said, nodding his head. "Now all we do is wait."

Ezzy laid the laptop on the log. The screen still glowed: a web page opened to the Skype web app.

Erwin sighed and looked up at Jeremy. "I still think this is foolish."

They had spent the last hour sending emails from Jeremy's

personal account and posting messages on social media. His current Facebook status read: "Met a really interesting man in my travels the other day. His name is Thaddaios Wyllt. I sure wish I knew how to get in touch with him."

Erwin wasn't particularly fond of those words.

"Jeremy! This is pure foolishness," the gnome argued. "There are humans out there who are just as dangerous as Thaddaios Wyllt, and I'm afraid you'll just be calling more attention to yourself."

"Even better," Jeremy said. "They can fight over the treasure the goblins have."

"Oh, Jeremy! You do not know the danger…"

"He's correct," Ellesmere said. "Humans and goblins have been thorns upon this realm for millennia. Inevitably, they will war with one another. Discern the truth. You'll know it too."

Jeremy and Erwin exchanged an awkward glance.

"Chronicler," she continued. "I'll admit there's a lot that can go wrong with this plan. But I'm afraid my heart could not take the alternative. I cannot imagine a world in which Mercurio didn't live."

There was more to Ellesmere and Mercurio than Jeremy had realized.

"Were you two like a thing at one time?" Jeremy said.

Ellesmere's eyes widened and her mouth curled to a frown. "A thing?"

Ezzy giggled and pulled her hand up to cover her grin.

"You know, like boyfriend and girlfriend, or married?" Jeremy said.

"Married? Mercurio and I?" Ellesmere said. Her shock turned to reflection. "No. We should have been. There was no one who would have objected, save Mercurio and myself." She laughed.

"What do you mean?" Jeremy said.

Erwin grabbed his pad and pencils.

"Had we both not become so involved with the Gift Giver's mission, we just may have married. In essence, we were both married to Nikolaos." She laughed again. "Everything we did revolved around him. My father wanted me to marry. The matchmaker chose several husbands for me. But how could I have ever devoted my time to anything except Nikolaos? Together we changed the world… Nikolaos, Mercurio, and I. And how could I have given my heart to any other, when I knew someone else already had it."

They all somberly stared at Ellesmere as she sighed.

"Had Mercurio gone to the matchmaker for me, I would surely have pursued it."

Ellesmere sat quietly for a moment, staring at the flickering flame of the campfire.

Ezzy placed a comforting hand on her shoulder. "Immatina, I knew there was more to your story with Mercurio."

Ellesmere smiled at Ezzy.

The familiar melody of Skype resonated from the computer.

Erwin jumped up and fell over the log.

Ezzy turned and grabbed the laptop.

"This is it!" Jeremy shouted. He helped Erwin regain his seating and then turned to Ezzy. "Don't answer it yet! We need to get in the tent and Birch and Grath need to be ready."

Ezzy ran to Jeremy's tent, and he followed. Birch and Grath made their way to either side of the tent. Erwin waddled behind.

Jeremy and Ezzy went inside, just as the Skype melody ended.

"It stopped," Erwin said nervously.

"That's good. We can call back. Now that he called us, the ID he's calling from is saved in the missed call list."

"What should I do now?" Ezzy asked.

Jeremy sat down, his back to the wall of the tent.

"Ok. Everyone ready?"

Ezzy placed the laptop in front of Jeremy so that the screen faced him.

I am ready, Gift Giver. And so is Grath. Birch said.

"I'm ready," Ezzy said.

Erwin stood at the entrance of the tent, biting his lip. Terror filled his eyes. Behind him Ellesmere watched.

"Alright, just click on this," Jeremy said, pointing to the missed call log.

Ezzy did as Jeremy said. The Skype ring started up. Outside, the koth warbled their bird-like song. Ezzy took her place behind the laptop, out of the camera's view.

Jeremy wanted to make sure that Wyllt had no way of figuring out where they were. He was confident in the security protocols Ee'azar had set up on the fancy Elven laptop. But he wasn't sure if Wyllt had some sophisticated way of using local sounds and land-marks to figure out their location. He didn't know if such a thing even existed, but he'd read enough books and seen enough TV and movies to be paranoid of that kind of technology.

The Skype ring ceased, and the image of Thaddaios Wyllt, surrounded by his henchmen, filled the screen. Wyllt sat confi-dently in a comfy-looking white leather office chair. The detective and the other two goons stood menacingly behind him. Wyllt smiled and shook his head.

"Mr. Goodson, you *are* full of surprises! If I didn't know any better, I'd think you missed me."

Jeremy swallowed and took in a breath. "Mr. Wyllt. I need to speak with you. But it has to be in private."

Wyllt raised an eyebrow, looked down at the screen through his bifocals, and laughed. "You know the old proverb, the grass is always greener on the other side of the fence? I say that's a poor man's way of looking at things. I much prefer to say the grass is greener where you water it. It's a much better way to look at things, wouldn't you say Mr. Goodson?"

"Mr. Wyllt, that's not what this is about."

"Oh. Really?" Wyllt said, leaning back in his chair. "This is just a social call?"

"No. But I'm not saying anything else until you're alone."

"You and your elf friends are quite clever. We tried paying a visit to your parents. I'm impressed."

"Mr. Wyllt, if you want to talk…" Jeremy licked his lips nervously and swallowed. "I'm going to have to insist that you're alone."

Wyllt smiled and laughed again. "I underestimated you, Mr. Goodson. It's alright if I call you by that, right? Being as we're not quite on a first name basis yet? Or is 'Mr. Goodson' reserved just for your students? Or how about Mr. G?"

Hearing the moniker his students called him come from the lips of Thaddaios Wyllt sent a shiver down Jeremy's spine. But he stifled it with a swallow and his best icy stare. "I don't really care what you call me." Jeremy said.

Wyllt leaned closer to the screen again, clasped his hands together as he rested on his elbows, and smiled. "Very well, let's just go with Jeremy."

The sinister look on Wyllt's face caused him to shiver again. Jeremy clasped his hand to his wrist and braced it against his stomach, hoping that would help him remain calm.

"Believe me, Jeremy, I don't underestimate people very often. And the strange thing is, I really, really like you." He rested his chin on his knuckles and paused long enough for another chill to run down Jeremy's back. Wyllt turned his head toward the detective. "Mr. Jaeger, go and pay Jeremy's parents a visit while we talk. I'm sure with some effort your team will figure a way to whittle down the defenses there."

Jeremy swallowed and looked at Erwin.

The chronicler shook his head as if to say, "I told you so."

"Tell Jau that I said he should go with you. He might have some insight." Wyllt then turned back to the screen.

His henchmen walked away, and the sound of an opening door followed the footsteps and a door closing.

"Very well, Jeremy. You've got your wish. Speak."

"How do I know they're not just hiding somewhere in the room?"

Wyllt rolled his eyes and sighed. "You're as cautious as I am. I appreciate that." Wyllt reached for his laptop. He walked around the room showing Jeremy the floor, corners, a small closet, and under the desk. He then set the laptop on the desk and sat back in his chair, legs crossed and hands resting in his lap. "Satisfied?"

Jeremy shook his head. He licked his lips again and drew in a deep breath.

"Mr. Wyllt, why… why do you want to go through the Veil?"

"Jeremy, we've already had this discussion."

"I'd like to have it again."

Wyllt sighed. "The world is a very unbalanced place. There are people out there who have far more ignoble intentions than me. I simply want to be prepared when those less scrupulous than I make their moves. And, in the meantime, if I can make a little money by controlling what others have, then so be it."

Jeremy curled his lips and jerked his head back. "Hmm. That was a… a more honest answer than I expected."

"Jeremy, I'm not as bad as you think I am," Wyllt said, raising and lowering his eyebrows.

"You threatened to feed my parents to your pet goblin!"

"There is that. But in all fairness, he's not a pet. He's more of an associate."

"Which is what I want to talk to you about," Jeremy said.

"About Jau?"

"Yeah. How much do you trust him?"

Wyllt slapped his hand on the desk and laughed. "Jeremy, I don't trust anyone. And I doubt I would ever trust a goblin."

"So, then what is this partnership you have? How is it a partnership?"

"Good question. Let's say that we both want the same thing. Eventually we'll get to a point where our interests will come into conflict, but until then, Jau gives me intelligence; leads to follow up on. That's how we found you."

"And what do you give him in return?"

"A place to hide himself. A network of connections. When we find a way to pierce the Veil, I'll take what I want and Jau's people will take what they want."

"Really? Has he told you about the treasure trove of magic items that his people already have?"

Wyllt's nonchalant, happy-go-lucky facial expression changed.

He wasn't smiling anymore. His lips straightened, and his eyes crinkled. He slowly placed his elbows on the desk and drew closer to the screen.

"Jeremy, why are you calling me?"

"Mr. Wyllt, I believe that goblin is using you. I know on good authority that the goblins have a reliquary of magic items in Kurgal."

"A reliquary? That's a big word for a fourth-grade teacher."

Jeremy studied the older man. He used confidence like a bully used his fists. This man was terrifying, but he didn't need Erwin's truth-finding abilities to know that he had hit a nerve. He decided to push a little more.

"Mr. Wyllt… did you know the goblins have been hoarding magic items in Kurgal for centuries?"

"Centuries, eh?"

"Has that goblin of yours really helped you… get very many items? What's he kept for himself? What's he told you about Kurgal?"

Wyllt didn't answer. He stared at Jeremy.

Silence. He'd hit a nerve alright!

Jeremy swallowed again, his confidence building. "Kurgal. You've heard of it, right?"

"Yes." Wyllt nodded.

"Have you been there?"

"No, I can't say that I have."

"Do you know where it is?"

"No. Do you?" Wyllt said, leaning closer to the screen.

"I do… I know exactly where it is. And I know that the goblin king has a nice collection of magic items."

"Jeremy, what are you getting at? What do you want from me?"

He hesitated. "A… a brief partnership. I'll lead you to Kurgal. You get to keep everything you find."

Erwin's eyes grew wide, and he frantically shook his head.

Jeremy tried to ignore the gnome's disapproval. "But there's one thing I get to keep."

Wyllt tilted his head to the side, raised an eyebrow, and pointed to the screen. "Jeremy, I've seen a lot of things in this world. Things that you've never even imagined. But I must say, you are one of the most surprising people I've ever met. You have a bold meekness that makes me believe you may one day inherit the earth."

Jeremy smiled nervously. "What do you say?"

"It's an interesting offer, to say the least. But there's something I just have to know. What is it you want from Kurgal?"

Erwin shook his head and hands again, mouthing, "Don't tell him."

"A ring." Jeremy said.

Erwin slumped his shoulders and smacked himself on the forehead.

"A ring? What kind of ring?"

"Mr. Wyllt, um… I'm sure a man like yourself appreciates secrecy. You can have everything else. I… I just want the ring. You must agree to that term."

"Color me intrigued, Jeremy."

"Do you agree?"

"I admit it is a very tempting offer. But I haven't survived as long as I have by having too many partners. As you may well be correct about Jau, you may have confirmed my distrust in partnerships. I'm more of a many minions kinda guy rather than a co-conspirator. It's less messy that way. On the other hand, it is a very interesting offer. I'll need some time."

"You have twelve hours." Jeremy tried to say matter-of-factly, but his false bravado came off a little strained and he squeaked out the last two words.

Wyllt laughed, reached forward and shut his laptop. His image disappeared, replaced by the words "Call Ended."

Jeremy closed the Elven laptop and took a deep breath. He smiled at Ezzy who sat across from him. She smiled back. But Erwin's seething expression drew his attention away from the girl.

The gnome pushed his way into the tent. "Jeremy Goodson, you are either a fool, a madman, or a genius, and I promise you that your chronicle will reflect the truth," Erwin said, balling one fist around his beard and continuing to stare at Jeremy with disapproval.

"Indeed," Ellesmere said. "We'll all soon find out which, won't we?"

CHAPTER 46
TO FATTEN
WITH FRIENDSHIP

"Do not be fooled by the goblin sages. There is nothing sage-like about them. They are cunning warriors who use knowledge and subterfuge as their primary weapons. But if you should corner one, beware they are as gifted with the sword as they are with their mind."

~ From *The Veiled Happenlore of the Master Construct* compiled by Fulbert Gisilfrid, a Chronicler of the Master Construct, Third Order, an alfargnym of Unterbaum.

Thaddaios Wyllt stood with his hands behind his back, gazing out the large picture windows of his penthouse. The buildings glistened as if the city that never slept had been covered in a sheet of ice. The sun had gone down, and Thaddaios needed to think.

Jeremy Goodson was an enigma. No… more than that, he was an enigma served with a side of annoyance. Thaddaios breathed a stifled laugh at his clever analogy of the schoolteacher-become-adventurer. He liked Jeremy. There was something endearing about him. His doggedness despite his fear was commendable. Was Jeremy's assessment of Jau true? Thaddaios couldn't be sure, but he doubted Jeremy had the bravado and guile to pull a con on him.

And that left Jau. Thaddaios was no stranger to the duplicitous nature of goblins. He'd heard about them from his father and grandfather. He knew the stories of how they once influenced some of the greatest empires through trickery and misdirection. But if Jau was playing him, what was his endgame? *Power.* It was that simple. For years he'd allowed that goblin to be a part of his inner circle. Jau was privy to most of Thaddaios's holdings, and with that the location of every magical antiquity they'd retrieved over the years. That goblin had used him to find and retrieve hundreds of magic items all over the world. Was Jau planning to one day take them all for his empire? Or was he looking for something specific? Jau had told him that the goblin empire had been stripped of all its magic. That elves had taken it from them. *Clever. Use my own agenda against me.*

And their most recent find, the elf that followed Jeremy. Jau had shown a very enthusiastic interest in that elf. He didn't seem to care about Jeremy or where he had entered the Veil. He was very clear about capturing the elf.

The elevator doors swished open. The reflection of Jaeger, Decoudreau, and Tufts stepping from the elevator interrupted Thaddaios's view of the city. Jau unsuspectingly led the trio into the living room.

The goblin climbed up on the soft white couch and smiled at Thaddaios's reflection.

"No luck getting past the Goodson's guards. There's at least three that I could see. And they are prepared. How'd it go with Mr. Goodson?" Jau said.

"They just don't know," Thaddaios said, still looking out the window. "Americana. They wake up and they just go about their business. Blinders on, they toil. They play. And they're content in their own little lives, uncaring..." He sighed. "...unwilling to look beyond their own circumstances to see that the world they so mindlessly cling to is much bigger and in grave danger." He turned away from the window and sat in the lounge chair, diagonal from Jau.

Jaeger, Decoudreau, and Tufts stood at ease behind the couch; behind the goblin.

"Selfishness," Thaddaios said. "That's why the world is the way it is today." He leaned forward and grabbed his coffee mug. A stark white rounded mug that blended in with the stark white décor. "I despise selfishness." He sipped from the mug, leaned back, and crossed his legs. He turned his gaze to the goblin.

"What's even more troubling is that we delude ourselves into thinking that we're not selfish. We wrap our selfishness in a blanket of misguided attempts to look good. Now, the Sawi people of Papua New Guinea. There's a culture that prides themselves in their selfishness." Thaddaios took another sip of his coffee and placed the mug back down on the white marble coaster. "In fact, their highest ideal is treachery. They call it *tuwi asonai man*." He laughed and smiled at Jau. "To fatten with friendship for unexpected slaughter."

Thaddaios continued to stare at the goblin, his lips turned upright with a disapproving smile. *Is that what you've done, you avaricious little devil? Fattened me up for the slaughter?*

Jau's lipless mouth made an uncomfortable and grotesque looking smile.

"It's funny, you know? This ideal. To the Sawi, a man who could trick an enemy into thinking they were friends only to kill him unexpectedly was called a legend maker. Ah, to be a legend. I'll drink to that." Thaddaios leaned in again for his mug and then tipped it slightly towards Jau. "To be a legend maker is a distinction of high honor and praise among the Sawi." He leaned forward slightly, clenched his teeth and intently stared at Jau. "Is that what you want to be, Jau? A legend?" He didn't let the goblin answer. A tactic Thaddaios often used to make those he interrogated more uncomfortable and get them off guard. "Will the goblins one day sing songs and praise of Jau'Asar; the one who restored magic to his people."

"Uh," the goblin nervously adjusted his position on the couch, "we don't really sing much."

"Is that right?" Thaddaios said, sitting back in his chair again. "You know, you've never told me much about your culture. What's it been, about eight years now that we've known each other, and I know so little about where you come from or your people."

"We don't normally find the time to sit around and talk, do we?" Jau said.

"No, we don't," Thaddaios replied.

"Wyllt, still, we've known each other for many years. I know your tactics well enough to know you're uneasy about something. Don't treat me like a child's toy and don't treat me like I'm one of your targets. Just ask of me what it is you wish to know."

Thaddaios's eyes narrowed, and he continued to stare intently at the goblin. Jau was hiding something, and now the treacherous rat was going to try to re-establish a level playing field.

"Kurgal," Thaddaios said sharply. "Tell me about it."

"Kurgal is where I was born. It holds the last throne of the Goblin Sar."

"And?" Thaddaios said.

"And what?"

"And what else?"

"What else?" The goblin tried to hide the nervousness in his voice. But Thaddaios's experienced ears picked up on it.

"Jau, I'm going to do you the courtesy that I give very few people who betray me."

"Betray you?" Jau leaned forward.

Tufts pressed his gargantuan hand down on Jau's shoulder. The man's sausage-like fingers spanned the goblin's chest, and the tips pressed into his abdomen. Jau eased himself backwards, guided by the immense man's hand.

"How much magic do your people have stored in Kurgal?" Thaddaios said.

"I told you. The elves stripped us of our magic centuries ago."

"How many magic items have you and your people acquired and now have stored in Kurgal?"

"Magic items?"

"Enchanted items, magical devices, magic relics? You know what I mean. Now who's playing games?"

Thaddaios scowled at the goblin, growing more impatient with him by the second. Had Jau been a man, he would have had him by the throat with one hand, and his Nighthawk 1911 or Ring of Ra pressed into his temple. But Thaddaios didn't trust being that close to the goblin. Jau was a crafty little devil.

"Wyllt, of course, we have some of those things. Kurgal is an ancient place. Why would you think otherwise?"

"Because you've never mentioned it before. You know my stance on magic. No one can be trusted with it."

Jau laughed. "Wyllt, you're a hypocrite. It's allowed for you to have all your protected warehouses all over the world, but no one else? Let's not—"

"Let's not what?" Thaddaios said, leaning forward again. "Let's not beat around the bush? Let's not be hypocritical?"

Jau laughed again, trying to hide his nervousness. The goblin's smugness was beginning to irritate Thaddaios.

"Wyllt, you speak of selfishness being a problem with the world, but you have built quite an impressive empire based on your own selfish goals. Only to always find yourself out maneuvered by the Rook."

Oh, that stung. The little ape knew he didn't like when people mentioned the Rook. Thaddaios wanted to scream at the indignant goblin. Instead, he took a deep breath and stood up.

"See now, Jau. That's what disturbs me most about our fraying relationship." Thaddaios turned and walked toward the picture window. "All this time I've made my intentions clear. Pragmatically speaking, what I do *is* out of selfishness. I live comfortably, very comfortably. I enjoy excellent food, lavish homes. But that is just a benefit of what I do. Ultimately, though, what I do is keep magic out of the hands of people who would use it to gain power."

"Wyllt, you're the self-proclaimed arbiter of magic! What gives you the right to decide who gets to use magic and who doesn't?"

"What gives me the right?" Thaddaios spun around and stared down at the duplicitous creature on the couch. "Oh, Jau. No one gave me the right." He poked his finger at his own chest. "I claimed it because no one else was willing to do so. The elves hid themselves with their own magic, leaving us behind. But magic can't really be hidden. We all know it's there. And from the time man first had its taste, we've selfishly scrambled to command it. From the Order of Orpheus, the Pythagoreans, the Knights Templar, the Masons, you and your kind, and all these other splinter groups that have formed over the centuries, we've killed for magic. My own ancestors… my own father did despicable and selfish things in his futile, vain hope to use magic and elevate himself to a place of power. And you and your people. How much magic have you amassed? Eight years ago when you came to me, I foolishly thought—"

"You thought I was just leading you to enchantments to help you with your own agenda?"

"Don't be stupid, Jau. Of course not. I've always known that this was a short-lived partnership. I figured one day we'd find ourselves at odds. But I thought your people were far worse off. You led me to believe you had no magic at all. That was my mistake."

"Indeed. So where does that leave us?" Jau said.

This is your last chance, Jau. Thaddaios turned and faced the window again. "Jeremy wants a ring that he believes is in Kurgal." His thumb gently rubbed against the ring he wore on his right hand. "Any idea what ring he's referring to?"

The goblin didn't hesitate. "No idea."

Thaddaios swung around, turning to Jau, raising his fist. His mint green eyes now glowed orange. The jewel in the center of the Ring of Ra matched their intensity.

Jau's eyes widened, and his lipless mouth descended into a grimace of shock.

"No idea?" Thaddaios said.

Jau scrambled to break free of Tufts's grasp. His fear-filled eyes intently stared at the ring.

Thaddaios frowned disapprovingly at the goblin. *This is going to get messier than I expected.*

"Mr. Jaeger, call Kripke and Kahn and let them know I have a mess for them to clean up. Then call Ms. Davenport and have her order a new couch and rug."

CHAPTER 47
THE MAN
BEHIND THE MASK

"I've only known the Second Gift Giver's appetite to wane when he was worried."

~ From *The Second Gift Giver Chronicles* compiled by Erwin Albowyn, a Chronicler of the Master Construct, Second Order, an alfargnym of Unterbaum

Twelve hours. Jeremy paced back and forth outside the campsite. He actually gave Thaddaios Wyllt an ultimatum. Well, not really an ultimatum… a deadline. Jeremy couldn't believe he'd done that without crapping his pants.

The others thought he was crazy. At least Erwin did for sure. Ellesmere was hard to read. She seemed cautious, yet hopeful. The Elven elder wasn't anything like Jeremy expected. This Ellesmere seemed more like the Ellesmere that he'd seen in the mimstone, and nothing at all like the one he met when Mercurio brought him before the Elder Council. Jeremy glanced at the matriarch.

Ellesmere and the others all sat around the campfire, waiting… chatting. His stomach fluttered and he couldn't eat. Nor did he want to sit any longer. His eyes wandered to Ezzy. She sat next to Ellesmere, reading a book. She didn't seem to have a care in the world. But man, she was beautiful.

The Skype notification chimed again. Jeremy's heart skipped a beat. His mind quickly switched gears from wanting to know more about Ezzy to hearing what Wyllt had to say.

Ellesmere pepped up and nodded to the laptop.

Ezzy quickly grabbed the computer.

Jeremy leaned over her shoulder to look at the screen. In the Skype Chat window, he read Wyllt's response: *Let's do this! Call me.*

"Let's do this?" Jeremy mumbled. He swallowed and licked his lips.

"What? What is it?" Erwin said nervously.

"He wants me to call him."

"Well, are you going to?" Erwin said.

"Yeah." Jeremy nodded at Ezzy.

She moved the cursor over to Wyllt's name.

"Wait!" Erwin shouted. "What are you going to tell him?"

Jeremy scrunched his face in thought and rubbed his fingers up and down the stubble that had grown on his face over the last few weeks.

"Well, I guess we need to have a meeting spot. Somewhere outside of Kurgal."

Ellesmere looked up at Jeremy. She said nothing. But the way she cautiously stared at him; almost squinting. Her mouth closed and drew to an emotionless flat line. It was unnerving. If Jeremy didn't know any better, he'd think that she was actually looking to him for answers.

"It would have been a good idea for us to discuss this first," Erwin said. "Because we have a problem. You don't have a way of getting to Kurgal. It's a day's travel from the nearest gatehouse." Erwin pointed to Jeremy. "But Eginoff will surely not let you in. I didn't even consider how we'd get you out of here without a writ of passage from the Council of Elders."

Jeremy looked to Ellesmere.

"No. We won't get one of those. We'll not find help in the council at this time," she said.

"Can't we use Nikolaos' Sack?" Jeremy said.

"No, it was on the sleigh. It's with Mercurio," Erwin paused to think. "We'll need to hike down to the nearest city and find passage to South America from there."

"What?" Jeremy stood up. "No. That's crazy. That'll take days! We don't have days. Mercurio doesn't have days. We need to go now. We'll have to have Wyllt come and get us."

"Jeremy, by no means! That man can never come close to a gatehouse, ever! Besides, without a frithstone they'd never make it through the Veil."

Jeremy reached into his pocket and pulled out the familiar green and white speckled glowing stone he'd received from Bartleby at the Argosy Bookstore.

"Frithstone? That's what this is?"

"Yes," Erwin said. "Without it you'd be going mad now, sick to your stomach, and frightened out of your mind."

Jeremy looked down at the glowing stone in his palm, trying to figure out how it could be of some use. Nothing came to mind.

"We could just leave the human here," Hamjil said.

Jeremy jerked his head toward the guardian. *Leave me here? Oh no, I'm not doing this again.* Jeremy frowned. "Human? Really? We've been here together for two days. Everyone else calls me by my name."

Hamjil crossed his arms and pursed his lips. "I—"

"And, no. You're not leaving me here. This is my plan. I'm Wyllt's contact. And he's our transportation and protection. We'll figure this out."

"Hear me, *Jeremy*," Hamjil said. "I'll not hear any more of your plan. My sole purpose is the protection of Elder Ellesmere. This plan of yours—"

"Hamjil," Ellesmere said. "You do a wonderful job of protecting Ezzy and I. But it is your job to protect us wherever *I* say we go. And we are going to rescue Mercurio."

The guardian tensed, and then eased with a sigh, as he crossed his arms. "Very well, Elder Ellesmere." Hamjil nodded to her and then looked at Jeremy. The guardian's scowl told Jeremy everything he needed to know. If something happened to Ellesmere, Hamjil would hold him responsible.

"We'll just have to hike far enough away and have Wyllt meet us there. How far from the gatehouse will the Veil affect people?"

Erwin sighed. "A one-mile radius from the gatehouse."

Over the next hour, they worked out a plan. Using Jar'iyu's laptop, they plotted a course far enough away from the gatehouse. Jeremy marveled at the complexity of the Elven laptop. He wondered what sort of magical technology it used to get an internet signal in the middle of the wilderness. He would've asked but being so close to Ezzy made him feel warm and nervous and it took all he could to focus on the task at hand.

Ezzy clicked away at the keyboard, masterfully navigating the laptop's OS and its apps. She was remarkable.

Finally, they were ready to call Wyllt. Jeremy gave instructions to Birch and Grath to break camp as soon as he finished the call.

They positioned themselves in the tent while the two koth resumed their positions outside.

Ezzy, sitting opposite Jeremy and holding the laptop, reached around the screen and clicked the call button. This time Erwin stood behind Jeremy, looking over his shoulder. After a few seconds, Wyllt's image appeared on the screen. The man leaned closer to the camera and smirked.

"I was beginning to wonder," Wyllt said smugly.

"Wonder what?" Jeremy said.

"Wonder how much longer you'd take to call me back. I'm a patient man, Jeremy. But even I have my limits."

"Why'd you call me?" Jeremy said, hoping Wyllt would give him the answer he was looking for.

Wyllt laughed. "As if you didn't know." He shifted position and sat back in the chair. "You've persuaded me. Do you have a plan to go to Kurgal, or were you expecting me to come up with one?"

"First, I'll need your word on the terms of this venture," Jeremy said.

"My word?" Wyllt smiled and leaned closer to the screen again. "Do you really trust my word at this point? Don't you want some collateral or something like that? Perhaps a child? Or a cache of magical antiquities to hold?"

Jeremy's eyebrows furrowed with confusion. He looked up at Erwin, who was no help. The gnome stood there nervously looking back with a face that said, "Don't ask me! You're the one who got us into this mess."

"Jeremy?" Wyllt said.

"Um, yeah?" Jeremy swallowed.

"Relax. I'm just joking." Wyllt wafted his hand at the screen, sat back, and leisurely rested his feet on the desk's top. "You see, I have nothing to lose here. And you have everything to lose. So, let's be honest. Once you and your gnome friend are in my presence, you belong to me. I can choose to allow you to lead the way to Kurgal or I can take you back here and interrogate the both of you. Hell, I can put a bullet hole in your heads and leave you where you lay."

Jeremy swallowed.

Erwin's fingers dug into Jeremy's shoulder.

"The fact that you've reached out to me for help means that you're pretty desperate. Let me ask you this. Where are your elf friends? The ones that rescued you from my *evil* clutches?"

"Um." Jeremy swallowed again and licked his lips. "Um..."

"It's okay, Jeremy. I know they're not with you. The question I don't have the answer to is why? And what does Kurgal have to do with this? So be straight with me."

Jeremy sighed and nervously looked away from the screen. *What should I say?* His eyes went from Ellesmere, to Ezzy, to Hamjil, hoping one of them could give him an answer. But they all looked to him; trusting him that he had the answers. The only thing that made sense was to tell the truth. But could he trust Wyllt with the truth? The silence of his thoughts seemed to linger on for far too long. He caught Ellesmere's careworn eyes, and she nodded to him assuredly.

"Jeremy. I have a lot to do. There are other magical strongholds to plunder, and I'm not quite convinced that Kurgal is worth my time today," Wyllt said.

"Mr. Wyllt. I don't... I'm not... I—".

"Just spill it. It'll be cathartic for you, and it just may lead to a lifelong friendship neither of us ever expected," Wyllt grinned. "You know what they say about the truth."

"Fine," Jeremy huffed. "Mercurio and the other elves are gone. They went to Kurgal to get something that belonged to them."

"This ring you mentioned?"

"Yes. But that was several days ago. They should have been back already."

"This is a rescue mission? The irony." Wyllt smiled.

"Mr. Wyllt, I don't care what you do in Kurgal or what you take from there. I only want my friends to leave there safely with the ring. You can have everything else."

Erwin gulped, and Jeremy felt another nervous squeeze on his shoulder.

"Your gnome friend doesn't appear to like that deal. But let me assure you both, I'll honor it." He pulled his feet off the desk and drew closer to the screen.

"I discovered recently that you were correct about my goblin associate. I'm curious to see what Kurgal does hold. And you, Jeremy Goodson, you may very well turn out to be someone I've been looking for, and I didn't even know it."

Wyllt shifted in his chair again. "See, you've cast me as the villain." Wyllt laughed and followed it with his best Cheshire Cat smile. "But the villain, I'm not. I think you've earned a bit of trust yourself here, Mr. Goodson, so let me tell you a little about me. I come from a long line of would-be wizards. Men and women who know that magic exists, who pursued magic to control and manipulate. My father, and his father before—and so on, you get the point

—they belonged to an ancient organization called the *Order of Orpheus*. Over the centuries, there have been many offshoots of this group, but the one that has had the most success, and succinctly done the most damage, is that of *The Black Swan*. I grew up in this organization. I watched as my father and his associates garnered for themselves magic from all over the world. There isn't a continent or country I haven't been to." Wyllt paused and lost himself in thought.

Jeremy looked to Erwin again, who continued to cautiously and uncomfortably watch the screen. He wanted to remove Erwin's tiny hand from digging deeper into his shoulder, but he ignored it for the gnome's sake.

"I saw my father murder, pillage, and steal from whoever he wanted, all for his own selfish ambitions. I saw the same in others whom my father warred with. And I saw what the desire for magic did to him and these others. One day, I remember it so clearly, it just clicked. This was wrong. This couldn't be how people lived. I was watching an episode of the Lone Ranger, the one where Clayton Moore played the man behind the mask. You remember him?"

Jeremy had no idea. He'd seen posters and clips of the old TV series, but that was way before his time. He smiled and nodded, figuring if he just listened and said nothing, Wyllt would eventually get to the point.

"As a child, I loved watching that TV show. 'A fiery horse with the speed of light,'" Wyllt said in his best announcer voice. "'… a cloud of dust and a hearty Hi-Yo Silver! The Lone Ranger, with his faithful Indian companion Tonto, the daring and resourceful masked rider of the plains led the fight for law and order!'"

Wyllt paused with a smile, lost in nostalgic thought. "Of course, these were the reruns of the 1970s. I'm not that old. So, I'm watching this one episode, and I finally realize… my father is the bad guy. This didn't sit right with me. I confronted dear ol' Dad that day. And his reaction is the reason I'm the man I am today. He slaps me across the face, then grabs me by the collar, pulls me up so that I'm standing on my tippy-toes, and he looks down at me and says, 'this is your legacy too. Son, everything our family collected over the centuries is so that you can one day rule this world, so that your sons can one day rule this world. We are Black Swan. It's in our blood. And with the magic of the ancients, we'll be kings and rulers. We'll make the laws. Our family will be safe at the top of the food chain.' The magic of the ancients. That's what he used to call it. He killed for it. Not to stop it from falling in the wrong hands, but to use it for his own selfish agenda. And that was the deciding point for me. I didn't want to be Butch Cavendish. I wanted to be the Lone Ranger. Dare I say, I once entertained the idea of wearing a mask."

He paused and smiled. "This is where you laugh out loud, Jeremy."

Jeremy forced an uncomfortable giggle. He found it funny, but Wyllt was so intimidating, he gave Jeremy the creeps.

"Jeremy, magic is much too powerful for any one person to possess. It needs to be protected. What I do is a means to an end. I exterminate those who use magic for ill-gotten gain. Which leads me to my next question. This ring you want, I need to know what it is. And I need to know why you want it."

Jeremy's telltale nervous swallow betrayed him again.

"Jeremy, I like you. And I'm starting to believe I can trust you. And believe me, my trust doesn't come easily. If you tell me you want this magic ring to protect your family or something noble like that, I have no problem letting you have it. Hell, if you tell me you want this ring to beat up a bully, I might even consent. But if you tell me you want this ring to seduce people into making a better life for yourself, you're out of luck. So tell me, why do you want this ring?"

"It's the Ring of Nicholas," Jeremy blurted. He forced it out fast, so it was out there.

"The Ring of Nicholas?" Wyllt furrowed his brow, tilted his head, and came closer to the screen. "Do tell."

"It's a ring that was made for Saint Nicholas a long time ago."

"Saint Nicholas? Santa Claus? Oh my." Wyllt laughed. "You've thrown me for another loop, Jeremy Goodson. The Ring of Saint Nicholas. My father said Santa Claus was real." Wyllt laughed again. "But what father doesn't tell his child that?"

Jeremy nodded, not knowing how to proceed.

"So, you want this ring..." Wyllt's eyes darted up and to the left as he put the pieces together. "And you have several elf companions. Jeremy, you... you want to become Santa Claus?" Wyllt grabbed his belly and laughed. Not just a giggle, but a full on, uncontrollable belly laugh that lingered too long for Jeremy's comfort.

The laughter was contagious. Jeremy could hear Wyllt's minions in the background.

"Jeremy, that is a... quite the... the... I don't even know how to phrase it. You've actually got me tongue-tied."

The laughter continued.

"So? So what if I want to?" Jeremy said.

"Jeremy, can you hear yourself? You can't even say it. Come on, let me hear you say it."

Those words sounded like a taunt to Jeremy. They caused a familiar pang in his stomach, like a ball had suddenly formed there. He knew that feeling all too well. He'd experienced it dozens of times as a kid, and he'd seen it as a teacher. Jeremy hated bullies. "What difference does it make if I say it or not? All I want from you is to help rescue my friends and get that ring! Like I said before, you can have whatever else you find."

Wyllt composed himself and leaned back in the chair again. "Jeremy, if you can't say it, then you don't truly know if you really want this. When I decided to betray my father and become who I am today, I owned it. There was no going back. When I was eighteen, I joined the Navy. I left against my father's wishes, but I told him. I went right up to his face and I told him, 'The next time you see me, we will be enemies.' I don't think he believed me. But I did. I believed it, and I made it happen. I joined the Navy with the sole intention of completing SEAL training and becoming one of the most highly trained warriors in the world. I didn't do it because I was a patriot. I did it for the training, for the experience. And once I figured I was ready, I left the Navy, and used my savings to hire a few mercenaries to help me intercept one of my father's raids. I became his enemy. What about you, Jeremy? What are you ready to become?"

Jeremy took a deep breath. Again, Wyllt was right. How could he become Santa Claus if he couldn't even say it out loud?

"I want to become Santa Claus." Jeremy blurted it out. It was quick, like taking off a band-aid quick. "I want to become Santa Claus."

Wyllt laughed again. "I'm sorry, Jeremy. I do believe you." Wyllt held his stomach and strained to stop laughing. "I really do believe you, but come on. The notion is ridiculous. Why on earth would you want to become Santa Claus?"

The awkward nervousness Jeremy felt around Wyllt was slowly turning to anger. He felt like he was dealing with a school bully here. Memories of the bigger, cooler kids pushing him around, making fun of him for still believing in Santa Claus in 6th grade; it all came flooding back. Only this time he wasn't going to just sit here and take it.

"Mr. Wyllt, why do you think I want to be Santa Claus?"

"I haven't the faintest idea. The very image of you in a red suit flying around on a sleigh pulled by eight tiny reindeer just seems silly."

"I don't think it'd be silly to the millions of children in the world. And I don't think it would be silly to the adults, especially in a world where so many people have lost hope. That's the real magic, Mr. Wyllt. The image of Santa Claus brings hope to everyone. It strengthens the spirits of those who have hope, and it ignites the spark of those who don't. And that's what I want to do. It's not just about being Santa Claus. It's what he represents."

Wyllt's brows furrowed, and he stared into the camera with icy intensity. Jeremy felt as if the man was weighing and measuring him. "Jeremy, you might just be the rarest of all people. The diamond in the rough. Have you ever seen a genuine diamond? One that hasn't been harvested from the earth?"

He leaned back in his chair, not waiting for Jeremy to answer. "If you didn't know what to look for, you might just miss it.

However, if the light in the mine is just right, you might catch a quick sparkle and know where to dig. When that diamond is pulled out, it's not all that pretty. A dirty, crystalline rock that then needs to be cut and polished. And that's the important phase. That's where the diamond gets its brilliance. It's cut in just the right way, with just the right angles so that the light can shine brilliantly through it. But if it's not cut correctly, the whole thing is ruined. See, that's what concerns me, Jeremy." Wyllt shook his head and tsked. "What happens to Jeremy Goodson when the cutting and polishing are done? Will we be left with just a rock, or will we have ourselves the next Hope diamond?"

"That's really not your concern," Jeremy huffed. "All I want from you is to help rescue my friends and get the ring."

"And I'm going to help you do that. But Jeremy, don't fool yourself. If you think we're going to part our merry ways once your elf friends are rescued and you have the Ring of Nicholas in your possession, you're sadly mistaken. There's something about you, Jeremy Goodson. You've merited my long-term interest, and whether you like it or not, I'm going to keep my eye on you."

A shiver slowly moved across Jeremy's back. The idea of having this guy around for any longer than was necessary was not appealing. "OK. So here's the plan. I've been thinking about how we can best infiltrate Kurgal. We—"

"Jeremy, stop," Wyllt said, holding up a hand and flashing his wicked smile again. "I tell you what. You let me and my men with all our collected tactical knowledge worry about how to infiltrate places, and I'll let you worry about how to deliver presents on Christmas Eve. Do we have a deal?"

CHAPTER 48

THE ELUSIVE ALTRUIST

"Thaddaios Wyllt traveled in a modern marvel of human engineering that would cause my Artificer brethren to scratch their heads."

~ *From The Second Gift Giver Chronicles* compiled by Erwin Albowyn, a Chronicler of the Master Construct, Second Order, an alfargnym of Unterbaum

The four-hour hike down the mountain to the rendezvous point was exhausting. Jeremy carried his backpack and staff, and that was enough for him. He felt bad that Birch and Grath carried all the other gear, but it didn't seem burdensome to either of them.

He and Birch practiced mindcasting along the way. It wasn't as hard or creepy as Jeremy had expected. In fact, it was quite fun. Birch made a game out of it that reminded Jeremy of "I Spy".

Erwin, Grath, Ellesmere, Ezzy, and Hamjil took up the rear. Jeremy often looked back and caught Ezzy's eye. She'd smile at him and he'd quickly snap his head forward. He felt awkward around her, and every word he wanted to say to her felt as if they'd come out all jumbled. Halfway down the mountain, Jeremy decided that this wasn't the time for romance. He needed to keep his head in the game.

They stopped at the rendezvous point; a clearing three miles from Eginoff's cottage. That gave them a two-mile buffer outside the circumference of the Veil surrounding the gatehouse. Trees surrounded the clearing on three sides. A lonely single lane road bordered its other side.

Jeremy plopped his backpack down and heaved a sigh of relief as he sat on a patch of dry grass. "Phew!" he said taking off his ball cap and wiping the sweat from his brow. "I haven't done anything like that in years." He leaned back on his hands and took a deep breath.

"Like what?" Erwin asked.

"Hiking. Down a mountain. In the middle of the summer."

"You live in a very big city." The gnome raised his eyebrow and held out his hands. "Surely you walk around a lot. You said you don't have permission from your government to use a combustion carriage."

Jeremy smiled. That was the most alien statement Jeremy had heard Erwin say. The gnome was well versed in English and even a bit of American pop-culture. But when it came to absolutes, Erwin seemed to want to classify everything and use very specific terminology. A car wasn't a car, it was a combustion carriage. An apartment building wasn't an apartment building, it was a multi-level, multi-residential structure. Jeremy could only imagine what his chronicle would be like when Erwin finished it.

"No, I don't have a driver's license," Jeremy chuckled. "And I do walk around in the city a lot. But that's way different than hiking down a mountain."

Birch and Grath snapped their heads up to the east. The others turned and looked in the same direction.

Ezzy stood up, holding her hand above her eyes, staring off into the distance.

Jeremy arched forward and did the same. All he could see was the orange and blue of the evening sky.

"Is that them?" Ezzy said.

"What? What is it?" Jeremy asked. He squinted to try and make out what they saw. But other than the clouds and the light of the setting sun, the sky was clear.

"I thought I heard something unusual," Erwin said.

"What is it?" Jeremy demanded.

"I believe it's an airplane. And it's headed right toward us," Erwin said.

"A plane? That can't be Wyllt. He can't land a plane here!" Jeremy scratched the back of his head. He thought Wyllt would be coming in a car or truck.

They all watched the sky. After a minute or so, Jeremy saw it; the silhouette of a plane among the orange and blue. It was descending straight towards them.

He waited a few seconds to see if it changed course. Its black metallic finish gleamed with the summer sun and continued in their direction.

Jeremy backed up. He reached down for his staff and pack. "Everyone! Back into the woods!" Jeremy turned and ran for the forest.

They each hid behind a tree, peeking out to see what would happen.

The rumbling engines and the whooping propellers grew louder as they approached, but Jeremy couldn't see the plane. *Was it invisible?*

A sudden whoosh of air and the dry dirt of the clearing formed a cloud. Branches and leaves swayed and shook. The whooping and whirring of the plane increased with a thunderous intensity. In the clearing, the shadow of the plane grew larger as it descended vertically to land.

How in the… Jeremy had to see this. He stepped out for a better look and he saw the shiny black plane, now with its wings tilted sideways and the propellers spinning above like a helicopter.

The plane landed with ease in the clearing, and the sounds of the propellers decreased. A door on the side of the plane opened and Wyllt, followed by his henchmen, jumped down.

It surprised Jeremy to see Wyllt dressed in full combat gear. He wore a black durag on his head, fancy looking black fatigues, complete with combat vest and utility belt. His men dressed similarly, but there was no doubt that the man wearing the horned rim glasses was Thaddaios Wyllt. His very countenance demanded compliance. Even the hulking mook who stood behind Wyllt didn't seem as imposing.

Wyllt and his men stood there, almost motionless save for the wind of the propellers causing the loose parts of their garments to wave.

What are they waiting for? Jeremy wondered, partially hidden by a tree. He was sure Wyllt could see him, but the men just stood there.

Jeremy stepped out from behind the tree and walked toward Wyllt.

The henchmen quickly switched their stance, pointing their guns at Jeremy.

He felt a tug on his shirt. Jeremy turned to find Erwin holding on and looking up at him disapprovingly.

"What are you doing?" Erwin said.

"What do you mean, 'what am I doing'? What's it look like I'm doing? I'm going to meet Wyllt. That's what we came here for." Jeremy pulled away from the gnome's grasp and stepped out into the clearing. He stopped, waiting for a signal. But none came. Wyllt and his men continued to stand there, guns pointing straight at him.

"Ah, geez!" Jeremy heaved a big breath and walked to meet Wyllt.

Birch and Grath appeared at Jeremy's side.

Halfway there, Wyllt holstered his pistol and raised his hand, turning his palm toward his men, gently waving for them to stand down.

They complied. Wyllt's hand rested on the handle of his holstered pistol.

Jeremy exhaled with some relief.

"I figured I'd give you and your friend a chance to shake the heebie-jeebies off before you came out," Wyllt yelled over the propellers.

Jeremy nervously took in the situation. His eyes darted around, glancing at the weapons and protective gear the men had, and then at the strange looking hybrid plane-helicopter.

"Well, let's not stand out here. We got some elves to save, right?" Wyllt yelled, motioning them to enter the plane.

This was it. Did he dare enter the lion's den? If he did, he'd indeed be as Wyllt said; this man could do with him whatever he wanted. All this really wasn't about Jeremy. It was about Mercurio. It was all the elf's idea. *I wouldn't be in this mess if it weren't for Mercurio.* Deep in his heart, he couldn't let Mercurio die without doing anything. He remembered the John Wayne mug his Dad gave him. *Courage is being scared to death but saddling up anyway.*

"Well, Mr. Goodson?" Wyllt said.

Jeremy blinked and took another deep breath. He waved for Erwin and the others to come, then grabbed onto the side of the plane's doorway and hauled himself up. Wyllt followed.

Jeremy looked around, taking in everything. The inside was stark white from the walls to the upholstered seats down to the tables and seat belts. The cabin was divided, with three seats when you first walked in; two directly across from the door and one to the right of the door. Another four seats in the back faced each other in pairs.

A pilot and co-pilot, dressed in the same gear as Wyllt's henchmen, sat in the cockpit.

"You didn't tell me you had lizard people with you," Wyllt said. "I'm afraid I only have enough seating for humanoids. But I'm sure we can rig something up in the cargo."

"They're not lizard people and they're certainly not cargo. They're called koth, and they have names."

"I wasn't implying that they were cargo. I just don't have anything for them to sit on or be strapped in up here in the passenger cabin."

Jeremy, we are not offended. We will be fine bracing ourselves here. We do not wish to leave you alone with Mr. Wyllt, Birch said.

Will you be safe standing during the flight? Jeremy mindcasted to Birch.

We will.

"They'll stand here in the passenger cabin with us," Jeremy said, taking the seat to the right of the door.

"That's not very safe," Wyllt said.

Erwin walked in, followed by Ellesmere, Ezzy, and Hamjil.

"They'll be fine." Jeremy tried out his false bravado again. It seemed to work.

"Very well." Wyllt nodded to the pilots. He then eyed Ellesmere and the other two elves. "Well, it seems you surprised me again. I'm afraid we don't have room for all of you. There's only one seat left."

"I won't need a seat. And neither will he," Ellesmere said, pointing to Hamjil.

"I'm afraid you don't understand. There are weight restrictions due to fuel. We're already going to have to refuel twice."

"I assure you Mr. Wyllt," Ellesmere said. "We will not slow down the flight, nor will we be in any danger during the flight."

Two of Wyllt's henchmen took seats in the rear.

"Ezzy, you sit back there with those men," Ellesmere said. "Hamjil and I will sit here." She pointed to the floor. She then leaned forward and made a graceful circular motion, spinning herself around and then sitting cross-legged to face the two seats.

Hamjil did the same.

Wyllt nodded to his large minion at the door.

He pulled the cabin door closed and joined the others in the back, leaving the seat next to Erwin, for Wyllt.

"Wait," Jeremy said. "Elder, you should sit in my seat."

"Jeremy, I will be far more secure than you are. Stay."

Jeremy sighed and sat down again.

With the door closed, it was remarkably quieter inside. The dull, steady whooping of the propellers was barely noticeable.

"All right, then. Our motley crew has assembled." Wyllt smiled and laughed. "Ortiz, let's ride!" Wyllt said, nodding to the pilot.

"Yes, sir!" the pilot said, spinning around in her seat.

"Wait. How do you know where to go? I thought you needed us to give you the coordinates?" Jeremy said.

Wyllt smiled.

"No. I already know where we're going. What I need to do now is keep my eye on you to see if you're the real thing."

"The real thing?" Jeremy raised his brow.

"The elusive altruist. A rarity among our kind these days." Wyllt stared at Jeremy with those cold green eyes and that smug grin.

Jeremy stared back, wanting to return the smile with one equally arrogant, but he couldn't. This man terrified him.

"I believe introductions are in order. You all know me. But I only know Jeremy and you don't know any of my crew." Wyllt crossed his legs, sat back in his seat, and turned his head to look at Erwin. "Let me guess. Is your name Mistletoe?"

CHAPTER 49

A LESSON IN LEADERSHIP

"The Son of None did what all other High Kings never did. He rose from obscurity and led his people into the glory that Odin intended."

~ From the *Chronicles of the High Kings of the Dweorg*, Vol. 30 compiled by Stenn Jorunn, a Chronicler of the Master Construct, First Order, an alfargnym of Unterbaum

Masaru willed his eyes to open, but they wouldn't. He only saw darkness. And all he could feel was the unrelenting pounding of his head. Throbbing, constricting, pounding in his head.

HE COULD FEEL his body again. The pain in his right side. His head throbbing. His body ached, but it was warm. Warmer on one side. The smell of smoke. The touch of hands. Small hands with sharp nails. They held something wet. He could feel it dabbing his face. He could feel the small fingers shove something sweet and gritty into his mouth. Then nothing again.

THE SMELL of smoke tickled his nostrils. A bright, warm light pushed through Masaru's eyelids. A bright darkness... a bright nothing. He couldn't open his eyes. Pain. Pain in his head. Pain in his side. A throbbing, aching pain that permeated every muscle in his body.

"Masaru," Turtak said. "Do not wake yet. You must sleep."

Masaru obeyed.

HE TOOK A DEEP BREATH. His ribs still hurt, but not as much as before. His neck and shoulders ached. It would be difficult to turn his head. But he had to see the source of the warmth. His eyes blinked open and tears formed from the strain. He slowly turned his head. A flickering fire burned brightly, and he squinted further from its intensity.

Masaru stared into the fire. He was glad to be alive. He didn't know where he was. He turned his head again and tried to push himself onto his right side. He couldn't. His body was stiff and the pain too much. He steadied his breathing and turned his head back to the fire again. The dancing flames entertained his mind as he drifted off to sleep again.

THE SNAPPING of the heated sap escaping from the burning wood woke Masaru up. He turned his head, loosening the stiffness in his neck. The fire still burned, but Masaru wanted to get up. He could tell he'd been laying there for a while. How many days had it been? He took a deep breath and rolled to his right side. Every muscle still ached. Bracing himself with his stump, he used his left hand to push himself up. Pain surged through him, and he winced. He pushed through it and sat himself up, back to the flames.

"Masaru," Turtak said. "You must take it easy."

The once soothing voice of Turtak now stung. The words of the Russian reading the letter echoed through Masaru's mind, and they pained him like needles under his nails. Turtak was responsible for what had happened. He had pitted the Russian prisoners against him. This he was sure of. But why?

"I could've died," Masaru grumbled. His throat was dry, and his voice was raspy.

"You did not," Turtak said.

"I could've."

"I told you, Masaru. Death would try to come for you. I did not allow it. I protected you as I always do."

"Protected me?" Masaru said through clenched teeth, filling those words with as much vitriol as his battered and bruised body would allow. "Those men would've killed me. You gave them the letter and my picture, didn't you?"

"Yes."

Masaru inhaled. Fueled by anger, he pushed himself to his feet, guarding his abdomen and right side with his left arm, ignoring all the pain. "Why? Why would you let this happen to me?"

"Masaru, what have you learned?"

"Learned?" Masaru stammered under straining breaths. "Learned? I almost died!"

"Precisely. You learned you could die."

"What? I already knew I could die! I didn't need to be beaten and tortured within an inch of my life to know that I could be killed."

Masaru teetered slightly, his head spinning. He grabbed a nearby tree.

"Careful, Masaru. Your wounds have not yet healed, and the poison in your body has not yet passed."

"What? Poison?" He found it more difficult to breathe. "They poisoned me?"

"No. Your own body has." Turtak paused. "The amount of gold in your blood. When they tried to shock you, much of it was burned away. Your body is reacting to its toxins and desperately trying to replenish what was lost. It will take some more time to recover."

Masaru slowly slid back down the side of the tree.

"If you drink the mixture I have prepared for you, it will help you recover faster."

A small tin bowl near the bedroll floated through the air. Masaru stared at it in disbelief. Turtak had never done anything like that before. The bowl rested next to Masaru's left hand.

He picked it up. It smelled horrible. It looked like the pulverized remains of an animal. Small bits of meat, plant matter, and what appeared to be the crushed wings of a large insect floated in a solution of blood.

"Awgh. What is this?"

"I will not tell you. You wouldn't take it if I did. Just drink it."

Masaru shook his head and obeyed, slurping down the vile concoction. It was chunky with bits of hard and soft parts. The texture alone was enough to make him want to throw it up. The taste, however, was sweeter than he expected.

"Masaru," Turtak said. "What have you learned?"

Masaru breathed deeply, straining to roll his eyes a bit, to show his annoyance. "I learned I could die," He said flatly.

"Is that all?"

Masaru thought for a moment. He remembered the first time he killed a man. Only a few weeks earlier. He remembered the power he felt that night; surrounded by darkness. Others panicking. And he in full control of the situation. The blade, guided by his hands, slicing through evil men, taking their lives. Those men were guilty of spilling blood out of selfishness. They would no longer prey on innocent people. His mind wandered to the prison. Those men were evil, too. And it felt good to know that he was the one who stopped them from ever doing evil again. Only he really didn't. For all he knew, those men were still out there. He had fought an army and lost. *I lost. Was that the lesson? Defeat? So what?*

"I lost," Masaru whispered.

"Yes."

There was silence as Masaru pondered that thought. He lost, but he didn't understand what he was supposed to have learned from this. "The task was impossible for one man."

"Precisely," Turtak said.

"Then why would you have me do it?"

"Masaru. Death is inevitable. It is something all creatures on Earth must experience. This battle was not your last. You will have many more. But you won't be alone. You will have a vast army of your own to command. And you must be willing to die for them as you ask them to die for you. You must learn from your experience. How would the battle at the prison have been different if you had your own army to command?"

"Much different. Those men wouldn't have escaped."

"Precisely. Your objective was to stop them. That is what you were told. My objective was different. I presented you with a situation you could not win. I wanted you to know what it was like to lose so that you would have a better understanding of what you will ask your warriors to do. And so that you understand what a captive in your possession is experiencing. Your experience these past four days will continue to teach you new lessons as you grow deeper as a leader and warrior."

"Four days?" Masaru gasped. "Is that how long it's been? Have I been unconscious that long?"

"Yes. Your wounds were many. And the lightning sickness made things worse."

"Lightning sickness?"

"The toxins from the gold in your body rapidly being heated. It is well known among your kind."

His kind? Masaru knew he was different. But if he was not a human, then what was he?

"My kind? When are you going to explain this to me more?"

"Masaru, I want you to see for yourself. Seeing is not the same as being told. I promise you. All your questions will be answered when you reach your homeland. The land where you were abandoned and found."

"Fine. At least tell me what's up with all this gold in my body. You seem to think it's normal. My doctors seem to think otherwise."

"You are not human. You've always known that. I don't want to discuss this further. You will learn more when you return to your homeland."

Masaru noted the rare inflection of anger in Turtak's voice. This was truly a sore subject he didn't want to discuss. But why? It wasn't worth pushing him. Masaru closed his eyes again, resolved to rest against the tree.

"The gold," Turtak said softly. "All beings born of magic have higher concentrations of gold than those who are not born of magic."

CHAPTER 50

ROLE PLAYING

"Thaddaios Wyllt found Jeremy's naivete refreshing… like a cat found a mouse refreshing. He'd toy with it before devouring it."

~ From *The Second Gift Giver Chronicles* compiled by Erwin Albowyn, a Chronicler of the Master Construct, Second Order, an alfargnym of Unterbaum

Jeremy swiveled the luxury seat around to look out the window of Wyllt's aircraft. The propeller spun faster and faster as the plane ascended. The wing slowly rotated, and the propeller tilted forward like something out of a Transformers' movie. Jeremy glanced over at Wyllt. Above the dull sound of the aircraft, Wyllt acquainted himself with the others. Jeremy didn't quite make out what they were saying. He became lost in thought. The imposing man wasn't all that imposing, physically. He was ordinary looking, like he could be the local grocer or clothing salesperson at a department store. But it was the way he carried himself that made his presence so overwhelming. His smile. The way he stared at you. How he'd slouch slightly; not in a poor posture way, but in such a way as to show you that he was weighing and measuring everything about you as he intently listened. It was creepy. Jeremy shuddered and turned to look back out the window.

What in the world am I doing? He wondered as he watched the aircraft's wings tilt forward, locking into a fixed wing. The aircraft sped off into the horizon, and Jeremy let out a little gasp.

"Pretty fantastic piece of machinery, isn't she?" Wyllt said.

Jeremy glanced back at the man and nodded.

"I assure you she's nothing magical. Just one of humanity's mechanical marvels. She's an AW609 Tiltrotor. Made right here in the good ol' U.S. of A. I had a few magical upgrades added," Wyllt said and then pointed at Erwin. "But what I wouldn't give to get one of these gnome fellas a chance to upgrade the engine, know what I mean?"

Jeremy didn't.

"You offend Odin," Erwin chimed in. "All alfargnym are not as mechanically inclined as you assume. As if the Allfather would have made everyone the same! That's like saying he made all men egotistical." Erwin shot a satisfied glance at Jeremy.

The co-pilot opened a cabinet next to where Wyllt was seated. He removed a small cart and rolled it in their direction, assuming the role of a flight attendant.

"I do have a lot to learn," Wyllt said. "No time like the present. We have a long ride ahead of us, so we might as well get to know each other a little better. This is former Kommando Spezialkräfte, sergeant Rafer Lang. Co-pilot, medic, rifleman, and cabin steward."

Lang smiled and nodded at Jeremy. "We have Coke, Sprite, Fanta, Château du Tariquet, a Château d'Yquem Sauternes 2005, and a Screaming Eagle Cabernet Sauvignon 2016. A selection of craft beers, including Westvleteren 12, Amber Bock, and Samuel Adams Leinenkugel. We also have spring water. What can I get for you?"

Lang was a strange sight; battle gear, gun holstered at his side, and a white towel draped over his arm.

"I'll just have some Coke," Jeremy said. He then turned his attention back to Wyllt. "I'd like to hear the plan. How are we going to rescue Mercurio and the others?"

"Well, that's going to prove rather difficult because we don't have any maps of where we're going. Going in blind is never ideal. But I'm confident we'll get in and out unscathed."

The commando flight attendant handed Jeremy a fancy goblet of Coke. Iridescent white star-shaped ice cubes bobbed within, contrasting with the dark caramel color of the soda.

Jeremy thought about Wyllt's statement. *Going in blind?* He was right. None of them even knew where the entrance to Kurgal was. And judging by the map, the mountain range was quite large. He turned to Erwin.

"Do you know anything about Kurgal? What it looks like? Where the entrance is? Something that would help us?" Jeremy said.

"I know many things about the Kingdom of Goblins." Erwin said. "I know that it's not a place anyone but goblins should ever enter. I know they do unspeakable horrors to keshaphim in there. Alas, I don't know the answers to any of your questions."

"I told you to worry about your job," Wyllt interrupted. "I'll worry about getting in and out of Kurgal,"

"I just assumed we'd follow you in," Jeremy said.

Erwin shot him a disagreeable glance.

"You see, Jeremy. This is why we need to leave the strategy to me."

"I know how to strategize. I've been playing D&D since I was ten. My Dad was our Dungeon Master and he made us strategize some pretty incredible missions. Once we had to enter this maze-like lair of a Rakshasa. And he had all these traps, illusions, and doppelgängers guarding the place."

Wyllt lifted an eyebrow and shot Jeremy a crooked smile. Not his Cheshire Cat smile, but more like the way you'd look at someone you pitied. All that did was fuel Jeremy's dislike of the man.

"Jeremy—" Wyllt said.

"Interesting fact about the Rakshasa," Erwin interrupted, looking up from his drawing pad. "The humans known as Hindu purported the attacks against their people by the Taotie as the spawn of their god Brahma, exiled from Brahmaloka after rebelling against their creator. The word Rakshasa comes from the Sanskrit word, Rakshama, which, strangely, means 'Protect me'." Erwin laughed.

"Gentlemen," Wyllt interjected. "While this is all so fascinating, we have more pressing issues at hand. If our mission is to be a success, each of you needs to know precisely what your role will be. Any deviation could result in failure."

"But there's more to the story!" Erwin said.

"I'm sure there is. But, as I already said, we need to stay focused on the mission at hand."

Erwin frowned. "Very well."

"OK. So, Birch, Grath, and I can take the rear," Jeremy said.

Wyllt smiled at Jeremy and shook his head.

"What?" Jeremy said.

"Jeremy, listen carefully to what I'm saying. You have no actual combat experience. Games of strategy are fun, but they're no substitute for the real thing. My men and I have trained for these events. We didn't sit around, rolling dice and arguing over whether the barbarian should kick down the door or have the thief pick the lock."

Jeremy frowned, shooting Wyllt a disapproving look.

Wyllt continued. "The reality of this line of work is that you need to make split-second decisions based on the intel at hand."

"OK. Fine. So how do we all fit in?" Jeremy said, whirling his finger around to indicate himself, Erwin, the two koth, and the three elves.

"We'll be one team, divided into operators and non-operators. Among the non-operators, we will need one to watch the bird while we're inside. We'll need someone standing guard at all times, and someone with Ortiz monitoring the comms and drone visuals," Wyllt said, lifting his drink to his mouth.

"I'd suggest leaving Erwin, Ezzy, Ellesmere, and Hamjil to do that," Jeremy said. He pointed to Ezzy. "She's really good with technology so she can run comms and visuals with Ortiz. Hamjil can stand guard. He's supposedly a really good fighter, and his skills might be good to have inside. But he won't go anywhere without Ellesmere."

Hamjil nodded in agreement.

"And what about me?" Erwin said.

Jeremy shrugged. "You can watch the bird, whatever that means."

Wyllt smiled and shook his head. "Jeremy, your naiveté is stunning... just stunning. Though it saddens me that our little endeavor will more than likely expunge that part of your delightful personality."

Jeremy gave Wyllt another disapproving look.

"Jeremy," Ellesmere interjected before he could retort. "While I appreciate you speaking on our behalf. There's no need. I have no intention of sending Ezzy or myself to Kurgal. There are ways, however, that I can support you that wouldn't include staring at a screen. I'll go into Kurgal with you, but I'll create a proxy for my essence to inhabit."

"What?" Jeremy's eyes widened.

"You might know it as a golem," Erwin interjected.

"No way!" Jeremy said.

"I assure you I do know how to create such a thing," Ellesmere said.

"My, my, my. This is going to be a lot more fun than I imagined," Wyllt said, taking another sip from his goblet.

"A golem?" Jeremy said. "Like... but how?"

"All Elders and most guardians learn how to create golems," Ellesmere said. "Elders, so we can protect ourselves when the guardians are unable."

"So cool!" Jeremy said. He leaned forward and glanced at Ezzy. She was facing the rear and he could hardly see her save for her elbow resting on the armrest.

The mook sporting dreadlocks, sunglasses and a durag caught Jeremy's glance. He raised his sunglasses, smiled at Jeremy, and then shot a quick glance at Ezzy. His smile broadened and he raised his brow, looking at Jeremy once again.

"Ezzy cannot," Ellesmere said.

Jeremy glared at the man. He turned back to his conversation. "Cannot what?"

"Ezzy cannot create a proxy. Your suggestion of her working the artifices is a good one."

"Great!" Wyllt said. "Now that just leaves you and your two dino-pals."

"Koth. They're koth. Not dinosaurs," Jeremy said.

"So, given the choice, what role in the party will you play?" There was a hint of mocking sarcasm in Wyllt's question.

"The three of us will go in with you. Birch and Grath are well trained in combat."

Wyllt stared at Jeremy. A piercing stare that made Jeremy feel as if he were being sized up; probed and scanned to see if he really had what it takes. His stomach twisted and he felt a chill run down his spine.

"I think Jeremy should stay on the plane with us," Erwin said.

Jeremy furrowed his brow and shot the gnome a disapproving look. *Not this again.* "Oh no I'm not. I'm going in. I've been training for this. I'm not going to be the one to *watch the bird* outside while you go in."

"Jeremy, don't be ridiculous. You've certainly shed a few pounds over the past few weeks, but you're no guardian," Erwin said.

Jeremy bit his lip. He wanted to scream. *How do these people have the right to tell me what I am and what I'm not?*

"I'm going into Kurgal. And they're coming with us," Jeremy said, whipping his finger around again to point at Birch and Grath. "Look at those two. Look at 'em! You can't deny that having those two in battle with you wouldn't be a good idea."

"I certainly wouldn't want to go up against them myself," Wyllt said.

"And they're sworn to us," Jeremy said, waving his hand back and forth between him and Erwin.

Sworn to you, Gift Giver? Birch mindcasted.

Just go with it, Jeremy said.

"Oh, they are, are they?" Wyllt said, raising an eyebrow.

"Yes. We… we saved their lives once. They have a, uh, life debt with us."

Life debt? Birch said.

Just go with it, please.

"This has all been very enlightening," Wyllt said. "Though, I'm inclined to side with the gnome on this one. I'm glad you believe in yourself. That's noble. Commendable, even. And I'm compelled to take you in with me, despite my own better judgment. But I want to say one last thing on this matter."

He leaned forward, holding his goblet in his hands, settling his eyes on Jeremy. His icy, probing stare seemed to peer into Jeremy's very soul. Jeremy swallowed and gritted his teeth. Though it were mere seconds, Jeremy felt as if he were in a staring contest before the man broke the silence.

"I've been hunting relics, gnomes, elves… you name it… if it's remotely esoteric, living or dead, I've traveled the world to find it. I've dealt with the scum of the earth. Men and women who would make your skin crawl and fill you with the desire to put a bullet in their head. And I've met fine, upstanding individuals who care more about helping their fellow man rather than whether they upgraded from a 50 inch TV to 70 inch. Point is, I've met a whole lot of people, Jeremy. But I've never met anyone quite like you. To say that you're special is an understatement. The world needs Jeremy Goodson, not Santa Claus. Sure, you can be both, and I surmise that you'd do a lot of good running around in the red robe. But I shudder to think of a world without you in it. That saddens me. Make your decision wisely, knowing the potential void you leave behind."

Erwin stared at Wyllt with a dumbfounded look. He then grabbed his pencil and started sketching the man.

"When I was seventeen," Jeremy said hesitantly. "I lost my sister. She killed herself. Do you know why she killed herself, Mr. Wyllt?"

Wyllt sighed and looked to Jeremy. A solemn expression. "I'm sorry, Jeremy. It's difficult to lose a loved one." He took another sip of his drink.

"She killed herself because she had no hope. No one around her knew how miserable she was inside. I'm her big brother, and at the time I didn't really care. In fact, I was one of the reasons she wanted to die."

Jeremy bit his lower lip and inhaled, feeling the too familiar sorrow seep in again. "I was supposed to protect her. But I ignored her... pushed her away. There was one day I remember, only a few months before she died," Jeremy swallowed as the memory flooded in. "She ran into my room, crying because she was upset about something..."

Jeremy paused. "I don't even know what it was. But you know what I did? I didn't even give her the chance to tell me. I yelled at her and told her to get out of my room. Get out of my room." Jeremy wiped a tear from his eye.

"Jeremy, I don't mean to interrupt your pity party here," Wyllt said. "But here's what I'm hearing you say. You feel bad about the way you treated your sister and now you want to punish yourself by placing yourself in a situation that could get you killed. That's what my dear ol' grandma would call stinkin' thinkin'."

Jeremy gritted his teeth and fixed his eyes on Wyllt.

"No, Mr. Wyllt. I don't think so. I'm doing this because I'm tired of looking the other way when the bully picks on somebody. I'm tired of being too scared to say something when I know something is wrong. And I'm tired of burying my head in the sand, pretending that everything will be all right when it isn't. I could have saved my sister, Mr. Wyllt. But I was too busy worrying about myself. I'm not doing that anymore. I'm going into Kurgal, I'm finding my friends and that ring, and then I'm going to start making plans for Christmas."

Erwin and Ellesmere stared at Jeremy. Ellesmere smiled and Erwin's mouth was agape again.

"And," Jeremy swallowed. "If I die in there, I want you to give the ring to my Dad. He'd do a great job as," Jeremy hesitated, still finding it hard to say the name. "… he'd make a great Santa Claus."

Wyllt smiled and winked at Jeremy before swallowing the last of his drink. He placed the glass down and clapped. "Bravo, Jeremy. Bravo."

CHAPTER 51

STOPOVER

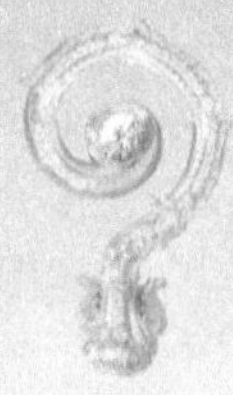

"One could not help but feel pity toward the pitied one known as Ezzy. But despite how her own people treated her, she had a passion for life and a love of reading. She found peace within the worlds of the books she read, feeling only whole in the comfort of their pages; that was until she met Jeremy."

~ From *The Second Gift Giver Chronicles* compiled by Erwin Albowyn, a Chronicler of the Master Construct, Second Order, an alfargnym of Unterbaum

The hot, humid air and the smell of gasoline exhaust and old grease greeted Jeremy as he departed Wyllt's plane. True to her word, Ellesmere had somehow, despite the added weight, made the plane fly more efficiently. They had stopped at Wyllt's private airstrip in the Florida Keys to refuel and stretch a bit.

Wyllt went into his office in the hangar, claiming that he was making arrangements to have another plane or a helicopter available so that they could quickly evacuate everyone after the rescue.

Ellesmere, Ezzy, and Hamjil walked around inside the hangar, talking. They didn't seem to mind the mechanic who kept staring at them.

"Uh, we're going to a costume party," Jeremy told him. "Pretty sick costumes, right?"

The mechanic nodded and smiled, continuing to listen to whatever he had playing in his red Skullcandy headphones.

Erwin enjoyed the fresh air outside the hangar. He sported an illusion that made him look like a tall skinny tennis player, complete with white shorts and headband. Under the circumstances, he stood out more than the unveiled elves.

Wyllt's giant mook, Tufts, stood guard outside the plane. Where the other henchmen were, Jeremy didn't know.

After walking and stretching, Jeremy decided to practice his staff. He wanted to be ready to fight the goblins. He found an open area of the hangar and broke into the first form; his muscles remembering each way to move the staff. He executed that form a few times as a warm-up and then moved into the next few forms he'd learned. Feeling confident in those forms, he wanted to try some of the advanced ones the guardians had started to teach him before they left. He found these much harder to remember. He paused, feeling awkward; knowing that he was missing something.

"Your foot's not in the right position." He heard her voice. Her soft, beautiful voice.

Jeremy turned around and found Ezzy standing there.

"Your right foot needs to point outward, not forward," she said.

Jeremy smiled at her. "Uh, OK. Let me try that." He broke into the stance, whirled the staff from his left to his right, and pointed his foot outward as he turned. She was right. It worked better that way. He stopped and placed his staff end down. "I didn't know you knew how to fight?"

"Well, I don't, really. Self-taught mostly. I like to watch the Orindin Swordsworn train. I can see them from my house. They're so graceful. Mercurio showed me a thing or two as well.

He always told Ellesmere that I needed to know how to defend myself in case the guardians couldn't."

"Huh. Do you want to be a guardian?" Jeremy said, realizing how stupid that sounded. *Idiot!* He felt himself blush, hoping she wouldn't see him for the imbecile he was.

Ezzy smiled. "No. They'd never let me do that." She looked down as if she was ashamed.

"Why? I'm sure you'd be good at it."

"How would you know? I gave you one tip and you think I'd make an excellent guardian?" Her smile widened and her cheeks reddened.

An inner warmth, different from the sweltering heat of the hangar, overcame Jeremy, and he felt lightheaded. "Um, well… uh," he swallowed.

Ezzy glanced to her left, and Jeremy followed her eyes. A large push broom lay in the corner. She started walking toward it.

"Before you make a judgment, you should gather as much information as possible," she said, smiling as she grabbed the broom by its handle. She stepped on the brush and then unscrewed the shaft. The two parts separated, and Ezzy hefted the handle up, taking a defensive posture. She swung the shaft around, feeling its weight and breaking into form. She moved through the same form Jeremy had been trying, only she did it effortlessly.

Slack jawed, Jeremy stared at her. *She's amazing!*

"Alright," she walked toward Jeremy. "Let's try this. I'll be at a disadvantage using this inferior staff, so go easy on me."

What is happening here? This girl seemed so shy before. Now she was acting all tough and flirty. *She* is *flirting, right?*

"Um, I don't know. What if one of us gets, uh, hurt?" Jeremy said.

"Well, like I said. Take it easy on me." She smiled.

Gosh! That smile. It's a weapon in itself. She wasn't serious, was she? How was this happening?

"Come on. Staff up," she said, nodding her chin at his weapon. Her curly locks bounced.

Jeremy reluctantly took the staff in both hands and moved into battle stance.

Ezzy slammed the broom handle down on his staff.

Jeremy instinctively pushed it up and away from him, stepping to the side. He assumed a defensive stance rather than counter striking.

Ezzy didn't hesitate. She whirled the makeshift staff around and went for a head-shot.

Jeremy flinched, stepping backwards and raising his staff to block the blow.

Relentless, Ezzy came after him, blow after blow, getting faster with every strike. Jeremy countered each one, stepping back or to the side.

They drew a small crowd as Ellesmere, Hamjil, and the tennis-ready Erwin walked over to watch. Jeremy didn't dare look at the others. He needed to stay focused on the unrelenting Ezzy. He followed her eyes, staring into them. Their beautiful light green color contrasted with her lush eyelashes. There was an undeniable attraction here. That made it difficult for him to do anything but defend her strikes.

"Come on!" She yelled. "Don't just keep backing up. You're starting to be predictable." She feigned a strike to his left, then took advantage of the opening on his right. The tip of the broom-stick rammed into his gut, and Jeremy winced, barely able to step away from her next strike.

"Come on *Santa*! Pretend I'm a goblin trying to steal your toys."

Jeremy looked at the crowd of spectators, trying to gauge their expressions. Did they know something he didn't?

Ezzy charged forward with a flurry of windmill-like attacks. Each jarring crack of wood on wood seemed more intense.

Sweat poured from Jeremy's brow. He pushed at her, deciding that this wasn't going to end if he didn't make his best effort. He wanted to take off his glasses and wipe the sweat, but he didn't dare. He brought his staff down on hers, and she smiled. She seemed to be exhilarated because he was finally on the offensive.

The two danced, exchanging strike and counter strike until exhaustion got the better of Jeremy. He was too winded to say anything, so he put up his hand and placed his staff at his side.

Ezzy backed up. She didn't seem tired at all.

Jeremy placed one hand on his thigh and arched over slightly, trying to catch his breath. He took off his glasses and used his forearm to wipe his brow.

"Good match," Ezzy said.

Jeremy looked up at her and nodded.

"Well now," Ellesmere interrupted. "If the two of you are done playing, I'd like a word with you, Ezzy."

"Wheels up in five minutes!" Yelled the fake detective.

"Yeah… good… match." Jeremy stood up. "Thanks, I needed… the practice."

Ezzy nodded and then walked over to Ellesmere. They walked back toward the plane, and Ezzy turned around.

"Hey," she called to Jeremy. "Do you like to read stories?"

Jeremy placed his glasses back on. "Um, do I like… to read… stories?"

"Yeah, you know… like books about things that aren't real?"

"Um, yeah. I love to read. You should see my bookshelves at home. They're, um, uh, they're filled with novels."

"Have you ever read Tristan and Iseult?"

"Um, no. I haven't. I've heard of it though."

"It's one of my favorites. I think I've read almost every version."

"Ezzy," Ellesmere said, clearing her throat. "Please come with me."

Ezzy frowned. "I'll lend you a copy later," she said and then waved timidly, leaving Jeremy with a smile.

That smile!

THIS CHILD! Ellesmere fumed. She was going to be the death of her! *The girl is smitten!*

Ezzy grabbed onto Ellesmere's elbow and they locked arms.

"Yes, Immatina?"

"This cannot happen," Ellesmere said, softly, but with conviction.

"What do you mean?" Ezzy said, looking back at Jeremy one last time.

Ellesmere tugged at her arm to get her attention. The two walked around to the other side of the plane, out of sight of anyone else.

"Child, don't play coy with me. You know precisely what I mean. Whatever romantic allusions or delusions you have about having a relationship with Jeremy Goodson need to be extinguished, here and now."

"Oh, Immatina. It's just—"

"Nothing! It's just nothing. Because that's how it has to be," Ellesmere said, turning Ezzy around to face her.

"Immatina, for as long as I can remember, you're the only one who even looks at me. He's the only other person who has said more than a sentence to me… ever! I… I…"

"Not more than three days ago you had a conversation with Bartleby the gatekeeper!"

"Yes, but it's not the same. He's a—"

"A what? An alfargnym? Makes no difference."

"Yes, but Immatina, Jeremy's different. He—"

"Ezzy, Little Heart. Listen to me. I can't pretend to know what it must be like for you. I'm saddened that you were born to bear this burden. But you must understand that whatever it is you wish to happen between you and Jeremy, it simply cannot. Jeremy has already made a mess of things. Once this is all over—"

"Over? What do you mean, over?"

Ellesmere stared into Ezzy's suspicion-filled eyes. She didn't know what to say.

"Wait. You don't really… what?" Ezzy placed her hand over her mouth. "You don't believe that Jeremy can do this, do you? This is…"

The gaunt expression on Ezzy's face was too much for

Ellesmere. She turned away, bowing her head and closing her eyes.

"This is all just a way for you to not have to deal with Jeremy anymore."

Ellesmere opened her eyes and spun back to Ezzy. How could she accuse her of such a thing?

"Child, no. It's not like that at all!"

"Then what is it?"

"Just because I think he's going to die in there doesn't mean I want it to happen. And even if he does survive, it still changes nothing for you. Jeremy has a long struggle ahead of him. He won't be accepted, even with Nikolaos' ring. And having you at his side will only make that worse."

The angry furrows of Ezzy's brow straightened. Her jaw relaxed as her expression grew from anger, to hurt, and finally sadness. Ellesmere's heart sank. She only wanted Ezzy to be happy. "Ezzy, I know this is difficult. You know I've tried to change things for you. But the council is set in their ways. Your father... he did something that went against the council. You are a persistent reminder of his transgressions. You..." Ellesmere didn't know what more to say. The girl's heart was broken. She'd give anything to mend it, but with all of her accomplishments and power, she couldn't. "Oh Ezzy." Ellesmere reached out and grabbed the girl for a hug. If words wouldn't help, she hoped a comforting embrace would.

Ezzy latched on and cried on her shoulder. Ellesmere's heart ached with Ezzy's.

"All right! Everyone, let's go!" One of the humans yelled. "We are clear for wheels up. Everyone in your seats."

CHAPTER 52
THE PRISON
AND THE PACIFIER

"Our shared world was once home to many species. Of those that perished in the futile pursuit of control were the centaur, the taotie, tengu, troll, naga, and dragon."

~ From *The Veiled Happenlore of the Master Construct* compiled by Fulbert Gisilfrid, a Chronicler of the Master Construct, Third Order, an alfargnym of Unterbaum.

Masaru hiked through the Russian wilderness, still not knowing his destination but following Turtak's directions.

Born of magic? Those strange words lingered in his mind. Turtak had always told Masaru that he was not like everyone else, that he'd been chosen for a purpose, and that his lack of a right arm was not a disability. All his life, Masaru proved that. But what did he mean, *born of magic?*

Turtak claimed that Masaru was a magical being. *Magic?* Masaru couldn't wrap his mind around that. It was a concept that he'd been taught was the stuff of fairy tales. And Turtak had never mentioned it before.

Masaru weighed those words. If what Turtak said was true, then Masaru had an unfair advantage over his peers. That was a disheartening revelation. He wanted to be the best, not because of an unfair advantage, but because he worked harder than everyone else.

He exhaled disappointment and reflected on his journey these past three weeks. How much of what he accomplished was because of magic and not simply his iron will? Masaru survived on his own, living off the land and conquering death. Well, that part he didn't do on his own. Turtak's lesson of knowing defeat had brought him to the brink of death. His unseen guide had saved him, nursed him back to health, and guided him further North in the Russian wilderness. But to what end? Curiosity jabbed at him, but his training held it at bay. Turtak had urged him to be patient and to look for clues along the way. This was a time for patience.

"Stop," Turtak said from behind. "We will set camp for the night. Forage for your supper and then rest."

Rest? Masaru had been resting for days. Despite his wounds and the poisoning, he had recuperated well. He felt fine. Perhaps having magic wasn't all that bad.

MASARU CUT a strip of meat from the rabbit roasting over the small campfire. The sun had set and Masaru took a moment to take in the tranquility of a land undisturbed by humanity.

An image appeared on the other side of the campfire. Masaru blinked and jumped to his feet, immediately falling into battle stance. He drew his katana and focused on the image. A creature sat, staring at the fire. Bundled in a fur coat, the hairless creature with long pointed ears sat cross-legged with a sword across its lap. Scale-like tattoo markings crowned his skull.

"Turtak?" Masaru said.

The creature looked up at him with those eerie dark, globular eyes. "Masaru, it is time."

Masaru considered his words; so strange to hear from such an inhuman creature. *It is Turtak!* "Time? Time for what?"

"It is a time of great transition, not only for you, but for the world. It is time for this part of your journey to end and a new one to begin."

Masaru noted his own breathing; heavy and uneven. Turtak had caught him off guard. He breathed in slowly, steadying his heart rate and his breaths.

"What... what are you?" Masaru said.

"Sit. There is much to tell you." Turtak waved his hand to the place Masaru had been sitting.

Masaru sheathed his blade and cautiously sat down. What did he need to be cautious of? This was Turtak, someone who knew Masaru better than anyone else. Someone who practically raised Masaru. But he was so strange looking. Turtak was smaller than him. And those eyes... void of pupils and as dark as night. They caught the reflection of the campfire, giving him an eerie appearance.

"Masaru, we may be physically different from one another. Two different species. But our peoples have endured the same indignities. Subjugated and enfeebled by those who felt threatened by our power. Hidden away in the shadows while humanity, a lesser species, is left to prosper. All manipulated by the blight; an enemy to both our peoples." The creature... Turtak sighed and turned his gaze to the fire. "My people, goblins, were stripped of our power and cast away in a prison to rot." He tossed a handful of kindling into the flickering flames, and then stood. "You, Masaru, are Dweorg; a once proud race of warriors, now lulled into a state of complacency. Your king is fat and lazy and his soldiers are soft and predictable. They shame your ancestry. This is your birthright, Masaru. You will be the one to free our peoples and restore us to the glory we once held."

"Why haven't you told me all this before? Why now?"

"Patience."

"I have been patient."

"Yes, but how much harder would it have been to be patient knowing this. How much sooner would you have pressed me to claim your birthright? I needed to ensure that this was done in my time, not yours. You have done well. And now you are ready. Tomorrow we will part ways. The next measure of your journey, you will walk alone."

"Why? Why can't we do this together, like always?"

"Where you are going, I cannot go."

"Why?" Masaru said.

"The Veil. It weakens me." Turtak walked away from the fire, then turned and looked up at Masaru. "It is what separates us. The Veil is the prison of my people and the pacifier of yours. Tomorrow you will pierce the Veil."

Masaru steadied his breathing again, fighting anticipation and anxiety. "And then what?"

"You will enter the land of your ancestors and claim your birthright."

CHAPTER 53
FAMILY DYNAMICS

"Each year the Lore Keepers publish a directory of enchanted items, called *The Almanac of Enchantments*. Details on the type of enchanted item, its abilities, its creator(s), and who its current owner are meticulously recorded within."

~ From *Appendix A: An Explanation on Magic from Lore Keeper Samil iyl Sayalla*

The Veiled Happenlore of the Master Construct compiled by Fulbert Gisilfrid, a Chronicler of the Master Construct, Third Order, an alfargnym of Unterbaum.

Jeremy walked onto the plane, still on cloud nine; the warm fuzzies tingling all over his body. He walked past Wyllt, who was already sitting. Jeremy sat and stared at the doorway, looking forward to seeing Ezzy walk through.

Erwin walked in and the visage of the tennis player faded.

"Felt good to stretch, didn't it?" Wyllt asked.

"Yeah," Jeremy replied. He glimpsed at Wyllt and then turned back to the door. "It felt real good."

"Getting pretty good with that staff of yours."

"You saw?"

"Security cameras. They're everywhere. I figure if Big Brother is watching, I should be too," Wyllt said with that pompous smile. "Your form's looking good. That elf girl wields a mean broomstick."

"Yeah." Jeremy nodded, his eyes wandering back to the door.

"Indeed!" Erwin said. "You two put on quite a show out there."

The two mooks walked in and took their seats in the rear.

Tufts still stood guard at the door.

Ellesmere and Ezzy stood in the doorway, with Hamjil behind them.

Jeremy smiled as Ellesmere walked past and Ezzy climbed in.

She didn't smile back. Ezzy didn't even look at him this time.

"Hey, Ezzy," Jeremy called.

The girl stopped and turned. She smiled, but it wasn't the same. It seemed put on. Her mouth formed a smile, but her eyes told a different story. She'd been crying.

"If you have that book with you, I'd love to read it."

She hesitated and then shook her head. "I don't have it with me." Ezzy turned and went to her seat.

What just happened? Everything seemed fine only minutes earlier. What had Ellesmere said to Ezzy to make her so upset? Jeremy furrowed his brow and looked at the matriarch.

"Ellesmere—"

"Jeremy," she cut him off. "I want you to have this." Ellesmere undid the clasp of her cloak and unfurled it from around her. Folding it in half, she reached across the cabin, handing it to Jeremy.

He stared at her; his mouth frozen in mid speech.

Jeremy leaned over and sheepishly took the cloak as if there was some cruel trick about to be played on him.

"Ezzy has the companion stone to go with my cloak. When we land, you may get it from her and choose whoever you wish to give it to."

"Companion stone?" Jeremy said.

"It allows a companion to see you when the cowl is drawn. It makes it easier to travel together."

"Cool," Jeremy said, glancing back to where Ezzy sat. He could barely see her arm and curly brown hair. She didn't look to find him. He looked back at Ellesmere. "Why are you giving this to me?"

"You'll need every advantage to survive Kurgal."

"I doubt it will fit, though. I'm a bit bigger than you."

"I had that cloak made when Ezzy was ten years old. I've always been worried about her." Ellesmere looked back to where Ezzy sat. "She always had a wandering heart with no place to wander." She turned back to Jeremy. "And I doubted she'd ever have a Veil cloak of her own. To my surprise, she was recently permitted to have one. Most likely because the council knew how much stress you and Mercurio put me under. They relented, for my sake. It didn't change how any of them viewed Ezzy. But they know I care for her as if she were my own, so they recently granted the commission of her Veil cloak. Yet, as I stated, I scarcely believed she would ever have one, so I commissioned this one when she was old enough to travel with me. It has *other* enchantments."

"Please fasten your seat belts. We are cleared for departure." The sound of the pilot's voice echoed through the cabin.

Jeremy sat back and checked his already fastened seat belt.

"Now, that is fascinating," Wyllt said. "Please. Tell us about these extra enchantments."

Jeremy frowned at the man.

"The Veil Cloak will expand to accommodate whatever it's covering. It will instinctively expand to the wearer's size and anything the wearer puts under it. It can also be pulled to whatever size I wish. I could hide the entire plane with a little help."

"That *is* an impressive cloak," Wyllt said.

"I had anticipated having to use it to cover both Ezzy and me. Perhaps that was a bit paranoid on my part, but it's only Ezzy and I, and no one else had the girl's best interest." Ellesmere glanced over at Hamjil who, judging by his frown, took some offense at this comment. "Oh, come now Hamjil. You know very well that if you had to choose between saving me and saving Ezzy, you'd not hesitate. It'd be me every time."

"Yes, but elder, that *is* my job," Hamjil said humbly.

"And protecting Ezzy is *my* job."

"Ah." Wyllt said. "Family. Don't you just love unusual family dynamics?"

The others ignored him.

Wyllt pointed to Ezzy. "What's the deal with that girl, anyway? Does she have some sort of disease? The way you're talking about her makes it sound like she's some sort of pariah."

"Our family dynamic is not of your concern," Ellesmere said.

"I didn't say I was concerned. Just curious," Wyllt said.

No one replied.

Jeremy swiveled his chair around, away from Wyllt and Erwin. He stared down at the folded cloak in his lap and then to the rear, trying to catch a glimpse of Ezzy. She was hidden, save for her elbow, among the high-backed chairs and imposing mooks.

He didn't feel like talking, so he took off his glasses, reclined his seat, closed his eyes, and waited for sleep to come.

CHAPTER 54

KNOCK BEFORE ENTERING

"In 6,266 B.C. the dweorg suffered their greatest defeat when the clanhold of Vidarheim was attacked by the dragons Shet and Magor as well as hordes of goblins and taotie. The intense battle leveled the mountain, plunging it into the Great Lake of Friga."

~ From *The Veiled Happenlore of the Master Construct* compiled by Fulbert Gisilfrid, a Chronicler of the Master Construct, Third Order, an alfargnym of Unterbaum.

For the first time in his life, Masaru was truly alone. Walking through the dense Russian forest for miles only amplified that feeling. Several times he stopped, asking Turtak if he was heading in the right direction. No answer came. It was a strange, hollow, mournful feeling. The voice he'd heard all his life was no longer there. Turtak warned him and told him it'd be a long time before they saw each other again. That was after he revealed himself. *A goblin? How strange?*

Masaru glimpsed the outline of a house in the distance. This was what he was looking for. He breathed in and readied himself to meet the gatekeeper. He'd been told that all he needed to do was ask for passage to Nidavellir. If the gatekeeper denied him, he'd have to hurt him. He hoped it wouldn't come to that.

Masaru crept up to the house. It was small, made of round stone and wood, with a thatched roof.

A streak of purple-gray fur dashed out from the other side of the house.

Masaru moved to a defensive stance.

Another streak followed, this one more gray than purple. It pounced on the other, and the two tumbled to the ground. They chirped and growled as they tussled in the dirt.

Masaru could barely make out their features. The fur, the likes he had never seen in that grayish-purple color on an animal, covered most of its body.

The door swung open, and a small, disheveled old man wearing a bomber hat with the ear flaps buttoned to the top walked out. His short, brown, fluffy beard covered most of the lower part of his face, and a pair of aviator-style sunglasses covered the rest. He wore what looked like an old cloth sack with holes cut out for the arms and head. Over the sack he had a blue vest with many pockets. Around his waist was a ragged, yellow… Batman utility belt? Masaru had seen kids with similar ones. Was this the gatekeeper?

The little old man yelled down at the creatures. They stopped and sat on the ground, resting on the back of their hands, panting. The creatures had large, black pearl eyes and a small, oblong, beak-like snout. They stared up at the old man with remorseful eyes.

He continued to scold them and then pointed inside the house. Masaru didn't recognize the language.

The dejected creatures slumped their shoulders and walked toward the door. The dark purple one trailed behind the other, stopped, and darted back. It grabbed for something on the ground, hidden within a patch of grass. Once in his grasp, he turned around and headed back for the door, dragging a dead mouse by its tail.

Once the creatures were inside, the old man entered the house, closing the door behind him.

What in the world was that?

Masaru caught a glimpse of pink flutter by his head. He turned and saw a winged creature. It glowed a pinkish-red color. Its wings silently flapping, it hovered there, cocking its head and staring at Masaru. It had the slender body of a woman with no visible genitalia. Wisps of pink, shimmering energy wafted off its head like long hair blowing in the wind. She stared at Masaru with large, dark eyes.

Masaru returned her gaze, unable to turn away. He couldn't believe what he was seeing.

Another of the creatures appeared at his other side.

Fairies! These are fairies. He had truly entered a place vastly different from anything he could imagine. In fact, he wasn't that imaginative to begin with. Masaru wasn't the kid that played with toys or watched TV. Turtak had taught him that those things were just distractions. But none of his studies prepared him to come face to face with a fairy. Why hadn't Turtak taught him about these things? About magic? It sure would be useful now.

"Hello," Masaru whispered.

The fairy hovered backward slightly and cocked its head to the side.

"Do you speak English?" Masaru said. He switched languages, repeating the question in Japanese, Russian, and Norwegian.

Each time the fairy cocked her head in the opposite direction, smiled and zipped around his head. The other one followed.

Hmmm… I wonder…

"Can you understand me?" He said, this time in the secret language shared by him and Turtak.

The fairies silently zipped around his head again.

Masaru followed them with his eyes until he became slightly dizzy.

Wait. He thought. *What if these are part of some warning system?* They seemed harmless, but he couldn't take the chance. He inhaled and steadied himself, focusing his eyes on one spot in the fairies' flight path, studying and timing its every move. Masaru eased his left hand to the sheath of his katana, slowly pushing the hand guard forward with his thumb. He drew the sword faster than the fairies could react. The blade sliced through the air, cutting them in half. Their remains fell but dissipated into golden motes of light before they could hit the ground.

Huh? He looked around for any remains, but they were completely gone.

Unsure of how to proceed, he watched the cottage for another hour before finally deciding to make his move. Masaru inched toward the cabin, careful not to make any noise. He approached the door, placed his hand on the knob, and turned it slowly, trying to avoid making a sound.

Click! went the mechanism. Masaru tensed, holding his hand on the doorknob, waiting for any sign that the occupants were alerted to his presence.

None came, and he resumed turning the knob, easing the door open.

Click! Another mechanism sounded. With the door more than halfway open, Masaru looked up to find a solid log moving his way. He jumped, trying to avoid it, but it caught him square on the side of his head, knocking him to the ground.

Stars and waves of energy exploded in his vision as he hit the ground. He wanted to push himself back up, but the blow had been too jarring.

In the doorway, he glimpsed a pair of boots. His eyes darted upwards, and he saw the Batman symbol on the belt. He wanted to get back up, but his head fought against it and his eyes slowly closed.

"Silly dweorg. You should have knocked," he heard someone say before he lost consciousness.

CHAPTER 55

A LESSON IN GATEHOUSE ETIQUETTE

"Dweorg possess the same magical potential as elves and alfargnym, but they are a stubborn lot. They refuse to learn how to manipulate magic beyond that of making weapons and armor."

~ From *Appendix A: An Explanation on Magic from Lore Keeper Samil iyl Sayalla*

The Veiled Happenlore of the Master Construct compiled by Fulbert Gisilfrid, a Chronicler of the Master Construct, Third Order, an alfargnym of Unterbaum.

Masaru awoke with a pounding in his head and a poking on his cheek. He fought to open his eyes against the blaring light that only intensified his headache. He turned his head slowly, and the poking on his cheek stopped.

The small purplish creature with the big black eyes stared at him. It hummed a high-pitched growl and poked its finger at his nose before jumping back.

Masaru squinted at the creature and pushed himself away. He

held his hand to his head and tried to stand up, but only made it to a sitting position.

"Ah! You is wake." Masaru heard a squeaky voice from across the room. He looked over and saw the strange old man use his short staff to hobble toward him.

Masaru jumped to his feet and withdrew his sword, ready for a fight. He concentrated his vision on the old man while glancing about to take in his surroundings and look for exits. The room was small and L-shaped. A wooden table, grayed with age, sat in the middle with two chairs tucked under it. Against the wall was a wooden counter that seemed too tall for someone of the gatekeeper's size. In an alcove was a large bed. Across from it, Masaru could see the side of a flat screen TV sitting on a stand. Windows with old, drab, drawn curtains were on every side except where the counter was. He took a quick glance backward and found the door.

"Silly dweorg. Didn't no one talk you about gatehouse? Why you hold your sword at me?" The gatekeeper smiled awkwardly.

Masaru was about to say something, and then he realized that the old man spoke in the secret language that only he and Turtak spoke. Masaru stared at him and turned his head to the side. "Turtak?"

"Huh? Turtak? That goblin speak? 'Renewed life,' I thinks. Or be it 'water bringer'? Haven't studied goblin long time! I not so good with other languages. I speak gnymish good, but others not so good. You speak gnymish?"

Masaru continued to stare at the old man. He didn't know what to make of him, but he certainly didn't trust him. An awkward silence persisted as the two stared at each other.

"Please, you sword, put it back in his sheath. Tell me, what be your destination?"

Destination? He's going to open the gate for me. Masaru stepped back and sheathed his sword.

"I'm ready to go," he said.

"Wait span." The old man's grin grew wider. "This must be

you first time this side of Veil. You lost from you group? Did friends not say how gatehouse work?"

"No," Masaru said.

"No?" The man giggled. "No? So, how you get long way here without know use a gatehouse?"

"I was only told where to find the gatehouse. And that I'm supposed to use it to get to Nidavellir."

"Ah. Now understands." He turned around and walked back toward where he was when Masaru first woke up. "Well, come, silly dweorg. You go."

Masaru walked up to the gatekeeper and watched as he raised his staff and pushed on the wall sconce. It tilted sideways, and the wooden counter slid along the wall about a meter, revealing a hidden stairwell in the floor. The gatekeeper hobbled down the steps, using the staff to brace himself.

Masaru followed him into the dark stairwell. He pulled his head back as the musty, trapped air flowed upward. A light switched on up ahead, revealing a turn that led deeper into the damp and musty bowels of the gatehouse. The winding staircase took several minutes to descend before the light intensified. *How strange.* It was as if they were walking into sunlight.

The gatekeeper led him into a room where the bright light emanated. A shimmering curtain of brilliant golden energy hung in the center. It lit up the entire room, exposing the brick all around and a pedestal beneath it. To its right was a control device with a large dial. Around its edge were twelve icons; mostly jewels but some were shapes. An inner dial had ten more symbols, circling yet another dial with ten other symbols. The little man turned the dial and placed his hands on two gold-handled levers. He stared at Masaru and sighed.

"Silly dweorg. What you wait for? You want go home?"

Masaru raised an eyebrow and sighed. He wasn't sure what he was supposed to do. Nothing was happening.

"Did log hit you braincase very hard you not remember anything? What you name?"

"Masaru."

"Masaru?" The gatekeeper scrunched his forehead. "What kind name is?"

"It's a Japanese name. It means victory."

"You parents new thinkers, huh? Not good to have human name. What you friends must think. Remember Elder Zohar words, 'bout humans… 'Leave them to kill themselves off.'" He nodded matter-of-factly, staring at Masaru with eyes that seemed to pity him.

Masaru knew that look all too well. He'd seen it in the eyes of his teachers and classmates most often. But it was a look that almost everyone gave him. Masaru didn't want their pity, or this old man's either.

"You ready go home?"

"Um, yes. I'm ready."

"You go now." The old man nodded toward the shimmering curtain.

Masaru stared into its rolling, hypnotic beauty and waited for something to happen. But nothing did.

"Silly dweorg. Go through, or you need rest you broken brain-case before go?"

Through? Was he supposed to just walk through it? Masaru sighed and took a step forward, reaching out with his hand to touch the Veil and push it aside. His hand went through the field of brilliant light as if it weren't even there. The Veil seemed undisturbed.

Masaru breathed in deeply, stepped up on the pedestal, and into the golden light. He blinked as the bright light of the Veil covered him. The transition disoriented him, and his vision swirled. He was in a completely unfamiliar room. This one was brighter, with white and gray marbled walls. A heavy wooden door, gilded in bronze around the edge, stood in front of him. In its center was a symbol made of iron. He focused on the symbol, trying to reorient himself and overcome the strange feeling that made his vision swirl and his head feel numb. A set of triangles blurred in a dizzying vortex before coming into focus. This was *the* symbol. The one Turtak had shown him many years ago. Five interlocking triangles. The same symbol he incorporated into the design of his katana's guard.

From the corner of his eye, Masaru saw movement. He instinctively tightened his grip on the hilt of his katana and turned to see what was there.

Two bearded men armed with guns stood to either side of the door. Beside one, a large black and gray short-haired dog laid with its head still on the floor. The men, dressed in aqua blue and dark green uniforms, wore simple, rounded helmets with their faces exposed. On one shoulder, the pauldron was crafted into the shape of a bird. The light of the Veil reflected off the blues of the feathers, picking up subtle hints of the dark green leather in the tunic beneath. Their guns were odd looking; the medium-sized barrel was shaped like an animal, its mouth the part where the bullets would come out. *A bear, maybe? A tiger?* He couldn't tell. They held their guns across the chest; one hand on the grip and the other under the barrel. Maybe some kind of shotgun? Masaru knew little about guns, and these were stranger than any he'd ever seen.

There was something about these men that was oddly familiar to Masaru. Their stout, squat shoulders and rounded features reminded him of his own. These were his people!

"Wayford?" One soldier said, taking a step toward Masaru.

Masaru stared at the soldier. He was plump, with a black beard speckled with… *Are those crumbs in his beard?*

"Wayford," the soldier said again, resting his gun on his shoulder and extending his free hand.

"What are you saying? I don't understand," Masaru said in English. He wondered if he should have used the secret language. But he was curious to see what the soldier said or did.

The soldier raised an eyebrow and glanced at his partner, then back at Masaru. "Yer not in the manethel no more. Is there a reason yer speaking that language?" He spoke in the secret language. At least it sounded like the secret language; a broken, stilted version of it.

Masaru shook his head. "I don't understand what you're asking me for," he said, this time in the secret language.

"I need to see yer wayford."

Masaru stared at him, then glanced at the soldier's palm, and then back again. *He wants something from me.*

"I don't have one."

"If ya lost it, yer gon have to wait here fer another one. It might take a day or two. What's yer name?"

"I don't have time to wait. I need to see the king immediately."

"You had a wayford to see the high king?"

"No."

"Well, if yer expecting a wayford to see the high king, that could take longer. Up to a fivespan, mayhaps. I'll have Gunnulfor get tidends up to Konungarhol. In the meantime, ya can stay in one of the visitor rooms or ya can go back to where ya came from and come back again in a sevenspan. I need yer name though."

Masaru studied the soldier, summing up his threat level. He and the other were slovenly and fat, but well armored. His eyes darted back and forth between the two, looking for a weakness. The other one had a reddish-brown beard, with a braid on each side. Masaru couldn't see the armor beneath the beard, but he judged by the way the black-bearded soldier moved his head, there wasn't much protection there. He'd have to be careful of the guns, but he was pretty sure he could take them both out before their fingers even reached their triggers. He'd give them one last chance.

As for the large dog, the thing barely moved. Though its eyes were now open and it looked up at Masaru. Its head was massive, reminding Masaru of a pitbull, only larger. Though it seemed docile now, it was no doubt a guard dog. He'd need to take it out first.

"I can't wait a week. I need to see the king now. Take me to him, now."

The soldiers looked at one another again and then turned back to Masaru. "Are ya of the mountain, or not?"

"What?"

"Are ya of the mountain, or not?" The soldier repeated, this time gritting his teeth and moving his gun from his shoulder.

The other soldier followed suit and the dog stood. It's massive head above the guard's waist. Eye's fixed on Masaru, the beast bared its teeth. A menacing growl rumbled from its sharp toothed maw.

Masaru drew his katana, stepped off the pedestal, and jabbed the blade down into the dog's skull, then up into the opposite soldier's neck. He turned, grabbed the barrel of the other soldier's gun and pushed it down. He swung his sword around, beheading the soldier before he could pull the trigger.

Golden light trickled from the gaping hole that once held the man's head. Masaru startled, stepped back and glimpsed the other soldier. Light trickled from his wounds as well. Masaru stared wide-eyed and perplexed as the light consumed the flesh, blood, and bone of both men and beast, leaving nothing behind save for their armor, clothing, and weapons and the dog's collar.

What just happened?

The urgency of the situation left little time to ponder. He looked around the small room and saw nothing more of interest. It was like the one he'd left, though the control panel was further away from the pedestal. He rushed to the door, and gingerly pushed down on the handle until he heard the tumblers click.

Masaru opened it slowly, exposing a gray and white marbled hallway with six wooden doors and a staircase at the end. Hanging between each door were thick, round, plate-like bronze lamps. In the center of each plate, a round, glowing white bulb lit the way down the gray cobblestone hall.

The air here was warm and toasty, void of the musty smell that greeted him earlier. Hints of lemon and other flowery scents lingered.

What was he going to do now? He hoped he wouldn't have to kill anyone else. Masaru looked to the remains of the dead guards and the blood-stained floor around them. *Why didn't the blood disappear along with the rest of their bodies?* He examined his hooded sweatshirt and cursed when he saw the splattered blood had formed darker stains on the black cloth. Masaru needed a change of clothes. Something that wasn't bloodied and something that made him fit in. He contemplated posing as a guard but concluded that he didn't know enough to try and blend in that way. If he looked like a traveler, he could at least feign ignorance. He closed the door to assess his options. If someone found the guard's remains, they'd put out the alert and come after him.

The shimmering curtain of golden light disappeared, startling Masaru. An empty pedestal remained.

Now what? He had no idea how to open it again.

Masaru removed his hoodie and used it to wipe up the blood, but it still left a stain. He used the last of his water bottle and t-shirt from his pack to scrub the floor clean. He threw the bloodied clothes on top of the guard's armor and then went and looked over the controls. The dial was identical to the other one, but he had no idea how to work it. He noticed each dial had the five-triangle symbol on it that matched the one on the door. Two of the rings were dialed to the symbol, but the outer one wasn't. He turned the ring so that all three displayed the triangle symbol at the top. Nothing happened.

With only one way out of the room now, Masaru opened the wooden door and stepped carefully into the hall, sword ready. There had to be some clothes in one of the rooms. He tried the first one, slowly turning the handle. The sound of snoring greeted him as he carefully opened the door. He slipped in without letting too much light stream in from the hallway. On the other side of the room, he saw a dresser with three drawers.

Perfect. He tiptoed across the room and slowly slid open the first drawer. Unable to make out any of the clothing, he grabbed a bundle and closed the drawer. On the desk, he spied a single jar. He removed the lid and sniffed its contents. It had the smell of spiced jerky. His stomach grumbled, forcing him to take it. He emptied the contents, returned the lid, and silently slipped out into the hall.

Masaru sniffed a piece of the jerky again, catching hints of salt and aromatic spices, but he couldn't tell what kind of meat it was. He took a bite and still couldn't tell. He unraveled the clothes, finding several light blue tunics, but nothing else. It'd have to do. But first, he needed a place to ditch the armor.

He opened the door of the next room, finding two empty beds and two more dressers. The dressers were empty. *Perfect.*

After stuffing the guards' clothing in the dressers and hanging their armor on some hooks he found in the room, Masaru was ready to get out of there.

He took off his belt, pulled the tunic he found over his head, and used the belt to make it snug around his waist. He shoved the extra tunic in his backpack and fastened the katana sheath back on the belt. With his sword in one hand and a piece of jerky in the other, he headed back into the hall.

Masaru ignored the other doors, making a hasty exit to the stairs. He estimated that he had been at least thirty meters below ground before coming to two great, thick wooden doors. Round at the top and gilded with bronze all around. The centerpiece, bisected by each door, was a large iron bird like the ones on the soldiers' pauldrons.

He grabbed the two handles in the center of each door, turned them, and pushed them open. A gust of icy wind and snow burst in. Masaru squinted and turned his head, peering up slightly to see the snow filled landscape. Looming in the distance was the tallest mountain Masaru had ever seen.

CHAPTER 56

CLOBBERING TIME

"Biomagical potentials vary between the keshaphim and are classified as such using the Togodumnus Scale."

~ From *Appendix A: An Explanation on Magic from Lore Keeper Samil iyl Sayalla*

The Veiled Happenlore of the Master Construct compiled by Fulbert Gisilfrid, a Chronicler of the Master Construct, Third Order, an alfargnym of Unterbaum.

Ding! Ding! The sound of the cabin bell pulled Jeremy from his sleep.

"All right, people. We're about to start our descent," The pilot said. "This is gonna be rough and tricky. So you stow-aways better hang on tight. Everyone else, make sure your seat-belts are fastened and your seats are in the landing position."

Jeremy rubbed his face, coaxing the sleep dust from his eyes. He put his glasses back on and looked to see if he could make eye contact with Ezzy one more time. She was still hidden among the mooks and the high-back seats. He swiveled his chair around and he felt it lock in place. The seatback automatically adjusted to move him forward. He looked over at Erwin. The gnome neatly placed his sketch pad and pencils in his satchel and looked up at Jeremy.

"Did you sleep well?"

Jeremy nodded. "You get any sleep?"

"Some. But Thaddaios and I had some very interesting conversations. I'm reluctant to say it, but I do believe that this was a much wiser choice than I gave you credit for, Jeremy."

"Whattaya mean?" Jeremy said, looking over at Wyllt.

The man smiled.

"Well, though I don't agree with his methods, he's been truthful about everything he's told us. He genuinely wants to see you succeed in this."

Jeremy glanced over at Wyllt, waiting for the man to say something. But he just continued to smile back at him.

"And you're sure of this?"

"I spoke directly to his pillow and to that pin he always wears. They were quite certain of his sincerity. His pin and I had an extensive conversation."

"His pin?"

"Yes, the Black Swan one on his collar." Erwin pointed to a flat, rounded pin on the man's collar; a black swan, its neck bent forward, and its wings fanned out, set against a dark gold background. "He let me hold it for a while. It's enchanted, which makes it a much more reliable source. Believe me, you'll be in excellent hands while you're in Kurgal."

Strange. He hadn't noticed that pin before. But even more strange was Erwin's newfound trust in Wyllt. Jeremy was still leery of the man. For all he knew that pin could be another deception, designed to mess with Erwin's ability to discern the truth.

The aircraft lurched and rumbled. Jeremy grabbed the armrests and braced for landing. He swallowed as the plane violently shook and teetered until it finally landed. Outside, he could see a rocky clearing surrounded by dense tropical trees.

Tufts was the first out of his seat, followed by the guy in dreadlocks. Tufts opened the door. Hot, humid air rushed in. Dreadlocks, his submachine gun ready, hung close to the door and peered out the side. Then he stepped out to the right, followed by Tufts to the left.

"All clear," Dreadlocks said.

Lang took Tufts' place by the door.

Sergeant Jaeger walked out next.

Jeremy unclicked his seatbelt.

"Wait," Wyllt said, holding his hand up and waving for Jeremy to stay seated.

Ellesmere and Hamjil stood up. Wyllt held his hand up to them, too.

The three mooks returned several minutes later.

"How's it look, Sergeant?" Wyllt asked.

"Good." Jaeger said. "Plenty of cover and concealment."

"Excellent. Let's go," Wyllt said, unbuckling his seat belt.

Ezzy walked up to Ellesmere and stood next to her while Wyllt and Lang exited. Hamjil went next, followed by the two koth and then the two elves. Ezzy never made eye contact with Jeremy. That bothered him. He'd never felt like this before with any woman. There was definitely something there between him and Ezzy. It wasn't gone, it was just being... pushed aside now. But why?

Jeremy put on Ellesmere's cloak. Miraculously, it fit him perfectly, going down past his knees. It was wide enough to wrap himself in, and the hood seemed big enough to fit over his head, though he didn't put the hood on yet. He was tempted.

The fresh and humid evening smelled of flora, fauna, and minerals. It was unlike anything Jeremy had ever experienced. He thought he'd gotten used to the wilderness in Colorado, but this was different. There was a mineral aspect to the air here, and it was far more humid.

Ortiz had landed the plane on the edge of a small plateau on the side of the mountain. Lush vegetation in the form of trees, bushes, and grass surrounded them for as far as the eye could see. Chirps, screeches, hoots, and howls echoed from every direction.

"All right, everyone. Before we set up, let's get organized," Wyllt called.

Everyone formed a circle except for Tufts. The big man walked over to the plane and opened the cargo hold.

"My men will set up the area," Wyllt explained. "This will be our Tactical Operations Command. We'll call it TOC. Ellesmere, Ezzy, Ortiz; you'll be set up inside the bird. If I call you on the radio and use the name TOC, it means I'm talking to Ortiz. If Ortiz is busy, Ezzy, you answer. Once we leave, we'll be using radios and call names that Decoudreau will assign you. Hamjil, you'll stand guard outside and you'll coordinate with Ortiz. Any sign of trouble, you cover her so she can get the bird humming and ready. I know your job is to protect Ellesmere, but the best way you can do that is make sure Ortiz gets this plane off the ground. As soon as we know which direction the entrance is, Jeremy, Birch, Grath, Jaeger, Tufts, Decoudreau, Lang, and I will head out."

The sound of struggle caught everyone's attention. Tufts emerged from the cargo hold with a goblin. The big man held a nylon cord attached to a collar around the creature's neck. Another restraint held the goblin's hands behind his back, bound to a thick belt around his midsection. Tufts kicked the goblin hard, and it rolled toward the group.

"What the——?" Jeremy said.

Tufts yanked on the cord, and the goblin flew back toward him. It grunted and lay stunned before it wearily pushed itself off the ground. The creature wore nothing save for a dirty towel that covered his lower half.

"Let me introduce my associate to you," Wyllt said. "This is Jau'Asar. You'll have to forgive his attire. Normally he's dressed in a fine Italian suit fit for someone I consider an associate. But today he's sporting the rags and restraints of a duplicitous snake." He discreetly nodded at Jeremy. "It's a good thing for us we figured out his plan. He's our ticket into Kurgal. Right Jau?"

The goblin sneered at Wyllt.

Tufts yanked the cord, and the goblin choked, straining its neck to find relief from the collar.

"Eh, I'll gladly show you how to get in," the goblin sneered. "I'm happy to deliver you all to my Sar. You'll all make fine subjects to experiment on."

Tufts kicked the goblin in the side, lifting him a few feet in the air and sending him to the ground. Jau'Asar coughed and struggled to catch his breath.

"Decoudreau will get our non-operators set up here," Wyllt continued. "We leave in an hour. If there's any gear you plan on bringing with you, it gets cleared by Jaeger first. This is a Direct Action Recovery Mission, not a hike. Only bring the essentials. Got it?"

"Yes, sir!" The mooks said together.

"Alright, let's do this," Wyllt said.

The circle disbanded and Dreadlocks led Ellesmere, Ezzy, Hamjil, Erwin, and Ortiz back to the plane. The other mooks went to the cargo hold, leaving Jeremy standing alone with Wyllt.

He knelt to go through his backpack.

"Jeremy!" Ezzy called.

He looked up, his heart beating a bit faster as he saw her in the doorway. Jeremy stood.

"Here!" She tossed something. Jeremy reached for it but missed.

Wyllt snatched it before it fell to the ground.

"It's the companion stone to Ellesmere's cloak." She shot a concerned look at Wyllt.

Jeremy placed his hand out to receive the stone.

Wyllt opened his palm and studied the ordinary looking white and brown rock.

"Looks pretty ordinary to me," Wyllt said. "Shall we try it out?"

"I'd rather not," Jeremy said, still holding his palm out.

Wyllt placed it in Jeremy's hand. He closed his fingers around it and nodded to show Ezzy he had it. But she was already gone. Jeremy opened his palm and studied the rock. It was ordinary. But who would he give it to? Birch? No. He could mindcast with Birch, allowing him to feel his presence. Grath? Maybe. But the only solid choice was Wyllt. *Oh boy.* If he hadn't already placed his life in this man's hands enough, giving him the companion stone to Ellesmere's cloak would only seal the deal.

"Jeremy, listen before—"

"Wait. You should take this." Jeremy handed the stone back to Wyllt.

Wyllt took the stone. "That's not what I wanted to discuss with you."

"I know. But I need to trust you to have my back in there."

"Listen, there's a fine line between being brave and being foolish. You can just as well be a part of this mission right here. I promise you Jeremy, if I find the Ring of Nicholas, I *will* give it to you. This is your last chance to back out, because once we head out there, you're in for the long haul."

"I'm going. I'm not backing down now. Not after coming so far," Jeremy said, resolved. He didn't want to argue about it anymore.

"Well then, come with me." Wyllt placed his hand on Jeremy's shoulder and escorted him over to the cargo hold. "Lang, hand me my duffel and the extra one."

The commando did as he was told. Wyllt walked over to the edge of the clearing and squatted. "We don't have any time for training. I'd have liked to show you how to use a pistol. But I'm not about to give you one in close quarters. You're likely to hit one of us. But with this"—he pulled out a belt with a small dagger hanging from it. He stood up and then removed the dagger from its sheath. "Tayanu's Dagger."

The shining blade reflected in the sunlight.

Erwin walked over and curiously stared at the dagger. He held his pad in his arms and began to sketch.

"This dagger belonged to an Elven warrior named Tayanu. I'm told he lived back when goblins were more powerful, before the elves defeated them. Tayanu had this dagger enchanted, especially for the fight against goblins. It was his backup weapon, but its enchantment works whether it's sheathed or held."

"What's it do?"

"It gives the bearer the ability to detect goblins."

"That's it? How's that going to help? We know we're going into a whole nest of goblins."

Wyllt handed him the dagger. "See for yourself."

Jeremy took it.

"Where's Jau?" Wyllt said.

Jeremy carefully scanned the area. He didn't see the goblin anywhere. His eyes widened and he felt a chill move across his spine as an impression formed in his mind. He turned and looked into the forest. He couldn't see Jau, but he knew the goblin was tied to a tree, about a hundred feet into the forest.

Wyllt must have noticed the shocked expression on Jeremy's face. "And?" he said, smiling.

"He's over there," Jeremy said, pointing into the forest.

"And? What state is he in?"

Jau was weak and scared. His side hurt from being kicked by Tufts.

"Whoa! That's amazing!" Jeremy said. "So weird. It's not even like I can see him there, I just know he's there. That's *so* weird!"

"If we have any gobs hiding within 90 meters of you, you'll be able to tell us: what they look like, how they're feeling, and what they're armed with."

"May I see the dagger?" Erwin said, placing his pencil behind his ear and holding his hand out to Jeremy.

"Like advanced radar," Jeremy said, handing the dagger to Erwin.

"Something like that. But don't expect me to start calling you Radar." Wyllt laughed.

Erwin took the dagger. "Tell me a little about yourself." He mumbled to the blade.

"We'll still have drones and cams with us," Wyllt continued. "But you'll be able to tell exactly where the goblins are. You'll relay that intel to Decoudreau so that he knows where to point the drone."

"I can do that."

"This is fascinating," Erwin said. "Oh, and a bit of advice to you Mr. Wyllt. Never let a Swordsworn Guardian hear you refer to him as an Elven Warrior. It is considered to be very insulting."

"Oh. Why is that?"

"Because they're not warriors. A Swordsworn Guardian does not seek war, they seek peace through force. They will never actively start a war, but they will gladly finish it."

Wyllt nodded his head. "Noted."

Erwin handed the dagger back to Jeremy.

"Thank you."

"I've got one other thing for you," Wyllt said, squatting down and reaching into his duffel. He brought out a rolled black cloth. He stood and unraveled it. It looked like a military shirt, similar to the one Wyllt and his mooks were wearing. He handed it to Jeremy.

Jeremy held it in front of him.

"Hmm," Wyllt said. "It might be too small on you. It's a large."

"Yeah. I'm an extra-large, even with the weight I lost these past few weeks."

"Lang!" Wyllt yelled.

Lang was on the other side of the camp. Going through his own backpack. He immediately jumped up and ran over.

"Yes, sir?" Lang said.

Wyllt grabbed the black uniform from Jeremy and handed it to Lang. "Take this. Remove the buttons and sew them on to that plaid shirt Jeremy has." He pointed to the blue and gray plaid shirt Jeremy had tied around his waist.

"It's not going to be perfect. You'll lose the ballistic defense of the dragon fiber in the blouse. But the buttons will keep you safe from heat and cold. You'll be good for any attacks up to two thousand degrees and below negative forty. But not from acid, arrows, or blades. We'll flank you and try to keep them away from you."

"Whoa! Seriously?"

Lang nodded. "I'll need your shirt."

"Huh?" Jeremy said, still stupefied by the overload of information. He wasn't prepared for this. What was he even thinking? Was he really just expecting to walk into a goblin stronghold with just his staff?

Lang pointed to Jeremy's waist. "Your shirt."

"Oh, yeah." Jeremy untied his shirt from around his waist and handed it over.

"OK. Let's get you loaded," Wyllt said. "Dump out everything in your ruck."

Jeremy, still feeling numb, did as he was told.

"You're packing as light as you can. I want you swift on your feet."

He and Wyllt sorted through everything, and Jeremy was left with a backpack containing a pair of night vision goggles, a multitool, a small first aid kit, mosquito repellent, mosquito mesh, two flares, two glow sticks, a map of the area, a compass, and a camelback. It was still heavy, but not nearly as heavy as the gear the others were carrying. The mooks were loaded down with heavy looking vests, backpacks, and weapons.

They were all ready to leave. The operators, as Wyllt called them, gathered at the edge of the clearing. Tufts had the restrained goblin close to him.

The non-operators were in position in or outside the plane. Hamjil stood guard by the door. Ellesmere, Ezzy, and Erwin stood in the doorway. Ellesmere stepped out and walked toward them.

"Oh, yes." Wyllt said, "you did say something about coming with us."

Ellesmere held out her hands, moving them around in circular motions toward the ground. She stopped and focused on an area closer to the plateau's edge before backing up a few feet. Kneeling, she placed her palms on the ground.

Jeremy heard a rumbling, and the surrounding earth shook. The plane wavered.

Ortiz appeared in the doorway, eyes wide. She looked to Wyllt for instructions.

He waved his hand, telling her to stand down.

"She's going to wreck the bird!" Ortiz yelled.

The dirt around Ellesmere cracked and rose into a slow, swirling cloud. The area in front of her started sinking in on itself. From within the sink hole a rock... no, a hand appeared; a massive hand made of gray rock pushed on the earth, as more rocks appeared. Another massive hand emerged, followed by a head and shoulders. Its head was the size... was a boulder! And its shoulders were massive, at least five feet across. It pulled itself from within the earth, took a step forward, and then knelt before the Eleven Elder.

Ellesmere placed her tiny hand on its gargantuan head, and she spoke. The golem trembled. Each rock that formed its body shifted slightly out and back into place. Ellesmere stood, and the gray and beige behemoth stood with her. The golem stepped forward and walked toward the group. It towered over everyone, standing at least nine feet tall.

"I am with you now," the gravelly voice boomed from the creature.

Jeremy noticed the head wasn't actually a boulder, but hundreds, maybe thousands, of smaller rocks combined to form plain facial features.

Amazing! Jeremy stepped closer to examine the creature. It reminded him of one of his favorite superheroes, the underrated *Thing* from *The Fantastic Four*. He wanted to reach out and feel all the intricate details of dark grays, light grays, and sandstone that formed an almost camouflage-like pattern. Each body part crafted perfectly, ready for battle.

"It is me, Jeremy," the golem boomed.

Jeremy jumped back. "I know... but this is just amazing. How'd you, uh—"

"Jeremy, we should be going. It takes a lot of energy for me to hold this form." Ellesmere said through the golem.

"Well, you heard the lady. Let's roll," Wyllt said. "We've got about a 19-klick insert."

Jeremy snapped his head from the golem to Wyllt. "Nineteen klick insert?"

Wyllt laughed. "You didn't think we'd just fly up to the entrance and walk right in, did you?"

Jeremy frowned. *Yeah, kinda. And I don't even know what a klick is!*

"Let's move!" Wyllt commanded.

Jaeger took the lead, bushwhacking his way forward into the forest with a machete.

Jeremy trailed just behind Grath and in front of Birch. They only made it about twenty feet into the forest before Jeremy stopped. His stomach churned and his chest tightened. He watched the commandos effortlessly trudge up the mountainside, and he himself felt woefully inadequate.

What is it, Gift Giver? Birch mindcasted.

Jeremy stepped over to the side and threw up.

I can't do this. Jeremy thought, as he heaved a second time.

PART THREE

CHAPTER 57

STRANGER IN A STRANGE LAND

"You may wonder of my disappointment in the dweorg. As I told you already, the elves sustain this world, but this responsibility was tasked to the dweorg by the Allfather. Sadly, the modern day dweorg have all but relented their tasking. They've grown complacent, sheltered away in their mountains, forsaking their oath to the Allfather."

~ From *The Veiled Happenlore of the Master Construct* compiled by Fulbert Gisilfrid, a Chronicler of the Master Construct, Third Order, an alfargnym of Unterbaum.

Wind and snow whipped all around Masaru as he trudged through the frozen landscape toward the mountain. He followed the barely visible cobblestone path that led from the Veil's entrance. Stinging cold nipped at his nose and cheeks, and his bare arm tensed with goosebumps. He regretted ditching his hoodie. He held his sword in his prosthetic hand and wrapped his flesh arm in the second tunic he'd stolen, keeping it close to his body for added warmth. Shivering, he pressed on.

After a ten-minute hike, Masaru spotted the entrance in the mountain. Triangular and carved from the mountain itself, the entrance stood twenty feet high and equally wide. Something moved at the entrance. It was hard to make out from this far, but it appeared to be two more guards. He could see the same blue-gray uniforms as the two he'd killed earlier. They stood up and moved into place; one soldier on either side of the entrance.

Masaru sheathed his katana and unwrapped the extra tunic from his arm. He pulled it over his head, wearing it loose like a poncho so that it would hide his prosthetic arm.

Drawing closer, he noticed that there were six shallow steps at the entrance. One guard stood at the top of the steps, while the other stood on the lowest rise. Another one of those short-haired beastly dogs sat beside him. This one's fur was bluish gray. Neither of the guards moved, or even acknowledged Masaru's presence. The dog, however, continued to eye him as he approached.

With his hand ready on the hilt of his katana, Masaru stopped a few meters from the first guard and made eye contact. The sentry slouched but said nothing.

Masaru's eyes shifted from the guard, drawn to the grandeur and architecture of the wrought iron triangular entrance. The dark metal contrasted beautifully with the dark gray of the mountain and the white of the snow. He breathed in the cool air and sighed. This was where he had come from. Only to be discarded by his people somewhere, not too far from this very spot; left in the snow to die because he was born different.

He glanced at the guard at the top of the stairs: a fat, slovenly dweorg with a bushy brown beard whose uniform barely fit. The other guard wasn't any better. What was with these people? It was just as Turtak said; the dweorg had grown fat and complacent.

Masaru approached the entrance.

The guards looked at him, then at each other. Neither said a word. The dog's eyes remained fixed on Masaru as he walked past the guards and moved further inside. A gentle breeze of warm air caressed his cold, numb face. He ran his hand along the walls of the spacious hallway; carved from the mountain itself, made smooth by master craftsmen centuries ago. The black rock sparkled from the light of large domed glass fixtures that lined the ceiling and bathed the hallway in bright light.

Thirty meters in, Masaru heard the sounds of civilization ahead. The hallway curved, and after another thirty meters, Masaru found himself in a large chamber with a balcony. A white stone staircase, leading down, bordered one side of the balcony. On the other side, a ramp led down to some unknown place. Above the staircase and ramp a white stone bridge with train tracks led from one tunnel into another. Beside the tracks, a walking path extended from the balcony into the tunnels. The path and tracks ran parallel to the balcony, separated only by a thick gray balustrade.

Several people stood on the balcony, talking. The sounds and smells of industry and commerce emanated from below. Masaru looked around for more guards, but there were none. He cautiously approached the people on the balcony, his hand still on the hilt of his katana. He pulled tightly on his makeshift poncho, ensuring his prosthetic arm remained hidden. Two women and a man stopped talking when the man nodded in Masaru's direction. His eyebrow raised from curiosity. A child eyed Masaru and then hid behind a woman.

"Ho, kunder! Ya back from the manethel?" The man spoke in the secret language with a thick accent much different from Turtak's. *Kunder? Manethel?* He didn't recognize those words.

Masaru wondered who this man was. *Man?* Could he call this person a man? He was a male; a male dweorg. But he was not a man, is he? How strange. Would he refer to Turtak as a man? No. Would he even refer to himself as a man? *One day you'll grow up to be a man.* He heard his adopted father's voice echo in his head. *I am dweorg. I'm not a man.* Masaru thought proudly.

"What say ya, kunder?" The male dweorg said.

Masaru didn't know how to answer. But he figured he better say something. "Yes, I've been gone a long time."

"Is he from the manethel or the alfarethel, moddy?" Said the little boy, looking up at the female.

The smell of baking bread and roasting meat crossed Masaru's nose, and his attention was pulled to whatever was below the balcony.

"Ah, I see. Yer clothes are a bit raggedy. And that sword a yers is a bit strange. How long ya been in out of the mountain?"

Masaru's stomach growled as he walked past the male to the edge, placing his palm on the flat handrail.

Below was a vast metropolis of stone, iron, and light. Buildings of all shapes and sizes were lined up in rows. Streets were filled with peop… dweorg.

"Hey, kunder. I asked ya how long ya been out of the mountain?"

"Um…" Masaru didn't have time for this. He turned back around and faced them. "I need to see the king. It's urgent."

"Urgent, eh? High King Unn?" The male said.

"High King Unn?" The female beside him interjected, slapping the male on his shoulder. "Do ya know of any other High King in Nidavellir?"

"Eh," the male said awkwardly, stroking his beard and laughing. "No, I don't."

Masaru studied him. He wasn't a warrior. He seemed like more of a laborer. His hands were calloused, and he wore an apron over his tunic.

"The steamsteed 'ill be here in a short throw," the male said.

Steamsteed? Masaru raised an eyebrow.

The others didn't respond.

"What tidends do ya bring our High King?" The male asked.

Masaru paused. He wasn't comfortable telling these three anything more. They appeared common; harmless. But any one of them could alert the authorities and he didn't really want to kill them.

"I have a message for all dweorg. But I have to give it to the high king first. Then everyone will hear it from the high king."

"Odin's Beard, kunder!" The male said. "Ya got me upedged! Must be faining tidends for ya to keep it so."

Masaru raised an eyebrow at him and then turned to smell the food from below. The jerky was good, but whatever that pungent smell was, it made him hungry again.

"I hope so," one female said. Then she turned to the other. "Could be bad tidends, though. A screamer maybe?" She said, frowning.

"Oh, Odin forbid it! I hope it ain't a screamer," the other female said. She then turned to Masaru. "It ain't a screamer, is it?"

Masaru stared at the female. These dweorg spoke the secret language, but they used words he didn't quite understand. *Slang words maybe?* Still, he didn't want to give any of them reason for alarm, so he just smiled and shook his head.

A hissing, rumbling sound emerged from the tunnel. The three bystanders looked in the noise's direction, as did Masaru. A train came roaring down the tracks. Masaru gasped and his eyes opened wide to see the horse-head-shaped locomotive barrel toward them. Cast completely in a whitish-golden ore, the contours of the horse head glimmered in the light as steam snorted from its nostrils. The train slowed and Masaru spied a barely visible conductor in a black engine room at the base of the would-be horse's skull.

"It's Sleipner! Moddy, it's Sleipner!" The child yelled excitedly, tugging on his mother's tunic.

"Yes. Yes, it is." She smiled.

The impressive steam engine came to a stop at the balcony's edge. Several ornate passenger cars lowered a set of small stairs. The balustrade lowered into the ground, and the handrail became a step that met with the first rise of the train's step.

Several dweorg exited.

The child tugged on his mother's hand and pulled her forward to be the first to enter the train. Masaru waited until all the others were aboard before he entered the passenger car. He nearly tripped; not just from his awe of the train, but because the rise of each step was shorter than what he was used to. They had built it for the stout legs of dweorg, not the long gait of a human.

The inside of the passenger car was lit with small, rounded lights that ran in three parallel lines across the ceiling: one line on either side and one in the center. Bench-like seats, designed to accommodate the stout frame of dweorg lined the sides of the car. Upholstered with a bluish-gray fabric, like the color worn by the dweorg soldiers, there was plenty of seating available as well as room in the center of the car for standing. It reminded Masaru a little of the Tokyo subways.

Five other dweorg were aboard. None were soldiers, and none seemed to be armed. They all glanced at Masaru with varying levels of curiosity and surprise.

Masaru stood and grabbed onto the overhanging handrail, noting that several of the other passengers continued to stare at him. He ignored them and stared out the window.

The train lurched forward, letting out a blast of steam that could be seen through the windows. Masaru stiffened his flesh arm and shifted his weight with the train's momentum. His tunic swung open and one of the dweorg sitting close to him glimpsed his prosthetic.

The dweorg took a second glance, tilting his head and raising a brow before looking Masaru in the eyes.

Masaru glared back at him and tugged the tunic back in place, maintaining his balance as the train sped forward into the tunnel.

He diverted his attention from the nosy dweorg to look out the window. A brightly lit gray cobblestone path, currently empty, ran parallel to the tracks.

Several minutes passed, and the train sloped upward, climbing higher inside the mountain.

The dweorg child knelt on his seat and looked out the window.

"We're almost there, Moddy!" He shouted.

"Hush. Bor. Yer not the only one here," the mother scolded.

Minutes passed, and the train exited the tunnel.

"Moddy, may I say it now?" the excited child said.

"Not until ya see Jörmungandr," she replied.

The train turned and offered Masaru a picturesque view that caused him to hold his breath in wonder. Hewn from the mountain itself was a three-tiered palace. Black pillars and walls glittered more intently than anywhere else he'd seen here. Columns, railings, and balusters of polished gold and silver reflected the palace's grandeur.

Masaru released his breath and leaned forward to get a better look out the window. Green marbled stairs on either side of the palace lead to each of the tiers. Soldiers stood at every level.

Before the palace, a grand gold and silver statue of a dragon mounted by a stone dweorg warrior stood as the centerpiece of a public square. Interlocking scales of gold and silver meticulously placed cast the dragon in frightening realism; its menacing eyes made of black jewels, its sharp teeth whitish gold. The dragon's outstretched wings spanned across the square, casting a shadow on the green marbled cobblestone below. A stone-skinned dweorg warrior with a golden jeweled crown and bronze armor sat upon the dragon's back. In his hands, a gold spear stuck into the dragon's neck. Red jewels depicted blood oozing from the wound.

"High King Rangvald!" The child cried out. "Thank you for saving us from Jörmungandr!" He smiled and looked to his mother for approval.

She returned the smile and nodded. "Thank you, mighty High King Rangvald."

Rangvald must be the warrior on the back of the dragon. *A true warrior*, Masaru thought. Not like the dweorg Masaru had met. He wondered if High King Unn was as disgraceful as his soldiers.

Other passengers on the train echoed the female, saying, "Thank you, mighty High King Rangvald."

To the left of the palace stood another statue. This one wasn't a dweorg, but it had the physique of a muscled human holding a golden spear. He was as tall as the palace and adorned in a shining, golden breastplate. He wore a golden, horned crown that extended over his right eye, like a patch. A bird, made of iron, sat upon his shoulder. His skin was a speckled medley of white, golden flecks and rose-pink tones that contrasted with the dark stone of the building it stood attached to. The man's legs served as the building's door-less entrance. The one-eyed king could be none other than the Norse god, Odin.

Opposite the statue was a shorter building. Like the others, it was carved from the black sparkling stone of the mountain. It stood only two stories tall, with ten pillars across its front that created arched entrances to an open plaza. To the rear of the plaza were three sets of large double doors.

What is this place? Masaru wondered. There was so much to take in. He'd been to big cities before, traveling with his adoptive parents to Tokyo, Beijing, Oslo, Rome, Berlin, New York, Chicago, L.A. and Las Vegas. But this was different. There was something surreal about this city carved from rock millennia ago. It bore the ancient architecture of the past, like Rome, but modernized and kept pristine. It was breathtaking and beautiful. There was so much light, it was hard for Masaru to believe he was inside a mountain. Light shined from everywhere; lamp posts, wall sconces, and from somewhere up above, like the sun.

Masaru craned his neck to see where the light was coming from, but the window and the angle made it impossible to see.

The train hissed and came to a gentle stop. The passengers rose from their seats to exit the train. Masaru walked out into a wisp of dissipating steam and onto a balcony. Though more ornate, with columns and architecture that matched the palace, this balcony was like the previous one. It had a descending white staircase on one side and a descending ramp on the other. Most of the passengers walked to the staircase. The child led his mother to a dweorg manning a small cart harnessed to a massive dog, different from the others he'd seen. The creature was lying down, but its head came up to the merchant's waist. Its dark, fluffy, golden fur produced a darker, poofy lion-like mane that almost hid its canine snout.

The merchant stood on the other side of the cart, working over a grill. The smell was wonderful: savory and pungent like spicy grilled chicken. Masaru's stomach growled again. The merchant was obviously selling the food, but he doubted the dweorg would take Russian rubles.

Masaru sighed as the merchant spooned the pungent red meat into a piece of brown flatbread. He handed it to the female, who then handed it to the child. The merchant served her a second helping. She paid him with a small, rectangular silver bar. Then she and the child walked to the stairs. The child sloppily ate his meal; a cube of meat rolled from the bread, down his cheek and onto his shirt before meeting its eventual destination on the floor. The boy ignored it and kept walking.

The train hissed, and Masaru turned around to watch the majestic steam engine pull away, revealing the grand architecture below. He looked up to find the source of light. A series of large mirrors circled the ceiling of the large cave. *A cave?* They were inside a cave. The notion struck Masaru as unbelievable. He sighed again and looked toward the high king's palace. Masaru tightened his grip on the hilt of his katana and breathed in deeply to clear his mind. Soon he would meet the high king.

CHAPTER 58
UNTO THE BREACH

"Jeremy didn't realize at first the true friend he would have in Birch. I surmised it was because it was difficult for Jeremy to wrap his mind around a koth being an intelligent being. I blame humanity's penchant for making the dinosaurs out to be the bad guys in their fiction."

~ From *The Second Gift Giver Chronicles* compiled by Erwin Albowyn, a Chronicler of the Master Construct, Second Order, an alfargnym of Unterbaum

Jeremy barely said a word during the six-hour trek up the mountain. All he could think about was getting killed. Would it be fast? Or would they torture him like Erwin said they were doing to Mercurio at this very moment? Where had all his bravado gone? What happened to not sitting on the sidelines anymore? He'd thrown up twice more along the way. And if that wasn't bad enough, as the sun set, he became the object of adoration for a swarm of mosquitoes. The repellent Wyllt had given him didn't seem to help.

The man tried to comfort Jeremy several times. Jeremy barely heard a word Wyllt said, catching only a phrase or two here and there. Something about this being a natural reaction for anyone without proper combat training and that it was all right to be scared. Was that true? Or was he just a spineless coward? Jeremy couldn't decide. Though he knew one thing for certain; he was an idiot for even thinking about going on this mission.

Wyllt wanted him to rest while he and his men did further reconnaissance. But how could he? Mercurio and the other guardians were being tortured at this very moment. Unless they were already dead. How could he be expected to get some rest? Sure, he was exhausted physically and emotionally. Every time he closed his eyes and gave himself to the darkness, an imaginary goblin emerged and killed him in some new way.

What is bothering you, Gift Giver? Birch said.

Jeremy had forgotten that the two koth lay beside him on a makeshift bed created from rocks.

I can't sleep, Jeremy mindcasted.

Shall I sing for you?

No. Just go back to sleep. You need to rest too.

If you allow me to lull you to sleep with a song, it may help. I can mindcast it to you. I know many songs with words.

Jeremy furrowed his brow at the strange notion. *Telepathic singing?* The wonders never ceased.

I suppose it couldn't hurt, Jeremy said.

I assure you it will not hurt.

Jeremy cracked a grin and laid back down, using his pack for a pillow.

Sayalla, home of the first born of light. Sayalla...

Jeremy's eyelids opened wide with surprise. He sat back up and looked at Birch with pure astonishment. The koth's singing voice was remarkable and hauntingly reminiscent of Nat King Cole.

... refuge to those who are lost. In time of darkness, in time of need. Come to Sayalla, to rest your weary head. Come to Sayalla and be welcomed by all. The elves... the alfargnym, faun, and koth... all may enter in peace.

Jeremy lay back down and allowed the beautiful, spine-tingling timbre of Birch's voice to push away any thoughts of goblins and death. Sleep finally came.

"LET'S GO, JEREMY," Wyllt said.

Sticky bits of dust and the faint light of dawn made it difficult to open his eyes. Wyllt stood over him, nudging him with his boot.

"Get your gear together. It's time to breach."

Jeremy's body fought against him. It ached with stiffness and begged for more rest, but Jeremy fought back and stood at Wyllt's side.

The man laid a comforting hand on Jeremy's shoulder. "You ready for this?"

No. Absolutely not. Jeremy's stomach twisted. If he had anything left in his stomach, it'd be gone now. He hesitated, and then nodded.

"OK. Get your comm gear from Decoudreau and something to eat from Lang. We leave in five; eat on the way." Wyllt patted Jeremy on the back and walked over to Decoudreau.

Jeremy followed him.

"Here you go, Santa Man." Decoudreau smiled and handed Jeremy a small black box.

Santa Man? When did he start calling me that? Jeremy opened the box containing a small black, earbud-style wired headset.

He examined the earpieces. It was obvious which part went in his ear. But there was another, smaller looking speaker on the outside and a small slot toward the back. Each earpiece had a small colored line next to the small slot; red on one ear bud and blue on the other.

"How's it work?" Jeremy said.

"What you mean, Santa Man?"

"I mean, how do I use this to talk?"

"It's cool. These things," Decoudreau said, pointing to the ear buds in his own ears, "they're on a private frequency." He took the box back from Jeremy and pulled out the headset. He then looked at Jeremy's ear and then back in the box, taking out one of the tiny antennae and placing it into the recess. He pulled out one of the foam tips and screwed it into place. And then repeated the process for the other one before handing it back to Jeremy. "Try it. Red is right, blue is left, okay?"

Jeremy removed his glasses and placed the earbuds in each ear. The ambient sound of the jungle dampened, and he could barely hear anything.

Decoudreau checked each ear, fiddling with the earbuds, making Jeremy feel uncomfortable as the man poked and prodded at him. He then connected the wire and small antennae to the box and clipped it to Jeremy's belt. He flicked a button, and the sounds of the jungle returned.

"Its state-of-the-art hear-through tech." Decoudreau boasted. "Those little mics on the outside pick up everything around you, but they suppress loud noises like gunfire and explosions, okay?"

Jeremy smiled and nodded.

"They also have bone conductivity, so once they're active, you can just whisper to talk. Let's do a comm check. Okay?" Decoudreau said, pushing a button on a small box in his backpack. "Gobstoppers. This is Omega-5. All signs sound off," he whispered.

Jeremy heard it clearly.

"Omega-1, over," Wyllt said.

"Omega-2, over," Jaeger said.

"Omega-3, over," Tufts said.

"Omega-4, over," Lang said.

Decoudreau nodded to Jeremy.

"What?" Jeremy mouthed back to him with a shrug.

Decoudreau nodded, as if he was supposed to know what the man was talking about. Jeremy thrust his hands forward and mouthed "What?" again.

Decoudreau smiled. He tapped on his ear with one hand, and held up six fingers on the other, mouthing the words "Omega-6."

Jeremy nodded and sighed. "Omega-6, check. I mean, over."

"TOC, this is Omega-5. Do you copy?" Decoudreau said.

"TOC, good copy, over," Ortiz said.

"All right. Let's move in," Wyllt said. "Omega-6, you're in the center between Grath and Birch. Ellesmere, you have the rear for now."

The pile of assorted rocks shook, clicking against each other and rolling into place, forming the massive golem that contained Ellesmere's essence.

Jeremy stepped toward his backpack.

"One more thing," Decoudreau said, placing his hand on Jeremy's shoulder. He took out a small, one-inch cube and fastened it to the drawstring of Jeremy's cloak. "This is your body cam. TOC can now see everything you see."

Oh good. Ezzy'll see me throw up again, Jeremy thought. He licked his lips and swallowed, trying to moisten his dry mouth and throat. But nothing worked. He knelt to grab his pack and noticed that the others had their night vision goggles on their foreheads. He nervously fumbled to unzip his backpack and take his goggles out.

With his backpack on, his staff in his right hand, and the goggles strapped to his head, Jeremy sighed nervously and walked to the others to take his place in line.

A small black drone whizzed by him. Jeremy barely heard it. If he hadn't caught a glimpse of it in his periphery, he would have barely known it was there.

Decoudreau, with his gun slung over his shoulder, controlled the drone from a wrist-mounted remote, complete with a large screen that reminded Jeremy of Pip Boy from *Fallout.*

The other soldiers had their guns ready. They all carried their heavy packs but marched as if they were carrying nothing. Jeremy envied them and their training. Another reason he should just stay here and let the professionals do their jobs.

They approached the mountainside, ending at a large rock face with two tall palm trees beside it.

Now what? Jeremy wondered. He didn't relish having to climb up the side. *Please let there be a secret entrance.*

Tufts dragged the goblin to the rock face.

"Omega-6." Jeremy heard Wyllt's voice come through his ear buds. "Remember, the second you get an impression of any gobs, you let us know right away."

Jeremy nodded.

"Copy that?" Wyllt said.

"Copy that," Jeremy replied.

Wyllt nodded at him again.

Jaeger took a position against the mountain, and Wyllt stood opposite him, against the rock face.

Wyllt motioned for the rest of the party to stand to the side.

"Let's go, defensive positions," Wyllt whispered.

Tufts dragged the goblin forward and aimed his machine gun at the bare rock wall.

"Say it," Tufts growled, tugging hard on the goblin's leash.

The goblin choked, cleared his throat, and then muttered something unintelligible.

The rock face between Jaeger and Wyllt cracked into dozens of smaller pieces. The two mercenaries crab-stepped to the side, making way for the forming entrance. The rocks settled to make an arched door frame, leaving an opening big enough to fit Ellesmere's golem. Light streamed from within.

"No gobs. A lighted tunnel, ten feet wide, and ten feet high," Decoudreau said as he studied the readouts on the monitor. "TOC, are you reading this?"

"Copy that," Ortiz said.

Wyllt shot the goblin a curious glance. "You said there'd be four guards here."

Tufts pulled the leash without giving the goblin a chance to answer.

"I… I did. They should be here," Jau said. "Maybe they know you're coming."

"Or maybe your intel is old. You haven't been here in over two years, right?" Wyllt said.

Tufts yanked on the leash again and the goblin choked.

"No!" Jau spat, futilely pulling away from the leash like one of those little capuchin monkeys arguing with an organ grinder Jeremy had seen in old cartoons. "It's been almost three years since I been back here!"

Wyllt frowned and then nodded at Jaeger.

The sergeant ducked and headed in first, disappearing to the left. Wyllt followed, disappearing to the right. Tufts, dragging the goblin, entered next.

Jeremy froze. His throat was so dry. He kept on swallowing, but nothing helped. *Oh, dear God, if you're listening, oh please, don't let me go in there. Help me, God.* His mind could only focus on the God he was always unsure of. The God he only went to in times of despair. A final, last-ditch effort to invoke the help of a higher power that he wasn't even sure existed. *Oh God, please. If you help me now, I'll... I'll...*

"It's clear," Jaeger said.

"Let's go, Omega-6," Wyllt said.

Lang gently pushed Jeremy.

Oh God, oh, God, oh God... Jeremy looked to Birch.

I'll be with you, Gift Giver. The koth's words brought no comfort.

Jeremy stepped into the cave. Dim light streamed from several flickering fixtures. His eyes focused on one of them. He gasped. Light came from an orb at the top of the fixture. Below the orb was a cage-like apparatus. Inside, a gaunt-looking fairy hung. Its head down. Wires connected its body to the orb above.

The drone drew closer to one fixture.

Ellesmere lumbered over to the fixture and examined the tiny creature. "Jeremy," her voice rumbled, "remove this poor creature from its prison. And the others as well." She pointed to the light fixtures along the passage.

"No!" Wyllt said, before Jeremy could even move. "We can save them on the way out. The longer we can refrain from doing anything that would get us noticed, the better off we'll be."

Ellesmere groaned. "Very well. I'll see this place razed one day. These goblins are despicable creatures."

"Alright, let's keep going," Wyllt said. "Stay in formation."

CHAPTER 59

ON THE PATH OF JUDGEMENT AND REDEMPTION

"Kurgal pales in comparison to the majesty that Badtibirra was. Kurgal, with the exception of the Sar's Throne Room and quarters, was designed differently. It was designed to be hidden and it was designed to pursue more despicable clandestine deeds."

~ From *The Veiled Happenlore of the Master Construct* compiled by Fulbert Gisilfrid, a Chronicler of the Master Construct, Third Order, an alfargnym of Unterbaum.

They walked for several minutes down the long mountain corridor. Jeremy looked behind, checking to see if Ellesmere's golem was still there. It was surprisingly quiet for something that weighed several tons and was made entirely of rocks. Jeremy stopped, alerted by an impression of three goblins further down.

He swallowed, barely able to speak. "There are three… three of them ahead of us."

Wyllt held up his fist, halting the group. The drone slowed but continued on.

"I have them," Decoudreau said. "Three gobs. Three sets of double doors. One left. One right. One in front. Each gob has a door."

"There's more," Jeremy said, feeling the impressions of several others beyond the doors. "Seven. F… f… four on the left door. Thr… three behind the center door."

"The left leads you up to the Hall of the Sar," the goblin said.

Tufts tugged on the leash. "The right?" he grunted.

"Down to the lower levels," Jau said through gritted teeth.

Wyllt turned and walked up to the goblin.

"Jau, you know Tufts as well as I do. He's a man of very few words. So, here's some advice. If you have any hope of not having your neck broken, then I'd suggest that when Tufts asks you a simple question, you reply with a thorough, informative answer. A good indicator would be, if you even think that your answer isn't thorough enough, it isn't. Just keep talking. Otherwise, I've a feeling that you'll wind up dead, or at the very least, a paraplegic before the day is over."

Jau sneered at Wyllt.

Wyllt returned the displeased glare with that cold, pensive stare of his; the one that gave Jeremy the chills.

"The door on the right leads to the lower levels. That's where the broodery, the barracks, and training facilities are. It's also living quarters for those of non-caste blood. The door directly in front is for the Blood of the Naga; research labs, living quarters, and stockpiles."

"Stockpiles?" Jeremy said.

Jau swallowed and shot a quick glance at Tufts. "That's where the sages keep the stuff they experiment with."

"And by *stuff* you mean living creatures they perform despicable atrocities on?" Wyllt said.

Jau hesitated and nodded.

"So where do you think Mercurio and the other elves are now?" Wyllt asked.

"Depends on whether Sar Borahsh is finished with them or not." Jau hesitated again, and Tufts jerked the leash, whipping the goblin's head backwards. Jau sneered and licked his lipless maw. "They, uh, could still be up in the Hall of the Sar, hanging in the Sar's Bane so that Sar Borahsh can delight in their torture. They could be in the holding cells, being restored so that they can hang in the Sar's Bane again."

Restored? Jeremy gulped, and his stomach turned.

"Or, if he's done with them, they could be in the stockpile. Their blood is valuable to the sage."

Wyllt sighed. "And the holding cells are below the Sar's chambers?"

Jau nodded.

Wyllt glanced down the hall and then back at the goblin.

"Oh, please don't say we're going to split up?" Jeremy said. "I can't—"

"No. We stay together," Wyllt said. "Splitting up would be foolish. What's your gut tell you?"

"Me? You're asking me?" Jeremy stammered.

"Yes. What's your gut telling you?" Wyllt repeated.

Jeremy looked down at his churning, aching belly. "That it wants to leave here, right now, as fast as we can,"

"You have that option," Wyllt said.

Jeremy gritted his teeth. "Ugh! I know."

"So, what's your gut tell you about where Mercurio is?"

How am I supposed to know? Jeremy said to himself. *I don't have anything that tells me where elves are.*

"He's in the Sar's Bane," Ellesmere rumbled.

"Very well. Then up it is," Wyllt said, nodding at Jaeger.

"Omega-2, you have thirty-mikes before clearance," Decoudreau said.

"Copy that," Jaeger said. He and Lang walked down the hallway.

Jeremy walked over to Decoudreau and looked over the taller man's shoulder to see the screen.

The drone hovered at a turn, keeping the three guards in view.

The goblin guards wore armor covering their shoulders, torso, forearms, and waist, but their feet and hands were left exposed. They each carried a polearm and stood outside the large doors. They looked so small compared to the halls and doors. *Why would such a small people design such large doors and passages?*

"I have visual," Jaeger whispered over the headset.

Jeremy intently watched the small screen, waiting to see how Jaeger and Lang were going to handle the goblin guards.

He heard Ezzy's voice over the earbuds. "Jae... I mean Omega-2's camera just went off."

Jeremy tensed.

"It's all good TOC. Keep your eyes on Omega-4's now," Wyllt whispered.

From the hallway, a small black blur landed on the ground, startling the guards. One guard looked at the other two. They exchanged curious glances, and one of them stepped forward. One guard nodded to another and said something in goblin. The other guard cautiously walked to the hallway where the black object came from and he disappeared off screen.

The two remaining guards studied the object from a distance. One of them used his polearm to prod at the black object. Nothing happened. Jeremy still couldn't tell what it was they were looking at.

The guard squatted and picked up the object. He turned to his partner and uttered something before pulling a string from the object and unfolding it.

A sack. An ordinary looking black sack. The guard opened it and looked at his partner again. He pointed inside and said something. The other guard held his weapon out and prodded in the sack before stepping in.

Oh, my gosh! Jeremy realized. *It's a sack just like Nikolaos'.*

The guard disappeared.

The other stuck his head in.

Lang charged from off screen, did some sort of fancy maneuver that seemed too fast for Jeremy's eyes, and wound up sitting behind the goblin, holding it in a one-armed headlock.

Lang stabbed it in the side of the neck and sliced forward. Blood poured out, and Lang pushed the goblin to the side. He grabbed the sack and opened it wider.

Jaeger appeared from within. "All targets eliminated."

"Let's go," Wyllt said. He motioned forward and walked down the hall.

The rest of the party followed. They found Jaeger and Lang standing at the intersection. The armor of one goblin guard lay on the floor.

Lang and Jaeger grabbed the dead goblin's armor and shoved it in the sack. Remarkably, it was just like Nikolaos'. It didn't seem to fill out or get heavier as they filled it.

While they worked on stuffing the armor in the sack, Wyllt stood beside the large double doors that Jau said led to the throne room. He put his ear to it.

"No gobs here?" Wyllt looked at Jeremy.

Jeremy grabbed the hilt of the dagger.

"No. Just here and here." Jeremy said, pointing to the central door and the door on the right.

Lang folded the sack and put it in his backpack.

Jaeger took his place in front of Wyllt and stood to the side of the double doors. Wyllt turned the handle and pushed one of the double doors open. Jaeger slid in with his rifle ready.

The door opened to a round chamber big enough to fit their group and then some. Four fairy lights lit the room. Opposite the entry doors, a large ascending staircase glittered with light reflecting off golden bricks that made up the center third of it. The other two-thirds had been carved from the mountain itself. Above the high, arching entrance to the stairs, a metallic gold sign hung from iron chains.

Tufts yanked on the goblin's leash. "What's it say?"

The goblin jerked his neck and cleared his throat. "To seek the Sar of Goblins is to seek judgment or redemption. Choose to enter wisely, for it is the Sar's will that determines your fate."

"Oh, isn't he a peach," Wyllt smirked. He nodded to Jaeger and then up the stairs.

Jaeger started up the steps, and the drone sped past him. The party followed him up. The steep staircase went straight up, with no end in sight. Jeremy's heart pounded harder with every step. He stopped after a few minutes.

"I see a landing up ahead," Decoudreau said.

Jeremy swallowed. "G…g.. goblins. Fi…fi…five of them," he stammered.

Wyllt held his hand up, and the party stopped.

"Come on. Tell us what we're up against," Wyllt said.

"Two… no three on the right. I think one is on the inside of the door. And then there's t… two more just ahead of them on the stairs. They're soldiers, armed with polearms, like the others we found."

"Door on the right. What is it?" Wyllt asked Jau.

"Holding area for those who are placed in the Sar's Bane."

"Okay. Give me details. What's it like in there?"

"Six cells. Usually two guards on the outside. Maybe two or three on the inside."

"How many flights of stairs is it from the throne room?" Wyllt asked.

"It's straight up. Maybe a hundred steps before you get to the entrance."

"OK, Omega-2. Omega-4. Same formation." Wyllt nodded up the stairs.

"Omega-5, you got anything yet?" Jaeger said.

"Four confirmed. Two guarding a door on the left. Two standing guard five steps up." Decoudreau announced.

Jeremy nervously rubbed his head and stepped to the side to lean against the wall. His hands trembled. He took a few deep breaths before sitting on the stairs. He felt a hand grab him by his bicep. Wyllt pulled him up, waived his pointer finger, and slowly shook his head no. He then raised his finger to his lips.

Wyllt nodded at the big man and went back up to take the lead position.

Tufts shouldered his gun and yanked the goblin to him. He removed a bandanna from his pocket with one hand and shoved the goblin down with the other. He placed his boot on Jau's back and then gagged him with the bandanna. The goblin didn't resist.

"Targets eliminated," Decoudreau said.

"Let's go," Wyllt commanded.

Jeremy jerked his head toward Decoudreau. He was surprised that Jaeger and Lang moved so fast.

The party resumed its hike up the stairs, meeting Jaeger and Lang on the landing, where the remains of four goblins lay. Lang and Jaeger stuffed the armor and weapons in Lang's bag of holding.

"Anything?" Wyllt looked at Jeremy and then nodded to the door. It was smaller than the other doors they had seen, only about five feet high and wide enough to fit a person.

"Ju… just the one," Jeremy said.

"Where's he positioned?" Jaeger asked.

"He, uh, he's standing against the wall. Right there." Jeremy pointed to the right of the door.

Jaeger finished helping Lang put the last of the remains in the bag. He pulled out his knife and walked to the door. Placing his hand on the handle, he slowly pressed it down. It clicked, and Jaeger swiftly pushed the door open, raised his knife, and lunged at the unsuspecting guard. Jaeger grabbed onto the goblin's polearm and thrust the knife up and into the side of its neck, all in a matter of seconds. He eased the body quietly to the ground before it dematerialized.

Jeremy cringed at the efficiency and expertise that man had with a knife.

Jaeger stood by the door as the drone passed him.

"Empty," Decoudreau said, repeating the word three more times as he flew the drone. "Got someone. One cell is occupied."

Ellesmere pushed her way forward, stopping to stand over Decoudreau and look down at the screen.

"Gaviryl!" She said, "That's Gaviryl. Get him out of there."

Lang moved into the room.

Jeremy stepped closer to watch from the door.

"Cell's locked," Lang said.

Jaeger searched the guard's remains. "I don't see any keys. Maybe they were on the others?"

Lang sighed and removed his backpack again. He took the sack out, opened it, and climbed in.

Ellesmere grumbled and disassembled.

"Ellesmere! No!" Jeremy cried out.

"She's OK Jeremy," Ezzy said over the radio. "Just watch."

Wyllt moved to block the door.

Ellesmere reassembled into two smaller, but equally menacing golems.

"Ellesmere, wait." Wyllt said, holding his free hand up. "If you make too much noise, you'll draw attention. I have no doubt you could pulverize me and that cell door. But you risk jeopardizing the others. If we don't have the key, we still have other ways to get him out quietly."

"Got it," Lang said, seconds before climbing out of the sack. He rushed to the cell, unlocked it, and stepped inside.

Wyllt moved to the side, and one of the smaller golems rushed in. Jeremy walked closer to the door to get a better view.

Ellesmere walked into the cell.

"He's alive. He's got a wound on his left side. It's covered with some dark yellow goop," Lang said.

Ellesmere placed her hand on the elf's shoulder. She spoke to him in Elvish, gently shaking him.

Gaviryl stirred and groaned.

Jeremy couldn't see his face.

"He's too wounded to come with us to find the others," Wyllt said. "The safest thing we can do is leave him here with both doors unlocked and grab him on the way back."

"We can't just leave him here," Ellesmere said. Her voice echoed from both golems.

"You put him and all of us in more danger if he comes up to the throne room with us."

"Fine. But at least leave him a weapon," Ellesmere huffed and turned her attention back to the Gaviryl. She spoke to him in Elvish.

He mumbled, and Ellesmere continued to comfort him in their language.

Gaviryl mumbled and groaned once more.

Ellesmere walked out, meeting her other golem. The rocks vibrated apart and reassembled back into one massive golem again.

"He's in the throne room," she said. "They healed him yesterday and rehung him there again today."

He's still alive. Jeremy brought his hand to his mouth and stumbled back against the wall. Relief washed over him but was quickly replaced by a numbness as he thought of the torture that Mercurio and the others must have endured. How many times were they healed, only to be tortured again? He sank to the ground, unable to move.

CHAPTER 60
DO OR DIE

"Female goblins are confined to the lowest levels of Kurgal. They are relegated to servants, breeders, infant caregivers, pukas, and experimentation."

~ From *The Veiled Happenlore of the Master Construct* compiled by Fulbert Gisilfrid, a Chronicler of the Master Construct, Third Order, an alfargnym of Unterbaum.

Even with the help of his staff, Jeremy's body fought against exhaustion. The stairs ascending to the goblin king's throne room seemed to never end. His mind flashed, and he felt the presence of dozens of goblins up ahead. He gasped and staggered to the side of the staircase.

Gift Giver, what troubles you? Birch said.

Wyllt put up a hand, and the party stopped, each on a different rise. "Jeremy, you got something?"

Jeremy trembled, wanting to speak. Several of the goblin impressions were heading toward them.

"G… g… goblins. Lots of 'em," Jeremy swallowed.

"How many?" Wyllt whispered.

"Um, I dunno… dozens maybe?" Jeremy's vision blurred. The goblins were heading down the steps. *Oh God. I don't want to be here. I… Oh God, please help me. Please. I can't be here.*

Wyllt grabbed Jeremy by the arm and straightened him up. "Listen, this is your do or die moment," Wyllt said, looking Jeremy in the eyes. "You get it together or give me the dagger and head back to the rendezvous point."

Jeremy's chest heaved with nervous breaths, almost to the point of hyperventilation. He cast his head down and put his hand to his chest.

Perhaps we should go back and get Gaviryl. Birch said.

"I… I… Birch, Grath, and me. We can go back and get Gaviryl," Jeremy said.

Wyllt stared at him; the man's mouth formed an emotionless straight line while those piercing green eyes probed his very soul. There was nothing noble about Jeremy's suggestion to take the two koth and get Gaviryl. Jeremy wanted to run. He needed to get out of here. This was no trick of the Veil. This was all him; his cowardice in overdrive.

Wyllt took the dagger and continued his probing stare, looking down on him. He couldn't look Wyllt in the face.

Jeremy took a step down and stumbled over his own feet. He regained his footing with the help of his staff and the wall.

"Twelve incoming," Decoudreau said.

"Go," Wyllt said to Jeremy. "You're on your own from here. Wait for us at the rendezvous point."

Jeremy used his staff to get his balance and continued down the stairs, not looking back, wanting desperately to get out of there.

He continued down the steps as fast as he could trying not to stumble; the two koth at his sides. With each step, his inner thoughts betrayed him, warring with one another. Thoughts of his death argued with thoughts of his cowardice. Humiliation chimed in, making him think of Ezzy. He'd never be able to face her now.

"Omega-2, Omega-3. Go right. Omega-4, Omega-5, left." Jeremy heard Wyllt say in his earpieces.

Jeremy yanked the earbuds out as if they were some foul insect stinging him. He couldn't run out of there fast enough.

They arrived at the landing where the holding cells were. Jeremy stopped to catch his breath and allow the koth to retrieve Gaviryl. Grath entered the room and seconds later emerged carrying the elf in his arms. Seeing Gaviryl reminded him of Mercurio. *Oh, man… what have I done?* He looked back up the stairs and swallowed. He couldn't go back up there. But that meant not saving Mercurio. *The others will rescue him.* He rationalized. *This is what they do. I was an idiot to even think I should be here.*

Jeremy stepped down and made his way to the stairwell chamber. He grabbed for the door handle.

Wait! Birch yelled in Jeremy's head.

Jeremy jumped and grabbed his chest. *Oh God… what? What?*

I can smell more goblins. They're outside the door.

Oh God, oh God, oh God, what are we going to do? Tears blurred his vision. Jeremy backed up against the wall. The chamber seemed smaller than before.

Grath and I will execute them. Birch said.

Grath laid Gaviryl on the ground.

Gift Giver, open the door and we'll run out.

Jeremy looked at Birch, hesitating.

Open the door, Birch repeated. His voice calm, yet direct.

Jeremy took a deep breath, placed his palm on the handle, and opened the door. The koth raced out. Jeremy stayed hidden behind the door, listening to the fight on the other side. Goblins yelled. Koth roared. Steel clanged against stone. And then there was silence.

Gift Giver. Come. It is over, Birch said.

Jeremy walked into the hall; armor parts lay in pools of blood. Grath and Birch dripped with blood from their claws and fangs. Jeremy closed his eyes and looked away.

Wait, Birch said. *There's more up ahead.*

"Oh, come on! I just want to get out of here already." Jeremy mumbled.

They're coming this way. From the entrance.

From the entrance? But how? We'd have seen them, Jeremy said.

This could be a trap, Birch said.

Oh God. No. Please, God. No. Jeremy hunkered against the wall. His head felt light, his vision flared, and the hallway spun.

Gift Giver. Are you well?

Jeremy stabilized himself with his staff and the wall. *Am I well?* Jeremy swallowed and mindcasted to Birch. *No. I'm not well. We're going to die here. Just like Erwin said.* He kicked the wall with his heel. *I'm such an idiot!*

Grath and I will execute those coming down the hall. You wait here. Birch went to one side of the hall, Grath the other. They looked at each other. Birch made a deep, knocking sound. Grath nodded and the two rushed down the hall.

Jeremy tried to control his breathing, inhaling through his nose. He laid his head against the wall and exhaled through his mouth. *Oh God, what am I doing here?* His emotions continued to rage, contradicting one another, arguing about what led him here until they all just focused on one thing. His sister, Ashley. *Oh Ashley. I'm sorry. I'm so sorry.* He sobbed and sank to the floor.

Jeremy! Run! Hide! Birch's voice broke in.

Jeremy jumped up gasping for air. His muscles tensed, all except his stomach, which twisted, making him want to double over. Sweat mixed with tears burned his eyes, and his hands trembled so much he could barely hold on to his staff. Jeremy grasped it with both hands and pushed himself away from the wall. His eyes darted frantically between the three doors before him. He pushed his hand beneath his glasses, wiping the sweat and tears away. Jeremy couldn't remember what the goblin said about the doors. He couldn't even remember which were the stairs that led up. *Left? Right? Straight? Straight, that leads up? No. The left leads up?* Jeremy grabbed onto the handle of the right door. He pulled it open and ran into a chamber like the one he had come from earlier. These stairs went down.

Jeremy. You must run! Hide. They're coming to you and we can't stop all of them! Birch's frantic pleas sent shivers down Jeremy's spine and he darted down the stairs, running, stumbling, catching himself a few times before he lost his balance, falling forward and tumbling down the stairs. He landed at the bottom of the stairs; his head slammed into the cobblestone floor. His vision flared and blurred, forcing his eyelids to shut, and the sound of his beating heart and gasping breath faded.

THE PAIN in Jeremy's knotted stomach woke him. He writhed and slowly opened his eyes, rolling over onto his back. He placed one hand on his stomach and the other on the cold cobblestone beneath him. *Where am I?* It was darker down here. Dim lights glared from the walls, spread far apart. His vision blurry; he could barely make anything out. Despite being disoriented, lying still on the cold, damp floor brought some comfort.

A scuffling noise came from down the hall. Jeremy stiffened. He wanted to turn his head to look, but he froze with fear.

It moved again.

This time, Jeremy jerked toward it. Something was coming. He rolled over and pushed himself to a kneeling position. Jeremy looked to the other side for escape, but something moved there, too. He couldn't make out what it was. *Oh, God! No. Please.* He looked to the left. It was still moving, creeping toward him.

Jeremy placed his hand to his face. His glasses were missing. He frantically felt for them on the cold stone floor. His fingers brushed the familiar metal, and he grabbed the glasses and fumbled to put them on.

He looked down the dimly lit hall. The outlines of dozens of goblins and their glowing yellow eyes stared back at him. He looked to the other side, hoping to escape, but he saw the same ominous sight skulking toward him.

Jeremy scrambled backward, to the steps. Feeling the first rise, he turned around to desperately crawl up.

Birch? Birch? Are you there? No reply.

He looked behind him. Dozens of goblins stared up at him. They carried no weapons, but Jeremy wasn't about to face them.

He crawled up the stairs, pushing himself to move as fast as he could.

"Are you a good witch or a bad witch?"

Jeremy froze at the sound of the familiar phrase spoken in unaccented American English. He swallowed.

"Crikey, look at the size of that one." Another voice said in a familiar Australian accent.

Several other voices giggled.

Jeremy slowly turned around and carefully sat on the next rise. He pushed his glasses up and wiped the sweat from his face. He swallowed and placed his glasses back on.

These were certainly goblins; big eyes, large pointed ears, lipless mouths, and green skin. But they were smaller and dressed in… Jeremy blinked, trying to make sure he saw what he thought he was seeing. They were all dressed in normal-looking clothing; some in t-shirts and jeans. Others in skirts and dresses. And their voices; they sounded like children… human children.

"Will you be my friend?" asked one in a pink shirt with a sparkly unicorn on the front.

CHAPTER 61

IN THE PRESENCE OF THE HIGH KING

"Before the Veil Accords, the dweorg heavily influenced the humans living in what is now called Scandinavia."

~ From *The Veiled Happenlore of the Master Construct* compiled by Fulbert Gisilfrid, a Chronicler of the Master Construct, Third Order, an alfargnym of Unterbaum

The guard made eye contact with Masaru, slowly scrutinizing him until his gaze landed on his katana. He turned and nodded to his partner. The lazy guard next to him looked up and stared uncaringly at Masaru.

Masaru casually passed by the building with the ten pillars. He took note of this guard. *He may be the only warrior worthy of holding a weapon in this place.*

The guard stood straight and scanned each visitor as they came in and out of the building or walked by. Masaru had seen dozens of guards around here and this was the best of the lot. Masaru was sure he'd be able to take him if he had to. It was the soldiers' guns that concerned him. He was fast, but he couldn't outrun a bullet.

As he passed the last pillar, Masaru wondered what went on inside. Dweorg of all sorts walked in and out, but he couldn't figure out what this building's function was. This wasn't his target though. He needed to focus on the guards at the palace. He'd been watching them for the last six hours, noting that they changed shifts every two. Curiously, the light of the spacious cave decreased as the day went on. It had been just as Masaru expected. Natural sunlight streamed through openings in the mountain and reflected off the mirrored surfaces along the ceiling.

He walked from the building with the ten pillars, up the wide, green-marbled steps that lead to the palace. It was even more impressive up close. Three stories tall; each level with its own balcony. Two guards and a guard dog stood at the foot of each staircase, with two more at each level. They'd been on duty for an hour now.

The king was on the third floor. Masaru had counted ten more guards and four more dogs there. This was going to be difficult. He had no idea how long the king stayed on his throne, but he assumed that, like most people, he'd retire for the day once it grew darker. Turtak was not here to help him, so darkness was Masaru's only ally.

Before entering discreetly, he decided to see how far he could get into the palace by normal means. He approached two guards and their dog at the foot of the palace stairs. They stepped closer, blocking the stairs, raising their guns to their chests. The dog stood in front of its master, unalarmed but waiting for further instructions.

"What business do ya have at the Great Hall of High King Unn?" One guard asked.

"I have a message for the high king," Masaru said.

The guard that spoke glanced at the other and then back to Masaru.

"Thor pound ya, kunder! Ya been in the manethel so long ya don' remember ya need to speak to Thane Uther?"

"I don't have time for that. Besides, the message is only for the high king."

"No tidends come to the high king's ear without first greeting the ears of Thane Uther."

It was as Masaru expected. How could he expect an audience with the king? But now he knew the procedure, and even more importantly he'd gotten a closer look at the security.

Masaru walked away and sat under the wing of the dragon statue in the public square. He'd wait for darkness.

SEVERAL HOURS PASSED. Masaru sat in the plaza on a bench by the dragon statue, continuing to observe the guard patterns. He ate the last of the jerky and gulped down his last water bottle. A sort of twilight had come, and the cave was now only lit by lamp posts and light fixtures along the buildings. Masaru carefully stepped from the shadow of the dragon's wing, following the shadows cast by the lamp-posts and other parts of the statue. He made his way to the rear of the building of the Odin statue and relieved himself there. He didn't want to, but he hadn't seen any public bathrooms. Masaru removed his boots and socks and then climbed to the roof and made his way across the top. Looking over, he spied two guards at the staircase on the palace's third floor. Beyond them, the throne room was dark.

He climbed along the wall of the mountain and over to the roof of the throne room. Summoning all his upper body strength, he peeked in and saw no one. He then climbed down, entering the dark throne room. Two doors, with light streaming from beneath each one, dimly lit the room's edge. The pleasant odor of roasted meat crossed his nostrils and grew stronger as he crept to the first door. He heard the muffled sounds of talking and the occasional clanking of metal.

Masaru slowly turned the door's handle, pushing it open enough for him to peek in. Light illuminated a large table covered in bowls and platters of food. His mouth watered. He saw three people sitting at one half of the table. The door hid the other half. Masaru's eyes immediately fixed on one individual; a burly dweorg robed in blue and black, his salt-and-pepper beard arrayed in tight braids, wearing a bronze crown upon his head. At last, he was in the presence of High King Unn.

Masaru thrust the door open and swiftly withdrew his katana. He ran toward the king and leapt over the high-back chair, toppling it to the floor.

A female screamed.

A child cried out.

Masaru landed on the tabletop. Plates, goblets, and bowls of food flung in every direction. He grabbed the king by the nape of his cloak with his prosthetic hand and shoved the tip of his katana to the king's neck, careful not to puncture the skin but hard enough for the king to feel the cold steel at his throat.

The guards to the king's sides pointed their guns at Masaru.

"Halt!" someone said.

The king's ruddy pallor washed to a pale pink, and his fear-filled eyes stared up at Masaru. "Wh... wh..." he stammered.

For months, Masaru had thought about what he would say at this very moment. He'd mulled it over, practiced it, rearranged the words to be sure they were clear.

"High King Unn, I am Masaru Hagen, a dweorg of Nidavel-lir. By right of blood, I challenge your kingship and calling to this throne. Today, you will defend your throne and your right to sit upon it." He yanked the king closer, adjusting the blade so it wouldn't pierce the king's skin. "Choose your weapon and defend your right to the throne."

"Wh... wh... ya, ya can't," the king said.

"I can. It is my right as dweorg," Masaru said.

The king swallowed and stammered unintelligibly.

"Choose your weapon now!" Masaru said, jostling the king.

"No!" A female voice said from behind. "Cease him now!"

"You shoot or step near me and my last breath will be used to plunge this sword into his throat, and you'll still have no king.

You'll have dishonored the laws of our people by not giving the king his right to defend the throne," Masaru said.

"He's correct," a male voice said from behind. It was matter-of-fact, devoid of emotion. "He has a right to the throne through upcalling of the kingship. And High King Unn has a right to defend it by his own hand. If anyone here halts him, once the upcalling has been made, the high king and his family will be dishonored."

"Grofr!" The female cried. "How could you?"

"How could I? It's my job as the High King's Mimir. I must advise him accordingly."

"Precisely! Yer the Mimir of the High King. Ya should put a halt to this now," she said.

"My queen, ya don't seem to understand. My foranswering is to the throne, not he who sits upon it. This dweorg, or any dweorg, has a right to upcall the high king."

"But, b… b… but no one… h… has… ever…" Unn stammered.

"Incorrect, high king," Grofr said. "The right to sit upon the throne has been upcalled twice. In either happening, the upcalled has lost. No one has ever ascended to high king of the dweorg by upcalling."

Masaru tightened his grip and tugged on the king's cloak. "Choose your weapon, now!" he said through gritted teeth.

The king's eyes drifted to the side, and he swallowed, focusing on the sobbing little voice.

"Foddy. Please, foddy. Please, don't hurt my foddy."

"Unn, no!" the female said, her voice turning from rage to anguish.

"I am Unn, son of Brynjar Dainn—" the king said.

"No!" The female sobbed. "No, Unn, no!"

"Foddy!"

"Unn, listen to me!" the queen screamed. "He's not of the mountain! Listen to his words! He's not of the mountain!"

"It would appear that he is dweorg," said the Mimir. "There is nothing of yore or lore that says his speech must be the same."

Masaru loosened his grip, and the king stood back, pushing his seat out. He raised his hands to the side, commanding the guards to give him room and stand down. "I am Unn, son of Brynjar Dainn…"

"Unn, no. Please…," the female begged.

"… High King of the Dweorg. And I accept yer upcalling," Unn declared. "Grofr, what are the terms of this upcall?"

The female and child continued to cry and plead.

"High King Unn, ya have accepted with honor," Grofr said. "By yer right as high king, ya have until the next sunset to call the time and place of this battle."

Unn's jaw tightened, and the king's eyes bore into Masaru.

Masaru saw a fire there he had not expected. He didn't know if this dweorg could wield a weapon, but he was not the pathetic coward Masaru had expected.

"At light's first entry, on the Balcony of Kings, by the throne I defend, there we will see if ya have what it takes to claim the honored throne of the high king of the dweorg," Unn said. He turned and left the dining room.

CHAPTER 62

ANYWHERE, U.S.A.

"The Goblin Sar will choose a mate to sequester until she gives birth. If a male child is born to the Sar, he will be raised in luxury and groomed to one day take the throne. Female children of the Sar are treated as all other females."

~ From *The Veiled Happenlore of the Master Construct* compiled by Fulbert Gisilfrid, a Chronicler of the Master Construct, Third Order, an alfargnym of Unterbaum

"Wait a minute," a goblin said in a child-like voice. He turned and looked at the others. "He's real, isn't he? That's a real human?"

"I want to touch him," said another.

"I want to hug him," said the one in the sparkly unicorn shirt.

"Yeah. He's big like a big ol' teddy bear," another said.

What is going on here? Jeremy sat on the stairs, staring down at the assembly of child-like goblins, looking up at him. "Who... who... are you?"

Their eyes all grew wide and they began to chatter at the same time.

"Wait! Wait!" A goblin in a Pikachu shirt said. He was taller than the others, but still shorter than Jau. "Shhhhh." He fluttered his hands up and down, trying to calm the others. They obeyed and all stared up at Jeremy.

"Wh… what do you… what do you want from me?" Jeremy said.

The goblins turned and looked at each other as if they had been anticipating this.

"Will you play with us?" asked the girl in the unicorn shirt. At least he assumed she was a girl. It was hard to tell them apart physically.

Jeremy stared at her and swallowed. "Play with you? What… what do you want to play?"

"We have lots of games. Come with us. You'll see," she said.

The others nodded their heads and spoke in unison. "Yes, yes."

"Come with us," another repeated.

Did he have a choice? Jeremy wondered. He turned and looked back up the stairs. He could run. But it was doubtful he could outrun them. And who knew what was up there waiting for him? Jeremy breathed in deeply and stood up. *Here goes nothing.* Slowly, he stepped toward them. They smiled and oohed. Some clapped and bobbed up and down in anticipation.

Jeremy noticed his staff at the bottom of the stairs. Did he dare grab it? He took a few more steps down, and the goblins backed up. He reached the bottom and slowly leaned down toward his staff.

A goblin darted at the staff.

Jeremy jumped back.

It grabbed the staff and pushed it up toward Jeremy.

He hesitated and slowly took the staff from the goblin.

"He's really big," he heard one say. Several others agreed.

"Come," said the taller one. He reached for Jeremy's hand, and Jeremy recoiled slightly. The goblin kept his hand extended, and Jeremy slowly reached to accept it. The creature clasped his hand snuggly and walked him down the hall. Its skin was smooth, but it felt awkward with only three fingers and a thumb.

What in the world is going on here? He looked behind him and the crowd of goblins were following him. They were of various sizes, but smaller than Jau and the guards he'd seen earlier. *Holy cow! These are goblin children!* Jeremy looked around at each of them, looking up at him and smiling, all clamoring for his attention. *Children.* His gift. Never did he ever think that his gift would save his life. But here he was, being shepherded down the halls of the goblin kingdom by a horde of goblin children. And they acted just like any children he'd ever met. In fact, too much like human children.

The goblin stopped at a door. "This is the game room," the one holding his hand said.

"You've got your own game room?"

"Yeah. I told you. We have lots of games," he said, opening the door.

Lights flickered and flashed. The familiar sounds of video games buzzed and beeped from within. Jeremy stepped into the large room. Video game systems and big screen TVs lined the walls. Tables stacked with board games filled the center. Two goblin children played *Dance-Dance Revolution* while another played *Pac-Man.* Four more sat at a table playing *Monopoly.* Jeremy stared at the scene; his mouth open in shock. He blinked his eyes, removed his glasses, and then rubbed them to be sure that he wasn't hallucinating.

"Come. Let's play," the goblin said, pulling him further into the room. "Do you like Super Smash Brothers?"

"I get to be Pikachu!" one yelled behind him.

"I'm Link," another yelled.

"Come on!" The one holding Jeremy's hand yelled. He let go and pointed to the Pikachu on his shirt. "You know I'm always Pikachu."

"Geez Jake, just because you have a Pikachu shirt, doesn't mean you always get to play Pikachu!"

The crowd ran toward a large screen. Some leaped over a couch, grabbing at the controllers on a coffee table in front of it.

He watched them with slack-jawed fascination, unable to believe what was happening.

Jake led him over to the huge TV. "Hey, there's only enough for eight players. Make sure you save a controller for him," he told the others. Jake then looked up at Jeremy and cocked his head to the side. "What's your name?"

"Um, my name? Um, Jer…" He hesitated.

"Do you have a name?" Jake said.

"Um, yeah. Just call me Santa."

Jake looked up at him with a scrunched brow. A smile slowly formed on his lipless mouth. "What? Like Santa Claus?"

"You don't look like Santa," said a goblin kid in a blue Spider-Man t-shirt.

"Well, I…"

"Yes, he does!" said the little girl in the unicorn shirt. "Look at his smile."

"Come on Sally! He doesn't even have a white beard," said the goblin in the Spider-Man shirt.

"Maybe he shaved. Just look at his smile," Sally said.

They all leaned forward and stared up at Jeremy. As ugly and as creepy as they were, there was something cute about them. He couldn't help but smile.

One by one, the goblin children smiled back.

"Oh, yeah," said the one in the Spider-Man shirt. "I see it now."

Others nodded and agreed.

The door flung open, and the goblin children all jumped to face the door. Jeremy stiffened and put his hand on his chest.

"Overseer! The Overseer is coming!" a goblin child said as he ran into the game room.

"Oh no," Jake said. "You need to hide." He frantically looked around the room.

Jeremy's heart pounded. He searched for some place to go, but there was nothing tall enough or concealing enough to hide behind or in. He could stand behind one of the large TVs. Then he remembered Ellesmere's cloak!

"Go! You have to hide," Jake said, pushing him toward a corner.

Jeremy thrust the cowl over his head and disappeared.

The goblins oohed and aahed again.

Jeremy walked over to a corner of the room to get out of everyone's way. The goblin children all assumed various positions of play, some at the video games and some at the board games.

The door opened again. An adult goblin walked in. Dressed in a black hooded tunic, he was noticeably different from the children. The overseer closed the door with one hand and surveyed the room. He had a muscular physique with black tattoos that made him look like he had snake-like scales on his forehead and bare arms. At his side, a sword in a gold and black scabbard hung from a thin, black leather belt. The overseer carried an electronic tablet in his hand. He stared at the children and then brought the tablet up and scrolled through the info with his finger.

"*Puka!* Organize!" the goblin overseer yelled—in English! Perfectly plain English, with a slightly midwestern accent.

The children stopped what they were doing, powered down the video games and TVs, packed up the board games, and formed three straight rows in front of the overseer.

"0-0-1, what is the capital of Nebraska?"

"Lincoln." Jake said. His accent sounded Midwestern too.

"Correct," the overseer said. "0-0-1 through 0-1-0, you will report to the gym for combat training."

Several goblins, including Jake and the one in the Spider-Man shirt, nodded their heads and marched out of the room.

"0-1-1 through 0-2-1, you will report to the store for economic training."

Several more nodded and walked out.

"0-2-2 through 0-3-1, it's time for your I.H.T. You'll be divided up into sibling pairs, in which you will learn all aspects of a typical American family. Follow me to your assigned areas."

What? Jeremy stared out at the children, neatly lined up,

listening attentively to the overseer. Each dressed in typical American kid's clothing. Playing American games. Talking like American children. It all made sense now. It was like those stories you hear about the Russian Sleeper agents! Jeremy swallowed and shook his head. He couldn't believe it.

Before the door could close, Jeremy rushed to follow the line of goblin children. The overseer led them down the curved hallway, past several other doors. Jeremy got the impression that there was some sort of central hub on the left, with smaller rooms because there were fewer doors on that side. The overseer stopped at one door on the right and walked in.

Jeremy placed his hand over his mouth, wanting to gasp at the sight before him. Dozens of houses on a typical street in Anywhere, America stood before him. Smells of freshly cut grass and grilled meat filled the air. Several adult goblins, wearing typical upper class, mid-western clothes, stood out on the porches while others stood on perfectly groomed lawns. Light, simulating the sun, shined down from the high dome-like ceiling.

"0-2-2 and 0-2-3. You are assigned to house Forty-Two, Sixth Avenue West. 0-2-2, your name is William Lake, but everyone calls you Will. Billy is the traditional nickname for William, but you hate being called Billy. 0-2-3, your name is Andrew Lake. Everyone calls you Drew, not Andy. You don't like being called Andy. Your parents are…"

The goblin overseer continued for several minutes, assigning each one to a home and giving them American names.

What is going on here? Jeremy thought. But the cold, hard truth was obvious. These goblins were training to infiltrate themselves into American communities! How many of them have already done so across America? And how did they hide themselves in plain sight? Had any of them ever been a student of his? Surely he'd notice a hairless, green skinned kid with only three fingers in his class. A chill moved across his spine, and he shivered. *Why are they doing this?* It was worse than he ever imagined.

He waited for the overseer to finish and followed him out of the fake neighborhood and back down the hall to another room.

Jeremy slipped in behind the overseer. He found himself in a replica of a typical school gymnasium. Another overseer, dressed identically to the first one, stood by the door. Ten goblin children, including Jake, had been assigned here.

The overseer he'd followed scrolled through his tablet again. He nodded to the other overseer and left. Jeremy found a corner of the gym and sat.

The children were divided into rows, spread apart from each other. The overseer led the goblin children through various techniques of blocking and arm locks.

Jeremy watched the young goblins. He had no idea what to do.

Birch? He tried mindcasting again. No answer. *Oh God, please don't let him be dead.* He remembered the earbuds. Jeremy shoved them in his ears.

"Anybody? Can you hear me?" He whispered.

No answer.

Oh crap, oh crap. They all can't be dead. But what about Ezzy and Ortiz? They were back on the plane. She should be able to hear him, right? Maybe it was the cloak? *Oh God, what am I going to do?* He looked at the goblin children. They were so much like any other child he'd ever met.

See, your gift is with children. Jeremy remembered Mercurio's words on the day they first met. *You have a bond with them that no one else does. When you look at a child, you see their wonder, their potential, their purity… when a child looks at you, they see something they can only explain as wonder. They are drawn to you. They can see your true heart.*

Jeremy swallowed, and a nervous energy swept over him. *My gift.* He thought. He stood up, feeling hope slowly push away his trepidation. *These goblin children are just like any other children.* Jeremy watched the overseer instruct them with military precision. He then looked to his staff, then back to the overseer. Jeremy walked over, raised his staff, and hesitated. *No.* He lowered the staff. *I need to convince the children first.*

CHAPTER 63
IN THE SERVICE OF THE MIGHTY SAR BORAHSH

"The Goblin Sar is seated by birth. If the current Sar does not have a male heir to the throne, one of the Excellencies to the Sar or the Lord of War will ascend to the throne. This is decided in battle, unless all but one of the candidates concede."

~ From *The Veiled Happenlore of the Master Construct* compiled by Fulbert Gisilfrid, a Chronicler of the Master Construct, Third Order, an alfargnym of Unterbaum

The overseer ended the combat training and escorted the goblin children out of the gym. Jeremy followed as they marched quietly through the halls, meeting up with the other children returning from their training. The overseer led them to the game room.

"You have sixty minutes for U.R.," the overseer told them.

Sally tugged on the overseer's robes. "Overseer, tell us about Santa Claus."

The excited children stopped what they were doing and quietly turned to the overseer. Their faces all wide eyed.

Jeremy brought his hand to his chest. *Oh no!*

The overseer looked down at the little goblin in the pink shirt. "Santa Claus?"

"Yeah. Santa Claus," she said.

"Why are you asking me this?"

"Uh, we was talking about Santa Claus earlier," Jake said.

The overseer looked suspiciously at Jake and then back to Sally. "Santa Claus is someone you should know about. He's important to humans. You will learn more about him in your Fourth Quarter training."

"Is he anything like the Santa Claus in the movies we have here?" Sally pointed to the TV.

"0-1-2 this is not the time for these questions. Use your Unsupervised Recreation time wisely. If you want to know anything about Santa Claus, watch one of the films we have here."

The overseer left and closed the door.

"Or I could just ask him myself," Sally smiled. "Santa! Are you here?"

Jeremy threw back his cowl and breathed a sigh of relief.

"He's here!" yelled one goblin.

The others stopped what they were doing and turned around.

"Where'd you go?" Jake said. He laid down the video game controller and walked over to Jeremy.

"I was here, just invisible," Jeremy said, smiling. His confidence was returning, but he still didn't know what he was going to do.

One by one the goblin children came up to Jeremy, forming a crowd around him.

"Listen, I need your help," he said. "Do you know, uh, the… the Goblin King?"

"Like in Labyrinth?" Sally said. "Jareth, the Goblin King?"

"Jareth! The Goblin King!" the one in the Spider-Man shirt shouted enthusiastically.

The crowd of goblin children giggled. Jeremy couldn't help but laugh with them.

"No, no. I'm not talking about a movie," he smiled. "I mean, in real life. Your king?"

"Sar Borahsh. He's the *emperor,*" Jake corrected. "He's more than a king. He's the king of kings. He's the mighty Sar Borahsh, Emperor of the Goblin Empire!"

"Sar Borahsh!" a goblin kid cheered.

"The Mighty Emperor, Sar Borahsh!" another yelled.

Oh boy. This is gonna be harder than I thought.

"Um, yeah. That's… who I'm talking about. Sar Borahsh. Something's wrong, and he… um." Jeremy swallowed. He felt the pressure on him now. He needed to get out of here. And he needed to find out if Wyllt and the others had succeeded. But how? "Wait. I need to do something," Jeremy said, stepping away from them and pushing the earbuds back in. He needed to test his theory about the comms not working while he was cloaked. "Hello. Is anybody there?"

"Jeremy!" Ezzy screamed "Peace and mercy! It's about time! Immatina! Jeremy's back on the radio!"

"Ezzy! Oh man, am I glad to hear you. Wait. What about the others?" Jeremy said.

"We haven't heard or seen anything for hours. There was a battle, and we lost all contact, except through Ellesmere. And then she lost contact when the goblins somehow caused her vessel to crumble. The only body cam that still works is yours. But that went out a little while ago and just came back on."

His suspicions were correct. Ellesmere's cloak blocked all incoming and outgoing transmissions.

"You've seemed to have made some friends with those goblin kin," Ezzy said.

"Yeah." Jeremy scratched his head. "That's kind of a long story."

"I've been watching. Do you really think you can trust them?" Ezzy said.

"I dunno. But I'm not sure I have a choice at this point."

"Ortiz has been trying to assemble a rescue team, but they're hours away. What are you gonna do until then?"

"I need to figure this all out. Hold on." Jeremy exhaled and rubbed his hand over his face. He glanced back at the crowd of goblin children, all staring up at him, watching his every move. He needed their help, but he had no idea what they could do or where their loyalties lay.

"I need to ask you all something." He walked back over to the goblins. "Do you know what's going on here? Why you have these overseers and all this training?"

They tilted their heads in unison. Then they looked to Jake to answer.

"Are you asking us our mission?"

Jeremy relaxed and smiled. "Yes. What is your mission?"

The goblins shuffled into lines and stood at attention, just as they had when the overseer came for them earlier.

"Our mission," they all recited, "is to serve the Mighty Sar Borahsh in restoring the Goblin Empire. We will do so by infiltrating human society and subverting them from within. We will become productive members of human society, attaining the highest levels of human government, education, and commerce."

Jeremy held his breath and then swallowed. *Oh man. This is really bad!*

"Wait, do you even know what that means?" Jeremy said.

Again, they looked to Jake.

"It means we'll one day take over the humans again and the goblin empire will expand under Sar Borahsh's rule."

They do understand. Or at least the older one does.

"B, but, I'm… I'm a human. You know that right?" Jeremy said, pointing his hand at his chest.

They repeated their wandering glances at one another before focusing on Jake.

"Well, yeah. But we thought that's why you're here. To serve Sar Borahsh and help us," he said.

Help you? "Hmmm…" *Yeah. Maybe that is why I'm here.* Jeremy paused and exhaled, making a puffing noise. "Exactly. I'm here to help you. But first, I have to help my friends. They're here somewhere in Kurgal, and they're hurt."

"Oh," Jake said. "What happened to them?"

"What happened?" said several others.

Your emperor's deranged! That's what happened to them. That's what Jeremy wanted to say. *Maybe that's it. Pepper it with the truth.*

"I'm sorry to tell you this, but your Sar is… sick. His mind… it's been poisoned."

The goblin children all gasped and their creepy eyes grew wide. Jeremy felt a tinge of guilt for lying to them.

"He's jeopardized his own plan. He's taken my friends hostage and done terrible things to them. And he's taken my ring. The one that gives me all my Santa powers."

The goblin children gasped.

"I need to help Sar Borahsh by rescuing my friends and getting my ring back."

"When you say friends, do you mean your elves?" the boy in the Spider-Man shirt asked.

"Um, yeah. Some of them. Some are humans and some are koth."

"Elves are evil, aren't they?" Jake said.

Oh boy. Jeremy swallowed.

"Yeah, they're our worstest enemies!" the boy in the Spider-Man shirt said.

An eruption of discussion spread throughout the room as the goblin children discussed the many ways in which elves are evil. All but one. The precocious little Sally stood there, hand on her chin, with her lipless mouth curled into a contemplative snarl.

"But wait," Sally said. "The elves, are they Christmas elves? The ones from the North Pole?"

The conversations dulled into silence as each child stared at Jeremy, waiting for an answer.

Jeremy hesitated. "Um, yeah."

"Oh no!" Sally said.

"Well, they can't be evil, can they?" Asked a boy in a neon green Under Armour shirt.

"We have to help them!" Sally said.

"Yeah, we'll help," Jake said, nodding vigorously.

"We have to save Christmas!" Sally yelled.

The others agreed.

Oh no, she didn't just say that, did she? Jeremy didn't know whether to laugh or to panic. *These kids have watched way too many Christmas movies!* This was perfect.

"Yes, we need to save the elves so we can… save Christmas." Jeremy held back a smile.

"Let's go rescue the elves!" Jake yelled.

"Oh no. No. That's too dangerous," Jeremy said. "The Sar's not the only one that has been infected. All the goblin grownups have been. The guards. Even the overseers. They've all been infected."

"Oh no," several shouted. Others nodded their agreement.

"We'll help!" Jake said, standing up straighter and looking at the others. They all shook their heads and straightened, too.

"Listen, if you do this, you can only listen to me. Your over-seers are going to try and stop you. The guards will try and stop you. You need to be willing to…" Jeremy swallowed. *What am I doing?* The realization struck Jeremy hard in the gut and his stomach tightened again. *Oh man, I'm using children to fight my battle. What is wrong with me?* Jeremy turned his gaze away from the goblin children and rubbed his forehead. *Idiot!*

"What?" Jake said. "What do we need to be willing to do?"

"Forget it," Jeremy said. "It's too dangerous. You could get hurt, and I wouldn't want that. I'll just have to find another way to rescue my friends."

"But we want to help," Jake said.

"We do," said several others.

Jeremy paused, closed his eyes, and rubbed his head again. Maybe this could work. Maybe he could do this with no one getting hurt or killed.

"Okay, listen. My friends are more than likely up in Sar Borahsh's throne room."

"The Hall of the Sar!" they announced with awe.

"Yes, the Hall of the Sar," Jeremy repeated. "I can get in there without anyone seeing me, but it's going to be tough trying to get the others out without being seen. All I need you to do is cause a diversion. Can you do that?"

"I think we can. What do you want us to do?" Jake asked.

"Is there more than one way into the Hall of the Sar?" Jeremy asked.

"The Path of Redemption and Judgment is the only way, unless you're a servant of the Sar," Jake said.

"What, like a servant's entrance?" Jeremy asked.

"Yes, in the Dwelling of the Sar. Only servants may enter."

"I get that. But how do you get to the part where the servants enter," Jeremy asked.

"It's just down the hall. Past America, and just before Great Britain," Jake said.

"If you come to Australia, you've gone too far," the one in the Spider-Man shirt said.

"Geez. You guys have little replicas of different countries you train in?"

"We're American puka. There are twenty training sites here," Jake said.

"Twenty! Holy cow! How big is this place?"

"I once walked to Russia," said the boy in the Spider-Man shirt. "It took me two hours. I missed my A.T. that day. The overseer punished me good."

"OK. Listen. I know I'm not a servant," Jeremy said, "but I think the best way to——"

"Jeremy, are you still there?" Ezzy said through the earbuds.

Jeremy jumped, forgetting that he still had the earbuds in. He held up a finger toward the goblins and then turned and walked away from them. "Ezzy. Sorry, I got distracted."

"Listen. Ortiz said that a rescue team is about four hours away. Ellesmere's created another vessel. She's going to wait at the entrance for them."

"Good, but I don't know how much longer I can wait. Mercurio and the other guardians have been here for days. If Wyllt and his men are still alive, they may not have much time, either. I'll keep you posted. You may not be able to contact me for a while. I don't think the walkie-talkies and body cams work when I go invisible. But I'll try and keep you updated. Okay?"

"Okay. Um, but Jeremy… please don't die," Ezzy said.

Jeremy paused. *Please don't die?* "I will. Uh, I mean, I won't… I'll try not to. I gotta go now."

"Bye," Ezzy said. There was a slight hesitation in her voice. He expected her to say something else, but no other transmission came.

Jeremy returned to the goblins.

"Who are you talking to?" Jake asked.

"Um, the others from the rescue team. But let's not worry about that. We need to focus. Everyone ready?"

They shook their heads and murmured various forms of affirmation.

"Okay, you…" Jeremy hesitated, pointing to the taller goblin. "Jake, right?"

"I'm Jacob," he said. "But I like to be called Jake."

"Like Jake from State Farm," Sally giggled.

They randomly introduced themselves. Jeremy could only catch a few names. The one in the Spider-Man shirt was named Craig. The other names blurred together, though he was sure he heard a Pete and a Melissa in there somewhere.

"Okay, everyone, you'll follow Jake. Jake, I'll follow you. When I go invisible, I'll grab your hand. If you meet anyone, you can't tell them about me. But you'll need an excuse why you're roaming around the halls."

"There would be no excuse for that. If a guard sees us, he'll send us back down here," Jake said.

"But we won't run into any of the guards going through the servant's section," Craig said. "Not until you get to the throne room. Then there'll be guards everywhere."

Hmmm. Jeremy pondered the situation for a second. "You guys are trained infiltrators, right?"

"Yeah, but we're not graduated yet," Jake said. "Craig and I are the furthest along, but we have another two years before we're assigned to an actual mission. Then we'll get our Illusory Implants and become real puka."

"Yeah, I can't wait," Craig said.

"Why not try it now?" Jeremy said. "You can pretend to be servants and get into the throne room. Cause a distraction there."

"No, that wouldn't be convincing. We're not tall enough. Without our Illusory Implants we only look like this. And we've only trained to be American children. I'm from Nebraska," Jake said.

"I'm from Minnesota, don't ya know," Craig said.

Others started repeating American states and cities. The overwhelming ramifications of these goblin infiltrators weighed heavily on Jeremy. If these children were being exploited like this, and they were successful in their missions… Jeremy couldn't even imagine the damage they could do. He couldn't allow that to happen. He couldn't allow these children, and dozens—probably hundreds of others—to be used in such a way. Jeremy sighed and looked at the door. First, he had to help the elves.

"Okay, let's try this." He counted the number of children. Twenty. "Do you think we can convince some other children from other training areas to join us?"

"Yeah. Easy. I can talk to Malcolm in Great Britain," Jake said.

"But we only have forty minutes of U.R. left before the overseer comes back," Craig said.

"Okay, let's do it. Jake, you sneak down to Great Britain and get them to join us. We'll give you ten minutes and then we'll meet you at the servants' entrance."

"What if the overseer comes looking for us?" Sally asked.

"I'll take care of him," Jeremy said. It seemed he'd gotten his bravado back. But when push came to shove, he feared it would reveal itself as false again.

CHAPTER 64
IN THE SERVICE OF THE HIGH KING

"The seat of the High King of the Dweorg can be passed from the reigning king to his chosen predecessor. In most cases it is passed to the Thane of Nidavellir. If the son of the High King is old enough, he will usually be appointed the seat of Thane of Nidavellir. However, any dweorg can challenge the High King for his seat."

~ From *The Veiled Happenlore of the Master Construct* compiled by Fulbert Gisilfrid, a Chronicler of the Master Construct, Third Order, an alfargnym of Unterbaum

"Yer plan is to become High King of the Dweorg?" Grofr asked.

Masaru ignored the question. He was more concerned with the *hospitality* they had offered him. Grofr and two guards escorted Masaru to his room for the evening. He scanned the luxurious chamber, noting all the exits and entrances. He'd been given all the amenities anyone could ask for. A large bed with red and blue pillows and black fur blankets, a spacious wardrobe, private bath, shelves filled with books, and a comfy-looking chair.

High King Unn had insisted that Masaru stay in the palace as his guest for the night. An odd request, Masaru thought. Though, after all the nights he'd spent in the wilderness, it would be nice to sleep in a bed. He doubted he'd get much sleep. He took a step into the room and ran his prosthetic hand along the smooth stone wall.

Grofr cleared his throat and crossed his arms.

"Yes," Masaru said, not making eye contact with the other dweorg. He made his way over to the large antique wooden wardrobe and opened the doors. It was empty. He slid his polymer fingers along the edges, using the amplified electrical signals to search for false drawers and hidden doors.

"Yer going to kill High King Unn.," Grofr said.

"Yes, I am."

"I'm not questioning ya. I believe it. He's never wielded his axe in battle. He's trained to use it, but I cannot remember the last time he truly practiced with it."

Just as Masaru expected. He wasn't impressed with the king. Even after he accepted his challenge. The king was soft, and he needed to die, or at least step down.

"Ya have blood on yer hands. I see it in yer manner, in yer eyes. That's why I'm here," Grofr said.

"To convince me to back down?" Masaru glanced back at Grofr, studying him before answering. The bald dweorg seemed an oddity to him. Slightly taller than Masaru, he was heavy set and broad shouldered. Unlike most other dweorg, he had a long goatee and not a full beard. The king's counselor, or what was it they called him - a Mimir?- seemed... stately for a dweorg. He wore a dark gray tunic with ornate blue and gold detailing at the cuffs and blue yoke that set him apart from the other dweorg Masaru had seen.

"No. There's no turnaround from the upcalling. That would be a dishonor. His wife and son would be made lower than a skogarmaor!" Grofr said, shaking his head. "I'm here to prepare ya. It's my berth as the Mimir to advise the high king."

Masaru tsked. "So, you're looking for a job?" He ran his hand along the walls as he walked toward the bed.

Grofr laughed. "No. I have a job. Hark back to what I said, I serve the throne, not he who sits upon it. I've no doubt ya will be the next high king. I just want ya to be sure ya know what comes with the crown."

This wasn't at all what he'd expected. He figured he'd challenge the king, the pathetic dweorg would call his guards or possibly even try to fight him himself, and Masaru would kill him. He wasn't expecting all these politics and rules. "Tell me about the challenge. What can I expect?" Masaru squatted and looked under the bed. There was nothing he could see.

"That's simple. At the appointed time and place, y'ill meet the high king. He'll try to put up a good fight, but I've no doubt y'ill have killed him in a quick span. Thirty-seconds, more likely. Then y'ill take his crown, and his axe, and sit upon the throne."

"That's it?" Masaru said, moving his hand across the floor to look for a trap door under the bed.

"Were ya expecting a coronation?"

"No," he said, standing up, "but—"

"I'm sure there'll be a crowd there. Once the guards go off berth, the word of an upcalling for the throne will be on everyone's ears. Y'ill have an audience. And once ya kill High King Unn, y'ill be able to address yer people."

Masaru scrutinized the hefty dweorg. None of this seemed to concern him. He was so matter-of-fact, speaking as if all of this was normal.

"How do I know he won't try to have me killed tonight?"

Grofr raised an eyebrow and stroked his goatee with one hand; the other hanging by his side. His eyes shifted to Masaru's prosthetic arm. "Yer an unnamed, aren't ya?"

"What?"

"Yer an unnamed. Ya were born here, but ya weren't raised here. That's why yer speech and mannerisms are so different. And the fact that ya don't know what an unnamed is, or that ya don't even know yer one, tells me a lot."

Masaru stepped toward Grofr, his teeth clenched and his eyes boring intently into the dweorg's. The adviser didn't flinch. "I am dweorg! I have every right to challenge the king! Just because I was cast out of here for not having an arm, my blood is still the same as yours."

"I never said that ya had no right. But yer going to need my help more than I thought."

That was true. Masaru didn't have Turtak to help him anymore. If he could trust this guy, he'd certainly prove useful. Masaru breathed in a calming breath and turned back to the bed.

"Besides, ya can't crown yer self high king with that skogarmaor name."

Masaru's brow furrowed and he turned to Grofr. "What?"

"That name of yers. It's a human name. If ya want the respect of yer people, you'll need a proper name."

Masaru had never thought of that. He'd always been, Masaru… even to Turtak. He'd have to think about that some more. But not now. Now he had more pressing things to find out about. "If the king isn't planning on trying to kill me tonight, why wait until tomorrow to fight me? Why not just get it over with tonight?" Masaru knelt to inspect the nightstand.

"Despite what ya think of High King Unn, he's honorable. If ya died before the upcalling, his honor would be in question. Y'ill be well protected tonight. And High King Unn 'ill spend his last night with his son and wife."

Was that supposed to make Masaru feel bad?

"They'll be yer responsibility now."

Masaru shot up, turning away from inspecting the nightstand. "My responsibility?"

"Yes. Another reason the high king accepted yer upcalling. If he didn't, and ya killed him anyway, his line would be dishonored, and his family would be displaced. They'd be made kaupmaor but treated more like skogarmaor! Living off scraps and skulking about like the svartalgnym. It'd be terrible for them."

"How is that my problem?"

"You evoked the upcalling! He accepted. What was his 'ill now be yours."

Crap! What am I supposed to do with a bastard and a widow?

"Can I give them to someone else? I don't want to be looking over my shoulder, thinking they'll be looking for revenge."

Grofr laughed. "Ya opened the closed book. Now all 'ill want to read it. There hasn't been an upcalling to the throne in ages. Y'ill be looking over yer shoulder more often than ya think."

Masaru grunted and sighed wearily. He wished Turtak was here. "Either way, I don't want the queen and prince getting in my way. What are my options?"

"Options? Few. No matter what, y'ill be responsible for them. And, for yer knowledge, Tarben, the high king's son, is not a prince. Our people don't have princes. He may have indeed been chosen as a successor to the high king at some point, but it more than likely would have been Thane Uther. Uther is who ya need to be on guard for. He'll not likely accept ya as high king. Y'ill need to hold him to his berth. Best way to do that 'ill be to do so with the other thanes present. That should be yer first order of business, to call a gathering of the thanes."

"Who are the other thanes?" Masaru asked.

"Thane Vidar of Thorheim and Thane Hjalmar of Valiheim. You are aware of the other dweorg strongholds?"

Masaru hesitated. "No."

"The high king rules the five mountain kingdoms of the dweorg. Of the five, two are no more and their memory lives on in their name. Each stronghold has a thane that governs, answerable only to the high king. It 'ill be most necessary for ya to meet with them right away. I'd suggest that be yer first order on the throne. Send a tidend to the thanes and call a meeting at a foretold time. There, y'ill assert yer authority to all three, upcalling each if need be. If the other thanes respect ya, Uther will have but no choice to do so as well. He won't like it. But he'll do it."

Masaru sighed and placed his hand on the hilt of his katana. This was going to be far more complicated than he ever imagined.

Grofr eyed the weapon and nodded. "What's her name?"

Masaru raised an eyebrow. "Her name?"

"Oh, come now kunder. A fine blade such as she must have a name. Odin had Gungnir. Thor had Mjölnir. And High King Unn has Skiljana. Ya can't go around killing with that sword and not give the kunder something to tell tales about."

Masaru looked down at the hilt of his katana. This blade allowed him to reclaim his birthright and restore his people. It was not only his redeemer, but his peoples'. "Lausnaril." He said, speaking the word that Turtak had taught him. The word in the dweorg tongue that meant redeemer.

"Ah!" Grofr said. "A fine name for a fine blade. Now that we've pushed that out the way, let's discuss tomorrow. I've arranged for a wearshafter to make ya more suitable clothing and for evenmeal to be brought here. Though I assume you'll think the food poisoned, correct? We'll share a platter and I'll eat the same food."

Tomorrow couldn't come soon enough, but a good hot meal would be nice. Masaru nodded his head and strode over to inspect the bookshelves.

CHAPTER 65
THE BANE
OF SAR BORAHSH

"To move a mountain, one must begin by moving stones."

Sar Eengurra

Jake and several dozen other goblins marched toward Jeremy and the remaining goblin children waiting outside the servants' entrance.

Jeremy removed his cowl and smiled. "Good job, Jake."

"Santa, this is Malcolm," Jake said, pointing to a similarly dressed goblin.

"He doesn't look at all like Father Christmas!" Malcolm said. His accent was clearly British. It seemed just as strange as Jake and his Midwestern accent.

"He's in disguise," Jake said.

"I am," Jeremy nodded. "You told him what happened to the Sar?"

"Yes, he did," Malcolm said. "That's why we're here. And to help rescue your mates."

"And to save Christmas!" Sally shouted.

The other British goblin children all nodded in agreement.

"So, you have a plan?" Malcolm asked.

"Yeah, we need a diversion. I'm thinking you, Craig, and Jake, being the oldest and tallest, are going to disguise yourselves as servants. The rest of you are going to cause several diversions. I want one of you to go up to the king's throne room—"

"The Hall of the Sar!" Sally smiled.

"The Hall of the Sar!" the others shouted.

"Yes, the Hall of the Sar." Jeremy nervously looked around for anyone who might overhear the boisterous children. "You'll enter through the main entrance—"

"The Path of Redemption and Judgment," Sally corrected him again.

"Yes, you'll go through the Path of Redemption and Judgment. Now remember, the Sar and his guards have all been compromised. Their brains are not working right and they've made some pretty bad choices. We need to work together to rescue my friends and help the Sar."

"And save Christmas!" Sally shouted.

Jeremy smiled. "Yes, and save Christmas. If anyone tries to stop you, you need to tell them that something terrible has happened down here."

"What do we tell them happened?" Malcolm said.

They all paused in thought.

"I'll tell them that Albert took my Snickers bar and ate it!" Sally said, sneering at another goblin in a red basketball t-shirt.

"I did not!" Albert said.

"Okay, Okay. That's enough, guys," Jeremy said in his calm teacher voice. "Sally, we need to focus on rescuing my friends. We'll see about your candy bar later. What we need is something really bad to tell them."

"Like a monster?" Sally said.

"Yeah, like a monster!" Craig said.

Several others agreed.

"Oh, I know," Jake said. "We'll tell them that the experiments from level two got out and are tearing things up down here."

"Yeah. That's a good one," Malcolm said.

"Especially since it happened once before. About two years ago. I'll never forget that day," Craig said.

"That sounds like a good plan," Jeremy said. "That's what you tell any grownups you see. And you have to be believable. Cry, scream, yell. You gotta sell it."

"We can do that," Jake said, nodding to the others.

They nodded back.

"All right, so Jake, Malcolm, Craig, you're with me. We need someone else to lead about ten of you up through the Path of Judgment and Redemption."

"Redemption and Judgment," Sally corrected. "It's called the Path of *Redemption and* Judgment."

This kid is too cute. "That's what I said." Jeremy smiled.

"No, you said *Judgment* and Redemption."

"Yeah, you did," Craig said.

Several others agreed.

"What's the difference?" Jeremy asked.

"That's not what it's called," Jake said. "It's called the Path of Redemption and Judgment."

Jeremy stared at the boy. "OK. I ge*t it*. But we're losing focus here. We need to stay focused. We need someone to lead the team to the Path of Redemption and Judgment."

Sally smiled and nodded at him with approval.

Several goblins raised their hands and called out, begging to be chosen.

"Jake, you know them better. You pick," Jeremy said.

Jake turned and looked at those raising their hands. He then looked at Malcolm and teetered his head indecisively. "I think Michael or Jason will do a good job."

Malcolm nodded in agreement. "Go with Michael. He's a bit older."

"Alright, Michael it is!" Jeremy said.

"At your service, Santa." Michael stepped forward.

"Fantastic, Michael," Jeremy said. "Let's move out."

They spent a few minutes dividing the teams, with Sally

insisting that she be on Jeremy's team. There were twenty-eight goblins. Jeremy sent twenty with Michael, and he took the rest.

Jeremy placed his cowl on, disappeared, and then grabbed Jake's hand. He opened the door to the servants' entrance and entered a hallway much like the others, but not as tall and wide. Halfway down on either side, there were doors. At the end, a staircase led upward.

Jake guided Jeremy without hesitation up the stairs. The long stairwell led to another door, and Jake stopped and pointed.

"The servants' quarters are in there," Jake whispered. "I'm not sure how many there are. But it's just a bunch of beds and trunks."

Jeremy pulled his cowl down. "Are you sure?"

Jake shook his head.

"How do you know for sure?"

Jake curled his lipless mouth to one side and shrugged. "I snuck up here once. I made it all the way up to the servants' entrance, just outside the Sar's throne."

"Why didn't you tell me that sooner?" Jeremy said. "That's good information to have ahead of time. Tell me about it."

"Oh, it's big! Sick, man! It's an actual dragon skull!"

"What?" Jeremy asked.

"The throne! It's an actual dragon skull," Jake said.

Jeremy sighed. "Tell me about the way up there. What will we see?"

"After we walk through the servant's quarters, there's a few rooms on the other side, in the hall. But I'm not sure what's in them. At the end of the hall is another set of stairs that leads to the Sar's personal kitchen. All the yummy food is there. It's so much better than the stuff we eat."

"Okay. What comes after the kitchen?" Jeremy said.

"Well, outside the kitchen is the hallway to the Throne of the Sar. But across from the kitchen is a room filled with the king's clothes and a couple of servants mending and washing them."

"Okay. And there's no guards around there?" Jeremy asked.

"There weren't any when I was there. They're all in the Hall of the Sar."

Jeremy nodded and thought about their next move. If the servants weren't going to bother them, then it was just a straight shot. But he needed to get the door of the throne room open without causing a scene. That's where Jake, Craig, and Malcolm would come in.

THE THREE GOBLIN BOYS, dressed in clothing they took from the servants' quarters, stood at the door to the Sar's throne room. All they had to do was open the door and bring the Sar a snack. Jeremy hoped it wouldn't arouse too much suspicion. But with the chaos that was about to ensue, it wouldn't really matter... he hoped.

Craig opened the door. Jeremy shielded his eyes from the bright light that streamed in. Jake and Malcolm walked in, holding trays filled with assorted finger-foods that looked like pastries. Two guards stood outside the door. With his cowl on, Jeremy followed the boys in and stood to the side, out of their way. He squinted, adjusting to the intense light that engulfed the throne room. The massive dragon-skull throne sat in the center. His heart beat faster, and he found it harder to breathe.

Take it easy. They can't see you, Jeremy reminded himself.

The sar stirred from atop his throne and looked down at Jake and Malcolm.

A fat goblin sitting below the throne uttered enthusiastically in a language Jeremy assumed was goblin. *Goblinese?*

Jake and Malcolm froze and looked at each other.

Come on boys, you can do this, Jeremy said to himself.

The king eyed the platters and licked his lipless maw. His excited expression turned to a sneer. He yelled something at the boys, scolding them, and waving his royal scepter around.

The fat goblin awkwardly stood from his seat below the throne and joined in the scolding.

Jake and Malcolm cowered, still frozen in place.

Oh no! What's the problem? Jeremy wondered.

The fat goblin pointed his sausage-like finger at the door and continued to yell.

Jake and Malcolm didn't move.

Move! Go already. I'm in! Just get out of here, Jeremy yelled inside his head.

Jake and Malcolm turned around and quickly left, leaving Jeremy to face the goblins on his own. A twinge of panic set in as he looked around. Below the throne were three steps that led down to the golden path. It led straight through the hall and out through an enormous set of ornate doors. Twelve armored goblins stood below the steps, and two more at the doors. To the left of the path was a wall of weapons and armor. In front of them sat three display cases.

Jeremy carefully stepped forward to survey the rest of the throne room. Opposite the wall of weapons, he saw a gruesome display. He placed his hands over his face and braced himself with his staff from the wave of anguish that washed over him. Mercurio, Ee'azar, Jar'iyu, Wyllt, Decoudreau, Jaeger and Lang, hung naked from long, ominous stone pikes jutting from the floor. Each pike pierced the side of its victim, going in through the front and out the back. They hung over a cross post that hindered them from sliding further down the pole.

Lang twitched and coughed up blood.

The goblin sar turned to watch. He laughed excitedly, and the two goblins below the throne joined in.

Jeremy swallowed. *How in the world am I going to get them out of here?* His insides twisted. He didn't know how much longer he could stand the turmoil. He needed to follow through with the plan, but he had no idea how he was going to get them down from the pikes. They had to be at least eight feet high, and the cross post they hung over was at least four feet down from the tip.

A dragging sound drew Jeremy's attention. A goblin, dressed similarly to the overseers, pushed a large wooden cart over to Lang. He folded down a set of steps from the cart's side, opened a cabinet-like door, and removed a metallic case. The goblin laid the case on top of the cart's flat top and opened it. Its contents glowed, lighting up the goblin's face. He pulled the object out. The glow came from a jar-like container attached to an odd contraption with gold, spider-like arms protruding downward. The goblin grabbed something else from the case and walked up the small stairs. He squatted making himself eye level with Lang's side and the pike that impaled him. He poured a handful of goop from a small bottle and rubbed it on both sides of Lang's wound. The goblin then took the glowing contraption and placed it on Lang's back. Its arms spread out around the pike, circling the wound. The goblin twisted a knob at the top of the contraption, and a small scream emanated from within. The glow faded.

Jeremy was too far away to see exactly what the goblin was doing, but he remembered Jau had told them that the Sar's prisoners were frequently healed to extend their torture.

Jeremy cringed and wanted to retch. But there was nothing left in him. He felt lightheaded. He took a deep breath and stared down at Mercurio. The elf was barely moving, save for his labored breaths. They needed Jeremy. It was time for him to saddle up.

CHAPTER 66
DIVERSION...
DESTRUCTION... DEATH

"When Sar Belshunu was the Goblin Lord of War he lured the Dark Elf Elder, Sidion iyl Nadal out from behind the Veil by making his presence known among the humans of Benin. Belshunu killed Sidion and claimed his ears and his dagger as his prize."

~ From *The Veiled Happenlore of the Master Construct* compiled by Fulbert Gisilfrid, a Chronicler of the Master Construct, Third Order, an alfargnym of Unterbaum

The sight of Mercurio, bloodied, impaled and hanging from a pike was more than Jeremy could bear. He needed to help them *now*. Jeremy closed his eyes and hoped the goblin children would cause the diversion soon. Under the veil of Ellesmere's cloak, he leaned against the warm stone wall of the throne room, next to the goblin torturer.

What is taking them so long? He wondered. Jeremy opened his eyes and peeked around the corner at the goblin on the throne. The so-called King of Kings, Emperor of the Goblin Empire. A wave of revulsion washed over Jeremy, and he swallowed. The king seemed barely a remnant of his former self; nothing like he looked on that night… when he'd killed Nikolaos. This one creature caused so much trouble, so much despair. Jeremy imagined how easy it would be to skulk up to his throne and kill him. First, he'd start with the guards, then his two cronies, and finally Borahsh. He could stab them without ever being seen. But could he really murder them like that? Jeremy didn't think so. He wished he could. He'd be doing the world a favor. Maybe he could if it came down to him fighting for his life. He sighed and hoped the impending distraction would be enough.

Next to him, the goblin torturer sat in a chair beside a cart, reading. Jeremy turned away, but the torturer's book drew him back for a second glance. A tattered and stained copy of *How to Win Friends and Influence People* by Dale Carnegie. How strange? And how disturbing! These creatures were truly hell bent on niggling their way into the human collective conscience and influencing humanity from within.

Screams from outside the throne room caught Jeremy's attention. The guards stepped forward into a defensive stance, polearm blades facing forward. The torturer stood up.

This is it. Jeremy swallowed. He grabbed his staff with both hands and readied it.

The doors slammed open, and the children ran in. They screamed, yelling something Jeremy couldn't understand. They looked genuinely frightened! *Nice job!*

Jeremy breathed in, raised his staff and slammed it as hard as he could into the back of the goblin torturer's skull. He whirled the staff back around and slammed it into the goblin's face as he fell forward. The torturer jerked backward and fell to the ground.

The children's screams echoed throughout the chamber. Jeremy watched as they ran down the golden path, yelling and pointing behind them. They were really selling it.

Jeremy draped his cloak around the cart, pulling it tightly around to extend its size. He pushed the cart over to Mercurio, took down the steps, and climbed up onto the gurney-like flat top. He gently tried to lift his friend off the tall spike.

A blood curdling roar came from down the hall, and Jeremy froze. He closed his eyes, took a deep breath and turned to see what manner of creature could make such a sound. When he opened his eyes, his body stiffened. An ape-like beast, almost as tall as the doorway and almost as wide, stood at the threshold. Its massive frame was covered in black calloused skin. In one hand it carried a limp goblin soldier. The creature roared again as it pounded the goblin into the floor. It then flung it to the side, sending it soaring into the wall. The soldier hit one of the lamps with a resounding *thunk* that repeated when it hit the ground. The creature thumped its chest and roared again before slamming its fist to the ground and launching itself toward the children.

Oh crap! What is that?

The children ran to the side of the path as the guards charged after the beast.

Jeremy wiped the sweat from his face, swallowed hard, and turned back to try and ease Mercurio off the pike. The elf groaned and looked up.

"Mercurio, it's me," Jeremy whispered.

"Jeremy?" Mercurio said weakly.

"Yeah, I'm going to get you out of here."

"No… Jeremy. You should…" Mercurio groaned again as Jeremy pushed him upward.

The slurping sound of flesh and blood sliding up the jagged pike sent a wave of nausea to Jeremy's already empty stomach. He lifted Mercurio faster, wanting to be done with it. As he approached the top, Mercurio's warm blood oozed onto Jeremy's hands and head. He heaved one final upward overhead press, and Mercurio was free.

In the background, the children's screams, and the creature's roar, combined with the sound of clanking metal, created a cacophony of chaos that Jeremy tried to tune out. He laid the elf down on the flat top of the cart and used his sleeve to wipe Mercurio's blood from his face. He looked behind to see if the children were safe. Sally stood at the servants' entrance, holding it open for the other children as they ran to safety.

Goblin guards fought to no avail against the mighty creature; their blades making no purchase against the hard sable skin of the beast.

Jeremy quickly retrieved the first aid kit from his backpack. He unrolled the gauze.

"No... no," Mercurio groaned and pointed to the side of the cart. "The... device."

"But I don't know how to use it," Jeremy said.

Mercurio grabbed the gauze from Jeremy's hand and pressed it to his wound. He cringed at its touch. "Quickly! I'm losing... too much... blood."

Jeremy scrambled to open the cabinet and remove the device. It glowed as soon as he opened the metal container. *Oh God, no.* Jeremy thought as soon as he saw the device's power source; a fairy trapped within the chamber, its hands bound on a gold cross-like mechanism. Manacles wrapped around each wrist, attached to gold wires that fed the spider-like legs below. Jeremy stared at the poor creature within. *How could anyone...*

Mercurio grabbed Jeremy's arm and pulled. "Now! Hurry," he grumbled.

Jeremy grabbed the bottle of goop from the container and opened it. He then moved Mercurio's hand away from the wound and poured the gelatinous liquid onto the elf's side.

Mercurio stiffened.

"The... back..." he moaned.

Jeremy guided Mercurio onto his other side to expose the bleeding puncture. He then slathered the goop over the wound.

Mercurio winced.

Jeremy picked up the device and sighed, sadly looking down at the tormented fairy.

"It's dead... already," Mercurio said. "There's nothing... you can do... to help it."

Jeremy gritted his teeth and placed the spider-like arms around the wound, just as he had seen the goblin do earlier. He swallowed. "I'm sorry," he whispered as he turned the knob at the top. The little creature within writhed and let out a tiny scream. Its glow faded, and the fairy went limp as the device's arms moved in circles around Mercurio's wound. The bleeding stopped as the hole closed.

"The other side," Mercurio said.

Jeremy repeated the process.

Mercurio slowly pushed himself up. He was weak and pale. The magic had healed his wounds, but it didn't give him any strength back. Jeremy could only imagine what the elf had gone through. Almost six days had passed.

"Jeremy…" Mercurio whispered. "You shouldn't… have come… here."

"I know. But I had to. Come on, we have five more people to rescue."

"You get them down… and I'll use the device to heal them." Mercurio said.

Mercurio stayed on the cart and held the ends of the cloak together while Jeremy pushed the cart over to Ee'azar.

"I see… Wyllt followed you…" Mercurio coughed.

"Um, not quite. I, uh, kinda invited him."

"You did what?" Mercurio winced.

"Yeah, I, uh, called him. Asked him to help rescue you."

"Jeremy, of all the possible… bad moves… you could have made… that was probably…" Mercurio seized up in a coughing fit.

Jeremy placed his hand on Mercurio's back to comfort him. "Yeah, I know."

Mercurio nodded to Ee'azar.

Jeremy climbed up the steps and lifted the elf down from the pike, spilling more blood onto his hands and head.

Mercurio applied the goop as quickly as his weakened body would let him. He then took the device from Jeremy and used it without hesitation on Ee'azar.

The elf stirred and let out a moan.

Jeremy felt something knock into him. He hit the cart and it tumbled over, sending them all to the blood-soaked floor. The cabinet opened, and dozens of other glowing containers rolled out.

He shook off the shock of the impact and looked around to see what had happened. A goblin soldier lay several feet away from him. And beyond the goblin, Mercurio and Ee'azar lay on the ground, exposed.

Jeremy pushed himself up and stepped over the goblin guard.

The monstrous creature stood in the center of the room, breathing, huffing, looking around, taking in the devastation it had caused. Goblin soldiers lay still all around. The light of the throne glistened off the monster's ebony skin and the bloody carnage surrounding it.

Jeremy looked up at the throne. The king and his cronies were gone. He searched for the children; they were gone too. Hopefully, they were all safe.

Mercurio groaned and pushed himself up, resting on his hands and knees.

The creature jerked its head towards Mercurio and leapt at him.

"No!" Jeremy yelled.

A bolt of gray and brown slammed into the creature, sending it to the ground. The monster rolled and slid into the steps leading to the throne.

It roared, and a fist of stone punched it in the mouth.

Ellesmere! Thank God.

Ellesmere's golem pummeled the creature with a flurry of punches.

The creature kicked, and Ellesmere soared backwards down the gold path.

It jumped up, beat its chest, and roared at the golem.

Ellesmere curled herself into a ball and rolled toward the creature. When she was upon it, she unfolded herself and leapt at it, sending the beast back to the ground and resumed the clobbering.

Jeremy grabbed Mercurio and helped him up.

"We gotta hurry!" Jeremy said. He helped Mercurio over to

Ee'azar, who lay unconscious on the floor. Jeremy looked around for the device. He retrieved it and brought it back to Mercurio.

Mercurio grabbed the dim canister of the device and ejected it. He picked up a glowing one, inserted it and the spider-like legs came to life. He set the device in place as Jeremy lifted the cart and rolled it over to Jar'iyu. He hefted the elf off and laid him on the cart.

Ellesmere rose from the fray and stared down at the unmoving body of the monster. She then lumbered over to Jeremy and the elves.

"Mercurio, are you alright?" she boomed.

Mercurio wearily looked up and smiled at the golem. "I knew you'd come around."

"Hmph!" she groaned. "Don't get ahead of yourself, guardian. We've still a long way to go. Let's start by getting out of here."

Ellesmere lumbered over to Wyllt and easily lifted his body off the pike.

"No," Mercurio said. "Leave him."

"I will not," Ellesmere said, laying Wyllt next to Jar'iyu.

"Ellesmere… those men are evil." Mercurio grumbled.

"They risked their lives to save you," she said.

Ellesmere lifted Decoudreau off the pike and laid him beside Wyllt.

"Mercurio, please," Jeremy said, taking down his cowl so the elf could see him. "I think we had Wyllt all wrong. We may not agree with his methods, but he's not as bad as we thought."

"He has you fooled," Mercurio said.

"No, Erwin confirmed it. Said that he wasn't lying."

Mercurio shook his head and sneered as he applied the goop to Jar'iyu's back.

"Santa!" Sally shouted from behind Jeremy.

He turned and saw the group of goblin children walking out from the servants' entrance. Sally ran towards Jeremy, her arms wide open.

Mercurio grabbed the nearest goblin polearm and weakly hefted it, taking a defensive posture toward the goblin children.

Sally gasped and stopped short; her eyes fixed on Jeremy; her smile disappeared as the girl's lipless mouth opened wide with shock.

Several other goblin children yelled "Santa" as they emerged from the doorway.

"It's okay," Jeremy said, holding up a hand to Mercurio. "They're with me."

Sally covered her mouth and stared wide eyed at Jeremy.

"Santa," she said slowly. "Are you alright?"

"Yes." Jeremy said.

"All that blood," Craig said.

Jeremy couldn't imagine what he looked like. He was covered in elf blood. "It's not mine. I'm OK."

Sally took her hands away from her mouth and continued her run. She leapt into Jeremy's arms and gave him a tight hug around his neck.

"Oh Santa, I'm glad you're OK," she shouted in his ear.

Jeremy hugged her.

She pulled away from his neck. "Did we save Christmas?" Her face lit up with her equally cute and grotesque, toothy smile.

Jeremy smiled. "Almost. We still need to find a few more of our friends and then get out of here."

Mercurio put the polearm down and returned to reviving the others.

"Why's your Christmas elf naked?" Sally asked.

Jeremy shook his head and stifled a laugh. "That's a long story," he said, lowering Sally to the ground. He then turned to Michael. "What happened?" He pointed at the fallen creature.

"Well," Michael said, "you told us to make it believable. So, we stopped in the Sages' laboratories first and we opened a few cages. We saw that big guy in a cage, and when we let him out, he started destroying everything."

Jeremy shook his head. "Well, you certainly did cause quite the distraction. I'm just glad Ellesmere was here when she was. Otherwise, your distraction would have been the end of us all."

Wyllt wearily sat up and surveyed the room. His eyes fell on Mercurio and he nodded a silent thank you.

Mercurio ignored him and moved on to Decoudreau.

"We need… to get… out of here." Wyllt croaked. He grabbed his throat and swallowed. "Water?" he asked.

"I'll get some!" Jake shouted.

"Good idea. You guys help Jake get enough water for everyone," Jeremy said.

"Jeremy. Your… radio." Wyllt struggled to speak.

Yes! That's right! Jeremy took a step and then activated the radio. "Ezzy! Can you hear me?"

"Jeremy! Yes. The rescue team is on its way. They said something about not landing, but fast-roping from the helicopter directly to the entrance."

"How are they gonna get in without Jau?" Jeremy asked.

"I don't know," she replied. "They didn't say."

Jeremy turned to Wyllt. "A rescue team is coming, but they can't get in without someone to open the secret door."

"As long as… Ortiz gives them… the exact coordinates," Wyllt placed his hand on his side and took in a deep breath. "...they'll be able to get in."

Jeremy relayed that information over the radio.

"Copy that," Ortiz said.

"We still have to find Tufts, Birch, and Grath, but I have no idea where to look. Birch isn't responding."

"Tufts…" Wyllt groaned and waved his hand, "… is dead."

Jeremy stared at Wyllt. He hardly knew Tufts at all, but a sense of remorse washed over him.

"Who's Tufts?" Sally asked.

Jeremy stared down at the little goblin. "Someone who risked his life to save my friends."

Jake and the other goblin ran in with corked bottles and handed them out to everyone.

Wyllt, Jaeger, Decoudreau and Lang took long swigs and then

wearily pushed themselves up. They gathered weapons from the fallen goblin soldiers and used whatever cloth they could find to wrap around their waists.

Wyllt wearily walked over to the other side of the throne room and stood before the display cases. "Jeremy!" he yelled. His voice was still strained. "I believe this is what you came for."

Jeremy met Wyllt at the display case and stared inside. On a red, plush pillow sat a gold ring with a single band of silver around its center. Etched along its surface were fanciful symbols unknown to Jeremy.

Wyllt smashed through the glass with the hilt of a dagger. "Take it… Santa Man," he said.

Jeremy looked behind him. Mercurio and Ellesmere stared at him. The elf curled his lips into the thinnest of smiles and nodded his approval.

Jeremy reached in and grabbed the ring. He examined it before sliding it on his right ring finger. He expected a surge of magic or a sense of supreme shock and awe. But it didn't feel any different from any other ring, nor did it make him feel any different.

"Let's go," Wyllt said. He turned and smashed the other case, removing a dagger from within. He then walked to the wall and removed the sword and its scabbard. Wyllt fastened it to one of the belts he'd gotten off the goblin soldiers. Then he slowly and shakily walked to the doorway.

CHAPTER 67

GETTING OUT ALIVE

> "Sidion's dagger was a rare dually enchanted item commissioned by him for the purpose of helping his people. It performs as a sort of compass, leading its wielder to anything or anyone it desires. No one or no thing could escape from Sidion, for the dagger would always tell true of its location."
>
> ~ From *The Veiled Happenlore of the Master Construct* compiled by Fulbert Gisilfrid, a Chronicler of the Master Construct, Third Order, an alfargnym of Unterbaum

The band of weary rescuers descended the stairs, heading toward the place the goblin children called the Sanctum of the Sages. They looked like a ragtag group of refugees from a *Conan the Barbarian* comic book. Wyllt and his men were barefoot and bloody, carrying polearms and swords, and wearing an assortment of torn cloth to cover their midsection. Decoudreau wore a set of goblin grieves around his forearms. Mercurio, Ee'azar, and Jar'iyu all wore goblin tunics and armor.

Ellesmere led the way, and Jeremy and the goblin children took up the rear.

"Mercurio," Jeremy called out.

The elf turned and waited for Jeremy to catch up. "What is it?"

"Do you think… Birch is okay?"

"I don't know. But I won't leave here without him or the others." The elf turned and looked behind at the group of goblin children following them. "Jeremy, what is your intention with these goblin spawn?"

"My intention?" Jeremy hesitated. "I don't know. But I can't leave them here. They're just as much victims as anybody. And… they're children. They need our help."

Mercurio grunted. "I recall having a similar conversation with Nikolaos many years ago. He'd often bring up the idea of bringing toys to goblin children, too. It seemed a most ridiculous notion. Of course, we argued about it, but logic won out. There was just no way to do it safely."

The idea was strange. But even more so, Jeremy wondered about these children and their knowledge of Santa Claus. It'd seemed odd that they'd even know about him, considering the goblin king's hatred for Nikolaos. It made Jeremy even more curious about the indoctrination process these goblin children underwent.

"Hey, Jake," Jeremy said, "what have you been told about Santa Claus?"

Jake looked up at Jeremy. "What do you mean?"

"How do you know about Santa Claus?"

"We've seen all of your movies. And when Craig and me did our 4th Quarter H.F.S., we had Christmas and New Years. We got lots of presents. But we didn't get to keep them once the simulation was over." He frowned.

"So, what'd your, uh, overseers tell you about Santa Claus?"

"Just that you were a big part of Christmas and that you bring toys to the children while they're sleeping on Christmas Eve," Jake said.

This made little sense to Jeremy. Borahsh had killed Nikolaos. Did the goblin children know that?

"And the older kids will tell us all about their training and simulations. We love to hear about the holidays they get to celebrate," Jake said. "My first H.F.S. was only a few months."

"H.F.S.?" Mercurio said.

"Housing and Family Simulation. I only celebrated Thanksgiving, Christmas, and New Years. My next simulation will be for six months, and I'll get to celebrate my birthday, Easter, Memorial Day, the 4th of July, and seasonal changes."

"But I don't get why you do the simulations like that?" Jeremy said. "Why not just leave you in there for a few years, that way you get the whole experience all at once?"

"It's quite brilliant," Wyllt interrupted. "It allows the adult gobs to *reprogram* them regularly, and at the same time allow them to flawlessly adapt to the culture. Devious little devils."

Jake looked at Wyllt with a disapproving glance.

"You see?" Wyllt said.

"No, I don't," Jeremy said.

"Let me ask you this, Jake," Wyllt said. "When was the last time you saw a child older than you?"

Jake squinted and then looked at Jeremy.

Jeremy nodded approval.

"Craig and I are the oldest now. We're both ten. We've been the oldest for two years now. Before that it was Jon and Andrew."

"And what happened to Jon and Andrew?" Wyllt asked.

"They went on assignment. And I guess that's when they got their Illusory Implant. Jon was training for Kansas and Andrew was training for Ohio."

"What are you supposed to do when you go on assignment?" Wyllt said.

"Whatever our parents tell us to. And we need to complete our mission. We need to attain the highest levels of power in our assigned field."

"You see, Jeremy, these gobs are just at the beginning. I would be willing to bet that the next level for your friends, Jake and

Craig, is full scale, chemically induced indoctrination. And I would guess that everything about them is being assessed. They're being poked, prodded, analyzed, and prepped for the best possible insertion into our society. Clever. I'd like to meet the gob that developed this sleeper program."

Mercurio looked up at Wyllt. "What you're saying is that these goblin spawn have been trained to live in human society just so that they could eventually take it over?"

"A little slow to the game, aren't you, Mercurio? But yes, that is essentially what I'm saying. In fact, I'm not actually the one saying it. You heard it right from the little gob's mouth."

Mercurio glanced at Jeremy and then at the goblin children. He stopped and studied each one. Then he looked back at Jeremy and shook his head.

Jeremy stopped. "What?"

"Remarkable." Mercurio said. "It's just like the human children. These goblin spawn are drawn to you."

"You're just noticing this now?" Wyllt said.

"Truthfully, I did notice earlier. But before my attention was drawn in other directions. And I am honestly not a scholar on human or goblin auras. But it's obvious. It's just like when I first saw Jeremy with the human children. Their auras are intermingling. You don't see that with any creature, unless there is a deep emotional connection."

Jaeger cleared his throat.

Wyllt nodded at the man. "I'm sure this is fascinating, but we've a long way to go and we still need to clear the hall to the exit," he said, stepping down the stairs.

Mercurio shook his head again. "He's correct. Let's keep going." He resumed walking down the winding stairs, leaning on the shaft of the polearm for support. "But the question remains, Jeremy. What is your intention with these goblin spawn?"

"Well, we can't just leave them here. You heard Wyllt. They're going to brainwash them even more."

Mercurio stopped short and held up his hand. He tilted his ear to listen down the stairs. The other elves did the same.

Ee'azar looked at him and nodded.

Wyllt held up his fingers and silently counted from two to five.

Mercurio held up ten fingers and then motioned for everyone to move to the sides of the stairs.

"Goblins! Nian Riders!" Ellesmere boomed. She sprinted down the stairs.

Mercurio gritted his teeth and snarled at Ellesmere before following her.

Jeremy looked down and swallowed hard. Three goblins riding armored creatures bounded their way. The gray and brown furred beasts, the size of grizzly bears encased in bronze, looked like a pack of hyenas on steroids. Each one gnashed its sharp fangs and growled at the sight of the golem. They charged on all fours with muscular haunches that looked powerful enough to tear through the golem's rock-ridden body. And behind the riders, an army of goblins marched toward them.

"Take cover and hold your ground!" Wyllt yelled. "Let them come to us."

Ellesmere's thunderous footsteps echoed with her battle cry as she came upon the riders.

One rider raised his arm and a blast of red light shot from a device on his forearm. The beam hit Ellesmere, and her golem crumbled into pieces. The light from within vanished. Hundreds of rocks fell like an avalanche, descending the stairs and under the feet of the creatures and soldiers. Many of them tripped, collapsing into the others and tumbling down the steps.

"Hit 'em!" Wyllt yelled. He, Jaeger, Decoudreau, and Lang ran down and attacked. Mercurio, Ee'azar, and Jar'iyu followed.

Jeremy watched as worn elves and men somehow summoned the strength for battle. He sighed and turned to the children. "Stay here," he said, raising his cowl and running into the fray. Jeremy slammed into several goblins with his staff, sending them back down the stairs. The war beasts roared. One bolted forward and landed on Lang. Jeremy pivoted to jab the beast, but Lang had already skewered it. Pinned to the ground by the creature's enormous weight, Lang used the polearm as a lever to push the bloody beast over. It slid off Lang's blade, spewing blood as it tumbled down the stairs and knocked into Decoudreau before it dissipated into golden light. Caught off guard, the man rolled with the beast's armor and landed hard against the wall several steps down.

"Back up!" Wyllt yelled.

Mercurio looked around. Blood dripped from his face, arms, and blade. He whipped his head around, tussling his long hair away from his face. "Ee'azar, Jar'iyu. Follow," he commanded before trudging down the stairs.

Another bloodbath. Jeremy had never seen so much blood in all his life as he had seen in the last day. He looked down the stairs. Barely moving goblins lay amid the armor of their already dead brethren.

Wyllt, Jaeger, and Lang backed up to the children. Wyllt looked around and spotted Decoudreau among the carnage.

"Cover me," Wyllt said as he sprinted down to his fallen henchman. He knelt beside the man, feeling for a pulse. Decoudreau stirred, grunted, and then smiled. Wyllt hefted Decoudreau up, and the man winced and limped forward.

"My knee. It's blown," Decoudreau said.

Below them, several steps down, Mercurio and the other elves stabbed the fallen goblins in their throats.

Jeremy's eyes were drawn to the oozing brownish-green blood of one goblin. It was darker than human blood. The creature twitched, choked and went still. Golden motes of light emanated from its body and joined with that of the other dead goblins. Amidst the blood and carnage, the stairwell filled with golden, sparkling light that slowly dissipated into nothingness. Only elves and men remained. Stained in blood and weak from torture and exhaustion, Jeremy couldn't help but wonder if they were going to make it out of Kurgal alive. *We made it this far, but we're not getting out of here, are we? There are more goblins down there just waiting for us.* He looked to Decoudreau, who limped down the stairs with Wyllt's support. *They're just going to whittle us down, one by one.*

"Jeremy!" Wyllt shouted. "Let's go! We've got a lot more ground to cover."

Jeremy breathed in and shook his head.

Lang came beside Decoudreau. Wyllt looked up, past Jeremy.

"Jeremy?" Wyllt said again.

Jeremy stared at Wyllt, but the man continued to look around.

"Jeremy!" Mercurio shouted as he ran up the stairs toward him. "Jeremy! Are you okay?" the elf shouted, looking around.

"Santa!" Sally yelled from behind.

Jeremy took in a deep breath again, realizing now that he still wore the cowl. Wyllt didn't have the companion stone anymore, so no one could see him. He took down the hood. "I'm okay. I'm right here," he said numbly.

"Jeremy! Don't do that again," Mercurio scolded. "By all means, use the Veil cloak. But be certain to let us know you're okay once we're clear of danger."

Wyllt glared at him. He didn't need to say anything. His perturbed glance said the same thing Mercurio said.

"Sorry," Jeremy said.

He felt little fingers grasping his.

"Santa," Sally said, looking up at him and tightening her grip on his fingers. "I don't understand what's going on. Where are we going?"

Where are we going? The words seemed to echo in Jeremy's head.

"Santa?" Sally repeated.

Jeremy squatted down to see her face to face. He swallowed and grabbed both her hands in his. "We still have a few friends to rescue."

"And then what?" She said.

Jeremy wondered the same thing. He awkwardly tilted his head to the side, breaking eye contact with her. He licked his lips and slowly looked up at her again. "I, I don't know," he muttered.

Mercurio placed his hand on Jeremy's shoulder. "We can figure that out once we're a safe distance."

"But I want to go with you, Santa." Sally said.

Several other goblin children agreed.

"We'll figure all that out later," Mercurio repeated. "We need to go now."

Jeremy nodded and smiled at Sally. He patted her on the shoulder and then stood up. "Let's go," he said, continuing to hold her hand as they walked down the stairs.

CHAPTER 68
BIRTHRIGHT

"The son of none was a true dweorg at heart. Knowing the will of the Allfather and doing whatever it took for him to restore his people to Odin's glory."

~ From the *Chronicles of the High Kings of the Dweorg*, Vol. 30 compiled by Stenn Jorunn, a Chronicler of the Master Construct, First Order, an alfargnym of Unterbaum

Masaru awoke at the knock on the door. He reached for his sword, lying beside him. Disoriented, he sat up and looked around, remembering now where he was.

A second knock and Masaru threw off the covers. "Come in," he yelled in English.

The door creaked open.

"Offsake?" A voice yelled through the open crack.

"I said, come in," Masaru yelled, this time in the secret language. By now he knew the secret language wasn't truly a secret language, but the language of his people, the dweorg. He wasn't sure what it was called, but he could speak it fluently with the exception of the myriad of slang words they used.

The bushy-haired tailor he'd met last night entered. "First light has broken," he said. "Here are ya clothes." He handed him a stack of folded, dark blue clothing.

Masaru hopped out of bed, accepted the stack, and laid the clothes on the mattress.

The tailor stood by the door, staring at Masaru.

Masaru raised an eyebrow. "I don't have any money for a tip," he said.

The dweorg's brows scrunched together and he stared intently at Masaru. "What's that?"

"I don't have any money. I can't give you a tip," Masaru insisted.

"I dunno what yer saying, kunder," the tailor said politely.

"What do you want?" Masaru said, gritting his teeth.

"If ya please. Try on the clothing I made ya. I want to be sure they fits."

Masaru hesitated, then looked to the folded, dark blue clothing.

"Go," Masaru said, shaking his head. "I'm sure it'll be fine."

The tailor squinted at him, looking astonished by the request.

"The clothes will be fine. Go," he said, pointing to the door.

The dweorg crinkled his face and *humphed* as he left.

Masaru removed the clean nightshirt they had given him and threw it on the bed. He grabbed his knapsack and went to the sink. It was filled with clear water, but there was no discernible way to empty and refill the sink. He placed his flesh hand in the water. It wasn't hot, but just the right temperature.

Masaru unstrapped his prosthesis and laid it on the table beside the sink. He then took off the black polypropylene sleeve that fit over his stump to help keep the prosthetic in place. From his bag he drew a small kit containing several cleaning solutions, lotions, and rags. The rags had seen better days. He threw them in a basket with his dirty clothes from yesterday. Using his flesh hand, he submerged the sleeve under the heated water and cleaned it with one of the soapy solutions. The water turned light brown and soapy and then became clear again. Masaru paused, staring at the sink and wondering how this was possible. He felt the water again. It was still the perfect temperature. He removed the sleeve from the basin and used his stump to hold the sleeve in place. Masaru wiped it dry with a clean towel. He poured some alcohol solution on a rag and used it to clean the collar and socket of the prosthesis. He then applied a lubricant to the same area. After cleaning his prosthesis, he used the soap and water to clean his arm. The last step was to rub the conditioner over his calloused stump. His doctors said that he was fortunate to have such tough skin because most people with prostheses have a difficult time with stump skin. It also helped that his artificial arm had advanced sensors in the liner that automatically adjusted to reduce friction.

He had a much-needed bath the night before but making sure that the prosthesis and his stump were cleaned regularly was integral to it working perfectly.

When everything was clean and completely dry, Masaru strapped on the arm and went through his calibration routine. He then dressed in the new clothes provided for him. The blue tunic had a fancy white yoke with silver detail. The tailor had made a long-sleeved black shirt for under the tunic, but Masaru decided not to wear it. He slid on the black pants and his old boots.

There was a knock at the door.

"Come in!" Masaru said, tying his boot.

Grofr walked in. "First light has broken. High King Unn awaits the upcalling."

"I'm ready," Masaru said, grabbing his sword and fastening his belt around his waist. The excitement of what was about to happen invigorated him. It wasn't the killing aspect, but that he had worked his entire life for this day.

Grofr and two guards escorted Masaru down the well-lit corridor toward the high king's terrace. "Y'ill walk onto the terrace from the right side. The high king's throne 'ill be on yer left. Approach the high king and declare yer intention a second time, invoking the upcalling to the throne for all to hear. Speak loud."

Masaru raised an eyebrow and directed a sideways glance toward the adviser. He seemed almost as eager for Masaru to kill the king as he was. "What's in this for you?" he asked.

"Hmm?" Grofr raised his eyebrows.

"I may be young, and I may be, as you all say, from the utangard, but I'm not stupid. You seem eager to have this done with and to have me be king, like Unn means nothing to you."

"I've told ya," Grofr said dispassionately, "I'm the high king's most trusted adviser. I know High King Unn. I know the law. And I'm mighty good at what I do. I predict outcomes and I advise the high king to do what is best for our people."

"Seems a conflict of interest. You have no loyalty to Unn as a friend? Once he's dead, you won't miss him?"

Grofr sighed and turned his lips to a melancholy smile. "It's much simpler than that. Yer lack of understanding of dweorg ways make ya see things through an utangard spyglass. Y'ill soon understand. And let's also say that I understand ya and yer intentions better than ya think. I agree with yer eye on mootish happenings and a change would be good for our people."

Ah. Masaru was right. Grofr had more than just a general interest in this.

"But don't cast me in a dark light." The adviser said. "Unn is my friend, and I will miss him. But our eyes never met on the same view for our people. If ya had not come, I forecast there'd be another. Now our people 'ill return to Odin's sake."

They rounded a corner and walked through a door out onto the terrace. The king's throne was to the left. In the distance, across from the terrace, hundreds, maybe thousands, of dweorg stood on the train platform. A hush fell over them as Masaru stepped forward to the edge of the terrace. Hundreds more dweorg filled the plaza and streets below.

Masaru turned and faced the throne. High King Unn sat

upon it, fully armored, with an enormous axe between his legs. Several guards stood behind the throne and the surrounding doorways.

To the king's left, his wife stood with their son. She held back tears, as did the boy.

On the king's right stood another dweorg, well dressed and armored, carrying a great spear. His long auburn beard covered his chest. He scowled at Masaru.

"That is Thane Uther," Grofr whispered. "It is rumored that if ya defeat High King Unn, Thane Uther 'ill issue an upcall to ya."

Masaru let out a slow growl and scowled back at the thane. Exhilaration surged through his body; a palpable energy coursing through his blood, fueling his rage. He breathed in deeply and then yelled for all to hear. "I was born unnamed, here in Nidavellir! Today I claim the name of Rangvald!"

Gasps filled the silent cavern.

"By my right of birth and my blood as a dweorg, I challenge you, High King Unn, for the throne!" Masaru's voice echoed through the still, silent cave.

"I am Unn, son of Brynjar Dainn, High King of the Dweorg!" He grasped the handle of his great axe and held the massive weapon above his head. "I accept yer upcalling." He faced his people and brought his weapon down. Unn rolled his shoulders, and his pauldrons clanked against his polished breastplate. His blue cape, outlined with black fur, slid off and onto the throne.

The queen sobbed and clung to her son.

Masaru drew his blade and approached the king.

Unn removed his crown and laid it upon the throne. He faced Masaru, hefting his battle-axe over his shoulder.

Masaru's nostrils flared with the thrill of battle.

The high king stepped forward several paces and stood ready.

Masaru studied the king, analyzing his stance and the way he held his axe. It appeared that Unn might actually know how to use the clumsy looking weapon. The axe was bigger than any Masaru had seen before. He doubted any normal human could ever lift such a thing. But Unn held it steady, waiting for his opponent to strike first. If he was any good with it, the king would have an advantage. Masaru inched closer. He lunged to the king's right, feigning an attack to see what Unn would do.

The axe swung down and to the side, stopping when Unn realized Masaru wasn't there. Though the king had missed, he regained his footing and kept the massive axe from slamming into the ground. Masaru feigned an overhead swing to the right. Unn countered in a surprising move, using the axe's head as a shield.

Masaru sliced the sword horizontally toward Unn, testing to see if he was weaker on his other side. The king evaded to the right and brought the axe down again. He stumbled forward two steps, trying to regain his balance and keep the axe's head up. Unn pivoted, bringing the axe back over his shoulder. *He's weak on his left.*

Masaru repeated the swing toward Unn's weak side. The king swung the axe down and arched to the right. Masaru evaded the axe by stepping around it and launching a sidekick into his opponent's chest. Unn stumbled; the heavy battle axe pulling him off balance.

Masaru spun with a roundhouse kick, ensuring that Unn wouldn't be able to regain his footing. The king tumbled to the ground.

Masaru pounced like a caged tiger being released for the first time.

The axe slipped from Unn's hand.

Masaru placed one foot on Unn's shoulder and the tip of the katana straight at the bridge of his opponent's nose. He stared intently into Unn's eyes.

The cavern was still, with only the sounds of the queen and the child crying.

Masaru applied pressure to the katana, pushing against Unn's nose. "Will you yield?" Masaru said through gritted teeth.

Several dweorg gasped in the background.

Unn's eyes flashed with terror at the sight of Masaru's razor-sharp blade.

"Yield, and you can live in exile with your wife and son," Masaru whispered.

Unn's eyes wandered from the blade toward his crying family. He focused back on Masaru, then toward his axe. His fingers stretched toward the weapon.

"I will not yield!" Unn yelled, reaching for his axe.

Masaru slid the blade from the bridge of Unn's nose, into his eye, jamming it past the ocular muscle and into Unn's brain.

Unn's body jerked, and Masaru withdrew his sword.

Masaru turned and bolted straight at Thane Uther. The dweorg's eyes went wide with shock and he brought his spear up.

Masaru bowled into the thane, knocking him off his feet and his spear to the ground.

The crowd gasped.

"Do you want to challenge me now?" Masaru shouted, holding his sword to the dweorg's throat.

The thane, eyes still wide with shock, swallowed. "No. No. I don't."

"*I* am your king now." Masaru gritted his teeth. "You serve *me!* If I hear one word of rebellion or discord from you, I will *not* hesitate to kill you."

The thane swallowed again. "Yes, yes, my high king."

Masaru sighed and turned, slowly taking in the sight before him. A multitude of his people stared at him from every direction. The queen gripped her son with one arm and wiped tears from her own eyes with the other. He couldn't see the boy's face, buried in his mother's lap.

On the throne, cushioned by Unn's fur cape, laid the high king's crown.

Masaru approached the throne and placed the crown upon his head. He then grabbed the fur cloak and walked over to Unn. He draped it over the dead king's body. Then he claimed Unn's battle axe and returned to the throne, taking his seat as high king of the dweorg.

Grofr stepped forward, facing the crowd gathered on the platform and in the plaza. "On this day, the five mountains of the Dweorg Kingdom has a new high king. High King Rangvald, son of none. May he reign with the wisdom and might of Odin."

CHAPTER 69
TIME TO
SADDLE UP AGAIN

"I have known Mercurio most of my life. I was assigned to the Gray Guard when I received the honor of Second Order, and my supervisor had the assignment before me. If it were not for Jeremy, Mercurio would not have only left Wyllt and his men in Kurgal, he would have finished them before he left the Hall of Goblin Sar."

~ From *The Second Gift Giver Chronicles* compiled by Erwin Albowyn, a Chronicler of the Master Construct, Second Order, an alfargnym of Unterbaum

Mercurio breathed a ragged sigh and tensed from the soreness of his muscles. Yet, it was not the time for rest. He'd have to summon all the strength he could to get Jeremy and the others out of Kurgal.

Jeremy stood beside him, watching Wyllt's men. Mercurio looked up at the young man and then down at the ring Jeremy wore; the ring of his old friend. A spark of pride ignited in him only to be dulled by the memory of Nikolaos. Despite all the tribulation they'd faced, Jeremy possessed the ring and now all they needed to do was get out of here alive.

One of Wyllt's henchmen listened at the double doors that led from the stairwell to the hallway. The man's aura was overwhelmingly red with courage, just like Wyllt's. These men were formidable fighters, and they were recovering remarkably well from the torture they had endured. The green of their auras were still muddy but getting better by the minute.

The man at the door turned to Wyllt and nodded.

"Standby for breach," Wyllt said over the communication device he'd taken from Jeremy. "Bravo Team is at the entrance."

Wyllt turned to Jeremy and nodded toward the female goblin spawn holding Jeremy's hand. "Send the little gobs out first," he whispered.

The indigo of Jeremy's aura spiked black, and his face crinkled with disapproval. He shook his head.

"They won't harm their own children," Wyllt whispered. "The little gobs will distract the big gobs and we'll get the jump on them."

Wyllt had assumed control of the group. Under normal circumstances, Mercurio would have objected, but now wasn't the time to argue. Besides, he needed to concentrate on finding the others and getting out of here in one piece.

The older goblin spawn nodded his head at Jeremy, his aura eager with yellow.

"But what if there's another one of those creatures out there?" Jeremy said.

"If there were, it wouldn't be this quiet," Wyllt said.

The goblin spawn nodded at Jeremy again.

"Fine," Jeremy said. "Let them go first. But promise me you won't let anything bad happen to them."

"We won't. If anything tries to harm them, we'll take care of it." Wyllt looked to Mercurio and nodded, looking for agreement.

"It's a sound plan," Mercurio said.

"Fine," Jeremy said.

Wyllt ushered the goblin spawn over to the doors. "On three,

Jaeger will open the door. Then you run out in a panic and head to the left, toward the entrance. The rest of you against this wall," he said, pointing to the area next to the door.

"No," Mercurio said. Wyllt's idea wasn't bad, but they weren't using their gear to its full advantage. "Ee'azar, over here with me," he said, directing him toward Jeremy. "We'll use the Veil cloak. Ee'azar on one side, me on the other. Jar'iyu, you stand ready with the humans against the wall. Wait for us to attack before you strike at the first goblins you see, and we'll try to get as many in here as we can."

"Good," Wyllt said. The orange of his aura dissolved to brown, and the green spiked with black. There was reluctance in his voice. The man wasn't used to having his authority challenged.

"We should also extinguish the lights in here," Mercurio said. "Give their eyes a few seconds to adjust from the light in the hall."

"Goblins can't see in the dark?" Jeremy asked.

"They can," Mercurio said. "But if they're going from light to darkness, they'll be at a disadvantage for a few seconds, and every second we get is an advantage to us."

"That'll put me at a disadvantage, too." Jeremy said.

"You'll be veiled," Mercurio said. "Now, help me with these lights." He walked over to the lamp and removed the glass fixture. He then disconnected the suffering fairy from the wires. Mercurio repeated the process for each lamp, gently handing each fairy to Jeremy.

Waves of black rippled through the blue of Jeremy's aura as he sadly gazed at each battered fairy. There was no way to help them. Their bodies had been broken along with their primitive minds. The best they could do was ease the poor creatures' suffering.

Mercurio retrieved all four fairies and quickly snapped each one's neck. He laid their tiny bodies in the corner.

With all the fairies removed, the chamber was dimly lit only by light that peeked down from the stairs.

Everyone did as ordered. The guardians and humans readied their weapons. Jeremy faced the doorway and disappeared under his Veil cloak, stretching it out to accommodate Mercurio and Ee'azar. Wyllt nodded at his lead henchman, who raised his hand and silently counted to three with his fingers. He then pulled one door open, and the goblin spawn ran out, screaming. The henchman left the door open, and they waited.

"There's more!" a goblin shouted from the hallway.

The goblin spawn continued to scream.

"Over here!" another goblin yelled.

Two goblin warriors approached the threshold, polearms ready. One slowly stepped in.

Wyllt held up a dagger, ready to strike.

Two more goblins appeared behind the first two.

As they carefully stepped into the chamber, Mercurio and Ee'azar let their polearms fall to the floor. The metal hit the stone and a loud clattering sound echoed through the chamber.

The elves launched themselves at the goblins. Mercurio grabbed hold of the first goblin and used his momentum to tumble with it to the floor.

The goblins in the rear ran in. Wyllt and Jaeger seized them.

Mercurio straddled the goblin from behind, sliced its throat, and then found a familiar opening in the side of its armor to slip the dagger into its heart. He jumped back up and faced the door. No other goblins entered.

Mercurio ran to the door and held his hand up to the others as he peeked out. He looked up and down the hall and saw nothing. He could still hear the sounds of the screaming goblin spawn in the distance. Mercurio wiggled his fingers, urging the others to follow.

"We were told that the laboratories are in there," Wyllt said, pointing to the double-doors directly across from the stairs.

"Let's go," Mercurio said.

"Wait," Wyllt said. "You're just going to walk in there blind?"

"My friends are in there. I'm not leaving without them," Mercurio said.

"I tell you what. My men and I will provide a little distraction for you. When Bravo Team blows the entrance door, it's going to make some noise."

"Mr. Wyllt, wait…" Jeremy said. "What are you saying? You're not gonna help us save them?"

"Jeremy, I agreed to help you get him and that ring," he pointed to Mercurio and then Jeremy's hand. "I've done what I said. Now I have one man dead and another wounded. Not to mention that we're in pretty bad shape and the fact that I've not received anything you promised me."

"I—" Jeremy stammered.

"No need to say anything. Knowing the exact location of this place is enough for me. I'll be coming back for sure. Now listen, we breech in twenty. We'll head back to the bird and wait for you there. I'll leave your radio just outside the entrance, after we breech. Contact me when you're safe." He nodded to Jaeger.

Jaeger started walking ahead. Lang, still helping Decoudreau, followed behind.

"Twenty minutes, Jeremy," Wyllt said as he followed his men down the hallway.

Jeremy shook his head and then looked at Mercurio. "We're not leaving Birch and the others here, right?"

Mercurio held his finger up for Jeremy not to say anything. He then counted to sixty, giving Wyllt and his men time to get further away.

Jeremy grew impatient and kept mouthing the word "What?" Mercurio ignored him and continued counting until he was confident that Wyllt was out of range.

"Yes, Jeremy. We are going to get them. We don't need Wyllt." Mercurio smiled. "We have you."

"What? I can't… what do you expect me to do?" Jeremy said.

"Jeremy, you have one of the most powerful enchantments ever created. And you have a Veil cloak. You are virtually unstoppable. Even if you show yourself, there's not a thing they can do to hurt you. You're going to put on the cowl, open that door, and walk right in there to rescue our friends."

"But what if they're unconscious? I can't carry all three of them." His eyes shifted to Nikolaos' Ring. "Can I?"

"Reconnaissance first. See if you can locate them and if they can walk. If they cannot, then we'll figure an alternative way to get them out of here."

Jeremy hesitated and looked at Nikolaos'… *his* ring again. He took a deep breath, and his aura intensified with red.

"Well, I guess it's time to saddle up again," Jeremy said, throwing on his cowl and disappearing.

One of the double doors opened and then closed.

CHAPTER 70

THE SANCTUM
OF THE SAGES

"The Gift Giver's Ring, once known as the Ring of Nicholas, is the most powerful enchanted item on our Shared World. Jeremy was unaware of the power he possessed when he placed it on his finger. He would have much to learn."

~ From *The Second Gift Giver Chronicles* compiled by Erwin Albowyn, a Chronicler of the Master Construct, Second Order, an alfargnym of Unterbaum

Jeremy slowly closed the door behind him as he entered the Sanctum of the Goblin Sages. That's what the goblin children called those creepy tattooed goblins wearing black robes: sages. But after the children explained what these sages did, it seemed to Jeremy that they were anything but sages. More like a strange amalgam of spy, mad scientist, and warrior.

The doors led to another wide hallway, this one leading left and right. Brightly lit with fairy light along the corridor, Jeremy could see that there was no one around. *Thank God!* But which way should he go? He could see more doors down both hallways. Looking down, he noticed the trail of smeared blood.

Jeremy drew in a deep breath and followed the trail to a single door. He slowly opened it and peeked inside. The large, round, brightly lit chamber had cells all along its perimeter and lab stations in the center.

"Intruder!" a goblin yelled and pointed at the door. Two other goblins looked up from their stations and drew their swords.

Jeremy slammed the door and stepped to the side.

Oh God, please don't tell me they can see me through the cloak!

Three goblin sages rushed toward the door.

Jeremy shimmied along the wall, up to the first cage, praying that they had no means to see him through the Veil cloak.

One goblin opened the door and cautiously looked around.

Jeremy's heart pounded.

"Nothing," the goblin peeked out the door into the hallway.

"I don't like this," another said.

Jeremy cocked his head, realizing he could understand the creatures. He audibly heard the strange language they spoke.

Jeremy looked at his ring. *It* must be translating for him.

"I don't know what's happening!" A goblin sage said. "Too much distraction for one day. Fortuitous that we have new specimens. But by the blood, we've had nothing like this happen before."

"It is odd," another replied. "When do you think the guards will be back?"

"*If* they'll be back. We may still be under attack."

"Bar the door. We want no more distractions."

One of them removed an odd-looking duck-bill shaped tool from a cart and wedged it under the door.

"That should hold," he said. "Now let's get back to work."

The three walked to the rear of the circular chamber to a workstation made up of a lab table, several cabinets, and strange devices. Jeremy adjusted his glasses and squinted to see what was on the table. A white and dark green... *Birch!* Jeremy's heart pounded against his rib cage. Anger flared from his twisting, empty gut. He breathed in, took his staff in both hands, and ran to the three goblins. He swung his staff, hitting one in the back of the head. The goblin jerked and spun around. Jeremy met him with a second strike that sent the goblin backward against the table.

"Blight!" another goblin yelled.

Jeremy struck him in his face and then in the stomach.

The remaining goblin pulled out his sword, backed up, darted his head all around and yelled, "You Blight!"

Jeremy lunged and swung his staff into the side of the goblin's head then whirled the shaft around to hit him in the gut.

The other two goblins stirred behind him.

Jeremy turned.

A goblin wildly swung its sword and charged in his direction. He brought his staff down to a defensive position to block the blade. When blade hit wood, a concussive wave emanated from Jeremy and sent the three goblins and Birch flying. Birch's body slumped to the ground. Goblins slammed against their workstations. One hit hard against a cage.

Jeremy frantically looked around. His heart still pounding, sweat dripping into his eyes. He took a deep breath, trying to calm himself. *What just happened?*

The room was now silent. Jeremy dashed to Birch's side. His friend lay limp but breathing. Birch had a strange mechanical collar around his neck, but no signs of injuries.

Jeremy examined the collar to figure out how to take it off. The device appeared to be made of several metals; gold, iron, and copper, Jeremy guessed. The most elaborate part of the device sat on the base of Birch's neck, along his spine. There were several boxes with buttons and holes that Jeremy couldn't make sense of. On the opposite side, pressed against Birch's throat, was a single silver box, with gold trim that looked like a fancy seatbelt buckle. It had no keyhole or release mechanism that Jeremy could see. In its center was a gold concave recess. He pressed it. Nothing happened. *A thumbprint reader?* Jeremy placed his thumb in the recess. Nothing happened. He got up and dragged one of the unconscious goblins to Birch and placed its thumb in the recess. The mechanism clicked and loosened.

The goblin stirred and let out a mild groan.

Jeremy slammed its head into the stone floor and pushed the goblin to the side. He watched, hoping it would not move again. It lay still.

Jeremy turned back to Birch and removed the collar from his friend's neck. It resisted coming off. Examining the area, Jeremy found a large-gauge needle stemming from the mechanism inserted into the back of Birch's neck. *What in the world?* Jeremy slowly slid the needle out. His stomach knotted up when he saw how long it was; it had to be at least four inches.

Blood trickled from the entry wound on his friend's neck. Jeremy pulled out the first-aid kit from his backpack. He removed some gauze and used it to apply pressure to Birch's wound.

"Come on, buddy," Jeremy said. He gently stroked Birch's warm snout. "You can wake up now." He sighed.

Birch didn't move but thankfully he was still warm and breathing. Jeremy used surgical tape to affix the gauze. There was nothing more he could do for Birch now. He was just glad that the koth was still alive. That gave him hope the others would be, too.

Jeremy stood up and walked to the cages surrounding the perimeter. The ones closest to Birch were empty, but to his surprise, the next one had three elves in it! It was set up like a jail cell with two filthy cots on the side walls and one in the rear.

"Hey! You guys okay in there?" Jeremy yelled.

No answer.

They didn't look like anyone Jeremy knew.

He examined the lock. Another thumbprint.

Jeremy ran back to the goblins and stopped. This wasn't a good idea to try and free them himself. *He needed* to get Mercurio and the others. Jeremy ran to the door, removed the doorstop and cart, and then made his way back to the door where the guardians were. He took down his cowl, knocked three times, and waited. Three knocks came from the other side, and Jeremy opened the door.

"Guys, come on. We need to work fast," Jeremy said.

On the way back to the lab, he told Mercurio and the other guardians what he found.

They entered the lab, and Jeremy secured the door in the same way the goblin had before.

"There's prisoners and creatures in here everywhere." He ran over and dragged a goblin to the first cage with the three elves. "They're all locked with thumbprint identifiers." He tugged the goblin toward the first occupied cell.

"Wait," Mercurio held his hand up to Jeremy. "Stop. Let's do this quickly. Ee'azar, Jar'iyu. Over there." He pointed to the two goblins laying on the ground. He walked to Jeremy and helped him raise the goblin's hand to the thumbprint reader.

"Thanks," Jeremy said.

The cell door clicked, and Mercurio opened it.

Jeremy followed the elf inside.

Mercurio laid his hand on the chest of the first elf.

"Is he alive?" Jeremy asked.

"Yes. Barely."

Jeremy looked around at the other two. "Who are they?"

"I've no idea. They're dressed in rags and I can't tell where they're from."

"Palgen!" Jar'iyu yelled. "Gaviryl, I found him. He's alive."

"Peace and mercy!" Mercurio said. He moved from one elf to the next, placing his hand upon each chest. "Jeremy, go look in the other cages and see if you can find Grath."

"OK." Jeremy exited the cell and went to the next one. This one had no cots in it and was darker than the other. In the corner a shadowy silhouette moved with the sound of ragged breathing. Jeremy couldn't make out any of its features. "Hello," he said.

Nothing.

Jeremy squatted and held on to the bars, trying to get a closer look. "Hello. Are you all right?"

The creature froze. Its eyes glinted eerily in the dark. It was smaller than Jeremy, about the size of a goblin but it had the shape of a small koth.

"It's okay. We're here to help you," Jeremy reached in.

The creature sprang at Jeremy, a small dinosaur with a snaggle-tooth snout, small eyes, and spiked fur on its back. It was fast and upon Jeremy before he could even react. Its jaws clamped down on his hand, but the ring forced it away, slamming it back against the wall.

Jeremy jumped back and dropped his staff. He fell to the floor and landed on one hand, while waving the other fiercely, incredulous to the fact that it was still in one piece. *Geez! What the heck was that?* He examined his hand. There were no marks.

"Jeremy!" Mercurio rushed out of the cage with his sword drawn. "Are you all right?"

"Um, yeah… but I have no idea what's in there."

Mercurio turned his head to see. "I'm not sure what that is. But it's hostile. Just move on."

Jeremy sighed, pushed himself up, and moved to the next cage. It was empty. The one after that was set up differently. Rather than one large cage, it comprised nine small cages, each holding a diminutive creature. Several were monkey-like, others lizard-like, and others… Jeremy couldn't liken them to anything he'd seen before. Two of them were covered in fur, with a large snout, long arms, and a tail they wrapped around themselves. Another was covered in callouses, like the huge monster they'd fought in the throne room. They all stared at Jeremy, still, as if waiting for him to do something.

The three lower cages appeared to be empty at first. Jeremy took a closer look. There was something in each one, but all he could see were balls of fur timidly curled up in the corner. Curiosity got the better of him. Boosted with confidence in the ring's power, he eased his hand into the cage.

The creature trembled.

"It's okay. We're not here to harm you. We're here to help." Jeremy reached his arm further in. He came in contact with it, feeling its trembling fur. He pulled it closer to the bars. Its fur was a grayish purple color, and it had two short legs and arms. It cowered, trying to cover itself as best it could.

"It's okay, little guy. I'm not gonna hurt you," Jeremy said.

It peeked out through its crossed arms, revealing two large ebony eyes and a short, rounded mouth. Jeremy had seen this kind of creature before. Several of them in Orindin and Sayalla, only this one was smaller. He stroked it along the short tuft of fur on its head and down its back. "It's all right. We're gonna get you out of here." He withdrew his hand and moved to the other cages. It looked to be the same kind of creature in each of the bottom cages.

"This place is sick," Jeremy stood up. "And I don't mean that in a good way." He walked over to Mercurio, who had opened another cell. This one contained an unconscious faun. "What in the world were these goblins doing?"

"Experiments. It's what they do. They're masters of blood magic and blood manipulation. They mix creatures to create new ones that will do their bidding," Mercurio pulled the faun to the center of the room.

"You mean genetic engineering? Just like they created Birch's people?" Jeremy said.

Mercurio laid the faun beside the three elves they found. Next to them were Gaviryl, Grath, Birch, and… Jeremy gasped. Two children! Human children!

"Yes, that is what your scientists would call it. The goblins have had centuries to master it."

"This is the last one." Ee'azar dragged a gnome over and laid him beside the faun. "That cabinet over there is filled with fairy batteries. There must be hundreds in there."

"And that one over there is filled with hundreds, maybe thousands of vials of blood from dozens of different species," Jar'iyu said.

Mercurio sighed. "I have no idea how we're going to get all of us out of here. We can't carry them all."

Jeremy's eyes were still on the children. The elves continued to talk, but Jeremy could only think about the enormity of what was happening. These goblins were *evil*. Children? They experimented on children. These poor kids. What had they endured? Where were they from? They wore rags. They appeared to be Hispanic. Maybe they were locals, kidnapped in the middle of the night by goblins. Jeremy could clearly see why Mercurio killed goblins with such extreme prejudice. They were truly despicable. But what about the goblin children? Would they inevitably grow up to be just as evil? Nurture versus nature, the age-old question. Did it apply to goblins?

"Jeremy," Mercurio said. "Are you hearing me?"

Jeremy sighed. "Um, sorry. What?"

"I asked you if you thought you could carry a few of the elves or the children."

"Yeah, maybe. I… uh, I haven't slept much in the past few days."

"Do you feel tired?" Mercurio asked.

Jeremy turned his head away from the children. He had to think about that question. He held his hands out and took mental stock of himself. Jeremy didn't feel tired. Still a little shocked by all that's happened, but not tired at all.

"Um, ya know… I actually feel fine. In fact, I feel pretty good, considering," Jeremy said.

"The ring," Mercurio said. "It has restorative properties as well. You'll only need to sleep an hour or two each day while you're wearing it."

"Seriously?" Jeremy said. He then glanced down at all the prisoners they had found. There had to be a better way to get all of them out of here. "Man, I wish we had the sack. What happened to it?"

"We lost much of the equipment we brought. I've no idea where they put any of our enchanted items. Our cloaks are gone too. And my sword… my father's sword." He sighed. "We don't have time to search this whole place."

"I could," Jeremy said.

"You can. But time is not on our side. We—"

The chamber rumbled.

"They've breached," Mercurio said. "Wyllt's second team is here."

CHAPTER 71

FATTENED FOR SLAUGHTER

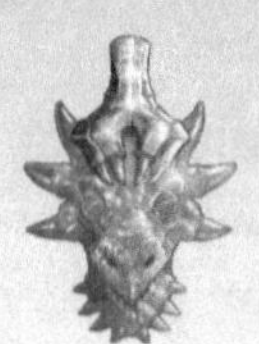

> Honor has no place among the goblin empire. They believe honor to be restricting. Instead, high ideals for the advancement of their species are interpreted by those with the power to impose their will. In essence, their mentality is to do whatever it takes to get what they want.
>
> ~ From *The Veiled Happenlore of the Master Construct* compiled by Fulbert Gisilfrid, a Chronicler of the Master Construct, Third Order, an alfargnym of Unterbaum

Sar Borahsh leaned on his scepter, clutching it tightly and gasping for air. He sneered at his warlord. He wanted to scream at him, but he could barely catch his breath. They'd been fleeing the attack for almost an hour now. How could his warlord have allowed humans and elves to invade Kurgal, his sanctum… his empire!

"My Sar," Alfash said. "Please rest. There are seats, and even a bed here. The warlord assures us we are safe."

Safe? I run like a rat in my home, and Qannu thinks us safe! Borahsh didn't have the air or energy to speak, so he just growled. He strained for a deep breath and leaned into his staff.

Alfash offered him his hand. Borahsh accepted and the Excellency helped him sit in the nearest chair of the small safe room.

Qannu, the Lord of War of the Goblin Empire, had rescued the sar and his excellencies as they fled through the back of the throne room. Together with six of the Sar's Fang, they made their way to a safe room hidden beneath the sar's bed chamber. The warlord stood by the door, whispering to the Fang, as Borahsh slowly regained his breath.

"You… imbecile!" Borahsh spat, glowering at the warlord. "How… could… you… allow this… to happen?"

The warlord turned from his conversation. Qannu's expression hardened, and he walked toward Borahsh.

"Forty-seven years," the warlord said calmly. "Forty-seven years we have planned for this day."

"What?" Borahsh grunted. "What are you… spewing?"

"Two centuries you've ruled," Qannu said. With one hand, the warlord easily knocked the sar's scepter from his hands. With the other he seized Borahsh by the throat.

The sar gasped and gripped his hands around Qannu's wrist.

"What?" Alfash yelled. "Stop it!"

"Stop!" Ubarat said. "Get your hand—"

Three of the Sar's Fang approached and turned their pole swords towards the Excellencies.

"How dare you question me about letting this happen?" Qannu said through gritted teeth. "*You* are the one who has destroyed this empire through gluttony and selfish ambition!"

Borahsh gasped. *No. This can't be happening.* He wanted to yell for his guards, for anyone to stop Qannu. But the warlord's grip tightened.

Qannu yanked Borahsh forward, whirled him around, and tossed him to the floor. The sar rolled and slammed into the wall. He laid there, straining to catch his breath, thankful for the air that now rushed into his lungs. A foot slammed into his shoulder and turned him away from the wall. Qannu stood over him. The warlord's cold, hard stare met Borahsh's terror-stricken eyes. He stepped harder on Borahsh's shoulder and drew his sword.

"One more year was all you had left, and you were going to die by my hands. It seems that day has been accelerated by today's events. The humans and elves were not a part of our plan. Borahsh, do you see clearly what you have done? That your single-minded compulsion has plummeted our empire into complete disarray? Humans breach our halls. Elves treat us as if we were mere insects. And you've allowed this for centuries, concentrating everything on killing a single elf and filling your fat gut."

"Mercurio—"

Qannu lifted his foot and slammed it into Borahsh's abdomen.

The Sar jerked wildly, expelling whatever breath he had left. He choked and gasped.

"You end here today. But know this before you die. Every vestigial part of your reign dies with you as well."

Borahsh heard a groan from across the room.

Qannu stepped to the side, revealing the source of the groan. One of his Fang held Alfash by the collar with one hand. In the other, he held the hilt of a dagger; the blade embedded into Alfash's gut. The Excellency doubled over, holding his hands to his stomach. Both Alfash and the Fang looked at Borahsh. Alfash's eyes were filled with pleas, but none came from his mouth. The Fang slid the knife up Alfash's gut and pushed the blade deep into his chest. Alfash twitched and gagged. The Fang removed the knife and the Excellency slumped to the floor.

"No. Please," Ubarat whimpered. "I'll serve you as Sar. I promise," the weak fool cried. "Please."

Qannu shook his head.

The same Fang that killed Alfash slammed his bloody knife into Ubarat's midsection, gutting him just as he did his counterpart. Ubarat sobbed with every groan and fell to the floor. He sniveled a bit more before he fell silent and his flesh and bone were consumed by his golden essence.

Qannu leaned down and struggled to lift Borahsh from the

floor. He slammed him against the wall. "The Goblin Empire rises this day. And when all the other pieces are in place a year from now, the world will say about us just as it did the Britons. The sun never sets on the Goblin Empire."

Qannu moved and Borahsh felt a searing, wet pain in his abdomen. He swallowed.

No. I cannot end here. I still haven't killed Mercurio.

"The Borahsh Dominion ends," Qannu said.

No. He felt the knife slide up to his rib cage. He could no longer swallow.

Qannu pushed, and Borahsh felt the tightness in his chest as his heart struggled to pump blood. Fear of the inevitable dulled the pain.

"The Qannu Dominion begins!" The six Sar's Fang exulted in unison.

Borahsh slid down the wall and onto the floor. The taste of iron and copper filled his mouth and he gagged.

Qannu's foot stood firm, inches away from Borahsh's face.

A bright white flash followed by a dull click blinded Borahsh. He blinked and strained to open his eyes. He could still see the faint, blurry foot of his betrayer. Borahsh choked, and blood splattered onto the warlord's foot. It trickled slowly down his ankle.

Borahsh felt his essence seep from his body. Before it consumed his flesh and bone, he choked his final word. "Mercurio."

CHAPTER 72
LIONS, AND TIGERS, AND BEARS

"Though many of the enchantments of the Gift Giver's Ring are innate and do not require the wearer to do anything, there are several that can only be activated through gesture and incantation."

~ From *The Second Gift Giver Chronicles* compiled by Erwin Albowyn, a Chronicler of the Master Construct, Second Order, an alfargnym of Unterbaum

Jeremy surveyed the laboratory. There were three flat-top carts. Two could be used to push the koth. One more could be used to push two elves and the three furballs. He could carry the children. That still left Gaviryl, one other elf, the gnome, and the faun unaccounted for. A guardian could carry one of them, but not all. Jeremy exhaled in frustration. There had to be a way to get them out of here. If Wyllt hadn't left, they'd have been fine! He pounded his fist against the lab table and cursed under his breath.

"Jeremy," Mercurio said, "come with me. Ee'azar, Jar'iyu,

secure this room and prepare everyone you can for transport out of here."

Mercurio hefted one of the unconscious goblins onto his shoulder and started toward the door.

"What are we doing?" Jeremy said.

"I've a hunch." Mercurio pushed the cart away from the door and removed the doorstop. He then pushed the cloak open and grabbed onto Jeremy's waist. "Put the cowl up."

Jeremy did as he was told. Mercurio guided him out the door.

"You notice how tall and wide these passageways are? And how most doorways have double doors. The room we just came from is the only single door in this passage. There's another set of double doors down the hall. We were told that this area is where the goblins perform their blood magic experiments. My guess is that whatever is in this next chamber contains larger experiments. Perhaps they're holding the b'hemayal in there? At the very least, maybe some more carts."

"The reindeer! I'd forgotten about them. Ellesmere said they've already returned to Orendin with the sleigh," Jeremy said.

"Well, that is good. Unfortunately, for us at this moment it doesn't help."

They approached the double doors. Mercurio slowly opened one. They inched closer to peek in. It was another lab, at least twice the width and height of the other. Mercurio's hunch was right. Cages filled with animals larger than humans lined the walls. It was like a zoo with elephants, bears, horses, and more. Along the center were workstations with various-sized platforms and assorted tools and devices. Some stations were in disarray, with tools strewn about. The bloodstained remains of goblin clothing lay on the floor.

Jeremy and Mercurio walked further in to discover more animals: lions, ostriches, and others Jeremy didn't recognize. There were also two larger carts. *Perfect.*

To the rear of the chamber, a large cage door hung open. It was big enough to have held the monster they fought earlier. This was, no doubt, where the goblin children had unleashed it from.

Next to the open cage, a silverback gorilla stared curiously at Jeremy. *Can he see me?* Jeremy wondered. He raised his hand and waved.

The gorilla didn't react.

"Take the carts into the hall." Mercurio ran out from beneath the cloak. He darted to the horse cage and used the goblin's hand to open it.

Jeremy pushed the carts, one by one, into the hall.

Mercurio herded the horses out to meet Jeremy.

"Now, go and free that elephant. Wait for us here in the hall, and then you can lead us to the exit."

"And what am I supposed to do with the elephant after I free it?" Jeremy asked.

"Ride it out of here," Mercurio said.

"You want me to ride an elephant? I don't know the first thing about riding any animal! What makes you think I'll be able to lead an elephant to the entrance?"

Mercurio shook his head. "Your ring. I told you it's very powerful. It'll protect you from harm. Wild animals can be quite dangerous, but your ring will keep them calm toward you and more amenable to your commands."

"So, what… now I can talk to animals, too?" Jeremy said.

"Not quite. It's not something I can teach you, nor do I have time to. We need to get out of here. You'll just have to trust me and see for yourself."

"Wait. What about that creature in the other lab? I tried talking to it and it tried taking my arm off!"

"Must be above average intelligence and more mature." Mercurio turned around and started down the hallway.

"Mercurio. Wait."

Mercurio stopped short and turned around. "What is it now?"

"In the other lab, there are several smaller cages clustered together. The bottom three have those purplish-gray creatures I saw in Orindin and Sayalla. I told them that we'd rescue them."

"Krodin."

"Krodin?"

"Yes, that's what they're called. I'll be sure to rescue them as well." The guardian turned and sprinted down the hallway.

Jeremy went back into the large lab. He stood just inside the door, surveying the creatures once again. He studied the elephant. An African, if he remembered correctly. It had large, fan-like ears, dark gray skin, and short ivory tusks. He turned to the lions. *Hmm… I may have a better idea.* He approached the lion cage and slowly extended his hand toward the bars.

"Hey there… kitty. It's all right. I'm not gonna hurt you. Come on over here." Jeremy stared at the lion, trying to send it calming waves. He had no idea how this worked.

The lion, a male, stood up and lazily walked to the front of its cage.

Jeremy startled and withdrew his hand. A sense of giddiness surged through him and he quickly put his hand back through the bars.

"That's it," he giggled.

The lion sniffed Jeremy's hand, then stepped closer, nuzzling the part of his mane beneath his ear against Jeremy's hand.

Jeremy giggled again. "That's it." He looked to the rear of the cage where the lioness still lay. "What about you? Come on over here," Jeremy commanded confidently.

She stood and stretched before sashaying her way over.

Jeremy took his other hand and gently rubbed beneath her ear.

"Yeah, this is going to be a much better plan," Jeremy smiled.

CHAPTER 73
OUT WITH THE OLD

"High King Frode, son of Asgar Brokir commissioned the Grand Throne of the High King as a gift to himself upon his ascension to the throne. Every High King after him complained about how uncomfortable it was, but none were ever willing to do anything about it.

~ From the *Chronicles of the High Kings of the Dweorg*, Vol. 30 compiled by Stenn Jorunn, a Chronicler of the Master Construct, First Order, an alfargnym of Unterbaum

"They are on their way, High King Rangvald," Grofr said.

The name didn't quite sound as strange to the new high king as he thought it would. He'd been Masaru all his life. Masaru Hagen. But that life was over now. And *High King Rangvald* felt right.

The crowd had cleared, and news of the new high king of the dweorg quickly spread. Rangvald did as Grofr had advised and ordered a messenger to each of the other clanholds with the message that a meeting was in order.

The throne felt awkward beneath the new high king. It certainly wasn't a comfortable throne. He found it hard to lean back and sit comfortably unless he slouched. It was a fine-*looking* piece of furniture made of dark wood and gilded in gold, silver, and iron, with a tall high-back that held a finely crafted symbol of the dweorg above his head. But no matter how he sat, it just wasn't comfortable.

Rangvald leaned forward, bracing himself with his elbows on his knees, and looking out over the king's terrace. He couldn't believe this day had finally come. Now he'd begin the next phase of his plan. But he needed to deal with a few other things first.

Ragna, daughter of Ivarr Skavithir and her son, Ivarr, son of Unn Dainn escorted by two guards, approached the throne. The former queen finally stopped crying enough so that Rangvald could talk to her.

"Your relatives. Tell me where they live." Rangvald leaned back and slouched uncomfortably on the throne.

"My father and mother live here, in Nidavellir."

"Thane Uther," Rangvald called.

Uther stepped forward from beside the throne. "Yes, High King Rangvald?"

"Prepare her parents to leave here."

Ragna gasped.

"They will go with her," the high king continued. "They can bring with them anything, and anyone else they want." He turned to his right. "Grofr?"

Uther and several guards exited.

"Yes, High King?" Grofr said.

"Who would be a good resource to find Ragna and her family a new place to live, comfortably, in exile?"

Ragna sobbed.

Grofr leaned over and whispered into Rangvald's ear. "High King. We discussed how they are yer responsibility now."

"I didn't say that I wasn't going to take care of them," Rangvald said aloud for Ragna to hear. "I just don't want them here. And I don't care who goes with them. Find them a comfortable place to live. And make sure that someone checks on them frequently to see what they need. In my estimation, that would constitute taking care of them."

"It 'ill be done High King," Grofr said. He ushered Ragna and her son away. "Take them to their former chambers and allow them to pack their belongings and anything else they wish to take with them."

Several guards walked to Ragna's side. She turned and faced the exit.

"Ragna," Masaru called.

She stopped.

Masaru leaned forward. "Ivarr, look at me."

The child continued to hide his eyes behind his mother.

"Ivarr," Rangvald said through gritted teeth. His voice was calm, but stern. "I said look at me."

Ragna pulled her child in front of her and lifted his head to look at the high king. The boy squinted through bloodshot eyes.

"Your father died honorably so that you could live. Remember that." Rangvald turned his gaze from the child to Ragna. "Don't raise your son to hate me. Raise him to respect the laws of our people. Raise him to respect and honor me. I don't want to have to kill him as I did his father. Don't make that mistake." Rangvald stopped speaking, allowing it to grow quiet, hoping to emphasize his words more with an intense stare and a slow nod. He shifted uncomfortably back in his throne.

Ragna inhaled and held her head high again. "It 'ill be as you have said, High King." She tapped her son on his shoulder and spoke softly to him. "This is our high king now." She paused. "You will… honor and respect him."

"When the boy has chosen his career, let me know," Rangvald said. "I will make sure he—"

Ragna stared strangely at the high king. Her brow raised and her lips pursed.

Grofr leaned over and whispered in Rangvald's ear. "Dweorg

do not choose their career. They are chosen for a career based on years of meticulous observation from parents and others in the community. However, all dweorg are required to serve for two years in the military before they're assigned to a career."

Rangvald sighed. "Whatever. When he's old enough to join the military, let me know. And keep me posted on whatever career you think he should be in."

"It 'ill be done as you command, my high king," Ragna replied.

Rangvald nodded to his guards, and they escorted the former queen and her son away.

Watching them leave, he felt a twinge of guilt, but he quickly extinguished it. There was far more at stake here than a woman and her child. Besides, he'd make sure they were taken care of. "I want to approve any final plans for Ragna and her son before they leave."

"It 'ill be as you command, High King," Grofr said.

Rangvald shifted awkwardly on the throne again, this time bringing both legs up to sit cross-legged. He exhaled in frustration. "Grofr?"

The adviser leaned over.

"How old is this throne?" Rangvald asked.

"It's from the Reign of High King Frode. Approximately twelve-hundred years old."

"Hmmph," Rangvald said bitterly. "I think it's time to do some redecorating. Get me someone who knows how to build a desk."

CHAPTER 74

LIKE A WHITE KNIGHT ON HIS STEED

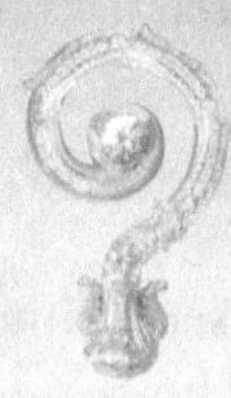

"It seemed that once Jeremy possessed the Gift Giver's Ring, it enhanced the gift he already had. This was something unexpected. At first, Mercurio kept that bit of information to himself…"

~ From *The Second Gift Giver Chronicles* compiled by Erwin Albowyn, a Chronicler of the Master Construct, Second Order, an alfargnym of Unterbaum

Jeremy sat high atop the elephant's back, hunching forward to avoid hitting the top of the doorway as they passed from the Sanctum of Goblin Sages to the main hallway. A parade of animals and assorted enchanted creatures marched behind him. Mercurio, Ee'azar, and Jar'iyu each rode a horse that pulled a cart with makeshift rigging to carry the unconscious prisoners. It looked like some sort of cosplay parade you might see at Comic Con.

Jeremy looked back at the strange parade he'd organized. Mercurio wasn't pleased that he had set the other animals free.

But once he knew Jeremy could control all of them, he saw the value in having them to help fight their way out if they had to.

As they drew closer to the exit, they came across more goblin remains. Jeremy had counted thirteen before he saw the light of day pushing its way into the dark and dusty hallways. His heart fluttered with exhilaration as they approached the exit.

"Stop!" Mercurio yelled.

Jeremy turned around. Mercurio waved his hand. The look on his face was cause for alarm.

"Stop!" Jeremy held up one hand and concentrated his command on all the animals.

They all stopped and looked at him.

Mercurio jumped off the horse and ran to Jeremy.

"This is all too easy," Mercurio said. "They may be waiting outside for us."

"Who?" Jeremy asked.

"Goblin soldiers. They may try to ambush us. Come down from there, and you and I will scout ahead."

Jeremy climbed down.

He put up his hands and commanded the animals. "All of you stay here." He didn't know if he had to use his hands, but it seemed the right thing to do. "And don't eat each other," he said. He wasn't sure if he had to reinforce that notion, but that too seemed the right thing to do.

The bear let out a growl and plopped his butt down on the ground. The lions laid down, the female resting her head on her mate's back.

Mercurio grabbed Jeremy's waist and led him to the entrance. Debris from the breach explosion was scattered over ten feet inside the entrance. Goblin weapons and armor lay among the carnage. But there were no signs of the others, not even the goblin children.

They walked out into the jungle, and the humid air intensified with the sunlight. It felt wonderful. Jeremy breathed in deeply, expunging the last remnants of the goblin kingdom's stale air from his lungs. He felt a tug at his waist, stopping him from moving any further.

Mercurio scanned cautiously, turning him around in a circle.

Jeremy saw nothing out of the ordinary except for the backpack that lay beside the entrance. *The radio!* Wyllt had left it as promised. He went to grab it, but Mercurio held him back. The elf continued to scan the area.

"Wait here," Mercurio said. "When I step out, take three steps backward and to the right."

"OK," Jeremy shrugged. *I guess you can never be too cautious.*

"Now." Mercurio stepped out of the Veil cloak, tensed and ready for anything.

Jeremy stepped back and to the right.

Mercurio's head slowly turned and angled to the side. His eyes shifted as if he heard something. He then took a deep breath and relaxed. "We're clear. I don't see or hear anything out of the ordinary. Yet, this still seems too easy. It's as if they're letting us leave without a fight. I don't like this at all."

Jeremy pulled down his cowl. "Don't look a gift horse in the mouth," he said.

"I doubt this is a gift. Something is wrong."

"Well, we don't have a choice. We need to go," Jeremy said.

"Agreed," Mercurio turned around and headed back into the cave.

Jeremy grabbed the pack and followed the elf. He opened the pack and pulled out the radio. Then shoved the earbuds in his ear, securing them just as Decoudreau showed him. Then he turned it on. "Can anyone hear me?"

"Jeremy!" Ezzy said.

"Jeremy, glad to hear you made it," Wyllt said.

"Yeah. We're out and heading down to you. How's everyone else?"

"All accounted for, Santa Man," Wyllt said.

"Ellesmere keeps pawing at me to ask you about Mercurio," Ezzy said.

Jeremy climbed back up on the elephant. "Let's go," he said to the parade before hitting the button to talk to Ezzy. "Mercurio's fine. We have the whole team, and more. We found a bunch of prisoners we're bringing back with us."

"Of course you did," Wyllt said. Jeremy could hear the sarcasm in his voice. "How many?"

"Seven," Jeremy said, ducking as he exited the cave. He took in an extra deep breath, savoring the moment and relief that this ordeal was over.

"OK. I'll arrange for extraction. But, Ezzy and Jeremy, you need to relay this message to everyone. It's going to take several days to get copters in and out of here to exfil everyone. We'll talk more about that when we see you at the bird."

"Sounds good," Jeremy said. "Oh. Mr. Wyllt, what about the goblin children? Are they with you?"

"Yes," Wyllt said. "They are. And they're eager to see you."

"Good. That's awesome," Jeremy said. *But now what?* He wondered. *What becomes of them?* And what about the others they left behind? "Oh, I forgot to mention," Jeremy said. "We found a bunch of animals too. I'm actually riding an elephant right now!" He laughed.

"I thought that was an elephant. Your camera's been a bit fuzzy since you left the throne room," Ezzy said.

"Yeah. An African elephant." Jeremy looked down at his camera. The lens was covered in blood. As was most of his clothing.

"Oh, come now, Jeremy," Wyllt said. "I'm disappointed. I truly expected to see you soaring out of Kurgal on the back of an emerald dragon. Or at least a spotted griffin."

Jeremy could picture that grin of his. He laughed.

The three of them spoke for a bit longer, before going radio silent to allow Wyllt to make arrangements to get everyone out of the jungle. Jeremy tucked the earpiece away, exhaling a great big breath of relief, and allowing the tension of the past few weeks to roll off him.

They'd done it. They got the ring and everyone was safe.

Well, everyone except for Tufts. He didn't know the man well, but a twinge of guilt and sadness dampened his jubilation. Jeremy's thoughts wandered from Tufts to the goblin children they'd left behind.

There were probably hundreds of them being brainwashed into the service of the mad goblin king. If he didn't do anything to help them, they could be his enemies one day. Especially with the grudge these goblins held. Jeremy was sure that he'd be on Borahsh's hit list now.

He'd be safe in Orindin for most of the year, though. Then he'd only have to worry about them coming after him on Christmas Eve. He was going to insist that Mercurio teach him how to fight. And he wasn't going to take no for an answer. He'd learn to use a sword and whatever martial arts they had. Heck, maybe he'd even start carrying a gun.

And then there was Ezzy. Jeremy couldn't wait to see her. Sure, the last time he saw her she'd gone from flirty to standoffish in a matter of minutes. Something must have happened between her and Ellesmere. But what would have changed? When he spoke with her on the radio, he could hear how happy she was to know that he was alive. It'd probably take some time to whittle down her defenses. But heck, now he had plenty of time. They'd be living in the same town and he was practically immortal now. *How cool is that?*

CHAPTER 75

THE SAR'S GAMBIT

"The best enemy is the enemy that does not know you exist."
~ Goblin Idiom

High atop the mountain known to the goblins as Kurgal, Sar Qannu stood on a ledge overlooking the entire countryside. He watched the odd caravan led by the human riding an elephant. Behind the Sar, a legion of goblin soldiers stood at the ready, awaiting his orders.

To the Sar's right a sage took pictures of the caravan below. Qannu tried to ignore the clicking and whirring sound, but the human contraption's sound was more irritating than that of the buzzing mosquitos. He tolerated it nonetheless.

Turtak made his way through the line of warriors and appeared at the Sar's side. "You're letting them get away?" he asked.

Qannu let out a satisfied breath and smiled. "Letting them get away? I'd say it's more like moving them into place."

Turtak nodded. "I understand the timeline has been changed?"

"Yes. The Borahsh Dominion has ended, and with it the vengeance oath is no more. From this day on, we will concentrate all the might of the Goblin Empire on regaining power. I take it that your return indicates your mission was successful?"

"Masaru has entered the Veil. Now we just wait to see if he succeeds."

"Do you doubt his chance of success?" Qannu said.

Turtak laughed. "No. He will succeed. I've trained him well."

"Good." Qannu nodded.

"The plan to assassinate Borahsh is ahead of schedule. What's your plan now?" Turtak asked.

"I believe this turn of events was fortuitous. If Masaru is successful, it will give both of us a chance to prepare for the final phase. And, it will allow us to work with the dweorg now rather than later."

"And what would you have me do?"

"Thaddaios Wyllt." Qannu sighed. "He's proven to be far more formidable and unpredictable. He discovered Jau'Asar's duplicity, so we have no one on the inside of his organization anymore. And I doubt he'll ever let anyone else in again. You'll need to stay close to him and his operatives. Find a weakness. Something we can use to shut him down so that he doesn't interfere with our plans for the new era. You and Jau'Asar will leave first thing in the morning to meet with the Rook. Your trip to Bilar will give you time to find out everything he knows about this man."

"It will be done, Sar Qannu," Turtak said.

Qannu stared at the human riding the elephant. This one was going to be a problem. Though the attack on Kurgal had worked in Qannu's favor, he didn't like the idea that this seemingly ordinary man was capable of doing what he did. And now that he had that ring, he was even more powerful. He could be the one that undid five decades of planning. This human had to die. That would prove to be a difficult challenge. He'd need to find this human's weakness and use it to crush him.

EPILOGUE

Outside the ancient oak where the Elven Council met, Jeremy paced back and forth. Anticipation caused his stomach to churn. A crowd of citizens from the various species that lived in Sayalla formed around him, separated by a wall of Elven guards that included Ee'azar and Jar'iyu. Fairies flittered above the crowd, taking in their wonder. Several small purple and gray furred krodin peeked through bystander's legs, curiously watching Jeremy.

The doors of the tree opened, and a guard appeared. "The council has come to a decision. They wish to see you now," he said.

Jeremy's eyes widened. He inhaled an exaggerated breath, puffing his cheeks up and exhaling loudly. *This is it,* he thought confidently. With Ellesmere at his side, and with all the trouble they had gone through, the council couldn't possibly say no... again. He walked through the double doors and onto the lift, wondering if the elders were going to impose any additional rules upon him. And what about Ezzy? What would they say about the two of them?

The lift came to a stop, and the doors to the Court of Elders opened.

Jeremy stepped inside and his eyes grew wide at the majesty of the court. He caught his slack jaw and snapped it shut before he embarrassed himself. He held a comforting hand to his chest and sauntered into the chamber.

Mercurio stood in the center, just below the nine elders.

Jeremy stood beside him and flashed Mercurio a smile.

"Jeremy Goodson," said Shirgha, the elder in the center. "We, the Council of Elders, have come to a unanimous conclusion. We were greatly influenced by the testimony of Elder Ellesmere of Orindin. She speaks highly of you and your actions."

Jeremy's smile widened a bit, and he nodded at Ellesmere. She nodded back but didn't smile. Jeremy had gotten to know her well enough to know that a nod from Ellesmere was as good as a smile.

"Nevertheless," Shirgha continued. "It is with some reluctance that we grant her request to allow you to take up where Nikolaos left off."

Jeremy swallowed and held his breath. He wanted to say something, but he knew that would just make things worse. *How could they…*

"Therefore, Ellesmere will oversee your transition and ensure that all protocols are followed. You are granted permission to do as Nikolaos once did."

Jeremy wanted to shout with joy. But he only allowed himself to smile.

"In doing so, you must understand this. You will awaken humanity's knowledge of magic. It is our sincere hope that humanity will change its course, and one day our peoples will live in harmony."

Jeremy opened his mouth to say thank you and give a speech. But the elder's hopeful expression changed as he turned to Mercurio. Shirgha's eyebrows tightened, and his lips flattened. Jeremy closed his mouth and swallowed.

"Mercurio iyl Sayalla. You have committed grievous infractions, mainly that of going against the express command of the

Council of Elders. There is no place for you in our cities, and you are therefore exiled."

Jeremy's smile turned into a gasp.

"You will leave the protection of the Veil, living out your remaining days in isolation. You will leave immediately with only the clothes you wear. You may not take with you any enchantments. You may say your farewell to your friends before you are escorted from here."

No. This can't be happening. Jeremy turned to Mercurio. The elf was smiling. Not a joyful smile. But a humble one… a satisfied one. *How could he not be angry?*

"Thank you, Elder Shirgha. I leave here today without regret. I thank all of you for the opportunity to have served as a guardian these many years."

Jeremy looked back to the council. They all sat there emotionless and resigned. All but Ellesmere. Tears trickled down her stoic face.

"Though I may have acted against the will of the Elder Council, I stand by my actions as a guardian," Mercurio said, his chin held high. "For it was those actions that brought Jeremy Goodson to you, and to the world. We will all look back one day, knowing that my actions were in the best interest of all peoples. When I took the Oath of the Swordsworn, I vowed to protect our realm. And my actions bringing Jeremy to you have done just that." Mercurio turned to Jeremy with a knowing smile. "Jeremy, it has been—"

"Elders!" A shout came from behind the council.

A guardian burst in from one of the back doors. "Forgive the intrusion!" He announced as he ran toward Elder Shirgha. "I have an urgent message." He handed Shirgha a slip of paper.

Shirgha quickly grabbed it and began reading it. His brow wrinkled, and his eyes grew wide. He then brought his hand to his forehead and leaned forward in his seat.

"What is it?" Ellesmere said.

Shirgha's mouth became slack, and he leaned back in his seat, holding the message limply at his side. "It's news... from the dweorg. Days... days ago..." He sighed and looked up.

"Shirgha! Do not keep this to yourself!" One of the Dark Elf elders yelled.

Shirgha straightened, composing himself. "High King Unn has been killed!"

Several gasps and exclamations of disbelief emanated from all around the court. Conversations broke out and the chamber became abuzz with chatter. Several elders demanded to know more. Who had done such a thing?

"Wait!" Shirgha shouted. "Hear me! There's more." He stood up and waved his hands for everyone to quiet down. When the room was silent, he turned to Mercurio with a grave look upon his face. The elder's eyebrows scrunched together, and his lips pressed slightly.

What did this have to do with Mercurio?

Shirgha lifted the paper to read it. "This, it says, is from their new High King. A dweorg named Rangvald."

Whispers moved like echoes, questioningly repeating the name.

"This is what he has to say," Shirgha continued. "I, High King Rangvald of the Dweorg, am giving you to the end of the Festival of Fimbulvinter of this coming year to shut down the Veil. If you do not do so, then the might of the dweorg will come upon your cities and we will tear the Veil down ourselves. This is not open for discussion."

Jeremy swallowed hard and closed his eyes.

The End
of Book One
of *The Veil Saga*

THE SHARED WORLD
Copyright 2021 • The Veil Saga by Steven A. Guglich
Once upon Gazelle Cartographer
Thorheim
Nidavellir
Vidarheim
Valiheim
Sadal
Balderheim
Gaslo's Gate
Rocherl's Gate
Sayalla
Janngate's Gate
Gate of Nikolaos
Fastwin's Gate
Nadal
Amyin
Astrala
Badhtierra
Fludeherl's Gate
Oriadin
Eliar
Zohl's Gate
The Gate of Argosy
Baldo's Gate
Kargal
Jayir
Brid
Ganzir
N
S
E
W

KICKSTARTER ACKNOWLEDGEMENTS

A special thank you to the following people who pre-ordered this book on Kickstarter and helped to bring this book to publication.

Jon Auerbach, Joel Babcock, Adam David Barnes, Brandon Baker, Robert Barbour, Chris Behrsin, Jan Birch, Daniel Hanson-Brown, Tricia A. Brubaker, Karen Bulgarelli, Dorothy E. Carlson, Kayla Carpenter, Joshua C. Chadd, Doylenn Chastain, Nickolas Chatterton, Flann Christenson, Ian Constantin, Esther Cordova, Hana Correa, Rob Crosby, Tom Dean, Tyler DeJong, Anthony Deyarmond, Jessica Deyarmond, Lindsay Dragoon, Jared Dreher, Lynn Duffey, Jimmy Durst, Russel Fisk, Timothy Fling, Christy Foster, Dianne Gardner, Robert Garrett, GhostCat, Crystal Gordeuk, The Grover Family, Debra Guglich, The Haverlock Family, Allie Henry, James Ingenito, Cari Jehlik, Jacob H. Joseph, Paula Kaledzi, Richard Keebler, Owen Kerschner, Claudia Klein, Nicholas Kotar, Aleksey G. Kovalyov, Samantha Landstrom, Anthea Lawrence, Mathieu Lefebvre, Brittany Lozada, Alex & Ruth Marquez, Connor Mayo, Gerald P. McDaniel, CJ Milacci, Richard Novak, Rachel Olson, Amy Overy, Jake Parrick, Jerry & Roberta Perlman, Gary Phillips, NeonPixxius, Darrell J. Pursiful, Arne Radtke, Paul Richter, Colby Rodeheaver, JF Rogers, Michael Rossano, Lazaro Ruiz, Josh Samples, Marilyn Schmidt, Rebecca Schug, Ernie & Adele Sehringer, Chris Session, Katherine Shipman, Kym Smith, Rob Steinberger, Michael H. Sugarman, Noah Jenkins, Natasha Swift, Francesco Tehrani, David A. Trotter, Carmen Troutman, Leslie Twitchell, Hector Villegas, Vitor Publishing, Andrew Webster, Jonathan Wells, and Robert Zangari.

ABOUT THE AUTHOR

Steven A. Guglich grew up in New York City. He lives in Williston, North Dakota with his wife, his four children, and his collection of books. He is an Elementary School Principal and is the 2020 North Dakota Principal of the Year.

In 2022, he and his wife launched Your Wildest Dreams Publishing, LLC to fulfil a dream born in the imagination of Steven's Dad, Stanley, and to publish Steven's books.

For more information on Steven's books, please visit www.stevenguglich.com